3

FROM R[illegible]

PART 3

The Key

V. E. Bines

ISBN: 979-8-7222-4757-5

SOUTHERN ARMORNIA

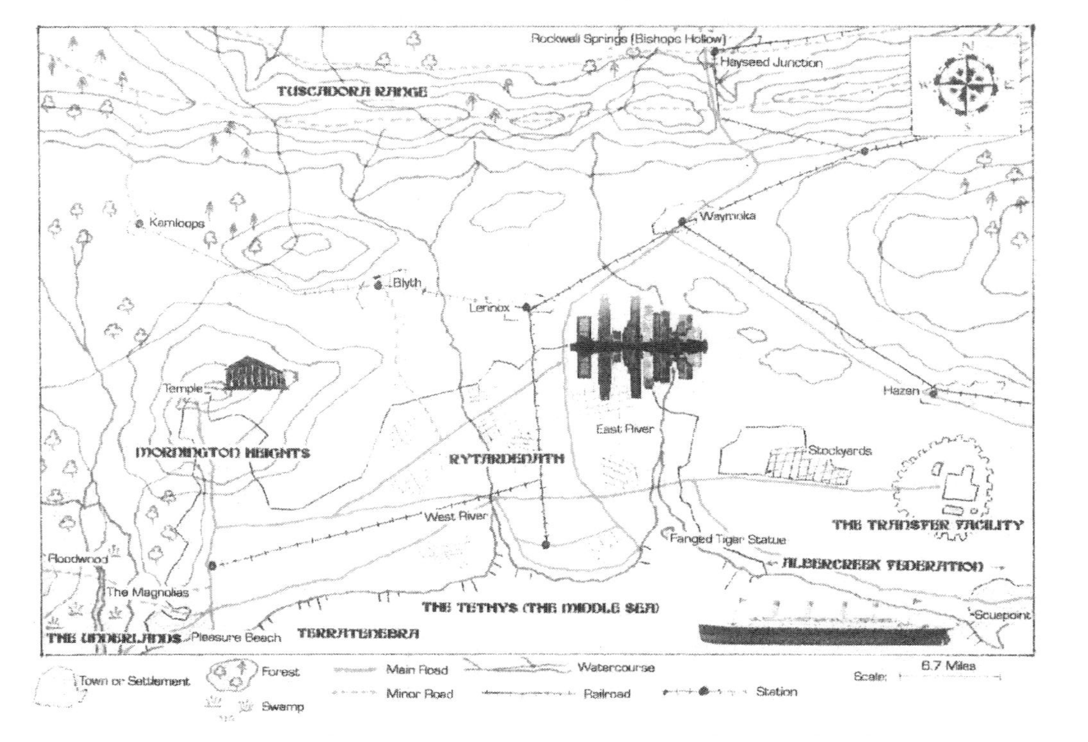

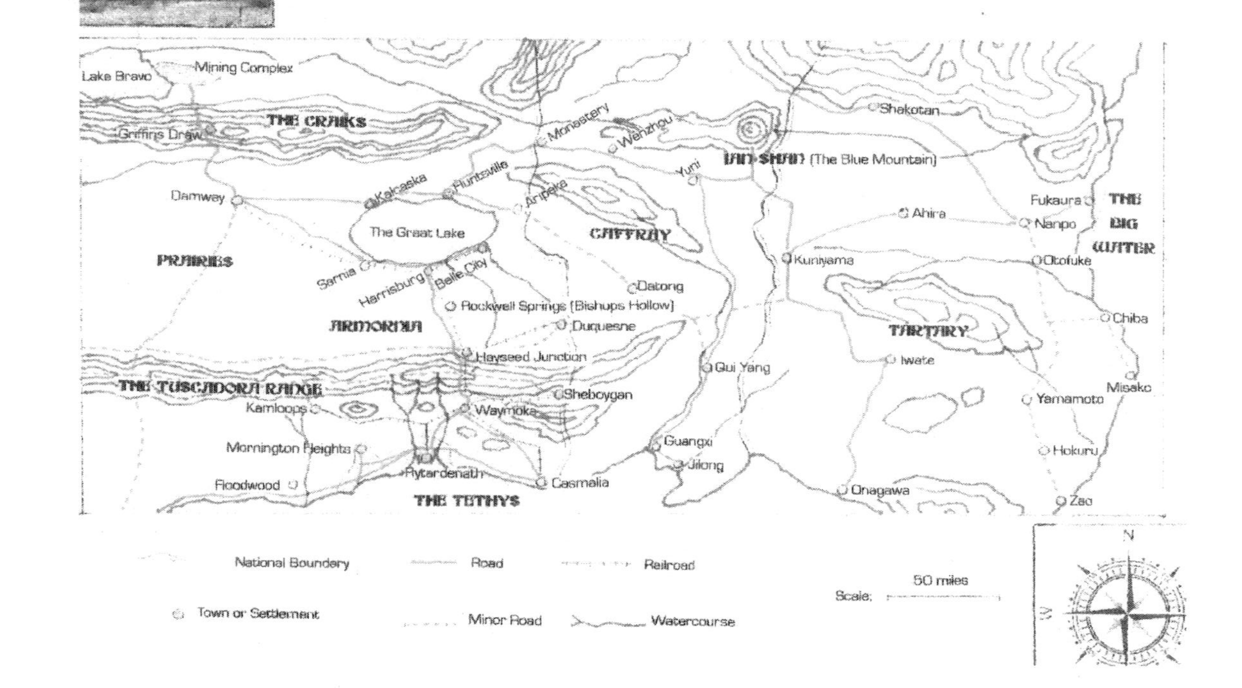
PANGORLAND (The Northern Continent)
Lake Bravo
Mining Complex
THE CRAIKS
Griffins Draw
Monastery
Wenzhou
Shakotan
IAN SHAN (The Blue Mountain)
Yuni
Huntsville
Kalcaska
Damway
Aripeka
Ahira
Fukaura
Nanpo
THE BIG WATER
The Great Lake
CAFFRAY
Kuniyama
Otofuke
PRAIRIES
Sarnia
Harrisburg
Belle City
Datong
Rockwell Springs (Bishups Hollow)
Duquesne
ARMORIKA
TARTARY
Chiba
Hayseed Junction
Gui Yang
Iwate
Misako
THE TUSCARORA RANGE
Sheboygan
Yamamoto
Kamloops
Waymoka
Guangxi
Mornington Heights
Jilong
Hokuru
Rytardenath
Floodwood
Casmalia
Onagawa
Zao
THE TETHYS
National Boundary
Road
Railroad
Town or Settlement
Minor Road
Watercourse
Scale:
50 miles
N
W

Contents

Characters in alphabetical order

ANN (HILDA HANNAH ARBERICORD) – age: 18/19. Dando's soul-mate. Horry's mother. Has *Crossed Over* and is now a *Dancer.*

AZAZEEL – The Dark Brother. Unnaturally conceived offspring of Aigea and Pyr. Originally part of one being with his brother Pendar.

BAU-ZHI – An exceptionally gifted child who guides Jack, Milly and Horry across Caffray to Ian Shan (the Blue Mountain).

BECCA (PEEPO) – age: 62/63. Showgirl and boarding-house keeper in Vadrosnia Poule. Comes from Armornia. Jack's friend.

BOIKO – age: 17/18. Duke's brother.

CHET WILSON – Boxing promoter whom Damask meets on her way to the mine workings.

COLONEL WAPSHOTT – age: 68/69. Historian and guest-house keeper in Damwey.

CURTIS – Becca's elder son.

DAMASK – age: 18/19. Dando's twin sister. Strong willed girl who rebels against the role assigned to all Glept women. Has an affinity with travelling people, particularly the Roma.

DANDO (THE LORD DAN ADDO) – age: 18/19. The Dan's second son. A young aristocrat who has a mysterious destiny to fulfil. Horry's father.

DANTOR (THE LORD DAN ATTOR) – age: 22/23. Dando's elder brother. Has become head of Clan Dan on the death of his father.

DOLL (ADELAIDE AGNETHA GOODHOUSEN nee APPLECRAFT) – age: about 51/52. A Nablan. Substitute mother to the Dan's offspring. Potto's daughter.

DUKE – age: 20/21. A gypsy boy. Damask's first lover.

ENNIS AND SPATCH – Ghostly children whom Dando encounters in the underworld.

FOXY (EVERARD TETHERER TROOLY) – age: 28/29. A member of the Nablan race. Dando's half brother through his father. A parricide.

FYNN – age: 16/17. Member of the Posse. Jack's lover.

GAMMADION (GUBBO THE GREAT) – age: centuries old. A powerful but corrupt wizard. The stealer of the Key.

GORTH – A fire-breathing dragon in the Caves of Bone.

HORACE (HORRY) – Dando and Ann's son. Is growing older at an unnaturally fast rate due to a curse Gammadion has laid.

JACK HOWGEGO – age: 23/24. Gay citizen of Drossi. Has been blinded by the bandit known as the Cheetah in revenge for a perceived wrong done to him and his brother by the boy's grandfather.

LETITIA (LETTY) – A fanged tiger.

LIN-JI – Solitary monk living on the border between Armornia and Caffray.

LORETTA – An inhabitant of Floodwood, a black community on the outskirts of Ry-Town.

MA BAKER – A procuress who takes prostitutes across the Craiks to the mine workings.

MABELENE – An inhabitant of Floodwood. Employed at the Dark Continent restaurant.

MATT – Drummer with the Posse.

MILLY – age: about 15 or 16. Damask's black maid. Former child prostitute rescued from a Gateway brothel by Dando. Idolises the one who saved her.

MEENA – Milly's cat.

MONA – A black cleaner at the Transfer facility.

MOTHER EULALIE – age: 82. Bishops Hollow's obeah woman.

PENDAR – The Bright Brother. Unnaturally conceived offspring of Aigea and Pyr. Trapped by his brother Azazeel, he has spent thousands of years under Gammadion's sway.

POTTO POTUNALIUS APPLECRAFT – age: about 72/73. Attached nibbler. Dando's former manservant and substitute father.

QUAHAUG – very old. Natural philosopher (scientist) of the Inshami race whose base is beneath Ian Shan where Azazeel also has his seat of operations.

RALPH – Tallis' dog.

STIGMORE FLETCHER – Train driver in Armornia.

TALLIS (PRINCE TALLISAND) – age: late middle. A lonely man who had spent most of his life on a quest for a mysterious object known as *The Key*. A musician.

THE DAN – age at death: 48. Dando's father and head of Clan Dan.

THE GREAT ONES (AIGEA, PYR, ROSTAN, BRON ETC.) - alien immortals of mainly hominid origin whose original purpose in coming to earth was to retrieve the Key and dispatch it to its intended place in the cosmos but who, once here, were seduced by the notion that, with the Object in their possession, they would have absolute power over the planet's inhabitants.

THE MINISTRANT – Caretaker in the temple on the summit of Mornington Heights.

THE POSSE – An up-and-coming pop group from Vadrosnia Poule.

THE RUNAWAYS – Close-harmony singers. Dando's rivals at the final of the *Go-Getter Game*.

TOM (THOMAS TOSA ARBERICORD) – age at his presumed death: 36. Ann's father. Cobbler and attached nibbler to Clan Dan, but also the high priest, the Culdee, of the Nablan race.

TYLER – Sheep farmer whom Damask marries on her way to the mine workings.

URSULA – Quahaug's great great granddaughter. Azazeel's mistress.

WINNIE – The leader of the Posse.

OTHER CHARACTERS WHO ARE REFERRED TO IN BOOK THREE BUT WHO DO NOT APPEAR

CLARKE – Becca's ex-husband.

DEMPSEY – Becca's younger son.

ORLANDO – age at his premature death: 30. Quahaug's great great grandson.

THE OLD ONES – alien immortals of mainly non-hominid origin. The original visitants from deep space who brought the Key to the earth.

Synopsis of Part 1 - The Valley

Chapter 1: Pyr and Aigea, two incorporeal beings posing as gods, are voicing grave doubts as to their continuing tenure of a small rocky planet, favourable to life, orbiting a minor star in the arm of an unremarkable spiral galaxy. They have been granted foreknowledge of a boy who may hold their fate in his hands although he is as yet unaware of the fact. On that same planet, a lonely man, a knight errant of sorts born out of his time, has been travelling for many years and at a certain point along his route arrives in the valley of Deep Hallow accompanied by his dog Ralph and horse Carolus. He puts up at an inn strangely titled *The Justification.* In days gone by his mother, Morvah, told him he could claim the soubriquet: *Tallisand, Prince of the Lake Guardians, Keeper of the Key* by right, but if he is a prince, it is a prince without a people, and as for the Key that disappeared long ago. At the inn he makes the acquaintance of the innkeeper, a Mrs Humpage, and is attracted by a fair-haired servant girl that he is informed belongs to the subject nibbler (Nablan) race *'oo do all the donkey-work roun' 'ere.*

Chapter 2: Tallis, his horse and his dog are provided with food, after which he retires to his room. Here he encounters another Nablan, a young man with an extremely truculent attitude. Tallis goes to bed but cannot sleep. Lying awake he thinks back to the beginning of his journey and his reasons for undertaking it.

Chapter 3: Tallis recalls his childhood in a poor mountain village far to the south. Despite their poverty his mother insisted that she had been born a king's daughter, one of a people who guarded a Treasure in the form of a Key which had the power to change the world when it was turned but was of such potency that there were few who could remain close to it for long without suffering the consequences. It was given into her nation's keeping by Pyr, known, among other things, as the Sky-Father, the Master-of-Winds and the Lord-of-Heaven. He had turned it for the present Age-of-Thought after having persuaded Aigea, the putative earth mother, to surrender it by professing his eternal love for her and suggesting they create an offspring of pure spirit between them. (Several thousand years before, this supposed goddess had also turned it, bringing about the Second Age, the Age-of-the-Heart). Tallis' mother explains that she was seduced by a corrupt wizard named Gammadion who, although he was supposed to be acting merely as errand-boy for another, persuaded her to steal the Key on his behalf because he believed it delayed ageing in whosoever held it, the more so the longer it remained in their possession. As soon as she does what he asks and the Treasure is surrendered, the lake beside which her people live vanishes and their kingdom is destroyed. Its citizens set out to recover what they have lost leaving Morvah along the way in a mountain fastness to bear and raise her son. When Tallis reaches the age of fifteen she tells him that it is his duty to follow and find his people, to mend what his father has undone and bring back the Key so that the Land of the Lake can be restored.

Chapter 4: Precipitously Tallis is launched on his quest when his mother begins to fear that the villagers are filling his ears with a different account of her origins and that he will no longer believe what she has told him. In the last act of her life she packs him off down the road and then relapses into a trance out of which, according to a strange voice that issues from between her lips, she will never awaken. At this point Tallis' recollections are interrupted by the noise of falling rain and the sound of an argument taking place below his window between some unknown persons and the obstreperous Nablan whose acquaintance he has already made. Day is dawning and he hears the Night Hymn to the Father being sung. At last he is able to fall asleep.

Chapter 5: In a luxurious house in the centre of one of the small valley towns, a member of the ruling Glept elite, the Lord Dan Addo, lies abed in the grip of a nightmare. This dream involves two narratives, one of burning which has its source in actual events, while the other concerns an enormous and threatening tunnel under the world. On waking, Dando, second son and heir to the Dan, a powerful clan chief, decides he must play truant from school and go on an expedition in an attempt to exorcise this recurrent dream. Despite having all the trappings of wealth and position (expensive clothes, opulent living quarters, numerous subordinates) the boy is not a typical scion of the philistine Gleptish aristocracy – among his passions are a fascination with books and cookery. The year is now well into its ninth month and it is the morning following Dando's seventeenth birthday. As he sets out astride the Dans' great black thoroughbred Attack and singing to himself (a somewhat ear-tormenting sound!) he dwells on his recent experiences as a military cadet - an Outrider - in the town of Gateway which lies at the entrance to the valley. Whilst there he has heard a scandalous story concerning his own father to the effect that he once married a nibbler woman who bore him a son. This has particular relevance for Dando as he also loves a Nablan girl, and it is for her sake that, the previous year, he refused to swear the oath of allegiance to his people which required that he put their good above all others. That is why he is currently residing in the little town of High Harrow instead of in Gateway or at Castle Dan, his clan's ancestral home, having been sent there, in deep disgrace, to study estate management. During his stay he prepares a meal for Father Adelbert, one of his teachers, and this worldly foreign priest is greatly impressed by the quality and originality of the dishes on offer. In fact Dando has been developing his culinary skills since a small boy and by now has reached a professional standard.

Chapter 6: On his way to the extreme western end of the valley our truant finds himself amid a confusion of lanes on the south side of the River Wendover. Here he has a strange encounter with a supernatural being in the form of a black dog. This is one of a class of elementals who came from outside the earth long ago carrying a Treasure they had stolen, (the very same Key that Tallis is seeking), and who chose to establish their hegemony on this particular planet. These entities, the Old Ones, are occasionally visible to the human eye and Dando has been blessed or maybe cursed with the ability to see them because of something which happened to him when he was seven years old. He hates this hag-ridden side to his life and yearns to be normal, as he imagines everyone else to be. Nevertheless, because of the confrontation, he is prompted to think back to his beginnings and to face up to harrowing memories which he is usually at pains to suppress. These concern a mentor named Tom, the Dans' Nablan cobbler, who was also, unknown to his masters, the high-priest or Culdee of the Nablan race and the intercessor between his people and Aigea, the earth goddess and object of their worship. Tom's daughter Ann shared a wet-nurse with Dando when they were babies and later played with him and with his twin sister Damask. In due time they became childhood sweethearts. Although the Lady Damask's people, the Glepts, ostensibly worship the Sky-Father she decides, at the age of six, that she would like to pray to the Mother on behalf of one of her sick friends. While Tom is away the three children go to his workshop where, as the young Glepts have discovered, an image of Aigea lies concealed in an annex behind a dresser and Dando is elected to conduct the ceremony. He is thus brought to the attention of the immortal who recognises in him one with a destiny to fulfil which if achieved might pose a threat to her own existence. A few months later, when he is just seven, she lures him away with ill intent to her shrine in the Upper Valley, the Midda as the Nablans call it, and he would have perished if Tom, who guessed the goddess's intention, had not rescued him. Because the cobbler has gone against her will in saving the little boy he incurs the wrath of his mistress.

Chapter 7: Three years of foreboding on Tom's part pass before Aigea engineers his quietus. Blamed for the death of the Dan's youngest son he is condemned to burn as a witch within the bounds of the immortal's holy shrine. Before the cobbler's arrest Dando falls ill and only learns what has happened to his friend once he recovers from the blood-poisoning he has contracted due to his sister's tattooing techniques. Subsequent to Tom's immolation he is plagued by bad dreams identical to the one that has spurred him into setting out on his present journey. His solution, both then and now, is to go to the Upper Valley which is at the heart of the nightmare and *face his demons* as he puts it. At twelve years old when he and his sister make the trip he ventures close to the immortal's lair and as a result the dreams cease; he cannot understand why they should have returned now after so long an absence. Before Tom's presumed death Ann disappeared off the face of the earth. In fact she had been spirited away by other Nablans to live with her maternal grandmother at the Justification Inn. Desperate to find her, Dando searches high and low, including, once he has become a cadet, in the brothels of Gateway, but without success.

Chapter 8: Reaching the Midda which contains the flat-topped mound known as Judd's Hill Dando brokers a pact with the Mother: *If I can walk round the edge of this hill and back to my starting point without straying, the dreams will cease for good and I will go free.* He is vouchsafed many visions as he makes the circuit which are intended to lure him into the centre where the Mother lies in wait, but he successfully resists these temptations and completes the course. Despite this the goddess still tries to do away with him, using her power over the forces of nature, and he only escapes by cutting one of his wrists and giving some of his blood to the earth, thus tricking the deity into believing that his life has been forfeited. Groggy and traumatised he returns to the place where he left the horse only to find that Attack has panicked and fled, laming himself in the process.

When he discovers his steed cowering beside the cliff that surrounds the Upper Valley he leads him back across many miles to Castle Dan but does not yet feel ready to face his father's wrath. Instead he leaves the horse in safe hands and continues on foot all the way to High Harrow on a rainy night, arriving, soaked and exhausted, in the early hours of the morning to be greeted by his faithful servant Potto.

Chapter 9: The unattached nibbler, Everard Tetherer Trooly, nicknamed Foxy, whom Tallis has already encountered in his room at the Justification has no idea as to his origins. He has been brought up by a goatherd on the border of the Dans' estates and does not venture down into the valley proper until well into his teens. When his sense of adventure leads him to the little settlement of Low Town in the centre of Deep Hallow he immediately falls foul of some Outriders, and, not understanding what is expected of him, is beaten for showing insolence to his betters. The military cadets, and by association the whole Gleptish race, earn his undying hatred for being responsible for this outrage. At the age of about eighteen Foxy leaves the valley and pays a visit to the Delta City, Vadrosnia Poule, which is situated near the mouth of the Kymer River. In this cosmopolitan metropolis he picks up revolutionary ideas and returns to his birthplace eager to launch a rising of the Nablar against their oppressors. He intends to do this by recruiting Tom the cobbler to his side. When the Nablan high priest is condemned to death he turns his attention to his daughter Ann who he hopes will eventually step into her father's shoes and, in order to protect her, goes to work at the Justification Inn. He is determined to keep his future priestess inviolate and is greatly disturbed by the fact that she loves the Dan's second son. While on one of his many poaching expeditions he sees Dando pass by on his journey to the Upper Valley and for a moment has the opportunity to kill him, thereby ridding himself of this obstacle to his ambitions. Inexplicably he fails to do so. He is also concerned that another member of the aristocracy, the Lord Yan Cottle, has designs on Ann, or Hilda as she is known at the Justification. The girl is just too beautiful for her own good.

Chapter 10: Pyr taunts Aigea over the failure of her latest attempt to do away with Dando despite the fact that it was very nearly successful. At the inn, where he is jokingly referred to as *Sir Knight,* Tallis wakes in the late afternoon and begins his daily practice on the kuckthu, the musical instrument by which he earns his living. As he plays he recalls the time when he came by the ancient proto-harp in the first place. On quitting the mountains of his birth he was lucky enough to be taken in by a philanthropist named Guyax who ran a commune. Abandoning his quest when it was suggested that the events his mother recounted told of something that had happened not recently but in the far distant past Tallis stayed with him for several years, married his daughter Prudence and only went back on the road after the romance turned sour. With great generosity he was given the kuckthu when he left. Since then he has virtually traversed the length of a continent and in the process crossed from the southern to the northern hemisphere. Leaving his room preparatory to eating an evening meal he finds Ann asleep on the stairs and recognises her as the girl who attracted his attention the previous night. Inadvertently he startles her and she retaliates by unleashing the latent magical powers she has inherited from her father. These act like a blow and send Tallis sprawling. Refusing to acknowledge that anything out of the ordinary has occurred he persuades himself that he must have been taken temporarily ill. It is a fact that through age and infirmity he is beginning to feel the need of a companion on the road and he actually unbends enough to ask the innkeeper for advice. She tells him that a hiring fair is taking place in High Harrow on the morrow where he might be able to recruit someone suitable.

Chapter 11: Since puberty Damask has been confined to the women's quarters of Castle Dan which are ruled by a phalanx of aunts, robbing her of the freedom she and her brother enjoyed in their childhood when she mixed with gypsies and travellers and roamed unsupervised throughout the valley. Constantly under the surveillance of a spy network of servants her way of life is severely curtailed until Dando brings her a small black girl named Milly, a child prostitute he has rescued from a life of exploitation whilst searching the Gateway brothels for Ann. Milly becomes Damask's maid and together they embark on a series of adventures in which Damask reacquaints herself with one of her lovers, a gypsy boy named Duke. On the day Dando visits the Upper Valley Damask is informed, late at night, of his misdeeds and, leaving her apartment at the castle, goes to investigate. She finds that the great horse Attack has indeed been injured while in the care of her brother and that Dando, to her horror, has apparently run away rather than face the music. The next morning she tries to get in to see her father on his behalf but is prevented by the mercenary soldiers with which the clan chief has surrounded himself.

Chapter 12: Meanwhile Ann has been leading her usual down-trodden existence at the Justification, slaving away from morning to night. She is finding life increasingly difficult because as she gets older and nearer to sexual maturity the magical potential she is heir to is becoming more and more difficult to control; since her father's death she no longer has someone to guide her in its use. She is especially afraid because Yantle (the Lord Yan Cottle) is threatening to take her as his *pet*, his concubine, and she fears she will employ *the gift* as it is known to protect herself. To utilise the power for her own benefit even if it means the difference between life and death is something her father told her she must never do. In the three years that elapsed between incurring the anger of the Mother and his unmasking Tom attempted to pass on knowledge, both old and newly acquired, to his daughter. He spoke of Dando and his intuitive feeling that the boy had some world-altering task to perform. He also warned her that a Culdee should never take a lover because his or her partner will incur the jealousy of the goddess. When young, however, he did not follow his own advice and in fact fell in love with and married Martha, a woman of the Nablan race, only to lose her when she died giving birth to his child. He also tells Ann of what he has recently become aware that the gods, the Great Ones, who hold the world under their sway actually originate elsewhere; they first arrived on the earth pursuing the previously mentioned Old Ones, and are in fact usurpers. These extraterrestrial newcomers started out as creatures of the flesh like themselves but, through an inevitable evolutionary process, left their physical bodies behind in the same way that a butterfly sheds its chrysalis. All intelligent beings in the universe have the potential to follow a similar path and are given the epithet *dancers* once they have *Crossed Over*. After their apotheosis they achieve immortality and are able to move unfettered among the stars. Pyr and Aigea, the Sky-Father and Earth-Mother, are two such lifeforms, as are, in a different sense, their unnaturally engendered children Pendar and Azazeel. Both offspring, who were originally one being, vanished soon after their creation, and it is a commonly held belief that, if they still exist, it is in the shadowy places deep below ground. Humans have progressed far enough up the ladder of life to be capable of casting off the cycle of death and rebirth, and Tom does not fully understand why they are rarely able to do this. He suspects, however, that the difficulty may lie with the Treasure that was brought by the aliens from somewhere in space and which, as previously stated, has taken on the appearance of a Key. The planet has been locked into a form of stasis by this Thing-of-Power and, although not it's original brief, it now determines, when turned, the nature of each new age. The fates of any beings who have held or manipulated it are inevitably linked to its ultimate destiny. Despite the Key's maleficent influence there are infrequent occasions when earthlings can make the already mentioned *Change* to a new type of existence. If an exceptional individual, whose mind has reached a certain level of spiritual awareness, lies close to death they may be able to overcome the interdict and achieve a *Crossing* before the end arrives. One day, so he has heard, when the curse is lifted, the whole human race will follow their example and then... *the great rocks will sing and the little rocks frolic like lambs.*

Chapter13: The next morning Tallis is up betimes in order to set off for High Harrow. He omits his usual morning prayers to the Lord-of-Heaven because of a feeling that the immortal has abandoned this valley and the ones who dwell therein and has shut his ears to their pleas. On arriving at the settlement's civic centre he leaves an account of his requirements with the town crier and then goes to wait at the King's Head Tavern for job-seekers to appear. Potto rouses Dando and tells him it is time to go to school but he rejects the suggestion and then sleeps through until noon. On waking he skips lunch and, leaving the house, crosses the river to the fair. Here he listens to the crier's message and decides that applying for the job as Tallis' companion could provide the answer to all his problems. He meets the *knight*, as he has become known, at the hostelry but the traveller's first impressions are not favourable even though, as well as offering his services, Dando promises to provide supplies for the journey and a pony to carry them; in fact the man is intimidated by the boy's obvious breeding and status. Dando returns, disconsolate, to his base at the Dans' town house only to be arrested by his father's men and escorted back to the castle. Tallis waits out the afternoon in High Harrow but receives no further applications for the position he is offering and so returns to the Justification. Later that night, going downstairs to use the privy, he finds several people in the inn yard including Mrs Humpage. They have been woken by the arrival of the Lord Yan Cottle accompanied by one of his servants. Yantle, as already explained, has had his eye on Ann for some time and wants to appropriate her for his own amusement but has been frustrated by the innkeeper's lack of co-operation. As a last resort he has come to abduct her by force and commands his man to fetch her from the hovel out back where she lives with her grandmother. The henchman returns dragging the girl along with him. Tallis intervenes despite realising that Yantle has one of these new-fangled weapons that he has only come across once or twice before – namely a gun. His life is suddenly in deadly peril until Ann, stretching out her free hand, cries "STOP!" As the gun fires it flies to pieces and Yantle falls mortally wounded. "Witchcraft!" a voice whispers in the ensuing hush. By threatening Mrs Humpage's life Tallis manages to rescue the young magic-worker from an inevitable reckoning and then flees with her insensible body across his saddle-bow towards High Harrow.

Chapter14: Dando spends the night in a cell in the Punishment Yard at Castle Dan and the next morning is taken before his half-mad father. The Dan tells his son that his patience has finally been exhausted and that the miscreant is to be relegated to the lowly role of priest; he will fill the post of house chaplain, a greatly despised position. Dando is conducted down to the cleric's quarters in the bowels of the castle and later goes through the ordination ceremony after his head has been shaved in order to conform to tradition.

Chapter 15: Aigea, examining the time-lines, believes that Dando is going to quit the valley in the near future and presumes that he has learnt what posterity holds in store for him. Pyr replies that although this latest idea of hers is complete nonsense, the fact remains that, if he does decide, for some reason, to leave, their potential nemesis will be far more vulnerable when out alone in the world and they will stand a much better chance of dealing with him there. Tallis, by now implicated in what appears to be sorcery and murder, understands that he and his charge's only hope of escaping from the valley is to seek out the young aristocrat who offered him assistance. After hiding by the River Wendover during the hours of daylight he finds his way to Castle Dan and makes contact with Potto. He is worried about Ann who has been completely comatose since the events in the inn yard. Meanwhile Foxy, who was elsewhere at the time of Yantle's death, returns to the inn and discovers what has taken place. He immediately sets out to track the runaways. Passing through High Harrow and on up the valley he realises that those he is pursuing took a turning towards the castle but loses the trail in the encroaching darkness. Potto, having talked to Tallis and learnt what has happened at the Justification confesses to his master that he knew of Ann's whereabouts all along. Dando goes to meet the traveller and is reunited with his long-lost love, following which he eagerly agrees to be true to his promise and provide everything needed for the road. When he makes clear his intention of becoming part of the expedition however Tallis does not welcome the idea. At a loss to think of any other way to persuade the man to change his mind Dando suggests that he should become the paladin's squire, something he has read about in books and family records, but in so doing does not explain that there is normally a commitment on both sides. The idea of having such an aristocratic youth at his beck and call appeals to Tallis' vanity and so he agrees. Dando swears an oath of fealty to the man. He then turns his attention to the task of getting everything together for the journey including *borrowing* Damask's pony Mollyblobs to carry the baggage. They set off northwards, the direction Tallis has been following all his life, and travel up a little-used track known as the Way-of-the-Shades. Dando and Ann - the girl having by this time recovered - walk close behind their leader holding hands. "Where in the world do you think we're going?" Dando asks her in a whisper and then, "to tell the truth I couldn't care less where we go." To himself he adds, *so long as I'm with you.* Damask and Milly, understanding that Dando has up sticks and left the valley, are both equally keen to follow, Damask because she sees this as a great opportunity to escape from her restrictive way of life, Milly for the simple reason that she thinks of the young man as her saviour and so worships the ground he walks on. In the absence of Mollyblobs they harness Phyllis, an ancient donkey, to their dog cart but then, instead of going north, mistakenly head east down the Incadine Gorge and so, without realising it, soon diverge from the way that the others have taken. Foxy returns to the castle once it gets light, resumes the pursuit and, through his tracking skills, discovers that the fugitives have taken the northerly route. At the same time the Dan is told that his son has absconded and, through his mercenaries' persuasive techniques, learns from Potto the direction in which he is heading. Reaching a spur of the moment decision the clan chief sets out, determined to recapture his errant offspring. Foxy, as he hides amongst the rocks halfway up the valley side, sees a troop of soldiers approaching with the Dan at its head. For him this man embodies all the injustices that have been heaped upon his people throughout the generations. He failed to kill the son but now that he has the father in his sights he is determined that there will be no hesitation. He draws his bow and with deadly accuracy sends an arrow winging its way towards the clan chief's heart.

Synopsis of part 2 – The Shady Way

Chapter 1: After fleeing from the Valley of Deep Hallow, Tallis, Dando and Ann, accompanied by the dog Ralph and the horses Carolus and Mollyblobs, head into high country. Tallis has learnt, while in the valley, of the fraught relationship between the two races that dwell there, the Glepts and Nablar, and is suspicious of Dando's intentions towards Ann. These misgivings are intensified when Foxy arrives, fires off an arrow that pins Dando's sleeve to the tree beside which the travellers are camping, in the process grazing his arm. He gives as his reason for so doing that he caught the two young people in a compromising position while Tallis was sleeping (in fact the boy was merely providing comfort during an emotional crisis that Ann is going through). To make matters worse Ralph has transferred his allegiance to the young Glept which leaves the knight feeling highly resentful. Now, delighted that Foxy has joined him,Tallis is ready to dispense with his so called *squire's* services altogether - such a relationship, he thinks, is in fact thoroughly archaic and will in no way further his ultimate purpose - but Ann, showing remarkable strength of character, pleads her loved-one's case and he is allowed to stay. However when they bed down for the night he is banished from the circle around the fire and so lies awake, cold and miserable, until, looking for a handkerchief in his pack, discovers a generous gift left there by Potto - the old man's life savings.

Chapter 2: Damask and Milly, driving their dog-cart which is being pulled by the ancient donkey Phyllis, mistakenly go east in pursuit of Dando and so leave the valley in the wrong direction. Travelling through Gateway and down the Incadine Gorge they fall in with a clown known as Pnoumi the Mog who makes his living by running a performing cat show. Having failed to hear any news of Tallis' party they put up at an inn in the village of Upend where they watch the clown's act. The next morning they set off for camp-sites on the River Kymer but Phyllis is not equal to the demands they are making on her and eventually collapses. The cat-circus caravan puts in an appearance, minus the cats, and Pnoumi offers to give them a lift to an animal doctor in Millfield, a small town on the Kymer Levels. They take him on trust but, once they are shut in the back of his vehicle, he sets off in the opposite direction. When night falls they manage to escape by means of a ruse and in a complete reversal of roles Pnoumi becomes their prisoner. On the way back to Millfield, driving the caravan, they come across Phyllis's corpse as well as the looted dog cart and then encounter a group of the Dan's mercenary soldiers who have been banished from the Valley following the clan chief's death. The troop's leader tells them of his assassination. The defenceless girls are about to be taken advantage of when they are rescued by a company of actors led by a character who calls himself the Grande Stupendo.

Chapter 3: As Tallis and those accompanying him continue their journey Dando is relegated to the bottom of their small hierarchy and is often on the receiving end of verbal abuse from Foxy. During the day the Nablan goes hunting, bringing back a varied bag for the despised Glept to butcher and cook. One night their camp is invaded by robbers. Dando, almost unintentionally, manages to kill two of them, thereby earning a certain grudging respect from both Tallis and Foxy. Eventually they arrive in Formile, a town on the River Burple, where they spend three nights at an inn. Here they learn that an oracle's shrine is situated further up the road, a place of pilgrimage for those wishing to consult Rostan, the presumptive god of the earth's core. While they sit talking on the inn's patio Dando asks Tallis for details concerning their journey including information about when they are likely to reach their goal. In response his master recounts the story of the Lake Guardians and his reasons for being footloose throughout most of his life. As he does so the wanderer at last tumbles to the realisation that the Glepts of Deep Hallow are, undoubtedly, a remnant of those his mother regarded as her people. He decides that he will visit the oracle in the hope of receiving guidance. Ann has had her confidence boosted by Dando's presence and is learning to gain control of the occult powers she has inherited, but at the same time Foxy, in their private moments together, is trying to persuade her to return with him to Deep Hallow. Tom, during the long conversations that he had with his daughter shortly before his betrayal, recounted the tale that Dando has already heard, of how the Dan, in his youth, once married a Nablan woman. He went on to tell how, when the man unexpectedly became Head of Clan and could no longer care for his young wife, she drowned in a pool by the isolated cottage he had built for her. Her child, the result of their union, disappeared. Tom was of the opinion that the youngster survived and that Foxy is that missing waif. Now, as a means of persuading Ann to turn back and retrace her steps the Nablan tells her that the Dan has been killed and that it was he who did the deed. A concerned Ann decides not to pass on what her father suspected, namely that the clan chief was Foxy's father, afraid of the impact that this may have on the young parricide. One night Dando, whose sexual frustration has been growing, wakes Ann while he is on watch and tries to persuade her to go apart with him.

Chapter 4: Damask and Milly join the Ixat Instipulators, the group of strolling players that rescued them from the soldiers, and Damask discovers she has a talent for acting. Pnoumi, by now terrified of the older girl, escapes from the caravan and disappears, leaving them in sole possession. When the players put on a show at Millfield they share the stage with a three-piece pop group named *The Posse,* the members of which are looking for a new lead singer, their previous one having succumbed to the lethal effects of an addictive health drink known as Dr Good's Elixir which is imported from the country of Armornia on the other side of the Middle Sea. Damask and their accordionist have a one-night stand. For several weeks the two girls tour with the actors until they receive news that Dando and his companions are travelling along the Northern Drift known in the Valley as the Way of the Shades, a road running through the hills to the west. They are advised to try and rendezvous with them at Formile, but when they get there find that the travellers have left over a week before. Learning that people going north are failing to return, Milly fears for Dando's safety and determines to continue the pursuit, while Damask, who has discovered that the route is not suitable for caravans and who secretly wishes to rejoin the players, refuses to accompany her. They part with a certain amount of acrimony and go their separate ways.

Chapter 5: Yielding to Dando's plea for a night-time tryst Ann casts a sleeping spell over Tallis and Foxy, but once they are alone together, instead of succumbing to his charms spends the time telling him not only of Foxy's origins but about his father's death and who was responsible. Dando's first impulse is for furious retaliation but she appeals to him to carry things no further as there is great wrong on both sides. It is not until two nights later that he prevails on her to come into his arms and they both loose their virginity. Soon the travellers experience their first snowfall of the winter but, despite the cold, from this point on Dando and Ann meet secretly during the times he is supposed to be on watch in order to make love. In the intervals between intercourse she explains her father's belief that the world is sickening because it has been in thrall to the Key for far too long. She also uses magic to heal Dando's voice, enabling him to sing properly for the first time, and teaches him, among other enchantments, to cast the sleeping spell. Having entered an increasingly hilly region and taken a road that leads them to a village called Labour-In-Vain the group discover that the place of the oracle, Toymerle, has been occupied by a bandit known as the Cheetah who specialises in abductions and that those who live along the pilgrim route are planning to recapture thc town. They are enlisted into a makeshift army which is heading for what may possibly turn out to be a small but bloody war.

Chapter 6: Damask, driving Pnoumi's caravan, goes in search of the Stips and on the way stops off to watch an open-air silent movie show. Here she encounters one of her female gypsy friends who tells her that a wedding is about to take place, the bridegroom being her old lover Duke. She visits the Petulengros' camp and tries to persuade him to elope with her but he refuses on the grounds that such a move would start a vendetta between his and the bride's families. Journeying onwards she eventually runs the acting troop to earth but finds there is no longer a place for her within its ranks. She therefore decides that her next port of call will be Vadrosnia Poule and on the way overtakes Pnoumi the Mog who, lacking transport, has been forced to carry just two baskets with him containing a greatly depleted number of cats. As she has always intended she returns his caravan and then continues down river on foot, meaning to take ship *Across-the-Brook* (over the Middle Sea) to Armornia on the continent of Pangorland.

Chapter 7: Milly follows the Northern Drift, the Shady Way, through back country in search of Dando with the aim of warning him that he may be walking into danger, but as she does so misses the turning to Labour-In-Vain that Tallis' party followed and thus, again, diverges from her quarry's route. Frightened by a bear she falls into a river and is swept downstream away from the road. Winning back to solid ground she carries on in the same northerly direction but across uncharted wilderness and eventually, virtually starving, comes upon a ravine blocking her path. Bizarrely she hears the sound of singing floating up over the edge of the cliff and, exercising great caution, creeps forward to investigate.

Chapter 8: The scratch force from Labour-In-Vain which Tallis, Foxy, Ann and Dando have joined travels onwards towards the Place-of-the-Oracle. The troop is led by a local man named Rhys who, as they journey, recounts certain legends concerning the Key and also tells Dando about the bandit brothers known as the Cheetah and the Panther, originally legitimate businessmen but who now make a living through extortion. The Cheetah has occupied the little town they are heading for while the Panther is based on a sea-girt piece of land known as Hungry or The Dark Island. Here he sacrifices captives to some supposedly carnivorous trees, believing that, by so doing, he can secure a safe haven for himself and his gang. The army reaches Toymerle which is already snowbound to find that the man in charge has gone hostage hunting and has left only a small number of gang members behind. Dando and Tallis accompany the Gopher, a member of the shrine's laity, into a maze of tunnels surrounding the underground basilica which is the settlement's main place of worship. They look down from a gallery onto an orgy taking place in the body of the church and see that one of the prisoners is being used for target practice by the outlaws. By speaking through a tube in the rock Dando frightens the bandits into fleeing out of the main door and into the town square where they are bested by Rhys's task force. He then rescues their victim, a twenty-two year old citizen of Drossi named Jack Howgego. Jack has been blinded in revenge for a perceived wrong done to the Cheetah and his brother by the boy's grandfather, a shipping magnate. Dando cares for Jack in one of the ransacked houses and, as the two young men, both from privileged backgrounds, get to know each other, they find they have much in common. They exchange confidences and Jack confesses that he is gay.

Chapter 9: Rhys and his cohorts, along with Tallis, Ann and Foxy (the Nablan has by now acquired a gun from one of the dead robbers) set off in pursuit of the outlaws who have escaped, with the intention of preventing word of the retaking of Toymerle from reaching their leader. Left behind in the settlement Dando keeps house and cooks for Jack while his new found friend goes out and about, learning how to find his way around with the aid of a cane. Tallis, trying to keep up with the others, overtaxes his strength and suffers a minor seizure. Ann helps him back to the town and puts him to bed in a house on the main square where he is looked after by one of the released female prisoners, giving her the opportunity to go in search of Dando. After she finds him they spend the night together before Foxy arrives and reclaims her. The girl, tired of dissembling, confesses to her protector that she still loves Dando and that her feelings are reciprocated. She manages to extract a promise from the

Nablan to the effect that he will not harm the boy, whatever transpires. Jack decides to leave for Drossi with the other kidnap victims but cannot persuade Dando to accompany him, while Tallis, more or less recovered, remembers his desire to consult the oracle. The Gopher tells him that the one who breaths the fumes in the Chamber-of-Breath, by which the god's message is conveyed, must be a priest. Dando, having bccn ordained in Deep Hallow, volunteers. He, Tallis and the Gopher descend to the oracle's chamber where Tallis asks for information concerning the location of the Key. The oracle speaks through a tranced Dando, giving an obscure and ambiguous answer. When they emerge from the basilica Ann recognises that her lover is still in the possession of Rostan. In order to rescue him she enlists the aid of the Earth-Mother, making use, as they make love, of the immortal's powers to expel the Fire-God from his body, but in the process also manages to shield him from the clutches of the summoned deity, thus incurring her wrath. Tallis is determined to continue the journey north and so the travellers prepare to depart. They are advised that the only negotiable pass through the mountains in the dead of winter is the one on the road that reaches the coast near Trincomalee, and that, because of the steepness of some sections of the route, they will have to leave the horses behind in the care of the victorious citizens of Labour-in-Vain.

Chapter 10: One foggy winter's morning Damask arrives at the end of the Green Dolphin Avenue, the causeway into Vadrosnia Poule. She makes her way across to the docks on the other side of town intending to board a ship that will take her over the Middle Sea to the northern continent of Pangorland, but is told that the country of Armornia on the far side of the straights has strict rules governing immigration. Instead she finds lodgings and spends a week sampling the delights of Drossi but in the process runs out of funds. Homeless and penniless she sells herself to a seaman for £12-10s, then falls foul of the local pimp and has to run for her life. She takes refuge in the house of a prosperous city big-wig and by impersonating an acquaintance of the family gains a meal and a bed for the night. The next morning she decides to quit the town but as she is leaving meets some young people who are going to a gig at an event known as the Solstice Festival. On the list of bands appearing she notices one she recognises, namely the Posse who are now backing a singer named Primo. After the concert she makes contact with Matt their drummer and he takes her to a shanty in the slum, built over water, where he was born and raised. Here they smoke reefers and sample Dr Good's Elixir. Damask wakes alone several hours later with a hangover and goes back to the festival site only to find that the entertainment has ended and the participants are already departing. Among the wagons driving away she recognises Pnoumi the Mog's caravan. She follows it down the road and later that day manages to persuade the clown to have sex with her, thus reinstating herself in his affections. On the morrow they take a road leading to the mountains which passes through several small towns, but have not gone far before Damask recognises Milly and Jack coming towards them on horseback.

Chapter 11: The presence of these two unlikely allies is explained by the fact that it was the blind boy who had fallen into the ravine that blocked Milly's path on her journey north. He had come to grief when the party of ex-hostages he was with fled from the Cheetah after meeting him on the road. The black girl rescues Jack and together they make their way to Toymerle only to find it deserted apart from several dead bodies buried beneath the snow. Hoping that Dando and his friends got safely away before the Cheetah returned and the weather worsened they leave to go east, the only route still open, on the two horses Carolus and Mollyblobs that they find abandoned in a small stable behind one of the houses. Descending to lower altitudes they are in the right location and at the right time of day to meet Damask and Pnoumi. Damask assumes command of the little band and under her direction all four set out towards Vadrosnia Poule.

Chapter 12: Tallis' contingent continue their journey northwards through mountainous terrain and steadily deteriorating conditions. Dando is almost out of his mind with impatience and desire because, in these circumstances which entail all the members of the group sleeping in close contact at night in order to conserve body heat, his love-affair with Ann has had to come to an abrupt halt. At the same time Ann is afraid that, as the daughter of the Culdee and having angered the goddess, she is attracting the attention of the immortals and putting not only her own life but also Dando's in danger. In addition she discovers that she is pregnant but confides this to no-one. In fact, instead of sharing her anxieties, she determines to leave as soon as it is feasible to do so. Eventually they come down from the mountains and reach the sea at a small fishing port named Gweek. The ancient wizard Gammadion, going under his street-performer alias of Gubbo the Great - the very same who stole and hid the Key thousands of years before – has come out of the north and crossed to the southern continent, believing, according to an insistent inner voice, that he will prosper there. Meanwhile, at sea, a pirate ship is prowling the coast near Gweek looking for rich pickings. The captain is none other than the Panther who, also on the urging of a voice within his head, decides to turn in towards the insignificant poverty-stricken settlement he sees on shore convinced that its inhabitants are hiding something of value. The travellers find accommodation for the night in one of the houses halfway along Gweek's main street and Dando, once more supposed to be keeping watch, persuades Ann to go up to a wood above the town in order to resume their relationship. After they have made love he falls asleep, giving her the chance to leave him a lock of her hair and take one of his before departing. Later Dando wakes to the smell of smoke and understandably concerned goes to the edge of the wood only to look down on a settlement in the grip of a fierce conflagration!

Chapter 13: Horrified and guilt-ridden, he manages to reach the burning house where he left Tallis and Foxy but discovers no trace of them. Presuming they, as well as his soul-mate, have been taken prisoner by the Panther he steals a boat and, at dawn, sets sail for Hungry Island where he remembers being told the gang have their base. There he spies on the raiders' camp and discovers an underground prison cell in its midst. Once night has fallen he works the sleeping spell that Ann has taught him on the guard and lets himself in through the prison door. He finds no sign of his friends but instead comes upon a young fisher-lad evidently earmarked as the next sacrifice to the trees. Now convinced that all three of his companions have perished along with the rest of Gweek's inhabitants he sets the boy free and takes his place, resigning himself to die when the ceremony of offering transpires two weeks later at the dark of the moon. Meanwhile in Pickwah, the most westerly member of the Seven Sisters League (a federation of city states along the coast of Terratenebra, the southern continent) a lowly lieutenant, Jory Trewithik, has seized power with the intention of carrying out a campaign of conquest. His first foray, he tells his followers, is going to be against the corsairs of Hungry Island in order to appropriate their ill-gotten gains and with this end in view he has recruited a bevy of magic-workers to deal with the threat of the man-eating trees. When time for the sacrifice arrives Dando is hung from a branch in the sacred grove, a heavy rock tied to his feet. By nightfall he is close to death but in his delirium hears a voice telling him that the task is not yet complete and that he must live to atone for his fault. For a long time Aigea has been determined to kill him and it is due to her wiles that he has come to this pass. Pyr, however, the Master-of-Winds, is opposed to her stratagem, believing that the boy will be more use to them alive at this stage. He raises a fierce storm which sweeps across the island felling trees, including those reputed to eat flesh. The next morning Trewithik's troops, who call themselves Axemen, invade, route the pirates and discover the sacrificial victim still in the land of the living although badly injured. They take him with them when they leave.

Chapter 14: During the Panther's raid on Gweek Foxy and Tallis had actually awoken just as the cottage they are occupying is about to be consumed by fire. They escape to the coast through smugglers' tunnels and then, with other villagers, make their way via a steep path to the neighbouring village of Praa. Ann, after leaving her lover an hour or two before the pirates' arrival, collects her things from the house where the others are sleeping and then climbs to the coastal highway, turning westward. At first light she encounters Gammadion walking in the opposite direction. As already stated he is acting according to an idea planted in his brain by Aigea which suggests he will encounter something on the road to his advantage. Despite the fact that her suspicions are aroused, mainly on account of the strange pendant in the shape of a manikin that he wears around his neck, Ann falls victim to his enchantments and is forced to tell him about her companions and the purpose of Tallis' quest. As a result Gammadion lays curses on both Tallis and Dando. Having arrived in Praa after an exhausting climb along the intervening cliffs, the refugees from Gweek, plus the two strangers, are provided with a meal by the locals, but just as he is being served Tallis falls to the ground, struck down by another stroke, this time a major one. Milly, Jack, Damask and Pnoumi, on their way to Drossi, discover that a circus tent has been erected on the outskirts of the city in place of the turn-of-the-year Solstice Festival and, the next day, Pnoumi and his cats join the show with Milly as assistant. On the evening of their arrival Jack takes the two girls to a nightclub called the Green Goat where they meet a singer and ex-movie star from Armornia named Becca. She offers them lodging at her rooming house. Damask, keen on continuing her acting career, gets a part with an avant-guard theatre company while Jack, who discovers that his mother committed suicide when she was falsely told that he had died, returns to the rackety existence he had been leading before his kidnapping. Soon their paths no longer cross and Damask learns that he is living in his grandfather's palace on the Grand Canal.

Chapter 15: The truth of the matter is that Jack has been abducted for a second time. The wealthy shipping magnate, Hiram Howgego, worried about how rumours of his past treatment of his grandson are affecting business, determines that they will present a united front to the world. Jack is captured and kept under lock and key in the mansion of Non Pareille. Once a month he is paraded before the townsfolk, his good behaviour guaranteed by threats of incarceration in an insane asylum. Jack manages to escape this *durance vile* by diving out of a window at night into the canal while most of the palace's occupants are absent at a banquet. He purloins a boat and drifts out to sea, ending up on a spit of land further along the coast where most of the town's rubbish washes ashore. In Praa Foxy and Tallis outstay their welcome. Tallis, although severely disabled by his stroke, is showing some signs of improvement. The mayor gives Foxy an old bath chair in which to transport the invalid and they set out eastward, the Nablan with the intention of encountering Dando and exacting revenge for his treachery in abandoning them to the fire. The country they pass through is too poverty-stricken to provide much sustenance and the mode of travel they are forced to employ imposes a severe strain on Tallis' health. When they reach a coastal manor house on an estate entitled Witteridge Acres and see an advert for an under-gardener pinned to the gate Foxy decides to apply. By this time Ann, increasingly burdened by her pregnancy and still in Gammadion's power, has lost all hope of rescue. The wizard has designs on her baby and, taking her with him, sets out for Drossi where, according to the promise still echoing in his scull, he is going to make his fortune. However, when he arrives, he finds that the magic workers Trewithik enlisted for his campaign of conquest and then abandoned when they were no longer needed have got there ahead of him and queered his pitch. He decides to travel further east and return later.

Chapter16: Aigea is furious with the Sky-Father for saving Dando. He explains his reasons for going against her will. At the end of three weeks the boy wakes from a coma to discover he is in a fortress high above the Axemen's stronghold of Pickwah, and being looked after by an old woman known as Squinancy. At first reluctant to re-enter the land of the living he overhears a snatch of conversation informing him that most of the inhabitants of Gweek escaped the fire and realises that therefore his friends may still be alive. His immediate desire is to set out to look for them but he is in no fit state to do so. In fact, as a result of Gammadion's curse, his lower left leg has become gangrenous and is amputated below the knee by an Armornian doctor, Raymond Spoon, using as anaesthetic Dr Good's Super Strength Elixir. The members of Trewithik's army, preparing to set out on further campaigns, feel, superstitiously, that Dando, having been given to the trees, is bringing them bad luck while he remains in their midst. Squinancy, afraid of what their leader may do if he is influenced by this belief, helps her patient to leave. She provides him with crutches and arranges a passage on a ship called the Cormorant which is sailing to Drossi. First, however, he is encouraged to consult Trewithik's seer who tells him that to fulfil his karma it is his duty to go *Over-the-Brook* to the northern continent. Far from well enough to embark on any such demanding journey, Dando nevertheless boards the Cormorant after Squinancy gives him a bottle of Dr Good's which she has already been administering to counter the agonising cramps that afflict him at night as a consequence of the physical trauma he has suffered. The ship is only a short way into its voyage when he is accused of being a *Jonah* by the master and put ashore.

Chapter 17: Dando struggles eastward on foot, making for Gweek, but soon falls foul of a den of thieves who destroy one of his crutches and rob him of his warm clothing, money and pack which contains the tincture on which he depends. Trying to exist by begging he reaches the town of Osh where he steals a bottle of Dr Good's Elixir Strength 5 from a patent medicine stall. He is arrested, whipped and spends a night in the cells. In the morning he is handed his crutch, boot and belt but also, as a result of some administrative muddle, the elixir he stole. Carrying on he is overtaken by crowds of refugees fleeing from the Axemen's advance. He finds that life as a crippled and penniless hobo is a much harsher business than it was for a privileged son of a powerful clan chief and he suffers his fair share of persecution and ill-treatment. It is only his helpmeet Dr Good's that enables him to stay true to his purpose although its regular use is causing him to become more and more addicted. On the brink of collapse he is given a night's lodging by a kindly farmer and his wife. Although they offer him permanent sanctuary he insist on continuing his journey and, once back on the road, it is not long before the drug runs out and then withdrawal symptoms kick in with a vengeance. At the absolute end of his tether he arrives on the quayside of a small harbour town where he hears a sailor aboard one of the moored ships playing a shanty on a penny whistle. Miracle of miracles, it is his friend Jack Howgego who, as soon as he recognises Dando's voice, comes ashore and enfolds him in an embrace.

Chapter 18: The rampaging Pickwah army manages to take Osh but Trewithik realises that he will need more men to have any hope of doing the same when they reach Vadrosnia Poule. It is at this juncture that the Cheetah, the outlaw from Toymerle, arrives and offers to bring reinforcements in exchange for the release of his brother, the Panther, who has been held prisoner since the Hungry Island episode. Foxy is employed as under gardener on the Witteridge Estate and finds that the work is greatly to his liking. In fact horticulture soon becomes his passion and supplants most of the ideas of revenge and revolution that up to now have obsessed him. Tallis meanwhile is in despair because of his incapacity, feeling all hope of continuing his quest has ended. By this time the eighth new moon of the year has entered the sky. Milly returns to Drossi after participating in a circus tour up river, minus Pnoumi but with one of his cats, a little seal-pointed creature called Meena perched on her shoulder. Not long after this, when putting up posters around the town for her theatre company, Damask stumbles upon the Great Gubbo's magic show and recognises Ann, now not far off her time. With Milly's help she manages to rescue the girl and they take her back to Becca's house. When Gammadion follows, Becca shuts the door against him. He returns at night and, standing outside, lays a curse on both the mother-to-be and her baby. As a result Ann goes into a violent and protracted labour which threatens to end her life.

Chapter 19: Jack abandons his budding maritime career and takes Dando under his wing. As they carry on towards Gweek he helps him through the symptoms caused by the withdrawal of Dr Good's. Because he has fallen in love with the boy he is eager to start a physical relationship and Dando, although initially repelled, is persuaded by feelings of gratitude and pity to allow the intimacies. One night the dog Ralph appears. At first Dando hopes that his long-time companions are also nearby but this proves not to be the case. Journeying eastwards, finding food becomes a problem. When they reach a small town where a marriage is about to take place Jack suggests that they crash the wedding breakfast. The meal is followed by dancing and Dando, who has always had a talent for the terpsichorean art, feels profound regret that he cannot take part. Jack encourages the boy to try some moves telling him he is going to make him practice until he becomes *the best bloody one-legged dancer this side of the Middle Sea.* In due course they arrive in Gweek and discover that Tallis and Foxy stayed at Praa for three and a half weeks but have now left. Somebody mentions the Witteridge Estate. By this time the whole country is on the move, fleeing before the Pickwah army, and there is a feeling of lawlessness and anarchy in the air. On the road again the two young men camp near yet another small town where they are caught in the act of kissing by a patrol man. He insists on taking them back to his command post which is crowded with local militia. It is just getting light as Jack is condemned to a day in the pillory for *corrupting civic morals* while Dando is left to the mercy of the off-duty vigilantes.

Chapter 20: That same evening Jack is told by the men who release him that they have given his *rent boy* a *good seein' to.* He goes in search of his friend and eventually, with Ralph's help, stumbles across him outside the town. For many hours Dando will not speak or allow any physical contact until Jack breaks through the wall he has erected by telling him he is not alone in his suffering, that he has undergone similar abuse in the past, both in a Drossi back alley and at Toymerle. He tries to get the boy to communicate and is encouraged when he eventually breaks down and, weeping, starts to talk. They continue on to the Witteridge Estate and find Foxy and Tallis in situ. Dando kneels before his half-brother and, in retaliation for what happened at Gweek, Foxy, ignoring his promise to Ann, smashes his gun across the other's face, breaking his nose, but in so doing settles the differences between them to the satisfaction of both. The Lord of the Manor, Witteridge of Witteridge Acres, appears on the scene and, recognising in Dando one of his own kind, arranges for his nurse to treat the boy's damaged face; he also invites the newcomers to accompany him a fortnight later when he moves to Drossi. Despite his injuries, Dando takes over the knight's care and, as a result, Tallis' growing awareness of his squire's worth increases by leaps and bounds. Also, on Jack's urging, the young man continues to practise his dancing which helps counter the feelings of intense worthlessness that now frequently sweep over him. After two weeks have passed the whole household sets out and, a short distance down the road, encounters an undisciplined rabble calling themselves *The Kymer Volunteers*; this amateur army has been formed with the intention of confronting the Axemen. Foxy immediately decides to join them.

Chapter 21: At Becca's house Ann's baby has not yet been born and a doctor, the best in Drossi, tells them he cannot save both mother and child – it will have to be one or the other. The girl, on being asked to decide, makes clear she is willing to sacrifice herself and the medic performs an operation with Becca's help. Afterwards Milly and Damask enter the sick room to say goodbye and hear Ann, with her last breath, give the baby the name Horace. As her life drains away she sees Tom, her father, standing by the bed. He tells her it is time for her to come *Over-the-Brook* and become *a dancer,* on this occasion meaning to take the next evolutionary step which should be the fate of the whole human race if it were not for the malign influence of the Key. Holding his hand, she goes through the *Change* and passes over into a new physical state, leaving her mortal remains behind. The army from Pickwah is now less than two weeks away from the Delta City causing many of its citizens to flee up country. Becca tries to find a wet-nurse for Horry but without success. In the end Damask puts the baby to her own breast and within a day is producing milk. They soon discover that the youngster is developing far faster than normal. Becca is familiar with the type of curse Gammadion has employed and realises that it will cause the child to become old before his time. The Witteridge contingent enters Drossi and arrives at the Lord of the Manor's pied-a-terre. In order to help Dando forget what has happened to him Jack takes him to the Green Goat where the boy performs his dance routine to much acclaim. Later they go on to Becca's house and Dando learns that Ann has died giving birth. The shock causes him to pass out. His last words before he temporarily loses consciousness are *So I killed her after all.* The next day the volunteer army that was intending to halt the Axemen's advance returns, having been defeated, and a wounded Foxy appears on Becca's doorstep. The group of friends decide that their only hope of survival lies in going down to the docks in order to obtain a passage across the Middle Sea. Meanwhile the enemy arrives and starts shelling the town. Amid scenes of mass panic the women, plus the baby, are allowed to board a clipper named Diamond while the men are turned away. Gammadion however, concealed in the crowd, does manage to embark. Jack leads his male friends out onto the dykes of the delta where he remembers an old barge is moored that he used to visit as a teenager. Our travellers and a crowd of other refugees, including the Posse and a group of Roma, board this venerable craft and put to sea. As darkness falls it begins to fill with water and they are only saved from drowning by the arrival of a luxury liner - the Behemoth. This vessel stops to pick up the barge's passengers having been directed towards them by Ann, whose powers to protect Dando have now greatly increased, and her father. Dando himself is reluctant to quit the sinking ship as he is afraid of what may await him on the Northern Continent but eventually does so for Ralph's sake because the dog will not leave him.

Intolerable,
The fire that love engenders,
Yet without it we would not exist.

Chapter one

"How do I look?" enquired Becca, anxiously adjusting her dress and pulling her jacket down. "Who'd have believed they wouldn't have such a thing as a smoothing iron on board?"

"You look triffic, just the ticket," Milly reassured her. Damask gave a cursory nod; she was more concerned about the baby Horry's welfare than the impression they were likely to make when they arrived at their destination.

"I've radioed ahead to the Rytardenath Port Authorities," one of the ship's officers told them, "they know you're coming."

"I must look the best for my public," insisted the showgirl, full of first-night nerves.

The Diamond's compliment had been gratified to realise that they had a celebrity in their midst. They made much of Becca and because of her past fame ensured that there was no unpleasantness when it came to granting permission for the rest of her party to land in Armornia.

"These are my personal assistants," she had stated firmly to the immigration official who came on board to check the new arrivals. "They are in my employ and are an essential part of my entourage."

Milly was continually worrying about the ones who had been left behind.

"Wot's 'appened to the Lordship," she asked "an' the three other geezers do you think?"

"I guess they got on another boat," replied Becca consolingly "we'll see them again soon. When I left home," she continued, " I closed up the house above Pleasure Beach and handed it over to a security firm. There won't be any problems when we get back."

"And when was that?" asked Damask.

"Not all that long ago." Becca's reply was given with an air of stating the obvious, yet at the same time she appeared vaguely uncomfortable.

The egress was cleared, the gangway extended and the show girl walked forward to accept the adulation that was her due. She came to a halt at the top of the ramp, taken aback by what met her eyes.

"Oh," she breathed.

To greet her on the quayside stood just a handful of middle-aged and elderly townsfolk making up in enthusiasm for what they lacked in numbers. It was not the welcome she had been expecting but, in the best traditions of show-business, she thrust out her magnificent bosom, placed one hand on her egg-timer waist and in the other waved a dainty handkerchief towards her fans.

"Hi folks," she called.

Damask, holding Horry, and Milly carrying Meena's basket followed her off the ship and stood waiting patiently while she greeted each admirer individually. Then, having asked regally of the man standing next to her, "Hail me a cab, dear," she disappeared with her luggage and the two girls into the horseless carriage that drew up, re-emerging to blow kisses out of the window as the vehicle drove away.

"Well, I suppose we gave them pretty short notice," she remarked plaintively to Damask and Milly as soon as they were on the road, "one shouldn't count one's chickens," and to the driver, "Decatur Drive honey – the shore end."

Dando, who, not long since, would have been able to claim the title of the Lord Dan Addo until disinherited by his father, leant on the taffrail of the great ship Behemoth and gazed back over the expanse of sea they had already crossed and into the past. On one side of him was propped the crutch that had become an essential part of his everyday existence since his left foot had been amputated by the doctor in Pickwah Fortress; on the other his master Tallis sat slumped fast asleep in a wheelchair. He knew that if he turned his head he would see, some way behind him, his half brother Everard Tetherer Trooly, commonly known as Foxy, perched high on a cabin roof busily scratching an intricate pattern onto the wood of his long bow, an anachronistic weapon in the setting of this steam driven vessel. Next to Dando's one remaining foot lay the large shaggy shape of the dog Ralph, far removed from the sights and smells with which he was familiar, but content to endure this alien environment so long as he could stay close to the one he revered. Of the fifth member of their party, Jack Howgego, there was no sign. Although robbed of his sight, this ever curious, ever restless young man had probably discovered, in the short space of time they had been on board, more about the workings of the huge luxury liner that had picked them up than his more able companions would have done throughout the whole course of the voyage. He might be anywhere among her many decks and promenades, making new contacts, poking his nose behind the scenes, metaphorically learning the ropes.

If our watcher had chosen to look north into the grey distance across the gently rippling sea he would have been able to distinguish a low coastline passing slowly by as the ship ploughed westward towards her destination. This shore had been in sight for the last three days but had barely changed in appearance throughout that period. Its hazy outline gave no hint as to what lay beyond apart from the fact that the occasional vaguely geometric shape suggested that the land was not uninhabited. Instead Dando turned his gaze downwards to the foaming wake being generated about forty feet below him and thought of Ann. Annie, his darling, his heart's ease, the other half of him, was dead; she had died giving birth to their child and every morning when he awoke he had to face up to the knowledge that he had been one of the wretches who had contributed to her demise. She was gone and now he was homeless indeed and would be for the rest of his life: she would never again lie in his arms nor he in hers. Not that it would have been possible for them to have lived together as man and wife, as he had once hoped, even if she had survived. Since their parting something had happened to him on the road during one endless day, something unclean, which he tried to dismiss from his mind because remembering the violation robbed him of any desire to go on. He was afraid now that if he touched anyone in a certain way he would pass on the defilement he had suffered and as a consequence must avoid intimate human contact. It seemed that, in the future, a solitary life was to be his lot.

He had not even had the chance to bid her farewell. As a result of their precipitate exit from the Delta City he had been prevented from going to where she lay. He should have crossed over to this Cemetery Island, Vadrosnia Poule's necropolis, and found her resting place; he should have been allowed to stand next to the structure in which she was interred, press his lips against it and weep for the happiness that was never to be, for the unfulfilled dreams, for the life with all its promise brought to a premature end, to weep until he lost the will to live through yet another interminable day. Instead he had run away to save his own unworthy hide. But yet there had been no choice. Back at the castle in Deep Hallow he had bound himself as servant to the man who sat at that moment asleep beside him; he had vowed to be faithful until he was released. Once already he had broken that promise. Now there was no question but that he must remain true to his word and put the other's needs and desires before his own. If Tallis, a man with the vague bearing of a knight errant from the old days, intended to cross the sea then Dando must go across the sea; if his master was looking for some mysterious object known as *The Key* then Dando must help him in every way possible however hopeless the search might be; if Dando had himself been set a task to perform on the northern continent then that undertaking must be elbowed aside in order to defer to his more important duty. A few days earlier when the huge ship on which they had embarked hove to beside their little floundering vessel he had felt a great reluctance to set foot on the ladder to safety, but had he remained below and committed himself to the waves he would have again reneged on his vow and that in itself would have been a betrayal.

In the midst of these meditations he was suddenly startled by a silvery scale being played on a pipe close to his ear. Jack had crept up behind him and was insisting on breaking into his sombre reverie; the blind boy seemed to have an uncanny ability to locate people in his dark world and to sense their state of mind.

"Come on, my bird," he cried after seguing into the first few bars of a lively hornpipe, "this brooding isn't good for you – snap out of it - stop your moping and stand up straight. It's time to dance."

The Behemoth, making her way back from a round-the-world cruise, was packed to the gunwales with her full compliment of holiday makers. She had been completely booked up months before the date of embarkation and there was not a single spare cabin to accommodate the war victims from the Delta City who had fled the fighting taking place in Terratenebra. In order not to inconvenience his more valued guests the captain had had an awning erected over a section of the third class deck and it was here that the refugees were expected to sleep. Fortunately the weather remained mild and the sea relatively calm. They were warned not to go below or mingle with the fare-paying passengers – a rule immediately flouted by Jack. Now the Vadrosnian led Dando to an uncluttered area at the front of the ship and urged him to begin his daily dancing practice. As the one-legged young man steeled himself to face the physical rigours that this demonstration demanded and launched into the elaborate sequence that he himself had choreographed, crowds of people jostled for position along the rails of the upper decks in order to look down on the spectacle. Word had quickly spread that a curious and original form of entertainment was on offer each morning during these last few days of their vacation. The voyagers had become jaded by the Behemoth's thirty-piece orchestra and her famous artistes; they had tired of the nightly dinner-dances which by now had become almost routine; the health spas, beauty parlours and fifty-foot swimming pool had also lost their charm. In contrast, here below them they witnessed a complete novelty. Not only had they never seen such dancing in their lives before but to see it executed by a performer who evinced no embarrassment in flaunting his disability before the world was a definite first. This boy from the Dark Continent with his unmentionable missing foot and single old-fashioned crutch, his unwashed hair and shabby clothes must either be very brave to run such a risk or else very stupid. Well perhaps he stood a chance of getting away with it out here at sea so long as nobody spilled the beans once the ship arrived in port.

As soon as Jack, Dando and Ralph disappeared forward, Foxy, the Nablan, climbed down from his perch and took their place by the rail. He had been turning over something in his mind ever since his return to Vadrosnia Poule after defeat in battle and he saw this as a good opportunity to solve the mystery. Tallis was still deeply asleep, his chin sunk on his chest. The old bath chair that had been his means of transport for several months had finally given up the ghost as Jack and Foxy lifted it up the ladder from the sailing barge on which they had escaped from Drossi. Once on board the Behemoth a steward offered them the use of a far superior conveyance.

"It's the only one we have," he told them, unfolding a state-of-the-art wheelchair. "We don't get much call for that kind of thing; we keep it just for emergencies. You're welcome to use it while it's not needed elsewhere. I presume the gentleman is only temporarily incapacitated?"

Foxy whistled loudly and tunelessly for a while without result. Giving up on this means of waking the sleeper he directed one or two well aimed kicks to the underside of the chair's footrests. This produced the desired effect. Jarred throughout his body Tallis lifted his chin and gazed blearily at the red-headed Nablan.

"Where's my squire?" he slurred.

Foxy jerked his head in the direction of the bow.

"Wi' that jessie up at the front o' the ship. Prancin' aroun' as usual."

"I need to relieve myself," complained Tallis, a querulous note in his voice. With a bad grace Foxy wheeled him to the heads and then, when they returned to the deck, brought up the subject that had been troubling him.

"Who be the father o' the Glept-woman's sprog?" he asked.

In the mad panic to evacuate Drossi in the midst of a bombardment by the Pickwah Army the female members of their small collective had been allowed to board one of the few ships prepared to give refugees a lift to the northern continent while the male members had been turned away. Left behind they had subsequently made their escape on the leaky old barge Gloriosa which had been about to sink and dump them in the drink when the Behemoth put in a fortuitous appearance. Where Becca, Milly, the infant Horry and Damask, the child's surrogate parent, were by now they had no idea.

Tallis looked at Foxy with complete incomprehension.

"I don't know what you mean," he said.

"I mean the one they call the Lady Damask." Foxy spat out the title contemptuously. "Who be the father o' her chil'?"

"Oh, you mean my squire's sister," replied Tallis, seeing the light. "No, you're wrong – it's not her child."

Foxy looked surprised. "Whose be it then?" he asked.

"Why poor Hilda's of course. Damask is looking after it because Hilda passed away. Very sad."

Foxy was dumbfounded. "Passed away? She be dead?"

"Yes, she died giving birth."

The powerful Nablan swung round and walked to the other side of the poop where he stood for sometime, his back turned, staring out to sea. Eventually he retraced his steps, a set expression on his face.

"It were he weren't it – he be the father."

"My squire? Yes. During our journey they were having relations. We didn't realise."

Foxy's normally freckled face became almost puce with fury. He opened his mouth but no sound emerged while his hands balled themselves into fists.

It was just at this moment that Jack and Dando came into view, making their way back along the deck, Jack's arm around his friend's waist to support him; as usual the boy was near to collapse after his tremendous balletic effort. Seeing Foxy standing next to Tallis Dando was reminded of some unfinished business. Ever since, in Drossi, he had had to accept the fact of Ann's death and his own part in it, he had been aware that Foxy, her long-time protector, should be told what had happened and that the account ought to come from him. As yet though he had not plucked up the courage to make a confession. Now one look at Foxy's face informed him that he had left it too late; the other already knew the truth. He realised he might have only minutes to live.

"Hilda. It be you that murdered her." His accuser spoke in a level expressionless voice, blue eyes filled with hate. "She died acos o' you."

"Yes, it was me," replied Dando quietly, "you can do as you please."

Foxy put his hand inside his jacket and took hold of his gun. But then Jack stepped between the two adversaries, Glept and Nablan, and spoke as only he was emotionally detached enough to do.

"Hang on a minute, you two!" he cried, arms held out to create a barrier and head turned towards Foxy, "don't you see you stupid man, you both loved her, but he loved her longer than you! And she loved him – they loved each other right from the start. It wasn't his fault she died. If you want to shoot anyone shoot me – he's suffered enough!"

The Nablan pushed him roughly aside and stared at Dando. Of his own choosing he had joined the forces ranged against the Pickwah Army. He had fought on the losing side and known the bitter taste of defeat. During the struggle horrific images had been indelibly printed on his brain. He had seen men riddled with bullets but still alive, men blown limb from limb by shells; he had witnessed fighters blinded but otherwise apparently unscathed and others coughing blood after breathing noxious fumes from cannisters that the Axemen lobbed into their lines. It came home to him that the youth in front of him, with his mutilations and physical debility, his truncated limb and single battered crutch resembled nothing so much as one of those wounded soldiers he had seen retreating from the fighting. The Glept had also been wounded, it appeared, but on a different kind of battlefield; the boy was engaged in some form of private conflict which was beyond Foxy's comprehension. There was something else that he could not ignore. Jack's words had started an echo in his mind, an echo from the past. *I know him all my life. We drink the same milk as babes. I knowd him longer than I knowd you. He were my sweetheart Foxy – I love he an' he love me an' he need me more 'n you do.* It was Hilda's voice that he heard. *Promise me you won't do he no harm* she had said. He had promised. Dando had abandoned his post at Gweek and consequently both he and Tallis had come close to being burnt to death, but he, Foxy, had also been guilty of bad faith, as evinced by the yellowing bruises on the boy's face; in his determination to wreak vengeance he had deliberately and knowingly ignored his pledge. It could not be denied that they had both broken their word. Then he became aware of something else which up to now he had refused to acknowledge: that, although pierced to the heart by his loss, he was not the only one bereft. *They loved each other right from the start.* Could that really be true? He got a sudden inkling of what the girl's death must mean to Dando. Turning on his heel he walked away.

A couple of days passed and the attention of all aboard the Behemoth was focused forward. The city of Rytardenath had come into view on the starboard bow and everyone crowded towards that side of the ship to get a glimpse of it. The refugees were told by a helpful crew member that they were viewing the greatest of all the conurbations to be found along the shores of the Middle Sea. "Ry-town's the governor," the man averred, "bigger 'n all the rest of the Albercreek towns put together." They had to take his word for it because the faint blurry smudge in the far distance appeared no more than a vague collection of vertical needles, the tallest towards the centre. It was only after several hours that these columns solidified into recognisably man-made structures: enormous buildings mounting far into the sky. As the ship closed with the land their size was emphasized by the minute but frenetic activity taking place at ground level. Tiny vehicles buzzed to and fro along the shoreline and a long string of linked carriages slid smoothly away around a headland. High above their heads the outlines of the giants faded and merged together as if lacking substance, for a widespread miasma hung over the city. In and out of the shadows and fog, well clear of the ground, little buzzing dragonfly-like creatures swooped hither and yon, some flying out over the ship; the southerners had never seen the like. Rubbish floated just below the surface of the waves and a low-level continuous roar crossed the intervening space from the heart of the city; the sheer presence of the place was overwhelming. The Behemoth reduced speed and made her approach with understandable caution for the sea was littered with numerous hazards both mobile and stationary. Between ship and shore several mammoth three-legged structures stood in deep water, one supporting a tower with revolving blades, another a flame-topped chimney which was contributing to the pollution. The liner slowed almost to a stop, waiting for a minute pilot boat to chug fussily out to meet her. Other boats also came to escort the returning prodigal into her home port - there were several workmanlike tugs, fire tenders shooting spouts of water high into the air and tourist boats full of goggle-eyed sightseers. The voyagers' ears were continually assaulted by a cacophony of horns and sirens from anchored vessels, but it was not until a smaller passenger ship passed by that the Behemoth deigned to deafen them with a greeting in her own resounding bass.

Two wide stretches of water to the east and west, probably river mouths, marked the city centre's boundaries and it was for one of these that the liner headed. On her way into harbour she skirted an island on which stood a massive gilded statue, several stories high, in the form of an animal supported on three feet, one forepaw raised in a threatening gesture, its jaws open in a snarl.

"Fanged tiger," said the same informative mariner, "Ry-Town's emblem. There's said to be a few still living wild in the forests to the west. Doesn't look exactly friendly does it."

The travellers stood staring in silence at the panorama, lost for words, as the ship approached her berth. Slowly the land closed around them, the great buildings enveloped them in shadows and the metropolis took them to its heart. Finally Foxy grunted, "Who would ha' thought it."

"Amazing," replied Dando in a low unemphatic tone.

Tallis just gazed up silently at the soaring skyscrapers, a blank slightly stunned look on his face as if he could hardly give them credence.

"Do you have any cash?" asked Damask, wondering how they were to pay the taxi fare.

"Sure, I've got a few dollars stashed away. Just remembered to bring them along at the last minute. The Heights are a swell place. You'll be smitten if it's anything like it was in the old days. Beach parties – soirées that last till morning – all day levees – there wasn't much that the folks didn't get up to, what with one thing and another."

"Why did you leave?"

"Well there was a situation developing that was making me nervous – and I'd just split up with my ex. Yes, that was it – unhappy love affair – needed to get away."

The high-rise blocks were gradually left behind as Becca's party progressed westward and, after crossing a bridge, they found themselves passing through leafy suburbs boasting wealthy-looking ranch-style houses spreading themselves beneath venerable trees in the midst of extensive grounds. The car had been gradually climbing since they left the city centre. Eventually they reached a point where it turned away from streets mounting to an even higher elevation in order to follow a long straight road on the left that ran down towards the sea. Having descended for about a mile and a half the show girl directed the driver away from this avenue into a small almost rural lane and after a few twists and turns they came to a gate. What lay beyond was hidden behind an extensive wall of bushes.

"Here we are," she said, paying off the cab man. "Home sweet home. Garden's gone a bit wild I'm afraid."

A bit wild was an understatement; they had literally to fight their way between vegetation that met across the drive before they came in sight of the house. When Becca caught a glimpse of her property she stumbled to a dismayed halt.

"Oh, my lord!" she cried, "what in the world's happened?"

The building, an imposing colonial mansion, still displayed signs of faded glory. The entrance, sporting a pillared portico, was very grand and, because the house boasted an extensive third story situated in the roof space, it appeared superior to others in the neighbourhood, but the general impression was of dilapidation. The windows were boarded up, the paint stained and peeling; the tiles had been colonised by moss while drainpipes and guttering could be seen to be in poor repair. When Becca went to open the front door and got out a key she found it swinging loose on its hinges.

"Looks like your security guards haven't been doing their job," remarked Damask.

"I guess I've been away longer than I realised," admitted the crestfallen star.

"Ooer," Milly contributed.

"I think Jack may have already visited this coast when he was crewing aboard the merchantman," said Dando, looking around the ship for his friend.

"Yes – but we didn't go ashore – strictly forbidden."

Jack had materialised beside the small group of migrants after yet another of his forays below decks and he now caught hold of Dando's arm in an attempt to pull him towards the top of a stairwell.

"Come on lad – we can't hang around here – we've got to make ourselves scarce before they round us up and chuck us in clink."

"What do you mean?"

"I mean we've got to get off this ship."

"Well shouldn't we wait and go with the others?"

"Do you want to be banged up for maybe six months or more and then deported at the end of the day?" asked Jack. "They're not going to welcome you with open arms you know. These guys I've met," he continued, addressing Foxy who had also returned, "have offered to get us off through the crew's entrance, but we must go now. Can you see the Posse anywhere around? Tip them the wink plus anyone else you feel needs a hand-up and tell them to get in line."

His vehemence persuaded the others that he knew what he was talking about. Tallis was helped out of his chair which was then folded and carried by Foxy while Jack supported the knight - *knight* being by now Tallis' established nickname - with an arm round his waist as he had often supported Dando along the many miles of road they had travelled together. They headed away from the open air, descending deeper and deeper into the ship. The members of the Posse, a three-piece band from the Delta City and old friends of Jack's, fell in behind, along with some Roma who also seemed to have got the message. The blind boy held his cane in his right hand and ran it along the walls and openings as they progressed downwards, his lips counting silently.

So that's how he finds his way around, thought Dando.

They passed through a door marked *Private* and then through another labelled *Crew members - 3rd and 4th rank – no admittance.* Eventually they came to a halt in a corridor filled with taciturn men, and a few women, all standing waiting patiently. One or two shot them inquisitive glances. A muscular individual appeared close beside Jack and put his hand familiarly on the boy's shoulder at the same time giving the thumbs-up sign.

"All arranged," he confided, "I've handed over the sweetener. They'll turn a blind eye."

"That's great Pedro," said Jack somewhat ironically, "I'll reciprocate."

When the man had gone Dando asked, "Have you paid money Jack – your own money?"

"What do you think I've been doing while you were lazing around on deck? I had a lucky streak – there's always a game going on in these places if you can run it to earth."

"You've been gambling? But how can you gamble if you can't see?"

Jack grinned. "Wouldn't you like to know!"

In due course a hatch was opened ahead of them and the sounds and the smells of the city wafted in on a faint breeze. The waiting deck-hands filed out onto a descending ramp followed by the travellers and from thence into a tender which ferried them across to a remote landing well away from the main debarking area. As the transport hove-to beside a vertical ladder fixed to a concrete wall the crew members took it in turns to climb the rungs and disappear over the top. Foxy went ahead with the wheelchair across his shoulders when it was time for the travellers to take their turn leaving Jack to give Tallis a bunk up and also lift Ralph onto the quay. For the second time since leaving Vadrosnia Poule Dando hesitated, seemingly reluctant to make the transition from ship to shore. "Where are you?" cried Jack. "Come on lad, you're holding things up."

Dando put his arm through the top of his crutch, took hold of a metal hand rail and heaved himself several feet onto solid ground. As his foot made contact with concrete something grabbed his attention and caused him to stop dead.

"Did you feel that?" he said to the others.

"Feel what?" replied Jack.

"The earth – it moved."

Jack doubled over with ribald laughter. Almost within reach barges piled high with huge lumps of some sort of mineral were being unloaded and lorries full of goods from the docks were pounding to and fro impelled not by horses but by internal combustion engines that emitted clouds of smoke into the atmosphere through funnel-shaped exhausts.

"Lucky you!" he said, and then, "Of course it moved, you nitwit. It couldn't not move with all this going on."

"No – I felt it tremble – like up at Judd's Hill that time. When Attack took fright."

"All it means is that you haven't got your land legs yet. Pay it no mind."

Foxy unfolded the wheelchair and gestured for Tallis to seat himself. Dando, bringing his attention back to practicalities, raised an objection.

"Don't you think we ought to return the chair - it's not ours."

Jack snorted in exasperation.

"Oh, for crying out loud birdy," he expostulated, "give us a break! How do you think we're going to take the knight along with us? Are you offering to carry him over your shoulder?"

"I can walk," said Tallis stiffly.

"No you can't. Not at the pace we're going to set. We've got to make ourselves scarce pretty damn quick - we've got to lose ourselves in this warren before the powers-that-be realise we've done a runner."

The three members of the Posse, also having disembarked, were standing nearby talking amongst themselves. Now Winnie, the group's founder, grabbed Jack's arm.

"We're gonna split man – take our chances. Hope to catch you later."

"Right you are," replied Jack, "next time we cross paths I expect to see your names up in lights. Best of luck."

He shook hands, lingering over his farewell to Fynn, the young fluffy-haired saxophonist. Matt the drummer and now lead singer nodded briefly from under his hood and then the three of them crossed the busy road and melted into the crowds on the other side.

"Come on," said Jack, "we'd better follow their example and make ourselves scarce."

They set off inland, swinging round the first corner they came to in order to get out of sight of the ship.

When Becca, Damask and Milly propped open the house's front door and penetrated the gloom of the hall the first thing that reached their ears was an ominous scuttling sound. Dust lay thick over everything and cobwebs brushed their faces. Numerous empty bottles littered the floor and there was an unpleasant smell of rotting organic matter.

"Where are my things?" cried Becca wandering from room to room like someone bereft. All that remained on the ground floor were a few broken-down bits of furniture. Upstairs the situation was slightly better. There were beds and, by some miracle, only one mattress had been seriously stained; the place at least seemed dry. Damask claimed a bedroom for herself and Horry and set about giving the baby a feed; breast milk was no longer all that was required; although less than four weeks old the child was already showing an interest in solid food. Becca pulled herself together and lifted her chin in a determined manner.

"Come on girls," she said, "why should we be beat by a bit of dirt? My mama wouldn't have let it get her down. She faced far worse in her life than a filthy house. *Don't just sit thar like a frog on a log* she would say, and this was a woman with twelve children."

She and Milly went downstairs, found brooms, dustpans and buckets in the kitchen and began work. The water supply was functioning and there was plenty of wood in the garden to feed the stove. More amazingly the phone was still connected. Becca put down her floor cloth, took paper and pencil out of her handbag and made an inventory.

"Give me Smyrna 252," she told the operator. "Is that the Meteor-Mart? Can you deliver today? The address is 1346A Decatur Drive. This is Rebecca Patternoster – put the things on my tab." She reeled off a long list of items ranging from food to bed clothes, then, having replaced the receiver, smiled triumphantly. "At least *they* remember me," she said. "I was always a good customer." Damask, coming downstairs, observed this transaction with fascination; she recalled the communication device in the silent film she had watched on the Kymer Levels and realised what a useful piece of equipment this *telephone* might turn out to be.

The streets of Ry-Town, set out on a grid pattern, were not particularly narrow, yet they gave that impression when contrasted with the enormous slabs of buildings hemming them in on either side. Everything at ground level was submerged in a murky twilight. Looking up, the party absconding from the Behemoth could see hazy sunlight penetrating the fog and striking the upper stories, but no beams reached to the bottom of the deep canyons. Street lights were shining and the windows of retailers and businesses along the roadways were illuminated so that shoppers could examine what was on offer. With surprise they saw that the clothes of the passers-by often had little decorative bulbs attached to them that sparkled on and off; it seemed to be the fashion to be lit up in this way and looked pretty enough. From a distance the lights were all you could make out of these pedestrians, but when they came closer one was struck by a certain uniformity of appearance: everyone was prosperous-looking and apparently glowing with health. The Rytonians, although not overweight, were well built with plump, rosy-fair faces, the children miniature versions of their parents. Everyone walked with a firm confident step as if they knew exactly where they were going, both literally and metaphorically. Did they look happy Dando asked himself? – no, not exactly - they looked determined. The immigrants drew many curious stares as they progressed further into the metropolis, the city dwellers regarding the little group from the southern continent with astonishment before quickly turning away, apparently embarrassed.

As soon as they came ashore the voyagers had noticed a change in temperature. Up above in the sunlight it might still be as warm as it had been out at sea but down here, although they were only in the second half of the tenth month, the air was frigid. Consequently clouds of vapour rose from gratings in the pavement beneath which ran some kind of underground conduits. The four newcomers realised they were desperately in need of thicker clothes. Dando felt grateful for the tatty military greatcoat he had been given by a kind-hearted farmer's wife during his journey along Terratenebra's northern coast, but wondered if he ought now to donate it to Tallis who crouched in his chair looking frozen despite his thick cloak. They had been walking for about half an hour, hardly speaking, when Foxy broke the silence by saying, "Where be we a-gooin' then?"

"Yes," said Jack, "it's about time we thought about that. I think we've sufficiently confused any pursuit."

"Well, I be confused, anyroad," said Foxy.

"Becca told us to ask for Peepo," went on Jack. "She said everyone would know her along this seaboard."

"Do you think they managed to get here alright?" wondered Dando.

Tallis, who during this whole perambulation had appeared stupefied by the avalanche of new impressions constantly bombarding his senses, suddenly came to life and began fishing in his pocket.

"I can give you an idea of bearings," he said bringing out the small disk of his compass and holding it on the palm of his hand. Under the glass the needle swung wildly and refused to come to rest.

"That's strange," said the knight, "move on a bit."

Foxy pushed the chair a few yards further down the road and Tallis made another attempt. Once more the needle would not settle and despite trying several different locations it could not be persuaded to give a consistent reading. Tallis looked at Dando with an incredulous horror-struck expression.

"It doesn't work any more," he cried. "It doesn't work this side of the sea! How am I ever going to find the way north?" The man seemed totally overwhelmed.

Feeling inadequate Dando hesitantly patted his shoulder.

"We'll find it," he said trying to sound reassuring, "we'll be guided by the sun."

But in fact, during the last few minutes, the sunlight, high above, had disappeared. The gloom of the streets intensified and now rain, mixed with hail, descended on their heads.

"That's marvellous," grumbled Jack, "what did we do to deserve this?"

"There's a place further down the road where we could shelter," Dando told him. "I think it might be a bar. There's people going in and out."

When they reached the premises in question they saw that there were two separate signs over the door: one, neon lit, announced to the world that they had arrived at *Dino's Diner -Top Class Eatery,* the other, non-electrical and somewhat faded, displayed the legend *Rytardenath Reading Rooms, Established Through Public Subscription*. On entering they found themselves in a cheerful mini-brasserie serving food and coffee to a number of patrons. At the back of this area there was a door marked *Library* leading through to another room. Jack bought them drinks - he seemed to have a copious supply of the local currency - and then made enquiry of the young man behind the counter.

"Have you heard of a night-club singer called Peepo?"

"Miss Peepo? That rings a bell. Wasn't she an actress in the silents? My ma's generation. I think I heard she went abroad."

"Do you know where she used to live?"

"Well – that's a poser. I'd guess at Mornington Heights – that's the place where most of the movie people used to hang out although they don't make pictures there any more – too smoggy."

"How would we get there?"

"Oh – just take the El from downtown."

Dando had been exploring out the back.

"There's a room with lots of books and some newspapers. There's nobody in there. I'm going to have another look."

"Drink your coffee first," ordered Jack but Dando had already disappeared through the door: books drew him like a magnet. By the time the others finished their drinks and had each been treated to a snack the rain had stopped. Jack went in search of his friend.

"Oh Jack, there you are." Dando was turning over the pages of a newspaper on a reading desk and seemed to have discovered something on an inside page. "Look what I've found."

"I can't look – remember."

"No of course - sorry. There's a picture of Becca and I think that's Damask and Milly in the background. It says *Hasbeen Star Flees Fighting*."

"Hasbeen Star!" repeated Jack with amusement. "Poor Becca."

"Yes – I'll read it: *Rebecca Patternoster, professionally known as Miss Peepo, came ashore from the clipper Diamond last night with other refugees escaping the unrest that has broken out across the Tethys. Peepo was one of the original pioneers in the early days of cinema and was also acclaimed for her few stage appearances during which she proved that she had a fine singing voice. However she left these shores shortly before the industry converted to sound. Although greeted on the quayside by a group of fans, director Magnus T. Battledore gave it as his opinion that she was unlikely to be able to revive a career that had begun to fade even before she voluntarily quitted the business. The foreign war has temporarily brought to a halt all trade with the southern continent. As a consequence there may be some shortages at steel manufacturing plants and in the automobile industry. The government are considering opening up old mines north of Damwey which could supply materials for the escalating conflict on the eastern front...* No there's nothing more about Becca – but it's her – I'm sure of it."

"Well that proves they arrived all right. The only thing we can do is go to this Mornington Heights place and ask around to see if anyone knows where she is. *Take the El from downtown* – what's that supposed to mean I wonder? Tear that page out – we might need it."

But this Dando resolutely refused to do.

By the evening several rooms at Becca's house were fit to live in. Beds had been made up and the meal which she sent out for had been eaten.

"Well there's still a heap to sort out," said the show girl, "But we've made a start. I'll visit the studios tomorrow and see if they can offer me anything. I believe it's all location work nowadays."

"Would they have anything for me and Milly?" asked Damask. "She's good at costume and make-up and you know what I can do."

Becca shook her head unhappily.

"I wish I could say yes," she replied, "I don't want to sound discouraging but it's a pretty hard business to break into and the acting side is an oversubscribed profession. As for you Milly..." she stared with concern at the young black girl. "Things ain't exactly the same over here as they were in Drossi, honey – Drossi was a very easy-going place you know – you've no ideah... You may have to get used to different attitudes – a different set of values."

Damask realised she had yet to set eyes on another dark-skinned person in Rytardenath. Everybody looked the same in this town – the same colouring, the same blooming state of health, the same age range – under sixty-five she guessed.

Where are all the old people? she inwardly wondered.

The next day Becca went to her former studio and came away with vague promises of an interview when the head of production returned.

"We'll put you back on the books," she was told.

"It's a hard business – a hard business..." she confirmed to Damask as they cleared out a flooded drain at the back of the house. Milly, who had been ineffectually trying to cut a way through the growth along the drive, suddenly appeared, flying round the side of the building, her face one big grin.

"They're 'ere!" she shouted dramatically, "the Lordship an' the rest of 'em. They've made it crorst the sea!"

Becca, her mind occupied with thinking about number of beds and the expense of supporting four more adults, set out to greet the new arrivals. Words of welcome were already forming on her lips and her hand was held out as she turned the corner of the house. The newcomers came to attention as she appeared: Tallis from his position slumped in a far superior vehicle from the old bath chair in which she had last seen him, Jack with his head on one side, trying to detect her approach by ear, Foxy, his concentration seemingly divided between their meeting and the state of the surrounding jungle and Dando leaning on his crutch, smiling in an abashed and diffident manner. Becca's hand flew to her mouth as she came in sight of this collection of crocks, misfits and cripples that made up the full complement of her Terratenebrian companions.

"Oh my word!" she murmured to herself.

For the first time she was seeing the southerners through Rytonian eyes and could not help but anticipate the dangers and difficulties that lay ahead for these foreigners in what was, to them, an alien and uncharted land.

"They don't know the half of it," she thought with concern, *"why for mercy's sake didn't I tell them before we left? Now it's far too late. I'll just have to do my best to protect them."*

Time to dance my lad,
Here's your chance,
Make with the moves, shake that ass...

Chapter two

Dando was back in Drossi, down by the Poule, fighting to stay upright as he was pushed to and fro by the sweaty, panicking crowd, every member of which was aiming to secure a place on one of the few ships evacuating people from the beleaguered city. The fact was he was dreaming of recent events, something that often took place when he first fell asleep, and in the dream he found himself up against a barrier on the other side of which he could see Becca, Damask and Milly walking away. He shouted after them and one of their number responded - one of the three. But then he realised he had miscalculated because there were four people in the small group on the other side of the wire. As this fourth person swung round in answer to his frantic cry he saw that it was not the night-club singer who faced him, nor was it his sister or the little dark-skinned maid who, three years ago, he had rescued from a life of exploitation. This was a girl with blue eyes, a pellucid complexion and a flowing mane of fair hair, someone utterly dear to him and familiar.

"Ann!" he cried with incredulous delight, "it's you – you're alive!"

The feeling was like being restored to health following a long illness, like spring's burgeoning after winter, and his heart leapt with gladness.

"***My love,***" she said smiling and retraced her steps, coming to a halt only about a foot away from where he stood.

"Annie," he exclaimed again and tried to reach her, but the barrier, made of sturdy metallic netting, blocked the way. The mesh was too fine for either of them to put their hands through, but the girl inserted her fingers into one of the gaps and he kissed the tips of her fingers, tears filling his eyes. These tears of joy turned, in the fraction of a second, to tears of bitterness as he awoke to find himself far from the Delta City and realised that the whole thing had been an hallucination - a sham. How could he have been taken in, even for a second, even when comatose, by something so phoney - how could he have allowed it to happen? She was dead, dead – the dream had been sent solely to torment him and now he felt doubly bereaved as the fleeting vision of an impossible reunion faded.

Dawn was still a long way off but he was afraid to go back to sleep. He tried to keep himself awake by recalling something extraordinary that had taken place the previous evening. It had occurred when he and Tallis had been left alone together. Damask and Milly were upstairs attending to Horry, Becca had walked down the road to renew old acquaintances with the aim of reviving her career, Jack, as usual, was missing having gone off to goodness knows what low dive, and, as for Foxy, he had retreated to a shed some distance from the house where he had discovered a full set of tools suitable for taming the surrounding terrain. Tallis decided he would like to retire early and Dando went with him to the garden room which had been assigned to him, (Becca had experienced some difficulty in finding space for all her guests). Having helped him undress, wash and get comfortably settled Dando prepared to depart, but Tallis waved his hand towards a chair by the bed saying, “Don't go.” The boy sat down and waited to hear what was required of him. For a long period the knight remained silent, apparently lost in thought. Then he stretched out an arm for the other's perusal.

“What do you see?” he asked.

Dando stared at the proffered limb in puzzlement.

“Your hand,” he said.

The hand, long and gaunt with spatulated fingers and prominent joints, was covered in dark patches. It was also wrinkled, the skin loose over the bones like a worn-out and ill-fitting glove.

“Old,” said Tallis, “I'm old. I've lost count of how many years I've been travelling. I've journeyed so far that the sun, which used to go before me as a guide, has been left behind and remains at my back even during the height of summer. I've traversed one great continent and now that I've crossed the sea I may have as far to go again in order to reach my heart's desire. If I finally discover the Key - if it even exists - how will I ever find the hardihood to return as I meant to do and take it back to the place from which it was stolen? Am I even the one for whom this quest was intended I wonder? I'm old, my boy, old. Coming to this enormous city where people live literally one on top of another yet not even your next door neighbour knows if you are well or at death's door has made me realise that I'm just an ant in a vast nest of ants like all the rest. I'm beginning to think I never had a special purpose as my mother believed. Even if

I've been singled out for such a charge it's now beyond my powers to carry it out; I haven't got time enough or strength to complete the task"

Dando was amazed and appalled by this speech.

"But master," he replied earnestly, "w-when I first met you in High Harrow at the King's Head you didn't seem old to me then and that was only a year ago. You're ill, not old. L-let me look after you until you're better and then we can go on together."

Tallis shook his head and wearily ran his hand down his face. Eventually he asked, "What would be the form of words I would have to use to bring your bondage to an end?"

"My bondage?"

"Your squiredom."

"From what I've read you would just have to say *I release you*, but don't master, don't. Let me go on serving you. You need me."

Tallis swung his legs over the side of the bed and, reaching forward, took one of Dando's hands in his.

"You have done your duty faithfully and well, Dan Addo, but the time has come for you to be your own master. Go your way and live life to the full. *I release you.*"

"Oh no," cried Dando, his face twisted with emotion, "this isn't right! I can't abandon you now – not now. You really do need me – more now than ever."

"But you don't need me, my boy, an old man whose sole purpose in life has been the pursuit of something illusory, who has led you on a wild goose chase."

A few months earlier, in the days following their departure from Toymerle, Dando might have welcomed this turn of events. At that time, deeply in love and frustrated by the need to keep his love hidden, he had longed for the freedom to take Ann elsewhere where they could live openly together. But now she was dead and a series of ghastly experiences had drastically altered his view of the world. The service that he owed Tallis seemed one of the few things that still gave his life meaning. Take that away and what was left to him? In the extremity of his feeling the young high-born Glept was suddenly granted a new clarity of vision.

"A wild goose chase?" he protested, "that's not true – I know it isn't true. If it hadn't been for you I would never have learnt who my people really are and that we both actually share the same purpose; I would never have taken up the search that the valley dwellers abandoned all those years ago. It does exist, the Key - others have told me so - and someone has got to find it if the world is to be saved. Whether it's you or me doesn't matter – we'll go together."

Tallis stared at Dando as if drawing strength from his ex-squire's sincerity and surprising conviction. Then he bestowed upon him a most unexpected smile.

"You almost persuade me my dear boy," he said, "but now I must rest – I feel I must rest for a very long time if I am to go any further. I think I would like to be left alone now."

Dando helped him back to bed and then went to the room he shared with Jack, got between the sheets, fell asleep and dreamt of Ann as already mentioned. On his rude awakening he noticed that the other bed was still pristine; his room-mate had not returned and in fact would not appear until the rest of the company were already sitting down to breakfast. During his conversation with Tallis he had put into words things he had not even realised he gave credence to, things that had been working away at the back of his mind like yeast in dough. He no longer knew if he was still Tallis' squire but whether he remained so or not hardly mattered. What he did understand was that he could not abandon the man, that there were ties binding them one to the other that were stronger than mere oaths. He would wait until Tallis had regained his strength, however long that took, and then put himself at his disposal ready to go wherever the knight desired. But in the meantime how was he to pay his way? How could he manage to earn some money in this strange new land?

"This is a great place for makeovers."

When Jack came in the next morning his appearance, as had happened once before in Drossi, was revolutionised. This time he looked the complete Rytonian, from his carefully remodelled hair to the cut of his shoe leather. There was a gold ring in his left ear and he was even wearing a jacket decorated with the little twinkling lights that seemed to be de-rigour for the local fashionistas.

"It's heaven here," he explained, " you can get almost anything done. A mere manicure if that's all you desire or a complete face job if you've got the money. Every other outlet seems to be either a beauty salon or a fitness club. How do I look?"

Dutifully his friends handed out the confirmation of his splendour for which he was angling. He certainly appeared stylish enough but when indeed did he not? Even after weeks on the road and in a condition of penury and near starvation he had still contrived to retain a certain elegance. How he did this in his sightless state had baffled Dando ever since the day they first met at the Oracle's shrine.

“By the way,” Jack went on after he had sat himself down and begun hungrily to consume an egg and ham casserole accompanied by biscuits and gravy brought from the local carry-out up the road, “has Becca told you? The day after tomorrow is the start of carnival week – the week leading up to Sahwain. It's the high point of the year on the Heights – loads of people come out from the city centre in order to take part. Everyone gets into costume – lots of parades – you see some of the really famous stars on the floats. Bands, concerts, dancing – it's a regular magnet for dancers (this directed at Dando). Oh, and there's an amateur talent contest that runs all week. Big prize for the winner I believe.”

Everyone turned to Becca; she had not said a word about this forthcoming fiesta. She looked back sheepishly as if caught out in some cringe-making misdemenour.

“Well folks,” she excused herself, “I guess I thought that as you've only just arrived you'd prefer to have a nice quiet time around the house instead of gallivanting off up the hill. This foolery ain't all it's cracked up to be. Why don't y'all just have your own little wingding here on the Eve of the Ancestors – dress up - light some Jack o' Lanterns – apple bobbing – that kinda thing?”

This was met by a long pregnant pause until the blind boy announced, “Well, I don't know about you but I'm going into town.” and to Dando, “Are you game birdy?”

Dando was granted a vision of Jack, alone, in the midst of a huge crowd trying to feel around him with his cane and being cursed for getting in the way.

“All right,” he said.

Becca became slightly more agitated at this development

“Children,” she cautioned, “this ain't a good ideah.”

“Why's that?” asked Jack challengingly.

“Well...” Becca hesitated and then added feebly, “you'll like as not get into trouble.”

When asked by Jack to explain this mysterious statement she refused to elaborate apart from telling them, “If you must go don't stand out – leave your cane and crutch at home.”

Milly brought two different concerns to Jack in the hope that he might be able to set her mind at rest. When she and the former hostage had left the Oracle's shrine in the mountains, having found it abandoned, they had been accompanied by two horses which they had rescued: one, Carolus, had been Tallis' own mount, while the other, the pony Mollyblobs, had originally belonged to Damask and so had started her journey in the valley of Deep Hallow. On reaching Vadrosnia Poule the animals were left in a livery stables by the causeway into the city and only occasionally ridden when she or Damask had a day to spare. Now, too late, Milly realised nobody had given them a second thought during the panicky escape from the doomed conurbation.

"Wot 'appened to the 'orses, do you think?" she asked Jack, having sought him out. "We forgot orl about the 'orses. I'm afraid somebody will 'ave stolen them. I 'opes they di'n't get bombed."

"They were good horses" replied Jack reassuringly, "valuable horses. I think whosoever's hands they may have fallen into will prize them for their quality. I reckon they'll be well looked after."

"Poor 'orses," commented Milly sadly.

Something much more serious as far as she was concerned was bothering her and was the real reason for approaching this one-time companion. Her attitude to the young gay from Drossi had changed somewhat since the time when they had travelled amicably together on the road from Toymerle. She could not help but feel grateful to him for having brought Dando back to her but wondered at the two boys' easy rapport. She knew that Jack was also in love with the one she adored and would have felt sorry for him had she not had an uneasy feeling concerning the extent to which this single-gender relationship had progressed; it was undeniable that the green-eyed monster was stirring in her breast. Nevertheless Jack was probably the only person who could answer the question that was burning her lips.

"Wot's up wiv the Lordship?" she demanded. "I know 'e's sad cos of 'is sweet'eart an orl that but e's carryin' on as if 'e's got ants in 'is pants. Back when you both turned up before we crorst the sea 'e woz acting kinda weird an' now yesterday as well. When I put my 'and on 'is arm an' 'e di'n't know I woz there 'e nearly jumped out orv 'is skin."

Jack scratched his head and wondered what to tell this young female. He was aware that she was only in her mid teens – an age when most girls are just beginning to learn about life and discover what it means to be a woman - but he had also learnt a little from Damask of her maid's character-forming early years. These had obviously given her a brutal lesson in the ways of the world and as a consequence she was probably more capable of understanding what Dando was going through than most.

"Something bad happened along the road," he told her, choosing his words carefully, "in a little town we came to. The whole country was on edge and we got ourselves arrested by the local gendarmerie because of what we were up to in private. I was put in the stocks and Dando..."

"Wot do you mean by something bad?" interrupted Milly. "Did they 'urt 'im?"

"Well yes – in a way. These men - they thought that because he was with me he was the same sort as me – comprenez? - and as a result they considered him fair game. I'm afraid they used him for their own amusement – all that day while I was in the pillory. He hasn't got over it yet."

Milly's mouth puckered in dismay.

"You mean they tupped 'im? Oh blimey! 'E don't know any fink about that sort of fing – 'e woz brought up real nice. Poor Lordship!" Her black eyes filled with tears and she turned away. After a long silence she suddenly looked back her face blazing with anger.

"'Oo were they then? Oo woz it wot done it?"

"Just men – ordinary men – probably pillars of their own communities."

"Well I know what I'd like to do to them!" cried Milly, the avenging angel. She seethed inwardly for a few minutes and then burst out, "Why di'n't you save 'im?"

Jack shrugged unhappily.

"I would have if I could. When I got to him it was far too late. All I could do was try and help him through the aftermath. He's getting better – in the end he'll come out of it – he'll come out of it stronger if I know Dando. Meanwhile you and I must do what we can to make life easier for him."

"Is that why you gets 'im to dance?"

"Yes – it's one of the positive things – that and cookery."

Soon they were into the week leading up to the significant thirty-first and when Jack and Dando set out for the carnival after an early lunch, Damask, carrying Horry in a sling, and Milly, dressed in her best, accompanied them. Foxy refused an invitation to go along; he was far too absorbed in the fascinating task of turning the wilderness surrounding the house back into the gracious garden that it had been in its heyday. The two young men went equipped with their cane and crutch despite Becca's warning; they paid no heed to her embargo because she had not backed it up with any kind of factual explanation. On climbing the long hill that was Decatur Drive and entering the centre of the satellite town situated at the top they found the festivities in full swing. Dando had his work cut out describing to Jack everything that was going on.

"There's floats with great big animals on them, made out of paper and wire I think. There's people dancing on the floats and in between them as well – a sort of synchronised dancing. Nearly everybody's wearing costumes but I'm not sure what most of them are supposed to be – something out of the movies I reckon. I can see someone standing behind a machine on three legs – he's turning a handle and he's got a cloth over his head. I think it must be one of the things they use to *make* movies. And here comes a float with a band – they're black – almost as black as Milly. They're the first black people I've seen since we got here."

"Yes, I can hear them," said Jack, "they're good."

The four companions made their way through the throng taking in the exotically foreign sights, sounds and smells that surrounded them. Amusements designed to eat money such as pin-ball machines and one-arm bandits were installed along the side-walks and in the squares. On an open area they came upon a dancing bear, a steer-roping display, a fire walker, a demonstration of bare-back riding and a plethora of stands selling cookies, candy and local delicacies. Dando, who had not been expecting to enjoy the hi-jinks and had thought he was there just for Jack's sake, became absorbed, despite himself, in investigating the fast food of a new continent. He discussed with Milly, who was the only one of their number to show any corresponding interest, ingredients he had never encountered before such as sweet corn, buffalo meat, chillies, squash and various varieties of bean. Jack, thoroughly bored, pulled Damask aside.

"Can you help me find the place where they're going to hold this talent contest? I've got an idea..."

The Glept and the young black girl, unaware that they had been deserted, moved from one purveyor to another sampling the fare on offer, (Jack had handed Dando a fistful of notes before they set off). Our connoisseur of the culinary arts talked to the stall holders, the majority of whom seemed gratified to be able to supply information about their creations, although at the same time regarding their questioner with not a little wonder. Some in the vicinity, however, appeared less than friendly and one woman, waiting to be served, turned to them in a distinctly hostile manner.

"What's that nigger doing out here on the street?" she demanded aggressively, jabbing her elbow at Milly. "Tell her to get back to the dunny where she belongs."

Dando was taken aback. He pulled the young girl protectively into his embrace.

"S-she's with me," he said, "she's my friend."

"You! How about you? Aren't you ashamed to be seen in that condition?" gesturing towards Dando's crutch and sole remaining foot. "Why haven't you been transferred?"

A few passers-by stopped and began to take an interest.

"Yeah," somebody interjected, "where are the vice-squad when you need them?"

"Transferred?" replied Dando, "Transferred to where? I-I don't know what you mean."

At that moment Jack and Damask came wandering into view and the interrogators, realising that the target of their jibes had acquired reinforcements, backed off hurriedly although they still stood staring balefully from a distance. The two new arrivals were unaware that anything disagreeable had been happening and Dando did not enlighten them. Nevertheless he was considerably shaken by this odd encounter.

Both his companions, his sister and his friend, looked slightly flushed on their return as if excited about something. Jack stroked Dando's arm like someone gentling a nervous horse.

"I've got something to tell you birdy. Don't jump down my throat when you hear. We've put your name down for the competition – starts in an hour."

"W-what competition?" asked Dando, mystified.

"You know – the talent contest – carries on all week – there's a big prize."

"What! Are you crazy?! No way!"

"I'm not crazy, you donkey. Why not give it a go."

"But I couldn't!"

"Yes you could – remember how you danced for us at the Goat."

"The competitors go by what's known as a *soubriquet*, a sort of nickname," chimed in Damask. "They asked us what yours was. Jack wanted to call you *Footloose* but I said, why not *Footless*. *Footless* instead of *Footloose* because you haven't got a foot," she added unnecessarily.

Dando gazed at them in utter horror, robbed of words. Jack put his arm around him and gave him a quick squeeze.

"Come on my lad – chin up – this is what it's all been about – this is what all your practice was in aid of. You'll slay 'em."

The talent contest, entitled *The Go-Getter Game*, was to be held in a large community hall more commonly used for what were known as health of body and mind sessions, or so they were informed by notices outside. When they entered they saw that a mass of chairs had been arranged facing a capacious stage, at the rear of which an almost full-sized orchestra was busy tuning up. Most of the chairs were already occupied.

"We sit at the front," said Jack. "The first three rows are reserved for competitors and their sidekicks. All you've got to do is tell the band what music you want and then wait for your name to be called. Just let them know the sort of thing you like. This being the first round they'll pick twelve people today, then tomorrow eight of those twelve, then six the next day, then four and so on. Meanwhile the losers have their own competition and the one that wins through will go up against the last one standing on the main stage – that happens on Ancestors' Eve. There's a panel of adjudicators but the final is judged by the audience."

There were just four seats left vacant in the front row. Jack and Damask placed themselves on either side of Dando as if they were afraid that any minute he might get up and attempt to escape. Instead he sat with elbows on knees and his head buried in his hands, apparently trying to block out what was happening. Milly gazed anxiously across at him. Why were they doing this to her Lordship when he so obviously hated the whole idea? She did not understand. At two o'clock in the afternoon the contest got under way and the first performers were called. These proved to be a cherubic trio of children who sang in shrill penetrating voices *Daddy Wouldn't Buy Me a Bow-Wow.* They received much indulgent applause plus a smidgen of salacious laughter. Following this, a woman took to the stage with a dog that unfortunately went on strike and so never revealed the clever tricks which were supposed to astound the audience. Still on the canine theme the next turn consisted of several animals who, on a series of signals from their owner, barked forth, very slowly, the tune of a simple well-known ditty.

Damask snorted contemptuously. "Not much to worry about so far," she opined.

But after this came the first dance act, a svelte-looking couple who moved together as one and were step perfect. The only quibble that could be made about their performance was that the whole thing was a bit clinical and uninvolving; nevertheless this was a challenge that had to be taken more seriously. Act followed act and the afternoon ticked away. Dando refused to pay attention; he still had his hands over his ears and his head bowed. There was a slight pause while the orchestra members attended to their instruments and then the compère cleared his throat and announced: "The Lord Dan Addo, performing under the soubriquet *Footless*."

There was a buzz of interest from the audience at this imposing-sounding name. They craned their necks to see what sort of exotic creature would appear. Jack dug Dando in the ribs.

"Come on birdy," he said, "you're on. Give it the works my love."

Slowly the boy rose and tucked his crutch under his arm; he had the air of a man going to his own funeral. He limped to the bottom of the steps leading up to the stage and began to ascend. As he came in view of the crowd there was an audible gasp, a universal in-drawing of breath. Dando made his way to centre-stage and stood gazing out over the sea of heads. After a minute or two he looked towards the orchestra as if to indicate that he was ready. However he found that it was not ready for him. The conductor had deserted his post and crossed over to stand in front of the adjudicators' table, speaking quietly but vehemently as if objecting to something about this latest contestant. It was quite a while before the man threw his hands up in the air – he had obviously been overruled – and walked back, frowning, to his podium. He raised his baton, the musicians struck up, and Dando went into his unique routine. Each competitor had eight minutes in which to impress the judges, but our young dancer managed to have the audience on his side in a far shorter time than that with the dazzling blur of movement he wove around the top of his crutch. The after images his brightly lit body left on the air as he leapt and spun created the impression of a fleeting misty inflorescence hanging above a wooden stalk, a vision of a rapidly-fading flower. He presented the onlookers with supreme athleticism combined with beauty of movement and most of them were already applauding before no more than two minutes had passed.

"How's he doing," Jack yelled; he had to shout in order to be heard over the audience's excited response. Damask, who had only seen this performance twice before and was feeling enormous pride in her sibling shrieked "Great, great." She held the baby up to witness his father's prowess. "Look Horry, look."

"That's my boy!" cried Jack, but then exclaimed in consternation, "What's happening? Why are they playing silly buggers?" for the band had abruptly changed tempo. A moment later they changed again, and yet again, with no apparent rhyme or reason. Four-four, five-four, even seven-four - one beat morphed into another, giving the performer an increasingly difficult rhythm to keep in sync with. The permutations continued – six quavers to a bar, eight quavers, three crotchets – the time-signature totally inappropriate for what Dando was trying to do. "A waltz!" exclaimed Jack, "this is ridiculous – they're out to sabotage him!"

He need not have worried; the young hoofer effortlessly adapted himself to each new measure and even seemed to enjoy the challenge. When he took his bow at the end, breathless and soaking wet, he was grinning from ear to ear. The audience rose in their seats to a man – from their point of view it was a forgone conclusion that this remarkable performer would go on to the next round. In the midst of the cheering and acclaim Dando hobbled back to his seat, his temporary elation soon fading. He again squatted with his head in his hands, breathing fast, while the *Go-Getter Game* wound to a close. After the last act had performed, the compère gave a long peroration on the quality of the entries and then read out a list of the twelve winners - Dando's name was not amongst them. There was an outburst of booing from the crowd on his behalf and, remarkably, a fight broke out a few rows back between two spectators, one of whom agreed with the verdict while the other was incensed by it. The southerners left the hall in silence. On the street outside someone passing recognised the rejected competitor and handed out commiserations.

"Hard luck, guy," he said to Dando. "You were definitely the best. They let their prejudices rule their judgement. Of course, even for those who get knocked out there's always the chance of being spotted by one of the talent scouts in the audience – the ones working for the big noises I mean – but I'm afraid in your case they wouldn't touch you with a barge pole – too controversial. The studio heads are pretty lily-livered when it comes to things like that," pointing at Dando's solitary foot, "but I admire your guts."

Feeling slightly bemused Becca's guests turned their steps towards Decatur Drive and after a few yards Dando heaved a deep sigh.

"Well – that's that," he said, sounding profoundly relieved.

"Not so fast – not so fast, birdy," retorted Jack. "You've forgotten the losers' contest. You'll stand a better chance there because it's up to the audience to decide each round. They've got some sort of contraption for measuring noise levels; they can tell who gets the most applause. If I have anything to do with it you'll be here tomorrow ready to go again and this time you'll be in it to win it."

"Oh Jack," groaned Dando, "have a heart!"

The losers' competition took place in a small subsidiary venue on the periphery of Mornington Heights and was normally watched by people who could not find seats in the main hall. This time however things were slightly different. Dando had already acquired a following – an enthusiastic group of supporters who had vowed to remain loyal after he was eliminated from the primary contest and who were determined to cheer loudly and long enough in the hall down the road to enable him to win through to the play-off. When they learnt that he was definitely going to participate they crowded into the rather shabby assembly rooms ready to raise the roof on his behalf.

On each morning, before the event, Dando was unable to eat and twice he was physically sick. Jack pampered him, insisting that he rest, delegating the tasks he usually performed on Tallis' behalf to Foxy, who objected indignantly to being dragged away from his work in the garden. As the competition progressed Dando expected every moment to be knocked out; he had absolutely no faith in his ability to reach the final, so, as far as he was concerned, the sooner the ordeal came to an end the better, performing at the top of his game night after night was proving a severe strain. Yet he had no notion of throwing the contest; it did not occur to him, once up on stage, to do anything less than his best, especially when his friends were counting on him.

On the third day he and Jack were waiting for the proceedings to start (Horry had had a slight attack of colic and so Damask and Milly had stayed at home) when something rather bizarre occurred. All at once the chairs on which they were sitting seemed to come to life and shift from side to side like restless beasts of burden moving from one foot to the other, while, at the same time, at the periphery of the hall, two massive framed paintings came crashing down from the wall on which they hung, narrowly missing the people sitting below. The audience reacted boisterously to this strange event with war-whoops, cheers and whistles while one youngster leapt up onto his chair and stood wobbling to and fro with his arms held out as if walking a tightrope. A loud buzz of comment followed.

"There," said Dando, immediately perking up (he had been sitting huddled into himself, the very picture of misery). "You felt it this time – I-I told you that the ground moved."

"Oh yes," answered Jack, already a rather smug mine of information when it came to Armornian affairs, "it evidently happens quite often. The local wise men – *natural philosophers* or *scientists* they're called - say that it's the effect of the weight of the buildings on the earth beneath. The rocky substratum is being compressed, so they tell us. Nothing to worry about."

His friend looked sceptical. "That's not what it felt like to me," he said.

Jack laughed. "So you're one of these people who thinks there's an evil influence at work?"

Dando shrugged and did not reply.

The devotees who had followed him from the main contest were noisy, vociferous and not very well behaved; at a guess they consisted mainly of teenagers in full scale revolt against their elders. The assembly room, normally a social club's meeting place, was inevitably provided with a watering hole. During the interval - Dando having escaped outside in order to forget the whole sorry business for a while - Jack decided to buy himself a drink. As he sat at the bar listening in to conversations around him he identified a group of his protege's followers by the din they were making. He swung round in their direction.

"From what I hear, you go for Footless," he interjected during a slight lull, "why's that?"

"He's cool!" came a chorus of voices.

"Why is he so cool?" he pursued.

This gave them pause until someone daringly piped up, "He does his own thing an' he don't give a shiz about what might happen to him."

"Really? I don't understand. What is it that might happen to him?"

A long silence followed broken by one or two embarrassed giggles. Then these kidults, scarcely more than children, began to talk amongst themselves once more, cutting Jack out of the conversation. He was left with the sense that there was an elephant in the room which everyone was too scared to acknowledge. That evening he discussed the matter with Damask and then asked Becca, "When you said you quitted Armornia because things were making you nervous, what did you mean?"

"Oh no, dear. I left because I'd just broken up with Clark."

"But Damask told me you originally said it was because something was worrying you."

"Oh well – I suppose it was the current political situation – but I'm sure things are different now," and she would say no more. Jack vowed that he would find out what was going on.

As the losers' competition progressed, the Footless Fan Club proved to be a thorough nuisance to the more restrained members of the audience. Nevertheless, with their rowdy backing, Dando was carried through the heats until it became obvious that he would be the one heading for a showdown with the main competition winner. It was at this point that rumours began to circulate suggesting that the whole endeavour might be called off – why this was so, no-one would say, although it was hinted that most could have told you the reason if they had chosen to be brutally frank. In fact nothing of the kind happened – it seemed that the organisers were nervous about voicing their true reservations on the matter for fear of inciting a widespread popular reaction and yet were unable to think up some alternative innocuous excuse for cancelling, so things went ahead as planned.

Here there is no light,
But along winding mossy ways
Verdurous shadows breath her name.

Chapter three

The morning of Ancestors Eve, otherwise known as Sahwain, dawned dim and misty. This was the time of year, the beginning, as some believed, of the Sky-Father's journey towards the depths, when the veil between worlds was supposed to be at its thinnest. It was the end of harvest, the start of nature's long hibernation and the reinstatement of the Beldam, Queen of Winter. It was on this night that the Feast of the Dead was celebrated, celebrated even among the cynical sophisticates that made up Ry-Town's beau monde. An irrational conviction persisted that after dark people's supposed multiple lives melded into one and you might well catch a glimpse of those who were no longer with us as they would have appeared in their earlier or later incarnations. A large bonfire had been built on the Heights and, the weather turning warmer, the talent contest hopefuls, along with a number of more established performers who were going to extend the show into a full evening's entertainment, moved outdoors to a nearby stadium in order to accommodate the crowds that were expected from the inner city.

Back at the Magnolias - that was the name of Becca's mansion - a baby-sitter had been employed so that everyone could be present to support their contender. Even Foxy deigned to accompany them. This was quite a concession on his part as up to now the garden had claimed his full attention morning, noon and night. As Jack and Dando got dressed before breakfast our latest convert to Ry-Town style tried to persuade his friend to smarten up a bit.

"It may be Ancestors Eve leibling," he said, stroking the boy's hair which by now had grown back to its full Deep Hallow luxuriousness, "but you don't have to actually look like one of the ancestors. The way you're wearing it is just not comme-il-faut at the moment. Let me take you along to Raymond's this morning for a trim. He's got his finger on the pulse."

But Dando would only compromise to the extent of allowing his friend to wash the offending locks and clip two jewelled studs to his ears. The rest of his outward appearance, including the military greatcoat, was part of the act, he explained. As soon as he was able, he made his escape to an as yet untouched section of the grounds and spent the day incommunicado, only emerging when Jack went to look for him as the time to set out approached.

When the refugees from Terratenebra took their seats in the front row of that night's venue the hum of conversation from the audience increased by several decibels. Flashbulbs exploded. There were a few screams from one section of the crowd.

"You're a celebrity, spatzi," said Jack, his arm around Dando's shoulders, "they're on your side."

"Not all of them," commented Damask; she had distinctly heard some hooting when a wandering beam of light came momentarily to rest on her brother.

Dando, although not happy, was no longer in denial. He had bowed to the inevitable and, despite a strong feeling of unreality, was prepared for what was to come. The fact that he had gotten this far amazed him and could not help but boost his confidence. He just hoped that, win or lose, he had the strength to see the thing through. The length of each session had been increased from eight minutes to ten and it had been explained that he would be expected to go through his routine both at the beginning and at the end of the evening. Well, at least tonight would be the decider; after this there would be no repeat performance and for that he was profoundly grateful.

Milly had managed to grab a seat next to Dando on the other side from Jack and sat with one of her loved one's hands in both of hers, angry and distressed that the Lordship was being made to suffer this ordeal night after night.

"He enjoys it," the blind boy had said when she tackled him about the matter a couple of days earlier.

"But 'e's always so mis'rable waitin' 'is turn."

"You just look at his face when he bows at the end. He loves it – it's good for him – and we both know why that's important." Milly was not convinced. How on earth could Jack be aware of Dando's expression anyway?

Lots were drawn, the rival act won and decided to go first. Over the period that Dando was clearing each successive competition hurdle none of his friends had given much thought as to who their man would be up against in the final if he got that far. Now they discovered that his adversaries were to be a quartet that they vaguely remembered from the first round. These opponents were four well-built young men, members of a close harmony group know as the Quickfires, who sang popular songs in sweet, beautifully modulated tenor and counter-tenor voices. They had become flavour of the month with the audience at the main contest during the latter stages and boasted a remarkably wide appeal. As Dando had his rumbustious aficionados who were determined to be in at the finish, so these singers - typical Rytonians in appearance - could claim their own band of slightly older supporters. The rival factions were already at each others' throats, exchanging insults, even before the evening got under way.

The orchestra opened the proceedings with an accomplished performance showcasing the several virtuoso soloists within its ranks and then the anchorman got down to business.

"Ladies and gentlemen, put your hands together for our favourite thespian; you've seen him in most of the cutting-edge wrangler movies of the past decade. I give you - Cole Hawlings!"

A loose-limbed untidily-dressed individual shambled onto the stage, a hand raised to acknowledge the enthusiastic applause. He bent his lanky frame forward in order to speak into the microphone.

"Hi folks. I'm just here to introduce you to these four guys that everyone has been talking about for the last few days. They're know as the Quickfires and if I know black from white they're heading for a quick-fire success. I think you'll understand why we're so excited about them when you hear what they have on offer. Come out here boys... here they come... Bob, Mac, Derek and Simon – collegiates to a man. Sit back folks, open your ears and get ready to be wowed!"

Whether the quartet quite lived up to this wholehearted endorsement of their talents was a moot point. They performed three songs a-cappella, ambitiously arranged, the third one being a well-known ballad full of patriotic sentiments. The audience sang along and voiced their approbation at the end. There was a large machine at the edge of the platform called a Cheerograph which allocated a number according to volume of applause. The two men manning it held up cards showing the reading. The Quickfires scored 235 points.

"And now," announced the compère, once again taking centre stage, "we have another treat in store for you. Straight from the set of her latest film which we hear is to be a talkie version of that famous old silent *The Immigrant's Wife* we are proud to bring to you in person... Miss Melissa Walters!"

He looked to his right and everyone waited for the well-known star to appear. They waited in pleasurable anticipation and then waited some more. After a while the master of ceremonies appeared to be listening to someone speaking from behind the screen that hid the side of the stage.

"You what?" he said, cupping his ear. "She's not? Are you sure? I understood she'd already arrived – oh, I see..." He turned to the audience apologetically. "I'm sorry ladies and gentlemen," he went on, "I thought Miss Walters was going to introduce our second contestant but it seems she's been called away rather unexpectedly and..."

"I'll introduce him!"

Becca had jumped to her feet and was already climbing the steps to the stage fluffing out her hair and smoothing her dress as she did so.

"I don't know if you remember me, people," she began, adjusting the microphone and addressing the crowd, "your moms and dads might. You won't recognise my voice unless you came to one of my stage shows because I left the movie business before the talkies began, but I know it like the back of my hand. I'm called Peepo."

"Miss Peepo!" cried just one or two older voices from the rear of the stadium.

"That's right – I've been over the Tethys for a spell but when I returned only about a week ago I brought a young man with me who has such a remarkable god-given talent that he's been able to surmount enormous difficulties in order to perform for you tonight. You know him as Footless but I am proud to call him my friend and hope I'll always be able to do so. Come on up here, sweetheart."

She smiled at Dando and beckoned him onto the stage beside her. Slowly he negotiated the stairs to stand at her right hand while his fan-club yelled their approbation. Becca pulled his head down and gave him a kiss.

"Good-luck honey chil'," she murmured.

Dando turned to the band and issued some last minute instructions concerning the sort of music he required. This was the self-same ensemble, the self-same conductor, that had tried to subvert his routine on the first day of the contest, but, at the time, instead of being put off his stroke he had been inspired. Soon after, he had made the changing rhythms, the succession of time-signatures, part of his act and these virtuosic transformations had become one of his trade marks along with the moth-eaten greatcoat and the contentious missing foot. So now he was ready to welcome any test of his abilities and was up for the worst they could throw at him. He knew that if he was going to have any hope of winning he would have to excel himself, because about a third of the audience had debouched from Ry-Town for the final, curious about the hype, and were consequently new to his act. They had been told to prepare for total amazement but instead had brought a large dose of scepticism with them; they would not have been surprised if this new phenomenon had turned out to be some provincial hick with delusions of grandeur. In fact as the spectacle progressed they were both charmed and delighted by his performance but also more than a little shocked.

"My dear – who would have thought it?!"

"Shouldn't such blatant exhibitionism be banned?"

"I suppose he's too famous by now for the authorities to step in."

"All the same you can't deny that he's really got something."

Despite their reservations they gave him a rousing ovation when he finally came down to earth and the Cheerograph men held up their cards: 229.

"Final round after the interval," announced the compère.

Becca's party adjourned to the stadium's green room as the show continued and conducted a post-mortem.

"You're going great birdy," encouraged Jack, squeezing his friend's hand. "It couldn't be closer. The next time will be make or break so give it all you've got."

"Cut down on the spins, bro," advised Damask, "try a few more jumps – that's what gets 'em all excited."

"Leave 'im alone," scolded Milly angrily. "'E knows wot 'e's doin' better'n you."

"Change nary a thing," advised Becca. "You're absolutely fine as you are."

Since the start of the evening Foxy had not uttered a word. Now he suddenly made a contribution to the conversation. "I don' think much o' they singers," he complained, "worblin' away like a chicken that's just laid an egg. They should know better at their age."

As for Dando, he said nothing at all.

When they came back into the arena for the return match the order was reversed – the young Glept got first shot. During the break he had been thinking hard about what had gone before and had come up with a few new ideas on how to make his act more compelling. Once again he had words with the band leader and arranged that after the opening bars the accompaniment was to be percussion and nothing but – a driving beat aimed straight at the gut. He approached the lighting engineer in order to ask for the stage illumination to be drastically reduced. All he wanted was a single spotlight which at the forth and eighth minutes would flicker rapidly on and off for several seconds. Then for a finale the entire orchestra was to come in but with the drummer still dominating. His plan was to match these dramatic innovations with wilder and more inventive gymnastics, a bravura performance taking his dancing to a whole new level. As he stood waiting centre stage for the music to begin he prayed to his unknown god, "Give me the strength, please give me strength. Grant that my body doesn't let me down."

It did not let him down. The audience were markedly more enthusiastic at the end of the sequence and roared their approval. The men held up their cards: 237.

Now it was the quartet's turn. They sang three more songs as agreeably and melodiously as before and were acclaimed as enthusiastically by a large section of the audience. But this was followed by an unforeseen hitch. The Cheerograph, which up to that moment had been working perfectly, failed to register the Quickfires' ovation; it seemed that something had gone awry with the mechanism and the needle would not move. When the master of ceremonies invited the crowd to repeat the applause, only to have the same thing happen, he decided, in desperation, to ask for a show of hands.

"All those who think that the Quickfires should win, vote now!" he cried.

A forest of arms shot into the air and the adjudicators peered anxiously out over the crowd, attempting to estimate numbers, before consulting together.

"Now all those who think that the contestant known as Footless should be the winner please make your intentions known!"

Another mass of hands shot up, some enthusiasts leaping up and down as if to make themselves more visible.

"Cheats!" shouted someone from the quartet's faction. "That lot over there are holding up two hands!"

"Footless comes from abroad," someone else yelled above the noise. "Isn't this supposed to be an Armornian competition? Who said he could take part?!" "Yes – why is he allowed in the running?!" a second onlooker shouted, and it did not sound, from this objector's disgusted tone, as if it was just Dando's nationality that was at stake. A few hostile elements began to chorus,"Off! Off!" and soon a whole section had taken it up. In the midst of this mayhem a young man leapt onto the stage, gesturing for the audience to give him a hearing. He then dropped a bombshell.

"The Quickfires have signed a recording contract – they signed it yesterday – they're no more amateurs now than the singers at the Met – they aren't qualified to compete!"

Total uproar followed this announcement. The organisers went into a huddle from which no-one emerged for a considerable length of time. The noise gradually subsided but was replaced by a chant - "Why are we waiting... why are we waiting...?"

At last the anchorman came to the front of the stage and held up his hands.

"The adjudicators have reached a decision. They consider that the objections raised are not serious enough to invalidate the contest," he announced. "The first two rounds will be declared null and void and everything will depend on the applause at the end of a third and final session. The judges will decide who has received the loudest ovation."

For the first time since the whole thing started Jack looked worried.

"What do you think, caridad?" he said gripping Dando's arm, "will you be able to go a third time?"

"I haven't got much choice, have I?" replied his protege with a slight edge to his voice.

"Yes you have," went on an anxious Jack, "you're not being forced. You could tell them you've decided to retire."

Dando shook his head and his mouth set in a thin determined line. All at once he seemed to have moved onto a higher plain mentally and the light of inspiration shone in his eyes.

"I'm not giving up now," he averred.

In contrast the Quickfires appeared thoroughly disconcerted by this turn of events. They were inclined to argue and when overruled took to the stage with sulky expressions on their faces. They repeated three of the songs that the audience had already heard in a distinctly lacklustre manner and received a rather disappointed cheer from their followers.

After a short break Dando climbed the steps for a third time prepared to make a supreme effort. His face was lit up by some sort of unearthly glow and the drummer, picking up on his elevated state, rolled out a thunderous beat, pulling a blast of energy out of thin air. The young amputee began his routine as he meant to go on and was soon throwing his fragile frame into crazier and crazier attitudes which went far beyond what appeared humanly possible. The ten minutes allotted seemed never ending to those who were rooting for him and they gripped their chairs in suspense as they waited to see if he would make it to the finish. Eventually the chief judge held up his hand to indicate that the time had almost elapsed. The band began their final coda and Dando leapt up and up until his legs reached high into the air, his body balancing vertically on top of his crutch while supporting himself on a single arm. He held that stance for longer than seemed credible until, dropping back to earth as lightly as a feather, he stood on his one and only foot and swung the crutch triumphantly up over his head, pointing towards the zenith - it was the same position only reversed one hundred and eighty degrees. The audience jumped to their feet and yelled in consort while Dando bowed low and then went lower still – falling to his knees.

Becca swung round to Damask who was sitting beside her.

"He needs us honey!" she cried.

Jack, already on his feet, caught hold of the younger girl as they sped past and all three rushed to the stage just in time to retrieve Dando as he collapsed into their arms.

It was at least five minutes before the boy opened his eyes to see a circle of concerned faces gazing down at him. Jack was supporting him while Becca knelt at his side dabbing at his sweating features with a towel. He heard Damask's voice coming from nearby and turned his head towards her as she said, "You've done it Do-Do – you've won."

"I've w-won?"

"Yes - they want to give you your prize. I'll collect it for you, shall I?"

"No – no." He made an attempt to rise but found it, as yet, too great an effort. Becca climbed to her feet instead and addressed the restive crowd.

"He's fine folks," she said, "Footless is fine. He just needs a few moments to recover. Bear with him – he'll be back with you in a trice."

And indeed very soon Dando, with Jack's help, was able to get up and limp forward to be presented with a silver trophy and a roll of parchment tied with a red ribbon. The audience cheered themselves hoarse while the various adjudicators and judges smiled sourly. The proceedings were wound up, the bandsmen packed up their instruments and left and, as the crowd began to disperse, the compère came and spoke into Dando's ear in a conspiratorial manner.

"Don't forget – nine-thirty tomorrow at the sponsor's offices. Good idea to have a financial advisor along with you – you want to make sure you get the best deal possible."

"Can you tell me what all that was about?" asked Dando of Jack as their party sat in the taxi that had been summoned to transport everyone back to the Magnolias.

"You haven't looked to see what you've won," said Jack. "Undo the scroll."

Dando untied the ribbon and stared uncomprehendingly at the hand-written script that was revealed.

I promise to pay the bearer the sum of $100,000, the said monies to be spent on financing the setting up of a business in accordance with the wishes of the winner of the Go-Getter Game. Further instalments to be paid as required up to a maximum of $300,000.

"I don't understand," he complained weakly.

"It's your prize-money birdy. Didn't I tell you?" Jack's face wore a wicked grin. "That's what it was all about – that's why it was called the *Go-Getter Game*. Now we've – I mean you've – got the cash to start your own company. How about import-export?"

"No," objected Damask, "that's out of his league – and anyway he wouldn't be interested." She also seemed to be in the know – in fact everybody appeared more genned up about this reward than the one who had earned the money in the first place by his super-human efforts. "I'd go for a shop selling decent clothes for kids," she added, "it's certainly needed."

Foxy broke his silence for the second time. "A plant nursery with a garden shop," was his remarkable contribution.

"A travel agency," said Tallis even more surprisingly. Nobody would have believed he knew anything about such commercial enterprises except for the fact that he had once let slip that he had come across something of this nature in his wanderings and had been aware that it could be a good money-making proposition.

"A *theatrical* agency," suggested Becca. "They're the ones that rake in the bucks, even during a recession."

"'Ow about a beauty parlour?" put forward Milly.

"Oversubscribed," answered Jack dismissing this last suggestion out of hand. The occupants of the taxi began a heated discussion between themselves on the merits of various ventures without noticing that the actual prize-winner had not spoken. In the end Jack became aware of whose hand he was holding and turned to his silent companion.

"What do you think birdy? Don't you reckon import-export would be the safest bet?"

"Clothes," said Damask.

"Plants," insisted Foxy.

"Travel," "Talent," "Beauty." The argument was about to restart.

Dando cleared his throat.

"I-I'm going to open a restaurant," he declared with such conviction that the others were reduced to silence.

It was the evening of the same day. Jack and Dando had retired to their room. On returning to Becca's place they had started to eat a celebratory meal, obtained as usual from the snack-bar up the road, but Dando was drooping with overwhelming fatigue and Jack had soon whisked him away.

"He's got to have his wits about him in the morning," he explained to the others. Once in bed, however, the blind boy seemed inclined to stay awake and talk in the companionable way that was their habit when alone together. He had several things he wanted to get off his chest.

"This catering lark," he began, "it's a pretty uncertain business, liebling. Running something like an eatery is chancy at the best of times. It all depends on reputation and if you put a foot wrong you won't have a leg to stand on"

Dando laughed. "Yes I'll have to succeed right from the off as I certainly don't have a spare foot to stand on. All the same I've been thinking about it for years - I reckon I could make a go of it."

"You know all about the food side, that's a given, but how about the finances? The place has got to pay."

"I'll ask Damask to help – she's good with figures. What's important is the location – somewhere fairly central but without too much competition."

"You weren't thinking of going into the city?"

"Yes – why not?"

"Risky, my love, risky. Better to stay out here on the Heights. Let the punters come to you. Folk are more tolerant out here, more laid back."

"I don't get it. What do you mean by risky?"

Jack frowned and did not reply right away. When he spoke, his mind seemed to have gone off on a tangent.

"This is a weird place, this Rytardenath," he mused. "From what I've gathered so far there's no slums, no ghettos, no crime, no red-light districts – nothing unsavoury. Despite the awful pollution, everything is otherwise prosperous and spic and span, and so are the people."

"Well, that's good... isn't it?" asked Dando uncertainly.

"There are no old people – or at least no one who appears old. Damask said the same. The citizens seem to spend at least half their time exercising and beautifying, trying to stay young for as long as possible. I thought that was great at first but now I realise there's no-one like you and me birdy – no people who can't see – no-one who can't walk. When you got up on that stage I think you were the only character most of the younger members of the audience had ever come across without their full compliment of limbs."

"Perhaps they know how to make people whole again," said Dando somewhat wistfully, "perhaps the old people live in retirement villages."

"I don't know," Jack shook his head. "All I know is it gives me the willies. Watch out, spatzi - stay out of the limelight."

Dando laughed again. "That won't be easy if the restaurant's the success I hope it'll be."

For a long time Jack did not speak until Dando thought he had dropped off, but then his friend remarked abruptly, "If you get invited to dance up town give it a miss."

"You don't need to worry," replied Dando, "I'm not going to dance again - not like that."

"But..."

"It was killing me Jack – I don't want to die just yet – not now I've got my restaurant."

"It was good for you, birdy."

"The restaurant will be good."

At this point Jack did go to asleep – Dando could tell from his regular breathing that he was dead to the world and, for once, had not fallen victim to the nightmares that often plagued his unconscious hours – but he was unable to follow his example. Although so weary that he had reached a state beyond exhaustion his mind was still keyed up thinking about the events of the day, while every muscle and joint in his body throbbed and ached. Finally he got up, slipped the greatcoat over his nakedness and went out into the chilly garden.

In the process of restoring the grounds Foxy had come upon an old wooden bench lost in the undergrowth and had moved it to the top of a bank at the side of the house where he hoped that eventually it would overlook a prospect of hoary moss-hung trees stooping above well-tended lawns and newly-established flower beds. Wandering round the corner from the back entrance Dando was surprised to find Becca sitting on this seat, dimly illuminated by the disk of a sullen red-complexioned moon that floated above the tree tops – there were no stars. He went and stood beside her and without looking towards him she reached out and took his hand in hers as if she needed the comfort of human contact. Dando had a sudden thought: that if Tallis could class himself as old then Becca was probably not much younger.

"No stars," he commented, wondering what his hostess was doing out here so late at night.

"Stars? We never see the stars honey," she replied.

"You never see them? How can people live without stars?"

Becca patted the seat beside her. "Come and sit down," she said.

"They didn't know me," she went on after a long silence. "They've forgotten the old stars – movie stars I'm talking about now. It's all johnnie-come-latelies and talkies, talkies. There's no artistry any more – the silents were universal."

"How long were you away?" asked Dando, repeating Damask's query.

"Oh, not long." She paused and then in a lower tone added, "Well if I'm honest – about ten years. I'm never going to get back into it now. I'm washed up and that's the truth." Her voice broke on the last word.

"No you're not!" Dando's reply was emphatic. Disturbed by her obvious distress he tried to think how he could bring comfort but was at first completely baffled. Then suddenly he had an idea.

"What about Drossi?" he reminded her earnestly. "Everybody was crazy about you in that town. Why don't you do the same thing here? Be a singer again. I'm sure they've got clubs like the Green Goat somewhere around. Jack could probably help – you can bet your life he already knows all the best places to hang out. And..." he was struck by a brilliant thought, "when I get my restaurant going you can be the resident artiste - we'll need some entertainment with the food."

Becca turned to him and by the faint light he could see that she was smiling.

"Well, what d'you know – I think you've hit the nail on the head there, sweet-pea. Not films – live performances. Why di'n't I think of that? I could probably get a spot at the Kelly Klub if ol' Whit is still in charge – we used to be pretty cosy at one time."

The ex-movie-queen had been sitting with shoulders slumped in a position of defeat. Now she pulled herself together and seemed to obtain a new lease of life, lifting her chin as if once more ready to face the world. All the same there was a certain pathos about this brave rallying of forces which struck Dando as sad. Why, he wondered, was Becca so alone on this, her old stamping ground, where she should have been well supported; why was there no-one around to look after her and take her part? Apropos of this he was aware that if Damask and Milly had any problems with Horry they consulted the show girl. She seemed to know a lot about raising children.

"Where's your family, Becca?" he asked diffidently.

"Ma boys? I've no ideah. They disappeared long since. They preferred their pappy to me and when we split..."

Her voice was full of bitterness.

"I-I'm Sorry," said Dando.

"No, honey – don't apologise, I'm not offended. If they'd been anything like you it would have been a different story but they took after their da – more's the pity. Well I guess I'd better make tracks – an' so should our world-beater after his tremendous day. Go to your bed, pumpkin, and get up bright and bushy tailed in the morning."

She kissed him and departed.

Dando sat for a long time staring at the smoky-looking moon. He was feeling guilty at the prospect of being happy. It was three weeks now since he had learnt of Ann's death and recently he had begun to believe that he was learning to live with the heartache in the same way that he lived with his missing foot; but then, every so often, the realisation of his loss would hit him like a newly inflicted wound, raw and bleeding, almost as if he had only just heard the news. At such times the self-same accusations would repeat and repeat in his mind like a series of nails being driven into a coffin: he had got her with child, he had arrived too late and had not been there when she needed him most, he had high-tailed it out of Drossi without even visiting her grave. "I'll never be free of this," he agonised and immediately knew that he did not deserve to be free. Such had been the tenor of his thoughts up until the previous night. But now in the last few hours everything had changed; a dazzling prospect had opened before him as soon as he had learnt that he was to be given money to realise his lifelong ambition. He had a reason to go on living now, a compelling reason, but, however rewarding his forthcoming existence might be, it would be a life lived without Ann, a life in which she would drift further and further into the past, maybe finally to be forgotten. Surely imagining that he could have a future in a world where she was forever absent was a form of disloyalty which could be classed as yet another breach of faith to add to those of which he was already guilty.

The moon had gone behind a cloud and with its disappearance illumination from above was cut off. Earlier in the evening there had been fireworks – man-made stars – but now the only light that remained - low down and to his right - took the form of an angry glare spreading upwards into the sky, generated by the looming presence of the city. In his immediate vicinity everything was shadowy and below him the garden disappeared into a darkness black as widow's weeds. At least that is what he would have expected. But there was something in the midst of the gloom which he could not quite make out. Dando left the bench and walked down the slope in front of him until he arrived at the edge of a row of trees. In the centre of his field of vision hung a patch of silvery luminescence whose location was hard to determine; was it nearby, within touching distance, or was it further afield? Perhaps his eyesight was playing tricks as a result of his extreme exhaustion. As he moved forward the light seemed to retreat before him leading him into wilder and wilder locales. He stumbled into a briar patch, the thorns scratching his skin and tearing at his coat. Brought to a halt he tried hard to extricate himself and it was then that he saw her; she was standing just a few feet away, shining like a tiny sun come down to earth.

"***My bonny lad,***" she said.

"No – no." He attempted to hide his eyes, but the brambles trapped his arm and immobilised him. "No – not again. Go away Annie – you're not real – it's just a dream – just a dream – I can't bear it."

"***Be you asleep then?***" she asked.

"Asleep? I must be – it can't be real."

In desperation he made a superhuman effort to escape and tore himself free, but in the process managed to score his skin so deeply that blood came welling out of the cuts. He went to walk hurriedly away, but then, behind him, heard her voice once more.

"***What night do it be?***"

"Night?" He paused, then turned back puzzled. "It's the last night of the month – the end of summer and the beginning of winter."

"It be the night of those that have gone before. The night when the veils are lifted. The night when you see clearer than any other night of the year."

"The Eve of the Ancestors – Sahwain. Is it real then? Is it really you? Where are you, Annie – where have you come from?"

"From as far as the stars – from as close as the beat of your own heart."

Her image hung in the miasma, a vision from another world.

"Annie – Annie," he cried again, and then piteously, "don't leave me."

"My love," she replied, ***"I'm here – I'll always stay beside you if it be within my power. But you mus' be careful, – there be danger - great danger – although Dadda and I will do our best to make it so the lock of hair I gave you protects you from what threatens."***

Dando put his hand to his neck. "You mean..." he began but then faltered as the manifestation darkened and began to fade into the night. ***"Go to your bed,"*** he heard the girl murmur.

"Annie!" His intensity called her back and she stood before him once more as if ready to do his bidding. "But I can't sleep," he pleaded, "that's why I came out here."

"Go to your pallet, my love. I'll help you."

When Dando, obeying, made his way back to the house and climbed between the sheets he found that a transformation had taken place. For the first time since leaving Gweek he was at peace with the world, almost as if another warm body lay next to his, as if loving arms surrounded him. He sighed, and gradually the unhappy tension that had been his companion for days, weeks, months past, melted from his limbs, temporarily taking his pain along with it. His skin felt as if it were being bathed in a sanctified balm and the very air he breathed was healing. He sighed again – a deep, deep sigh – and fell into a fathomless oblivion, only to awake the next morning determined to believe that the whole night-time experience had been a figment of his skewed and exhausted imagination.

There's one who walks beside you,
In addition to those already there.
Tell me, is it a man, a woman or is it...?

Chapter four

"Where is he – where is he – where is he? Lost – lost – lost..."

"Ha-ha, wife! I know where he is! You can find out these things if, like me, you look down from above – not when you look up from below as you do. I look through air - you look through the sod."

"Where is he then, husband – where is he?"

"I'll give you three guesses."

"Is he in the place of the oracle where that witch so foolishly crossed me? (I soon got even with her). No, I see that he is not. Is he on the Island where he would have died but for your stupid intervention? No not there. Is he in the fortress on the Outcrop? - is he in the city by the River's Hand? He was but he has gone. Or is he across the water in the place where the fleshed ones gather as densely as the stars at the galaxy's hub – is that where he is?"

"Stop wife - as usual you don't play fair – that's five questions you've asked me!"

"Ah – it's that last one – I see - you've as good as told me how to find him! Now I know what to do – I'll make the thing happen there that would have happened anyway in the course of time. It will take about half an orbit to accomplish but I'll start right away."

"No – as I've already told you, if you kill him now, you will have done the most foolish deed in the entire history of our race. Let him live - let him find the treasure – it's his destiny – and then we can take it from him. After that you can end his life if you so desire."

"But can you imagine what would happen if he turned it, or worse, if he took it far away from this planet where we are trapped for all time? No, I will act according to my own lights, husband. This is a quarrel that has been long in the making; it's mine and mine alone and no one, let alone you, should interfere. And

remember – we are not the only ones to have an interest – don't forget the dark son who holds his own brother in thrall, the one who was cheated of what he desired. He may prove stronger than either of us if the seeker gets too close to the Caves of Bone. Better that the wretch should die right here and now."

"I remember - how could I forget."

When Dando went for his interview with the contest's sponsors in one of the high-rise buildings on the other side of the West River he took both Damask and Becca along as advisers: Damask for her financial astuteness, Becca for her knowledge of local currency and prices. But when it came to decisions about location, type of property, suitable personnel, fixtures and fittings, he needed no assistance. The men with the money were startled to receive a detailed briefing from this very young yet disabled man, all explained without the aid of notes. It was not long before they forgot his age and physical state and started dealing with him as respectfully as they would anyone who obviously knew his onions and was their equal in business nous when it came to setting up this particular project. A couple of hours later the three petitioners retired triumphant with the wherewithal to put the whole enterprise in train.

Dando could not bear to waste a minute in realising his lifelong ambition. That very day various calls were made, including one to an estate agent, another to a reputable builder, a third to a company supplying kitchen equipment and a further one to a furniture warehouse. In no time at all they had been apprised of a newly-erected premises actually situated on a corner of Mornington Heights' topmost square just below the point where the land reached its highest elevation. From the upper floor of this building there was a fine view across the outskirts of the city towards the vast towers at its centre. The construction-workers moved in immediately, followed by painters and decorators. Soon the kitchen was taking shape in accordance with Dando's long-cherished scheme which, for the first time, and mainly for the benefit of others, he had been persuaded to set down on paper in black and white. Initially the rather inadequate plumbing was removed and replaced by a more cutting-edge system after which came the installation of stoves and ovens, work surfaces and storage units. Then the tools of the chef's trade were acquired, the pots and pans and implements whose quality Dando insisted should be of the finest. Becca, Jack and Milly had a hand in designing the eating area on the first floor. Despite his blindness Jack was not going to be deprived of the opportunity to give advice on the sort of ambiance needed to attract the current in-crowd. Eventually they settled on a décor which was stylish yet unobtrusive.

Within a matter of days Dando began writing menus and interviewing possible employees. It was now in particular that he regretted the absence of his precious box of herbs and spices which had been lost to the fire at Gweek. He voiced his concerns and as a result someone directed him to a poky little emporium up a nearby side-street that proved to be a veritable treasure-house when it came to the flavourings needed for his recipes. Milly lent a hand in creating the waiter's uniforms and even invented one for herself. She had spent the past year growing up. Her friends, being so close by, had barely noticed the change, but since the start of their journey she had altered considerably and could no longer be described as a recalcitrant and rather kooky child. On the contrary, in the last few months she had blossomed into a beautiful young woman well on the way to confident adulthood.

"I c'n take orders," she informed Dando. "I c'n talk posh wiv the best of 'em. Let me 'elp in the dinin' room."

"Why not," replied the budding entrepreneur.

Damask purchased several ledgers and set about keeping the books in the tiny cubby-hole that was to serve as an office.

Such initial preliminaries occupied the new owner for at least fourteen hours a day. He returned to the Magnolias merely to sleep and was therefore seeing very little of Tallis. This worried him and gave rise to the suggestion that the knight should spend the day at the half-constructed restaurant where he would be under observation and his needs necessarily catered for. Tallis was nothing loath. Once installed inside the front window of the premises he enjoyed watching the progress of the project and was not slow to offer advice. His spell as a musician with no means of musical expression had finally ended. It was a red-letter day when Jack came back from an investigative foray up town gripping the neck of a large guitar-shaped instrument which looked as if it had been left out in the rain: it was ancient, battered and filthy dirty.

"Here," he said offering it to Tallis, "I picked this up – would it be of any use to you?"

Tallis took it from him with distaste, but when he tried strumming its few remaining strings a rich mellow chord awoke beneath his fingers. He had been in danger of a misjudgement; this was apparently an aristocrat fallen on hard times. It was nothing like the kuckthu of recent fond memory, but there was a similar exoticism about it that suggested that it had come from afar.

"It needs a lot of work," he replied tentatively.

"Let me have it for a bit," said Jack, "I'll see if I can find somebody."

He took it away with him and a week later brought it back transformed. The wood had been cleaned and varnished, the keys replaced and the twelve strings restrung. With it came a small bow.

"It's called a cithona," Jack told him. "I've been informed it's normally played with this," flourishing the bow, "but evidently you can also use a plectrum, whatever that is."

"I've got one," Tallis answered.

From that point on he was no longer idle as he sat in the restaurant overlooking the upper square but spent the time feeling his way around this new music-maker, mastering the intricacies of its harmonics and gradually persuading his stiff finger joints to loosen up. Whether he was playing it as its creator intended he had no idea but it was not long before his skills began to return and he found ways of adapting his old repertoire to this unfamiliar instrument. The fitters and other workmen, slaving away from morning to night in order to have the place ready for the winter holidays, appreciated this accompaniment to their efforts.

"Once we're in business you must carry on playing," Dando told him. "I thought a while ago that it'd just add the finishing touch to have music with the food. Jack's offered to take part - he's found himself some sort of flute to replace his old penny whistle – and Becca says she could have a go at singing for us when she's got an hour or two to spare."

On one particular evening during the time they were going through these preparations the afor-mentioned lady waylaid Dando as he was on his way to bed.

"Come into the front parlour, sugar. I've got something to show you."

Entering the room his eye was immediately caught by an object on the table. Lying there he saw a plain but exquisite silver pendant set with a smooth, semi-precious gemstone within the depths of which a tiny storm of nameless colours swirled. The piece was obviously of some antiquity. Becca pressed a concealed catch and the front sprung open to reveal a hidden compartment.

"My grandmama's locket," she explained. "What you keep inside it is supposed to bring luck and protection to the wearer. I wondered if you'd like to have it?"

Dando looked at her questioningly. Why should she want to relinquish something which, even ignoring what it might fetch at auction, must yet be of sentimental value?

"It's a place where you can keep treasured mementos," Becca went on earnestly, "precious memories of someone dear to you. I thought you might have a use for it, sweetheart."

Dando blanched and his hand moved protectively to his throat.

"Yes – you understand me. That little braid you've got round your neck is going to fall apart real soon – it's awful raggedy and dirty. Let me untangle it and clean it for you – then you can put part in here," indicating the locket, "and the rest somewhere safe. I promise you I won't let it come to harm and when you get it back I believe it will be a boon to your well-being."

"But..." cried Dando, his emotion clearly visible on his countenance.

"Trust me, honey, trust me. Sit down there – let me see what I can do."

For more than a minute the boy stood irresolute; then he obeyed her. Becca set to work, tugging, teasing and occasionally snipping with her nail scissors when the tangles proved to be too obdurate. Eventually the plait was freed and Becca held it up in front of him between thumb and forefinger. Dando gazed his fill; it was the first time he had set eyes on it, apart from in a mirror, since that night of joy and terror when he had discovered it wound around his fingers. There was no sign of its original colour: sweat and dirt had turned it a dark brown and it looked like a bit of unidentifiable rubbish that has got caught up in a drain grating.

"I'll have it ready for you by tomorrow," promised Becca, "I won't lose even a single hair"

Dando repossessed it, held it to his lips and then handed it back.

On setting out for the restaurant the next morning, after a sleepless night, he was feeling horribly exposed. It would not have surprised him if some terrible disaster had occurred during the course of the day, so much did he feel that his good fortune was tied up with that little tress. For the whole period he was away from the house he was on tenterhooks and by evening could hardly bear to wait for leaving-off time before he returned. It was with a sense of dread that he went and tapped on Becca's door. The show girl opened to him, then, smiling, took him by the hand and led him to the parlour table. There, in pride of place, lay the open locket and inside it was curled, like a tiny animal asleep, a silvery strand that gleamed in the light.

Dando put out a finger to touch but then withdrew his hand as if afraid of disturbing it.

"It's hers," he said wonderingly, "it's really hers."

"Here's the rest, honey," said Becca, "in this envelope. I've braided it as before."

Dando took the envelope and after looking within stowed it safely in an inside pocket.

"Thankyou, thankyou," he cried fervently, "I can't thank you enough!"

Becca closed the locket's compartment and held it out to him by its chain.

"Let's put her back where she belongs, and where she can protect you," she said.

Dando stooped and Becca fastened the chain around his neck.

"There you are, sweet pea," she comforted, "she'll be safe now and so will you."

He smiled a watery smile. "Thankyou, thankyou – you're so very good to me."

At last everything was complete; the eating-house was up and ready to go. Forty-eight hours before the grand opening the name Dando had chosen for his treasured enterprise was painted above the frontage: the restaurant was to be called *The Dark Continent*. On the day in question a few minor celebrities, acquaintances of Becca's, were persuaded to grace the new venture with their presence. More significantly, as the time approached, a queue of local people formed along the pavement outside Number Three Top Square. Curiosity in the neighbourhood had been piqued and some that remembered Dando from the talent contest came to see whether he was going to make a go of this new enterprise or finally fall flat on his face. Among the prospective patrons was a group of his teenage supporters, many by this time equipped with crutches of their own. One young man even attempted to dance in the street in imitation of his idol although as aids he had two metal elbow crutches, nothing like Dando's old-fashioned wooden support. The press attended in force and the new owner did his best to answer, perhaps too openly, their intrusive questions: "How old are you? Where do you come from? Why are you here? What do you think of Ry-Town? What's happened to your foot? Are you dating?" As soon as he was able, he escaped back to the real business of the day: food preparation. Tensions could not fail to be high in the kitchen as every member of staff knew that this was make or break time for the new undertaking;

a slip-up now might prove disastrous. But by eleven o'clock that night they had seen the last satisfied customer out the door and everything seemed to have gone smoothly. It was now just a question of clearing up and making provision for the morrow.

Damask and Becca had eaten a meal on the house and stayed while Damask dealt with the takings. Then they returned to the Magnolias, accompanied by Jack, who had turned up from goodness knows where. Going down the hill Becca bought a copy of that evening's edition of the local rag. Prominent on the front page was a banner headline and article referring to the eatery's opening and below it a further report. She was understandably appalled: *TITLED RESTAURANT OWNER, 18, ALREADY FATHER!* yelled the streamer. There was a photo of Dando in his kitchen whites gazing rather foolishly at the camera after which ran the following: *Our new infant phenomenon, winner of the Go-Getter-Game and known as Footless to his many fans, confided to me the tale of the tragedy that has blighted his young life...*

"Oh my word!" gasped the showgirl.

"What does it say?" demanded Damask and Jack.

Becca read out the offending column.

"Don't let Dando see it," ordered Damask.

"Too late," replied Jack, grim faced. "Someone will have rubbed his nose in it, you can bet your life - people are nice like that."

"Well don't let him know *we've* seen it."

When Dando eventually came back to the house, long after midnight, he was tight-lipped, silent and responded to their congratulations with a slight grimace. However, he had learnt his lesson. From then on he was extremely wary of anyone working for the media and confined his dealings with the press to the occasional advert placed in one of the more up-market magazines.

Not that the restaurant needed publicity. From day one it became a rip-roaring success, personal recommendation spreading like wildfire across the city. The people who had attended the opening through mere inquisitiveness went away deeply impressed and soon came back with friends and relatives in tow. As well as the slightly passé celebs, recruited by Becca, the establishment's patrons began to include important producers, directors and several major movie stars. The menu Dando served up was like nothing else to be found in the Greater Rytardenath area. Although not the slightest bit precocious or fanciful, it could not help but seem highly exotic to the Armornian palate because it came from the hand and imagination of someone totally out of step with the local cuisine. As far as Dando was concerned he was just offering good honest food of the kind that one's mother is reputed to make but very rarely does. However, this was not the impression the menu conveyed to his Ry-Town customers. He included a few Terratenebrian regional plats out of interest, Cloud Watcher's Crumble amongst them, and some of the snacks he had learnt about from fairground fast-food outlets as amuse bouches, but his signature dishes were all of his own invention and therefore completely original. At first he did not realise what a sensation he was creating in modish epicurean circles.

Becca and Damask both had difficulty picturing Dando in the role of head-honcho at the restaurant; they doubted he had the personal authority to command a business composed of a number of gifted and therefore somewhat idiosyncratic and unconventional men and women. Jack however begged to differ.

"If you think that, you don't know your brother," he told Damask. "You may imagine that he's an easy touch, that he's soft as butter – yes - but there's a core of steel in there somewhere - there has to be for him to have come this far. Lots of people, if they'd been through what he's been through, would have given up long ago."

In fact, once the Dark Continent had been in existence for a few weeks, those involved as employees or suppliers realised that Dando ran a tight ship and was not prepared to tolerate passengers. If one of the sou-chefs failed to come up to his high standards he very carefully explained where they were going wrong. Once, twice he would do this; then, on the third occasion, if there had been no discernible improvement, he would dismiss the offender out of hand despite not raising his voice or appearing to get angry in any way. There was never any problem in filling the vacancy: applicants were clamouring at the door.

The new restaurant's clients had to set aside their preconceived notions concerning what was decent, what was fitting and seemly, when they entered its portals. After all, this eating house boasted a one-legged owner, a black girl on almost equal footing with the patrons and an old man in a wheelchair who played background music while they ate, occasionally accompanied by a blind boy on a flute, all things totally at variance with Rytardenath acceptability. Also there was, would you believe it, a live dog ensconced just inside the main entrance; the Department of Health would not be too happy about that; animals and eating establishments did not mix. But this was part of the attraction, the very proscribed nature of what was on offer adding a spice of danger alongside the other exotic spices

Dando used in his cooking, and as a consequence drawing in the crowds.

Very soon the business began making money hand over fist and Dando was eager to share his good fortune with the rest of the small collective who had done so much to help bring about his triumph. Nevertheless he realised that this had to be accomplished in as tactful a manner as possible. To Damask, Milly and Tallis he was able to pass on a share of the profits in the form of bonus wages while to Becca he gave a regular generous emolument in exchange for their keep. Instinctively he knew he could not hand Foxy money directly; instead he set aside a lump sum which he instructed Becca to donate in small regular amounts to the horticulturist for *work in the garden*. When he offered Jack some of his wealth his friend grinned and patted his top pocket.

"No need, patootie, I'm flush – but thanks all the same."

Dando wondered, with a certain amount of disquiet, where Jack's money came from.

Every so often, even as far out as Mornington Heights, an earth tremor *shook the windows and rattled the walls*. It was a strange sensation, almost as if for a few minutes the ground liquidised and began washing around like the sea. These incidents never lasted long - it was just a question of hanging on to some nearby support and waiting for equilibrium to return. Occasionally there was minor damage. For a laugh Dando offered free meals on the nights when such shocks occurred but this soon proved to be an uneconomic proposition – they were happening far too frequently. When the minor quakes started to take place nearly every other day there was some public unease. Eventually a statement was issued by the powers-that-be and broadcast over the radio: *Seismologists working for the Department of Home Affairs assure listeners that the recent increase in substrata activity is just temporary. The government has the matter well in hand and as soon as they have eliminated the cause of the disturbance the situation will begin to stabilise. However citizens are warned to be on their guard and to report any negative manifestations.*

Over the next couple of weeks this mysterious prediction appeared to come true: things calmed down but left behind a residue of static electricity. People became quite used to getting minor shocks off common household objects.

Dando was a hands-on cook; he was not prepared to sit back and play a merely supervisory role. But he found that coping on one leg and a crutch while preparing dishes in a hot, steamy, crowded kitchen where everyone was working flat out and rushing to and fro at a rate of knots was incredibly difficult. He began to feel he was just getting in the way, that he was a hindrance to others, and his mood, which had been euphoric, gradually darkened. Jack would have picked up on this if he had been around, but the group was seeing less and less of him as the days wore on. Eventually Becca noticed that their young high-flyer was not displaying as much joie-de-vie as formally and tried to discover the reason. Dando was reluctant to reveal the cause of his angst but she was incredibly persistent and managed to worm it out of him.

"Yes my dear," she said after he had explained, "I guess I know what you're feeling but I reckon I could put you on to someone who might help. I've been thinking you ought to go and see this guy ever since we got here all those weeks ago. Can you spare a morning? Tomorrow's the day the restaurant's closed isn't it? I'll give him a call and if it's ok I'll take you over there."

Becca, on Dando's advice, had gone up-town looking for cabaret work and had been lucky enough to be given a spot at the Kelly Klub, despite the fact that her old friend Whit was no longer the owner. Coincidentally she found she was sharing the bill with none other than the Posse, on whom the man in charge had also been prepared to take a chance, as waifs from beyond the Tethys seemed to be all the rage this season. Both group and show girl were having a modest success. She also occasionally sang at the Dark Continent. With wages coming in it had been possible to get one of her two old cars, which had been mothballed since before she went away, out of storage and fit it for the road. It was in this vintage vehicle that she and Dando set out to drive into the city.

Hidden here and there at the base of the massive skyscrapers lay some remnants of an earlier, gentler age: an intrepid explorer might still come across two or three story brownstone buildings that had escaped the developer's bulldozer. Becca brought her car to a halt in front of one of these houses and then led the way up the path. They were greeted by a thin nervous man who ushered them quickly inside and then looked suspiciously up and down the street before closing the front door. He conducted them through the house to a flight of steps that descended into what was apparently a coal cellar. On the wall in front of them, once they reached the bottom, were shelves holding a collection of tools, tins and glass bottles. The man pulled out a loose brick from the wall onto which the shelves were fixed, inserted his hand into the cavity, gave something a quick twist and then stood back as the whole wall, shelves and all, swung aside. Walking forward, he switched on a light and turned to invite them to follow.

"There you go, honey," said Becca, "Solly here has got what you need. While he's fixing you up I'll mosey on down to the club and make arrangements for tonight. I'll be back in about half an hour."

When she returned after thirty-five minutes Dando was just coming out of the door of the house carrying a large brown-paper parcel. He dumped this, along with his crutch, in the back of the car before sliding into the passenger seat.

"You decided not to wear it home?" commented Becca.

"No. I'll show you what it's like when we get back. What an amazing place! He's got hundreds of bits and pieces – legs, arms, feet, hands - eyes and ears even – and all made by himself. But why all the secrecy?"

"Well..." began Becca; she seemed suddenly tremendously uneasy about something. "Solly must feel it isn't wise for too many people to know what sort of business he runs – you see it's not strictly legal I'm afraid. I don't think... No... it'd take too long to explain."

Dando turned to her and grinned.

"No matter," he said. "If this works you'll have done me an enormous favour – I'll be eternally grateful."

All his companions were on hand, even Jack, on their return and they gathered round in order to view Dando's new purchase. He disappeared behind a convenient door while they waited patiently for about five minutes. Then he emerged, crutchless, his heightened colour hinting at substantial embarrassment.

"What do you think?" he asked diffidently.

Milly was the first to find her voice.

"Crikey!" she exclaimed.

There was a combined murmur of astonishment from the others present. What they were witnessing was a substitute limb, a prosthesis, which Dando had strapped onto his stump in lieu of his missing extremity but...

"Honey chil'," moaned Becca, "I meant for you to choose something that looks like a *foot* – a proper foot – not a weird piece of scrap iron."

Well might she exclaim. The replacement appeared to be nothing more than a twisted metal blade, a scribbled zigzag line, and bore no resemblance to a human body-part whatsoever.

"But look Becca," cried Dando eagerly, "I can walk without help – I won't need my crutch anymore – or even a stick. I can run even!" and he demonstrated up and down the room. "This is springy – miles better than the wooden legs I tried – he told me it was his own invention."

"You won't be needing my arm anymore either," said Jack quietly, a rueful smile on his lips. Dando glanced keenly at his friend. He was wise enough by now to understand what the other was feeling and there was a complex mixture of emotions in his heart.

The next morning he set out jubilantly for the Dark Continent's kitchen buoyed up by a conviction that he would now be able to cope with even the most gruelling of conditions. The first thing he did on reaching the restaurant, however, was to have the old wooden crutch mounted on the wall in the dining area, just over where Tallis sat and played. It had been a good friend.

Although Dando could now walk with confidence and even take to his heels if necessary, his body would never regain the youthful vigour which he had hardly been aware he possessed in the days before his suicidal dice with death. By this time he had reconciled himself to the fact that the pain in his joints and the cramps in his muscles were part of him now and would remain so until he reached the end of the road which was probably far closer than had once been the case; there was no use complaining, you just had to live with things as they were and get on with life. He tired easily, felt cold all the time, became nauseous after only moderate exercise (as he had already reluctantly admitted, his virtuoso dancing has almost killed him) and if any infection was going round he was sure to catch it. These disabilities were a secret that he kept hidden as much as possible – to friends and acquaintances he tried to appear in reasonably good shape. The two people who could have read him and understood what he had to endure were both absent; namely Ann, whose mysterious reappearance at Sahwain he still refused to acknowledge, and Jack – well, they hardly ever saw Jack these days. Tallis was unaware that anything was wrong and, as for Damask, her mind was elsewhere: Dando was just her brother, too close to be seen clearly. Foxy ignored him most of the time and even Milly tended to accept his state of health at face value, assuring herself that her Lordship was fine now that he had his restaurant and his new foot.

As stated Jack was rarely present at the mansion, but occasionally he would put in an unexpected appearance and then disappear just as rapidly. One morning around dawn, the young man from Deep Hallow opened his eyes to see the Vadrosnian sitting, fully dressed, on the edge of the second bed in the twin-bedded room apparently staring fixedly at him from behind his shades. Dando had to remind himself that his friend was blind and that therefore his smile of greeting was wasted. Instead he swung himself round and leaning forward took the boy's hands in his saying, "Jack – I've missed you." In response Jack changed beds and came and sat beside him.

"I've got to talk to you, birdy," he began, "it's about you and me." He seemed to be in a very serious mood.

"Oh," said Dando, "you're not going to tell me anything bad I hope."

"Not bad, but not really good either. You see..." he stopped and for an extended period made no attempt to continue.

"How can I see," said Dando, "unless you tell me."

"It's you and me, my love. You're the one – you always will be, above all the others – you blow me away. But I'm not cut out for celibacy – do you get what I'm saying?"

Dando ducked his head.

"I can't Jack – I just can't."

"No, no – I know spatzi, my little bird – I'm not asking you to. But in that case – do you understand?"

Dando thought for a while then nodded slightly awkwardly, squeezing the other's hand. "I think I know what you mean Jack but it doesn't matter. You're my friend – you'll always be my friend, whatever..."

Jack embraced him and held him close for a long time. Then he rose, blew a kiss, and went out the door. Those he passed a few minutes later as he climbed Decatur Drive might have caught a self-justifying mumble with which he seemed to be trying to still a guilty conscience: "Now he's doing so well he doesn't need me – I've got my own life to lead after all..."

Milly was concerned about her appearance. As the only female member of staff in the dining area she felt that it devolved on her to uphold the reputation of the establishment. She wanted her hair to look just right, she wanted to use the tones of make-up that suited her complexion and, when not wearing her uniform, she wanted the latest fashions. But, on calling in at a local beauty salon to book an appointment, she was met with indignation followed by threats of physical violence. In high dudgeon the owner unceremoniously showed her the door. The same thing happened as soon as she set foot over the threshold of a nearby dress shop. Because Becca had done her best to shield her guests from some of the more brutal realities of Ry-Town life it took her a while to realise that as a result of a mere accident of birth, the fact that she had been born with a dark skin, she was persona non grata in the Albercreek Federation: people of her race were treated here in much the same way as the Nablar had been treated in Deep Hallow. The awareness that her friends would be accepted into this society while she would not came as a bitter blow, so much so that she was *like a one-eyed cat peeping in a sea-food store.* Rejection was to be her lot on this side of the Middle Sea and all that remained open to her if she left the restaurant was the role of a mere menial or drudge condemned to perform the dirty jobs that nobody else would tackle. The idea was so hurtful that she could not bring herself to confide her unhappiness to those around her; instead she nursed her shame in silence and told no-one – no-one that is apart from a middle-aged coloured woman whom Dando had employed to work her way through the mountains of washing-up each evening.

"Mabelene – 'ow on earth are we s'pposed to keep ourselves lookin' nice? When I went to get me 'air done they chased me away. You've got nice 'air – 'oo does it for you?"

"You wan' get your hair prettified, gel? Come longa me this evening when I go back to Floodwood an' you c'n call in at ol' Miz Trubshaw's. She'll be fixin' to do it for you – like she does for all the black folks – bin doin' it fer years. You c'n stay wi' me overnight so long as you don't mind sharin'. My man's bin taken up north to work in the mines."

"Mabelene's arst me to go 'ome wiv 'er," said Milly to Damask. "She sez I c'n get me 'air done an' maybe be fitted out wiv some nice clothes as well. Termorrer I c'n come back fer the second 'alf. I won't be there at lunchtime but I'll be in time fer the evening shift. C'n you tell the Lordship?"

Out of respect Milly never normally spoke to Dando directly when he was filling the exalted role of head chef. Damask passed on the message.

"Will she be all right?" worried the restaurant owner, "I don't know anything about Mabelene except that she's a good worker."

"She'll be ok," replied Damask, "Milly's got her head screwed on right and can look after herself. She doesn't need mollycoddling."

When the restaurant's front door was finally locked, sometime around the witching hour, the little black girl waited outside in the street while her new friend disappeared into the yard at the back. When she emerged she was pushing an old, impressively large, bone-shaker of a bike. At the rear of the machine a metal rack was fixed, obviously designed to hold luggage. The vehicle was not equipped with lights.

"My man picked it up at the dumps," said the black woman proudly. "S'prisin' what you c'n find there. Some white folks got more money than sense. You'll have to sit 'stride this bit at the back. It's mostly downhill."

As far as Milly could tell their journey was undeviatingly downwards. She sat awkwardly on the metal rack, her feet just clearing the ground, her shoulders level with the woman's substantial buttocks, as they free-wheeled westward out of Mornington Heights, touched the affluent coastal district at one point, swept over a bridge spanning an invisible river and into a swampy area *all set about with fever-trees*. The road metamorphosed into a muddy path slightly raised above the country on either side. Glancing into the gloom as they swept along Milly began to notice the presence of dim lights here and there, coming from behind the windows of squat, almost invisible shacks: the forest appeared to be dotted, throughout, with mean little log cabins built amongst the trees. At a certain point Mabelene pulled up abruptly and turned back towards her passenger.

"This is where us darkies live," she said in an authoritative voice, "in a place the rest have no use for. We keeps ourselves to ourselves down here and don' tell no-one else our business. We're not askin' for no white folks to come snoopin' round, showin' us what we can and can't do. In the rest of Ry-Town we have to act pitiful, we have to bow an' scrape an' crawl an' lick people's asses but here we please ourselves. What you see tonight you keep quiet about, gel, else you won't git asked no more."

Milly nodded solemnly, then nodded a second time with a slightly nervous smile. As they penetrated further into the swamp the cabins became thicker on the ground, almost as if they were entering the outskirts of a small town. Then suddenly the track turned a corner and they were faced by a veritable glare of light as they arrived on the periphery of what was obviously the centre of the built-up area. Rows of lanterns hung overhead and they could hear lively music being played. As her eyes adjusted, Milly saw a crowd of people thronging an extensive square, some dancing, some just strolling to and fro, the women wearing brightly-coloured skin-tight dresses, the men in dark zoot-suits with flared trousers and padded shoulders. The ground was partially flooded and fountains of spray were being kicked up underfoot but no-one seemed to mind; everybody appeared young and full of life. Milly looked on with wide eyes; she had never seen so many people of her own colour together in one place before.

"Wot's goin' on?" she cried.

"Oh, it's an Aunty Patti Party – happens every seventh day on the night before the holiday."

"'Oo's Aunty Patti?"

"She runs the local joog joint. Come on gel – it's late – if you're gonna call at Miz Trubshaw's in the morning you'd better git your beauty sleep. You c'n see the rest of the township tomorrow before we head back up to the Heights. My cabin's yonder."

Mabelene's dwelling, constructed over raft-like foundations, had nothing to distinguish it on the outside from any of the others in the area, but, within its walls, the floor space was almost entirely taken up by a king-sized bed with impressively carved headboard and baseboard. It was so large that one imagined the cabin might have had to be extended to accommodate it.

"Where d'you think we found this?" asked its owner, patting and adjusting the pillows, obviously intent on exciting envy.

"The dumps?" suggested Milly.

"Yes you're right! I guess you know more than you let on. Took us three days to git it home. It'll sure be nice to share it with someone again. It's bin real lonesome lying there since my man got taken away."

Milly slept soundly that night and after breakfast (a soul-food combination of fried chicken, turnip greens and black eyed peas) she spent an hour at the hairdresser's and came away more than satisfied that she could now hold her own with the restaurant's fashionable clientèle. She was also measured for some new clothes similar to those she had seen the girls wearing in the square the night before. After she emerged Mabelene took her to a certain cabin where she could buy beauty aids including make-up specifically designed for darker shades of skin and to another which sold herbal remedies for all sorts of conditions and ailments. There was also a tobacconist purveying other substances beside run-of-the-mill cigarettes (Milly eschewed these offbeat alternatives and acquired some shag, a small pipe and matches).

"An' if you needs a little help with your romance," Mabelene told her, pointing out a tiny isolated cabin built on a slight rise, "that's where our local obeah man lives. He c'n sell you a love potion any hour of the day or night, an' if you've got a rival or a deadly enemy you want rid of he c'n deal with them too, but you've gotta play fair with him – you've got to let him see into your soul."

Milly, taking all things into consideration, decided to give this magic-worker a miss, despite a slight feeling of regret in respect of the love philtre option when she thought of Dando's usual affable indifference towards her.

At about four thirty in the afternoon the two women climbed aboard the ancient bike and set off for the evening shift at the Dark Continent. It was hard work for Mabelene peddling uphill and sometimes they both had to get off and walk. Not far along the track Milly's hostess brought the machine to a temporary halt in the same place where she had stopped on the way down. For a second time she swung round in order to impart some important information.

"Now you've slept in the Underlands, gel, you're one of us. If you're ever in trouble we'll do our best to help. But you have to know the right words to use. When you're needy, go to one of our people and say, *Do you sell Aunt Patti's biscuits here?* Can you remember that?" Milly repeated the words.

"Good. Then if you've picked the right person – not all coloured folks are in on the deal – you'll hear them reply, *Sure chil', come right on in,* an' you c'n be certain that they'll do all in their power to aid you."

Milly could not see how, with her influential white friends, she would ever have a use for such information, but she stored it away anyway – you never knew.

When they dismounted behind the restaurant Mabelene patted her on the shoulder.

"From now on you'll always be welcome in Floodwood, gel. Come at the end of the week an' join in Aunty Patti's Party - come an' get your hair prettified. Then afterwards you c'n keep me company in my big bed. You'd like that, wouldn't you?"

"Not 'arf!" replied an enthusiastic Milly, pleased to be invited back. However much of an outcast she might feel in the rest of Rytardenath it was apparent that there was one place at least within this hostile environment where she could be at home. Although not exactly rosy things were beginning to look up. Her spirits soared.

Yesterday's revenant,
Forever whispering
'Might have been... might have been...'

Chapter five

The midwinter festival had come and then departed in a riot of moneymaking.

"I know it's a big thing round here – Yuletide I mean," Dando said to his sister as they tidied up the restaurant after a party that had gone slightly over the top, "but I think I preferred the way we used to do it at home. It was more serious somehow – quieter and more serious – you had time to think. I don't reckon that here they really believe the Year-Child makes a haypeth of difference to how things turn out. They don't even have a proper Year-Child anyway – just a silly doll that costs the earth."

For a month or two the temperature in the city had fluctuated around freezing and Ry-Town's streets were lined with brown hillocks of slush as its citizens headed for the hills to play in the snow. Then spring began tentatively to put in an appearance, although the change was barely noticeable inside the huge centrally-heated and air-conditioned towers. Foxy, with characteristic hardihood, had continued to sleep in the garden shed throughout the winter and carry out his renovations. His latest project was to build a wooden summerhouse near the back door of the mansion.

As time wore on the enthusiasm of Dando's fans showed no sign of abating. All through the cold weather there was a small gang of them hanging around in front of the restaurant, some apparently having come from quite far afield, armed not only with crutches but also with banners depicting a small silhouetted figure minus a foot alongside the letters NQPP. These disciples were always ready to clamour for autographs and break into cheers as soon as the proprietor appeared. He found this devotion highly embarrassing and also rather worrying when he considered the effect it might be having on his regular customers.

"I think it could be putting people off," he confided to Jack during one of the blind boy's infrequent visits, "but I don't know how I can stop it."

"The price of fame," replied Jack. "You're their idol, chickadee – their role model."

Dando pulled a face, then asked, "What does NQPP stand for?"

"The Not Quite Perfect Party. That's what they call themselves, your admirers."

Foxy lodged in the garden shed, whatever the weather, mainly because he preferred, as his living accommodation, a close approximation to the cave that had once been his home. As a consequence he saw little of the other occupants of the Magnolias, save at mealtimes. However, one night, when Horry had gone to sleep and seemed unlikely to stir for several hours, Damask quietly left the house and set out to beard the Nablan in his den. She carried an electric torch - one of the many Armornian innovations she had eagerly adopted on their arrival - so that when she came to the ancient hut and opened the door she was able to shine it around the interior. She found that Foxy was lying on some sacking on the floor surrounded by gardening equipment. He had not undressed and was still wearing the leather britches and sheepskin jacket he had acquired at Toymerle, but his feet, dirty and calloused, were bare. Damask stood over him, directing the beam down onto his sleeping face.

"Hallo goat boy," she said, (She had recently learnt a little of his history from Dando).

Foxy opened his eyes, stared into the glare of the torch, then, without reacting or seeming to move in any way, managed, somehow, to produced his deadly little pistol.

"Who be there?" he demanded.

"Don't shoot," said Damask, "it's only me. I thought praps you might be in need of some company."

"Company?" retorted Foxy, "I be asleep. Forwhy should I want company?"

"I thought you might be lonely," she went on, "all by yourself out here."

"Lonely? I don' be lonely on my own – I be used to it – this be the way I allas live – all my life."

"You've never had a friend? - a girl friend?"

Foxy's deep blue eyes, bluer than a midsummer sky, gleamed in the light of the torch as he attempted to see beyond the beam. Fractionally he shook his head.

"I don' goo in fer that sort o' thing," he said.

"What not at all?"

"Not soo's you'd notice."

It was Damask's turn to shake her head.

"How strange," she said. "Does that mean your heart's been broken?"

Foxy put his hand to his wrist and cocked his head on one side as if listening.

"It be whool, far as I c'n tell."

"Can I feel?"

He did not reply but raised no objection when she switched off the torch, knelt beside him and, disregarding his wrist, slipped her hand inside his shirt. They remained like that, still as statues, for a long spell while she imagined she felt a faint beat under her palm measuring out his life span. When she moved her hand lower to the belt of his britches he took and held it in his own preventing her from exploring further.

"Howd ye hard – I towd you, I don' fare to do that kind o' thing," he repeated.

It was a while before he released her. Once he had done so she stood up and switched the torch back on, shining it up into her own face.

"I like you," she said. "You and I could go a long way together. If you change your mind I'm not far away – just give me the nod."

In reply he did in fact nod but then followed it up with a shrug and a shake of the head which apparently referred to his current state of mind. After that, lying down, he faced away from the door, resolutely ignoring her and recomposing himself for sleep. Damask let herself out of the shed. She was not discouraged by such an outcome; in fact she had a strong feeling that this was not an end but just the beginning.

Forty eight hours later, in the early evening of the one day of the week that the restaurant closed its doors and most of those involved were at the house, they were startled by a throaty rumble rapidly approaching along the road.

"Blimey," cried Milly, staring down onto the drive, "it's Foxy. Wot the flippin' 'eck 'as 'e got there?"

"I gave him his money yesterday, " said Becca as she stood beside her, "I guess he's bought himself a second-hand machine and the clothes to go with it. He looks kinda neat, doncha think?"

Foxy came to a halt outside the entrance to the mansion and revved the powerful motorbike once or twice. He was staring up at the window of the nursery where Damask stood looking out with Horry in her arms.

"I be a-gooin' along the coast," he shouted. "I be back afore morning. You c'n come if you wan'."

"Give me a minute," she replied.

A short while later she emerged, minus her charge and suitably dressed. Slightly self-consciously as if knowing all eyes were upon her, she swung her leg over the vehicle's pillion, taking her place behind Foxy. Once more he revved the engine and then, throwing it into gear, roared off down the drive towards the road. In the listeners' ears the sound of the vehicle rapidly faded leaving, as the only proof of its existence, the faintest of blue exhaust fumes hanging in the air.

On the selfsame day, but about half an hour later, a cheerful ringing of bells announced the arrival of two cyclists at the Magnolias. Dando, who just happened to be coming out of the front door at the time, was amazed to see that one of them was Jack.

"Jack, don't tell me you can ride that thing?!"

"Why not? The tricky bit is learning to balance, but after that it's child's play. Fynn goes ahead of me making a noise and all I have to do is follow – nothing to it."

Dando realised that the second cyclist was the Posse's fluffy haired young saxophonist with the prominent nose. So, was this Jack's latest squeeze?

"What are you up to?" he persisted. "You can't kid me you're now a devoted fitness fanatic; that's just not you at all."

"We're members of the Rytardenath Push Bike Club," replied Jack, po-faced. "We believe in non-motorised transport – we're protesting against the increased mechanisation of society," but as he said this Dando detected a curious humorous twist to the corners of his mouth as if he were finding it hard to contain his merriment.

"Oh, I see," replied the Glept dryly, "and I'm the the king of Belturbet. Pull the other one."

"He thinks we're having him on, Lollipop," said Jack to Fynn in mock sorrow, "the cynicism of the younger generation shocks me to the core. Unbelievable, absolutely unbelievable!"

This time he could not prevent himself from bursting into laughter; he seemed to be in a very light-hearted mood.

"Well, so long as you're happy," commented Dando with a slight hint of bitterness, maybe even jealousy, in his voice.

The amused expression disappeared from Jack's face.

"I'm only as happy as you'll allow me to be, birdy," he answered quietly.

Dando did not react for a moment or two, but then reached out and touched his friend's shoulder. Nothing more needed to be said. Fynn, meanwhile, had been pretending a tremendous interest in some of Foxy's garden improvements; he did not speak but seemed ill at ease, his extreme youth suggesting a thin-skinned vulnerability.

After about a month and a half at the Magnolias Ralph and Meena, Tallis' dog and Milly's cat, had at last become friends. From the start both animals had been individually drawn to the wilderness of the garden which had prevailed when they first arrived and then, after it became more orderly under Foxy's administrations, to the woods beyond. Inevitably their paths frequently crossed giving rise to many a kerfuffle during which Meena spat and swore, her normally sleek fur bristling. When occasionally she turned tail instead of standing her ground Ralph gave chase enthusiastically, his eager tongue flopping out of the side of his mouth. This headlong pursuit usually ended with Meena streaking up a tree and Ralph sitting below whining in disappointment. Maybe it was deliberate provocation on her part, maybe she just missed her footing, but one day, having climbed aloft she came hurtling down from the branch where she had taken refuge to land fairly and squarely on Ralph's back. The dog gave an astonished yelp and took off at a mad gallop around the garden with Meena clinging on grimly, her claws entwined in his rough coat. Eventually he lost momentum and slowed to a walk, at which point his rider dismounted and strolled away, tail waving, much as might a fare-paying passenger on alighting from a bus. The next time she fled the same thing occurred and this again might have been an accident, but, when it happened a third time, it became obvious that she was doing it deliberately. Ralph now knew what to expect and was no longer so startled - he began to treat the whole thing as a game. The human inhabitants of the house became quite used to seeing the two animals together, Meena perched atop Ralph as if she were a bare-back rider at the circus. It was apparent that these representatives of two traditionally antagonistic species had declared a truce, realising there were mutual benefits to be gained from co-operation.

Now, however, a new element intruded. Meena's normally slender figure began to swell at the waist and after a while it became obvious that she was in the family way. The father's identity remained a mystery and in the absence of any obvious candidate the blame was laid at the door of some wandering Armornian hobo who had seduced the susceptible young maiden in passing with his itinerant charm. Milly purchased a basket, furnished it with cushions, and installed it next to the kitchen stove in order to provide suitable quarters for her cat's lying in, but, when the time arrived, Meena chose to have her kittens in a cupboard beside Dando's bed.

For two weeks all remained quiet. The cat, although not a particularly attentive parent, turned up often enough to keep her babies happy. Various members of the household, Foxy among them, came to admire and to remark on the surprisingly diverse coats of the five new arrivals, none of them looking quite like their mother. Only one visitor received a less than enthusiastic welcome: Ralph stuck his nose into the cupboard and then backed hurriedly away as he was met by a low hiss; in her maternal state Meena's inter-genus friendliness seemed to have temporarily evaporated. On the fifteenth day after the birth a small head was to be seen peering round the cupboard door, soon to be joined by four more all attached to torsos that were still a bit wobbly on their pins. From then on peace and quiet were permanently banished from the room. At night Dando lay self-sacrificingly on the bed while the kittens happily rampaged to and fro, treating his body as a playground, until eventually they curled up within its nooks and crannies and went to sleep for several hours. In contrast he was soon suffering from sleep deprivation.

"Why don't you move them into the kitchen, honey?" suggested Becca. "You need a good night's rest, working so hard. There's a nice basket there that Milly bought."

"I'm ok," he replied. "They could get hurt if they get too close to the stove. Wait 'till they're a bit older."

In actual fact he was fascinated by these totally innocent creatures - so helpless, so trusting and with such an appetite for life. As soon as they were weaned Meena, harking to the call of the wild, lost interest in her family and spent a lot of the time away. It fell to Dando to feed them, to change the earth in their dirt tray and to keep them out of trouble. When one, the runt of the litter, fell ill, he cared for it tenderly, carrying it round in his pocket, and rejoiced when it recovered. On one of his rare nights at the Magnolias Jack lay on the other bed listening to the thunder of tiny paws (it was perhaps significant that the kittens avoided trespassing in *his* vicinity).

Eventually he was induced to remark, “What is it with you and animals? They all seem to make a beeline for wherever you are. Do they know something we don't?”

Damask too, experienced a certain amount of exasperation when she witnessed her brother coming down the stairs followed, in single file, by a procession of miniature felines on their way to the garden. She noticed that he had the grace to appear somewhat abashed.

“I've just started taking them outside,” he explained apologetically in passing, “but they need to be watched – they're not grown-up enough yet to be left on their own.”

His sister, who was looking a trifle harassed and put upon, gave a disgusted sniff.

“How about your son?” she exclaimed crossly. “When did you last come to visit him? Wouldn't it be a good idea to take him out for a change? I could do with a bit of help in that department - I've got things of my own I want to get on with but having child-care responsibilities means such stuff has to go by the board!”

Dando's normally pale visage lost whatever remnant of colour it possessed and his expression became shiftily uneasy.

“I've been very busy,” he excused himself guiltily, “the restaurant you know.”

“But you've got time for that,” she countered, indicating the kittens milling around his foot.

Two days later Dando was to be found standing outside the room that had been designated as a nursery, a martyred expression on his face. From within came the sound of Damask's raised voice.

“Attitude! Attitude!” she was shouting. “It's attitude all the time with you, twenty-four-seven. Is it any surprise I'm pissed off?!”

Dando put his hand to the door – hesitated – then pushed it open. He was confronted by a tableau consisting of three individuals so absorbed in acting out some small domestic drama that they were completely oblivious to his presence. In the background he could see Becca employing glue as she sat at a table mending some toy or other while a small boy, blue eyed and flaxen haired, stood centre stage, glaring before him at nothing in particular, his lips in a furious pout. Damask was bending forward with hands on hips staring down at the miscreant.

“Why, for once, can't you behave?” she reprimanded her charge, “That's the third thing you've broken this morning. We're not made of money. You're a wicked boy – a wicked boy - I think you do it deliberately.”

In answer the child stuck his four Nibbler digits between his teeth and produced a retching sound as if he was trying to make himself sick. He looked up defiantly.

"Not impressed," scolded Damask, "not impressed in the slightest."

"Best ignore him," chipped in Becca, "my Mama always said..." but her Mama's words of wisdom remained unspoken as the door creaked and those in the room realised for the first time that they had a witness to their little altercation. Dando found himself the focus of three pairs of eyes. The child, whose thumb was still in his mouth, pulled it out with a pop and proved that he had a certain command of language by remarking, "Oo are you? - wot choo wan'?"

After an uncomfortable pause Becca decided it was up to her to break the silence.

"This is Dando," she began, "he's..." but the young man in question, greatly puzzled, interrupted her by asking, "Where's the baby?"

Wordlessly Damask gestured towards the boy, thus confusing her brother further, for the infant who was the centre of everyone's attention bore no more resemblance to a babe in arms than does a two-year-old child.

"But he can't be..." exclaimed the astonished Dando.

Damask looked helplessly at Becca who put her work aside and stood up.

"We need to have a little heart to heart darling," she said. "There's a lot you don't know – should have been told long before this. Let's take Horace out into the garden - he hardly ever goes out - and give this girl a much-needed break. It's a nice day."

They descended to the ground floor. On the way Horry possessed himself of their visitor's hand, looking up inquisitively into his face with azure eyes.

"Are you my da?" he asked. "My mam says Dando's my da."

Damask, apparently with a need to monitor the forthcoming conversation, followed them outdoors and, as Becca installed herself on Foxy's bench, gesturing to Dando to sit beside her, took up station behind them. Horry ran off to play with Ralph who was loitering nearby; the dog, when not absent on one of his garden forays, was never far away from the restaurant owner, following him from house to place-of-work and place-of-work to house day in and day out. The young man turned to look round at his sister.

"Does he think you're his mother?" he asked, thoroughly bewildered. "Surely this isn't Annie's baby... our baby?"

“No, not Damask,” said Becca, “that's one of the things we've got to talk to you about.”

“He thinks he sees her – Ann,” contributed Damask in her usual blunt fashion, “I catch him staring into space and speaking to someone who's not there. He's certainly got a vivid imagination.”

Dando's jaw and hands clenched; he looked both angry and afraid and muttered something under his breath too low for the others to catch.

“Long before this I wanted to pass on what the poor sweet told us before the end came,” went on Becca, “I wanted to tell you when you first arrived in Drossi but I was afraid of making things worse than they already were and Damask thought that it wasn't a good idea.”

“She was delusional,” said the girl.

“I don't reckon that's true.”

“Curses, possession, divine retribution? What other explanation could there possibly be?”

“It's about time we came clean...” and Becca pointed down the slope to where the child was romping, “this young man needs to know what we've known all along - he needs to understand...”

“Yes tell me,” said Dando taking a deep breath as if nerving himself to face something he had hitherto tried with all his might to avoid. “I think I can guess some of it already.”

Damask made an exasperated noise and walked off.

“She was in a pretty bad way, bless her, when your sister came to the rescue,” began the show girl, “the baby almost here and her half-starved. She seemed to want to confide in someone and before long we heard what had happened. She believed that her troubles started up in the mountains when you were at that shrine – that Place-of-the-Voice as they call it. She told us she had had to save you from one of the great ones, the god that's supposed to rule the fiery lower depths, and in so doing the immortal they call the Earth Mother became her deadly enemy.”

“Yes, that's right,” said Dando, “I was incredibly stupid and got caught - I don't remember how - I don't remember any of it at all. Evidently Ann managed to set me free, but by making use of Aigea's power to do it she mortally offended her. At least that's what she told me.”

“Something the girlie explained was that her father had been a priest in the goddess's service...”

“Yes - that was Tom...”

"...and having inherited his gift she believed she was acting as a magnet, drawing the deities' attention towards you by means of her presence. For some reason which she did not fully understand, the Mother and the Sky-Father were searching for you and she decided that as long as she remained nearby there was a chance they would track you down through her proximity and work some mischief. Because of that she made up her mind to leave. Of course by this time she knew she was expecting."

Dando shook his head, a stricken look on his face.

"I was blind," he muttered, "deliberately blind. I should have realised..."

"The goddess was still angry with her, Ann said, and as soon as she was on her own she brought down a terrible retribution on her head. Through some kind of sorcery she caused the poor girl to fall into the power of a powerful mage who enslaved her. This was the one we rescued her from when your sister came upon them together in Drossi..."

"He was really creepy," a third voice broke in - Damask had returned. "His skin was like marble, dirty marble, and he had all these creases in his face that had picked up the dust – as if it had been happening for years and years and years..."

"He had the power to force her to tell him your story, about where you both came from and where you were going. He learnt about Master Tallis and about you honey-bunch. He seemed to fear you, Ann said, and because of that he cursed the knight by head and you by foot and when we took her away from him I believe he cursed the baby in the womb and her in the bearing of it."

"You mean...?"

"Yes, little Horace is still under the hoodoo. That's why he's growing up so fast and there's nothing any of us can do about it because, as my mama told me, only the one who casts the spell can lift it. I know what you're going to say..." she was addressing Damask now who with a scowl was making plain her disbelief, "...but you can't deny the evidence of your own eyes. So you see," turning back to Dando, "it wasn't you who brought about her death, sweetheart. You mustn't keep blaming yourself. The doctor said it wasn't a natural labour – we all knew that – even you..." gesturing towards Damask. "It was that ill-wisher who did for her."

Dando, who had been staring at his hands, looked up, a bleak expression on his face.

"Even if she died because of him I'm to blame for the baby's being here at all."

"That's not a cause for regret – giving life should always be a matter for rejoicing."

"Well," said Damask as if she felt it was time to bring the conversation to an end, "I'd better take him in for his tea," and she went to collect Horry.

When Dando was alone with Becca they sat companionably together for some time without saying anything more. He looked sideways once or twice as if wondering whether to broach a difficult subject. At last he plucked up the courage to begin.

"Along the road from the valley," he ventured, "she would often say she heard her father, Tom, speaking to her (You know he died – but did she tell you how?). I thought it was just wishful thinking on her part but now a similar thing keeps happening to me. I know she's gone – I keep telling myself she's gone – but then I hear her in my dreams – almost every night – saying words I don't understand. How can I lead a normal life if this carries on? I thought eventually I would learn to live with the loss but she won't let me. Am I going mad do you think?"

Becca smiled pityingly at him but did not reply.

Dando remained silent for a while as if he found it too difficult to continue. At last in a low voice he confessed, "I even thought I saw her once in the real world – just down there – on Ancestors' Eve. It looked exactly like her except she was sort of lit up in an unearthly kind of way, and afterwards... well, it's the only time since we parted that I've felt really happy. Was it all inside my head?"

"But I thought you were happy now – now that you've got the restaurant. Wasn't that your dream?"

Dando shrugged, his face shadowed.

"Yes," he answered sadly, "I s'pose it was."

A while later after a pause long enough for their thoughts to have moved on to other things he suddenly broke the silence by remarking, "Damask doesn't believe this stuff about curses."

"Damask's afraid," replied Becca.

"You really think that this," indicating his missing left leg, "and Tallis," putting his hand to his head, "and Horry, and Annie..."

"My dear, if you'd grown up in the back of beyond like me and heard the old stories people used to tell, you'd know such things exist. That ju-ju man, he worked evil on you for some reason which none of us really understand. I'm afraid he may come back and try again. We know he was in Drossi earlier but he could be anywhere by now. Take care and be on your guard."

"People are always warning me of danger and yet nothing ever seems to happen."

Becca smiled at him and touched his hand.

"All the same watch your back, honey chil'."

From this point on Dando found time to visit the nursery when the restaurant was closed and take Horry out for walks either in the grounds or down towards the sea. The little boy accompanied him eagerly.

"You're my da, ain't you?" he frequently repeated as if needing to get something straight in his head. "My mam says you are."

On about the fourth occasion that he broached the subject Dando at last answered him.

"Do you really see your mother? When you see her what does she look like?"

He waited for the reply with great trepidation.

"She looks nice."

"But what colour hair has she got? Is it like mine?"

"No, not like yours."

"Is it like this?" and Dando very carefully brought an envelope out from his inner breast pocket and opened it so that Horry could look inside.

"Is that hers?" the little boy enquired wonderingly.

"That's what I'm asking you."

"It was like that but it were all loose an' there were a lot more of it."

"And what colour were her eyes?"

"Sorta blue. She tol' me things."

"What did she tell you?"

"She said she was sorry she couldn't look after me. She said you'd look after me until it was time for you to go away. She said you'd got a job to do but you'd try an' come back when it was all over."

Dando nodded without speaking. He stared silently into the middle distance for a while. Then putting his arm around the child he pulled him to his side.

"She was a lovely lady," he said, "but I think that what you're seeing can't really be real."

Now that her brother was taking an interest in his son Damask presumed he would go at least halves with her in the child-care stakes. Every other evening, or so it seemed, she appeared at Dando's bedroom door, holding Horry by the hand. "It's your turn tonight," she would say and without further ado be off with Foxy on the motorbike until the early hours. Dando would then wash and change the infant before tucking him up in Jack's vacant bed, following which he would lie awake in the other bed getting used to the idea of being a father. Was he prepared once more to risk his poor battered heart in the line of fire? Was he ready to lower his guard sufficiently to let in a new kind of love and to do this while the old love still haunted him? He did not know if he had the guts to lay himself open to the possibility of further mental suffering when his physical disabilities were making life hard enough already. In the night he often heard the child murmur and sometimes he imagined he caught another voice answering as if a third person might be there with them in the room. After their little chat and probably because of what he, Dando, had said at the end of it, Horry never spoke of these night-time manifestations and for the same reason, neither did he. As for himself the dear remembered tones often echoed within his head when he was about to fall asleep but there was always some type of distortion in operation, a kind of faulty reception that meant he was unable to understand what was being said. As he had told Becca in the garden he half suspected that the hereditary Dan madness was catching up with him at last.

On top of the substantial hill named Mornington Heights lay a piece of open ground, virgin bush that had not yet succumbed to modern development. In the midst of this scrub-land, on the highest point, stood a squat grey building constructed of huge ashlars and surrounded by a colonnade of thick dumpy columns. This edifice dominated the flimsy more impermanent structures that were gradually creeping up the sides of the hill towards the place where it was situated. The church or pantheon - whatever you chose to call it - gave the impression that it had been in existence for centuries and, despite its weathered condition, seemed as indestructible as the hill on which it stood. What it was doing there, completely out of keeping with the adjacent conurbation, was a total mystery to any of the companions who cared to glance upwards. From the Dark Continent, situated on the top-most square, it took only a five minute walk to arrive by the entrance and sometimes, on the rare occasions when things were getting slightly on top of him and he felt certain that the staff could cope on their own, Dando would excuse himself, fling his coat over his whites and slip out in order to climb the stony path that took him past the blackened circle where the Sahwain bonfire had been lit to the building's location. Its appearance reminded him of a painting that had hung in the main hall of Castle Dan. This enormous gloomy canvas had depicted ruinous architecture of a bygone age set in a romantic unfamiliar landscape and he had always understood that it represented the ancient abandoned city of Belturbet.

Having reached the temple he would open the unlocked door, enter, and be at once immersed in a calm untroubled atmosphere that began to work wonders on his stressed-out state of mind. He would seat himself in one of the simple wooden pews and allow the peace and quiet of the place to flow into his soul. The interior gave no clue as to whether it had been dedicated to a particular deity. There were no figurative representations of any kind on the walls, in fact very little embellishment at all apart from a large circle at the far end bisected by an s-shaped line which made him think of the double D symbol that he still carried on his shoulder, placed there during Damask's near fatal (for him) foray into tattooing techniques. Although the walls bore very little decoration, on the floor at his feet lay many identical tapestried cushions, provided to make kneeling less painful. While he sat and meditated, his eyes roved idly over the single design depicted, wondering at its significance. Eventually, curiosity getting the better of him, he stooped and picked up one of the hassocks, realising that what he was seeing was an extremely intricate embroidered maze. As he examined it more closely he found that it was possible to make out details of the motif. Around the edge there were three entrances to the labyrinth, two false that soon petered out into dead ends and one that led him deeper and deeper into the complexity until he was in danger of becoming lost, unable to go either forwards or back to his starting point. Subsequently, each time he visited the church, he sought out one of the kneelers in order to make another attempt at solving the puzzle. What tempted him to continue, what led him on, was the goal placed in the centre of the maze as a reward for those who did not falter but were stout-hearted enough to make it through to the end. There in the middle a symbol was depicted, the idea of which had become very familiar to him over the past year: the prize was in fact an elaborate, convoluted representation of a key. For a week or two he worried away at the problem until, after many false starts, came the day when he penetrated to the heart of the mystery and arrived at the centre. It took several more attempts before he felt confident of getting it right each time he tried, but from then on the solution appeared to be indelibly printed on his brain.

During his first few trips up the hill to the ancient building he never saw a living soul, although there were always candles burning and flowers in vases scattered about inside to prove that someone beside himself visited the place. But then one day as he entered through the main door he was confronted by a small grey-haired woman standing facing him halfway up the central aisle. She seemed thoroughly at home in the temple, almost as if she belonged there, and he got the strangest feeling that she had been waiting for him.

"I imagine you're acquainted with Manfred Quahaug's design by now," she said in a voice that had a remote antiquated quality about it, "as you've been here several times already."

"On the cushions?" replied Dando. "Yes, I've been studying it. What does it mean?"

"Prior to the wars Manfred was a member of the general assembly. He showed the design to me just before he went east – that's when I had these made. But as to what it signifies, that you'll have to find out for yourself." She paused for a moment and then added, "I was told right at the start that you would be coming."

"You were told? - who by?"

Wordlessly she gestured towards the far end of the church.

"Are you the caretaker?" he asked.

"Caretaker? Well I suppose that is what I could be called when there is something or someone to be taken care of, such as yourself."

"But how do you know me?"

"You were spoken of, or rather written about, long years ago."

"Really? - and what was written?"

"That you have a task to complete that will mend the world."

"I don't think that can be me."

"I know it is. The object you are meant to find is waiting for you along the road and, besides that, you carry the mark for those with eyes to see."

"What mark?"

"There's a design engraved upon your body as there is on that of everyone who is singled out for an extraordinary destiny. Be bold, be fearless, be of good cheer and you will win through."

"But that's just something my sister did and, anyway, I'm afraid I can't be very cheerful."

"Ah – you are smitten by sorrow but it is needless – needless. Have you never asked yourself if perhaps she did not die?"

"Do you mean Annie? But they buried her!"

"The body – that was not her. Most men and women do actually die and move on to their next fleshed incarnation, but there are a few, a very few, who, when on the point of death, refuse that end and are strong enough to break free of mundane matter and join the cosmos. They call such people *dancers* and the process *Going-Over-the-Brook*. One day, when you have found what you are looking for and have completed your mission perhaps everyone will be able to follow that same path. On that day, the old writings say, *...even the mountains will give voice and the minor hills in happiness disport themselves.* I see her now, your loved one, she is with you, and you will learn to see her too in time when you are no longer prevented - you will be together once more."

She smiled and, for a moment, laid her hand gently on Dando's arm, so gently that he was hardly aware of the touch; then she passed him by and went out the door; he sensed a faint breeze on his cheek as she did so.

"Where is it?" he called after her, "this thing I'm supposed to find?"

"I cannot tell you," her voice floated faintly back, "the burden is yours and yours alone. When you have found it that will be only the beginning."

"Wait!" he cried.

"Look for one of my people," came a whisper on the wind, "he will help you."

Although reluctant to take what she had told him about the after-life seriously - what he had understood of it anyway - Dando hoped he might meet the woman again on a subsequent occasion but, in fact, only saw her once more after this first encounter and in vastly different circumstances. From this time onwards, indeed for the rest of the period he was at the restaurant, he invariably had the temple to himself. Because of this he came to regard it as his own personal sanctuary, a special space where, for a short period, he could find peace of mind. During the time he was within its walls he felt he occupied an older and wiser world than that which normally surrounded him and because of this his meeting with the woman began to seem more and more like something encountered outside the everyday passage of time.

Jack returned to the Magnolias only very occasionally now and purely to check on Dando's well-being. One night, very late, he entered their room to find the former scion of a noble house hunched on the edge of the bed, rocking to and fro, his jaw clenched. Persuading him to lie down the boy from Drossi brought his clever hands to bear and quickly massaged the pain away.

"This rocking - is that what you do when you get cramp and I'm not around?"

"I get by."

"Mmm. Looks like I need to turn up here more often."

Having sorted out one problem Jack, brush in hand, began on another: tackling the tangles in his friend's flowing locks.

"You don't look after your appearance, patootie," he scolded. "Why do you let yourself get in this state? You care for the knight – why don't you do the same closer to home?"

"Oh you know," replied Dando grinning sheepishly, half ashamed, "I had a very decadent upbringing: I was waited on hand and foot and never allowed to attempt anything for myself. Disgraceful I must admit."

"Well it's time you took responsibility," scolded Jack, "you're a big boy now."

The next day Jack appeared at the eatery with his antique silver flute, and, in harmony with Tallis, spent the evening entertaining the diners. Afterwards, when everyone else had departed and he and Dando were companionably finishing up leftovers, he broached a subject that he did not seem able to keep away from for long: "I think I've almost got to the bottom of what this town is about, birdie, although persuading people to talk is like getting blood out of a stone. They're all so horribly afraid – afraid of appearing to criticise, afraid of sticking their heads above the parapet in case they should get them knocked off."

"Ok," said Dando after he had waited unavailingly for revelations, "come on then – what's the secret? Spill the beans – don't hold out on me."

"Give me a few more days spatzi. Then I'll come back to you with the whole grisly tale and it won't be pretty I can promise you that. Meanwhile have you realised that the NQPP is spreading like wildfire?"

"The NQPP?"

"Your fan-club, moron, although it's become much more than that now. There are cells cropping up all along the coast – not just in Ry-Town. It's turning into quite a political movement – there's a lot of disaffection and some pretty powerful people have been muscling in; it seems to have united a whole range of disparate elements that have been at daggers drawn up to now. The Not Quite Perfect Party is dedicated to nonconformity and imperfection in all its aspects and they've been holding rallies and organising marches. There's even been a call for elections - evidently there haven't been any for some twenty years or more although they're supposed to take place every five. The authorities are maintaining a low profile but I don't know how long that will last."

"Are you serious?" exclaimed an appalled Dando. "What on earth can I do?"

"Sod all, my love. It's out of your hands – it's out of all our hands – but keep a weather eye open. If storm clouds seem to be gathering make yourself scarce."

The exotically dressed man with the lined yet ageless face stood outside the door of the Dark Continent staring up at the sign. Round his neck hung a jointed silver pendant in the shape of a small human figure that, as he moved, seemed to writhe in frustration. While he stood irresolute his thoughts churned and roiled in a morass of uncertainty. Was this really the place where the wretch who presented a threat to his very existence was to be found? If that was the case then he had gravely underestimated his opponent. He had imagined from the description he had dragged out of the pregnant girl that the pathetic creature he had to deal with was an effete, cosseted child of privilege who would soon falter when presented with any serious hardship; the black spell he had cast should have been enough to lay him low once and for all. Instead it seemed his victim had made his way back from the very brink of death, had dragged himself to the edge of the Middle Sea and was now to be found on the Northern Continent, several steps nearer to the precious thing that he, the rightful owner, had not yet had the opportunity to put beyond reach. Whether the whelp knew the purpose for which he had been brought here, (the fact that he was involved in this catering lark suggested that he did not) he still remained a most palpable danger. Well now the time had come to meet him face to face; only then would he be sure whether this frail instrument of fate was the one destined to bring about a reckoning. If that were true - if the boy was likely to be the means of his undoing - then he must deal with him irrevocably once and for all.

Gammadion, professionally known as Gubbo the Great, adjusted his robes, tugging them straight with both hands. No-one was actually watching in the dusk but if anyone had observed his movements they would have noticed the patterns on the material swirl and mutate strangely under his touch. From one of his bottomless pockets he brought forth a comb with which he attempted to tidy his rather wild-looking hair that seemed to stir and move of its own volition like the tentacles of an undersea animalcule. He then produced a handful of money which he crammed into a purse taken from another pocket. After that came a strangely shaped hat, again marked with shifting patterns, an elegant malacca cane and a cigarette case. Thus equipped he composed his features and drifted towards the restaurant's front entrance.

"Excuse me my dear, if it's at all possible could I have a word with whoever's in charge?"

Milly jumped in surprise. The voice came out of dimness, out of a secluded corner of the dining area where she had no memory of having seated or served anyone. It was as if her sight suddenly cleared or a light was switched on and for the first time she saw the table, the dirty plates and the anonymous-looking man who up to that moment she had failed to take note of.

"Pardon me, his something not to your liking?" she asked, gathering her wits, "Hy'm afraid hy may have been somewhat remiss in clearing away."

"Not at all, not at all. It's just that I think I've met your patron in the past and I wish to complement him on the excellence of the meal."

"Hif you care to wait a minute hy will pass on your message and see if he has a moment to spare." Milly was standing on her dignity in her dealings with this diner feeling slightly put out that Dando should be expected to come running at the behest of such a nonentity. She went down to the kitchen.

"Can you let the boss know that one of his customers has asked to see him?" she informed the maître-d. A few minutes later the man himself appeared before her, slightly flushed, a fish slice in one hand.

"There's this geezer wants to say 'allo," she told him, "shall I tell 'im you're busy?"

Dando looked worried.

"Is anything wrong?"

"'E sez 'e finks 'e knows you."

The head cook and bottle-washer stripped off his apron and removed his toque. Running his fingers through his hair, he mounted the service stairs and then pushed his way past the swing doors into the dining room. Once on the other side he came to an abrupt halt. *A face like marble – dirty marble...* Damask's remembered words returned to him with a sudden greatly enhanced significance. Whereas for Milly the man had been almost invisible, as far as Dando was concerned he dominated the room, appearing to draw all eyes towards the table at which he was seated. Warily the young man walked forward, stiff-legged, like a combative dog. He felt as a tribesman might feel on approaching an age-old enemy for the first time with whom he has an inherited quarrel.

"You asked to see me?" he said coldly.

The other looked downwards at the place where Dando's left foot should have been.

"You've come a long way," he remarked.

"No thanks to you," replied Dando in a low voice.

The two stared at each other for sometime, recognition within both pairs of eyes. Eventually Dando delivered himself of an ultimatum.

"I think I must ask you to leave this establishment," he said.

The surrounding hum of conversation and rattle of cutlery died away while Tallis, who had been playing soft music on the cithona, stopped to listen.

"If I go now," answered the magician, "you'll never see me again and that might be to your disadvantage."

"What do you mean?"

"Besides the fact that you are yourself disabled I believe you have a son who also has a disability – in fact a most unusual disability. If you'd agree to take that infant and the old man," indicating Tallis, "and in particular yourself back across the sea to the land from whence you came, I could turn his life around, I could cure him – it would take only a few minutes."

"Are you out of your mind?!" cried a furious Dando. "You think I'd let you anywhere near Horry?! I wouldn't trust you further than I could throw you! You keep away from him. Go away and stay away and what's more get out of here right now!"

"Without my intervention he will die – die before he's twenty. You will bury your son just as you have already buried your woman."

A scarlet mist rose up in front of Dando's eyes. He lunged blindly and instinctively forward, propelled by a burning anger, but then, the next moment, cried out in pain and fell down clutching his left leg. Gammadion had stretched out his hand and the metal prosthesis strapped below Dando's knee had suddenly started to glow red hot. As the boy writhed on the floor the wizard disappeared down the main stairs to the door. Even in the midst of his agony Dando had the presence of mind to gasp, "Follow him Milly! Follow him! See where he goes." Milly dithered for more than a minute, conflicted, then, too late, hurried outside. When she returned she found Dando stretched on a sofa surrounded by a group of solicitous customers while the artificial foot from which he was now parted lay on the carpet where it had burnt a smouldering hole.

"Are you 'urt?" she cried.

"Where is he?" he panted trying to sit up, his face contorted. "I shouldn't have let him go."

"'E's vanished," she reported, "there's no sign of 'im anywhere. 'E's turned 'isself invisible I reckon. Are you orl right? What c'n I do?"

Yes the restaurant owner *was* a danger. Now that he had seen him – this weak, uncomprehending, crippled child – he knew that, despite his apparent helplessness, he presented a substantial threat. He must find a way to eliminate him. But first he must go to the cave where he had hidden his treasure away many years ago after it had become impossible to carry it with him any longer without incurring physical and mental damage. Gammadion, the corrupt wizard, stood in the darkness on the open land above the town, keeping well away from the ancient temple, and wove a distance spell. He drew his robes around him, put his hand to his head and speaking a word of power flashed north faster than the speed of sound.

Although he went like the wind he had a brief moment or two to remember the first time he had entered these climes by boat many years – centuries - aeons ago (travel, by means of spells, was ineffectual over salt water).. Then he had been full of triumph at securing the talisman that he believed would grant him immortality. Given a second chance and knowing what he knew now would he still go in search of the world-changer? He knew he would not; all those treadmill years, those mill-wheel years, grinding, grinding, wearing away his soul until all that was left was the mummified body still going through the motions. This was not immortality, this was just prolongation of life and now it was far to late to move on to his next incarnation if such a thing had ever been possible and far too late to join those lucky few who had discovered a way to flout the prohibition against evolutionary progress and go *Over-the-Brook* as they called it. Sometimes he felt that all he wanted to do was to find rest and an ending, yet, even after so long a time, he still feared the extinction that this might entail.

Now he was at the cavity in which he had chosen to hide the object all those many years ago. Everything appeared the same as on the day he had left it here, apart from natural changes due to the passage of time. He lowered himself into the shaft searching for the shelf where it should be lying. He found the ledge but on it was nothing but dust. The Key was gone!

Life altered considerably for Tallis after this episode. Up until the mysterious stranger's visit (could this really be the man his mother had once identified as her seducer and who would prove, in that case, to be his biological father?) someone had been delegated, each day, to push him to and from the restaurant in the wheelchair. But then, on the night of the wizard's incursion, the conveyance had been commandeered in order to take the injured Dando back to Becca's and its normal occupant had been left to return by whatever means lay in his power. To his great surprise he found he was quite capable of walking the distance to the house although it was over a mile.

The next morning the young restaurateur insisted on getting up, against the advice of his female companions and, despite the angry burns on his leg, indicated his intention of setting out for the Dark Continent. “He may come back,” was his excuse. “I need to be on the spot.”

It was obvious he was not going to get there on foot. Although it had been retrieved cooled and unharmed from where it lay his prosthesis would not be an option until his stump had healed He asked Becca if she could run him up the hill in her car but she refused point blank.

“You're in no fit state to go anywhere for now,” she admonished, “nor for many days to come. There's just one place for you at present and that's bed. That leg must be hurting you considerable.”

Dando shrugged and turned his eyes towards Tallis in mute appeal. The knight hesitated a moment, then said, “You can have the chair if you like,” adding rashly, “I'll push you,” as Becca heaved an exasperated sigh. Damask also volunteered to assist and so, between them, over the next few days, they ensured that the young man reached his place of business each morning and at least managed to carry out his supervisory duties. The knight found this exertion tiring but not overwhelmingly taxing. Eventually Dando, after expressing his gratitude, insisted, once again, on strapping on his blade and making the trip under his own steam. Tallis was left with much food for thought. Never, since leaving Gregory Guyax's commune, had he stayed for so long in one place as he had in Becca's imposing mansion on the outskirts of the great city of Rytardenath. It had been despair that had immobilised him. He had felt that everything was up, that he had come to the end of the road and that the purpose to which he had devoted his whole life had vanished into thin air. He convinced himself that his body was no longer capable of carrying him any further and that permanent infirmity had him in its grip. But now he realised that he had merely been ill as the boy had suggested; it was the sickness, the sickness in his head, that had afflicted him, paralysing his limbs and numbing his mind, and now the mere passing of time was effecting a cure. Health and strength were beginning to re-establish themselves – maybe not in full measure but in a sufficient degree to allow him to take up his quest once more. This understanding led to a more profound question: did he still have a quest to return to?

Back in that upland valley, the strange inimical place yclept by some the Lap-of-the-Mother and sacred to the eternal female, he had acquired a squire, accepting his fealty carelessly, almost reluctantly, and for many months had placed no value on his quiet and uncomplaining service. Now he understood that he had been a fool not to appreciate his good fortune and had even begun to wonder if he had been entertaining a paragon of virtue unawares. Recently he had also asked himself if, after all, his sole purpose in the world had been to alert this boy to a task that belonged to him and him alone and that it was his, Tallis', duty to pass on the torch, namely the quest for the Key, and then retire from the race. But if so it was surely a poisoned chalice, not a torch, that he had in his possession. For the love that he now bore the young man he would not hang this encumbrance around his neck; he wished to spare him the strange predetermined ordeal that such a search would entail and allow him the chance to lead a normal life.

Age catches up with everyone in the end, as Gammadion had once explained to Morvah, and its symptoms are plain to see: the steeplejack becomes vertiginous, the singer's range diminishes and in the artist's eyes his colours start to fade; the film-star's looks desert her, the actor cannot recall his lines while the writer's facility with words begins to fail. There was no denying, despite his renewed energy, that he, Tallis, was personally over the hill and on the downward slope - his body often reminded him that this was the case - yet it seemed only yesterday that his mother had hurried him into taking his first steps along the road leading out of the mountains. A life consisted of but a brief span he realised, much shorter than he could possibly have imagined when he quitted the place of his birth at the age of fifteen. Then he had been as naïve as the young people who now surrounded him, imagining a great stretch of existence lying ahead. What he had personally gathered at this late stage, but they in their innocence had not, was in how short a space they would become like him, far past their prime. When he looked into Dando's face, still showing traces of the child he had been not long before, yet already marked by the hard knocks he had taken along the road, he thought how soon, how very soon, the brightness would be dimmed; how quickly the light would fade. Surely the boy did not deserve to waste the brief period allotted him in some possibly fruitless and dangerous hunt in which he could well become the hunted. In Tallis' heart a determination to resume his travels began to grow, to take the weight onto his own shoulders and expend what was left of his life on this task, stealing away like a thief in the night without telling a soul. It was his hope that then the quest would revert to its original protagonist and his young friend would be left in peace to run his restaurant and find some kind of enduring happiness, no longer enmeshed and ensorcelled by a mysterious supernatural mission.

On the fourth day of the fifth month a major earthquake hit Rytardenath. One of the older skyscrapers down by the docks collapsed and two or three others suffered extensive damage. Six people were killed (the death toll would have been much higher had it not been a rest day) and for a brief spell life in the city was disrupted as clearing up and repairs were put in train. Nevertheless the general mood seemed to be upbeat and congratulatory. *CRISIS AVERTED!!* screamed a headline and underneath: *The authorities have dealt with the threat through exemplary vigilance and now business can proceed as usual.* The members of the Magnolias' small commune got the impression that the majority of local people thought their government had been instrumental in avoiding a worse disaster. This was utterly puzzling, but then the immigrants were beginning to find that everything about this city was puzzling. Ry-Town could best be described by that old saw: *a riddle wrapped in a mystery inside an enigma.* At the Magnolias gutters had fallen, tiles were dislodged and a couple of pipes fractured. The plumber was called. Dando's restaurant was unaffected.

At first light about a week later, after a particularly uneasy night during which lightning flickered and thunder rumbled around the horizon, a lone cyclist came wobbling up the drive towards the Magnolias. As he dismounted his left trouser-bottom got caught in the bike-chain and he hopped desperately for a moment before both he and the machine came crashing to the ground. Freeing himself from the tangle he crawled up the steps to the front door in order to hammer frantically on the outside, at the same time crying, "Let me in! Let me in!"

It was sometime before a metallic clinking indicated that Becca, in curlers and dressing-gown, was in the process of unlocking. On the threshold she discovered a dishevelled young man, his face streaked with dried tears and his hands clasped in front of him as if in supplication. There was a fey half-crazed look in his eyes. "Let me in!" he repeated.

"Why, it's Fynn," she cried in surprise, recognising the young saxophonist from the Posse. "Are you on your own? Where's Jack? Isn't he with you?"

"He's been arrested – they've all been arrested. I don't know where they've taken them. I'm afraid they're going to be killed, or something much worse than that. Hide me – hide me please!"

Becca's hand flew to her mouth; she looked the very picture of guilt.

"Oh my word!" she gasped.

At that moment a distant engine noise was heard rapidly approaching the house. The boy swung round in terror but it proved to be only Foxy and Damask astride the motorbike, returning from one of their night-time excursions. They came to a halt before the portico surprised to find someone about outside at this early hour.

"What's going on?" asked Damask.

"Fynn says Jack's been arrested," replied an appalled Becca. "This is dreadful – I knew something like this was bound to happen. He wouldn't take my advice about staying at home."

"You knew!?" cried an indignant Damask. "If you knew something was going on why didn't you tell us? All we've had from you are vague hints and warnings. I'm still pretty much in the dark."

"They've all been taken, all of them," put in Fynn shakily, making a great effort to regain his composure, "the whole boiling lot of them. Please let me in."

Becca moved out of the way to let the new arrivals by and then invited everybody into the parlour where she plumped up cushions and gestured for them to seat themselves. Damask and Foxy took up position on the chesterfield, his arm possessively around her shoulders.

"The Push-Bike Club didn't really have much to do with bikes, did it," remarked Damask to Fynn. He shook his head, his features creasing in distress.

"I was playing with the group, yesterday evening," he answered her in a breaking voice, "I didn't get to the club till after midnight. By that time there were floodlights outside and someone was yelling through a megaphone. *Moral Turpitude* it sounded like they were shouting, whatever that means, and something about re-education and treatment. The clubbers were told to come out with their hands up. There were guns. I saw the girls and boys loaded into vans – I saw Jack..." He buried his head in his hands. A little later he looked up, his face haggard and haunted, adding, "I didn't hang around – there's a list of members – they'll be searching for me..."

"You're safe here, chil'" comforted Becca.

"Who be the lot that nabbed them?" probed Foxy, "be they the filth?"

"They had vans labelled *Vice Squad*; they were wearing some kind of uniform."

"Don't tell the Lordship!"

Looking round they realised that while they were talking Milly had joined them, already dressed to go out. She had heard enough of Fynn's story to react in horror, her eyes wide with alarm.

"If 'e realises somefink's 'appened to Jack 'e'll prob'ly do sompthin' daft like tryin' to rescue 'im an' get 'imself into trouble," she continued.

"Stop talking crazy, honey," said Becca, " of course Dando must know – Jack's his friend. In fact I'll go and find him right now – I think he's up already."

Dando was in the kitchen with Tallis and Horry preparing breakfast.

"We must do something - we must find where they've been taken!" was his shocked reaction on hearing the news. "Would it be the local police station? Let's go down there at once and find out."

"No sweet-pea," replied Becca, "you don't know how things are ordered round here. I do – or at least I did. You go to work as usual. I'll head up town – I know who to ask. Better if you don't get involved."

"But I can't just sit around while Jack's in trouble!"

"I'll let you know as soon as I discover something – I'll phone the restaurant."

So, that morning, Dando, Tallis and Milly climbed the hill to the eatery on Mornington Heights and set about getting ready for the midday opening, but their hearts were not in the task. Dando lived on his nerves all day waiting for the phone to ring and when, by evening, it had failed to do so he despatched the others back to the

Magnolias to see what they could discover, exacting a promise that they would pass on anything they learnt. Meanwhile he began unavoidable preparations for the morrow. It was after the last staff member had departed and he was left alone in the first-floor dining area, giving the place a final once over before leaving, that he almost jumped out of his skin as a thunderous knocking came on the outside door. He was only halfway down to the ground floor when something heavy slammed once, twice, thrice against the central panelling and the structure, which had not been designed to withstand such an onslaught, burst off its hinges. Immediately the restaurant was filled with black-clothed men, some carrying weapons, who pushed past him up the stairs and began tramping to and fro overhead. The sound of breaking glass and crockery came to his ears along with banging and crashing as if chairs and tables were being thrown around. Dando rushed after them.

"What are you doing?! What are you doing?!" he cried.

"You're being closed down," a voice answered from behind and below him. He turned to find himself confronted by an individual imbued with unmistakable authority. "Law enforcement order number three six nine," barked this man, "dealing with premises employing unregistered aliens, status of said premises consequently illegal under the meaning of the act. Resistance is futile."

"I'm not resisting!" cried an anguished Dando, "stop them – stop them breaking everything up!"

"They're searching for evidence. Come downstairs – I need some details before you're removed."

"What do you mean? Are you arresting me?"

"Arresting? - we don't use that word." He pointed towards Dando's lower body. "You're physically challenged and shouldn't be out on the streets unsupervised. Removal is for your own good, besides the fact that the civil authorities have asked that they be allowed to question you on a matter of public order. You're being taken into protective custody and may eventually be given the chance of a better life."

Dando gathered himself together, glancing rapidly around as if looking for a convenient escape route - he was all ready to spring into action Then above him a figure appeared holding a very persuasive-looking truncheon while, below, his interlocutor produced a gun and used it to beckon him downwards. Both exits now being cut off it appeared that he had no choice but to obey. With his heart beating fast and feeling greatly outnumbered he acknowledged defeat and, raising his hands in the air, began - extremely reluctantly - to descend into the unknown.

The worst know what to believe,
The best are not so sure.
The bird circles endlessly.

Chapter six

I think it's nearly ready... I think if I push really hard in this direction... yes that's right... it's like giving birth... keep going, keep going – it's coming, it's coming...

"Dadda – what can I do? I go to tell he things but he won' listen. What use can I be to he if he turn away? I try to warn he an' now it be too late – I be afeared, much afeared."

"Don' 'ee fret, sweetheart – the danger be great I know but the greater the danger the clearer the path I see laid before him. It mus' come to this pass, to this extremity, I think, before he can go forward."

"But why do he turn away, Dadda? It do grieve me so much because of the love that were once between us."

"He still loves you my hinny – there's nothing more sure – an' that's why he's afraid to believe – afraid that it may all be a trick of the mind. Also I think that she from the Midda, the Earth Mother, and he from the sky, the Lord of the Winds, are blocking his eyes and ears to things beyond the flesh. Stay with him an' in the end his heart will shew he the truth."

Tallis and Milly left the restaurant and returned to the Magnolias, mid evening, with the aim of hearing the latest news concerning the goings on at the Push Bike Club and maybe, in the process, clearing up the mystery surrounding many aspects of life in Armornia which had puzzled them ever since they came to the country.

"For heavens sake head for home and see if there's any word from Becca," Dando had instructed, "perhaps she couldn't get through on this line."

At the house they came upon Damask having supper alone in the kitchen while Fynn lay asleep on the parlour sofa.

"He's worn himself out," she told them. "He spent all day leaping up and down, peering out of the window one minute and pacing to and fro the next – he wouldn't eat anything. No, I haven't heard from Becca – she should be at the club by now but because of what's happened I doubt she's there – I'm sure she'll be back later and then perhaps she'll be able to tell us what's going on. Foxy? Oh he's out in the garden somewhere – he never cared much for Jack anyway I'm afraid, although, since he's got to know him better, he's a bit more kindly disposed."

For want of an alternative the Magnolia's occupants fell into their usual routine, and, as on most evenings, Tallis, after partaking of a nightcap, decided to retire. He no longer needed Dando's assistance in the basic tasks of undressing and washing but the young man still made a habit of looking in on him when he finally returned to the house in order to check on his welfare and to douse the light. The knight appreciated this kindness and anticipated his visits in much the same way as he had once, as a child, looked forward to his mother's goodnight kiss. On this particular occasion however he woke from a long doze to find that, although it was well past midnight, the lamp was still burning. Had Dando forgotten to call or had he returned so late that he had gone straight to his rest thinking that his presence would not be required? For a long time Tallis lay irresolute until, with a groan, he put his feet to the floor and, taking the light, went to investigate. Silently opening the door to Jack and Dando's room he was confronted by two unoccupied beds; the boy was not there. Tallis was loath to disturb the formidable Damask, especially as he knew she would be sleeping in the nursery, so instead went to Milly's quarters on the first floor and discovered her curled up like a dormouse in a nest of untidy bedclothes. Shaking her by the shoulder he whispered, "I don't think our head chef has come back yet – I'm rather concerned."

Milly was deeply asleep and he had to repeat himself twice before she understood what he was on about, but, once she got the message, she was galvanised into action.

"I knew this would 'appen!" she cried rushing around flinging clothes off and on with a total disregard for modesty, "'e's gorn an' done sompthin' stoopid, I bet yer. I must go to the restaurant an' see wot's up."

Before he could react she was downstairs, out into the garden and had disappeared along the unlit drive. Tallis wondered if he should follow but got the feeling that by the time he had dressed and puffed halfway up the hill he would meet her coming back. He decided to wait. All the same it seemed like an age passed in the quiet house before he heard her feet on the gravel and she panted into the kitchen, having obviously run both ways. He waited to hear what she had to say but for a long while all she would do was stare at him with tragic eyes, her chest heaving. Eventually he asked gently, "What's the verdict?"

"It's busted!" she gasped hoarsely.

"What's busted?"

"The front door – an' everythin' inside is busted too. Orl 'is lovely plates an' stuff, an' the curtains pulled down an' the work benches an' the cupboards an' the tables an' chairs..."

She seemed to run out of words.

"But where is he? Is he all right?" Tallis' heart went cold within him.

"The lights woz on but there weren't no-one there – I called... I went upstairs..."

Milly burst into tears. Awkwardly Tallis embraced her, patting her on the back; it felt very strange to have a young woman, indeed anyone, in his arms after all this time. When her sobs subsided he asked diffidently, "Were there any signs – you know – of violence?" What he meant was: *did you see any blood?* Milly understood him. Her mouth tightened but she shook her head. "I dint see none," she whispered.

Just then there came the noise of a key in the lock and Becca entered through the front door. At the same time Damask descended the stairs. She had obviously not been sleeping but had stayed awake listening for the sound of the show-girl's car.

"What have you found out?" she demanded before their hostess had even had time to put her bags down or take off her jacket. Becca made a little querulous noise of protest in her throat. She was looking her age – tired and worn out.

"It's not just Jack wot's gorn now," cried Milly leaping in, "the restaurant's been messed up an' the Lordship's disappeared. Oh Lordship, Lordship..." She repeated the words under her breath in an anguished mantra.

Becca shook her head as if nothing further would have surprised her.

"I knew it," she said and then, "I went everywhere I could think of. No-one was prepared to say anything except for one guy who took pity on me and murmured as I was leaving – *the Transfer Facility."*

"What's that?" asked Damask.

"Well – there's a big hospital to the east of the city – beyond the stock yards. It's government run – things go on there..."

"What sort of things?"

Becca grimaced but did not reply.

"This really isn't good enough!" stormed Damask, thoroughly frustrated and in a mood to start laying down the law, "you've got to tell us what you know. There's something wrong with this place – something bad enough to have given you a reason to cross the sea and live with us in Drossi. *Transfer Facility, Transfer Facility* – what does that *mean*?!"

Becca stared at her for well over a minute; then sagged in capitulation.

"Come into the parlour," she said, "I'll try and explain."

Fynn woke in surprise to find his bedroom being invaded and took a while to gather his wits. By the time he had done so Becca was well launched on her account.

"About twenty years ago or more," she began, "Rytardenath and the other towns of the Albercreek Federation were set to elect a new administration. The campaigning generated a lot of heat because things had been kinda bad for some time: the crime rate was soaring, there was drugs-related gang warfare on the streets and lots of unemployment. Also the public health system was being strained to the limit trying to cope with the chronically sick and aged. For a long while power had alternated between two main parties with nothing much to choose between them and now they were both pretty much discredited. It was at this point that a third force appeared on the scene. These newcomers described themselves at first as a purity league and then later as the Party of Light, but to their adherents they were simply *The Whites* which was a pretty good name for them because they saw everything in terms of black and white, good and evil. They were a sort of religious fundamentalist movement and their contention was that the city had fallen under a malign supernatural influence. Wickedness was stalking the streets, they said, in the guise of ordinary citizens and it was the duty of all right-thinking men (they didn't include women) to run these idolaters to earth and deal with them by any means possible."

"When you say 'idolaters'," asked Damask of Becca, "do you mean that people were supposed to be worshipping some kind of evil god?"

"The Whites are adherents of the cult of the Maiden. They dug up the old story that's often told at Yuletide about the two divine brothers, the ones named Pendar and Azazeel, who were once a single entity and who when they were separated became each the antithesis of the other. It was the dark brother, they claimed, who was worming his way into people's hearts like a deadly disease in order to further his purpose of bringing the whole of our great city under his sway. By the gracious favour of the Maiden, declared the Party of Light, the pure in spirit had been granted a vision explaining how this terrible plan was to be thwarted. When they announced that they intended to contest the election the governing classes couldn't stop laughing; they marvelled that these red-necks could imagine that they would be able to take even a single seat. But this just shows how out of touch with the general mood the top people were because the ordinary man and woman in the street had paid attention to these newcomers who seemed to be putting into words exactly what they themselves had been thinking for some time. They listened to their message and bought the whole package, hook, line and sinker. The Purity League was swept into power with a huge majority."

Becca had a sudden fit of coughing. She turned to Damask croaking, "Can you get me a drink, honey - the bottle in the cupboard by the stove. Does anyone else want anything?"

Her listeners, their concentration broken, looked round and for the first time noticed that Milly was missing. No-one had remarked her going. Foxy had taken her place as early morning light crept through the windows.

"Ok," Becca continued once they had settled themselves again. "Now we come to what I'm afraid is the bad part. As soon as the Whites had the reins of government in their hands they set about making their position impregnable. They put their own men in charge of the police and the army and then declared a state of emergency during which the normal democratic processes were suspended. That's still in force today. After that they announced they were going to start rooting out the evil that had the capital in its grip. They began with the criminally insane – there was one particular prison where they were confined. These were obviously people who had sold their souls to the Dark Brother, they said, and they proposed a radical solution. Part of their belief system, which they share with many others, is that after death the individual progresses to another life, is reincarnated so to speak, but they differed from the majority in thinking that if, before the end arrived, the person was sufficiently penitent for past sins they had committed, then the slate was wiped clean. This was similar to the old ideas about heaven and hell, but applied instead to their next manifestation in a human body. It would be granting such pathetic victims of demonic possession a favour, they said, to facilitate their rebirth as whole and uncorrupted individuals and at the same time rid the town of a cancer that was poisoning its very lifeblood. And so they set about putting these poor crazy people to death – they called it *transference* and the hospital they built in order to carry out the procedure they named the *Transfer Facility*. After that it was just a short step from the criminally insane to ordinary criminals. Soon the jails were empty. From there they moved on to deviants, the chronically sick and the harmlessly mentally ill and then to anyone handicapped in any way whatsoever. Finally they declared that people over a certain age were a drain on the public purse and therefore obviously a weapon employed by the evil-one to weaken society. Surely it would be a kindness to spare them their final wretched years. It was then I decided to leave." Becca fell silent and for a long while no-one spoke. Eventually Damask asked, "And what about now you've returned? What are things like now?"

"I had hoped that they might have satisfied themselves; that they might have decided that they had finally cleansed the city and that the slaughter would have come to an end, but from what I hear nothing could be further from the truth. It's the frequency of these recent earth movements you see which the scientists say are caused by the weight of massive buildings on the substrata. The Whites evidently don't agree with that diagnosis, they think that Ry-Town still contains those that are aligned with the Prince-of-Darkness, in proof of which the ground revolts at having to bear the imprint of their feet. As a result the machinery of government is now directed towards identifying these people and wiping them from the face of the earth."

"And is that why they've taken Jack and Dando?"

"It seems likely. Both boys belong to categories they thought they had dealt with long ago – Dando's seriously disabled, and of course Jack..."

"But why didn't it happen sooner?"

"Well, for a long while I believe Jack slipped through their net - he's never been easy to pin down as you know - and Dando – Dando was just too famous it seems. The Party of Light have lost most of the popularity they had when they first took office. They're terrified that someone may appear who will unite the opposition, take up arms even, and lead a revolt that could sweep them from power. I think they see the NQPP as that threat but until now they've been reluctant to act for fear of bringing about the very thing of which they are most afraid."

"But what can we do? How can we save them?"

Becca shook her head looking distressed.

"I don't know," she muttered but then went on, "There's one faint possibility. You've got to understand how this thing works. It's all gotta be legitimate and above board. There's a lot of bureaucracy involved. In fact, apart from those convicted of a crime, the candidates for transference have to sign a consent form before the procedure is carried out."

"What!" cried Damask, "but surely no-one would do that?!"

"You don't understand the pressures they bring to bear; I don't think anyone's ever actually been known to refuse. Nevertheless friends and relatives can intervene. If we go to the Department of Health and lodge a complaint, giving good reasons for our objection, they're duty bound to listen. There's a remote chance we might bring about a postponement, even get the thing rescinded."

She sounded the very opposite of hopeful.

"Come on then!" Damask leapt to her feet ready to start out right away only to have Foxy pull her back down.

"Howd ye hard," he said, "it be only just after dawn."

"Yes," said Becca, "they won't be open till nine."

"Wouldn't it be better to go straight to the hospital?" asked Tallis. "You say it's to the east of the city?"

"You'd never get past the guards at the check-points - there's only one road in and out - and when you arrived what could you do without a permit? No – better to wait until eight o'clock and then I'll run you up town in the car. But we've got to get our story straight. Perhaps we could play on the fact that the boys are both foreigners – that they were planning to leave soon anyway - but then they might say they shouldn't have come here in the first place..."

"If you'd told us this sooner," cried an outraged Damask, "they could have been up and gone by now. Why on earth did you keep it a secret?"

Becca faltered and turned away, her eyes filling with tears.

"I guess I didn't want you to know what a bad place this is – I hoped everything would turn out all right... I was ashamed..."

Milly was on her way to Floodwood. She was running for the most part but slowed to a walk when she needed to catch her breath. The road seemed never-ending – if only she had Mabelene's old bike to speed things up. At last she found herself on the bridge that led to the half swamp half forest of the Underlands in which her people made their home. At the first cabin she came to she knocked frantically and as soon as the door opened a crack blurted out the words she had been taught: *Do you sell Aunt Patti's biscuits here?* She only had time for a brief look at the face within, a glimpse of the whites of someone's eyes, before the door was slammed shut. She moved on to the next shack only to have the same thing happen. On her third attempt there was no reply although she was sure she had seen a light in the window as she approached; if there had been such a thing it had been rapidly extinguished. But the fourth door she beat on opened and stayed open. An elderly man stood silhouetted against the light, not saying anything. Milly repeated the magical phrase.

"Who is it, Obadiah?" a woman's voice called from within.

"It's a chil' needin' help."

"Well tell her to come on in! Don' keep her standin' there you ol' fool!"

Wordlessly the man moved aside and Milly pushed past him into the shack. Within she found a bright room warmed by a wood fire, a room which at first glance appeared to contain all the necessities for a simple yet pleasant life. A heavily built but upright woman in a shapeless dress took Milly by the hand and invited her to sit down at a homely kitchen table.

"Have you come far honey?" she asked. "Here, sup some milk - fresh today. I see there's something weighing on your mind. Don' tell me till you're ready."

"I'm ready now," cried Milly, "there ain't no time to lose. C'n you 'elp?"

"If it's in our power we will – us folks need to stick together. But what's your trouble chil'? Is it one of your kin?"

"It's my friends," Milly struggled to keep back the tears. "They've taken them to the... to the trans... trans..."

"Transfer Facility," supplied the old man.

"Oh my lamb," the woman put a comforting arm around Milly's shoulders, "you're getting' worked up over nothin'. It's only white folks need to fear the 'cility – black folks just go there to do a job. There's plenty of other places we have to be wary of but not that. Your friends will be back with you before you can turn round."

"But they *are* white," protested Milly wretchedly.

This was followed by a shocked silence. The two old people stared at her as if she were a strange new species that had just crawled out from under a stone. Eventually the woman said coldly, "Black folks don' make friends with white folks."

"But they *are* my friends!." She was crying in earnest now. "We came crorst the sea together. The Lordship saved me when I was just a nipper – I must save 'im now – I mus'..."

"P'raps you'd better tell us your story," said the man seating himself at the table. So Milly, with a horrible feeling of vital minutes slipping away, explained about her early life, about the valley of Deep Hallow, about the long journey north and about her dear Lord who for the last three and a half years had held her heart in thrall.

"Mmm," said the woman when she had finished, "I mind my mama tellin' me that our people came from over there in the long ago where you say you come from, but I guess it were the white folks what brought us here against our will, else why should we have up and left our homes? I still say that nothin' good c'n come of white folks and black folks mixin' together."

"But this young girl has asked for our help," put in the man, "an' it'd put shame on us if we turned her away. What c'n we do for her?"

"Well – there's the 'cility bus."

"Dog my cats – I'd forgotten! Yes, girlie, there's a bus – goes from the bridge 'long the road. Takes the folk from here every morning that are employed at the T.F.. Loretta used to catch it – she cleaned the wards up to a year ago. Say Loretta, where's your pass? Give it to the girlie – she's just got time to get there if she hurries."

For an agonising few minutes Milly waited while the woman rifled through several drawers for the pass which she had put by and kept safe even though she had no further use for it. Eventually it came to light and Milly almost snatched it from her hand as she ran out of the door. The old man shouted after her, "Show it to the driver and at the check-points. The people on the bus can tell you where to go when you get there."

"She hasn't the ghost of a chance of bringin' them out alive," he said to the woman in a lower tone as they turned and went back into the cabin.

"An' that's as it should be," replied his wife.

Following his surrender Dando's arms were pinioned behind him and he was taken down the stairs and out into the cool night air. There he was loaded into a vehicle marked *Ambulance* but which looked more like a prison van, as a grill was in place between the driver's cab and the rear space and bars were fixed across the one and only window. Within he discovered a bench along either side and when he had awkwardly seated himself on one of them, a man who had previously invaded the restaurant climbed up and sat opposite, watching him silently and intently. On exiting the Dark Continent Dando had noticed two motor bikes parked nearby and another van. Now as the vehicle within which he was imprisoned jerked into motion he heard their engines wake to life and follow down the road. It was hard to get any clear idea of where they were headed from what could be seen through the front grill or the small aperture well above eye-level, but after a while he began to glimpse lighted windows flashing past practically overhead and realised they must be among tall buildings. Eventually he got the impression they were entering an enclosed space, a tunnel, from which they emerged into some sort of square tightly hemmed in by high featureless walls. The van drew up, the back doors were flung open and a voice barked "Out!" Dando looked to his companion for help but the other just stared back expressionlessly and did not move. He half stumbled, half fell out of the door, greatly hampered by the fact that he could not use his hands. He was then immediately grabbed and marched through an entrance into a reception area where, although it was the middle of the night, there was a crowd of people, almost exclusively male, milling around, whose attention was immediately focused on the newcomers. Here he and his captors were delayed for some time while communication was established by phone with a location elsewhere in the building. This situation was horribly reminiscent of another time and place when he had been defenceless and at the mercy of a gathering of men, but a continuing wave of indignation lifted him high above any apprehension and carried him through to the point when he and his keepers were summoned by a public address system and he could escape the intense scrutiny he was under. Once on the move their first port of call proved to be a lift, followed by several flights of stairs from which he was escorted into a nondescript room, its very lack of any defining feature lending it a sinister air.

A small moustachioed man was sitting on a muddy-coloured chair at a muddy-coloured desk in front of a muddy-coloured tiled wall. There were three more chairs, soon occupied by two men and a woman who silently filed in through a second door. Dando was left to stand in front of them, a lonely vulnerable figure, his hands still cuffed behind his back. Yet, buoyed up by his sense of outrage, he was the first to speak.

"Why have you trashed my place?!" he cried in anguish, "W-why?! It's a complete wreck! W-what earthly reason did you have? All that work gone to waste...!"

He had to struggle not to break down when he remembered the pitiful state of the restaurant's ground floor as he had last seen it. The four faces behind the desk looked startled at being on the receiving end of this infuriated remonstrance.

"It's not our job to answer questions," replied their spokesman as if trying to seize back the initiative. "You've been handed over to us because you're suspected of inciting others to cause a breach of the peace. If it wasn't for that you would have been dealt with by the Department of Health and Human Resources – a straightforward case I would have thought." He gazed pointedly at the boy's artificial foot.

"I don't understand," Dando replied, taking himself in hand and realising that he would be best served by appearing calm and rational. "I haven't been doing anything wrong. I haven't been inciting whatever it was you said."

It was the turn of the only woman to speak. She immediately gave the impression that she out-ranked her fellows.

"I believe you're in charge of this rabble that call themselves the NQPP?"

"No," said Dando, shaking his head.

"It's your image they carry on their banners."

"That's their business, not mine. What have you done with my friend?"

"Your friend...?"

"You arrested him and all the other members of his club last night." Again he was in danger of allowing his emotions to overwhelm him.

The four interrogators conferred together. Dando caught a few odd words: "...mopping-up operation... Vice Squad... perversion of accepted standards... modification..."

"Where have you taken him?" he demanded passionately.

"If you have an enquiry concerning a certain exercise carried out yesterday in order to bring a group of deviants into line you'll have to go to the Domestic Threat Reduction Agency – it was their assignment you're referring to I believe, not ours."

"And how am I supposed to do that?" He turned his head aside and downwards to indicate his manacled arms.

"If you co-operate with us we may be able to make a concession and allow you a certain limited freedom to lodge your complaint with the Agency"

"Well, where do I find it, this reduction thingy? Is it here?"

His questioners seemed surprised that the boy did not know the name of their august institution.

"This is the Bureau of Homeland Security," said the small man with an expansive gesture that took in the whole of the enormous building into whose guts Dando had presently been swallowed, "the DTRA is further down the road."

The woman, beginning to display a certain amount of impatience, turned to her colleagues.

"We're getting off the point. Explain to the detainee what we require of him."

"We're offering you an alternative option to transference," said the moustachioed man to a mystified Dando. "All we're asking you to do is to make a broadcast denouncing this movement you were instrumental in starting – this NQPP."

"But I told you – I didn't start it."

"Well, what's this name that's bandied about among the leaders? I think it refers to you."

"Footless," contributed the man on his left who up to that point had not spoken.

"Yes – Footless - a most subversive title – flying in the face of everything that's decent."

"If you'll use your influence to urge them to disband," put in the woman who obviously could not bear to take a back seat for more than a moment, "and if you'll endorse government policies, we'll make it possible for you to continue in this life, despite your infirmity, although it will have to be a long way from here. If not we'll hand you back to the DHHR for transference."

"T-transference – I've heard that word more than once. What do you mean by transference?"

"You aren't familiar with transference?" The four faces behind the desk regarded Dando as if they thought he must be a little weak in the head. Over the next few minutes it was made clear to him what sort of fate the City of Rytardenath reserved for its undesirables. He was suitably horrified.

"You want me to say I agree with killing innocent people? N-never... I would never..."

"To condemn a dissident organisation that advocates criminality and to endorse the merciful metamorphosis of those whose quality of life has been permanently compromised and who will therefore benefit from moving to a new mode of existence."

"By killing them."

"The good of society as a whole is paramount and besides, the candidates go of their own free will, they always give their permission before the procedure is carried out. In their next incarnation they get a fresh start; they leave behind all the misery of body and mind they have experienced here and begin anew."

Dando was very far from being persuaded by this argument: *Jack said he thought the truth was going to be ghastly,* he remembered, *but I don't reckon he knew the half of it.* Out loud he asked, "Who decides? Who says who will live and who will die?"

"You don't need to worry about that - there are tried and tested methods – categories have been very precisely defined - nothing is left to chance. If you do what we ask you'll be throwing in your lot with those on the side of light. All right-minded people need to pull together at such a time as this." She seemed to think that this clinched the matter. Dando, however, put into words a concern that had been bothering him ever since his bereavement.

"How can you be so sure they will go on - be reincarnated as you put it? How do you know that anyone survives death at all? Have they ever come back to tell you?" In saying this he felt he had got to the heart of the matter.

Up until that moment there had been a certain air of complacency exuding from the others in the room as they explained their government's long-standing policy to this defiant yet powerless delinquent, but now their whole attitude changed. The four members of the Department of Homeland Security stared at Dando as if he had uttered a blasphemy. It was sometime before the woman found her voice and then she spoke with a cold contempt mingled with a kind of nauseated aversion.

"Evidently we're wasting our time. It's quite obvious that you are a true servant of Azazeel. This town will never be purged until you and your kind have been eliminated for good and all. You pollute the very ground you walk on and it's no wonder the earth rises up. Come my friends!"

The officials swept out leaving Dando momentarily alone until he was collected once more by the men who had originally brought him to that place and taken down to the prison van masquerading as an ambulance in the courtyard below.

"Do you think praps it ought to be a man who does the talking?"

It was nearly eight a.m.. The group at the Magnolias was trying to decide who they should send to the Department of Health with their petition for clemency. Damask, although secretly convinced that she could put the case better than anyone, was yet cautious enough to take gender bias into consideration. Becca surveyed the three possible candidates - Tallis, Foxy and Fynn - and shook her head.

"No, honey, I reckon it'd best be just you and me and it's about time we hit the road - we need to arrive soon after nine."

They set out immediately in Becca's vintage car but having once reached the vast anonymous government building that was their goal they were met with delay after delay. They became increasingly frustrated as they were passed from one sub-section to another, in none of which a single person admitted to knowing what they were advocating. Eventually they were told that they were at the wrong location entirely and that they needed the Bureau of Homeland Security which was in another part of town. They hurried back to the car and set out, but on gaining this almost identical block were sent on to the Domestic Threat Reduction Agency which in its turn tried to shift responsibility back to Health and Human Resources, the place where they had started this convoluted journey. At each location they were required to fill in a sheaf of forms and told that no decision could be reached until an investigation had been carried out which might take place on the following day or might not, depending on staff availability. By the end of the afternoon they were thoroughly dispirited, feeling, for want of any better alternative, that they would have to begin the whole process again on the morrow.

Returning to the mansion they found Horry in a terrible mess, each of the men having expected one of the others to take responsibility for his care. Damask flew into a rage and gave all three a piece of her mind. Having relieved her feelings to a certain extent she came to a decision.

"We're not getting anywhere at all. I'm going to that hospital with Foxy this very night, guards or no guards. We'll go on the motorbike. We'll find them don't you worry. Pray heaven they won't have been stupid enough to sign anything before we arrive!"

Before it's ready
The preparation is long and arduous,
But then one gulp can swallow a town.

Chapter seven

Back in the van, Dando found himself, this time, alone. The handcuffs had been removed but so, under enormous protest, had his prosthesis and he was thus rendered virtually helpless. As the vehicle swayed and sashayed down the road he stood unsteadily on his one remaining foot, clinging stubbornly to the window bars, trying to catch a glimpse of where he was being taken. In due course the central skyscrapers faded into the background and a bridge was crossed, bringing into view a vast conglomeration of factories, workshops, storage yards and workers' housing which in the early morning light appeared grimly functional with not a trace of greenery to relieve the starkness. Then an almost overpowering stench of ordure heralded mile upon mile of what he took to be stockyards. On the few occasions that the engine idled the distressed lowing of literally thousands of animals came to his ears. For the first time he began to feel truly apprehensive.

By and by they reached a barrier, the back door was thrown open and someone looked in on him for a second ot two before slamming it shut. The vehicle lurched forward for about half a mile before reaching a second checkpoint where the road penetrated a high metal fence. At this cordon they were waved past without further inspection and, finally, Dando saw the place for which they were making. Three tower blocks lay ahead of him, set fairly far apart, and these were connected at ground level by a sprawl of single-story temporary-looking structures covering a wide area. Off to the left he could see a windowless rectangular building with a huge chimney rising from its centre which o'er-topped everything else in the vicinity. The complex seemed to reach out and envelope him as they approached, suggesting he was penetrating the streets of an autonomous self-regulating town with its own dictates and strategies. A uniformed man in charge of a wheelchair awaited him by the door at which the van eventually drew up and in a matter of minutes he was being whisked down a confusion of corridors to an elevator within the base of one of the high-rise buildings. “Where are you taking me?” he asked the official as they were transported skywards but the other stared straight ahead and pointedly ignored him.

Leaving the lift on one of the upper floors they passed the door to a room through which he could see a group of invalids - some in chairs, some on trolleys - being harangued, with messianic fervour, by an intense unintelligible individual. Dando was then abandoned by his conveyor in a corridor where several bewildered-looking people appeared to be waiting for something to happen. Here he was eventually approached by a young man holding a clip-board who asked his name, enquired into his origins and then went on to try to obtain intimate and embarrassing details concerning his physical condition.

“What's the point of all this?” Dando protested fretfully, “is it really necessary?” meaning, *if you're going to finish me off why not stop messing about and just get on with it.*

“This is a primary induction exercise,” the pen-pusher replied, rather pompously, “we'd like to know a little bit about you for our files before you have your medical examination.”

Medical examination! A team of white coats awaited him in an adjoining room and here he was told to strip and stretch out on a table. It was made clear that the procedure would take place with or without his consent and that there was little point in refusing to submit. Two men bent over him from either side and compared notes as they engaged in a thorough scrutiny of his body. His limbs were manipulated, lenses were applied to his eyes, all his other orifices were probed and his pulse, lungs and scar-tissue commented on. This was done without any acknowledgement of his participation until he began to feel that he might as well be a piece of prime steak on a butcher's slab for all the attention being paid to him as a person. As they worked, one of the men (a doctor?) threw single word evaluations over his shoulder to a clerk who was taking notes:- “Good – compromised – untenable – useless.” Dando realised that whatever it was they were looking for he was not coming up to scratch. At long last they finished with him and instead of having his clothes returned he was offered a hospital gown. It was in a state of shamefaced humiliation that he was taken once again into a lift and from thence to a large ward where, although provided with a meal of sorts, he was subjected, in the course of the day, to the usual indignities suffered by the bed-ridden.

Milly sat in the oddly named *'cility bus* as it skirted the northern edge of the city. She had arrived at the bridge just in time to clamber aboard and the driver gave her pass a mere cursory glance. The other occupants of the bus, middle-aged black women for the most part, were more curious however.

"Where do you come from, my sugar?" asked the large female beside her who was taking up more than half the seat, "I've never seen you around Floodwood before."

Milly thought fast.

"I'm Loretta's niece," she replied. "I needed a job so she said I could 'ave 'er pass an' take 'er place."

"That's strange – I never knew she had a niece. But baby, Loretta left more than a year ago when it was all getting a bit too much for her. Not the work mind – she just weren't happy. So there won't be a vacancy far as I know."

"Oh," said Milly. She relapsed into silence for a few minutes. Then, "I've got to get into the trans... trans..." There was a faint hint of desperation in her voice.

"Why's that?"

Milly shook her head.

The woman examined her more closely.

"Are you up to mischief?"

"No missus."

Her neighbour turned her broad dark face away and thought for a few minutes.

"I don't know what your game is but if you really want to find out what it's like inside I could take you in as my intern – it's been done before. You could say you want some work experience. But you'll have to promise to stick close to me and behave yourself. If you wander off I'll have the alarm raised in two shakes of a lamb's tail."

"Yers I promise," averred Milly fervently.

"OK – I'm Shona. And you're...?"

Milly gave her name and then another silence ensued.

"Where do they take the people they're goin' to trans... trans..." Milly asked hesitantly.

"You mean the set-up that gives the place its name? That's in Block A. I don't work there, thank goodness. I'm in Block B, but the people I do for are hardly any better off than those others. They're all white folks of course, praise the Maiden."

It did not take Milly long to realise that her companion was not being entirely unselfish in offering to facilitate her entrée into the hospital. As soon as they arrived and reached the block where the work was intended to take place the young girl was handed a bucket, broom, scrubbing brush and bar of soap while Shona stood nearby gossiping with one or two of the other cleaners.

"We're not 'lowed to talk to the patients," someone else told her as the forthcoming schedule was explained, "not even if they speak first. Jest keep y'head down an' concentrate on what you're doing. Did you bring any lunch? Oh well, somebody might be able to spare you some of theirs if they're feeling generous."

As the hours wore away Milly scrubbed, wiped, dusted and swept along corridors and in and out of wards becoming more and more impatient at the constant supervision she was under. How was she to bring help to her dear Lord if she was being watched all the time with not the slightest chance of slipping away? As she understood it she was not even in the right place to start looking for him. According to Shona they were working in Block B while the actual location where the transferences happened was in Block A. She looked in frustration at the many signs, some augmented by arrows, mounted on the walls. Throughout her few short years of life no one had bothered to teach the little abused child her letters and as a consequence the notices, which probably contained valuable information concerning the place where she wished to go, might as well have been in some foreign tongue for all the sense they made to her. Up to this point in her career she had cheerfully accepted her illiteracy but now, for the first time, felt her deprivation keenly. It was not until after midday that she was able to get away from Shona for a few minutes. The pile of rubbish they had collected – used dressings, needles, uneaten food, sweepings from the floor – had been put into sacks and then into a wheeled bin which she was instructed to take down by elevator to a side-door and from thence to the trash-site where the refuse was sorted.

"And make sure you come straight back – remember what I said about raising the alarm."

When she reached the location in question no-one was about. She saw that there were bays to accommodate various types of garbage:- paper, plastics, clothes, metal and so on. Metal! An area solely devoted to the storage of scrap-iron was situated at the end of the line and lying right at the front of it, slightly apart from the rest of the discards, she noticed something that resembled a twisted black blade with leather straps attached. She recognised it – it was her Lordship's artificial foot! For a moment Milly's heart almost died within her and then began beating nineteen to the dozen. She picked up the prosthesis - it was surprisingly heavy - and held it to her breast. Why was it here? What did this mean? She was struck by a horrible sense of foreboding. It was almost as if she had discovered a remnant of his actual body – a hand say, or an ear – which in that case would mean that he was... Her head whirled, she broke into a cold sweat and thought she was about to faint, but from this weakness grew a new dogged determination. She would find her dear Lord – (she would!) - whether he was alive or... she had to face the possibility now... whether they had done away with him. And even if he were dead she would rescue him from their clutches, she would save his dear body so that they could do it no further harm. Meanwhile, if she did not want the hue and cry to start, she must hide what she had found, get back in the lift and return to Shona.

"This is the last one."

Each storey of Block B contained two wards and, having started at the top, they had been working their way gradually downwards cleaning them methodically floor by floor. Now they were just above ground level and Milly was feeling extremely tired. She was not used to such relentless physical activity, not used to labouring for so many hours at a stretch. It was a relief to know that the end was in sight. When they reached the final ward Shona began sweeping round the beds on one side, starting near the door, while Milly dealt with the other side from the far end, by now expert in achieving the maximum effect with the minimum of effort. When it came to number of patients this unit was fuller than most. During the course of the day she had become used to seeing chronically sick people, many of whom looked to be at death's door, but it came as a shock to find that here those she passed as she worked appeared to have nothing wrong with them apart from the fact that they were under some kind of physical restraint and were connected to fluid-filled plastic bags placed on stands beside the beds. Also they were all, without exception, young. As instructed she kept her head down and avoided fraternisation, but nevertheless could not resist at least one curious glance at each detainee as she passed. On reaching the fifth bed along it was as a result of such a glance that, quite involuntarily, a single word exclamation was jerked from her lips.

"Jack!"

"What's that honey?" asked Shona who was almost on a level with her as she worked in the opposite direction. "No – nothing."

She looked to see if the boy – her friend - Dando's friend - had responded to the sound of his name but his head was turned away and he did not seem to have heard her. There was something peculiar about the way he was lying. She saw that his wrists, like those of everyone else in the ward, were shackled to the metal frame of the bed, and that some form of drip was being fed into his veins. As she worked her way round to the other side she was shocked to find that the glass eyes which usually gave his face a semblance of normality were missing. Because Shona was so near she did not dare make a second attempt at attracting his attention but moved on and by the time they had finished cleaning had had no further chance to reveal herself. As they left she was assailed by a tremendous sense of guilt at abandoning her erstwhile companion when he was so obviously in dire need, but what else could she do?

Now it was time to return to the area where the bus would be waiting to carry them back to Floodwood. On leaving the building their names were noted and they were handed an emolument, while a distinguishing badge and overall that had been distributed on their arrival were collected. Shona, a lot fresher than her acolyte who had definitely shouldered the lion's share of the work, chatted to another crony as they walked within the gathering dusk towards the stop. Milly loitered, falling farther and farther behind. When she was sure that the two women were sufficiently absorbed in their conversation to have forgotten all about her she turned off the path and found somewhere to hide. From there, concealed from the road, she watched to see what would happen. Sometime later she heard her name being called, once, twice, thrice, but nobody came back to look for her. Eventually the bus's engine started and it moved off round an adjacent corner. Milly, at last alone, set out to trace the long and confusing route circling the outside of the buildings which would eventually lead to the trash-site she had visited earlier and to the little side door that, if she was lucky, might still be unlocked.

"I be feelin' fare middlin' about this." As Damask and Foxy donned their leathers ready to leave for the hospital, the Nablan voiced his reservations.

"Well," replied Damask, "I know you never liked Jack much – nor Dando, for that matter, but I can't just sit around doing nothing. We should have gone straight there hours ago."

Foxy demurred. "It don' be that – I don' be a-thinkin' like that anymore, an' you an' me, we can't let these furriner fellows have it all their own way; but there be roadblocks they do say."

"We'll jump them – we'll be past before they even see us coming. With luck the guards'll be half asleep at this time of night." (It was about eleven thirty).

Her companion looked at Damask with reluctant admiration.

"You've got a heart hully like a man, gel," he commented.

Filling the motorbike's gas tank from a reserve can they set off towards the city, passing through its centre and out the far side over the East River bridge. As the highway swerved south-east a large sign gave directions to other towns in the Albercreek Federation but, beneath it, a smaller board with the legend *Livestock pens - Abattoir – Hospital (T.F.)* indicated a road leading straight on.

"That's the way," shouted Damask into Foxy's ear as she clung to his waist. "Remember, if you see any checkpoints, go flat out."

Sure enough at the end of a long straight stretch they came in sight of some lights illuminating a small guardhouse. Outside was an obstruction - a wooden barrier - but it was raised.

"There's one!" cried Damask, "go, go, go!"

Her companion opened the throttle and his machine leapt forward. As they approached, two men came hurrying out of the building shrugging on jackets. The bar began to descend but the bikers were passed before it blocked their way. From well behind came a series of loud reports: someone was firing at them but they were already out of range. Damask laughed jubilantly.

"Done it!" she crowed.

But now they saw another obstacle that they would have to contend with. A high metal palisade stood in their way with just a small gap where the road passed through. This time the barrier was down.

"It's just wood," shouted Damask," it can't stop us. Keep going."

Luckily she was right and as they hit it the bar broke and flew up into the air. However what they had not bargained for was a snake-like object a few yards further on stretched across the road at ground level and bearing an array of wicked-looking spikes. Foxy jammed on his brakes but too late. As they crossed this booby trap their tyres exploded, the motorbike slewed sideways throwing them off and both machine and riders skidded across the road surface side by side until they collided with a high concrete kerb. Damask's shoulder bore the brunt of the impact and she heard something crack. So far so bad, but she soon discovered that Foxy was even worse off. When, gathering her wits and calling his name, she managed to drag herself woozily over to where he lay she found he was out cold; it was his head rather than his shoulder that had made contact with the immovable object. Her left arm hanging limply, she knelt above him slapping his face with her right hand and urging him to, "Wake up, wake up!" A crunching noise heralded a pair of booted feet which arrived on the other side of his body. She looked up at what seemed like an immensely tall figure, realising at the same time that gasoline was leaking from the bike's ruptured fuel tank and spreading all around. She saw that the man was smoking a cigarette.

"Watch out" she warned urgently, "the whole place could go up!" at the same time making an attempt to pull Foxy away from danger with her one functioning arm. Two more cops arrived pistols in hand.

"Ok," ordered the first man, "refusal to stop, damage to property, aggravated trespass, exceeding the speed limit - you're guilty of all those and that's just for starters. On your feet ma'am – we're taking you in."

"You can't..." began Damask and promptly passed out.

Dando could not help but notice that a lot of the people in his ward were old - some very old. Of these several appeared to be wandering in their wits. Various nonsensical monologues were being conducted up and down the room. The senior in the next bed engaged him in earnest conversation.

"The government's stolen the sky," he was informed, "I found out about it – that's why they put me in here – so's I wouldn't tell."

"Really?" responded Dando accommodatingly, "Last time I looked it seemed to be still there."

"Ah – that's just a trick – artificial."

Someone a few places away was calling out repeatedly for "Rosie! Rosie!" while numerous other occupants continually coughed, mumbled and moaned, sounding very far from well.

One of the more composmentis of the inmates proved to be a sharp-faced weasely-looking creature pinned by one arm to the bed opposite. He grinned at Dando.

"All batty as fruit cakes, this lot," he said cheerfully, making the corkscrew gesture against his head with his one free hand, "'cept me of course. My trouble is I was a bit too light-fingered for their taste. What are you in for?"

Dando frowned, trying to make sense of the last few hours.

"I don't really know why I'm here," he replied cautiously, " but it may be because they think I started some protest group or other."

"That doesn't sound likely to me unless it's classified as criminal – far as *they're* concerned it all has to be done by the book. Are you chronically ill? Have you got any bits missing?"

Well – I don't think they're too happy about my having only one foot."

"*Footless!* Don't tell me you're the famous *Footless!*" The man laughed, apparently highly delighted at this revelation.

Dando shrugged in embarrassment, then asked, "Do you know what's happened to the people from the Push-Bike Club?"

"Come again?"

"My friend's a member of the Push Bike Club – they've arrested them."

"Hang on a minute, I think that rings a bell, - is it that bunch of queers you mean? Have they finally cottoned on and rounded them up? Jiminy! They won't be heading for the chop like us but I wouldn't want to be in their shoes. Block B, first floor - there's a special ward catering for homos - they've recently found a new way of dealing with them. This is block C."

"Aren't there three blocks?" enquired Dando.

"Yes – Block A – that's where they do it – that's where they launch you into the hereafter."

"How would I get to Block B?"

"The blocks are all connected at ground level – you just have to follow the signs, but it's a long way. How're you gonna get there? Hop?"

Throughout the day Dando lay and observed the ward. There were quite a lot of comings and goings in and out. Mounted on the door to the corridor he noticed a small square box with an array of buttons. The cleaners and nurses punched a number onto this keypad when they wanted to leave and presumably there was something similar on the outside. He watched and waited and in the end his patience was rewarded. The matron in charge had a station in the form of a small cubicle halfway down the room. As the day drew to a close activity lessened until she sat there on her own occupied with some desk-bound task. At the same time supervision of the patients, most of whom were unconscious or asleep, had almost ceased. He decided that if he was going to make a break for it, it must be now or never. Manoeuvring himself to the edge of the bed he lowered his single foot silently to the floor and then, performing a balancing act, arranged the bed-clothes as best he could to make it look as if a body were still in situ. After that, observed with interest by the self-confessed larcenist to whom he had been speaking earlier, he went down on hands and knees and crawled as quickly as he could to the last bed in the row, the one nearest the door, concealing himself beneath it. He had hatched a plan of escape but its success rested entirely on whether he could solve the problem of getting through the door and whether the two wheelchairs that he had seen sitting in the corridor when he arrived were still there. Suddenly he was startled by the face of an old woman that appeared over the edge of the bed under which he was hiding and looked down at him. "Hello sweetie," she cooed. Dando held his finger to his lips. The bed's occupant lowered her voice.

"If you're going to play down there dear, don't get dirty, otherwise I'll be in trouble with your mommy."

Dando smiled, nodded and then shrank into the deep shadows by the wall from whence he could obtain a good view of the door. He guessed that there would be a change of shift sometime during the small hours and sure enough soon after midnight a new nurse came into the ward and went to relieve her colleague. A little later the off-duty matron passed him on her way out. There was nothing wrong with his eyesight and he observed intently the input of a six digit number – 131297 – onto the keypad. The woman's replacement made a cursory tour of the room and then retired to the cubicle to read a magazine. When he was fairly confident that no-one was watching Dando slid out from under the bed, hauled himself up by the door handle and punched in the number he had witnessed. The lock clicked once and he was free. Manoeuvring quickly around the open door he shut it quietly behind him and to his relief found that his memory had not played him false: in actual fact there were three wheelchairs parked against the wall. Out of these he discovered one that was designed to be propelled manually by the occupant. He did not know which floor he was on although he was definitely well above ground level so set off in this new conveyance in search of a lift.

How was he to avoid being caught? He was wearing practically nothing – a hospital gown no more – and being wheelchair-bound there was no way he could pretend to be a member of staff. He felt it would only be a matter of time before he was spotted. But even if the mission failed he had to try – he had to find Jack. He came to some elevator doors, thumbed the call button and sat and waited, hoping against hope that the lift would arrive empty. Into his mind at that moment, almost as if someone had prompted the thought, came a recollection of the times he had spent on watch when travelling the Shady Way. Those were the hours during which Annie had been with him, the hours they had spent secretly together. Memories such as these were very precious but also exquisitely painful, partly because he believed she was now lost to him forever and partly because their guiltless lovemaking had since been overlaid by the remembrance of the horrific and degrading assaults he had experienced on the way to Drossi which had been etched ineradicably into his memory. But what had been remarkable about those idyllic nights with his lover was the fact that they were never discovered together. She had been able to cast a spell, a spell for sleep, which ensured that their jealous companions did not wake while they were in each others' arms. When they lay, sated and happy, exchanging intimate confidences, she had told him, or rather taught him, how to work this magic. There were also other spells which she had taken the trouble to explain: spells for mind-reading, spells for divination, spells of ward, spells for healing and concealment. Yes – concealment - she had shown him how it was possible to hide even when in full-view. That last – he had made an attempt to learn how the magic was worked, although he had never had a use for it up to now and was not even sure he could recall the details after so long. He vaguely remembered that you had to pass your hand over and around your head and body as if bringing into being a masking veil while reciting:-

Black as night,
Dark not light,
Mind unclear,
See not here.

Yes that was it, and it went on:-

Bright, not bright,
Sight, not sight,
Mirror bend,
Vision end.

It had taken him quite a while to memorise this doggerel – the nonsensical words had made him laugh and Annie had got impatient with him - how light-hearted he had been in those days. But now as the elevator, fortunately vacant, stopped at his floor he thought he had got it more or less straight in his head. There was no way he was going to be able to try the bewitchment out in a less threatening environment, it would be a case of getting it right at the first attempt or not at all. On entering the lift he put what he could remember into practice and by the time ground-level was reached felt convinced that on the way down he had woven the spell as accurately as his memory would allow. Miraculously it seemed to work because, although he encountered various people on his passage from one block to another and, without exception, they all altered course to avoid colliding with his chair, they seemed greatly preoccupied and appeared barely to notice him.

Block B, first floor. With the help of another lift he travelled upwards and then saw a door ahead of him with a key-pad similar to the one he had already used. Did each ward have its own code or did the same digits apply to all? Holding his breath he punched in 131297 and after what seemed like an age heard the lock click open. He pushed the handle down and entered. Inside, the lighting was very dim but he got the impression that the room was fairly full and as unsupervised at this hour of the night as the one he had just left. Slowly he wheeled himself along between the beds looking from side to side, searching for a familiar face. The patients were hard to distinguish, some just anonymous humps under a pile of blankets, but luckily it did not take him long to find what he sought. The blind boy was lying on his back apparently staring at the ceiling, but he was staring with eyeless sockets and his wrists were fettered.

"Jack! Jack!" whispered Dando urgently, manoeuvring the chair as close as he could to the side of the bed. There was no response. He tried again.

"Jack! It's me Dando – I've come to help you."

Again he got no reaction. The boy lay as still as a statue, barely seeming to breath. Suddenly Dando remembered the spell – the spell of concealment. What had Annie done to cancel the magic? Oh yes, he had done it himself before now - just a neutralising click of the fingers, that was all. Quickly he suited the action to the thought and then spoke again, "Jack – it's Dando – I'm here."

Jack's head turned slowly in his direction. On his face was an expression of such eloquent suffering that it pierced Dando to the heart.

"Birdy – is that you?" whispered his friend unbelievingly.

"Yes, yes!" Dando replied, gripping one of Jack's manacled hands. He discovered a tube inserted into the back leading from a plastic bag on a stand. "What's this? What's this stuff? What are they doing to you?"

"You wouldn't want to know."

"Yes I would! No more secrets Jack!"

"They gave us a lecture – they explained – they made out they were doing us a favour."

"Yes – but what is it? Tell me."

"Well," Jack swallowed and took a deep breath, "they call it *drug-induced castration* or *chemical emasculation*, but you might be able to think of a more bog-standard word if you put your mind to it. It's supposed to ensure we'll never be naughty boys ever again. Do you get my meaning?"

With a cry of disgust Dando yanked the tube away.

"Too late, birdy – too late," mumbled Jack, but "No!!" exclaimed Dando, refusing to countenance this. With the freeing of the tube came a spurt of blood which he staunched with a corner of the top sheet. At that moment the door burst open and a woman entered followed by four men. To Dando's amazement he recognised the female who had cross-questioned him at Homeland Security not twenty-four hours earlier. What was she doing here, this apparatchik? Had somebody told her where he was? A nurse whose presence he had not registered but who had obviously put in a call for help came running forward.

"Thank goodness you've arrived," she cried, "here he is! I didn't see him come in – he just appeared. I phoned right away. Look what he's done!"

At first the authority figure ignored Dando and pointed at Jack.

"Why is this one on the deviants ward?" she demanded. "Don't you realise he should be with the visually challenged? Get him over there at once. And you..." she began, turning to Dando, then hesitated as if a new thought had just occurred to her.

"No – just a minute," waving her hand towards the boy on the bed, " we were looking for one more to fulfil this week's quota – he'll do."

"But he refuses to sign – that's why he's here."

"Hasn't anyone told you? - those with a visual impairment are naturally exempt from signing. As for him," indicating Dando, " get him back to his rightful place and make sure he doesn't go wandering again."

She walked away muttering about sub-standard staff and untrained personnel while two of the orderlies began wheeling Jack's bed towards the door.

"Hang on!" cried a horrified Dando, "what are you saying? - that you have a quota for murdering people?" There was a ripple of reaction up and down the ward, while the eyes of the nurse and the other two men widened. The official turned and came back. She seemed to see the young man properly for the first time.

"I know you, don't I," she said. "You're that trouble-maker from the NQPP. That gives me an idea. Come into the office – it's just along the corridor - I'd like a word." and she led the way as if expecting him to follow. Dando, in fact, did just that, eager to discover where Jack was being taken, but once outside found that the two men, the bed and its occupant had already disappeared.

"You're a trouble-maker," repeated the woman when they were alone together, " but perhaps at this late stage you might still co-operate and do what we want if I explain things more clearly. Yes, we have a quota – government edict two two one, subsection fifty. It varies - is regulated - according to the birthrate. You see, because of our very high standard of living there's always a danger that population growth will get out of hand. So besides our cleansing operation we have to keep a check on numbers..."

"W-which means that you just go ahead and kill more people!" Dando, appalled, could hardly believe what he was hearing. Was there to be no end to these abominations?

"Transfer," replied the official, "and only those with a poor quality of life. They have to give their consent."

Dando sat back, robbed of words. He had suddenly tumbled to the fact that this signing business was the second time in the past year and a half he had heard a story of people going willingly to their deaths – of course he could not help but be reminded of the voluntary sacrifices to the trees on Hungry Island. Were these brutal terminations just another act of propitiation, then, to some sort of obscure demigod? "Well you're not going to do it to my friend." he exclaimed, "he's not going to put his name down on paper for you or anyone!"

"As I explained, there is an exception made for the visually challenged. A verbal agreement is all that's required."

"You want one more this week?" Dando was suddenly seized by an irresistible reckless impulse that, because of his anger, he found impossible to deny. "W-where's the paper? I'll sign your stinking form so you can fulfil your s-stinking quota!"

"You're volunteering?"

"Yes – instead of Jack!"

Wordlessly the other fished in a desk, found the relevant document and hurriedly filled in blanks on either side of a foolscap sheet. She then pushed it across to Dando indicating the places where he should write his name. Dando complied. The woman slipped the completed form into a drawer and then called in the two remaining men, instructing them to, "Take this young man over to the T.F. - room 25. That's been vacant since yesterday I believe - and tell your colleagues that the other one won't be needed." She looked at Dando with an inquisitive almost envious expression.

"It's been an interesting experience meeting you," she remarked, "even though you're hopelessly wrong-headed and on the side of the enemy. Pity this is goodbye. I could do with a few more original thinkers around here. You've no idea how dull it can get sometimes..." she hesitated as if about to say something more relevant but then turned and vanished through the door. After a short pause Dando was taken in hand by the orderlies. His fury had rapidly melted away leaving him detached and curiously numb. He understood the implications of what he had just done but was overcome by a sense of total unreality. He watched, as if from afar and at a great distance, his transportation across to Block A and installation in a single room on the tenth floor which appeared to contain all the luxuries of a five-star hotel.

After penetrating once more into the hospital complex Milly had become hopelessly lost. For the past few hours she had been wandering along a maze of corridors staring at hundreds of doors, mostly shut. Behind one of these her dear Lordship must be hidden away but how was she ever going to discover which one? Her eyes were permanently blurred by tears as she blundered heedlessly around corner after corner, long ago having given up trying to figure out her location. All she knew was that she was failing him, failing him, when his need was at its greatest. In the beginning she passed quite a number of people; they gave her curious glances but left her alone. She was wearing a cleaner's overall that was several sizes too big which she had discovered hanging on a peg, and carrying a mop and bucket she had found beneath it. The main thing was that she was the right colour for a cleaner – the staff on the lowest grade were without exception black - and although her presence in the middle of the night was something of an anomaly in that place, the habitués of the hospital had learnt the value of not asking too many questions.

She probably would have gone on for several more hours in this manner if something unexpected and totally bizarre had not occurred. It was when she came to a fairly deserted part of the complex where very few people were about that she was startled to hear the noisy sound of casters behind her and, turning, noticed a bed being wheeled along the corridor by two men. She stood aside to let it pass and was even more surprised to realise that she recognised the occupant. That fashionably cut dark-blond hair and the beautifully manicured hands shackled to the bed frame were unmistakable; it could be no-one but Jack. She waited a moment or two to let the men and their passenger get well ahead of her and then fell in behind. After a somewhat torturous journey the porters pushed their charge into a large service lift. Milly hurried to catch up and, entering the elevator, stood at the side trying to merge into the background. One of the men looked at her with raised eyebrows asking, "Which floor?" She shook her head and did not reply. After waiting a moment he shrugged and pushed the button for the fourth level. When the lift stopped she slipped out ahead of the other occupants and made to walk away but then, while they were busy with their charge, concealed herself down a side turning hoping against hope that they were not intending to come round that particular corner. Fortunately the conveyance trundled past, keeping to the main corridor, and again she set out to follow. On this level there was not a soul to be seen and consequently she had to stay a long way back to avoid raising suspicion. Eventually she discovered that the bed's progress had been halted before a door and the two men were standing beside it talking to a nurse. There was a chinking as something was done to Jack's fetters.

"You won't get that through here," the woman was saying, "that's a deviant's bed. This is a chronic ward – different width. You'll have to transfer him. Did you bring the paperwork? Oh, that's typical. No – don't go back – I think I've got some blank forms. Come on in for a moment."

The three figures disappeared through the doorway. Milly, seizing her chance, darted forward. She saw that the manacles were still on her friend's wrists but had been unlocked from the bed-frame. What luck!

"Jack! Jack!" she hissed urgently, "get up! get up quick!"

The boy turned his head slowly towards her.

"Who's there?" he croaked. He seemed to find talking difficult and his words were slurred.

"It's me, Milly. Get up – before they come back! Quick! Quick! We've got to get away."

She grabbed his arm and tried to pull him off the bed by main force. In fact she did manage to haul him far enough toward the edge so that he lost stability and tumbled awkwardly to the floor. The shock of the fall appeared to shake him out of some sort of psychotic trance so that he climbed unsteadily to his feet and stood there swaying. Milly caught hold of the chain attached to one of his wrists and began to tug him, stumbling, along the corridor towards the corner.

"There's a lift – if we get it goin' before they catch up they won' be able to follow straight away. Quick! Quick!"

Reaching the lift shaft she found that the elevator was still in place and the door was open. She pulled Jack inside and pushed a button at random. The door slid to and they were immediately on the move coming to rest several floors higher up.

"I di'n't want to go this way!" wailed Milly, "I wan' to go down!"

"Press the bottom button then," muttered Jack fretfully. His exasperated tone suggested he was thoroughly disgruntled at being forced to take part in this escape attempt. Milly did as she was bidden and with much clanking the elevator began to descend, passing floor after floor. After what seemed an age it finally came to rest and the door opened.

"Where are we?" cried Milly, "it's awful dark!"

The light from inside the lift faintly illuminated what appeared to be a huge pile of furniture just a few feet away but beyond that she could see nothing.

"There's tables an' chairs an' mattresses an' desks an' dustbins an' brooms an' mops an' I don' know what else. I can't see the top of the heap – I can't see the ceiling - I can't really see nuffink at all."

Jack walked forward; he had suddenly acquired an interest in what was going on. "Find me some sort of stick," he ordered, "a broom handle'll do." Milly set out to search for what he wanted but, as soon as she found it, the lift door began to slide shut and the mechanism to hum.

"Oh cripes – that's torn it" she cried, "they've pressed the button upstairs, they'll be comin' after us. We've gotta scarper but I can't see a bloomin' thing."

"Take my hand," said Jack and, broomstick at the ready, led the way into the dark.

"There's an exit somewhere ahead," he informed her as he conducted her unerringly between invisible mountains of stores. "I can smell it. It opens onto the outside. We must be in the sub-basement or the sub-sub basement I reckon. Tell me if you see a light."

Milly strained her eyes but the two of them were still enveloped in inky blackness by the time Jack's broom-handle made contact with the bottom of a flight of steps. They began to climb and went on climbing for a considerable stretch until they were brought up short by what felt like a wall across their path. Jack investigated.

"It's not a wall, it's a door – a very large door. There's a bar."

At that moment, in the distant, they heard the sound of the lift descending.

"They're comin'!" cried Milly.

Jack lent on the bar and it gave beneath his weight. Very slowly the obstruction moved outwards and they passed through.

"Can you see anything?"

"There's a sort of glow. I think there's more stairs."

"Well – we're in the open air – don't you recognise the smell?"

To both their noses came the unmistakable tang of Ry-Town's smog mixed with the faint stink of the stockyards. As they paused to get their bearings the heavy door swung shut behind them and they heard the click of a lock. Any hope of returning that way was now out of the question.

"Come on," urged Milly, "I know where there's another door – they won't be expecting that. They'll think we've scarpered – they'll think we're trying to get away from the place double quick. But we mus' get back in an' fin' the Lordship."

In the forefront of her mind lay the realisation that in rescuing Jack she had been diverted, perhaps fatally, from her main purpose. *But that's wot 'e would 'ave wanted me to do,* she reminded herself, thinking of the one she adored. *'E would never 'ave left the bloke in the lurch. 'E'd try an' 'elp 'im even if it meant puttin' 'imself in danger.*

As they mounted another flight of steps to ground level Jack was shivering. Like Dando he was wearing nothing but a flimsy hospital gown and now that his temporary spell in charge had come to an end he was rapidly reverting to a state of despair.

"It's all up with him," he jerked out miserably as Milly hurried him along. "He came looking for me and walked into a trap. They'll finish him off – no question."

But to Milly this was great news.

"You've seen 'im? 'E's alive?"

"He was, up to about an hour ago. But for how much longer I wonder."

"Where woz 'e?"

"First floor, Block B. He could be anywhere by now."

"I mus' fin' the side entrance where I woz before."

The light of the not yet risen sun was beginning to fill the sky by the time Milly, leading the way, located the trash site that she had visited twice already.

"There's a door 'ere," she told him, "an' this is Block B I fink. It's just up here... Oh..."

The door which had previously swung open when she pulled it towards her now stayed firmly shut. Jack also tried to effect an entrance. "You're out of luck, I think," he said.

For a few moments Milly was struck dumb with disappointment. Then she rallied.

"We'll 'ave to wait. Someone will come – praps Shona will' open it from inside when she gets 'ere for work. We'll 'ave to 'ide where we c'n keep an eye on wot's goin' on."

Opposite the garbage bays were a few roofed concrete storage bunkers which did not seem to be in use. It was in one of these that Milly had earlier hidden Dando's prosthesis after she had discovered it amongst the trash. She guided Jack inside, reaching up to pull his head down so that he would not hit it on the low ceiling.

"Look what I foun'," she said, putting the replacement foot into his hands. "They'd chucked it away in the rubbish. It made me fink 'e might be... you know... but now you say 'e isn't."

Her eyes filled with tears again at the thought.

Jack held the twisted metal blade for a long time, running his fingers gently along its curious zigzags. He opened his mouth to speak but the words seemed to stick in his throat. Then, swallowing noisily, he articulated.

"It's all over," he announced in fatalistic resignation, "where we're concerned. You – me – Dando. We might as well give up now and admit we've come to the end of the road."

At the Magnolias the morning dawned bright and sunny with a fine early summer's day in prospect. Tallis, Becca and Fynn had reached an impasse when it came to discovering the whereabouts of their missing friends; they had no idea what to do next apart from wait for news. As well as a deep anxiety on behalf of Jack and Dando they could not ignore the fact that Milly had now been gone for over twenty-four hours while neither Damask nor Foxy had returned. After breakfast Becca suggested that, as it was such a nice day, they should take Horry out to Foxy's newly constructed summerhouse which was not far from the back door and which contained a phone extension. The precocious child had got up in an obstreperous mood, angry that both his principle carers were absent.

"Where's Damas' – where's my da?" he groused.

"They'll be back soon," promised Becca, devoutly hoping that this would be the case. Fynn, who seemed to like children, or maybe it was just that he was nearer in age to Horry than to the rather intimidating adults two generations above him, picked up a big shiny red ball that had been abandoned on the summerhouse's veranda.

"Come on," he said, "come and keep goal for me. An' then we c'n go down through the trees an' see if there's a pond at the bottom." He looked to Becca for permission.

"Surely," she encouraged. "y'all go right ahead, honey. But bring him back in time for his luncheon. We'll have it out here. Praps we might have heard something by then. I feel so helpless," she added, turning to Tallis, "if only I knew someone else I could ask. Do you think I ought to try the ministry again?"

Tallis shook his head. A feeling of dread had been growing in him since the previous evening and he did not trust himself to speak.

With them in the little house were the two animals: Meena and Ralph. In a typical cat-like manner Meena appeared detached from the general perturbation. Since her maternal duties, which had never unduly concerned her, had come to an end she had been leading a remarkably laid-back existence. Her kittens, without exception, had gone to live wild in the woods, adopting a feral independent way of life. Ralph, on the other hand had spent the early part of the day deeply moved in spirit on his friends' behalf. He had returned to the mansion in a distressed state on the morning after Dando's disappearance and nobody knew where he had been or what had been happening to him. While Meena sat sphinx-like and inscrutable on top of a tallboy by Becca's shoulder, her paws tucked neatly beneath her, the dog paced restlessly along the drive every five minutes only to return in short order and plump himself down at Tallis' side. Even when immobile his attention was directed eagerly and unwaveringly towards the gate as if he expected the absentees to appear at any moment. Now, though, as the day wore on, both animals seemed unaccountably on edge, staring, wide-eyed, at nothing in particular and twitching nervously as each small sound from outside came to their ears.

Damask opened her eyes onto the sight of iron bars a few feet in front of her through which she could make out two patrol men lounging, half asleep, at a desk. The next thing she became aware of as she tried to move was a shooting pain in her left shoulder. She realised she was lying on an extremely narrow bench and just below her and to one side Foxy was stretched out on the floor. They were occupying some sort of cell, probably in a roadside guardhouse, because the entire area, including the part where the men were sitting, was very limited in size. Trying to ignore her injury, despite the faintness that came and went with the pain, she climbed down and, kneeling, examined her companion. His eyes were open but he was gazing blankly and uncomprehendingly at the ceiling.

"Hey fellow," she whispered giving him a nudge. The Nablan blinked a couple of times and, as if spurred into action, slowly raised his hand to his head. His pupils were dilated and underneath his red hair she could see a large patch of blackened congealed blood. Getting to her feet she went to the bars and tried to attract the attention of the somnolent officers.

"You there!" she called, "my friend needs a doctor."

One of the men stretched and gave vent to a tremendous burp. On the table beside him lay a dirty plate. Yawning he got to his feet and shambled towards her.

"What's that?" he mumbled.

"This man needs a doctor," she repeated. "He's concussed. There's a wound on his head. He may be very ill."

"Can't do anything now," the cop replied. "We're waiting for the paddy-wagon that'll take you to headquarters. When you get there they'll deal with it."

"But how long will that be?"

"Couldn't say – sometime this morning." He gestured towards the window where light was just beginning to show. Running a finger round the inside of his collar he then went to the door, looked out and lit a cigarette. Damask realised that if anything was going to be done about their injuries it would have to be by her. Her first concern was the terrible dragging ache in her shoulder which seemed to be aggravated by the weight of her useless arm. Gingerly she explored the area with her fingers and quickly decided that her collarbone was broken. Fortunately she was wearing belted trousers and so, by removing the belt and buckling it at its greatest extent, she made a sling which she put over her head, sticking her arm through the loop. This helped to relieve the pain to a certain extent. After this she turned her attention to Foxy. Very gently she probed his wound trying to ascertain the state of the bone beneath. To her great relief his bullet-like skull seemed to be whole and intact. His dark blue eyes - somewhat clouded - turned towards her.

"Ow!" he protested, "that hurt gel! What be you a-doin' of?"

"You hit your head," she replied. "Do you remember what happened?"

He frowned as if trying to penetrate a thick fog.

"The Glept an' his fancy man – be they in hospital?" he groped.

"We were on our way to rescue them. There was a crash – you were hurt – now we're being held by the police."

"How 'bout the bike?"

"Write off."

For a moment Foxy looked as if he was about to burst into tears, then, surprisingly, he reached out and took her hand.

"We be alright, gel, 'long as we stick together," he said.

It was not until after midday that the police vehicle arrived, they were loaded into it and set out towards the city.

"Your appointment's at one o'clock so you'll be served lunch at twelve. Would you care to make a choice of courses?"

A tall thin man in the familiar garb of an assistant cook was standing by the bed holding out a printed bill of fare. Dando examined it and blinked. The type of plats on offer would not have disgraced the menu of an exclusive restaurant. Here he was, waiting to be executed, and they were offering him haute-cuisine – it was surreal.

"My appointment?" he enquired, "is that when they're going to do it? - is that when I'm going to cash in my chips?"

The man looked uncomfortable. "I'm just here to take your order, sir" he said.

Dando re-examined the list of dishes.

"You cook these on the premises?" he asked.

"Oh yes – we got an award for the best hospital food in the whole of the Greater Armornia area last year. Everything's fresh – new supplies delivered daily." As he spoke the caterer swelled with pride.

Dando sighed and subsided back against the pillows.

"Some other time," he said and then realised that that did not make a lot of sense under the present circumstances. "If you could just bring me a glass of water?" he substituted.

There was a clock on the wall, its hands pointing to five to ten. Three hours to go. Left alone once more he shut his eyes and actually drifted into a dose. He began to dream and at the start of the dream found himself back on the Northern Drift with Ann in his arms. Then in an abrupt shift of focus he was hanging in the tree on Hungry Island and for a moment endured the tug of huge opposing forces. He dreamt about his restaurant but absurdly it seemed to be situated aboard a ship and the ship was sinking. He dreamt of the temple on Mornington Heights in what must have been a previous era because several processions composed of chanting white-robed votaries were making their way up the hill towards the place of worship. Afar off, where the giants of Rytardenath should have dominated the skyline, he could distinguish only smoke from the cooking fires of a small coastal village situated between two rivers. Penultimately he saw a great stretch of land spread out like a map and a soot-belching machine, hauling trucks, travelling south towards a depression in the earth, the sight of which chilled his blood. Once again he dreamt of Ann and awoke calling her name.

This time an elderly man was staring at him from the foot of the bed dressed in priest's vestments.

“You've reached the final day of your present incarnation,” the cleric informed him, “I've come to prepare you for your transference.”

Dando looked at him warily.

“You need to make your peace with the Maiden,” the man continued. “If you do that rebirth is guaranteed.”

“Make my peace?” This seemed totally irrelevant to his situation. “I don't know what you're on about. This *Maiden* you speak of – as far as I know we've never had a disagreement. In fact I don't recall ever having met the lady.”

His visitor frowned; he had obviously expected a more humble and submissive attitude from an individual about to face the ultimate sanction; instead he had an uneasy feeling that he was being mocked or made fun of in some way.

“You need to confess your sins in order to ease your passage into the next life,” he explained severely, “otherwise you may fall between two stools and end up in purgatory, or else find yourself greatly disadvantaged when you are reborn.”

“M-my sins are no concern of yours.”

Dando gave his answer in a low voice on account of his disquiet and after that refused to speak again. Eventually the priest went away.

At precisely twelve fifty, two porters arrived in his room, one of them pushing a trolley, onto which they indicated that he was to move. Soon he was travelling at a smart pace towards his date with destiny as light fittings flicked past overhead counting down to zero hour. It was not that he was afraid, he decided, although his heart was beating a little faster than usual and he was suffering from a certain shortness of breath; he simply felt sad that his existence was now going to be terminated when he had just realised how much remained to be done. If this was to be curtains as far as he was concerned he would not be able to help Tallis the Wanderer on his quest, he would not be there to care for his young son or even know if Jack were safe. As for discovering the whereabouts of some mysterious object, if that was what he had been meant to do, he would fail by default. Set against this was his belief that to die now would mean the end of struggle, separation and sorrow. He did not know what to make of stories of multiple incarnations but merely hoped that in death he might find some kind of peace, and, as it is termed, closure.

The room where they eventually arrived presented a severely clinical appearance. In the centre stood a narrow upholstered table, fixed on one side to a thick metal column that, slightly further up, supported a large machine projecting like a canopy overhead. Dando was ordered off the trolley and onto this table where he was secured firmly in place by straps round his wrists, waist and one remaining ankle. He lay there staring at the apparatus above him while various mysterious preparations took place nearby. There was a murmur of conversation between the personnel present but nobody spoke to him directly. As a nurse swabbed his arm he tried to catch her eye, feeling he needed a modicum of human contact before the lights went out for good, but, without exception, all the surrounding people avoided the embarrassment of looking at him directly. As the songwriter says: *the executioner's face is always well hidden.* A young doctor arrived at his side, a hypodermic syringe in one hand.

"This is going to sting a little," he said to a space about a foot or two above Dando's body. "You may initially experience a dry mouth."

The boy tensed, preparing himself for the fatal jab, but it never materialised. On a stand at the doctor's elbow a kidney dish was placed, containing various small instruments. The medic, holding the syringe at the ready, looked sideways, a puzzled expression on his face. From the dish rose a metallic rattling, an incongruous sound in that quiet theatre. Glances were exchanged between his subordinates. The next moment small confetti-like flakes of plaster began drifting down from the ceiling and a low reverberation commenced several stories below, growing rapidly louder as if some huge juggernaut were approaching, causing the floor to tremble. The shaking intensified and became so violent that those in the room grabbed hold of something near at hand in order to prevent themselves from falling. Then suddenly, with a deafening report, a crack appeared in one of the walls, stretching from floor to ceiling. This resulted in the doctor's hand holding the hypodermic to convulse with shock so that its deadly contents spurted harmlessly into the air. From this point on Dando was unable to make sense of what was happening to his surroundings. All he was aware of in that moment of extreme danger was the locket containing Annie's tress on the chain around his neck which for the moment felt as if it was throttling him. The world seemed to go completely mad and all he knew was that he was being thrown around by some tremendous force, with no idea as to whether he was on his head or his heel. He felt weightless, as if he were falling from a great height and at the same time the thongs binding him to the table cut into his wrists and ankle. Time remained in abeyance and only reasserted itself when movement ceased, gravity was reinstated and the overwhelming noise gradually faded to be replaced by a sort of titanic creaking and groaning. He tried to move, he tried to discover why he appeared to be suspended face downwards over an abyss, but the bonds held him fast. He could not even be sure, while he hung there, if it had grown completely dark or if, instead, he had lost the use of his eyes.

I see fissures, cracks,
A waste of fallen towers.
I hear heart-rending lamentation.

Chapter eight

"You'd better get away from here – you'd better get out in the open."

As day dawned, Milly crouched in the concrete bunker at the trash site, Jack beside her, her eyes focussed on the small side door to the hospital which she hoped against hope someone would come to unfasten so that she could resume her search for Dando. But long minutes turned into hours and as time wasted away not a single soul appeared. Eventually she realised that her companion, in his inadequate hospital gown, was shaking with cold, or maybe from reaction to what had been done to him.

"'Ang on," she said, "there's a 'ole load of clothes over there wot's been thrown out. I don' know why cos most of 'em are quite decent."

"Probably their owners are now sprouting wings and a halo," replied Jack cynically, presumably referring to the outdated idea of heaven and hell, his teeth chattering.

"I'll find you sompthin'"

She came back with her arms full of various garments one of which, a scarf, she used to tie Dando's prosthesis to her waist while her companion began carelessly to dress himself in those she handed over, demonstrating none of the careful fastidiousness that he would habitually have shown. After having indulged in this small spurt of activity Jack huddled down once more on a low wall just inside the bunker, only occasionally cocking his head to listen to what was happening outside as something appeared to attract his attention. What Milly, observing him, found most disturbing was that he no longer seemed concerned that his facial disfigurement - the shameful thing that, normally, he had been careful to hide – was on display. Remembering having seen a box of spectacles among the rubbish, she went and scavenged a pair of sun-glasses on his behalf. It was late in the morning when, apparently apropos of nothing, he offered her the afor-mentioned advice.

"You'd better get away from here – out in the open, if you know what's good for you."

Milly looked at him in surprise.

"Wot d'you mean?"

"Haven't you noticed? Haven't you seen them? I've heard them – passing overhead. There's something up - something weird."

"No," said Milly, "I don' know wot you're on about."

Jack sighed. "Pyr give me patience," he muttered, "birds, girl, birds! They've been flying above us all morning – flying out to sea. If I were you I'd avoid any tall structures. Get out in the open and stay there 'till it's all over."

"You fink... like last time?" answered Milly, "you fink...? Wot do you fink?"

"I think you should get away from the hospital, but don't follow the birds – give the water a miss for the moment and go inland to a bit of open country."

Milly hesitated, wondering whether to take him seriously.

"But wot about the Lordship?" she asked at last.

"Beyond your help – beyond anyone's help I shouldn't wonder."

Again Milly dithered, then, suddenly convinced by his certainty, made up her mind.

"Orlright," she agreed, "it don't look as if we've got any chance of getting' in anyhow. I'll do what you say but we mus'n't go too far an' if sompthin' does happen we mus' come straight back as soon as it's over. P'raps if the ground moves like las' time the door'll come open of its own accord an' we'll be able to get inside. Are you ready? – let's go."

At this Jack shook his head and turned away with a dismissive gesture only to discover that now she had determined upon action, the black girl was prepared to put her foot down.

"I'm not goin' wivout you – you've gotta come too."

There was a silent battle of wills which Milly won. Slowly, reluctantly, Jack rose and stood there holding out his hand like a helpless child. Milly took his hand.

Almost as soon as she found a piece of wasteland to the north of the hospital on which they could take refuge Milly became aware, through the soles of her feet, of a rapidly increasing vibration and, in no time at all, she and Jack had been thrown to their knees and then full-length on the ground. Milly clung to her companion, her face buried against his chest, and it was not until the shaking, surging and overpowering cacophony had ceased that she dared raise her head. Then she took one peep, cried, “Strike a light!!” and hid her eyes once more. Jack waited patiently until she had gathered the courage for a second look before asking, “Well?”

“It's not there,” she whispered in awe, and then, “we shouldn't 'ave left.”

“What do you mean?”

“We shouldn't 'ave come. It's not there – the 'orspital – like it woz – there's only bits left – bits and pieces. Oh dear... oh dear... Where is 'e? Where c'n 'e be?”

Jack disentangled himself from her arms and stood up with the help of the broom handle.

“Haven't you got it into your thick head yet?” he complained petulantly, “ it's not a question of where is he – the sooner you realise that the better. He just *isn't* – he *isn't* anymore.”

“No,” replied Milly, “you're wrong. I'm goin' to find 'im.”

She walked backwards away from Jack, angry at his negativity, intending to leave him behind, but then, touched by his forlorn expression and obvious helplessness, returned to lead him.

When what was obviously an earthquake struck, Damask and Foxy were being transported, under arrest, to Rytardenath. They had passed the stockyards and had just topped a rise from which one of the best views over the city was to be obtained as, from that high point on, the road ran unvaryingly downhill until the bridge across the East River was reached. It had been a car rather than a van that had come to collect them, which meant that, sitting in the back, staring down the muzzle of a gun levelled by the officer in the front passenger seat, they had a good view ahead as the driver slammed on his brakes exclaiming “Holy shit...?!”

Although it had ceased to move forward the vehicle in which they sat was still in motion as it stood there, bouncing and bucketing, rocking and rolling as if over a grossly uneven surface. But that was not what had caused the man to blaspheme. No, it was the almost unbelievable spectacle that met their eyes as they surmounted the hill's brow which prompted him to give vent to a grossly inadequate expletive. The fact was that at that very moment the famous skyline which tourists came many miles to see had begun to fragment. The great monoliths, the buildings of two hundred stories or more which gave accommodation and employment to thousands of city dwellers, were melting away in slow-motion that bright summer morning like icebergs beneath a tropic sun and it was all happening solely to the accompaniment of a faint rumble because they were far too distant for the full roar of disintegration to reach them. The occupants of the car sat transfixed long after the world had ceased its crazy highland fling. If they had heard about this cataclysm from a third party they would have been unable to give it credence, but now the proof was there in front of their eyes; without the shadow of a doubt Ry-Town the Great was no more. All that remained, all that could be seen against a stormy background through gradually subsiding clouds of dust were some massive white mounds gleaming in the last of the sunshine like the waste heaps from some Brobdingnagian quarry.

The officer at the front was no longer pointing his gun, had in fact put it back in its holster.

"What on earth was that?" he said in a small empty voice like an infant whose treat has been cruelly confiscated. In contrast, his companion suddenly started banging his head repeatedly on the steering wheel moaning hoarsely, "Oh my God! Oh my God..."

Damask's hand crept into Foxy's and they exchanged an incredulous glance before she turned to the rear window to see what was happening in that direction. There she was presented with a sight that galvanised her into action.

"Look out behind!" she warned urgently, "there's something coming!"

The driver's eyes flicked to his mirror and took in momentarily the dark tsunami sweeping down on them from the rear.

"It's the stock!" he cried, "they've got loose!" He gunned the motor and the car leapt forward. From then on it was a race to see if they could outpace the oncoming tide of stampeding animals that threatened at any moment to engulf them. Going flat out they flew over ruptures and crevasses in the road, almost taking wing, until...

"The bridge is down!" gasped the man on the right.

"Can't stop," shouted the driver and they bombed on towards the river where it was quite clear that the central section of the crossing that would have taken them into Rytardenath had collapsed and the carriageway leading to it had fallen, creating a descending ramp onto mud.

"Where's the water?" cried policeman number two. At this point an onlooker would normally have expected to be met by a view of an extensive blue expanse, wide and deep enough for medium-sized ships to navigate, but now the river bed was exposed and the stream reduced to a mere trickle.

"Hold onto your hats!" yelled the driver.

Damask and Foxy clung to whatever presented itself – the Armornians had not yet got round to inventing seat-belts – as the automobile headed downwards, leapt off the end of the ramp and landed with a tremendous splash in a morass of water, gravel and sludge. The wheels spun, then got a grip and they were carried a respectable distance away from the broken road before finally inextricably bogging down. However, with this ultimate spurt, they had progressed far enough forward to be out of danger. The cattle that had been pursuing them came heaving and tumbling onto the river bed in their turn where they wallowed, thrashed and kicked, gradually piling up into a living dying hill of flesh.

One of the policemen had been injured: his head had made contact with the windshield as they landed on the mud. The second man was solicitously attending to his wound and neither were paying any attention to the other occupants of the car, their erstwhile prisoners. Foxy struggled with the door beside him, eventually forcing it open and he and Damask climbed out. The ooze beneath their feet was firm enough to stand on and they walked a few yards away before stopping to take stock of their surroundings.

"We ought to go back and see what's happened to Dando and Jack," said Damask with marked reluctance, glancing up at the riverbank. Foxy was equally unenthusiastic.

"Your shoulder need treatment, gel," he replied, "an' my head's whooly burstin'. We be wunnerful sickly at the moment an' no use to anyone. I reckon if they be still alive after all this they'll come out o' it wi'out our help. They'll make for base same as we oughta do."

"You mean the Magnolias? That's right over the other side of the city. How do you suppose we get there? You saw what happened."

"Mayhap we could go roun'. If we walk this way," pointing in the opposite direction to the river's flow, "we c'n cross over to the narth an' then come back down."

"OK," answered Damask. An eerie mist smelling of smoke was beginning to roll up river, so that both middle and far-distant objects became obscured. The fog was occasionally lit from within by bright flashes. They both looked towards the car but there was no sign of anyone emerging. Turning away they set off together along the muddy alluvial bed and, as they splashed through the mire, they seemed to need the comfort of linked hands. It was about half an hour later, while they were still forging upstream, that they came round a bend in the river's course and discovered what had happened to the water. A chasm lay across their path, a gaping rift, and palely on its farther side a great flood could be seen falling vertically into the bowels of the earth.

"Oh well," said Damask after they had stood for a while staring in amazement at this newly-created niagara, "we've got no choice now. We'll have to go towards the centre of town and hope our luck holds. P'raps if the devil looks after his own we'll find our way back."

For the first few daylight hours the sun shone down benignly on the Magnolias seeming to make a nonsense of the feelings of apprehension shared between several members of the household, but then, just after midday, a shadow fell over Mornington Heights, interposing itself between the source of light and the planet that it nourished. Becca, having brought out the makings of a picnic from the house, looked up at the sky and, fearing a deluge, went to call Fynn and Horry in from their play, while Tallis, sitting just inside the summerhouse door, gazed uneasily heavenwards. Meena also came to the door and stood looking out, her tail lashing from side to side, while Ralph crouched whining. It grew darker still until for a moment the light seemed to fail completely during which Becca and the two boys almost fell into the room. Then, a breathless pause, a rumble, a heave, a flash of lightning and they saw by its gleam the walls of the main house in the act of tumbling outwards. Becca screamed, Horry bawled and the summerhouse took it into its head to become a toboggan. It slid down the slope at the side of the mansion, removing itself from danger, until it ended, still in one piece, amongst the trees at the bottom; the fact that it had held together on its journey a tribute to Foxy's workmanship. (Later it was discovered that while, in that short-lived instant, the whole of Central Rytardenath had collapsed, the little cabins in the area known as the Underlands or Floodwood had also managed to survive. They had ridden out the convulsion like boats at anchor in a muddy harbour and had come through unscathed despite a few of the surrounding mangroves being swallowed by the swamp and the sea encroaching on one side.)

The wooden building had come to rest at a slightly tilted angle but otherwise appeared undamaged. Becca stood in the doorway hanging onto the frame for support as if this was the only way she could remain upright.

"My house!" she cried, staring up the slope, "what's happened to it? It's all fallen apart!"

Fynn bent and looked under her arm towards a gap in the trees through which other properties could normally be seen.

"Like yours isn't the only one," he said.

"Why did they tell us we had nothing to fear?" moaned Becca, "I thought they said they had it under control!"

"At least we're still alive," contributed Tallis.

"But what about the others?" and in that moment all thoughts turned towards the missing members of their fraternity whose destiny now seemed doubly uncertain. Soon, however, more pressing concerns intruded. Horry was still grizzling and Becca set herself to offer comfort while Fynn demonstrated a surprising bravery by quitting the shelter and walking up the hill to examine the remains of the mansion. Left to his own devices Tallis was struck by a strange and disturbing thought: according to the tale that his mother had spun him all those years ago, the powerful talisman, the object of his quest, had trailed havoc in its wake as it travelled north in the hands of Gammadion the robber. This earthquake therefore – could it be a sign that the Key was near by?

It did not take long for Becca to pull herself together sufficiently to notice the food scattered about the room. She retrieved as much as she could and shouted for Fynn to return.

"I'm not letting this go to waste. Heaven knows where our next meal will be coming from."

Late in the afternoon, when Horry had fallen asleep, Becca and Tallis visited the house and at some risk to themselves managed to rescue a few essential items, one of which was a small safe in which the takings from the restaurant were stored. They spoke little and only about practicalities. Their hearts were heavy and their minds preoccupied with dwelling on the unknown fate of their absent friends. The storm that had threatened the little satellite town before the onset of the cataclysm had passed over with only one short spiteful hail shower to mark its going. Fynn wandered out to the front gate and then, turning northwards, set off up the hill. Around six o'clock he returned, pale of face and strangely subdued. It was fairly obvious that he had been crying.

"What did you see?" they asked him.

"I looked over towards the city," he replied bleakly. "Like there's a lake of fog lying quite low down and the buildings should be sticking up out of it but they're not. The Heights are a total mess – everything's collapsed. The people that are still alive seem to have gone completely gaga, they're walking around talking to themselves. I saw several dead ones..." He pressed his lips together and the tears sprung anew to his eyes. After that he went and sat on a stool in the interior of the summerhouse, head bowed forward, arms wrapped around his body. “I don't know what else to do,” he muttered when Becca laid a concerned hand on his shoulder.

As the day wore on towards evening the showgirl, with Tallis' help, did her best to make the little pavilion habitable. No one admitted that they were waiting... waiting for... they dared not put it into words. All they knew was that as the clock ticked on towards the day's ending their faith in a positive outcome gradually died. At sunset Tallis went for a last look down the drive, then came back and shut the door. He caught Becca's eye and fractionally shook his head. Horry was made comfortable on the one and only put-u-up and they finished the picnic leftovers for supper before preparing to lie down themselves. Becca spread some blankets and pillows on the floor that she had salvaged from the house and, as there would be no privacy, they decided to sleep in their clothes. She left a solitary lamp burning, a sort of desperate last ditch beacon of hope, but this was not conducive to slumber and it was as they lay wakefully listening to each other's breathing that there came a single bang on the door. Fynn leapt to his feet before the others had time to move and tore it open. Two unrecognisable figures, one supporting the other, stumbled forward and collapsed into their midst.

What's the matter? Am I dead? Is this a tomb? No, I can still feel, I'm still here. Well, where am I then and where is everybody? Was it a quake? If so it must have been the mother and father of all quakes because the whole place has gone completely haywire...

Thus Dando - now that gravity had re-established itself and a certain degree of sanity had returned to the world - tried to figure out the import of the extraordinary series of events that, with only the slightest heralding, had just occurred. Some catastrophic upheaval had taken place during which the surgical structure he was attached to had tumbled several stories and come to rest upside down jammed between two pieces of wreckage. It appeared that the inner framework of the tower block into which he had been taken had collapsed while the outer walls were still largely intact. But what had happened to the people in whose midst he had been lying only moments before, the people who had been about to put him to death? By some miracle he was still alive and unscathed whilst they... Slowly it dawned on him that his survival was not miraculous in any way but was as a direct result of his placement within the robust metal construction which had maintained its integrity in the midst of chaos and had protected him from debris during his fall. It had withstood the plummeting wreckage of floors, partitions and equipment, providing a secure shelter even as everything else was rent asunder. But now, unless he could escape its confines, the piece of equipment that had proved his salvation would yet spell his doom; he must regain his liberty if he was to go on living. He twisted and tugged, wrenched and struggled, a hard-fought campaign, until his already damaged wrists were bloodied once more. The battle lasted so long he had almost given up hope of release when all of a sudden something gave way and his left arm was free. After that it took only a matter of minutes before the other straps were undone, allowing him to lower himself onto the business part of the topsy turvy machine. His eyes had become adapted to the darkness by now and because of this he thought he could detect a faint gleam of light coming from over to his left. He slid sideways in order to peer downwards but then shrank back into his refuge. The bed on which he had been lying in the operating theatre now projected over his head providing a roof of sorts and this proved its worth, as, after an ominous rumble, the debris above shifted slightly and huge chunks of concrete came hurtling down, crashing onto the metal umbrella and bursting apart. He waited timorously until all seemed to have settled before he dared have another look.

On this second attempt he was given a longer breathing space in which to interpret his immediate environment. There was certainly some light to see by and he could make out the shadowy shape of massive blocks and girders above and below, presently motionless but tumbled precariously one on top of another so that they looked as if they might shift at any moment; the scene beneath was almost a mirror image of that overhead, his haven having become trapped between two substantial beams while the rubble that could have buried him had ended up much further down. Were there any other survivors, he wondered, had anyone else come through? He tried a few half-hearted *'helps'* with little hope of a response. Nevertheless, listening intently, he thought for a moment he heard someone shouting or screaming, but the voice came from so far off, almost on the threshold of hearing, that he felt he might have imagined it. Apart from this faint sign of life the only other sound was the trickling of water. The light was penetrating from somewhere lower down, giving hope that there might be a route to the outside world at that level. What would Damask do - what would his intrepid twin sister have attempted in a similar situation? Yet again, as if the recollection had been induced, he was struck by a memory from the past. He brought to mind the day when the two of them, idiot children that they had been, had undertaken a risky climbing odyssey over the outer walls of Castle Dan. Against all the odds they had returned in one piece from that expedition. It seemed doubtful that anyone would come and seek him out if he remained here and waited; it looked as if he was being asked to embark on a similar hazardous scramble. Well, nothing ventured, nothing gained. Perhaps, given a tremendous amount of luck, he might manage to lower himself through the interstices in the ruins without causing a further collapse and win to the exterior. It was worth a try. As he reached out from his shelter and found some initial hand holds he thought of Jack. The last time he had seen his friend he had been within the base of one of the other tower blocks, both of which, he was convinced, had been severely damaged. That the young man could also have survived the havoc and still be in the land of the living seemed remote in the extreme.

Sometime later Dando wriggled past some smashed light-fittings, then over a projecting ledge onto a flat piece of concrete and finally out into the open air before lying panting. After a few moments he rolled onto his back and found his vision limited as the sky above him and all of the surrounding area was hidden behind a blanket of fog, thick enough to knit with.

"Made it!" he grunted but was immediately reminded that he had used these very same words when duelling with the Mother up at Judd's Hill less than two years before. On that occasion, although he did not know it at the time, the matter had been far from resolved. Perhaps it was not such a good idea to jump the gun and count chickens before he was absolutely certain they had hatched. Anyway all he wanted to do now was rest and recover and forget some of the grisly sights he had seen during his descent to safety.

After a while he began to hear a cacophony in the distance coming from some unidentifiable source: a humming, clattering sound which increased in volume from moment to moment. He got painfully to his knees and in so doing noticed an oddly-shaped shard of wood lying nearby, broken off from goodness knows where. He picked it up, assessing its strength, measuring its length. Here was a stroke of luck – if he was not very much mistaken this would serve as a walking aid, a very rough approximation of a crutch. No sooner had this notion struck him than he acted on it and found that he could just about manage. He limped in the direction of the growing noise and as he picked his way forward over a shambles of broken building blocks a human figure, standing at a slightly higher elevation, emerged from the fog. Dando stopped abruptly because, in this shape that began as a vague outline and solidified into three dimensions, he identified a recent adversary of his: it was the masterful woman who had first questioned him about his connection to the NQPP and then sent him for transference. She currently cut a rather sorry figure compared to the last time he had seen her: her clothes were ripped and her exposed flesh streaked with dried blood. In her hand she held a rectangular black box with a projecting metal rod at one corner and as he watched she lifted it to her lips and began to speak. Then, before he could retreat, she looked up and he knew immediately that he had been recognised. She lowered the device, whatever it was, and addressed him in an accusatory tone.

"It's you! So I'm not the only one from the Facility to survive."

"No," said Dando, "I thought maybe *I* was the only one."

The woman put up her hand to her furrowed brow and turned away as if having an internal dispute with herself. Then she began shaking her head like someone who has been told an extraordinary truth that they find almost impossible to accept.

"You!" she cried again as if completely outraged, "It's you! This is all because of you! I should have realised. You've been saved by the evil one at the expense of..." and she waved her hand helplessly in the direction of the invisible ruined city as if robbed of words.

By this time the approaching noise had become deafening and suddenly overhead something large and menacing loomed out of the murk. Dando cowered, but then realised that what he was seeing, up close for the first time, was one of the delicate dragonfly-like creatures that had been swooping amongst the skyscrapers when they first arrived in Ry-Town.

"What d'you mean!" he shouted, feeling he had to understand her, as a hatch cover slid back and a jointed steel ladder came dropping down from the hovering machine. The woman collapsed the aerial on her communication device and stuffed the apparatus into a bag that was slung across her body. She put her foot on the bottom rung of the ladder, then turned towards him.

"I'm leaving, but don't think this is the end!" she yelled above the sound of the engines. "You'll pay – we'll make you pay! Before we've finished you'll regret that the transfer didn't take place - you'll wish you were safely off into your next life!"

A moment or two elapsed as she swung into the air, ascending as the ladder was retracted, then she and the helicopter were gone and he heard its roar fading into the distance. He was left feeling thoroughly unnerved by this encounter and quickly set out to find a way down off the hospital ruins, trusting that intense activity would dull the memory of what had just occurred.

-----------.

By the time Jack and Milly reached the edge of the scene of devastation that had once been the Transfer Facility and had begun dodging around fragments of wrecked buildings strewn haphazardly across the terrain everything more than a few feet away had vanished.

"I can't see where I'm goin'," she informed Jack, "It's orl foggy. Some people are prob'ly still aroun' but 'ow c'n we tell?"

"Stand still," commanded the blind boy, his confidence reviving now that his navigational skills were needed once more, "stand still and listen."

Holding their breath they both strained their ears trying to pick out any faint sounds within the silence that had descended over the land now that the holocaust had come and gone.

"I can't hear nuffink," murmured Milly, her voice sounding unnaturally loud in the stillness.

"Shhhhhhh," cautioned Jack, and then after a minute or two, "there's someone shouting a long way off. There's water not far away. I can hear an engine, up in the air. And there's something moving in that direction." He pointed forward with his arm slightly raised.

"Come on then," urged Milly, beginning to clamber upwards over the treacherous detritus in the direction that he indicated. Jack followed, once more using the broom handle to feel his way, while she scrambled up ahead of him until, with a sharp intake of breath, she ceased to move.

"What's wrong?" he called.

For a moment there was no answer, then came the reply, "It's 'im – like on the flags!"

"The flags?"

"Like on the flags of the en... kyoo... en... kyoo..."

"NQPP?"

"Yers! Lordship! Lordship!"

Jack groaned.

"You're calling him back from the dead, woman. It's a ghost you're seeing – a ghost conjured from your own imagination."

"No, it's 'im – it's really 'im! Lordship!"

"Let me touch him – then I'll believe you."

But Milly was right, for as the pale silhouette that she could see within the fog, reminiscent of the NQPP's logo, came closer it transformed into a creature of flesh and blood. Dando emerged from the miasma on single leg and substitute crutch, proving he was incontrovertibly in the land of the living. He was grinning with embarrassment in response to the girl's rapturous cry.

"Milly – Jack - where have you sprung from? How on earth did you get here?"

His greeting was both awkward and gauche and as he passed by on his way down the slope he made the fundamental mistake of patting the girl on the head. Then his expression sobered as he swung himself towards Jack. On reaching the boy he took him by the shoulders, drawing him into a close embrace. Jack, his normal swashbuckling manner totally in abeyance, brushed the other's cheek with his lips but let his hands hang by his sides, allowing himself to be hugged without responding.

"Birdy," he muttered brokenly and then to himself, "alright, I believe."

Dando drew back and examined his friend critically.

"Jack – it's great you and Milly are ok, despite everything."

"Are you kidding!" replied Jack, but then added, "What does it matter anyway, now that the world's come to an end."

"Look wot I've got," interrupted Milly slightly sulkily, swinging a cloth bundle down from her shoulders and beginning to unwrap it. "I knew you wosn't dead. 'Ere's some clothes – warmer 'n that thing wot you've got on – an' see, I foun' that ol' coat of yours among the res' of the stuff, the one wot you're so fond of. Besides that, 'ere's that funny foot you wear – they'd put it out wiv the trash."

Dando exclaimed in delight.

"Milly – you're brilliant! I never thought I'd see those again!"

Milly nodded, but having already experienced a condescending pat, felt she was being praised for filling the role of some sort of faithful hound.

Quickly Dando dressed himself and strapped on his prosthesis, before hurling the shard of wood high into the fog.

"Come on," he said, "from what someone said I think that this place may become rather unhealthy in the near future - we need to get away. We'd better try and find our way back to Becca's."

"Go towards the sea," advised Jack, "I think now it'll be safe. If things stay quiet you'll stand a better chance in that direction."

"Aren't you coming?"

"What's the point?"

Dando clicked his tongue. "For god's sake Jack," he admonished, "don't be so stupid. I'm sure it's not as bad as you make out. I don't reckon they could have done what you told me in just a few hours. It would take a lot longer."

"Leave it," admonished Jack, "I don't want to talk about it."

Dando put his arm across Jack's shoulders, part comfortingly and part in order to guide him, while Milly fell in behind. They skirted the ex-hospital, making their way south, passing one or two other lost souls whom the havoc had spared, before coming across a wide wave-troubled deep stretching away into the fog.

"That's funny," said Dando puzzled, "where's the road? There's supposed to be a road running along the coast before you get to the sea."

Jack walked forward a few paces, bent and dipped his finger in the water before putting it to his mouth.

"Salt," he said, "you'd better find yourselves a boat – I don't reckon you'll get any further by land."

"Heavens to Betsey! It's Damask and Foxy!"

The occupants of the little garden retreat had jumped back at the invasion of their refuge, giving the intruders a wide berth as they landed in a tangled heap on the floor,. The new arrivals were plastered in some sort of clay or loam which had dried to a pale ghostly coating all over their bodies so that they appeared scarcely human. Plucking up courage Becca stepped cautiously forward and, stooping, examined them more closely. Under the muddy carapace she became aware of leathers - jackets and trousers. On the head of the first anonymous figure she saw a fuzz of light-brown hair, while the second - the one who was lying on his stomach with face turned to one side - possessed a freckled cheek and chin. She knew them! - it was their two intrepid bikers returned alive! Exclaiming in delight she bent to raise the girl only to have the other intervene to stop her.

"Watch out," croaked Foxy in a voice more husky than he had ever had occasion to use before, "her shoulder be broke. You mun't try an' lift her by her arm." He scrambled to interpose himself between the two of them.

Taking heed of his warning, Becca carefully placed a coverlet over Damask who appeared to be unconscious and made no attempt to move her.

"I'll get some water," she said and immediately wondered where it was to come from.

"There be a spring," croaked Foxy, displaying greater knowledge of the grounds than the mistress of the house. "It be in the woods close to an old oak tree. We need a bucket or something."

He made an attempt to stand but then staggered sideways clutching his head and crumpled to the floor.

"No honey," said Becca, "you stay here. I think I'll be able to find it."

Fortunately the spring was unpolluted and still bubbling up amongst the trees although its position had shifted slightly. With the help of its limpid waters which she brought back in a kettle the two casualties were washed and their wounds dressed, after which Damask was provided with a more substantial sling. It had not taken her long to come round from her swoon and they then had great difficulty in persuading her to rest. She was ready to leap into action, not recognising that this was obviously well beyond her capabilities at that moment. Foxy allowed his head to be bandaged and accepted some painkillers that Becca always carried in her purse.

"Did you find out what's happened to them – Jack and Dando I mean?"

Fynn was so anxious to hear the answer to this question that he jumped in long before the showgirl considered her patients were in a fit state to talk.

"Poppet," she protested, "be considerate. They don't want to be bothered just yet. They're plum tuckered out."

"No," chipped in Damask, addressing Fynn and refusing any longer to lie down, "We didn't – we came a cropper and got arrested before we even reached the hospital. It's taken us all day to get back here after the earthquake helped us escape. We went north up the East River which has now disappeared down a hole in the ground and then tried to cross over. Every road we came to was blocked, there were fires all over the place and when at last we got to the river on the other side the bridges had all disappeared. But something had happened to the water level there as well. We managed to make our way to the west bank and then we waded up a creek which led in this direction. That's where we got so muddy. The others haven't returned then?"

Fynn shook his head as if he did not trust himself to speak and relapsed into misery.

The night was dry and mild and, because their numbers had increased by two, Tallis decided to sleep outside. Fynn soon joined him. The smoky fog that was blanketing the city had not yet extended as far as the Heights and looking up from where he lay the knight could see a few faint stars; this was a sight that had been missing from the skies above Rytardenath for many a long year due to both air and light pollution. The quietness that now brooded over the highways and byways was also something unknown within the experience of most of its citizens. Tallis fell uneasily asleep and stayed that way until daylight returned. Then he opened his eyes to find someone stooping over him gazing down - it was Dando.

"You're alive my boy!" he gasped, raising himself on his elbows and staring unbelievingly upwards.

"So they tell me," smiled his ex-squire - the devoted Ralph was already gambolling round whimpering with delight.

"The others? Are they...?"

Dando gestured towards the drive where Jack and Milly were just turning in through the gate. There was a flurry of movement as Fynn leapt up from where he had been lying and hurtled towards the new arrivals. "Capitaine, mon capitaine!" he cried and flung himself into Jack's arms clutching him fiercely. The blind boy merely staggered back a pace or two and did not respond. Fynn immediately insisted on taking over his care from Milly and solicitously shepherded him towards the comfort of the summerhouse at the same time pouring out his heart in a torrent of words. When they had all gathered within doors there was much rejoicing as it was realised that their numbers were now complete; even Meena deigned to rub round a few ankles.

"Who'd have thought we'd all end up safe and sound," exclaimed Becca looking them over one by one, "not like..." she waved her hand in the general direction of the city. "It sure is a marvel we're all here together."

The three newcomers were badgered for the tale of their adventures. Jack remained silent, apparently finding a detailed account too tedious to embark on, but Dando and Milly did their best to oblige. On making their way south from the hospital ruins, they explained, they had happened upon open water much sooner than expected but had been lucky enough to find a drifting dingy with oars aboard. They had put to sea and overnight had made their way past the southern extent of the destroyed metropolis until, with the dawn, they reached the Pleasure Beach area.

"The whole coastline's changed," explained Dando, "we came past drowned buildings. There were lots of things floating – animals – people..." he shuddered. "It was dangerous in the fog especially once it got dark. Jack was good at working out where we were. We had to navigate by ear until the sun rose."

"But how did you escape from the hospital?" asked Damask, "how did you find Milly and Jack?"

Dando grimaced. “It's a long story – it's complicated – I'll tell you later.” He glanced towards the blind boy as if needing his permission to continue.

“Come on, y'all,” said Becca, “he'll explain when he's ready - give him some breathing space. How 'bout we go up to the house again? We might yet find some food if we shift stuff and get into the kitchen.” She already seemed reconciled to the loss of her property.

Again Tallis was the only person prepared to accompany her. Damask and Foxy were still laid low by their injuries while Milly could barely stay awake. Jack, installed in the summerhouse, refused to move and Fynn would not leave him. As for Dando he had melted away; no-one saw him go but a little later they realised he was missing.

“I guess he's gone to look at his restaurant,” surmised Becca glancing in the direction of the Heights. “If he's hoping it's still in one piece he's in for a shock, poor lamb. It'll be the same for anyone who's still in the land of the living - trying to get over what's happened and put things back together again.”

She knitted her brows at the thought of the hundreds, nay thousands, of surviving Rytonians whose lives had been so violently disrupted and dismantled in just the passing of one brief moment.

The burden is yours.
No use complaining my son,
However long the road.

Chapter nine

"***So-ho, my lady! You've catapulted a thousand thousand fleshed ones into the hereafter and flattened the warren they were so proud of, but the one you targeted has escaped yet again and is getting nearer to achieving the thing you most fear. What have you to say for yourself?"*** (A sound as of thunder echoing amongst the peaks of alien volcanic ranges.)

"***Ha ha! You've become a laughing stock to our people, wife. A powerless figure of fun. Thankyou for providing so much entertainment."***

(Rumbling – grumbling. Then a roar like the sound of prodigious precipices clashing together at the instant of a planet's dissolution.)

"***Mm – very scary, I don't think! Speak woman! Tell us what you plan, what your next damp squib is going to be."***

(More rumbling, then...) ***"Mock on husband, mock on. At least I'm not sitting on my arse doing nothing, like some I could mention. Although it may have escaped your attention, there's another who desires what I desire. He's already proved useful to me and has much to lose. I will speak with him, the ancient calcified one, as I did once before; I shall reveal myself and then we shall see what we shall see. Being of this world he is more likely to know how to deal with the wretched good-for-nothing than we who come from afar."***

"***You think so? I know the man; he's but a shadow of his former self – a hollow mockery from which all the juices have been sucked. By stealing the Periapt from my keepers, which I understand has since been stolen from him, he imagined he'd achieved immortality on his own terms. Immortality? - I'm breaking up! And this is the one who will do your dirty work? In your dreams, wife, in your dreams."***

"Wait and see. Contain your impatience, husband, and observe; you may be surprised."

"Surprised? - I doubt it. Right from the start I suspected that both you and the thief were hand in glove, but, by now, I reckon your lap dog is on the verge of extinction."

Dando stood in the upper square examining the shattered wreck that was all that remained of his pride and joy and as he did so a wet nose pushed into his hand: Ralph had followed him from the Magnolias. In actual fact he did not need the comfort that the dog was offering. He had been under no illusion as to what he was going to find when he reached the site of the Dark Continent; he had seen too much despoliation in the last twenty-four hours to believe that his own premises, already damaged when he was taken into custody, would be spared. No, he had climbed the hill because something had been preying on his mind ever since he, Jack and Milly had disembarked at what was, before that morning's drastic transformation, Ry-Town's most fashionable resort. As he set foot on shore he had glanced upwards and on the skyline seen the ancient temple that had brooded unchanged over Mornington Heights for so many generations. He realised that the shrine, which for centuries had withstood the ravages of time, had finally succumbed during the major earthquake's few dramatic minutes and was now substantially damaged. Judging from the silhouette that still stood out against the sky the roof appeared to have slid sideways while quite a number of columns had fallen. Despite this, the outline of the building was little changed, giving the impression that the sanctuary was less of a write-off than many of the more modern structures farther down the hill.

Now, as he stood before the remains of the restaurant, a few people close by were wandering aimlessly while others, on the far side of the square, rooted with fierce determination amongst the rubble. There was a faint whiff of corruption in the air.

I'll see if there's anything worth saving when I come back down, he thought to himself deciding to postpone an investigation into what remained of his property; for some reason it seemed a forgone conclusion that his first priority should be a visit to the temple. He felt almost as if he were answering a call as he turned away from the built up area and, passing the point where recent development came to an end, set out to climb through untouched scrub land.

When he reached the top of the hill he lingered for a while absorbing the atmosphere, more alive up here to the missing urban roar, a sound which had been so all-pervasive in the past that after a period those living within the environs of the city ceased to notice it. In contrast he was now intensely aware of the wind's faint sighing and the twittering of a few local sparrows.

"Poor Ry-Town," he murmured, thinking not, at that moment, of the town's hapless inhabitants but of the almost abstract idea of a great metropolis destroyed. Eventually he approached the pantheon and, stooping, surveyed what he could of the interior. Why had he been drawn here? Who had summoned him? It was the absence of noise that enabled him to catch the sound of a feeble voice coming from within and to make out the words, "Are you there?"

"Yes, yes, I'm outside," he replied, "who is it?"

"Over here," called the voice.

"Stay Ralph," he ordered and taking his life in his hands – the second time in twenty four hours that he had braved a weakened and impaired building – he crept beneath the tilted roof and began to find a route through spaces between dislodged ashlars. Despite the damage, he felt the same calm atmosphere within that he had experienced previously, a sensation of being outside time. This was short-lived however for suddenly he was arrested by a sight that caused him to catch his breath in dismay. The woman, the one he thought of as the spirit of the place, lay on the floor a few yards distant, but only the top half of her body was visible; her lower torso and legs were hidden – pinned - beneath one of the temple's fallen columns. He could not begin to imagine what injuries she had sustained nor what she must be suffering, for she was conscious, that was plain. Kneeling briefly beside her to assess the situation he declared, "I'll get help!" and was about to rush back down to the square when she caught his hand in a surprisingly strong grip.

"No, don't go," she answered, "I need to prepare myself. I need to get ready to join the dance – human contact can be important at such times."

"But I must find people to move this off you," indicating the column, "strong men with a winch. Then we can take you for treatment." *But where?* he asked himself, remembering the state of the collapsed hospital.

"No, by no means - one place is as good as another for what is coming. I'll stay where I am."

She gave a small gasp and shut her eyes as a spasm shook her body. Dando, at a complete loss but anxious to please, could think of nothing more appropriate than to sit on the floor and continue to hold her hand. All his instincts were urging him to act; it was very hard to comply with her wishes and remain quiescent. After a while she looked towards him and said in a weakened voice, "You don't have to remain silent – we can talk."

He thought back to the last time they had met. Then she had claimed to be in possession of esoteric knowledge that could well have some bearing on his future. In the present circumstances he was reluctant to raise selfish concerns but eventually asked:-

"Have you got something to tell me?"

"No, nothing. But you can put a question if you wish."

He paused, then enquired hesitantly, "What's your name?"

"I have no name anymore. I am known as the Ministrant – the Helper – the Tool. I have waited for you to come."

"But how long have you been here – I mean in the church during the time before the earthquake?"

She smiled, a smile which quickly changed to a grimace of pain.

"For a while," she said falteringly, then, turning her eyes upwards added, "a long while."

"Does it hurt you to talk?"

"That does not signify."

"Who *are* you?"

"My kinsfolk..." - she suddenly began to speak surprisingly fluently as if giving voice to a long-prepared speech - "...came from over the sea, like you. Our home was a city to the west of the great river where we lived for thousands of years. Because most of our history was peaceful and prosperous we were given leisure for other things besides the mere maintaining of life; the scholars amongst us had time to accumulate a vast store of knowledge. We were famous throughout the lands for our erudition and people came from far and wide to sit at the feet of the sages and philosophers in the assembly. Our town was a place of pilgrimage, as illustrious as the Lap-of-the-Mother."

"Belturbet!" cried Dando, seeing the light. The Ministrant nodded then groaned slightly as if the movement pained her.

"But eventually the climate changed. For years there were endless rains and the river o'er-topped its banks, reclaiming the plains that it had covered at various periods in its history. Because the crops were frequently inundated food was in short supply and the people were starving. Then, as if preordained by some all-seeing deity, a nomadic tribe arrived outside our gates. They had a king at their head but he was old and frail and not long for this world. On their journey they had consulted the oracle in the mountains and had been instructed to change their direction of march in order to come and tell us their strange story. They were wandering the earth, they said, in search of a stolen object which had once been under the sway of the Lord-of-Heaven. He had appointed them its long-term guardians but they had failed in their trust. Their intention now was to recover this Thing-of-Power and return it to its rightful place so that their land could flourish once more."

"I know about that," said Dando guiltily, "I was told that they were my people. They were the ones who did not give up and stay behind but continued the quest." He sounded as if he felt solely responsible for the defection of those of his forbears who had decided to remain in Deep Hallow.

"Yes, I think you were told correctly. Anyway they asked us for advice – for aid. Their concerns were brought before the assembly which sat in extraordinary session while the visitors were temporarily excluded, and after a period set aside for contemplation each member spoke his or her mind. The consensus was that the story concerning the Talisman, a talisman in the shape of a key that had the ability to rule the ages, could be taken as essentially true. The fact that it had been stolen was also believed by most. Because of this theft it was understood that the present age would be extended beyond its normal span and, as such, was thought to be to the benefit of our nation. But there was one member, the one named Manfred, whose conclusions were at variance with the rest."

"The man who designed the cushions!" interrupted Dando in wonder.

"Yes – that's right. He was young then, a maverick, and was not popular with the other councillors, but I think he was probably the most brilliant of those present. It was accepted, he said, that, on this planet, the Key had assumed the role of initiator of each new age. Because of this he gave it as his opinion that when the time for the next turning came and went without result the world that was in thrall to this Thing-of-Power would show signs of disruption and climate upheaval, the present floods being possibly a foreshadowing. Nevertheless, if the Key were found, he who regained it should think very seriously before instigating another turning. The Object came from outside, he went on, and was wholly alien to the earth; no-one knew its true purpose. Each time it was turned the planet fell further under its sway. In his opinion, if left to continue this endless repetitive sequence it would ultimately bring about humanity's downfall. It should be dispatched to the place for which it was originally intended, far away from here, where it might prove a blessing rather than a curse, and only then would our species start to live life to the full."

"After he had had his say there was an angry buzz of disagreement from the others. Eventually the chairman spoke out on behalf of the majority. *That the Key comes from outside is not disputed,* he stated, *but in our opinion it has been a remarkable boon to humanity. The present age, the age of thought, has enabled us to acquire extensive knowledge and if it continues, who knows what we may achieve. There is certainly an argument for preventing a further turning but not in order to banish the Power-Bringer from the earth – that is out of the question. As life on the Levels has become untenable I suggest that our people join with the wanderers and assist them in their search. But then, if we can come upon this Key, the most responsible measure would be to take it into our possession and lock it away for all time.* Thus the council decided and Manfred was overruled. And so our citizens set out to accompany the so called Guardians to the northern continent, but with their own agenda, which was at variance with that of their supposed allies who thought that the two nations shared a common purpose. Belturbet was deserted, and the first company to arrive on these shores built this monument to act as a beacon for those that followed; my people became know as the Inshami on this side of the Tethys, and occasionally, to those with whom they quarrelled, as the Bunyips. Many are the tales told of the seekers, their travels and conflicts in the succeeding years, but suffice it to say that eventually the Key was found..."

"It was found!" exclaimed Dando in astonishment.

"Yes... yes... and then lost again; but for a while we had it in our hands and that's why, although we possessed it only briefly, several of us have lived beyond our normal span. I..." the woman broke off abruptly, apparently struggling for breath, and again Dando went to rise in order to bring help and again was prevented. The presiding genius of the temple took a great gulp of air and regained her voice.

"I'm ready to leave. Soon I'll go *Over-the-Brook* if I have understood aright how to free myself from the flesh. Look to my people – they will tell you what I have omitted."

"But why...?" began Dando and immediately broke off.

"Ask – ask – there isn't much time."

"Why, (his face paled and twisted with anxiety) did the one who sent me to be transferred say the quake was all my fault?"

"That wasn't strictly true. Nevertheless you were the reason it took place."

"You mean it happened in order to save me? Surely not!"

"No – it was intended to kill you but the plan misfired. If you wish to go forward you must accept that fact but it's a heavy burden to bear for one so young."

"So you really think it was all because of me?"

"Yes."

"Shit!"

He turned his head away, shocked at this revelation. Eventually he looked back and apologised saying, "But why, in that case, have I been singled out? - Why do I matter?"

"Why you - why me - why anyone? Only the one who was there at the beginning could tell you that," and she looked towards the circular symbol at the end of the church, half dark, half light, on what remained of the wall. Wearily she shut her eyes as her breathing became more erratic; Dando thought he could hear a faint rattle at the base of her throat. After a while she made a concerted effort to speak once more. In a whisper she warned:

"You won't make old bones – the sickness that will be your undoing is already at work."

Dando's face darkened. "I don't understand - what do you mean?" he said.

"Your time is limited, why do you linger here?"

"I'm waiting for my master."

"The task is yours not his. Also, while you remain, the ruler of the earth's surface knows where to find you. She may whisper untruths in your ear so that you will continue to doubt and not be able to take courage and inspiration from the presence of your loved one."

"My loved one - Do you mean Annie? But she's dead – don't try and tell me she isn't."

"You misunderstand – as I told you before she has merely shed the body."

The young man pondered this sombrely for a moment then said stubbornly, "Nevertheless I'll wait."

After this the Ministrant lay still and quiet for so long that Dando began to feel uneasy and looked sharply into the face of the injured woman. He discovered that she was bending on him a tranquil, otherworldly regard. Gradually a strange but familiar sound intruded; he was hearing her voice again but it seemed to be coming from within his own head.

"***Can you hear me?***" she said. He realised that the question was not directed at him. ***"Are you near?"*** A long pause followed. ***"Oh my dear, it's you. Please help me across, the time is already ripe. But first perhaps you have a message for the Seeker?"***

Her eyes switched towards Dando and she spoke once more with the aid of the flesh.

"She says she will always keep you in her heart. She says she is waiting."

As she broke off her whole body trembled and her hand holding Dando's convulsed, went limp and almost slipped from his grasp.

"Don't die, don't die!" he cried.

The woman's eyelids fluttered - her mouth gaped. "This is not... death..." she gasped. For a few moments she stretched out her free hand towards something above her that only she could see, until, with one last shudder, it fell back to her side. At the same time she ceased to breath.

Dando sat unmoving by the body for so long that when he eventually released his hold he was aware that her skin had grown noticeably colder. He stood up and tried to pull her out from under the column but failed miserably. He needed help for such a task but was unlikely to find it among the local citizenry: no-one was going to be bothered with this particular corpse when so many lay trapped, some not yet dead. If anybody was to come to his aid it would have to be the ones presently residing in the Magnolias' grounds. He composed her body to the best of his ability then set out to walk the distance to Becca's door quite forgetting his resolution to search the restaurant.

It was as he descended the hill with Ralph at his heels that he began to feel ill. Two and a half days had passed since he had had any real sleep and he was totally shattered. Also, he was beginning to suffer from a pounding headache as well as a painful sore throat and it looked as though his metaphorical prediction that the hospital might prove unhealthy for him could turn out to be all too literally true. Mentally he was greatly perturbed by what had occurred. He had never watched anyone he cared about die before, if in fact that is what he had witnessed. It had not been an easy thing to experience. Then there were the words that had come, through the mediation of the Ministrant, from some unknown source: *I will always keep you in my heart – I am waiting*. Remembering the message now, he found it profoundly disturbing, especially at a time when he was trying so hard to resign himself to a solitary life.

What the woman had told him created new questions without supplying answers. If the Key had been found then where was it? Was it really alien to the earth and if so what was its true purpose? How was he supposed to act if it ever fell into his hands? Should he turn it? destroy it? Take it *outside,* whatever that might mean? And these people from Belturbet that were supposed to help him – did they still exist after all this time? His head spun and he staggered slightly under the weight of his confusion.

Becca was at the gate of the Magnolias when he returned.

“Honey,” she said, “some soldiers have been here looking for you. We told them we didn't know where you were. Don't stand in the road – come inside where you can't be seen.”

With eight people and two animals crammed within the summerhouse, both to greet him and satisfy their curiosity, the little pavilion felt as if it was about to explode. Damask, beginning to regain some of her normal vivacity despite the pain from her strapped shoulder, stared curiously at the new arrival.

“What have you been up to bruv? Evidently you're on some kind of wanted list.”

She regarded her sibling with increased respect.

“I'll have to go, otherwise you'll all be in trouble,” said Dando, ready to beat a hasty retreat despite the fact that his legs were about to give way.

“No my dear,” urged Becca, taking his arm, “I think you're safe for the moment - we put them off the scent. We've decided we're all going to leave tomorrow. There's no food to speak of here an' not enough room for everybody, besides the fact that there's unburied bodies – lots of them – in the buildings up on the hill. Could get really nasty. I'm gonna take y'all home with me. It's a fair way but when we get there I guess we c'n make a fresh start. Meanwhile we saved you the last of the leftovers. I got into the kitchen and rescued a tub of cobbler I bought a couple a days ago and Foxy managed to find some peaches and strawberries in the garden. I've also got the restaurant money for you in my safe.”

“But there's a woman - she's up in the temple on the hill, pinned beneath a column, although, before I left her, she lost consciousness and stopped breathing.”

“Then you can't do anything more for her baby. What you need to do is get some rest – but first I'll give you your money and something to eat.”

A little later after he had toyed wearily with the food and eventually pushed the plate aside Dando asked, “You mean you're inviting us to your home town? Where is it?”

“It's a backwoods place called Rockwell Springs – a good way north of here.”

“North,” he repeated looking at Tallis.

“You go to sleep now, sweet pea. Tomorrow we'll head down to the station and see about tickets.”

The next morning Dando awoke with a streaming cold; he sniffed, sneezed and hacked in a most unheroic manner. Even when the immediate infection cleared up as it did after a few days he was left with a persistent cough that he could not shake off. Sometimes when attacked by a paroxysm that practically raked his lungs from top to bottom he would bring up a gobbet of phlegm laced with blood. His reaction to this disturbing phenomenon was the same as with anything concerning his compromised body: he just gave his usual fatalistic shrug and tried his best to make sure no-one else discovered what was going on. After all, he was well aware that, in the present extraordinary circumstances, he was unlikely to find himself in line for any pharmaceutical advice. Meanwhile Becca's quest to buy train tickets had met with a marked lack of success. The line was blocked by landslides, she was informed; several trains were trapped. If she wanted to travel by rail she would have to get herself to Hayseed Junction on the other side of the Tuscadora Range although the road that led there was also in a bad way. She might find things still functioning beyond the highlands but the phone lines were down so they could not tell for certain.

“It's a mighty long stretch,” the showgirl told her charges, “and I'm pretty sure the buses won't be running. As for going by car...” If the carriageway had crumbled motorised vehicles would be worse than useless.

After a pause Fynn piped up. He seemed to have been waiting for Jack to speak but when the blind boy remained sunk in gloom he said shyly, “There's bikes.”

The others looked at him in surprise.

“Bikes?”

“The Club. We all had bikes whether we rode them or not. Like they were kept in a wooden storeroom in the middle of a car park. I don't think they'll have been damaged.”

“But honey,” cried Becca appalled, “I can't ride a bike!”

“It's not difficult – after all even Jack could do it,” he gazed anxiously at his mentor. “There were some three-wheelers, some tandems and some with seats for passengers. If we come to places where the road's broken up we can lift them over."

The upshot of this was that Fynn and Milly made several trips to the site of the Push-Bike Club and brought back enough machines to accommodate all nine of them. For Milly, despite her time on the back of Mabelene's bone-shaker, this was quite a challenge, and during the numerous return journeys she was not particularly impressed when Fynn demonstrated how easy bike-riding could be by throwing in a few wheelies for good measure. Throughout the next day she and Becca had a stab at mastering a couple of single-seater models, while it was agreed that Damask and Horry would occupy a side-car attached to a bike peddled by the recovering Foxy. Tallis also sat in one of the side-cars while Dando did his best to provide the power. Finally, Jack took a seat behind Fynn on a tandem, although persuading the unhappy Vadrosnian to play his part was nigh on impossible at first. Before they left, Dando climbed the hill once more and managed to find some dried foodstuffs hidden in the partially destroyed restaurant's storeroom which had been overlooked by looters. These they took along with them – even such basics were better than nothing. The animals were not abandoned. Meena clung tenaciously to Milly's shoulder as they set out while Ralph took up a position by Dando's rear wheel and tirelessly kept pace even on the downward slopes although at times he was going flat out. Warily watching for the military as they said goodbye to the suburb known as Mornington Heights they took to the hills and began their odyssey, pushing the bikes on the upward slopes and free-wheeling down the descents. It was hard and hot work in the almost unbroken spell of sunshine that had set in, especially when they came to places where the road surface was damaged or had been covered in bank slippage, but at the approach of night they blessed the fact that the air temperature was comparatively mild for the time of year as they slept out under the stars.

The stars! Once more Dando had the glory of the night sky above him, unmasked by pollution, while by day the stunning blue dome dotted with delicate fleecy clouds gave his heart a lift. Just to be surrounded by the natural world once more - the trees, the scent of plants, the wind in his hair, the small creatures that often strayed onto the road ahead of them - was balm to his wounded spirit and he was profoundly grateful. He looked at Tallis to see if he felt the same way but the knight was uncommunicative, closed in on himself, and Dando could not tell what he was thinking. Because he wondered if the man's strength was equal to the journey they had set out on he treated his master with careful consideration and refused his help when pushing the bike up the steeper gradients. Milly had similar concerns. She had recently tumbled to the fact that Dando was not at all well. She did not like the sound of his cough and wished she could put him to bed for several days in order to dose him with a mixture of hot lemon and balsam, an infallible remedy according to the girls at the Spread Eagle. Watching him tenderly from a distance she saw that, even when he imagined he was unobserved, he would still place a hand politely in front of his mouth when afflicted. This, she thought, was a sure a sign of a true gentleman and enhanced his standing to an even greater extent in her eyes.

On the longer ascents the company would sometimes call a halt halfway to the top and sit for a while soaking up the sunshine and talking of the future.

"Is there anywhere we can get jobs in this place we're going to?" asked Damask of Becca.

"You won't need jobs," she replied, "I'll look after you."

"But we don't want you to keep us," said Dando, "that wouldn't be right."

"Well, you can help on the farm if you like ("There be a farm?" exclaimed Foxy, considerably interested). All that money you gave me from the restaurant - I've still got it. We should be able to manage."

"But that was meant for you," Dando protested, "not to spend on us. I've got money."

Another time, mindful of the story the Ministrant had told him, Dando asked Becca, "Where did your people come from? Have they always lived in the place that we're going to?"

"Oh no, honey, my granpaw's paw came down from the north originally and met up with other folks coming from the east and west – it's what they called the great migrations. Most of the people of Greater Armornia came that way, except the darkies – they came from the south I guess."

"And was there anyone here before you arrived?"

"Haven't you heard of the Madderhay Wars? Yes, we had to fight for our land."

"Against whom?"

"Against the aboriginal people, against other immigrants like ourselves and chiefly against the Bunyips - they were the ones that caused us the most trouble."

"I've heard that name already. Did people think they were spirits? - Old Ones?"

"They were called that because at night they were supposed to glow in the dark like ghosts – or maybe it was their weapons that glowed – they had powerful weapons that didn't just kill; even if you escaped being blown-up they could make you sick. Also they seemed to be able to vanish at will. But we were many and they were few because a lot of them had already left the country before we arrived. The story went that their wise men had gone east looking for some precious metal buried in the earth that would help them build ships that could sail to other worlds. One day the rest just stopped fighting and followed after them. It's said that you can still come across a few living in old lava tunnels beneath an extinct volcano in the land of Caffray - did you know there's a war going on there at present? - but I think that's just a story spread by some deserter who went awol from the fighting, spent the night in one of the cave mouths and whose imagination was working overtime. Anyway none of them have been heard of around here for a long long spell but if you want proof of their existence you can always pay a visit to Damwey, the city on the plains. That was their capital in the short while that they ruled the area, although now it's partially deserted. Twice a year the wranglers drive their herds that way. Damwey's short for Dead-Man-Walking."

"But what's this war about that you say's happening right now?"

"About? Wars don't have to be about anything honey, although of course an excuse is always found. Humans need wars – it takes the pressure off for a while. Without wars things start to fall apart."

"But what sort of pressure do you mean?"

"The pressure of being human."

Foxy - picking up on something she had mentioned earlier - asked, "Herds? Do you mean the stock we saw in Ry-Town?"

"Yes – the cattle ranches are on the prairies, northwest of the grain belt. From Damwey the drive used to follow a trail east and then, after the animals arrived at Harrisburg, they were brought down by train to the coast. Goodness knows if that'll ever start up again."

When they finally arrived at the station called Hayseed Junction half the residents of Rytardenath seemed to have got there ahead of them. The place was heaving with displaced persons apparently hoping to find a refuge further on up the line. It was a fight to get close enough to the track for a glimpse of the train that was standing beside the platform. When they managed it their hearts sank, for they could see that the carriages were already filled to capacity. People were hanging half in and half out of windows or clinging to the outside while others were up on the roof. Tussles were taking place between those who had already secured a seat and those who were trying to supplant them. Becca turned to a man in uniform who was looking on helplessly, having apparently given up on any attempt to bring order out of chaos.

"Where's this train going?" she asked.

"All stations north through the grain belt, then along the branch line to towns around the Great Lake. A lot of people have holiday homes up there. Change at Harrisburg if you want the Damwey terminus."

"Will it be stopping at Rockwell Springs?"

"Surely. But you haven't got a hope in hell of making it this trip. You'll have to wait."

"When's the next train?"

"There's no next passenger train although there'll be a few hauling essential freight – this is the only one carrying passengers at the moment. If you want to make the trip north you'll have to wait until it returns. Day after tomorrow if you're lucky. We can't take those," pointing towards the bikes. Becca clicked her tongue in exasperation.

"What a dern nuisance," she said, turning to the others, "we're going to be stranded here for ages and with all these folks wanting a ride there's no guarantee we'll even get on next time."

Horry tugged at Dando's sleeve.

"Wanna see the chooka-train, daddy," he pleaded, "take me to see the chooka-train."

Dando directed a wry grin at the others, gave his habitual shrug and then, obeying orders, began pushing his way through the crowds with his son in tow.

"Come on gel," said Foxy to Damask, "let's go an' look at the engine. Her'll already hev steam up. General McLoy – that's her name I hear. They say she's a flyer!" He was almost as eager as the little boy.

In the end they all went to inspect the hissing, fire-eating monster at the head of the string of carriages, which was ready, at the throw of a lever, to get a grip on the rails beneath its huge wheels and, unleashing its might, jerk the whole cavalcade into motion. When they arrived they found the fireman up in the cab shovelling coal while the one they took to be the driver was standing by his machine with his back towards them, oil can in hand. Having finished the task he was engaged upon he turned and as he did so one and all were struck by his singular appearance. He was a small man, below average height, but with a strong athletic body. His face was classically proportioned and although his hair appeared dark and on the long side his skin was without a blemish. His most striking feature was his pair of wide, violet-coloured eyes which had a sort of luminosity about them. Surveying the audience that confronted him his face wore a completely impassive expression so they were doubly surprised when he suddenly removed his little pork-pie hat and almost swept the ground with it in a deep bow.

"Miss Peepo!" he said as he straightened up, gazing directly at Becca. The showgirl patted her hair as if afraid she was not looking her best and pulled down her jacket.

"Peepo," she said, "yes, I guess that's what I used to to call myself. You remember me?"

"Madam," said the engine driver, an expression of enormous respect on his face, "I was your greatest fan."

Becca's own face broke into a startled smile.

"Well, that sure is nice of you dear, but it's a long time since I was actually in the studios. Things have changed quite considerable recently I hear."

"Not for the better," insisted her admirer. "Your movies – ones like *God's Own Country* and *Butterflies in the Rain* – they'll never be equalled."

"You remember those? Well I never - that's swell. What's your name honey?"

The small man gave another bow.

"Stigmore Fletcher at your service. Before I changed my career," indicating the engine, "I was also involved in your line of work – in a minor way."

"Really? Strange our paths never crossed."

In no time at all Becca and the engine driver had plunged into an exchange of show business reminiscences during which they became oblivious to all else around them. The others spent some time admiring the great steam-powered locomotive and then drifted aimlessly away, to end up sitting at a distant on a raised grassy bank where they could view the departure of the train. It was there that Becca found them after an increasingly frantic search.

"Heavens to Betsy!" she cried, "Where have you been! I've been looking all over for you. Stigmore's agreed to take us on his engine, but you must come right away!"

"On the engine!" cried Foxy, sounding as if all his dreams had come true at once.

"Yes, on the back part where they keep the coal. There's room he said as long as we don't mind getting dirty."

Oh, the astonishment on the faces of the hopeful travellers standing nearby when they saw certain of their number as well as two animals being helped up onto the engine's footplate by the driver of the train, and oh, the pride in the breasts of those fortunate ones as they found themselves in this privileged position. Becca, along with Horry, was actually invited into the cab by Stigmore who seemed disappointed that he had not got a red carpet to spread beneath her feet; everyone else had to make do with the open tender partly filled with coal and just a piece of tarpaulin to protect them from the elements. The bikes were left behind.

"All aboard!" shouted the guard and blew his whistle. The locomotive cleared its throat, gave a shrill scream and vented the first puff of steam in a rapidly increasing series. With much clanking of couplings and metallic groaning the great machine heaved the whole circus forward and the journey began. It did not take long for the companions to wish themselves inside one of the passenger-carrying carriages, however crowded. Although the passing landscape looked stunning in the early summer sunshine the temperature was decidedly cooler on this side of the Tuscadora range and now, with the train's onward rush, they had to withstand a gale of more than seventy miles an hour so that they were soon chilled to the bone. The warning about dirt also proved to be all too apt: sometimes it seemed that more smoke than steam was issuing from the funnel. The group in the tender huddled together, trying to retain as much warmth as possible while at the same time attempting to keep the soot out of their eyes, ears and nostrils. Dando felt indignant on Tallis' behalf: surely the driver should have recognised that an elderly man such as his master, obviously not in the best of health, ought to have been offered the same protection that Becca and Horry were enjoying. Fynn was worrying about how this discomfort might be affecting Jack's state of mind while at the same time Milly, lending a helping hand to a scared Meena who was still gripping her shoulder, wondered if Dando could withstand the harsh conditions without coming to harm. Despite the exhilaration experienced when travelling at speed with nothing between themselves and the open air it was a relief to these three concerned ones when the train pulled into a station and they were given a temporary respite from the buffeting.

Stigmore seemed to be under instruction to halt the train at every settlement they came to, however small and humble, and at each stop it was a forgone conclusion that some passengers would get off, making room for others to get on. Becca watched these boarders with interest, her curiosity piqued.

"Tell me, honey," she asked of the driver who was gazing back along the row of carriages with possessive pride, "why are those guys carrying picks and shovels and those round things on their backs? Do they work for the railroad? Do they mend the track?"

"No," he replied, "nothing to do with us. They're prospectors. They're travelling to the railhead near Damwey from where they'll find some transport to take them into the mountains. I guess they're hoping to find Xoserite. If they do they'll be rich men."

"Cozer...? Cozer...? What's that dear?"

"Xoserite? It's the new wonder material – used in everything from bridges to armaments to drugs. They'll need a whole heap if they're ever going to rebuild Ry-Town. Since the supply of raw materials from across the Tethys dried up, they've been exploring the prehistoric mines on the other side of the Craiks. It's Xoserite they're looking for although no seams have been struck in this region so far; up to now the only known source has been in the far east. They discovered its potential a mere two years ago."

"My word," said Becca, still a trifle mystified.

The train ploughed on and very soon an unexpectedly bucolic side to Armornia was revealed as they began passing through a pleasant undulating landscape not unlike the remembered woods and fields of Deep Hallow. The temperature started to rise.

"D'you think where Becca comes from is like this?" Dando mused as they stopped at yet another halt beside the inevitable grain elevator. "From what she said I imagined something really primitive – kinda rough and ready. But this is nice."

"Don't make premature judgements," Jack suddenly remarked. Those of the company who had been at the Magnolias during the earthquake and had only been in contact with the Vadrosnian over the last few days looked at him in surprise. Since his return from the hospital he had spoken so rarely that they had started to wonder if he had lost the use of his tongue as well as his eyes.

Eventually, when the train drew to a halt for the umpteenth time and it was already late in the afternoon, they saw Becca alighting from the cab with Stigmore's help.

"Come on folks," she cried gazing up at them, "we're here. This is Rockwell Springs – home sweet home."

They climbed down in their turn, joining quite an exodus; evidently a number of people had reason to stop off at this small town, for town it was, bigger than most of the places they had passed through up to now.

"It's been an honour," replied Stigmore when Becca thanked him profusely for coming to their aid. "If I can be of assistance to you or your friends in the future I will be more than happy to oblige. When they get the other trains back into service the General and I will be hauling freight on this line. I'll be passing through here at least twice a week. Just come down to the toll-gate and make yourself known."

"I won't forget," said Becca, "and if you ever have time to call, I live in Camelback Avenue, the one with the poplar trees. Number sixty seven."

As they left the station among the rest of the travellers, Becca leading the way, no-one noticed a man of millitary aspect also alighting, apparently on furlough from the eastern frontier and dressed in camouflage fatigues. He fell in at the rear and followed them into town. It was an odd fact that the random splashes of colour on his battledress appeared to change shape as he moved. If they had been alerted to his presence they might also have remarked his lifeless stone-coloured skin and the deep pits of his eyes opening onto a strange vacancy. As it was, diverted by the novelty of the locations they were passing through and listening to Becca's reminiscences concerning her girlhood in this town, they overlooked him completely.

The showgirl conducted them across the centre of the pleasant little burg, past small stores that despite their diminutive size appeared to stock everything under the sun, past a barber's, a bank, a tiny picture-house, the police station and jail, a car-repair shop and funeral parlour. Eventually they reached the suburbs on the other side of town and began following a straight road that surmounted two steep rises. Halfway along Becca stopped in front of a white-painted clap-board house that stood out from its neighbours on account of the extra care that had been lavished on its exterior.

"Here we are," she said proudly, "I had this built for my Mama when I started to make good money, but sadly she wasn't with us long enough to appreciate it; she passed in the year of the hurricane."

Preceding them up the drive she fished in her bag for a set of keys, but before she could insert one into the lock, the door was flung open and a deafening racket issued from within, made up of the shouts of children, the clatter of pots and pans and the crying of babies. A man in his mid-thirties stood just inside the entrance running his eyes over the new arrivals.

"Hi Maw," he drawled, "we've been expecting you."

"Curtis!" gasped Becca and then fell silent, robbed of words.

"Yup," continued the young man, "long time no see. Dempsey's here too with his family – we didn't think you'd mind. We had to leave the city – lost everything in the 'quake."

"Clarke?" mouthed Becca, "is he here?" She grabbed hold of Milly who was standing beside her as if to avoid collapsing completely. A shadow passed over the other's face.

"Paw was in the Jade Tower when the quake happened. We don't think he survived. From the reports no-one else did."

"Oh my word!" exclaimed Becca.

By this time every window in the two-story house had become populated with faces while behind Curtis a further group of residents, both young and old, stared out curiously.

"Who's in there with you?" breathed Becca, barely able to articulate.

"Well there's Tracy's and my kids and Dempsey's and Jo-Beth's too and also some of their poor little friends who've lost their folks and didn't have anywhere to go. Then there's Tracy's people and Paw's brothers and sisters – all the aunts and uncles – and of course there's Grandma Morris and some of *her* friends. It's a bit of a tight squeeze – the kids are sleeping on the floor – along with the animals. But we c'n find room for one more – just *one!*" He stared rather coldly at the group behind Becca. Jack, who was at the tail end of the procession of new arrivals, had already turned and was walking back in the direction of the station.

"Come on," he muttered to no-one in particular, "we're not wanted here."

Fynn and Tallis, taking the hint, followed him out of the gate to be pursued in turn by Damask, Foxy, Dando, Ralph and Milly while Horry, in contrast, darted past Becca towards the house and peered through the doorway, trying to catch a glimpse of the children he could hear but not see. She caught hold of his hand and pulled him away, muttering as she did so, "Sorry boys, got things to do – return later..."

"We should have stayed on the train," grumbled Jack as they made their way along the road, "this place is hopeless."

"No Honey," answered Becca hurrying to catch up, "there's somewhere else – my mama's *old* place – not far away. But it may be a bit neglected. We'll have to cross the line – and then go down the hill."

They trekked back towards the high street and on towards the railroad. Once over the track they became aware of something they had not noticed before, that the ground fell away quite steeply to the east and that a crazy patchwork of jerry-built cabins as well as a few trailers were crowded together below them, some in poor repair, others apparently abandoned.

"This is the old town," said Becca, "Bishops Hollow it's called. The folks from here that did well moved across the tracks and built themselves new places on the higher ground - as did I (proudly). But quite a few hung on, and of course the coloured folks weren't allowed to settle in Rockwell, they only came over to work. I reckon it'll get a new lease of life now that all these homeless people are looking for somewhere to stay."

Scrambling down a steep track the travellers eventually reached the shacks. The buildings were arranged in no particular order and Becca guided them through various meandering alleyways until they arrived in front of a low rambling structure built of tarred wood, whose extent they could not at first determine because it seemed to have been greatly altered and added to over the years until the original cabin was buried deep within later additions.

"Here we are," said Becca, "this is where I grew up – the Quackenbush place – that was my mama's maiden name. My paw didn't have a home of his own when they got married so they moved in here. Over the years we became a large family but there's no-one left now. I was the youngest by a long chalk and some of my older brothers and sisters passed before they were fully grown. We couldn't afford a doctor you see, we had to make do with what the local obeah-woman handed out." She produced another key from her purse and unlocked the door. This time there were no unexpected occupants to greet them, in fact the cabin seemed to have been deserted for some time. Inside it was very dark and there was more than a hint of dampness in the air. The furnishings, from what they could see of them, were sparse and the few carpets threadbare. Becca conducted them on a quick tour, pointing out bedrooms, a low-ceilinged living room cum kitchen, empty store-rooms and the outhouse where the privy was situated. There was certainly plenty of space, in fact enough to get lost in.

"You jest make yourself at home sweethearts," she invited, "and I'll go into town before the shops shut and buy some supplies. Will you come with me honey?" to Milly.

Once she and the black girl had left, the others stood around, awkwardly waiting for someone to articulate. Eventually Damask spoke her mind.

"What a dump!" she exclaimed. "Everything's filthy and the beds aren't fit to sleep in. How long are we going to have to put up with this do you think?" She seemed prepared to write the whole place off. But meanwhile Tallis had gone exploring on his own account while Dando began to investigate the kitchen facilities. Eventually the knight came back with news.

"That end is on a higher level than this," he explained, "you have to go up some steps. I think it's a bit warmer and dryer."

Acting on this information Fynn took Jack on a search for suitable quarters, although the disconsolate young man refused to share a room - he insisted on having one to himself.

"Where be this farm her were on about?" remarked Foxy, and then to Damask "Come on gel, let's find somewhere to shack up."

"Me too," chipped in Horry, "I wanna room."

"OK," agreed Damask reluctantly, "I s'pose we'd better make the best of it."

Meanwhile Dando had run to earth some cloths and brushes, lit lamps, discovered a water pump and started to get the kitchen into a fit state for food preparation. Milly returned alone carrying two heavy bags.

"She's gorn back to the uver 'ouse," she informed them, "cos she wonts to be with 'er family. It's donkey's years since she's seen 'er sons she tol' me an' 'er grandkids never o' course. I don' fink she'll 'ave much time for us now they've turned up." She heaved the bags up onto the kitchen table, meanwhile remarking to Dando, "She din't seem to know much about proper cookin' – the kind of fing you do. I 'ad to tell 'er wot you'd need but she said she'd pay for it."

Dando set about firing up the stove.

Night fell. The desultory activity within the shanty town faded while, as the hours passed, even the rowdy racket issuing from the local shebeen became muted and eventually died away. There was no street lighting, the only illumination in the narrow lanes came from the stars and a moon not far off its first quarter, for the sky was clear. The alleys were full of shadows and among them was one that moved forward in a purposeful manner. When this vague shape arrived outside Becca's ancestral home it disappeared into the dark recesses beneath the eves on the opposite side of the street, and soon a small spark of light, like the tail of a firefly, appeared out of this inkiness and crossed over, beginning to waver in, out and around the blackened walls as if searching for somewhere to perch. Eventually it settled in one particular spot, its tiny gleam picking out a piece of damaged timber that had worked partially loose from the rest. In less than a moment the shadow had darted across and seized this warped stave; there was a single sharp CRACK!! as it broke off, the light blinked out and thief and trophy vanished around the nearest corner.

Sometime later the shadow, alias Gammadion the Necromancer, climbed out of Bishops Hollow on the side away from Rockwell Springs and took a footpath that led through open country into a stand of trees. Reaching a clearing, the dark figure foraged for kindling and built a small fire which was then set alight through the simple expedient of pointing an index finger at the sticks. The wizard was still wearing his military disguise and anyone observing him in passing would probably have assumed that, having become used to bivouacking, the soldier preferred an outdoor billet to sleeping under a roof. When the fire was burning brightly he pulled the piece of tarred wood from one of his capacious pockets and holding it before him began a monotonous incantation that ended with a single sharply barked command in an unknown tongue, after which he drew back his arm and threw the fragment into the flames. Immediately the fire was dimmed and clouds of dark smoke billowed into the air. Gammadion coughed, waving his hand before his face, then broke into a laugh.

"So it begins my lady," he gloated, " this is what you wanted – you and me both. I heard your voice once more and on your urging returned to deal with that troublemaker. Perhaps soon we'll be free of him for good and I'll be able to recover the Death-Denier and find the answer to this endless existence." He brooded for a few moments and then added in a lower tone, "if any answer actually exists."

I dreamt of dying,
Then awoke feeling fulfilled.
How crazy is that?

Chapter ten

Over the next few days Dando set about cooking for his companions. He was a little uncertain as to how many he had to cater for although there were two he was pretty sure he could rely on. Foxy had not been slow in tackling Becca about a job on the farm which she owned and had been introduced, with very little delay, to the manager of the enterprise. The man had been surprised to be thus approached but was quite prepared to give this potentially willing worker a try out. Damask, after complaining, "I can't sit around here on my hands all day," accompanied the Nablan as he set off on his first morning, intending to make herself as useful as she was able around the steading despite her injured shoulder, while at the same time assuring the man in charge that she did not expect remuneration. In the weeks that followed the two of them were usually regular attenders at the meals that Dando provided. Jack and Fynn, in contrast, often opted out of eating all together as the blind boy immediately began to patronise the local grog-shop, known as Bo's Bar, and passed most of the latter part of the evening there before returning home in an inebriated state after it closed at midnight, an anxious Fynn in attendance. Tallis got into the habit of disappearing for long periods, while Becca spent nearly all her time with her sons and their wives and children over in Camelback Avenue. Horry was also there most days and Milly, accompanying him, became, all too soon, an unpaid servant to the Paternoster family. Nobody seemed keen to remain in the Butchers Hollow cabin longer than they could help although the quality of Dando's cooking acted like a magnet and often drew them back there to eat at some hour of the day or night. This meant that he had to be on call nearly all of the twenty-four hours and spent more time than anyone else in the rambling old dwelling.

"What's the matter with that stove?" enquired Damask on the third day of their stay.

“There's nothing wrong with the stove,” replied Dando somewhat annoyed.

“Well, every time we come back here the place stinks of smoke and you can't see to think. The walls are made of wood you realise – could go up like a Drossi Candle.”

“I don't think so – it's damp,” Dando reminded her.

“Yes, damp and depressing.”

Dando turned the matter over in his mind. He had to admit she was right about the pollution, he could have sworn that there was smoke hanging around inside the building although where it came from was a mystery. As evidence he had the fact that its presence, along with the all- pervading moisture, was doing his cough no favours, no favours at all. Nevertheless he could have put up with far worse conditions in order to do what he loved, that is practice his culinary skills. The task he was engaged upon was cooking in its purest form, he believed. It was not done for profit, nor to impress people, nor to get his name in the papers, but just to provide meals of the highest quality in order to send his friends away replete and satisfied. Normally, such an exercise would have filled him with a quiet delight, but he suddenly realised after about a week that the joy he had experienced in the past was absent. He was struck by a terrible anxiety. Had his devotion to his craft deserted him? Had he lost the ability to care? That night he was unable to sleep but instead lay coughing and sweating until morning broke.

Feeling he needed a lift, he decided, after he had tidied up one night, to go and join Jack and Fynn down at the bar. Out on the twilight street he needed no map to find his way, the raucous din issuing from the place to which he was bound acted as sufficient guide. As soon as he walked into the gritty tavern that smelt of unwashed bodies and stale beer, he got the impression he was entering the haunt of all the greatest losers in a losers' community. Most of those present, mainly male, looked down-at-heel if not positively shabby and already, mid-evening, were considerably the worse for wear. Dando went to the bar and ordered a drink (one sip was enough to tell him that this was the pukka rot-gut spirit, probably made in some illegal local distillery), and then looked round for Fynn and Jack. He discovered them sitting at a table in the midst of a collection of disreputable characters who formed by far the noisiest group in the room. Fynn quickly spotted the new arrival and putting his mouth close to Jack's ear passed on the information. Jack raised his head, almost like a dog sniffing out a bone, and called a greeting.

"Is that you birdy?" he shouted above the din. "Slumming it a bit, aren't you? Be careful the vibes don't rub off – you could get contaminated."

"Shut up, Jack," replied Dando inserting himself into a narrow space on the other side of the table from his friend. He realised that the blind boy was already half cut: beside his elbow were several empty schooners and he was apparently matching the more seasoned topers around him drink for drink. As the boy raised his glass Dando noticed that he was still wearing the metal fetters with which he had been manacled whilst in the hospital.

"I thought he'd had those removed," he said to Fynn.

"The chains," answered Fynn, "he insisted on keeping the bracelets."

"As a reminder," put in Jack stretching out his wrist and turning it this way and that. "It's the latest fashion – prison bling – to die for don't you reckon?"

There was an old man at their table who seemed slightly more inebriated than the rest. He was talking non-stop at the top of his rather quavery voice and the others were largely ignoring him apart from telling him every so often to "pipe-down Josh, for pete's sake". Dando watched him in puzzlement. There was something familiar about his appearance; he wondered if he might have come across him along the road. But then he realised that the man reminded him of someone he had known in earlier days: he was the spitting image of his father's uncle, his own great uncle, a rather unprepossessing individual that he remembered vaguely from his childhood. He tried to make out what the fellow was saying but all he could hear was the one word *tricked*, constantly repeated. He got up and walked round until he was able to tap the speaker on the shoulder. "Can I buy you a drink?" he asked.

The man turned and stared blearily, trying to focus. His clothes were ragged, his straggly grey beard stained with nicotine and his eyes red-rimmed.

"I was interested in what you were saying just now," said Dando, "but I couldn't hear properly. Let me buy you a drink and we can go over there where there's less noise."

The old man seemed finally to gather his wits about him and realise he was on to a good thing – not only was a free drink on offer but also he had found an attentive listener for once. He followed Dando to a secluded corner table and when the boy returned from the bar carrying two double whiskeys launched immediately into a long peroration.

"I've made a study of it," he assured Dando earnestly, "it's taken me years – I've travelled – all over – they were my ancestors after all. I often wondered when I was growing up why nothing ever went right for us. They were tricked, that's what happened - all those centuries ago – if it hadn't've been for that, everything would have been quite different."

"I see" said Dando courteously although this was far from the case.

"If they hadn't been tricked I wouldn't be here now – oh no – I'd be a long way away down south and I'd have my own land – a nice little farm. I've never owned anything in my entire life, you know – my family was dirt poor."

"But how were they tricked – your ancestors, I mean?"

The man assumed an air of sage erudition.

"That's quite hard for most people to understand - but me, I've studied it – I've done an investigation I tell you, and wrote it all up. There's a song which my ma used to sing – it was called Pyr's Piece:-

Oh where are you going to sweet love of mine,
To look for Pyr's Piece 'neath the dark o' the pines,
Neath the pines neath the pines where the sun never shines,
Oh my love she has vanished away."

He sang several verses in his old weak voice, then looked pointedly at his empty glass. When Dando returned with top-ups he continued, "They called it Pyr's Piece, meaning a coin you understand not an acreage and definitely not a key although that's what my gran said it was, but she was goin' a bit weak in the head. I believe it was lots of coins, a huge treasure-trove of gold and silver and jewels, and it was stolen from among us, from our land where we lived in the south, and when we finally tracked it down a vast distance away those we thought were our allies took it for themselves and our luck went with it. I'm the last... the very last..."

"But who were they, these people who tricked you?" Dando enquired, feeling short changed by this abrupt ending to the story although suspecting he was not going to get a second chapter; the man's head had fallen forward onto his skinny chest and he began to snore loudly. Reaching across, Dando moved his glass, then put a hand on the other's arm and gave it a gentle shake but without result. There were several unanswered questions he would have liked to put but it was fairly obvious that the old boy was out for the count. He wondered if anyone bothered to see him home at the end of the evening or if he even had a home to go to. He found a five dollar bill about his person and, folding it, stuck it into the down-and-out's shirt pocket.

By now the noise in the tavern had redoubled. He became aware that Jack was up on one of the tables, supported by Fynn, singing a familiar sea-shanty:-

"*There is a flash packet, flash packet of fame,*

From Ry-Town she hails and the Dreadnaught's her name..."

He was slurring the words and teetering unsteadily to and fro; it seemed likely that in a matter of minutes he would crash to the floor. From this point on, the evening markedly deteriorated, until at chucking-out time Dando had to help Fynn carry a comatose Jack back to the cabin. After this he felt no desire to repeat the Bo's Bar experience. It was no fun watching Jack get wasted and in retrospect he found the idea of again encountering the old man who resembled his uncle vaguely off-putting; he decided he did not want to hear anymore about his tales of being *tricked*. But this meant that, after the last meal of the day, he passed most of each evening alone in the smoky-smelling shack, Damask and Foxy having taken themselves up the hill in order to sample Rockwell Springs' night life, and the smoke seemed to weave a dark mist about his brain, blocking out the light.

When he was not in the bar Jack was the only other member of their group to spend the greater part of his time in the cabin. During the day he stayed in his room listening to old shellac records played on a huge wind-up gramophone equipped with a horn that he had found hidden away in some dusty corner, accompanying them moodily on his flute which had been retrieved from Becca's partially collapsed mansion, and repeating the same tracks over and over again, especially a bluesy jazz piece that he seemed never to tire of. Meanwhile Fynn went out and about on various errands. Jack no longer used a stick to find his way around but relied on the young saxophonist to lead him, even if it was just the few feet from his bedroom to the kitchen table. Fynn had become indispensable to him and yet he seemed to find the boy's presence intensely irritating. Dando would hear him telling him to *scram!* or occasionally, crudely, to *fuck-off!* One minute he was driving the young man away and then the next calling him back in an accusatory manner as if his carer had deliberately deserted him. After some time Dando could stand this no longer and tackled Jack about it, taking the opportunity while Fynn was off in town searching for the somewhat exotic brand of cigarettes his *Capitaine* was partial to.

"Why are you so hard on Fynn?" he wanted to know. "You're not being fair – he worships you."

Jack gave a snort of derision and then said sneeringly, "More fool him!"

Dando stuck his hands deep in his pockets and turned his back on the other.

"Just because you're feeling miserable," he said over his shoulder, "that doesn't mean you've got to make everyone else miserable too."

"What? Am I making you miserable then, birdy?"

"Hmph – I don't need any help."

The very next morning when Fynn and he passed each other on the way to and from the urinal, the boy asked Dando for advice.

"You knew him before I did," he said, indicating the window of Jack's room through which doleful music was floating, "and you were with him in the hospital. He's like got this idea that he's – you know – that he's no good in bed anymore."

"Yes," replied Dando, nodding.

"He says dreadful things, like that when he spent time with his mother she told him the cat had been *seen to. That's what's happened to me,*' he said, *I've been seen to.* Then yesterday he said he was only fit to be fattened up for the table because he'd been caponised, gelded – what they do to farmyard animals he said. Surely that's not true – is it?"

"No," answered Dando, "I don't think so. I think it's all in his head."

"Then like, what can we do about it?"

"Leave it with me – I've got an idea."

It took quite a rallying of forces for Dando to drag himself up out of the despondency, the smoky despondency, into which he was rapidly sinking and apply his mind to the problem that Fynn had brought into the open. He did have an idea of how to solve it but it would require Jack's cooperation. He went to see him.

For the first few minutes after he entered his friend's glory hole the boy from Drossi ignored him completely, busying himself by industriously rifling through the pile of discs beside the record player. On the bedside-table were two empty whiskey bottles and one less than half-full; there was also a glass and a packet of dodgy-looking cigarettes. Dando, being blessed with a large fund of patience – larger than Jack's at any rate - and knowing his entrance could not have gone unnoticed, was content to wait. He looked down on the young man feeling compassion and exasperation in equal measure. Eventually the other heaved a deep sigh and without turning remarked, “Well birdy – to what do I owe the pleasure?”

“I just looked in,” Dando answered, “to see if you needed anything while Fynn's not here.”

“What I need,” said Jack crossly, “you wouldn't be able to give me and what you can give I've got too much of already. I just want people to go away – can't both of you see that?” His voice was harsh with self-pity.

“You're not doing yourself any favours, Jack,” pursued Dando, “you're not eating properly. Starving yourself isn't going to provide answers.”

“I haven't got any appetite.”

“Well if you didn't drink so much you might feel hungrier.”

“Oh-ho – so you're trying to take away my one remaining pleasure. That's the game is it?”

“Don't be a fool! I just wondered if you realise it's Fynn's birthday in three days time – he told me – he's going to be seventeen. Don't you think we ought to do something?”

“Oh, not a party for fuck's sake!”

“No, not a party.”

“Well what?”

“I thought I could organise an exclusive dinner for the both of you – not any old meal but a tailor-made menu – like I used to do at the restaurant when people were out on a special date.”

“An exclusive dinner served up in this God-forsaken hole! That'd be something to see.”

“Yes – but why not?”

“I'm not sold on the idea – in fact I think it's crap.”

“It's just what you could do with lad – it'd be something different to think about. If you won't do it for yourself do it for Fynn and me – humour us – it'll be no skin off your nose.”

“Why for you?”

“I need something different to think about as well.”

“When did you say it would be?”

“Three days' time. I think everyone else is going out – it would be just you and him.”

“Not you?”

“I'll be your waiter – and chef of course. Will you do it?”

Jack ran his hand through his hair, a sullen expression on his face.

"It looks as if I'm being railroaded into it."

"Good, good. Just one thing – no alcohol between now and then..." and Dando beat a hasty retreat before Jack had time to voice his indignation.

He hung around outside the front door and grabbed Fynn on his return from town.

"Did you know," he informed him conspiratorially, "that you're going to have a birthday in three days' time? I'm arranging a surprise date for the two of you, you and Jack, a dinner date, so you've got to act as if you didn't know anything about it."

"Like I certainly didn't up 'till now!" replied Fynn, "my birthday's well later!"

"I reckon this one'll be your official birthday - all important people have two per year."

"Oh, ok - if you say so - but how will that help Jack?"

"Wait and see – and meanwhile keep him off the booze if you can."

Dando headed for the upper town to buy the supplies he needed for the meal. He went first to a good fruit and vegetable merchant and after that to the general store with the highest reputation. From there he carried on to a well-stocked druggist and bought some rather outlandish substances one of which cost a bomb. He drew up a menu, worked out a timetable, then headed for Camelback Avenue to beg some freshly-laundered table linen. Becca had something to say to him after she had dug out what he needed.

"With your permission, honey, I'd like to take Horry to see this person I know – Mother Eulalie she's called – a coloured lady. She's the one who came to the aid of my own mama when she had young 'uns. She's in her eighties now but still practising. She might be able to help with his – you know – with his problem. He's such a big boy now – he plays most of the time with Dean and Hank and they're all of five years older than him."

When Dando returned to Bishops Hollow the showgirl insisted on accompanying him.

"I'm afraid I've been neglecting y'all honey," she said. "I jest want to come an' see how yeez are getting along down at the ol' place. Milly tol' me she was worried about you – she thought you hadn't been feelin' too well lately."

"I'm all right," replied Dando, "we're all getting on all right – except for Jack."

"Oh yes – the poor guy." Becca shook her head. "I remember when he was a leading light on the Drossi scene – a real tearaway mind you. Of course he could still see then..."

At the cabin she sniffed suspiciously.

"Must be comin' in from outside - some folks got a barbie goin' I reckon." She took note of Dando's purchases. "Looks like you're about to have a celebration."

"It's just a little meal *a deux* for Jack and Fynn," Dando explained.

"Well we all realise what's going on there – my mama wouldn't have approved – but what the heck – things are different nowadays – love is love after all. Anyway I'm glad everything's fine with you honey – I'll see you soon," and she beat a hasty retreat back to Rockwell Springs and the grandchildren.

The significant day arrived and Dando began preparations early. He started by paying a visit to the local slaughterhouse, by-passing the butcher. In Ry-Town, as the owner of the Dark Continent, he had gradually become inured to such blood-soaked locations and now made his purchases in a purely professional manner. It was good to be busy – a relief to have something to take his mind off... off what? Perhaps he was feeling guilty because of the suggestion that he had been the cause of the earthquake which killed thousands. But no - that idea was so monstrous that he found it almost impossible to accept. This low mood did not seem to stem from that, he was just experiencing an unfocussed dread as if there were a dark shadow about to descend on his head heralding something indefinably awful. Yet, as he did not normally believe in premonitions, he also tried to dismiss this idea and find another explanation for why he was feeling so jumpy and on edge. Meanwhile he worked doggedly away in the kitchen determined to bring all his best skills to bear, and to apply a certain esoteric knowledge that he had acquired from a fellow enthusiast during the few months that he had been running his restaurant.

At eight o'clock, the appointed hour, Fynn and Jack appeared at the door, Fynn giving a convincing impression of someone completely in the dark about what was about to happen, following which Dando showed them into a side room where he had laid a table with Becca's best cloth, napkins and cutlery. Two flutes containing a light sparkling wine awaited them. He left them alone for about five minutes before bringing in the starters: a choice between avocado halves and asparagus rolls, both served with a honey and onion relish. Then came very small dishes of pasta, coated in a purée of cream-cheese, basil and ground almonds and after that the main course. Dando was busy pouring thimblefuls of spiced vin-du-pays as Jack took his first mouthful. He masticated for sometime in silence before asking,

"What's this?"

"Oysters," said Dando.

"Uh-huh," Jack shook his head, "this isn't shellfish, it's meat."

"Prairie oysters," said Dando and smiled mischievously, "but it's the sauce that's important."

"What's in the sauce?"

"Caramel, figs, herbs, ginger and something that's going to remain my secret."

Jack went on eating. Eventually he commented reluctantly, "It's good," and added some pleasant remarks directed at Fynn to which the boy eagerly responded. Again falling silent he waited until he had completely cleared his plate before remarking ruefully:

"I think I get it spatzi – this food's supposed to make me feel horny, right?"

Dando laughed. "If I've brought it off it's just a very special, exclusive, no expenses spared meal. Tuck in and enjoy – don't go looking for what isn't there."

"I don't trust you, caridad."

"Well, that's your problem."

By the time the dessert was served Jack had visibly relaxed. He had even unwound sufficiently to tell an extremely off-colour shaggy dog story of which he had a large supply, at which Fynn laughed so dutifully that one felt that he might have slightly misunderstood the clever denouement. Dando brought in two pretty china dishes followed by a bowl containing a coffee and chocolate torte sprinkled with a remarkable coating of fine gold dust. Fynn stared in amazement.

"Wow – awesome!" he exclaimed and then began to describe what he was seeing for Jack's benefit.

"So you're giving me gold now already!" Jack sniggered, "what are we going to end the meal with – lion's todger dressed in unicorn cum?" Despite this apparent cynicism it was possible to detect a faint renewal of hope in his voice, a hope that had been absent for some time.

"No – but I've got a drink you might like to try."

When the sweet was finished Dando came back with two small goblets, a bottle of clear green liquid and a jug containing iced water.

"You put a measure of the drink in the glass," he explained as he followed his own instructions, "and then place a sugar lump in this strainer on top. Pour some water through it till the stuff in the glass goes cloudy. Enjoy."

He retreated to the doorway and stood watching until he saw Jack reach out and grope for Fynn's hand. Then he slipped away, did the washing up and retired to his quarters.

Some time later he heard the two young men pass his door; they were talking in low voices and Fynn was giggling.

"We need a rope Lollipop..." Jack was saying and in reply Fynn assured him, "...I've got one..." Then they went out of ear-shot as they entered Fynn's room and the door slammed.

Dando lay fully clothed on his bed staring into space. He should have been delighted that his elaborate scheme had born fruit but instead experienced nothing but a feeling of anticlimax. About an hour passed before Damask and Foxy returned – they had been to see a movie at the miniature picture house – and again he caught snatches of their conversation as they made their way to the other end of the building.

"There's five more acres in the lower forty I've got to plough," came Foxy's voice, "we're going to sow it with rape this autumn as long as we get rain. The land's drying up without it."

"Rape!" Damask guffawed, "chance'd be a fine thing!"

"Rape *seed* – it's grown for the oil – looks a picture in the spring..."

Their voices faded away but despite this Dando put his hands over his ears as if to block out what he had just heard. The word *rape* had set up reverberations in his brain causing him to draw his knees into a foetal position as his memory conjured intolerable images. Up to now he had shrunk from using this explicit term to describe his hideous experience of a few months back at the mercy of the Terratenebrian militia, yet now he began to wonder if perhaps it was right to give the thing it's proper name, however distressing he might find it. To think that once he had been naïve enough to imagine that it was impossible for such a violation to be visited on someone of his own sex. What a dummy he had been! When night fell, sleep again eluded him.

The next morning on leaving his room he encountered Jack and Fynn dressed for a journey, their possessions packed into an odd assortment of bags. Fynn was positively scintillating while Jack radiated a quiet happiness. The blind boy put down his luggage and enfolded the Glept in an embrace, pulling him close.

"I don't know how to thank you my little bird," he murmured into his ear, "I owe you more than I can say. You've shown me what an idiot I've been over the past few weeks. You've given me my life back." "You did the same for me once, Jack."

"Anyway, we've made up our minds – Fynn and I are going to head for the bright lights. We don't like it here – there's something weird about this place – it's just a feeling but we've both got it. Don't you feel it? We've decided to take a vacation up at Belle City on the Great Lake."

"Belle City?"

"Yes, you know Belle City – you've heard the song: *Belle City Belle?*"

Dando shook his head. "No, I don't think so," he said.

"Well, it's a happening place – the place to be. There's quite a scene going on there and we thought we'd investigate. What we both want to know is, *Will you come with us?*"

Dando's heart felt heavy as again he answered in the negative.

"Oh, come on spatzi – why not? Cut loose for once and shed your inhibitions. It'll do you the world of good."

"I can't," said Dando.

"Why?"

"I've got to wait for Master Tallisand."

As he spoke he wondered what he was saying. The words seemed suddenly meaningless yet he clung to them like a drowning man to a lifeline. Finding him immoveable Jack and Fynn made ready to leave but not before Jack drew Dando aside in order to impart some information and issue a warning.

"Knowing you, my love," he said, "I don't s'pose you've noticed what's going on right under your nose."

"What do you mean?" asked his friend.

"It's your sister and the foxy gentleman. With anyone else I'd say they'd be blind not to see – even I'm onto it – but you – your head's always in the clouds."

"What are you talking about?" repeated Dando, somewhat put out.

"Well, they seem to have sort of got it on together – have done for some time of course but now it's getting quite steamy I think."

"So? - good luck to them."

"Ah, but you told me a story once – you told me that your father had a relationship and that therefore this Foxy fellow was your half-brother. OK – so she's your sister – then wouldn't that mean that he's her half-brother too? I don't know what your attitude to that kind of thing is but you'd better make sure they're using some sort of safeguard."

Dando looked surprised as if this aspect of the situation had not occurred to him.

"Damask doesn't need me to teach her the facts of life," he said.

"Yes, but does she know what you told me?"

"Not exactly."

"Well, she ought to be put in the picture – even if he isn't. By the way birdy – I haven't said this before – I'm really sorry you lost the restaurant – really sorry."

Jack and his paramour set off to catch the north-bound train which came through at midday and Dando went along to bid them goodbye. The train, crowded as usual, pulled into the station and a few people got off, leaving room for others to get on. Jack swung their luggage through the open carriage door then turned and caught Dando by the shoulders.

"We'll report back in a few weeks time, patootie," he said, "take care of yourself."

He gave him a kiss while Fynn also offered a quick shy peck – then they were gone. Dando trudged back to Becca's cabin feeling abandoned and alone.

Although such a thing had been completely unknown south of the Middle Sea Foxy had taken to mechanised farming like a duck to water. The set-up at his new place of employment was a mixture of arable and livestock but he was engaged purely on the crop-growing side and this suited him down to the ground as he was most at home cultivating the soil. He doted on the powerful tractors, the larger the better as far as he was concerned, and lovingly tended to their every need, keeping them in tip-top condition. When he drove one of them into the tractor-shed at night he refused to quit until the machine had been thoroughly cleaned, oiled and refuelled ready for the morning. Meanwhile Damask had to contain her impatience as she hung around waiting for him to finish. In recent days, when he had finally put everything to bed, they had not left the farm on shank's pony. It had been during one of the very rare rainy mornings that Foxy, at work in the hay barn, had shifted a few old bales and had come across a dusty, dropping-encrusted motorcycle, up to then hidden from view, whose name could barely be distinguished beneath the dirt.

"It be a Chapman 370!" he cried in amazement, "they only make a few hunderd of those – it be whooly worth a packet. I wonder if the singing-woman know it be here?"

"Oh yes," Becca said nostalgically when they informed her what they had found, "that was Clark's. We used to go riding on it when we were kids – before everything went wrong – glory days – glory days. No – I don't want it – it'd bring back too many memories. If you can get it going again honey, after all this time, you'll have earned the right to keep it."

Foxy did not need to be told twice. Evening after evening he stayed in the barn and worked on the bike, practically dismantling it before setting out to clean and reassemble the parts. When at last he felt that everything was as good as he could make it he filled the tank and then called Damask to come and witness a resurrection. She arrived toting a large dose of scepticism.

"Are you sure you know what you're doing?" she asked.

"Watch," said Foxy.

He swung his leg over the bike and stamped on the kick-start lever. The engine chugged for a moment then died. Four more times he tried with the same result until on the sixth attempt the machine suddenly burst into life with a roar. Foxy revved it over and over until he was satisfied that the regeneration was permanent before letting it subside into a throaty idling.

"Comin' fer a ride gel?" he invited in quiet triumph.

Dando waited his chance to get Damask alone. As a result of what Jack had told him he had woken up to the fact, rather late in the day, that his sister ought to be informed of her kinship to the man with whom she was spending most of her time.

"This is something that Ann told me which Tom told her before... before... you know what..." He grimaced uncomfortably and then went on, "It's about us and Foxy – and about father. But if I tell you, you must promise not to tell Foxy – I promised Ann..."

"Go on, then..."

"Promise."

"Oh, alright – if it'll make you happy."

"Well, evidently, when father was about our age..."

He recounted what he believed to be the truth of Foxy's origins and subsequent life history, as nearly as possible word for word as he had heard it, expanding on what she already knew, only omitting the telling detail of whose arrow had fatally wounded the Dan. When he finished he waited for his sister's reaction, fully expecting the tale to be met with incredulous resentment or indignant disbelief. Instead, to his surprise, Damask listened quietly, almost sadly, and then said with a shake of the head:-

"It's ok bro - if that's true and it may well be as far as we're concerned, you don't need to get your knickers in a twist. I know why you've told me but there's nothing happening with me and Foxy when we get between the sheets."

"Nothing?"

"Nothing – nada – zilch. Haven't even got to first base."

"That's not what Jack believed."

"Well, Jack was wrong – not that it's any business of his after all."

"Oh well – then I s'pose it's ok – but, as I said, don't tell Foxy what I've just told you."

"Why not?"

"I can't explain, but there's a good reason – and Ann made me promise."

"So there's more secrets?"

Dando's lips tightened and he frowned painfully; Damask noticed that his shoulders were slightly bowed as if something were weighing on him, not physically but spiritually. She shot him a concerned, questioning glance that spoke volumes and suggested that, on the rare occasions when she bothered to pay attention, she could read her brother's emotional state better than anyone.

"Are you ok, Do-Do?" she asked.

"Yes, of course – don't you start fussing too!"

"Well – don't forget – I'm around if you need someone to talk to."

The fact that her relationship with Foxy had remained purely platonic was not for want of trying on Damask's part; she had been strongly attracted to the Nablan from the moment they met, he rang all her bells in a multitude of ways, and she had imagined that he felt the same way about her, yet when it came to getting down to the nitty-gritty, to the mutual physical exploration that should precede the sexual act, he shrank away like a prepubescent girl.

Damask and Foxy regularly slept together, meaning to say they shared a bed – but that was all. He would allow her to indulge in a little foreplay and even seemed occasionally to enjoy it. In return he would kiss her but only in the most abrupt and perfunctory way, a kiss such as you might received from your maiden aunt or an uncle twice removed. Occasionally she was allowed to do such things as sticking her tongue in his ear, chewing on his nipples or sucking his grubby toes and this would sometimes result in an erection on his part but when she tried to take advantage of it he pushed her away.

"Leave me be," he would grunt.

She was not allowed to get anywhere near his cock and if, at any time, she did so he would turn over and present her with his broad backside as if that were the end of the matter.

The farm-manager had a good reason for clearing out the hay barn. It could not possibly have escaped the attention of anyone living in Rockwell Springs or even Bishops Hollow that accommodation in the two halves of the little town was at a premium. A constant stream of people - refugees from the ruined coastal city - were passing through on the railway or the main road at that time, many of them looking for overnight lodgings before moving on. Each evening every spare bed on both sides of the tracks was soon spoken for and this left a number of travellers without a roof over their heads. The manager, with Becca's approval, saw an opportunity to make a small profit by hiring out shakedowns in his barn for half a dollar a night. Latrines were dug, straw mattresses and buckets of water provided – that was the sum total of the amenities on offer. His two most recent employees were roped in to help promote this venture, the Nablan by providing and changing the bedding straw and cleaning up after the visitors left, Damask by taking the money. They got used to seeing a new set of strangers each evening before they departed for home, but one day, one fateful day, the queue that formed in the twilight by the barn door contained two travellers whose faces were not unfamiliar - not to Damask at least.

"Duke!" she exclaimed in astonishment, "and Boiko too! Look Foxy," to her companion who, having recently been forced to reverse roles and wait for her at the end of the day, was standing nearby at a loose end, "these are friends from home. You remember the Roma who used to visit the Valley? Well here's two of 'em turned up like the proverbial bent sixpence. Where's Kizzy?" she asked of the one who had been her long-time lover and who was now looking from her to Foxy as if trying to fathom their relationship.

"Kizzy not here no more," replied Duke, "Kizzy pass on in seisme."

"You mean she's...? But where are the rest of you?"

"When the seisme happen Roma camped by sea. Sea come right over us – many people drown. Boiko and me, we get swep' out, but man with boat save us. When we get back nobody there. We looking for the ones still living. Think they may have come this way."

"Oh, that's not good – I'm so sorry. Go into the barn and stake your claim – I'll come as soon as I'm done."

The swarthy young men disappeared through the door into the dim interior while Damask prepared to deal with the next in line. Foxy, feeling marginalised, stared first at the girl and then at the dark doorway, an ominous scowl on his face.

"Who be they two?" he demanded.

"As I said they're old friends. Weren't they on the same boat as you when you crossed the Tethys? – that's what Dando told me. I'll probably go and get reacquainted when I've finished here. You might as well get on the bike and go home – I'll follow later."

"What – you mean you'll walk back?"

"Yes – that's what I mean." She gave him a challenging look.

Foxy moved away but only in order to observe from a distance. When he saw her dispatch the last of the applicants and follow them into the barn he hurriedly returned. As he came through the door he caught sight of Damask and one of the gypsies in what, to his eyes, appeared to be a passionate embrace. Neither of them noticed his approach until he seized hold of Damask's good arm and dragged her away, not letting go even when he got her outside. Damask let out a shriek of indignation and followed this with angry protestations.

"What the hell do you think you're doing?!!" she cried, struggling to break free. Foxy held on grimly – he was by far the stronger of the two.

"You be my woman!" he answered menacingly in a low growl, "not some dirty pikey's!"

"Your woman! Well, you've got a fine way of showing it!"

"You want I to shew you? Come back to the house – I'll shew you!"

Damask eyed him for several moments in wild surmise.

"You're not kidding? All right then, I will – but it'd better be worth it!"

Dando, feeling even more miserable than usual, was tidying up after an evening meal that had been mainly wasted. He could not understand why Damask and Foxy had gone straight to their room without eating on returning from the farm. He had called them but there had been no response. Suddenly he heard voices outside the front door speaking in a foreign tongue that sounded vaguely familiar, after which came a peremptory knock. He went to answer.

"The Principessa – I want to talk to Principessa!"

With amazement Dando recognised Damask's old flame Duke and behind him his brother Boiko, standing with a rifle over his arm.

"Hello – fancy seeing you two after all this time," he exclaimed, and then, "you want Damask? She's in her room. I could call her I s'pose..." Something about the travellers' expressions told him that all was not as it should be and he hesitated to allow them over the threshold. But the next moment a shoulder made contact with his shoulder and Foxy, wrapped in just a shabby dressing gown, elbowed him aside.

"Get out!" the Nablan was shouting as he passed through the door, "get lost! You don' belong here! If you're not gone double quick...!"

"I want Principessa!" demanded Duke, and then at the full extent of his lungs, "Principessa!! Principessa!!"

"Go screw yourself!" cried Foxy, lurching menacingly towards the gypsy, and in a trice the two men were rolling on the ground at each other's throats.

"Fair fight – fair fight!" cried Boiko, hovering anxiously on the periphery, "fight with fists!"

Hardly any time had passed since Dando opened to the new arrivals but already a crowd was gathering; the citizens of Bishops Hollow appearing to have a sixth sense when it came to the possibility of a dust-up. A couple of burly men pulled the two contestants apart and to their feet while the rest slow-hand-clapped shouting "Bare-knuckle! Bare knuckle!"

Duke stripped off his shirt, Foxy his gown, and, to the edification of the onlookers, the two men began trading blows with the utmost ferocity. The gypsy could claim an advantage in height but soon the Nablan's superior weight and muscle power began to tell in his favour. Twice - three times - he rocked Duke back on his heels until with a straight left to the jaw the other went sprawling. Foxy turned contemptuously and began to stump back towards the cabin.

"Look out!" cried Damask who was now standing beside Dando in the doorway.

Staring at Foxy's retreating back and now on his knees, Duke had seized the rifle from a scared-looking Boiko and raised it to his shoulder. Reacting to Damask's warning Foxy flung himself full length on the ground, rolled, and in less than a heartbeat his deadly little pistol, appearing as if by magic from his near naked body, was out, up and aimed. Both guns fired simultaneously but only one missile found its mark: with the last of his strength Duke staggered to his feet, only to collapse backwards into his brother's arms mortally wounded. For a moment the world held its breath, then the crowd burst into excited uproar while a few of its members rushed off to fetch help. Foxy got up and stood irresolute, his gun-arm hanging limply by his side. There was another pregnant pause followed by a long howl like a banshee as Boiko gave vent to his grief. “Morto!” he cried in anguish, and then, pointing at Foxy with a shaking finger, “assassino!!”

“It was self-defence!”

Damask, who had arrived on the scene also only half dressed, stepped past a transfixed Dando and went and stood side by side with her bed-fellow ready to defend him to the last ditch. But by now a grossly overweight policeman had taken centre stage. He waddled forward and held out his hand.

“I'll have that,” he said. Instead it was Damask who took possession of the gun and then handed it over, Foxy giving it up to her without a murmur.

“He was going to shoot him in the back,” she protested, “he had to defend himself.”

The crowd began jabbering amongst themselves; it was not clear whose side they were on but it seemed that the opinion of the majority was that the interested parties should retire to the police house to sort things out while a doctor was summoned to certify death. Foxy was formally arrested as also was Boiko, who, having produced a knife, had to be restrained from carrying out retribution there and then. Everyone set off for Rockwell Springs apart from Dando. He was left alone with the body and went to fetch a sheet to cover it and a mop and bucket to clean up the blood. By now it was far too late to do anything else.

The time was well past midnight before Damask returned alone.

“Murder!” she exclaimed with great indignation. “They're going to charge him with murder. It was obviously manslaughter.”

“Is there going to be a trial?” asked Dando.

“The circuit judge comes round next week. You saw what happened – you'll have to be a witness. We must get a lawyer.”

Over the next week and a half Dando was left virtually alone in the cabin. Damask was busy organising Foxy's defence while Becca pulled what strings she could on her employee's behalf. In the midst of such a crisis nobody was sparing much thought for the young disabled man on the wrong side of the tracks. Milly came occasionally to check on her idol's welfare but was invariably moodily rebuffed and who could blame her if she then returned to sixty seven Camelback Avenue where she was at least valued for her housekeeping abilities. Tallis appeared infrequently, merely to eat and sleep, but was more usually absent pursuing his own mysterious ends. Our inspirational chef, our ex-dancer, did not even have the animals for company during his long days and even longer nights because almost from the start they had refused to come under the roof of the old dwelling. He fed them in the yard, after which Meena would disappear for hours on end while Ralph sometimes accompanied Tallis but more often than not hung around outside the back door, whimpering, whining and occasionally howling as if he felt his beloved human was in danger. The time was long past when Dando might have found the courage to break out of his inertia and make a dash for healthier climes. One dog at least had become his constant companion: the black dog of depression clung to his shoulders giving the whole world an alien and dispiriting aspect so that nowhere seemed to offer any better alternative to what he was experiencing in that dank, creaking, smoky old shack.

The law ground on its inexorable way and, despite his friends' best efforts, when Foxy's trial took place just a few days later he was convicted of second degree murder, satisfying neither the revengeful brother nor anyone else. The verdict earned him a sentence of ten years hard labour at the new mining project north of the Craiks. The Nablan's demeanour throughout the proceedings had been one of grim stoicism; he seemed to accept the justice of the verdict, unlike Damask who immediately tried to find out if it were possible to lodge an appeal. The answer she received was vague in the extreme and before she could do anything more about it events overtook her. In three days time, it was announced, a freight train would be coming through carrying convicts en route to a penitentiary outside Damwey, after which a certain number would be transported across cattle-country and over the mountains to the excavations. Foxy, or rather prisoner 45882, would be going with them.

"He wants to see you," said Damask.

"Me?" replied Dando, startled. Apart from playing his part as witness at the trial, he had tactfully stayed well away from the defendant. Relations between himself and Foxy has not always been easy and he did not want it to appear as if he was deriving any kind of satisfaction from the downfall of a rival. But now, with a certain amount of trepidation, he obediently made his way to the jail, wondering what was about to transpire.

Everard Tetherer Truly had always impressed the young Glept as indomitable: a free unbowed spirit. He had never imagined he would see him brought low, humbled and humiliated. But now as Foxy shuffled towards the bars of the tiny cell, legs hobbled and wrists cuffed together in front of him, clothed in prison pyjamas that were both too big and too tight at the same time, he realised that the thing he had not been able to envisage had come to pass. It was something he had no desire to witness and he felt profound shame that he was being asked to do so. All the same the Nablan appeared determined to ignore his personal situation. As he came forward, although he cut a sorry figure, there was the same challenging gleam in his eye that had always been present in his dealings with the young aristocrat. The only difference was that a humorous stamp had now been added. When he spoke it was with surprising friendliness and insight.

"I be a-gooin' narth," he said as if this departure was of his own choosing, "mayhap I'll not see you for a while, or maybe never. I wan' you to have somethin' of mine – the mo'bike. You may find it come in useful for you an' the knight – I know he be still a-lookin' for this here Key."

"B-but aren't you going to give it to Damask so she c'n keep it for you when you return?" Dando replied, astonished.

"Her don' wan' to do that – I ast her – her has other ideas. It be in the barn over at the farm. I fix a spare tank to the rear – there don' be many gas stations hereabouts."

"I've never driven anything like that in my life."

"Her'll shew you what to do."

Dando cast around for some way to express his thanks.

"I'm very grateful," he said hesitantly, "but w-why me? I sort of thought... I thought you didn't like me very much."

The Nablan directed at him a level apprising gaze from his piercing blue eyes.

"I bin cogitatin' a bit since I come in here," he said gruffly, "I reckon no-one can help who their father be – I never knowed who be *my* father – mayhap he be a duzzy owd rogue for all I know, or maybe a murderer. Mayhap I take arter he."

"You're no murderer," said Dando and meant it, at the same time thinking *shall I tell him?* This might be the only remaining opportunity he would get to enlighten Foxy about his parentage, but for a long while he had been of the opinion that he was the last person that should take on this awkward and delicate task. Anyway he had promised Ann that he wouldn't. All things considered it seemed better that the half-cast young man should never know the nature of the crime he had been guilty of on that day over a year ago when they had quitted the valley.

A long silence hung between the two of them until Foxy broke it by saying abruptly, “Well – goo'bye.”

Dando reached through the bars and shook the fettered hand.

“I hope...” he began but tailed off. Then, “I think Damask's still working on an appeal.”

“I be a-gooin' ter serve my sentence,” replied Foxy obstinately, “I know what's right.” He looked directly at the other with a strange almost compassionate expression. “Don' 'ee fret too much for our Hild – I mind that that were meant to be. An now you ha' the boyee to solace you.”

“You mean Horry?” replied Dando faintly, and when, a few minutes later, found himself outside the jail could not quite remember how he had gotten there.

When the time came for the train to arrive which would take Foxy away, Dando walked up to the station alone. After a longish wait a line of freight wagons pulled by none other than the General McLoy came puffing into sight and at the same time a van appeared from the direction of the town and the obese policeman and two of his deputies unloaded their prisoner, still in chains, and brought him down to the side of the tracks where a couple of open trucks crowded with men in identical overalls marked with arrows had come to a halt. They hoisted the Nablan aboard and secured him to a bench next to a long line of other convicts. Dando cast around to see if anyone else had come to make their farewells. Tallis was absent, which was not wholly unexpected, but where was Becca? where was Milly? and where in heaven's name was Damask? He looked up and down the line and suddenly caught sight of a head which, for a brief moment, poked out of one of the box-car doors before being quickly withdrawn. He walked alongside the track.

”Push off bruv,” a voice hissed from within the car as he drew level, “you'll give me away.”

“What on earth are you up to?” he demanded.

“What does it look like? I'm taking a ride, that's what.”

“But you can't...”

“Of course I can – he's not going alone. You'd do the same.”

“What do you mean?”

“If it was her – if she was in trouble – you would have gone along – wouldn't you? Don't try and stop me.”

As usual the reference to Ann caused Dando's heart to skip a beat.

"But sis..." he protested.

"Get lost, Do-Do. Go and tell him. Tell him I've got another gun – I got it last night from the farmer - he's on our side - and tell him I'm going with him – I don't care what he's done. I tried to tell him yesterday but he wouldn't believe me..."

Dando stared up at his sister. She was dressed for travel and had a rucksack by her feet. She looked utterly determined. He tried to think of something else to say but instead, when she waved him away, walked back to the trucks containing the prisoners, caught Foxy's eye and pointed meaningfully along the train. The Nablan bent forward, looking down the line of rolling stock and then turned back to the front, an unreadable expression on his face. The locomotive remained stationary for about five minutes more while the guard in charge of the prisoners exchanged pleasantries with the three cops, after which it gave a throaty toot indicating immanent departure. Dando stood back and, as it started to move, lifted his hand. Foxy was unable to reciprocate but kept his eyes fixed on the young man until a curve in the track meant that other following cars blocked his line of sight. By the time the one that the Glept had visited earlier came level the train was travelling at speed. Dando glimpsed his sister for a moment as it swept past: she was leaning out and grinning while throwing him a kiss and shouting something that he could not quite catch. Then all that was left to him was a rapidly shrinking image of the caboose as the train disappeared into the distance. Now he could choose between turning left into Rockwell Springs in order to discover the reason behind Becca's and Milly's truancy or, instead, returning forthwith to Bishops Hollow. In fact there was only one possible course of action as far as he was concerned: the old cabin drew him like a wasp to honey or more accurately an unsuspecting fly to flypaper as he drifted over the tracks and down the slope to the shanty town without any apparent volition.

When he reached his goal he went indoors and wandered into the kitchen. There seemed little point in preparing a meal because he did not think anyone would be coming to share it with him. The centre of his being felt mangled as if someone were trying viciously to destroy his heart's essence; it must be because he had just lost two more people who were important to him in a number of ways.

Perhaps the railroad is going to carry everyone away in time, he thought wretchedly. *Is that what happens when you live beside the tracks?*

As a result of his insomnia he had been hearing the cry of trains passing through the little town almost every night now - those long lonesome trains whistling down. They both called to him and repelled him in equal measure.

I try to do the right thing, he agonised, feeling as blameworthy as he had done on the voyage to Hungry Island, *I try to walk the line and leave the world a better place but somehow a spanner always gets chucked in the works. What's the matter with me? Why am I such a liability to those around me?*

He groped his way to Jack's vacated bedroom, the atmosphere so thick he could barely see where he was going. Yes, it was as he remembered, there was a crate in the corner full of bottles. He took possession of as many as he could carry and staggered back to the kitchen half blinded by fumes that got into his eyes and deep into his lungs. He opened one of them - the cork came out with a full-of-promise pop - found a glass and poured himself a libation.

Sitting at the table he drank his way through one bottle and then through another. After he had opened a third he began to lose his grip on reality, unsure if he were awake or asleep. Eventually his head sank onto his arms and he began to dream. The dream started with smoke – thick smoke rising all around, issuing from some fiery source far below. Wisps and plumes were waving, twisting, coiling, twining and, as he watched, these metamorphosed into writhing naked bodies which were constantly in motion, because, with an understanding taken from his own experience of pain, he realised that insupportable agony would not allow them to remain still for more than a moment. He saw that the shapes were in the process of weaving an image from their torment – it was no surprise to realise that the whole of his vision was being taken over by the stark shape of a death's head, the vacancy of its eye-sockets beckoning him into an endless pit of suffering. As he plunged towards the blackness a primitive instinct for self-preservation intervened causing him to tear himself out of the nightmare so that he resurfaced spread-eagled on the floor of a nocturnal kitchen feeling sick and with his head spinning. He made to heave himself up, only to encounter broken glass; the tumbler and one of the bottles must have been knocked off the table as he fell. By the time he had gotten to his feet his hands were bleeding and he could sense wetness on the side of his head. He staggered to the sink in order to wash and wrap cloths around the cuts, then in a nauseous state groped his way to his room and sat down on the edge of the bed.

Slowly, monotonously, thoughts, against which he had no defence, paraded through his brain like a persistent toothache and repeated themselves in an endless succession as if they were the hook of a hideously catchy song. Meaningless – the whole enterprise he was engaged on was meaningless. He might as well have stayed in Deep Hallow and endured his father's harsh justice rather than travel all this way. His entire life seemed without purpose come to that. Who were they kidding, the ones that had told him he had a special destiny to fulfil? In taking notice of such rubbish he was acting like a moron – and a big-headed moron at that. All he amounted to was the spoilt brat of a petty tyrant, an ungrateful son who had done nothing to earn the privileges that had been heaped upon him. And now he could not even lay claim to this manufactured persona because he had become a nobody, a nothing, and one moreover that seemed to spread ill luck wherever he went. Why had it taken him so long to figure this out? Even his great romance - the love that at one time had seemed so strong that it would outlast the ages - now struck him as naught but a sham. What proof did he have that it had been anything other than lust, pure and simple on his part, or a childhood infatuation that should have been allowed to die a natural death? And to think that he had had the temerity to imagine she, Ann, could love him in return – him - a member of the race that had oppressed her people for numberless generations; she had probably just been dazzled by his pre-eminence or else too afraid of the consequences if she refused him. His heart felt as if it was putrefying within his living body and, as his last life-line snapped, a light that had been so much a part of him that he had barely recognised its actuality blinked out leaving him swimming in the depths of a pitch-black lake, a lake of ink, with no sight, no smell, no touch and an unending pitiless silence, an eternity of estrangement.

Eventually he got to his feet and went to the back door. It was some unnamed hour of a cloudy windless night but, once outside, there was just enough light to see by. Dully he searched around the yard until he came upon two spare cans of gasoline that he remembered Foxy kept there. He picked one up and, removing the cap, began to pour the liquid over the outside walls of the shack. When the first one was empty he started on the second, working his way around until he had completed a full circuit. There was a small amount of gas left in the can. Having turned the final corner into the street so that he came level with the main entrance, he upended it over his own head and stood there dripping.

They don't know zip,
The poets that sing of love.
I could teach them a thing or two.

Chapter eleven

The clickety-clack, clickety-clack of wheels over joints gradually slowed while the squeal of steel on steel gave warning that the brakes had been applied. Damask realised that the train was coming to a halt amid arid grassland not far from Harrisburg. Ahead of her she could hear some sort of rumpus, the sound of shouting and barking. She was about to stick her head out of the door of the car to see what was going on when a pile of what she had taken to be discarded rags in the corner came to life. A man - a gaunt colourless creature of indeterminate age - pulled himself upright hissing, “Railroad Bulls! Time to take a powder! Now! – while you've got the chance!”

He hurled himself out into thin air and hit the ground at speed while the train was still in motion. Damask, more cautious, squinted along the line, only to see a group of cudgel-wielding security police descend like vultures on another hobo as he jumped down from the train and commence to belabour him unmercifully. The rest of the cops, running parallel to the tracks in company with a pack of wolf-like canines, were coming closer every moment. Making a split-second decision she flung herself and her baggage out of the car and after rolling down a bank found herself in a ditch at the bottom. Getting to her feet she retrieved her bundle and fled, an armed bruiser close on her heels. Even as she ran she was aware of other fugitives doing the same thing, all trying to put as much distance between themselves and the railroad as possible. It was not long before the chase lost impetus and the bulls called their dogs to heel and, having checked the cars for any remaining illegal travellers, retreated towards some buildings standing beside a crossing gate. The engine let off steam, gave its usual ear-piercing scream and got under-way once more. Damask turned to watch as the train, among whose long string of wagons were coupled the two open trucks carrying the convicts, moved off down the line.

Once it was in motion, most of the freight-hoppers dispersed obliquely towards the highway that bisected the tracks at this point. Damask stood still, fighting back furious tears, determined not to give any onlooker in the surrounding dried-up landscape the satisfaction of seeing her cry. All the same she remained in the same spot for several minutes biting her lip and rapidly blinking her stinging eyes while swallowing hard. It wasn't fair, it bloody well wasn't fair that before she'd even had the chance to smuggle the newly acquired gun into Foxy's hands or even prove to him, once and for all, that he hadn't been deserted, she'd been forced into this precipitate abandonment. The distance between where she stood and the train was now increasing with every puff of the engine and clank of the attendant rolling stock.

"I'll not let this scare me off," she vowed, knitting her brows in a determined manner, "I'll follow the rails to the end of the line, then find out where he's been taken and get there under my own steam. I don't care how far it is or how long it takes me."

She skulked north-west for about half a mile until she was sure she was out of sight of the crossing, then returned to the tracks and began walking along the ties, gradually adjusting her stride to their spacing. And it was in this manner that she progressed over the next six days before the rails ran out and she came in sight of buffers, water-tanks, fuel dumps and low warehouses signalling that she had reached the terminus. Pretty soon she saw some trucks and cars standing in a siding which she recognised as the ones that had carried both herself and the prisoners away from Rockwell Springs; otherwise there was no sign of any recent activity, the place seemed deserted. Far over to the left beyond the huddle of buildings at the end of the line she noticed a grim featureless wall that was probably the exterior of the penitentiary that had been mentioned at the trial. Was Foxy there or had he already embarked on the second half of his journey towards those excavations where he would serve out his sentence? She felt both lonely and desperately in need of advice from someone who knew something about the country ahead of her. Also by this time she was reeling from hunger and so tired she was almost on the point of falling asleep on her feet, as she had barely allowed herself any time out, day or night, on her journey. It would soon become vital to get some proper rest.

At this juncture she stumbled round the corner of a storage shed and came upon one of those old-fashioned covered wagons which trains and automobiles were rapidly supplanting. But this was no ordinary conveyance: the wood of both chassis and wheels was highly varnished and bore a decorative incised pattern while the cover itself was dyed with a variety of garish colours. Within the front opening a small woman dressed all in black could barely be made out against the dark interior. It was not until she spoke that Damask realised anyone was there.

"Well gal," the little lady said, "how did you manage to get here ahead of the rest?"

"What d'you mean?"replied Damask, at the same time thinking that this person, apparently very old yet with bright beady eyes that belied her antiquity, reminded her of the Roma matriarch who at one time had told fortunes in Deep Hallow.

"Ain't you one of the gels I hired for the job across the Craiks?"

"I might be," said Damask cautiously.

"Well, is you or ain't you? I understood they was all acomin' by the weekly passenger train an' that's not due for half a day yet."

"You're going to the mining complex – the place where they're searching for this stuff – what's it called - cozerite or some such thing?"

"Sure, that's my destination. There's a drastic shortage of females in those parts. Even if I say so myself it can be pretty lucrative for those who've got the cojones to cash in. You're an attractive woman, even if you're not one of the ones I hired – why don't you come aboard?"

"How much do you pay?" asked a hard-nosed Damask.

"That depends on what sort of an impression you make. My best girls can earn up to twenty a day. I'm pretty generous."

Damask glanced back down the track and then in the other direction towards the increasingly broken country to the north. She put up a hand to stifle a yawn.

"There's a bed inside," suggested the woman, "if you want to catch up on some zees. I'm not goin' anywhere until the train gets here an' that won't be for a while yet."

It took only moments to decide. Damask put her foot on the step and swung herself up into the wagon while the procuress shifted sideways to allow her access, at the same time giving her an appraising smile. "Sweet dreams," she said.

Coming woozily back to consciousness a good while later Damask awoke with the impression that she was lying in the middle of a springtime field and being deafened by a raucous dawn chorus: the air was full of chirpings and twitterings. Then she realised that her world was lurching and swaying beneath her to such an extent that shc had to grab hold of the bunk on which she was lying to avoid being rolled out of bed. At the same time her nose was assailed by the smell of perspiration overlaid by numerous perfumes combining every note imaginable from floral to musk. It was only at this point that she opened her eyes to find that the wagon was rapidly filling with young and not so young women as more arrived every moment.

"Do you mind!" she groaned, lifting her head and pushing her hand through her hair, "I'm trying to sleep!" but no-one paid her the slightest attention. There was a mixture of laughter and petulant protests as the girls hauled their luggage on board and tried to find a corner they could call their own. Damask's presence was finally acknowledged as she was told to - "Shift up honey – you can't have that bunk all to yourself."

"Hey Ma!" someone else shouted, "how we s'posed to all fit in here? There ain't room to swing a mouse let alone a cat an' that's a fact. I gets the megrims real bad if I'm overcrowded."

"Ma Baker, Ma Baker!" chimed in a third, "tell the others they'll have to sit up on the box."

"We gotta make room for Mary-Lou," a fourth voice contributed, "coz you know how she's like to pass out or worse with the phobics, an', besides that, what about food? - we're all so hungry our stomachs are rubbin' against our backbones."

The little old lady in black turned round and fixed them with a gimlet eye.

"If y'all jest stop fussing and fighting y'all'll see there's a seat for every last one of yeez," she scolded, "and if you looks in the cupboard up at the front here you'll find something to eat. The sooner youse settle down the sooner we'll git started, an' the sooner we gits started the sooner we'll git where we're a-goin'."

This produced little effect but after a while the whole shebang jerked into motion and the protesters had perforce to anchor themselves somehow or end up on the floor. The vehicle, drawn by four bony nags, bumped and swayed along the trail and very soon not only Mary Lou but a number of the other girls, after having eaten, were taking it in turns to be sick over the tail-board of the wagon. Damask was not involved in this misery. She had always considered herself a pretty good sailor when taking trips in Dando's little dingy and now she had this confirmed as she found that the irregular motion was not a problem for her. Instead she fell into conversation with the other owners of strong stomachs who were feeling slightly smug at their superiority over their wussy sisters.

"Who are you doll?" enquired their spokesperson, a young woman of ample bosoms and several double chins, decked out like a carnival queen, "I've never seen you in or around any of the joy-houses in Belle City."

"No, that's not where I come from," replied Damask absent-mindedly before moving straight to her main concern. "That train," she said, pointing back down the track, "the one that got here before the one you were on – it had some prisoners on board. Do you know if they've been taken to the place where we're going?"

"No ideah - you'd better ask Ma – she knows near 'bout everything."

Damask clambered across legs and other body-parts until she reached the driving bench and looked down on the straining backs of the draught-horses. The madam was sitting perfectly upright gripping the reins. Damask bent forward and shouted her question into the woman's ear. Ma Baker turned, shot her a penetrating glance, then invited her to sit down beside her.

"I've bin wonderin' why you decided to come along," she said. "When I looked you over a second time I could tell you wasn't like one of my regular gels. I reckon someone you're sweet on – your intended, perhaps – was a convict on that train, ain't I right?"

Damask acknowledged that her surmise was substantially correct.

"Well – where would he be now? Possibly in Damwey Penitentiary but as you've decided to take up my invitation I believe you know he's not going to remain there."

Damask allowed that she had hit the nail on the head.

"In that case he'll be headin' 'cross the Craiks, same as us. They use the cons to do the dirty work at the excavations – life expectancy's not that great I guess. One of my clients is a trucker – he's the one who does the transporting. They'll get there well ahead of us, us havin' only four horse-powers as you c'n see. You're not the first girl I've come across who decided to folla her man, but when you gets there what are you expecting to find?"

Damask, cautious, confessed that she had not had time to think that far in advance.

"Well, have you heard of buying a prisoner out?"

"Can you do that?" the girl asked eagerly.

The little woman shook her head disparagingly.

"It's possible, but if you're thinking of raising money through the profession I c'n tell you that, on your own, you'd have to service the whole camp for nigh on ten years before you earned enough."

Damask decided to ask what would be expected of her when they reached the end of their journey. "Do we sleep with the prisoners?" she inquired.

"The prisoners!" Ma laughed mirthlessly, "where would be the profit in that? No, the prisoners make their own arrangements. It's the guards, the overseers, the soldiers and the scientific guys who'll be our customers. Think you're up for it?"

It was not long before the covered wagon left the plateau-lands behind and began to climb in grim earnest. Mother Baker brought out her whip and laid it on enthusiastically, encouraging her team in a shrill elderly treble while the horses strained and struggled, their hooves slipping on the uneven rocky surface. In the end she pulled up and stuck her head into the interior.

"Ok girls – here's where you gits off – gotta lighten the load."

She was met by a chorus of groans.

"Oh ma'am – please have mercy!"

"I'm really not well..."

"I ain't got the strength to take to ma feet..."

"If I hoof it I'm bound to git left behind..."

The old woman sniffed her contempt.

"Fresh air and a walk is just what you need – exercise will soon set y'all to rights. Come on wimin, show a leg!"

There was no gainsaying as far as their captain was concerned. A bevy of harlots were ejected onto the road, their finery crushed and stained, and a sorry procession shortly trailed in the wake of the lumbering wagon, its members breathing the chill mountain air. This did, in fact, cure their upset stomachs although most were presently panting as the slope steepened. That night only the feeblest were allowed to sleep under cover; most of the rest made the best of the space between the wagon wheels, while the toughest and strongest, among whom Damask numbered herself, lay down at some distance from the van and settled themselves on beds of heather with a covering of blankets that the old woman provided.

On the seventh day of their journey the road topped a rise and there in front of them lay a shallow declivity at the bottom of which were signs of habitation.

"Back on board gals," commanded Ma, "an' smarten yeez up. There's probably the opportunity to do some business in this neck of the woods if things are the same as when I was last here."

The settlement, viewed from above as they descended into one of its few streets, conveyed a raw unfinished impression; Damask got the feeling that it had not existed for very long and might well vanish in the near future if circumstances so ordered; such a place could surely not be their ultimate destination. Along its wide main thoroughfare were a number of saloons, three hotels, two stores, one farrier but, as far as she could tell, no private dwellings. The first store they came to had an array of tools for sale: picks, shovels, trowels, spades, crowbars, augers, such-like implements. There were also large pans and various items of camping gear. As they passed, a man was coming out of the door weighed down by a mass of equipment.

"Where are we?" Damask asked of their leader. "A few weeks ago I saw people on the train with this sort of stuff."

"Griffins Draw," explained Ma Baker. "It's here to serve the local settlers but also the independent prospectors that come searchin' for Xoserite on their own account. There's supposed to be a seam runnin' through the Craiks but no-one's turned up the mother-load so far – not even at the government run excavations on the other side of the range. They've discovered various alternative deposits but no Xoserite. If, by some remote chance, they find what they're looking for then all the other minerals will become redundant. Sooner or later though I reckon they're gonna decide that the whole enterprise is a waste of time an' then everything will come to a halt"

Ma Baker reined in her horses in front of the third hotel along the street – a rather flashy establishment that had an extension that looked as if it might be a dance-hall. She disappeared inside and was gone for some time before emerging and encouraging the girls to alight.

"He says he's got space for everyone as long as he gets his cut. It's on a fifty-fifty basis but I'll see you don't lose out. There'll be lots of people in town tomorrow for the monthly market and hoedown – plenty of dollars on the loose. Go an' sign in – you're on the first level – two to a room. If you gets a bite you'll have to take it in turns."

The hookers flocked through the door with Damask bringing up the rear and feeling somewhat extraneous. Ma Baker put out a restraining hand.

"I haven't actually asked you whether you've ever done this sort of thing before?" she said.

"Once," replied Damask.

"Well, you'd better come up to my room when we're settled. I think you need a few words of advice before starting out on your career as a pro. For instance what do you know about...?"

That evening the girls dolled themselves up to the nines in their best bibs and tuckers and lounged on couches in a snug next to the bar. Every so often a man would come through from the adjacent room and ask one of them, in a most old fashioned and courteous manner, to accompany him upstairs. Damask sat with the rest but, by midnight, no one had spoken to her and she got the impression that this neglect was not just due the fact that she was unable to compete with the others in the clothing and make-up department.

Throughout the next day a procession of utilitarian buckboards carrying couples, families and a host of single men, as well as a number of droves, invaded the town, the incomers drawn one and all by the rare chance, in this lonely mountainous region, to make and spend money in the temporary market as well as sampling the entertainment on offer. The hoedown was due to take place in the hotel's ballroom, the large shed-like building Damask had noticed on their arrival – evidently it did service during the rest of the month as a court house and auction venue. The thought of attending a dance took Damask's mind back to the grand balls she remembered from her childhood at Castle Dan. She had not cared over-much for such goings-on but now she was granted a vision of her brother: tall, dressed in black and brown velvet and groomed to perfection by Potto, stepping out with all the grace of a born dancer. Poor Dando – could he still be living in that sinister, smoke-filled shack in Bishops Hollow that she suspected had been having such a detrimental effect on his state of mind?

When the time arrived for the hop to begin the band struck up and most of Ma Baker's flock were soon invited onto the floor. Even Damask was whirled away by a taciturn young man who asked her for dance after dance before timidly enquiring if it was permissible to retire to one of the hotel bedrooms. She agreed after making clear that this was to be a purely businesslike arrangement: Ma Baker had told her that when it came to her particular firm she had strict rules about length of assignations and number of climaxes allowed per session: more than two and the johns were expected to pay double. It was as they rested after the first bout of love-making that Damask noticed a faint flickering glow outside the window. She brought this to the attention of her customer and to satisfy her he got up and went to look. The next moment he was galvanised into running, trouserless, out of the door and she heard him yell "FIRE!!" at the top of his voice as he tumbled down the stairs. The blaze had taken hold in storerooms and stables at the rear of the premises and, after everyone at the dance had rushed to extinguish the flames, it was discovered that the main casualties were two of Ma Baker's horses and the mobile bawdy-house with its gaudy cover which was left a blackened smoking skeleton. The next morning the little woman gathered her troop of good-time girls together and gave her verdict on their situation.

"Well chickens – I guess we're stranded here for the present, at least until I can find alternative transport. But don't despair, trade seems to be pretty brisk in this neck of the woods and Charlie's happy for us to stay on as long as we continue to make money. If y'all rally round and do your bit I don't think we'll fare too badly."

Most of the girls were amenable to this new set up but for Damask it meant complete frustration. Day followed day and her routine consisted of little more than lazing around trying to look alluring as she waited for somebody – anybody – to approach her and take the bait. Hardly anyone did. She began to hear murmurings from the other girls that she was not pulling her weight, causing her to wonder what it was about her that repelled the shabby, plebeian travellers and farmers that called at the hotel. Although she herself was thoroughly mystified, the ostracism she was experiencing would have come as no surprise to any uninvolved bystanders in the vicinity. They would have immediately understood that it was her self-possession, a perceived presumption of superiority, which was obviously the legacy of her patrician upbringing, that the prospective patrons found intimidating. Like brother like sister, she was not normally introspective and rarely gave any thought to what impression she was making. Now, however, she had the leisure to ask herself what was wrong and even to consider consulting the procuress on the matter, but as she was not intending to make prostitution her permanent career it seemed barely worth the effort. What bothered her more, now that Ma Baker seemed to have given up on the idea, was how she was to get to the mine-workings over the Craiks where she imagined Foxy was being set to work. Could she make it there on her own, she wondered. She consulted Charlie Seeburg, the owner of the hotel, concerning such a journey, but the advice she received proved discouraging. The route was physically demanding and also dangerous he told her: bears and mountain lions roamed the canyons and a lone traveller ran the risk of being attacked. There were also the remnants of aboriginal peoples - cave dwellers - clinging on in some of the more remote locations – they could pose a threat. Was anyone else planning to travel that way? Not as far as he knew; not in the near future.

With no solution to her problem in sight she sank into a despairing lethargy which was only slightly alleviated a few days later when her dancing partner of a week before reappeared and monopolised her for two whole evenings. Almost incidentally, in between bouts of copulation, she learnt that his name was Tyler, that he was a sheep-farmer in a small way and sold wool and mutton to various scattered communities. It sounded a tough life. After their second night together he abruptly disappeared without saying goodbye leaving her to endure another unproductive and embarrassing procession of days. It was as she sat slumped in a chair during the next weekend, so bored that she began to wish she had followed Dando's lead in cultivating a taste for reading, that she was summoned to the hotel foyer and found a red-faced, bare-headed Tyler standing waiting for her, fingering his hat. Nervously, with a jerk of his whole body, he indicated that they should go outside. His buckboard was parked in front of the hotel entrance and she gathered that he wanted to take her for a ride. Nothing loath she climbed up onto the box and they set out along the main street. It was when they were about half a mile outside the frontier town that she began to wonder where they were headed.

"Hey – slow down," she cried, grabbing hold of the reins and bringing the horse to a standstill, "what's the idea? Where are you taking me?"

The man again removed his hat and holding it upside-down on his lap bent his chin to his chest so that his mumbled reply was directed into the crown. Damask caught just one word – *Marry.* She stared at him in astonishment.

"Say that again," she urged.

His vocalisation was just as inaudible a second time around. She saw that she would have to be the one to put into words the substance of his response.

"Are you asking for my hand in marriage?" she said.

Still not looking at her he gave an abrupt nod.

"Well I'll be...!"

For a long spell that was all the reaction she could summon. Finally she managed to marshal her thoughts.

"Look here," she said, her mind leaping ahead, "this isn't the right way to go about a thing like that. If you're talking about weddings, some sort of priest has to be involved at the very least. And what about my stuff? That's back at the hotel – I'm not leaving without it. Come on – turn around – let's do the thing properly."

"Do you, Tyler Matherson, take this woman, Damask Danieldottir (a name she had trawled from the remembrance of a story Dando had once read her) to be your lawful wedded wife...?"

"Do you, Damask Danieldottir, take this man, Tyler Matherson, to be your lawful wedded husband...?"

To officiate at the ceremony they had co-opted an itinerant preacher who was passing through Griffins Draw at that time, despite the fact that he had evidently spent the whole of the previous evening in one of the saloons and was now snoring the effects away in the local bunk house. They dug him out of the sack and hurried him, slightly befuddled, across to the hotel foyer. The rest of the congregation that assembled to support them consisted of Ma Baker, her kindly disposed tarts, the somewhat bemused hotel staff and a few other residents who just happened to be present in the lounge. Damask felt uncertain about the legitimacy of the proceedings but no-one else appeared to be bothered. Shoes were thrown, the couple were encouraged to jump the broomstick and the newly-weds drove away amid a hail of rice.

Initially, as they departed, Damask was buoyed up on an intoxicating cloud of euphoria - after all she had never been married before. They had progressed several miles down the road before her immediate excitement wore off and she began to feel a certain queasiness at her impetuosity. She was struck by the thought that involving herself in matrimony – matrimony! - to this unknown young man was perhaps the very last thing she should have allowed to happen. All she had wanted over the last two weeks was to escape from Griffins Draw and cross the Craiks to the mine-workings beyond. But now, she had gotten herself embroiled in a relationship with all manner of ramifications and possible unforeseen consequences.

When will you learn to look before you leap, she inwardly scolded, adding for good measure: *that's what people have always told me – that I'm too impulsive by half. But, what the heck - anything's better than stewing in that god-awful hole – it looks like I'll just have to make the best of it. Maybe things'll turn out all right in the end if I keep my head and use a bit of nous.*

The crests of the mountains got higher, the land closed in around them, the trail beneath the buckboard's wheels became fainter and more precipitous. One minute they had walls on either side, the next they were teetering on the edge of a sheer drop with practically nothing between themselves and the possibility of plunging into a shadowy crevasse. Tyler spoke softly to his horse in order to calm it but then the next minute used the same reassuring pacifying tone to Damask with nothing to distinguish between the way he addressed animal and wife. She got the feeling that as a result of the ceremony they had recently shared he had incorporated her into his world, and now regarded her as just another appurtenance, no longer adjudged a separate individual. However, at least he seemed to have lost his shyness. He began to explain how his life was ordered and in what way she would be expected to fit into it as his partner and helpmeet.

"I'm off on the hills most days, keeping an eye on the free-range critters. You'll look after the ones in the corrals – not that there's many at this time of year but plenty during lambing. I've recently bought a range for the kitchen, the most up-to-date model. I git in supplies once a month but you'll be able to raise chickens and grow a lot of your own stuff in the garden; the soil's pretty good close to the cabin – that's why I chose that spot. I'll teach you how to shear. On the meat side I kill some of the stock myself – that's for customers within a radius of twenty miles that I c'n reach the same day – and some I deliver alive-alive-o where they have the facilities for slaughter. Twice a year I drive a hundred beasts over to Lake Bravo – they've got a standing order – an' I think I may be able to up that in the near future because they're expanding the correctional unit – more mouths to feed."

"Correctional unit?" said Damask, "do you mean the place where the prisoners are kept?"

"Yes, at the excavations. There's a lot of lags serving out their sentences there. By the way you'll have to take my place as you find it – no time to sweep or clean at the moment, or to mend clothes for that matter – and of course with..." He broke off abruptly as if having second thoughts about what he was about to say. Damask scarcely noticed.

"You go to the mine-workings!?" she exclaimed, "when?"

"Well, the next delivery falls in a couple of weeks time. Takes me five days to git there an' three to return."

"I'll come with you!"

Tyler turned and looked at her for the first time since leaving Griffins Draw. His face registered astonishment.

"What in heavens name for?" he said.

"Oh... no particular reason – just interest."

He did not reply immediately but shook his head in a conclusive sort of way. Eventually he muttered, "Not on," and followed this up with a slightly suspicious sidelong glance.

Several hours later they came upon a gentler landscape in the midst of the surrounding rocky fastness. Damask stared down at an expanse of rolling moorland covered in ling and turf, an ideal place for raising sheep. In the distance she made out a small isolated structure, a basic-looking cabin, representing just a single human footprint in this otherwise untouched wilderness.

"Got the land cheap," Tyler informed her, "previous owner went bust. It's taking a while to pay off the debt."

It was when they pulled up before the cabin that Damask received the shock of her life. As the buckboard came to a halt the front door opened and a boy of about ten stood there clutching some sort of ancient fire-arm while behind him three more children ranging in ages from eight down to around two peered shyly out. They were all wearing clothes that were dirty and in a shocking state of disrepair. Tyler took a deep breath and spoke in a voice that shook slightly:-

"Hi kids – back safely. Here's your new ma, just as I promised."

The children looked at Damask with grave suspicion. The man swung himself down and held out his hand to help her dismount but she ignored the gesture and stuck to her place.

"Just a frigging minute!" she exclaimed, "what's going on? Are these yours? You didn't tell me you'd got children!"

Tyler looked away. "If I hadda done," he said, "I di'n't think you'd 'a' come."

"You're darn right I wouldn't! Get up here. We need to talk."

For a few moments there was a stand-off; then saying, "Ok kids – back inside - I'm going to show your mom around," the man took his seat in the wagon and drove down to the nearest corral.

"They're good kids," he assured her, "no trouble. Ryan's the eldest – he looks after the other three - Ethan, Trey an' Gracie-Jordan - when I'm not here. Thought p'raps you'd be able to teach them their three Rs – never got no book-learnin' myself."

"Do you mean," replied Damask, "that you've been married before? What happened to their mother?"

"Gone."

"You mean she's dead?"

Tyler looked as if he might be about to concur but then, meeting her eye, lost his nerve and decided he could not dissemble.

"She lit out," he stated shamefaced, "went off last spring with a peddler who came by when I was up in the hills or so I was told. I traced them as far as Kamloops. I guess she couldn't take the isolation."

"So you've already got a wife." Damask gave vent to her indignation. "Looks like what you persuaded me into back at Griffins Draw was a complete farce - or do you belong to one of these sects that advocates polygamy?" (how many of the attendees at the ceremony had been au fait with the true situation she wondered?)

Even more sheepishly the man shook his head. Damask suddenly realised that she had discovered an escape route.

"Well," she said, "I'm afraid I can't agree to live in sin on a permanent basis - my standing in the local community would be severely affected. I'll stay here until you go north and then I'll come with you to this place – what did you call it? - Lake Bravo – and make my own arrangements to travel on."

She found it hard to maintain her stance of spurious anger and disguise her overwhelming jubilation at this turn of events.

Over the next two weeks, as she shared his lonely existence, Tyler also started to experience a certain relief that she was not going to become a permanent fixture in his life. Damask, he discovered, had little interest in housework, was a hopeless cook and knew nothing about vegetable growing or mending clothes. She got on quite well with the children but his aspiration that she might help to educate them came to nothing. In the long run there was only one thing he could definitely claim for her - that she was good in bed. So when, on the prearranged date, he rounded up a portion of his flock and set out to drive them to the mine workings across the mountains he was more than happy for her to accompany him.

Deep night – clear – starry.
Lie in my arms
As the trees whisper together.

Chapter twelve

"Stop! Stop! my darling – don't do it! Oh no my sweet one! Please – please listen – I be here my love – right beside you. It's her – she ha' made that magic-worker fog your thoughts an' bring you to sorrow. It's not real – none of it is real. Come away my love – please hear me – just this once..."

Dando fished in his pocket for the box of matches that he kept there for stove-lighting. He struck one, the last one in the box, and then, shutting his eyes, threw it forward. There was an instantaneous muffled explosion accompanied by a hot breath that scorched his face. He recoiled reflexively, aware of a savage glare through his eyelids emanating from about a foot in front of him. It took just a moment to register but longer to fully realise that, although he was only inches away and his body was soaked in inflammable liquid, the flames had not reached him. This was not what he had intended. Well, it was easy enough to remedy – one step forward, one small step, and he would be engulfed. He nerved himself to perform the fatal action but for some reason stayed rooted to the spot; just at that moment he was unable to make such a suicidal move – it was almost as if another were holding him back. He stood there in full view, gas can suspended from his fingers, while all around doors flew open and people came rushing out with buckets full of water and brooms at the ready; fire was a frequent hazard in Bishops Hollow. He would have remained like that, immobile, until someone found time to deal with him had not two small hands grabbed hold, hauled him into a nearby alley and from thence towards the periphery of the settlement.

"Come on!" cried a desperate Milly, "come on Lordship – you gotta get away. We've gotta 'ide – outside the town – come on – come on..."

"No," rasped Dando, resisting all the way and pointing across the tracks towards Rockwell Springs, "there... there..."

"Wot d'you mean?"

Dando gasped, opening and closing his mouth like a stranded octopus. At last he managed to croak, "Becca...!"

"Orl right," replied Milly frantically, "but come on luv, for goodness sake. I'll bring 'er."

When the little black girl returned about half an hour later with the owner of the doomed cabin in tow Dando, smelling strongly of gasoline, was sitting against a tree in the hideaway she had found for him, his head tipped backwards, his eyes closed, the very picture of prostration.

"I brought 'er," she announced.

The boy looked at them uncomprehendingly for a moment before clambering groggily to his feet. "Becca," he began, "I..." then faltered.

"I tol' 'er wot 'appened," butted in Milly hurriedly, "I tol' 'er that the 'ouse burnt down but you managed to escape."

"Thank the Lord for that," said the ex-star. "The ol' place ain't much of a loss. We can soon replace it. I suppose it was an accident just waiting to happen."

"B-but you don't understand," mumbled Dando, barely audible, "I did it."

"What do you mean pumpkin?"

"I-I started the fire."

"Oh my word – did something go wrong with the stove?"

"No – I did it. I meant to start it."

Now that the spell-bound shack was in the process of being reduced to dust and ashes the pall that had weighed so heavily on his mind over the last few weeks was beginning to lift and he started to think rationally once more; yet when he opened his mouth it seemed almost as if someone else were speaking through him.

"'Ee's not well," Milly hastened to interject. "I don't fink 'e understands wot 'e's sayin'."

"Yes I do understand!" croaked Dando.

A number of expressions chased themselves across Becca's face, beginning with shock and ending in deep concern. "Fire-starting!" she said at last. "Does anyone else know?"

"I fink they all do," replied Milly. "I fink they saw 'im. That's why I brought 'im 'ere," indicating the spinney within which they were concealed.

"Mercy!" exclaimed Becca. "Fire-starting's a lynching affair in Bishops Hollow! He's gotta light out for somewhere safe – they mustn't find him."

"But I've p-promised to wait for my master." The words were no longer meaningless.

"'Ee's gorn," said Milly, "that's wot I come to tell you – look at this," and she showed Dando an envelope with his name on it, explaining breathlessly and in a hurried gabble how it came to be in her possession.

It seemed that two days previously a boy had knocked at the door of sixty seven Camelback Avenue bearing a letter addressed to *The Lord Dan Addo, presently residing in the Quackenbush Homestead, Bishops Hollow.* He had passed it to Becca saying, "The old guy wants you to give it to the young guy in a week's time, not before."

"Who are you, honey?"Becca had replied, "I seem to know your face. Don't you work at Lenny's Stables over Macon way?"

The boy had agreed that yes he did and, when questioned further, told them that a while back Tallis had come to them looking for a horse. They had had nothing to offer apart from a young palomino that no-one up to that point had been able to break. Lenny had put forward a proposition: if the gentleman could tame this tearaway and accustom it to the saddle he could have it at a knock-down price. Tallis had accepted the challenge and after much patient work had at last managed to pacify the beast sufficiently to be allowed to climb on its back. Immediately he prepared to depart. Lenny, however, according to the boy, had been dubious: "I reckon by now I can tell a wrong-un," he had said to no-one in particular, shaking his hoary locks, "an' Paco's a candidate if ever I seed it. But if he wants to take the risk..." This gave Becca and Milly much food for thought – so that's what their wayfarer had been up to during his long absences!

They decided to go over to Macon to find out if what they had been told was the literal truth and to enquire which direction Tallis had taken. Dando realised that this concern for the knight was probably the reason they had not been present at Foxy's departure.

"We ast Lenny 'ow long ago it was since 'ee left," continued Milly, "an 'ee said it were the day before yesterday an' that 'ee woz travellin' north. When 'we came back we wondered wot to do wiv the letter. You," turning to Becca, " thought we ought to stick by wot the knight had said to the stable boy an' 'ang on to it for a week, but I weren't so sure. Anyway, I kept thinkin' about it. I noo," to Dando, "you'd want to see it as soon as possible. Las' night I couldn't sleep wiv worryin' so I got up an come down 'ere, an' it's a jolly good job I did too!" She stared at the young Glept in a horrified and accusatory manner, her lips trembling. In reply, pale-faced, he held out his hand for the missive. The two females stood by silently as he opened it and perused the contents. As he did so they were shocked to see tears begin to run down his cheeks and this immediately caused Milly to weep in sympathy although she had no idea why he was so distressed.

"What is it, honey chil'," asked a concerned Becca and wordlessly he passed her the piece of paper. This is what the show-girl read out:- *My dear boy, by the time you get this I will be several days down the road, having once more taken up the challenge that I have neglected for far too long. I realise now that it would have been more fortunate for you if you had never known of my existence. Against my better judgement I involved you in the toils of a quest that should have remained my own concern entirely and as a result you have suffered grievously. But maybe it is not too late to mend matters. I have already released you from your oath, now I give you your life back. Do not waste it as I have done. Forget about me, forget about the Key, and find some kind of lasting happiness if you can. For my own part I will always keep you in my heart. With my most fervent gratitude for services rendered – your friend - Tallisand of the Guardians.*

There was a long silence until Becca again exclaimed, "Mercy!" under her breath.

Milly looked wonderingly at Dando. "Oh Lordship," she said, "you're free."

"No!" replied Dando, angrily wiping his eyes, "I'm not! How can I let him go off on his own like that? How will he manage? He's still not well – even if he won't admit it."

Milly did not respond but her expression suggested that she knew of someone much closer to home that such a statement could apply to.

"Well," said Becca, "I can't bring myself to believe you deliberately set light to the cabin unless you were having some sort of brainstorm or somesuch but, whether you did or no, you've surely gotta get outa here - it ain't safe for you to stay a moment longer. But how? Train or bus would be risky – someone might see you boarding." She thought for a minute. "What you could do with is a car or a bike, - Clark's motorbike! - How about that? It's up at the farm."

"You gave it to Foxy," Milly reminded her.

"Well, he won't be wanting it where he's gone, poor guy."

"Actually, Foxy passed it on to me," admitted Dando, "but I don't know how to work it."

Becca looked at him in surprise. "He gave it to you? Lan's sakes alive! Why did he do that I wonder?"

"He said he thought I might need it," replied Dando rather coldly.

"Well I can show you the basics honey. Come on – it's only just down the road."

Dando hesitated, looking in the direction of Rockwell Springs.

"If I'm going after Master Tallisand I must take Horry with me," he said. Both women were dismayed at this idea.

"Oh no, honey," Becca assured him, "he's quite happy where he is – I'll look after him for you."

The young man's mouth set in a thin obstinate line and his dark eyes flashed with determination in his tired and anxiety-ravaged face.

"I'm his father," he said, "he's my son. If I follow Tallis I may never pass this way again. He's got to come."

Becca lowered her voice. "You know he's not right. I took him to Mother Eulalie and she said that, unless that juju-man dies, or unless he lifts the spell, our little boy'll only live a quarter of the years that a normal person would, if that."

"All the more reason."

The showgirl frowned in frustration but, turning to Milly, instructed her to, "Go and fetch Horace love. Say he can have a ride on the motorbike. And bring clothes and food and water for washing; I think there's still some of Clark's stuff in my bedroom cupboard. I've got to help this crazy guy clean up and show him how not to kill hisself."

Inside the barn Dando's first attempt at mastering the bike resulted in his shooting straight into a pile of straw, which at least provided a soft landing. On the second attempt he never moved at all but slowly keeled over sideways. Patiently Becca explained about changing gear, about the clutch and the throttle and even gave a demonstration. "Takes me back," she said wistfully. Gradually he began to get the hang of the super-charged machine, finding, to his surprise, that his prosthesis was not a great hindrance, and by the time Milly returned with Horry and a couple of his pals who had decided to come and see their friend off on his journey he felt more or less in control. Both he and Becca were surprised to realise that the girl was wearing a back-pack and sporting similar clothing to the protective gear she was bringing for Dando's use. She also had a little passenger: Meena was clinging to her shoulder.

"I'm comin' wiv you," she told the boy, responding to his puzzled expression, "you don't fink I'd let you go alone!"

"What!? But you can't Milly."

"O' course I can. How do you fink you'd manage wiv Horry all by yourself? I c'n sit on the back like Damask did an' 'old 'im between us; Meena c'n go in the pannier."

("I wanna ride - I wanna ride on the mo'bike!" Horry shrilled.)

"But I don't know where I'll end up – maybe the ends of the earth..."

"Then I'll be wiv you on that endless journey – there's nowhere else I'd rather be."

Dando sighed and his body relaxed in weary defeat.

"Have it your own way," he muttered.

Donning Clark's old leathers which were paradoxically quite a good fit he discarded the ancient military greatcoat to which he was so attached. He did this with enormous regret but it just would not have been a practical garment for motorbike riding. As the four disparate characters prepared to depart they were joined by an unexpected fifth. Ralph appeared and took up a position by the back wheel. Milly looked down at him in surprise. "So, you're comin' too are you, mate?" she said, "I fort you'd gone wiv the knight." At this point Dando produced a well-stuffed wallet and attempted to hand it to Becca. "For the cabin," he said. Becca pushed it away.

"Oh no, my dear. You're going to need every cent of that I reckon. I didn't keep the restaurant's takings in my safe at the Magnolias through all your troubles for them to end up with me."

"But I owe you..."

"Honey chil' – I've got my boys back – despite losing their property they're pretty well loaded. Like a lot of clever people they invested their money away from the coast because of certain indications that things weren't quite right in Ry-Town, and now it's shooting up in value. They'll see I lack for nothing. As for the cabin – it's been empty a long while now - I reckon it was time for it to go. Even though it's no longer there, precious memories can't be destroyed."

Her advice was to follow a rough track from the farm that would eventually lead to the main highway. "By then you should be well away from prying eyes," she told him. "After that the road keeps close to the railroad tracks until you get to Harrisburg. Then you can either go east to Belle City or north-west to Damwey across the plains."

"Not due north?"

"The Great Lake's in the way."

"Perhaps we could take a boat."

Speech dried up. There was so much more to say but no words left with which to say it. Dando broke the silence: "T-time to go," he barked abruptly, his eyes again suspiciously moist – since escaping the fire he had been feeling like weeping every time his mood darkened. Meanwhile he straddled the machine and then indicated the pillion seat behind him, ordering Milly aboard in a peremptory manner: "Get on if you're coming and Becca'll hand you Horry."

Once his passengers were in place he fired and revved the engine. The show-girl raised her hand while Horry's two little friends waved enthusiastically. Dando called goodbye then let in the clutch far too fast so that the bike practically leapt into the air as it took off down the road, its roar drowning out any further communication. A panicky glance in his rear-view mirror revealed three hard-to-distinguish figures rapidly dwindling away to nothing. It had been a very unsatisfactory parting and as he bade farewell to that well-intentioned and forgiving woman, leaving her half obscured in dust, his remorse redoubled in intensity.

Gammadion the wizard, still wearing the curious piece of jewellery around his neck that took the shape of a silver manikin, stood before the burnt-out shack in Bishop's Hollow and rejoiced. A number of passers-by also paused to survey the smoking, stinking ruin and it was to one of these that he feigned concern over the fate of the occupant.

"A real tragedy," he sympathised, "and so young, so young. But insanity is no respecter of age."

The local – a calloused-handed working man - stared at him blankly.

"I don't get ya bonzo," he said, "folks round here rarely waste much sympathy on fire-starters, the only regret we have is that he didn't pay for his crime. It was sheer luck that we managed to stop it spreading."

"Not pay for his crime? I thought he died in the fire?"

"Well, we all saw him standing there at the start, with flames all around, an' we reckoned he'd bought it. We fought like the dickens to get things under control, but afterwards when we looked for a body we found absolutely nothing and no-one has seen hide nor hair of him since."

"No remains? Are you sure?"

"You're welcome to look for yourself fella, but I promise you you'll draw a blank."

Gammadion ducked away into an adjacent passage and hastened to shake the dust of Bishop's Hollow from his feet. Could it be true? Had the reprobate managed to escape yet again? He had been so certain that this time his scheme would work. And she – she had been relying on him. He had assured her that he knew how to rid her of her bête-noire. What could he do now to make up for his failure and avoid retribution? If the boy had survived then he would be free, once more, to resume his search for the Object-of-Power, while at the same time he himself was no nearer to discovering where it had been taken. All he knew was that it must still exist somewhere because his longevity depended on its survival and if it had been destroyed he would be dead by now. He had been so deliriously happy after she had spoken to him because she had offered to help him in his search once he had disposed of the troublemaker, but now he would have to begin again right from the start and he was tired... so tired...

It was a rough ride on the dirt track for the first several miles and Dando learnt a lot about handling the bike as he negotiated the uneven surface, changing gear frequently. Once they reached the highway he could afford to put on a little bit of speed but had to be careful not to outpace Ralph who was running alongside. Every so often he brought the vehicle to a halt so that the dog could rest and recover. Meena the cat, huddled in one of the saddlebags on top of a pile of underclothes, had an easier time of it. Milly leant her cheek against Dando's back, squeezing Horry between her loins and the young man's lower torso. The little boy did not object; he was cosy in that position and the noise and hypnotic motion soon rocked him to sleep. Eventually the day drew to a close.

They stopped at a small settlement and looked around for somewhere to stay. The search was harder than they had anticipated despite Dando's willingness to pay whatever charge was required. It was made clear at most of the houses they tried that although he and Horry were welcome, Milly's accommodation was a different matter entirely. In the end, at the last place they called at, they had to pretend that she was a servant, Horry's nanny, and even then she was required to sleep in some kind of garden shed detached from the main building. When something similar happened on three successive nights Dando became increasingly angry. Milly tried to calm him down, saying it did not bother her where she slept, but his nerves were raw, almost at breaking point, and she began to fear he would do something stupid and get them all into trouble. It was at this juncture that they met the prospector along the road.

Traffic on the north-bound route was light for the most part and mainly local, but occasionally they came across travellers on foot, their dusty and worn-down appearance suggesting they had been slogging it for some time. One or two stuck out their thumbs as they passed, gazing after them hopefully, though heaven knows how these hobos thought they were going to fit onto a motorbike that was already over supplied with passengers. This particular man, however, was walking towards them from the opposite direction and as they approached he held out his hand in an authoritative manner. Dando came to a halt – it was time, anyway, to give the faithful Ralph a breather - and waited to hear what the traveller had to say . The man unloaded an enormous knapsack from his back bristling with tools and impedimenta and let it fall at his feet.

"Here you are," he announced bitterly, "going cheap: pickaxe, shovel, crowbar, pan – all yours for twenty bucks – though why you should want them beats me. Digging for profit's a mug's game. This Xoserite don't exist, that's what I've decided, an' those deluded fools that are still looking for it are on a hiding to nothing. I'm heading back 'crorst the Middle Sea, war or no war."

The bike-riders, curious, examined his kit.

"What's that?" asked Dando, indicating a large greenish bag, very much stained.

"The tent? - You want the tent? Four dollars, take it or leave it."

"How big is it?"

"Big enough for three."

"Can I have a look?"

Having examined components which when assembled would have formed a sort of miniature yurt Dando paid the asking price, at the same time declining the implements with thanks. The prospector manqué gloomily shouldered his pack once more and, with a few more dejected comments ("I handed over my claim to a young panhandler – much good it'll do him, poor fool – he'll end up like the rest of us, dead in the water, mark my words"), limped off along the road.

"Now we're self-sufficient," declared Dando, sounding both aggrieved and justified at the same time.

That evening they found a suitably secluded site and, with some difficulty, he and Milly erected the tent between them. Then the young man invited his companions to enter but declined to join them. "I'll sleep out here," he said, "it's warm enough."

In fact the nights were becoming unpleasantly sultry while during the day the country round about baked in steadily rising temperatures. In these latitudes it looked as if it had not rained for weeks.

"I fort it woz supposed to get colder when you went norf not hotter," Milly complained. She was worrying all the time about Dando's mental and physical health and kept him under constant surveillance. At night, through the canvas wall, she often heard him coughing and once, when he seemed to have been tossing and turning restlessly for hours, she ventured to his side. "Are you 'urtin'?" she asked anxiously.

"No," he replied shortly.

"Can't you sleep?"

"Course I can't sleep if you come and ask stupid questions – I'm all right – leave me alone."

She returned to her bed but with none of her uneasiness allayed.

At each town or village they came to they asked if anyone had seen an elderly man on a gold and white horse but the answer they were given was invariably in the negative.

"I know he's got his compass to help him," pondered a worried Dando. "and it probably works ok now he's away from big buildings. On a horse he wouldn't have to stick to the road, he would be able to go straight across country. What I'm afraid of is we might get ahead of him without realising it. We could do with a map."

This was quite a long speech for the Glept to employ at this stage of their journey. Most of the time he remained despondently taciturn, answering a concerned Milly in monosyllables if at all, which meant she could not help but be aware of his misery. Horry on the other hand was cheerfully voluble, thoroughly enjoying this unexpected holiday and passing comments on everything that caught his eye. Even at night when Milly put him to bed with a folded blanket beneath him to cushion the hardness of the ground he continued to chatter.

"I seed a chooka train wiv one, two, three, five carriages t'day. The chooka train an' us had a race – we beat the chooka train! Did you see the chooka train?"

There was a pause as if he were waiting for a reply from some third party.

“Meena came outa her bag. She came an sat on my lap. Daddy said she had to go back in her bag – he said she might fall off... Yes, I did, cos daddy was cross, I put her back but she wouldn't stay. Did you see the baby deer? I went to have a wee-wee by the side of the road an' a baby deer was there havin' a drink from a pond. I don't know where his mummy was. You're my mummy aren't you? My Da thinks you're dead. I tol' him you weren't loads of times but he says for me to be quiet. You aren't dead are you...? Why can't daddy see you...? Did you see the two doggies in the town we drove through? One was getting' on top of the other an' the one underneath was trying to bite the one on top...” and so-on night after night until Milly begged him to stop.

“But my mummy comes an' talks to me when I go to bed an' so I talks back to her.”

“Well talk to 'er in your 'ead, mate – I'm sure she'll 'ear you. I don't think she'd want you to keep people awake.”

When the little boy had finally dropped off Milly lay staring up into the tent roof. Eventually, feeling extremely foolish, she cleared her throat and spoke into the dimness.

“Horry's mum - Lordship's sweet'eart – are you really there? Annie – that's 'is name for you isn't it? 'Ee's very sad now cos of everythin' wot's 'appened an' I'm pretty sure the magic man put a spell on the buildin' 'ee woz in which got inside 'is 'ead so that it still isn't right. I can't do nuffink on my own but we could 'elp 'im if we got together. He tol' me once about the time when one of them invisible ones took over 'is body an' you rescued 'im. Could you do that now? - could you take someone over like that? Praps you could use me to show yourself to 'im? If 'ee knowed you woz alive I fink he'd be 'appy again.”

As they approached the northern margins of the cultivated land they began to come across similar sights to those they had gotten accustomed to in impoverished and war-torn Terratenebra, namely unattended fields and abandoned dwellings. The soil here was parched and the crops irretrievably shrivelled, of use neither to gods nor men. Many local farmers appeared to have fled precipitously, trying to outpace the famine, leaving nothing behind but a few items of furniture and the occasional forgotten possession in their deserted houses. Those that remained gazed at the travellers hollow-eyed and stretch-lipped as they passed, their apathetic children pitifully thin with swollen bellies.

"It makes me feel rotten to see 'em," said Milly, "when we're pretty well supplied. I feel we oughta give 'em sompfink."

"I know what you mean," agreed Dando, " but the little we could offer wouldn't do them any good in the long run and if we did that we'd soon be starving too and no use to anyone. We've got to make our stuff last out until we get to Harrisburg."

"At least wiv orl these empty 'ouses we c'n stay under a roof for a change."

A lot of the dwellings appeared to have been ransacked after the owners' departure so entry was not a problem; nevertheless Dando and Milly could not shake off the feeling that they were trespassing when they appropriated one for a few hours, however strong the temptation to take a break from camping. On one particular evening, once they had consumed their fairly meagre supper, Dando went to the room he had chosen for his solitary rest. He looked at the grubby, dusty mattress on the iron bedstead and felt reluctant to commit himself to it. He knew what would ensue during the long reaches of the night: stretches of pain-filled wakefulness alternating with the occasional nightmare-haunted doze. Instead he sat in a reasonably comfortable chair by the door and, because he had not expected to, immediately fell asleep.

He was awoken by an awareness of someone busy about his head as they tied a blindfold round his eyes. Stiff with suspicion he raised his hand to snatch it away only to be halted by a voice from the past that temporally turned him to ice.

"***No – don' 'ee peek my love,"*** it said in those oh-so-familiar tones that had never failed to move him, ***"we're going to play a game. There be no harm in it – no harm at all."***

Almost without thinking he caught hold of a slender wrist, obviously feminine, and held it to his cheek while his heart turned somersaults in his breast.

"Is that you? N-no it can't be. Annie – i-is it really you?"

He pulled the hand close to his mouth and buried his lips in the palm. It twisted out of his grasp but then whoever owned it moved round to the front and, taking his hands in hers, tugged him out of the chair and guided him towards the bed.

"***There be nothing to fear, my bonny lad."*** The beloved voice spoke from only inches away and he felt a warm exhalation on his face. ***"There be no harm – come an' lie wi' me."***

He obeyed as if in a dream, (but this was no dream!), subsiding onto the bed, his limbs temporarily liquidising, while someone so well known to him that they shared a part of his soul joined him there, crouching above him, kissing his face and reaching inside his clothing to caress him. Automatically he responded, touching the well known contours of an unclothed body, sensing her wealth of hair feather-light against his skin, rediscovering the shape of her, the taste and smell of her until, at last, his hand came to rest between her thighs and he discovered she was aroused and ready for sex.

"D-do you want me to, Annie?" he whispered into the darkness.

"***Yes my love, yes – this is how it was meant to be.***"

He loosened his belt and unzipped his fly, releasing his member which was already stiff with desire, then took her into his arms, reversing their positions so that he was on top. She rose to meet him, giving a small moan of welcome as he thrust into her, while he laughed and wept and gasped for breath all at the same time.

"Annie! Annie!" he cried.

Afterwards he must have slipped into a deep healing sleep that lasted several hours because when eventually he came to himself he was not sure if he was alone or whether the one with whom he had earlier been united was still beside him. He reached across and discovered warm flesh, placing his hand beneath a breast. He felt a heart beat and also the soft regular breathing of a familiar body – it seemed she was with him yet - but something had changed; his more sensitive mental feelers told him that things were profoundly different and out of kilter. Flouting the prohibition that she had imposed at the start of their interaction he put his hand to the blindfold that was still tied tightly around his head, tore it off and saw... Milly!

The shock propelled him out of the room, out of the house. He ran several yards until his trousers ended up tangled round his ankles and he measured his length on the ground.

It was much, much later and dawn was breaking before he plucked up the courage to go back inside; to enter the room where the unbelievable had happened. Milly was still there, naked, fast asleep on the bed, mouth slightly open, hands by her sides, relaxed fingers curled inward like the petals of a half-opened flower. In this posture she looked little different from that twelve or thirteen year old child he had encountered nearly four years earlier in a Gateway brothel. He knelt down beside her and, leaning forward, breathed in her body odour. Here was confirmation of the miraculous: Milly's natural fragrance was exotically spicy, entirely distinct from that of the other who had apparently been present at the commencement of the night. After a while he rose, found a bedspread in a cupboard and used it to cover her. But the touch of the cloth brought her partially awake and she stretched luxuriously looking up at him in drowsy contentment.

"Lordship," she mumbled sleepily, and then, "did it work?" She felt around under the spread seeming to sound out her body section by section until a sudden grimace suggested she had come upon a certain part that was somewhat tender. "Yes it did," she said, frowning disapprovingly, "Blimey - I fink it did."

Dando drew in his breath sharply, forced to face up to astounding implications.

"Milly!" he exclaimed incredulously, "w-what have you made me do?"

"Ain't you 'appy?" Her eyes widened in consternation at his reaction. "I fort you'd be so 'appy if I... if she..."

Dando turned away. Suddenly all he yearned for was solitude to allow himself time to work out what he was feeling. His thoughts were in turmoil, his mind a total confusion. But here was Milly needing a response and needing it now.

"H-how did you make it happen?" he asked in a strained voice. "Tell me about it right from the start."

Milly sat up in bed and pulled the coverlet around her.

"It woz the nipper wot got me goin'," she complied, pointing towards the room where Horry was lying asleep, "every night 'ee carries on sompthin' chronic before 'ee goes shut-eye – I 'spect you've 'eard 'im. 'Ee says 'ee's talkin' to 'is ma. Then I got this idea from wot you tol' me 'appened up at the oracle place, about how these people who don' 'ave no solid bodies – people like 'er in the valley an' 'im up in the sky an' also your sweet'eart an' 'er da – people like that c'n go inside uver people's bodies if they wants to. I fort that if she used my body she could let you know she woz still around. I spoke to 'er but di'n't 'ear nuffink back until, when I put 'im to bed a few nights later, Horry said that she'd tol' 'im she would come to me when I woz out cold an' 'ave a go. She did come didn't she?"

"Don't you remember anything?"

"Not a fing."

"It was the same for me that time at Toymerle."

Dando kneaded his forehead and took several deep breaths. His feelings of fear and perturbation were slowly beginning to dissipate leaving him light and almost stupid with wonder.

"She did come," he said slowly, "your idea worked. She was here, although only present to certain of my senses."

"An' 'as it made you 'appy?"

"Well it's bloody hard to accept that it actually happened at all, an' you shouldn't have done it, but yes, I think I know now she's really still alive as people have been telling me for ages. I can't try an' pretend any longer although apart from that one night at Sahwain I'm not able to see her for myself. Horry sees her I think and also a few other people can – the woman in the temple for instance. It gives me hope that one day I may also... that we may..."

"An' does it make you 'appy?"

He did not trust himself to speak further but gave the briefest of nods, at the same time reaching out to squeeze the young girl's hand. He was well aware that he had a lot more to thank her for than she realised. Those other demons that had been plaguing him for months since he had suffered abuse on the other side of the Middle Sea had been stripped of most of their power now that he knew he was still capable of normal physical relations.

From this point on when they camped Dando no longer exiled himself from the tent but slept within alongside Horry and Milly. Also, when taking advantage of one of the abandoned houses, if they found only a double bed in situ he and Milly would share it. Gradually it came to pass that, for companionship, they slept together even when other accommodation was available. All the same they observed strict propriety, dressing and undressing separately and avoiding physical contact as much as possible: they were as shy with one another as two travelling salesmen forced to share a room in an overcrowded motel. But things were not destined to continue in this manner. One day very early in the morning Milly awoke to find herself in a sleeping Dando's embrace. How she had gotten there she had no idea, but, held by the one she loved above all others, she felt completely safe for the very first time in her short but troubled life. After a while Dando also stirred and, becoming aware of the situation, reacted with an almost silent gulp. As he woke fully he remembered that a similar thing had happened to him when he and Annie were children. They had been lying asleep, side by side, on the grass outside the abandoned cottage and had come back to consciousness with their arms around each other; it had been one of the things that had made him realise, even though still pre-pubertal, that he was already in love and therefore committed. Now, over the next half hour he and Milly remained in the same position, not daring to say a word for fear of having to confront the implications of this new state of affairs.

It was when they reached Harrisburg and decided that they had enough money in hand to stay at a guest house for a few nights that Dando found the courage to suggest that his and the girl's relationship should be put on a more conventional footing.

"Milly," he said after she had crept into his bed (they had started the night in separate rooms for propriety's sake), "you did me a great service a while back, something far beyond what I deserved, and now I'd like to do something in return. Is it true - do you like me a little bit more than just as a friend?"

The girl smiled up at him, her answer plain to see in her glowing eyes.

"Well, I sort of feel the same way about you. When two people like each other like that it usually ends up with... well you know what I mean."

The light went out of Milly's face as it twisted into a grimace.

"You mean it ends up with fucking," she said in disgust.

"Don't call it that."

"Well that's wot it is – fucking – just ruddy fucking."

Dando gazed at her sadly. It was brought home to him as never before how seriously she had been traumatised when just a child.

"You know Milly," he said quietly, "what was done to you in Gateway – that was all wrong – very badly wrong. But it doesn't have to be like that. It can be beautiful, this fucking as you call it, though I'd rather call it making love. What I had with Annie..." He trailed off overcome with emotion. Milly, with a quick change of mood, looked up sympathetically, at the same time stroking one of his mutilated hands, now berry-brown from the constant sunshine.

"I unner'stand," she said.

Dando made a concerted effort to pull himself together and put his point across.

"What you call fucking is when you feel most alive Milly – it's how our bodies were meant to be used. If you do it of your own free will with someone you care for... I really can't explain..."

"Would it make you 'appy if we did it?"

"I think it might make both of us happy."

"But wot about 'er?"

Dando stayed quiet for a long time. At last he said, "She'll understand."

Milly was silent in her turn until eventually she offered her compliance in a very small voice. "Orl right, but don' be rough."

And so they made love and, remembering what he had learnt during his and Ann's fateful coupling at Gweek, he was very gentle and stopped when she asked and continued only when she was good and ready until, as the climax approached, she began to urge him on. Both participated in a wild sensual crescendo which ended in a shared ecstatic orgasm and, as she came, maybe for the first time in her young life, she gave a great crow of triumph and raked his back with her nails in an ecstasy of sexual pleasure. He rolled to one side, withdrawing from her, trembling slightly.

"You know Milly," he said wincing a little, his words accompanied by a wry, rather rueful smile, "I think you've got the picture. I think you've taken on board what I was trying to say."

Horry was digging holes in the greyish sand of Harrisburg's lakeside beach. Dando and Milly, holding hands, sat looking out to – no not to sea – although you could have been forgiven for thinking that that was the case as the water stretched all the way to the horizon. Only the lack of salt in the air and the minuscule size of the waves that lapped the shore gave any clue that this was not a marine environment.

"Do you think there's such a thing as a livery stables round here?" pondered Dando, "that's where he would have gone if he wasn't just passing through - I'm referring to Tallis. You don't see many horses in this part of the world."

"You mean like where we left Carolus and Mollyblobs in Drossi?" answered Milly. "We could ask Mrs Greening, she puts up the boys from the round-ups when they comes into town though she says it doesn't 'appen much now as she's 'ad to raise 'er prices."

She had become aware, when talking to their landlady, that even this prosperous northern town with its ready supply of water was starting to suffer from the effects of the drought that had the hinterland in its grip. "The lake levels have never been so low," she was told.

Acting on advice, they found what they were looking for on the west side of the built-up area: a businesslike little concern, and with it came some information that caused them enormous gratification.

"I remember the mount more'n I do the rider," the head groom explained when he had learnt what they were after and taken them into his office. "A white and gold palomino; hard to forget; here we all reckoned that that hoss came straight from the Dark Brother's realm; none of us could have the mastery of him apart from the one who brought him in an' I guess even he was half afraid of him. I told him he was playing with fire but I don't think that was something he wanted to hear. They left about a week ago. Where was he going?

Well, when he lit out he took the road west. That's the one that ends at Damwey up on the plains. After that it's just rough trails as far as the Craiks. He said something I didn't really understand - that he needed to go west in order to get back onto the correct northern bearing. Do you know what he meant by that?"

"Have you got a map?" asked Dando eagerly, "one that shows the land north and south of the Middle Sea?"

"You mean the Tethys? Well, it just so happens you're in luck – I use one to plan my holidays – I like a bit of boating when I've got time to spare, an' not just on our local lake."

He found a large folded sheet in his desk and spread it out.

"Look Milly," said the boy after he had puzzled over it for some time, "there's the Southern Continent and there's Pickwah, only they call it Pickery on this map. It must be Pickwah because there's Osh a bit further along, only they call it Oshery. Do you remember I told you about when we came through the mountains and it was all snowy. We couldn't go over the high pass that would have taken us to Pickwah – we had to go over a lower one that eventually brought us down to Gweek..." He stopped abruptly and swallowed a couple of times before taking a deep breath and continuing. "Master Tallisand was quite upset that he couldn't keep going straight north and then of course he got ill and Foxy took him further east and after that we all ended up in Drossi. Well look here – do you see - if we'd managed to get to Pickwah and had then put to sea there, we would have reached Armornia round about this area and then if we'd carried on north, dead north, the route would have brought us to this Damwey place." His finger by this time was at the top of the map.

"Did you say there were mountains higher up?" he asked the groom.

"Yes, at the edge of the prairies."

"And then what?"

"Another lake I believe and mines that are being run by the government. They're starting to open them up to look for this Xoserite stuff. When they find it we're all going to be living in the lap of luxury so they say. But I guess that's a long way off now after what happened down on the coast."

"Do you see, Milly," cried a triumphant Dando, "Damwey is where Tallis is intending to go and we must go after him and catch him up before... before..." He stumbled, not sure what he had been meaning to say.

They filled the tanks *full of this gas-i-leen,* both the main and the spare, called a reluctant Horry away from his latest group of friends and set out. Soon after starting they passed through the town of Sarnia at the west end of the Great Lake following which the road began to climb and continued to do so for several miles before reaching level ground. After topping the ascent they found themselves crossing an apparently endless plateau so that they were constantly at the centre of an unchanging disk whose rim was the circling horizon.

It's even bigger and flatter than the Levels, was Milly's thought.

Although they were travelling at an average of twenty miles an hour or thereabouts, for all the difference their progress made to the surrounding scenery they might as well have been standing still. The world was reduced to two colours: brown and white: brown for the baked earth and sere grass beneath them and white for the burning bowl above. The only variation in this monotony were the balls of tumbleweed bowling along to left and right before a steadily rising wind.

Just as they began to wonder if the plains were entirely uninhabited and that they were going to have to sleep out in the open with nowhere to replenish their stocks of fuel, food and water they saw a mirage of man-made structures materialise in the distance and, a little later, drove into a tiny settlement consisting of two rows of false-fronted timber buildings facing each other across a wide – very wide – unmade roadway.

"Diner thattaway – flop-house t'other end," advised a laconic character gesturing wearily over his shoulder when they asked about places to eat and sleep. The accommodation was utterly basic - palliasses on the floor - the food limited and the prices astronomical but they were just grateful to have walls once more around them to protect them from the gale that had arisen and was growing stronger hour by unchanging hour. The next day they stayed put, visibility outside having been reduced to a few feet by the fine dry powder that had been lifted into the air. Twenty-four hours later the wind dropped and they were able to continue. And so the pattern of their days was set as they travelled first west and then north-west towards the ancient prairie capital of Damwey.

Dando and Milly's relationship was in its infancy and they were both feeling their way cautiously forward. The girl, after suffering years of ill treatment, had to get used to physical contact that was in no way threatening while Dando occasionally allowed himself to be cosseted without displaying his usual irritation. Among the concessions he made was to take the cough syrup that she purchased from a Harrisburg drug-store and to explain, when she expressed concern, how to help him, as Jack had done, by massaging the cramps away that still plagued him nearly every night. She also took great delight in attending to his hair and nails. Between them, however, stood the thought of the third who might be observing even their most intimate moments so that when they made love it usually started in an extremely tentative manner almost as if they had to ask permission before beginning.

"Why do you do all this for me Milly?" asked Dando eventually when, from some place they passed through, she conjured up a pot of salve and administered it each day after discovering that his stump was suffering from chafing.

"Cos I loves yer," she answered bluntly, "I knows you can't love me."

Dando looked somewhat shaken by this bald statement but attempted to correct it.

"That's not true," he said. "I spose you're thinking of Annie. Annie and I grew up together – she was like another part of me. When I thought she's gone it was as if that other half had died and I would never be whole again. I do love other people – very much - only it's a different kind of love from what I had – have – with Annie."

"But although you said you woz 'appy, you're still sad cos you can't see 'er."

"Of course."

"I wish I could make it so's you could see 'er."

Whenever the wind rose visibility became limited and they had to practically feel their way forward. Sometimes they passed groups of bony-looking cattle, dimly observed, standing with lowered heads, tails towards the gale.

"'Ow on erf are they managing to survive?" asked a concerned Milly. "There's nuffink for them to eat an' there's no water far as I c'n see."

"I'm wondering why we haven't caught up with him yet," worried Dando, his thoughts on Tallis rather than the local livestock, "the only thing I can think of is that he's travelling by night as well as by day. We haven't heard any reports of him staying in the places we've passed through. And of course we're probably going a lot slower than he is because we have to think of Ralph."

Despite their leisurely progress they sometimes overtook even more tardy wayfarers such as an ancient horse-drawn wagon or an old out-of-date automobile which was rocking along in a dust cloud of its own making. It was after they had experienced two calm clear days and had their spirits lifted by a road sign on which was painted *ROUTE 9 - DAMWEY 30m* that a rider on horseback passed them going hell for leather, easily outpacing the motorbike. As he went by he shouted something unintelligible and pointed rearwards. Dando brought the bike to a halt and they looked back to see what all the fuss was about. A sight greeted them guaranteed to freeze the blood. The whole of the eastern sky was a uniform black while the horizon, in that direction, had vanished completely. High in the air and appearing to lour over their heads were the tops of great massy grumous clouds, their interiors momentarily lit a lurid red before the sun was overtaken and extinguished by their advance.

"Blimey!" cried Milly, "wot is it?"

"I don't know," replied Dando. "It looks like the end of the world. We'd better make a dash for it. Ralph, come here..."

Bending he put his arms around the dog, an animal almost as heavy as he was, and heaved him up on to the gas tank in front of him.

"Lie down Ralph, lie down...!"

Then, gunning the engine, he opened the throttle to its full extent, selected first gear and let in the clutch. The bike shot forward. It was in this manner, bombing down the road at almost seventy miles an hour, with passengers both in front and behind, that Dando brought his charges safely to the outskirts of Damwey and took refuge, not before time, in the first dwelling to offer hospitality.

Five minutes after getting within doors the storm hit. The force of the blast shook the building they had chosen while the noise almost deafened them. Above the wail, shriek and roar of the wind they could hear wild bangings and clatterings as everything fragile or not securely tied down broke loose and went flying through the pea-soup air.

"It's not rain it's dust!" cried Dando unnecessarily as the gale attempted to lift the roof off the guest house they had chosen. Inside, the electricity supply soon failed and their hostess, looking scared, brought out a few battery operated lanterns and torches. There was little they could do but huddle into chairs in the tenants' lounge and stare out of the window at – nothing. The world and all it contained had been temporarily wiped from reality's slate while domicile and occupants were enveloped in a swirling snarling chaotic stramash.

Horry sobbed and Dando took him on his lap to comfort him, jigging him up and down as if he were still a baby.

"Don't you worry," he said into his ear, "nothing's going to happen. Mummy'll look after us."

Horry rested his head on Dando's breast looking up at him through tear-hung lashes.

"She says you've got to be careful," he replied. "She says you're getting close."

"Close to what?" replied his father, but in actual fact he thought he understood only too well what was meant. Just one glance at the walled city of Damwey as they approached across the plain had told him all that he needed to know. There, in full view, could be seen the vaguely classical architecture with which he was already familiar, and there on the skyline were numerous time-damaged roofs and towers built from substantial blocks of stone: it was the temple on the summit of Mornington Heights multiplied a thousandfold. And when they arrived and found much-needed accommodation on the periphery, something else took his mind back to the same ancient building and what he had discovered there. He immediately recognised the labyrinthine, maze-like nature of this place and begun to wonder if, because of his knowledge of a two-dimensional design he had studied on a cushion intended as an adjunct to devotion, he had the solution to a three-dimensional puzzle being presented to him here in the real world. Without ever having previously visited the ancient burg he thought he could tell anyone who asked that, if two entrances existed on the east and west sides of the town, then they were red herrings as far as penetration was concerned, while the street leading from the gate in the southern wall, the one that they had entered by, was the only possible route to the centre.

"I'll go and look tonight," he decided, shouldering his burden, "storm or no storm."

Long exiled underground,
It's the buzz I get playing with souls
That makes it all worth while.

Chapter thirteen

As soon as he was sure Milly and Horry were asleep Dando got dressed, tied a scarf over his nose and mouth, picked up the brightest of the lanterns and crept downstairs. The storm still raged but was not blowing quite so ferociously as in its first crazy abandoned onset. It had settled into a steady background wuthering interspersed with occasional lulls that seemed unnaturally quiet in comparison to the uproar of the past few hours. He was surprised to find both Ralph and Meena sitting by the front door apparently waiting for him to descend and as he approached they looked up expectantly.

"It's not nice out there," he told them, "I don't think you'd like it."

The animals, if they understood him at all, were undeterred: Ralph gave an eager bark while Meena contributed a tiny meow. They were each of them saying unmistakably, "Let us out please."

Dando shrugged and opened the door. They pushed through almost before there was room, Meena leaping over Ralph's muzzle in order to get first in the queue, then turned in the direction he was intending to take. Instead of disappearing into the murk, however, they stood a few yards distant as if waiting for him to catch up. In the street, not surprisingly, there was no-one else about. The night air was as full of dust as ever and the lantern's illumination did not stretch very far. The noise the wind made as it whistled and moaned around corners of buildings sounded rather like the crying of lost children or the lamentations of the damned.

As he set off Dando knitted his brows and conjured an image out of the past. He was thinking back to the time when the restaurant was in full swing - to the time when, if he needed a break, he would set out to visit the pantheon on top of the hill. He recalled sitting in one of the pews of this ancient building and holding a hassock on his lap, studying the intricate design with which it was decorated. You entered the maze at the bottom, presumably the south, he recalled, in order to go, firstly, straight forward, passing two right turns before taking the third, after which you continued veering right, twisting through a sort of chicane, until you emerged very close to the eastern extremity. Next you found your way back around many more confusing corners almost to the western outer limits...

He directed his steps in accordance with these recollections and subsequently arrived in a tiny claustrophobic square in which all the houses appeared to be deserted and boarded up, some in very poor repair. The gale here was being forced into a kind of whirlpool and scraps of paper, dried-up vegetation, all kinds of rubbish were swirling round and round in an endless futile maelstrom. So, where was he supposed to go? Was it that tiny unlit alley straight ahead that he had to take or was it the street diagonally off to the left, partially blocked because a building had collapsed? He did not know, he could not recall, and worse, he was not even sure he could retrace his steps if he tried to go back. A twinge of panic hatched in his breast as he realised that his memory was failing him. It was at this point that a small voice made itself heard above the bellowing of the wind.

"This way," it called.

He looked in the direction from whence it issued but all he saw was Meena, sitting on top of a pile of rubble, staring at him.

"What?" he answered, feeling a complete idiot, only for Ralph's head to appear over the edge of the pile as he heard a doggy voice repeat, "Come this way."

Was he hallucinating? At a complete loss and for lack of any alternative plan he went towards the two animals and they immediately turned and set off in a purposeful manner, occasionally looking back to check that he was following. And so, from that point on, despite a ticking off from the more rational part of his brain, he put his trust in these non-human companions, going where they went, allowing them to be his guides, and every now and then, when one corner followed another so closely that for a moment or two they passed out of his sight, hearing those strange zoomorphic voices telling him to, "Come this way."

It was another square, a bigger square but one equally dark, ruinous and deserted that they brought him to. The cat and the dog sat in the centre of the cobbled area and gazed at him with satisfied expressions as if congratulating themselves on a job well done. During his approach to the place he thought he had heard faint music ahead of him – a honkey-tonk piano and raucous voices raised in song – but this died away, and when he arrived he was confronted by some kind of ancient faded hostelry completely blacked out. The name, despite missing letters, could just about be deciphered by the light of his lantern; the tavern was called *The Blue Mountain Saloon.* It did not look as if it had been in use for many a long year. So was this it? Was this the place written in his stars? He looked at the animals nonplussed and Ralph seemed to sense his state of mind for he came and pressed his head against his groin. Meena rubbed round his solitary ankle but then trotted over to the tavern where she stretched up towards the door handle and glanced back over her shoulder needing no words to convey her meaning.

Dando walked across and stood indecisively before the inn for a long time, his hand partially raised. What was he getting himself into? Could this be a trap laid for him by his enemies? The place was surrounded by a sinister aura emanating mainly from its neglect and he got a sudden intuition that, in the past, it had once been a magnet to all and sundry but had later been shunned for some peculiar reason. At last he opened the unlocked door and entered. He found himself in a hall with a reception counter to the left, thick with dust. Opposite this a murky entrance led through into a large public room which included a small stage. As far as he could see the shelves behind the bar were empty and the chairs around the tables dotted about the room were tipped forward as they would have been each day at closing time but Dando got the feeling that they had not been moved for decades. Just in front of the stage stood a piano, but when he lifted the lid he found that a number of keys were missing and, of the ivories that remained, most were horribly warped and discoloured. He struck several notes only to be answered by a discordant twang. Until that moment he had imagined that he and the animals were the only living things in this silent inn but as the reverberations died away he could have sworn he heard an answering noise from up above. He held his breath and was rewarded by a grating sound followed by a low moan coming from somewhere overhead. Ralph had also heard it because he looked upwards and growled.

Nerving himself to face something unpleasant, Dando went back into the hall and ascended the stairs to the first floor. There were several numbered doors leading off a corridor and it was presumably from behind one of these that the noise had come.

"Is anyone there?" he called.

He was not sure if he caught a reply. If there had been anything then it was barely audible. Ralph, who had climbed the stairs at his heel, put his nose to the ground outside one particular door and scented through the gap at floor level.

"Is that where they are, Ralph?" said Dando. He knocked politely only to be answered by a sound that he could not identify.

"Are you all right?" he enquired, "do you need help?"

This time there was no response, just a squeaking noise that might have been made by bed springs. He tried the handle but the door seemed to be locked or jammed, inaccessible from the outside. He remembered a row of keys on a board behind the counter in the hall and so went downstairs to see if he could locate a spare one for room number twelve. The hooks on the board were labelled and, yes, there was one marked twelve at the end of the row. No, that was not strictly true, his key did hang there on the last of the designated hooks, but next to it he noticed another, presumably number thirteen. All the keys were uniform in size and design apart from this end one, suspended in the shadows. It was massive in comparison to the rest and its shape appeared antiquated yet oddly unfinished. Dando removed the itemised key from its hook, then, without understanding why, also took this odd-one-out and put it into his trouser pocket. Back on the landing he laid a restraining hand on Ralph's back, inserted key number twelve into the relevant lock, turned it and again gave the door a sharp push. It swung open and he was assailed by an odour of such pungency that he recoiled a step or two before holding up the lantern in order to reveal a figure lying on a filthy bed stained with blood and faeces. The man, (it was a man), lifted an arm and, reaching out towards him as if making some last desperate appeal, moaned, "Please, please..." In this barely human apparition Dando recognised the wanderer to whom he had pledged allegiance almost two years previously.

"Master!" he cried, stepping alone into the room (for obvious reasons Ralph had backed away as soon as the door opened), "what's happened to you? How did you get like this? Where are you hurt?"

But all Tallis could manage in reply was a mouthed "M'boy... m'boy..." before shutting his eyes and apparently lapsing into unconsciousness.

Frantically Dando cast around for some means by which he could bring help to his liege lord. The first priority seemed to be water. He saw that the man's lips, although stained with blood, were dry and cracked and, on touching his forehead, realised that he was burning up, probably severely dehydrated. He went in search of a tap but when he ran one to earth it did not work and re-entering the bar he found a few empty bottles but nary a full one. Returning upstairs he discovered that Tallis was breathing shallowly and unnaturally fast. Dando's common-sense told him that unless he could get him quickly to a medical practitioner the prognosis was dire to say the least. Standing beside the bed, not sure if the knight could hear him, he explained what he intended to do.

"I can't go away and leave you – I might never be able to find this place again without help. I'll have to take you with me – carry you – perhaps the animals will show us the way. I'll be as careful as I can."

He bent down, put one arm around Tallis' shoulders and the other under his knees and, summoning up a great deal of resolution, lifted him and staggered down the stairs. Ralph and Meena were waiting beside the open front door. "Find Horry, Ralph," he panted as he came into the street and then to the cat, "find Milly, puss - find Milly - find your mistress."

The lady in question woke at dawn to discover Horry fast asleep and Dando missing. His clothes were gone and the place beside her felt cold. She knew that towards morning he frequently became too uncomfortable to remain lying down. She had become totally familiar with the catch in his breath, the sudden involuntary movement that told her that pain had once again invaded her lover's damaged body. Bed for him at such times was no longer an option yet rising seemed to provide little relief. Watching him in concern while pretending to be asleep she would notice the small grimace he allowed himself when he stood up and steeled himself to face yet another day. So was he downstairs? Descending to the ground floor she looked in the lounge, in the dining room, even in the kitchen but he was nowhere about the place. She began to feel worried. If he had had some reason to leave why had he not told her? Was it possible that he had gone for good? Maybe he thought he would be doing her a favour by continuing his journey alone, but surely he would not just walk off and abandon his young son? Maybe he had left a message with their hosts. The guest-house was run by a Mr Wapshott assisted by his unmarried niece and Milly was about to go up the service stairs and invade their privacy when the front door burst open, Dando tripped over the threshold and, landing on his knees, knelt there coughing, Tallis still clutched in his arms; Ralph and Meena hovered outside. As she stooped to offer a helping hand he registered the girl's presence, and, in a husky whisper, instructed her to, "Go an' phone for a doctor, Milly, quickly! And get some water – lots of water! If you don't he's going to croak – no doubt about it."

Tallis was laid on the bed she had recently vacated. A mug was held to his lips but he seemed too far gone to drink. More water was heated in a copper and Dando removed his master's filthy clothes and carefully washed his bruised and lacerated body before sitting down by the bed to keep watch. Eventually, after a long delay, the physician who had been summoned by the girl's anxious call arrived and spent some time probing and examining while a concerned Dando and Milly looked on. With a certain amount of ceremony he finally delivered his verdict.

"I've found several broken bones," he told them, "but that's not the problem. I believe he's got internal injuries – I detect bleeding. He needs hospital treatment but there's no such thing in Damwey and he's not up to travelling. The next few hours will be vital. We'll get some fluid into him and I'll give him a painkilling injection; then I'll come back this evening to see how things are progressing."

As Milly let him out of the front door he stared at her meaningfully and shook his head.

All that morning and most of the afternoon Dando sat by the patient's bedside waiting for Tallis to show some signs of life as Milly came and went, liaising between the sickroom and their perturbed landlady while also dealing with Horry, who wanted to know why they were not going for their usual ride on the mo'bike. Eventually the knight's eyelids fluttered and he moved his lips as if trying to speak. Dando bent forward the better to hear him.

"M'boy," came a weak sibilance, "I meant for you to go somewhere of your own choosing, to live life and find your own way in the world."

"Yes," his squire replied, "that's what I'm doing. This *is* what I choose. But master, how did you get injured? Why were you at the Blue Mountain Saloon?"

Tallis seemed to have to search his damaged frame for strength before he could reply.

"The horse..." he whispered, "it took me there... I was given no choice. Then when I wouldn't dismount it tried to buck me off. It reared... threw me... hooves... trampled underfoot... I dragged myself upstairs... the door was open but, when I went in, it slammed shut behind me. I thought no-one would ever come."

He heaved, choked and Dando saw fresh blood on his lips. He wiped the patient's mouth with a cloth saying, "Don't try and talk – you need rest. The doctor will be here soon."

The doc returned, looked the patient over but said very little, his expression grave.

"Aren't you going to set the broken bones?" asked a concerned Dando, remembering his own experience.

"Not yet – let's get him through the night. I'll do what I can for now. Back in the morning."

The long hours dragged by emphasised by the slow tick of a grandfather clock in the hall. Dando continued his vigil, rejecting Milly's suggestion that they exchange places. He did not feel like sleeping because he was suffering from a sharp intermittent pain in his lower left side; it was almost as if he had recently been wounded in that area. He shifted uncomfortably on the chair, got up and limped to and fro, putting a hand to his hip, only to discover the bulky piece of metal he had thrust unthinkingly into his pocket almost twenty-four hours earlier. He pulled it out, experiencing immediate physical relief and sat down to examine it. It did not look as he remembered. Although still massive, it now glowed a dull bronze and the metal shaft had a perforated design of leaves and berries. Even as he watched it seemed to go out of focus for a moment. He blinked, rubbed his eyes and as the image sharpened again he saw it had changed dramatically. It was still a key but now no bigger than his palm, a fine filigree work of art in some form of precious mineral that drew his eye down through one layer of ornamentation after another until he felt he had to come up for air or else be lost forever. His hand closed around it and he placed the other on top as if he had captured something alive that might fly away at any moment. He now knew why he had been led through that maze of streets to the long abandoned hostelry and also why Tallis had been taken to the same place by his capricious mount. But as far as the knight was concerned the journey had ended in disaster whereas for him... He opened his hands to see that the object had altered shape once more. The dimensions of this mysterious entity seemed to be continually in flux. It was such a miraculous discovery and he became so absorbed in examining his prize that at first he failed to notice that Tallis was awake and watching him. All at once, realising that the man's eyes were open, he hastened to share his discovery.

"Look master! – it's what we were searching for! – it's the Key-of-the-Ages! - I'm sure of it! It was hidden at that inn - goodness knows why or by whom. Here it is – see...!"

Tallis stared for a minute or two and then held out his hand. Dando placed the object within it and was astonished to witness it metamorphose into a thing of dull metal such as might be used to unlock a storeroom door behind some humble dwelling. Tallis studied it for a moment or two but then seemed to find even its small weight too much to bear and let it fall onto the bed.

"So it's been found," he murmured, faintly animated, "my mother wanted me to take it back to the place where it came from. She thought that if I did that, things could be returned to the way they were before it was stolen."

Dando cast his mind back to his own traitorous ancestors, the ones who had remained behind in the valley of Deep Hallow and also to the tale he had been told by the drunk in Bishops Hollow.

"Perhaps you could do it when you recover," he said uncertainly.

"No," replied Tallis dully, "but you could m'boy. If you take it to the Land-of-the-Lake then my life won't have been in vain." Suddenly his pale half-dead face took on a horrid avidity and he panted with eagerness. "You will do it won't you? Promise me you'll do it!"

"Yes, yes," said Dando anxiously, patting his shoulder, "don't excite yourself. I'll do it – I'll carry it for you. But first I've got to make sure you get well." After that he remained silent for a spell, before adding, "It sort of keeps changing shape but it doesn't seem to be affecting the world around it like you said it did in the beginning."

"Perhaps it knows it's going home," whispered Tallis as he sank back with a strange pulsating sigh and shut his eyes, his body so still that he barely appeared to breath. Dando watched as before but, because he had experienced two sleepless nights - the second time this had happened to him in quite a brief period of time.- he inevitably drifted into a doze. It was much later that something brought him back to consciousness, only to discover his patient in the midst of a crisis that could have been building for some time. Tallis' was trembling uncontrollably and gasping as if he had just run a mile. His eyes were wide open in fright and when he realised Dando was awake he stretched out his hand mouthing "Hold me!" and then almost inaudibly, "It's you! – not me. It was you all along..."

Dando, racked with guilt at his dereliction, shifted onto the bed and, lifting the knight, took him into his arms. He clutched him while convulsion after convulsion shook the invalid's frame as he fought to retain his grip on life. It was a battle that was inevitably going to end in defeat. The time between seizures lengthened until eventually he went rigid and shuddered climactically before his mouth fell open and he gave a last despairing wheeze. Then it was all over. The body Dando was holding appeared to have suddenly gained in weight, bringing about a realisation, however much he would have wished to deny it, that he was embracing a corpse. Despite this he was unable to relinquish his grip but held on ever more tightly as if in this way he would not have to fully acknowledge what had occurred. As he did so he rocked to and fro weeping silently and unstoppably, watering his master's hair with his tears. It was thus Milly found him, sometime after dawn, and with many a soft word managed to persuade the boy to lay Tallis down, but when she tried to embrace him in his turn he jumped up and dodged away as if his distress was too deep for consolation. “I don't understand!” he cried.

Not until several days later when the funeral rites were over and the deceased had been committed to earth in an overcrowded cemetery did he relax his veto on being comforted. Then he finally allowed himself to be taken to Milly's bosom where he lay permitting his sorrow free reign.

“Why, why, Milly?” he lamented, “It just doesn't make sense. This was his story – not mine – and now it'll never have a proper ending. His whole life seems to have been rendered totally meaningless.”

“You fink life 'as to 'ave a meaning?” she answered, bitterness which had built up over many years of oppression coming to the fore. “I don' notice that many people's lives 'ave meaning - mos' don' seem to know what to do wiv themselves in between getting born and dying so they hitch up wiv someone an' 'ave kids to fill in the time. In fact orl they seem to do is try an' leave someone behind when they go to take their place – jus' like bein' on a merry-go-round - the same fing over an' over.” “No, no!” Dando shook his head emphatically. “Life should be a journey – you start somewhere and then you leave from somewhere else, further down the road.”

“An' then wot?”

“I don't know.”

He lay silent for some time while Milly allowed him space to think.

“Anyway,” he said after a while, “I'm going to take it back to this Land-of-the-Lake as he wanted – as I promised. It's the last thing I can do for him.”

“But fink 'ow long it took the knight to get 'ere. All 'is life nearly. It might take you the rest of your life to go back.”

“Ok – so it's a long way – I accept that.”

“But s'posin' you gets ill – you might you know.”

“I'm not going to get ill!” There was an indignant edge to his voice.

Milly looked at him with love but shook her head at the same time as if she were close to losing patience.

"Wot about your sweet'eart," she reminded him, "s'posin' she says no?"

Dando did not reply but his face took on a stubborn, mulish expression. Eventually he brought the conversation to an end by adding:- "I said I'd take it and that's all that matters."

Despite this talk of the Key and what he intended to do with it, the shock of Tallis' passing coupled with the bureaucracy that had to be attended to after a death meant that it was sometime before he discovered he had mislaid the very object with which he was so concerned. He had just begun a rather frantic search among his possessions when on removing the used sheets from the death-bed Miss Wapshott heard something fall to the floor. She brought it to her boarder.

"Did this belong to the dead gentleman?" she asked.

"Oh," cried Dando, greatly relieved, "yes, it did - I promised to take it back to the place his people came from."

"You'd better have it then. I reckon his folks'll be wondering where it is. Looks like it might be the key to his strong-box."

At that particular moment the Epoch-Changer was impersonating the releasing device of a humble padlock but no sooner had it returned to Dando's possession than it became intricate and decorative once more. Hiding it in his fist he took it through to where Milly was giving Horry a bath.

"Here, Milly – hold this a moment."

In Milly's hand the Key transformed into an object of barbaric splendour while in Horry's, despite the fact that he promptly dropped it into the water, it became a brightly-coloured plastic toy. "Strange," Dando thought when he was again in possession and once more alone, "it alters for each new person that touches it but it's only when *I've* got it that it changes all the time; it's never the same for more than a few minutes together. It's almost as if none of the shapes are real because it's afraid to remain in one form for long in case I should cotton on to its secret."

He stared at it – marvelling - hardly able to comprehend that what his master had been seeking for so long was now in his possession. Was it true what he had been told – that it conferred everlasting life? He certainly did not feel as if he was going to live forever. As he looked he experienced a sense of disconnection from the normal run of events until, the realisation that it was he who was holding it and not Tallis, rekindled his grief and in an attempt at alleviation he threaded the precious thing onto the chain around his neck which already held the locket Becca had given him. "That'll keep it safe", he muttered and then, "I will take it master – I'll take it! I'll do exactly as you would have done if you were still here and could have fulfilled your mother's wishes."

The storm had finally abated and a prolonged shower laid the dust. The world was transformed and the next day dawned bright but autumnal with a cool nip in the air.

"I fink we might be goin' to get more rain," said Milly, "they say they've bin 'avin plenty down souf."

The bike was serviced at a local repair shop and Dando asked for the tanks to be filled. Their possessions, such as they were, were packed into the panniers and their clothes given a new lease of life through their landlady's laundering and mending expertise.

"I'm leaving with Horry tomorrow," Dando told Milly, "but I think you ought to go back and find the others. I can't expect you to come with me on such a crazy expedition. I believe the railhead is situated not far to the east – you could travel by train via Harrisburg."

"Crazy?" said Milly, "it's you wot's talkin' crazy. I'm comin' wiv you an' Horry like I said. Try an' stop me."

"All right – but this Key's really my business and no-one else's. Heaven knows where it might lead me."

"Yes, and you're *my* business – someone's gotta look after you – an' the nipper o' course."

Dando looked at her in comic exasperation then smiled.

"I can see there's no getting rid of you."

"Not on your nelly!"

He managed to purchase another map in one of Damwey's few remaining shops and showed Milly the route they were to follow. There was a cattle trail heading almost due south, one that they could use at the start although later it seemed to lose itself amongst a waste of highlands, the westward extension of the range that ran to the north of Ry-Town.

"If we can get over those hills we should be able to cross the sea to Pickwah, although when we arrive on the other side, if it's getting cold, we'll probably have to turn in the Drossi direction." The thought that he might yet see Gweek again and maybe even his home valley gave him a strange frisson.

The evening before they were due to set off Milly called Dando into Horry's little room and then instructed the child to, "Tell your daddy wot you just told me."

Horry stared at Dando with big eyes and stuck his thumb into his mouth.

"Come on," urged Milly, "tell 'im what she said, your ma - don't be afraid - 'e won't eat you."

It took a lot of persuasion to get the little boy to talk and, even so, he offered up his contribution in a rushed and barely audible mumble.

"She says you're wrong to go south – she says it has to be taken outside, a long way away. She says you mus' look unnerneath the earth."

"Did you put him up to this?" cried Dando, so angrily that a frightened Horry started to cry and had to be comforted.

"No, of course not," answered Milly once she had pacified both of them, "'e jus' come out wiv it."

"Anyway," the young man commented later, "it doesn't make any sort of sense:- *taken outside – under the earth* – what's that supposed to mean? Perhaps Horry might care to explain."

"Don't be daft – 'ee don' know eiver – 'e's only a kid."

"Well then..." concluded Dando. He sounded vindicated, as if Horry's lack of understanding made the whole conversation up to that point a waste of time.

Milly felt it her duty to hand out a bit of plain speaking at this point, though when the young father was the recipient she rarely did anything else.

"You'd better woch out," she scolded. "If you keep scarin' 'im like that 'e'll probably never let on about anyfink again. Remember, 'e's the only one 'oo 'ears what she says."

Dando brooded gloomily for a bit but eventually acknowledged that she was right.

"I'm sorry, Milly. P'raps I'd better go and tell him a story. Then maybe he'll forgive me."

That night Dando and Milly shared a proper bed for the last time in who knew how long. Since his arrival at their house Mr and Miss Wapshott had been turning a blind eye to the fact that their paying guest appeared to be sleeping with his child's nanny; between themselves they agreed that, all things considered, males of his age have powerful urges which could get out of hand if not satisfied. The next morning it so happened that Milly was the first to wake, just as pre-dawn light was starting to creep through the curtains. She raised herself on one elbow in order to study the unconscious figure beside her, thus indulging in one of her favourite pastimes: examining her lover's features in detail as he lay asleep. She noted the finely drawn lineaments of his face animated by the faint movement of blood beneath the skin, and could not help but delight in the clean contour of his jaw, visible beneath his rather sparse growth of beard, the slender slightly misshapen nose and the expressive mouth in whose line could be read the tale of practically everything he had experienced over the past few months. At the same time she marked other examples of his beauty such as his high cheekbones, his finely-drawn silky brows, his luxuriant wealth of regrown raven-coloured hair and the smooth complexion overlaid by a deep tan which at present hid his normal pallor. Just to have him this close brought her intense happiness, although she could not help but feel how fragile such happiness might turn out to be: a heart once given away, so the old song says, will come back broken like as not. As she watched he swallowed in his sleep and she saw the delicate muscles move in his throat. Having recently witnessed Tallis stretched out dead and cold in the mortician's parlour she was suddenly granted a vision of Dando similarly lifeless. Horrified she pulled the covers back in order to doubly reassure herself of his living, breathing presence and this was enough to rouse him briefly so that he opened dark eyes, looked up and gave her a trusting smile, before sinking back into insensibility.

A few hours later, when all their preparations were complete and they were ready to leave, it was discovered that Ralph was missing.

"I think I know where he is," said Dando to Milly. "I believe he went there yesterday and the day before as well. Don't let Horry wander off – I'll be back shortly."

He was right in his surmise. The dog was standing stock-still by the side of Tallis' grave and as Dando approached he turned his head, an expression of pain, you might almost have said of guilt, in his golden eyes.

"Yes, fellow," commiserated the Glept, putting out a comforting hand, "he's gone – we can't bring him back. You knew him long before I did. You could tell me things about him I didn't get the chance to learn. What adventures you must have had together before you reached Deep Hallow! I'll never hear about them now that he's died. Come on, Ralph – we're going to do what he would have done if he'd been spared – we're going to take the Key back to the place it was stolen from." Dando went to walk away and after a moment's hesitation during which he lowered his nose and sniffed the newly turned earth the dog followed.

It felt strange reversing direction and heading back the way they had come - going south seemed wrong somehow, almost like a betrayal. The cattle trail, formed by the hooves of thousands of animals, was not the ideal place to take a motorbike. The machine and its riders were thoroughly shaken up and made slow progress over the rugged terrain; Dando worried about whether the bike had been built to withstand such rough treatment. Gradually, however, they got used to the irregular motion and in other ways things began to improve. During the last few days there had been several showers and, almost overnight, the prairie had turned from brown to green. Soon they were surrounded by the scent of sagebrush and mesquite born to them on a gentle northerly breeze. The huge firmament above presented a benign aspect adorned at it was by a heavenly mountain range of cumulus clouds that progressed in stately fashion along the horizon. On some days, however, these banks built up into awe-inspiring cordilleras of cumulonimbus which had a tendency to spill across the sky and dump heavy downpours on their heads.

"Look Milly," said Dando one afternoon, bringing the bike to a halt and waving his hand towards the north-east, "isn't it magnificent!"

"Wot you on about?" demanded his puzzled passenger.

"The clouds – girl – and the rainbow! Turn round! Most people never bother to look up – they miss all sorts of beautiful things. Don't you think that if we could go and live up there all our problems would be solved?"

"They wouldn't if the clouds're made of dust!"

Dando laughed. "No – you're right – but I don't think these ones are."

They sat and gazed for sometime until Horry, no longer rocked asleep by the bike's soporific motion, began to complain at their inaction. Dando gunned the motor but before he could put it in gear Milly clutched his arm and then, moving her hand to his chin, pulled his head back so he was forced to stare up at the zenith.

"Look," she cried, "wot's that?"

As they watched, a white line, apparently made of cloud stuff, was being drawn rapidly across the sky above them from north to south. Occasionally it disappeared behind a more conventional cloud only to re-emerge on the other side and continue to extend itself towards the horizon at the same inexorable pace.

"How weird," exclaimed Dando. "I think there must be something at the front that we can't see because it's too far away."

"If there is it's goin' like the clappers!"

"Could it be one of those little machines that used to fly among the buildings in Rytardenath?"

"They never went that fast."

In a very few minutes whatever it was that was making the contrail had vanished into the south while the line it left behind gradually widened and blurred before dissipating completely.

"Weird," said Dando again, running his finger around beneath his necklet before restarting the engine. Not so much during the day but almost every night now he was irked by that chain, rarely able to forget he was wearing it. Sometimes it seemed too tight, sometimes it irritated his skin, sometimes the delicate little piece of metal he had threaded onto it lay like a ton weight over his heart. When the chain had born nothing but the locket it had never troubled him; it was only since the Key had been added that it had begun to be a problem.

"Does my neck look sore, Milly?" he asked his companion the next morning, not having a mirror for self-examination.

"You've got a red line," she told him, "it goes all the way roun'. I should take that bloomin' fing orf an' put it in yer pocket. It's obviously wot's causin' it."

"No, that's not on. If I did that I might lose it – I can't risk that."

"Well, you'll 'ave to put up wiv it then."

The following day, soon after daybreak, some cattle appeared out of the dawn mist, coming from the south, with two mounted cowboys riding herd and a third, driving some sort of mechanical all-terrain vehicle, bringing up the rear. One of the horsemen stopped briefly beside the bike to exchange a few words.

"Howdy partners," he drawled, "where you headin'?"

"We're on our way to take ship across the Middle Sea," replied Dando, "does this road lead to the coast?"

"I guess so 'cos that's where we've just come from," said the wrangler. "Grazed the dogies on bladderwrack down by the sea during the drought but then the water decided to get it's dander up and swalla the land – lost at least half of them."

The man spoke laconically of something that, despite his insouciance, had obviously been a major setback for himself and his colleagues. Between his teeth he clenched a slender wooden toothpick that waggled up and down as he spoke and his distance-bleached pale-grey eyes gazed out from beneath a sweat-stained hat brim with calm fatalism. Dando's face lit up with the sort of admiration which can sometimes evolve into hero-worship given time.

"That must have been quite a blow," he said, empathising like mad.

"Sure was."

"Were you able to make any money from the carcasses?"

"Nope."

There was a brief silence.

Then - "Is there anywhere for flying machines to land in this direction?" Dando asked respectfully, "We thought we saw one go overhead yesterday."

"Nope – not so far as I know."

"How long will it take us to get to the coast?"

The cowpoke gazed with disdain at the motorbike.

"On that thing a few days," he replied. "Taken us weeks to come t'other way. It was a while before we could git goin' and then some of the stock got scattered in the forest – spooked by a fanged tiger I reckon or maybe a panther – had to round up the ornery critters."

"There's a forest?" said Dando surprised; they had not seen a single tree since leaving Harrisburg, "I thought this sort of country carried on right to the sea."

"Nope," replied the herdsman, refusing to elaborate and presenting them with his weathered profile while the pick did an independent dance between his lips. He remained for a while lost in thought until, removing his hat, he re-creased the crown and settled it back on his head. Then, with a "S'long folks" he dug in his spurs and galloped off after the cattle and his motorised companion.

"What a chap!" exclaimed Dando, "a real *son of the sage* as they say."

Milly sniffed.

"All show," she said disparagingly, "you won't be seein' 'is sort aroun' much longer. It's the one on the fing wiv the engine that's doing the business."

"You're such a wet week, Milly," replied Dando in mock sorrow, "do you enjoy destroying my illusions?"

"That's wot I'm 'ere for."

Soon the hills came into sight, range upon range, much higher than the ones they had crossed on the way to Hayseed Junction and all of them cloaked in a dark green blanket of vegetation.

"Trees," said Dando, "he wasn't kidding. Are we going to make it through do you think?"

"Wot about these tigers?" replied Milly, "'ee woz sayin' sompfink about tigers. I don't like the sound of that."

"Don't worry – when they hear the row that this bike makes they'll give us a wide berth."

The road, more of an earthen path really, wound gradually upwards and very soon arboreal growth o'erlapped the passageway limiting their ability to see more than a few yards ahead. What sunshine there was penetrated the leafy ceiling in isolated shafts of light within which danced swarms of tiny midges resembling constantly moving clouds of precious metal. When Dando cut the engine to give Ralph a rest they were surrounded by the solemn silence of the forest broken only occasionally by a solitary bird call or the staccato rattle of a woodpecker. There seemed to be a wide variety of plant species along their route and as they climbed higher the trees got larger until every so often they came upon a true giant around whose huge trunk the path had to diverge.

"I never knew something living could be this big," said Dando, his voice hushed in wonder. "How old is it do you think?"

Such enormous entities had equally enormous roots that occasionally created barriers across the path and over these the motorbike had to be lifted. Dando drove cautiously keeping a weather eye open for such hazards but almost inevitably the moment came when his attention was distracted and as a consequence the front wheel shot skywards and they all ended in a heap on the ground. No one was hurt but when he picked the bike up and turned on the ignition there was no responding roar.

He tried several more times until Milly pointed to the fuel gage - it was registering empty.

"But I thought I still had a spare tank full," said Dando, "I asked the man to fill both tanks before we left Damwey."

"P'raps 'ee di'n't unnerstan' wot you meant," replied Milly, "Foxy put that other tank on 'isself you remember."

"I went for a pee," Dando lamented, "I should have stayed and watched what he was doing."

"Oh well..." commented Milly, rolling her eyes.

Dando looked back the way they had come and then forward towards the unknown distance yet to be travelled.

"We're sunk," he moaned, "there's probably not a hope of getting more gas until we reach the coast."

"Well, we'll 'ave to walk then," said the practical Milly.

"What, and leave the bike?"

"No choice."

"But just supposing we find there's a small town up ahead with some fuel on offer after we've left it behind. I think we've nearly reached the top. Perhaps we'll be able to get a sight of what's to come from up there. I'm not abandoning it just yet."

Consequently they progressed upwards for a short distance until the path began to meander to and fro and pass one or two side turnings. Dando stopped to think before clicking his fingers and pulling a small item from his pocket.

"Milly," he said, "c'n you go in front an' find the way using this. It's Tallis' compass - I kept it as something to remember him by but now it may come in really useful. It works like this – see. Keep an eye on it and make sure the road we're on continues to head south."

So, when they set out once more, Milly walked ahead with the compass, gripping Horry by the hand, Dando came behind pushing the bike, a curious Meena peeping out of one of the panniers, while Ralph brought up the rear. Now that they did not have the noise of the engine to protect them the young man thought uneasily about the kind of wildlife that might inhabit these remote regions. It was hard work manhandling the machine up the long slopes but eventually the gradient became less steep and this made things a mite easier. They were well above the plains by now and, presumably, at an even greater elevation in relation to the sea which they understood lay ahead of them. The wind of altitude roared through the branches overhead so that the trees threshed and flailed, constantly in motion. Dando, doggedly propelling the motorbike forward with both hands and staring at the ground, suddenly caught sight of something out of the corner of his eye which caused him to jump and turn defensively. What, momentarily, he thought he had seen was a small imp-like creature rolling and tumbling along in an animated manner as if it had discovered some novel mode of locomotion. When he looked full-square, however, it resolved into nothing more than a scrap of shiny black plastic being swept forward before the wind. Ralph, who had also been taken by surprise, pursued the piece of rubbish barking wildly until Dando called him to heel.

"It's all right Ralph – it's litter – nothing but litter – although how it got right up here I can't imagine."

"When will we know if we've reached the top?" asked Milly, "we don' seem to be goin' up or down."

Dando got out the map he had bought in Damwey and unfolded it.

"It looks as if there's a road running along the summit of the hills," he said, "a sort of ridgeway. We should reach a crossroads sooner or later and after that we'll know we're over on the other side."

It was when they rounded a bend in the path that they came in sight of another stand of the huge conifers that were apparently indigenous to this range of hills. The track passed through its midst and, within the grove, picked out by a dramatic sunbeam that had somehow managed to find its way through the branches overhead, stood a stationary vehicle.

"It's a car," said a surprised Milly, "some sort of sports car I fink – though it's got a back seat – they don't usually 'ave that. 'Oo does it belong to do you s'pose?"

Drawing nearer they realised that a long, low, open-topped coupé awaited them on the road, predominantly black in appearance but with a red and orange flame motif painted along the side; this gave the illusion of flickering in the dappled continually shifting shadows. The engine was ticking over, a deep powerful throb, and its whole shiny futuristic veneer suggested a machine that had only just left the factory.

"I don' see 'ow it could 'a' got up 'ere," continued Milly greatly puzzled, "the parf's not wide enough mos' of the time, an' look at it – there's not a mark on it - it's not even dirty."

"Well," said Dando, "it may have come by the other route along the top of the hills. Anyway, it's parked on the crossroads I was telling you about. There's someone at the wheel – perhaps he'll be able to help us."

As they came within speaking distance a man, lounging in the driver's seat, turned and gave a brief acknowledging nod almost as if he had been expecting them.

"Hi," he said in a pleasant baritone voice, "have you had a breakdown?"

They saw an individual of about forty or so with regular features, a receding hairline and piercing intelligent black eyes. In some strange way his clothes, smart but casual and at the height of fashion were all of a piece with the ambience of the car. He gave the impression of someone who has done well for himself in the world and is, as yet, in the prime of life. Dando came to a halt, breathing hard. He was finding pushing the heavy bike more and more of a trial, and, even though they were now on the flat, was well aware he would not be able to continue for much longer. He bestowed on the stranger a rather twisted smile and replied "I'm afraid I've been stupid enough to run out of gasoline."

"Out of gas? Well, that's not hard to remedy. I can give you a lift to the nearest pumps and then find someone to bring you back here. Shouldn't take long."

"What, all of us?" Dando looked doubtfully at the back seat of the vehicle where a large black and white striped animal - he could not be sure of its species - lay asleep.

"I'm afraid I've only got room for one – Letitia takes up a lot of space as you can see."

Dando felt somewhat wary at this suggestion, uncertain as to whether he could detect some underlying unvoiced intention.

"Well, I can't leave Milly and Horry here all alone," he replied mistrustfully, "I'm afraid I'll have to decline your kind offer."

"In that case I've just remembered, there's a can behind the front passenger seat. Have a look – I think it's about half full."

Dando gave him a hard, suspicious stare but at the same time noticed that there was indeed a fuel container on the floor over on the near side between the front and rear seats. He went to walk round the back of the car to get within arm's reach of the vessel but before he could do so the man leaned over and flung open the door behind the driver's seat.

"Don't mind Letty," he said reassuringly.

Milly and Horry watched as Dando stepped into the vehicle and stooped to retrieve the can he had been offered, but were not prepared for what happened next. The large torpid creature on the back seat - not any kind of domestic animal but something more on the lines of the massive statue they had seen when entering the harbour at Rytardenath - came to life and, rearing up, enveloped the boy in its front paws. In a trice it had dragged him down out of sight while the driver slammed the door shut and turned to his controls. A thundering sound assaulted their ears, quickly overlaid by a high-pitched whine as a swirling cloud of dust billowed out from between the wheels. Then, instead of moving forward, the car, or rather craft, lifted vertically into the air, propelled by some kind of jet-based boosters under the chassis, following which gaps between the front and back sections of the vehicle were augmented by rudimentary wings which opened outwards on either side.

"Lordship!" cried Milly, hardly able to believe her eyes, "My love! Dando!"

"Daddy!" yelled Horry, but if they were answered the reply was completely drowned out by the engine's take-off roar as the machine gained in height before changing direction and vanishing over the tree tops before heading south. In less than a minute its noise had faded and died leaving the child and the black girl clinging to each other in horrified amazement.

We start out as star stuff,
As glowing particles of carbon.
It's anyone's guess how we'll end.

Chapter fourteen

Dando kept perfectly still, not daring to move a muscle, hardly daring to breath. As far as he understood it, he had merely entered the back of the stranger's car in order to retrieve the can that he had seen on the floor by the nearside door. He had just been about to pick it up when something out of nowhere had landed on his shoulders and by its sheer weight had born him down until he ended up lying half on and half off the rear seat. Claws tore at his clothes and he felt a cold breath on the nape of his neck. Then, with a possessive rumble, the unknown creature seized the back of his head in its jaws. He was gripped so tightly that he thought his scull was about to crack.

"Gently does it Letty!" came the voice of the driver of the car and then casually, "I'm afraid the sugarplum can get too enthusiastic at times – just lie quiet and she won't harm you."

Dando shrank into himself, pretending inanition, and slowly the vice-like grip slackened.

"Que fuerte! – she seems to have half undressed you – drop it! drop it! there's a good girl."

The voice was unctuousness incarnate but underneath held an unmistakable threat. What form it took Dando could not imagine. This was a powerful wild animal sharing the back of the car with him, he had felt its strength, and it seemed incredible that the stranger possessed the sort of dominion that meant he was obeyed without hesitation. Nevertheless this seemed to be the case. Like a well-trained dog, the creature released its hold and drew back giving him space to turn his lacerated head and get a view of his attacker. He was confronted by a huge black and white striped mask equipped with protruding incisors that were almost like tusks and the most extraordinary ruby-red eyes. In response to his movement the lips writhed into a snarl, wrinkling the nose and exposing more wicked-looking fangs, and once again his face was caressed by its breath, a breath straight from some frozen nether world, as frigid as if its entrails were made of ice. He noticed that the animal was wearing a heavy collar buckled around its neck although it was not restrained in any way. The man in the driver's seat fished under the control panel and brought forth a grubby towel which he tossed across, blithely ordering the great animal to, "Sit down Letty, you naughty girl!" He received instant compliance.

Dando dabbed at his wounds, at the same time ascertaining that the vehicle was in motion and that a transparent canopy had closed over his head. The light that penetrated through this shield was extremely bright and nothing other than sky was visible.

"Why..." he managed to rasp, then stopped as words failed him.

"Unavoidable," came the insouciant reply. "You were obviously not willing to accompany me alone and abandon your companions. But now you're here I hope you'll make the best of it and we can get to know each other better."

Dando, furious, thought of Horry and Milly left high and dry, miles from the nearest refuge, and also of the fact that he had been snatched away from the start of the journey he had embarked upon before it had barely begun. He determined to remain silent - not sure, anyway, that if he did speak he would make an awful lot of sense. The man in the front seat did not seem to care. He turned to his controls humming a little tune. After a while he said, "I believe you are a lover of atmospheric phenomena?"

Dando did not reply.

"Look over the side and you might see something that will surprise you."

Again his prisoner pretended not to hear, but a little later when the driver was busy with some instrumental adjustments he took a surreptitious peep through the window. What met his eyes took his breath away to such an extent that he had great difficulty in stifling an exclamation. Vaguely aware, even when he was being half mauled, that the craft had left the ground, he now saw that they were not just aloft but high up, in fact they were above the clouds! Previously, except when it was foggy, he had experienced clouds as transcendent heavenly images, a diffuse ceiling above his head, well out of reach; he had never expected to find them forming a floor beneath his feet. The vessel, the space-ship, the what-you-will, was forging ever upwards into a crystal clear stratosphere under a rapidly darkening sky where stars were beginning to appear. He saw that the cloud layer which had always appeared wholly detached from the earth, did in fact cling to the surface of the planet and curved with it, creating a blue, green and white opalescent pattern.

"It's a ball!" he said in wonder, totally forgetting his refusal to communicate, "it's a big shiny ball hanging in space, yet most people down there think it's just land and sky!"

"Ah, you're speaking of the body known as Terra," replied a voice that immediately brought him back to reality, "I see you're beginning to understand. There are trillions of others like it in the grand scheme of things but this one is somewhat out of the ordinary. All the same, what happens on this little pebble is not of any great significance. That's why that object you carry around your neck might as well be handed over to someone who could make better use of it elsewhere, don't you agree? Hold Letty!"

Dando found himself immobilised once more, in the grip of claws and teeth, while the driver lunged across the back of the front seat in order to snatch the Talisman away. What happened next was a shock to both of them. As the man's hand made contact with the chain which held both locket and Key his whole body convulsed grotesquely as if an electric shock had passed through it and he was flung backwards against the instrument panel. The flying machine's steady upward progress became violently disrupted and it began to execute a series of wild aerobatics that caused Dando and the predatory creature next to him to tumble every whichway before they ended up wedged between the seats in a confusion of arms, legs and furry body parts. A crazy few minutes followed until the driver managed to pull himself together sufficiently to put the craft back on an even flightpath once more. Then he turned his attention once again to Dando.

"What by all that's profane was that?!" he cried, "What have you got there next to the Periapt?!"

Dando struggled out of the animal's clutches, suspecting, by the pain in his shoulders, that he had suffered further damage. His hand closed protectively over his sacred trust.

"Y-you can't have it," he panted, "I promised... I promised..."

"Oh yes – you promised that nonentity with illusions of grandeur that you would take it back to some mysterious country no-one has even heard of and which probably never actually existed."

These words so accurately reflected Dando's own darkest imaginings that he burst out with, "How do you know that that's what I think? How could you possibly know that I like clouds?"

"How do I know? Well, I have my spies. Even if I say so personally I believe I understand you better than you understand yourself. I'm aware that not a minute goes by without your remembering what you think of as the betrayal of your friends and suffering physically as a result of what happened when you attempted to make recompense for that betrayal. I know too that you think the death of your master can be laid at your door because instead of concerning yourself with his welfare you spent the time in that shanty town selfishly brooding over your own troubles. And what about the woman? You blame yourself for her death as well, don't you? In fact when it comes down to it you're just a mess of self-indulgent guilt."

"Stop – stop! Don't..." cried Dando, feeling as if not just his body but his soul was being stripped naked. "Surely you can't... Who are you?"

"Me? I've been credited with many identities in my time but you can call me Kenneth if you like – Ken is as good a name as any for what's in train." The driver's eyes, so bright that they seemed to burn, bored into Dando. "But what happened just now?" he continued, "Ah – I think I understand – you have a physical fragment of that very woman, the one you believed was your lifelong soul mate, there in the pendant. It's the relic which is protecting the Catalyst. All I need to do is eliminate her and then it will no longer retain its power."

"Do her harm," cried Dando, "and I'll...!"

"You'll what?"

They stared at one another in silence, his abductor calmly and Dando in such mental turmoil that he was robbed of words.

"Shall I show you?" the person who gave himself the commonplace name of Kenneth eventually suggested, "shall I demonstrate how useless this journey you have just set out on would have proved had you continued? What would have taken years off your life I can cover in a single night, much as the one I trusted and who betrayed me achieved when fleeing in the opposite direction. How often has that eel managed to wriggle through my fingers over the centuries. It's hardly worth bothering with him now apart from the pleasure of exacting vengeance."

"Now see – my little car is levelling off and soon I shall begin to take her down to another part of the planet south of the equator. *Equator*, I don't suppose you even know what that means do you? I'm doing this just for your benefit my friend so that perhaps you'll change your mind about keeping such a dangerous thing in your possession. By the way, I expect you're wondering why I haven't grounded you by confiscating that..." indicating Dando's prosthesis.

"No point really, and – besides - you and I don't want to start off on the wrong foot, do we? Hee, hee! That wouldn't do at all," and he shook with laughter.

Dando's captor brought his craft earthwards once more and visibility became virtually zero as they descended through layer upon layer of dense brume. A dim diffuse light was all that lit up the interior of the car making it hard to see anything at all, but the young man did not need illumination to be only too well aware of what must unquestionably be a member of the species classed as *fanged tiger* sitting bolt upright at his side, practically leaning against him. He could not ignore its presence because one of its massive forepaws was planted weightily in his lap, pinning him down, practically crushing his genitals. He dared not move: any attempt to shift his position brought forth a rumbling growl accompanied by a cold foetid breath that fanned the whole of his upper body. As it squatted close by, the great creature's head o'er-topped his own by a significant margin - it really was a huge animal, one that was quite capable of killing him with a single blow if it so chose. Eventually the flying machine broke through the base of the cloud ceiling and he was able to glimpse what lay below. A panorama of twisted, tormented hills met his eyes, stretching off into the murk, unrelieved by water, greenery or any sign of human habitation. But it was not this desert alone that caused his insides to contract. Off to the right he saw a great dark depression interrupting the chaotic expanse: a huge sinister bowl was visible, completely circular in shape. He got the strangest feeling that he had encountered such a place once before in a dream. It was on the edge of this mysterious feature that Kenneth, or whatever he chose to be called, brought his flying machine to earth while the canopy above their heads dissolved.

"Here you are," the pilot said, as if expecting to be thanked. "We've done it in less than twelve hours. It *does* exist and this is where you would have ended up if by some miracle you had managed to finish what you started. This is the place where the World's-Bane was secreted at some time in the far distant past."

Dando did not reply, but, because the tiger appeared to have temporarily relaxed its surveillance by crouching to maintain balance as they came in to land, he stood up for a moment, gripping the seat, wondering whether to believe what he had just heard. *If he had completed his journey...* He thought back to that day when he and his companions had sat in the Formile inn-yard listening to Tallis' account of the thing for which he was searching and heard his explanation as to why he was involved in this long and arduous quest. The knight had described his mother's country as a kind of sun-drenched arcadia, a place of lush green grass and trees hung thick with fruit or blossom. Sparkling wavelets had lapped a pebbly shore so he said and there had been a palace surrounded by velvet lawns and crystal fountains, a dwelling fit for a king. Dando also remembered talk of orange groves and cypresses, of white stones on the crest of a hill, of wide expanses of blue water across which voyaged small ships with crescent sails. And what was he now being offered? Somewhere so forsaken and unwholesome that it looked as if it lay under a curse. But perhaps that was indeed the case - perhaps when the treasure was stolen all virtue had leached out of the terrain. Maybe the Land-of-the-Lake had been just an artificial construct, unable to exist once the enabling Object-of-Power had been removed from its midst.

Cautiously he reached for the offside door handle, making his movements as smooth and as unobtrusive as possible, and released the catch. Then, as the door swung open, he slid along the seat and lowered his metal foot and right leg to the ground, redistributing his weight, so that he stood outside the vehicle. He deliberately avoided looking back but sensed that the tiger had also shifted across in order to keep him within reach of its claws. There was no question but that he was still a prisoner although just to be quit of the flying car was a relief. He took a deep breath and surveyed his surroundings. The air in his nostrils smelt somehow thin and exhausted, speaking of a land where life has long been absent. As a result of the tiger's attentions his clothes were in rags and he shivered as his wounded flesh was exposed to temperatures not far above freezing.

"Why should I believe him," he muttered aloud, "this could be anywhere – anywhere at all."

"I assure you that this is the place you were aiming at." The voice came from close at hand and he realised that Ken had also quitted the car and that their shoulders were practically touching. "Look behind you – don't you see the standing stones - the palace ruins? - and there in front, in the middle of the bed - that's the islet on which the Catalyst was once hidden."

"The bed?" said Dando.

"The bed of the lake – this area before us. So now I've shown you what a waste of time your expedition would have proved to be we can change direction, start back and..."

"I must go," said Dando.

"What?"

"I must go to the island – I promised..."

"But I can assure you you'll find nothing there that will make it worth your while."

"I-I must go." His voice held a mixture of defiance and despair.

Dando's abductor remained silent for some time as if weighing up the pros and cons of such an action before announcing, "All right – have it your own way."

"You'd let me?"

"I'm not going to say you nay, but I warn you, it won't turn out how you expect. In fact the outcome could prove so grotesquely amusing that I can't find it in myself to object."

Dando did not wait for the man to explain what he meant or to change his mind but hurried forward to where the land took a dive into the shadowy basin-shaped depression. He stepped onto the slope and immediately lost his footing, hurtling down as if on a playground slide and coming to rest only when the ground levelled out. The nature of the lake bed, although the colour of a diseased liver, was as smooth and slippery as glass.

"Go Letitia," ordered Ken and the tiger, apparently in its element, bounded nimbly down the same incline. Meanwhile Dando was struggling to recover equilibrium. As soon as he did so he slipped once more, his metal prosthesis unable to secure any purchase on this treacherous surface. As he fell he flung out an arm and saved himself from total collapse only at the expense of ending up half across the tiger's back. He was so convinced that such impertinence would earn immediate retribution that he shrank inwardly, expecting a ferocious attack, but to his great surprise the animal just stood there like a patient beast of burden waiting for him to regain his balance. Realising that there was no way he was going to get any further without help he summoned up every scrap of courage he possessed and, wrapping his fingers around the tiger's collar, heaved himself up. In this manner, with his elbow resting between its shoulder blades, he found he was able to stand. Now all he needed was to get moving. Feeling utterly foolish he gave the command: "Walk on!" - an instruction that might have been obeyed by a well-trained and docile carriage horse, but by this wild, unpredictable creature? - never in a million years. Yet the tiger *did* walk and Dando walked beside it, holding tightly to its collar in order to avoid another tumble. In this way the two of them crossed the floor of the strange adamantine crater that centuries before had possibly been under several feet of water. As they progressed he became aware that certain lumps and bumps which were threatening to trip him up were in fact the fossilised remains of small aquatic creatures. The ground was littered with them, a mass of ancient living things petrified into unnatural attitudes suggesting that they had met sudden and violent ends. In the midst of this killing field and growing ever more distinct against the sky as they approached stood the little hill that he was beginning to believe had once been home to the Sky Father's most precious jewel.

Eventually they got close enough for him to make out detail and, sure enough, he saw that, indeed, there was a building on the summit of the knoll. Could it be? - could it!? *A little glass-walled structure... a belvedere or gazebo... rainbow coloured... an aura of elusive gold...* He remembered, almost word for word, Tallis' description of the shrine his mother has said occupied the island in the centre of the lake. He now realised that the knight's version of the tale as recounted to him by his parent must have been extremely faithful to the original because there it still stood, exactly as described, a fragile construct, apparently unaffected by time's attrition, a little transparent summerhouse through which the light passed almost unimpeded. Dando was gobsmacked. "Holy moly!" he whispered to Letty, (he felt the need to communicate if only to his non-human tormentor). "Is it real? Do you think it's been waiting here all these years for us to arrive? What are we supposed to do now?" In reply the tiger crouched down with a defiant snarl, a ridge of hair standing up along its spine and its gem-like eyes glowing red for danger. It was obvious that the animal did not intend to approach any nearer to the place that confronted them and that therefore, if he meant to proceed, he was going to have to do so alone. He shuffled a few feet forwards, looking upwards, then stopped. There was something so balefully pristine about the pavilion's cool flawlessness, standing in stark contrast to the surrounding desolation, that it appeared to have reversed the natural processes of entropy. This was unnerving. It took a great deal of resolve on his part to begin the climb up the steep denuded side of the hill, going on all fours to avoid falling. He found himself half wishing that the tiger would intervene and drag him back down to his starting point.

When he reached the top and stood upright before the door of the little temple he noticed that the ornate roof o'er-topped his head by only a few inches and that, to enter, he would have to stoop. He remembered that Morvah, Tallis' mother, claimed that when standing on the self-same spot she had felt unseen forces beating against her and had believed that she was within touching distance of a divine being's sanctum. He thought that he knew better. Lord Pyr, the entity that the Glepts had long worshipped and who's storm had saved him from the tree on Hungry Island, was not the personification of the heavens as so many believed, any more than Aigea embodied the earth. His mentors, Tom Arbericord and the Ministrant who tended the temple, had believed that these immortals were something else entirely, that they originated from far away, from some inconceivably remote yet strangely familiar place and had once been creatures of the flesh like themselves. Because of this understanding, the manner in which the building impressed him was vastly different from how it had impacted on Morvah. He sensed its supernatural nature yet also felt a strange affinity drawing him towards it. He knew, somehow, that if he wanted to take the next step on his long, wearisome journey he must not refuse this challenge but engage with the mystery.

All the same what was that next step to be? As he recalled it Morvah had found the Key-of-the-Ages on the outside of the structure; she had not had to enter in order to retrieve it. He ran his hand over the surface of the door facing him but discovered no opening device or means of achieving access. In doing this, however, the minimal pressure which he exerted was enough to make the barrier yield slightly which showed that it was not fastened and the resulting gap seemed to invite him inside. Instead, he recoiled in fear. For a moment it was as if he were confronting that gingerbread house he had heard of in childhood where some hideous hag waited to gobble careless youngsters up, skin, bones, juicy entrails and all. Conquering this dread meant steeling his nerves to an even higher level. With a kind of groan he took a pace forward over the threshold and, as soon as he was within, heard the door click shut behind him.

Tallis' parent, a princess as she would have had it, had seen mirrors and multiverses at this stage when she looked through transparent walls. He, conversely, found that he was standing at the right-angled crossing point of two lengthy corridors which, he was not surprised to discover, bore absolutely no relation to the building's outer dimensions. Yet he understood why she had thought there were mirrors. The mysterious passages, lit by widely spaced ceiling lights, looked exactly like the illusion that occurs when two reflecting surfaces are placed opposite each other. In such a case an impression of tunnels is created, tunnels whose ends are forever hidden from view behind the reflection of the observer. But these passages were not reflections. He could see the extremities, or rather not see them, because the corridors carried on to the vanishing point both behind and before, trapping him in the midst of hallways that could be immeasurable. He looked round for the portal through which he had entered but it had disappeared as completely as if it had never been. He had no choice but to pick one of the four possible routes and go down it, hoping against hope that by doing so he could find his way back to the outside world.

That outside world had been a quiet but not entirely silent place. Here, in contrast, there was a complete absence of sound so that, when he started to walk, the click of metal and the squeak of shoe leather struck him as a shocking intrusion. He had not gone more than a few yards when he became aware that the walls on either side of him were being interrupted by identical door-like panels occurring at regular intervals. For a brief moment he thought he had discovered a means of escape until he saw that none of them was equipped with a knob or handle. He leant his weight against one or two without result. Plunged once more into a jittery gloom he carried on, counting as he went: – 101, 102, 103... 262, 263, 264... giving each rectangular shape a blow as he came level and wondering continually if he should have chosen one of the three other alternatives. All the way along his route elements repeated themselves so relentlessly that after a while he felt he was making no significant progress but was walking on the spot. It was almost by accident that, when he had to stop, as he did frequently to clear his lungs, he noticed that what he had taken to be an identical door in one of the darker stretches of corridor was not, in fact, an exact copy of those he had already passed. It differed in that there was a design depicted on it at eye-level, a design that was strangely familiar. He saw a circle bisected by a sinuous line dividing light from dark similar to the one he wore tattooed on his shoulder and also the one he remembered from the wall of the pantheon on Mornington Heights. Hope sprang anew, especially when, going closer, he realised that this door contained something that none of the others could boast – namely a keyhole!

A keyhole but no key. As usual he discovered that it was fast shut and. in his utter frustration, bent forward to beat his head against the panelling. But, in so doing, the chain around his neck swung free and the two items it held tapped gently against the surface in front of him. He straightened up and put his hand to his throat, becoming aware as he did so that, all unprepared, he was maybe on the brink of having to reach a momentous decision. It took just a matter of moments to undo the chain and remove one of the objects it carried before replacing it round his neck. He examined the Game-Changer with rapt attention noticing that it had assumed the most basic of shapes: a simple brass shaft with a ring at one end and a row of teeth at the other. He inserted it into the waiting hole and discovered, without any great surprise, that it fitted perfectly. How easy it would be, how tempting, to complete the manoeuvre by giving it just a simple twist. Instead he stepped back several paces and clasped his hands behind him as if to negate the temptation to act.

He tried to recall everything he had heard about this Thing-of-Power: *the time of the next turning has come and gone - the earth is sickening - it must be kept safe for future generations - it will prove ultimately destructive - it has to be taken outside – an age of gold.* There was no consensus, one statement appeared to contradict the next. He realised he was sweating. In desperation he thought back to the reason he had decided to come here in the first place: it was because he intended to fulfil his master's wishes. So what would the knight have done? He knew that Tallis had been determined to obey his mother. She had told him that if he returned the Key to its resting place - the Key she had helped to steal - then the Land-of-the-Lake would be restored and everything would be as it once was. Well here he, Dando, was, and here *it* was, but nothing of that nature had occurred. Was it possible that by applying torque to the little object in front of him the miracle would actually take place - would the waters begin to flow, the earth bring forth and the dead return to life? He felt a sudden conviction that, by hook or by crook, his master would not have passed up the opportunity to bring about such a transformation however remote the likelihood of a favourable outcome and that, therefore, now the man had gone to his grave, Dando, the faithful squire, must act in his stead.

"It's the last thing I can do for him," he repeated, as if trying to convince himself.

Stepping forward he took the Key between his fingers. Even so he hesitated for long minutes before, holding his breath as he exerted the minimum of pressure, he rotated it anti-clockwise. The mechanism clicked over like something in frequent use and the door unlocked.

He could never be quite certain as to what followed. His fleeting impression was that the walls around him splintered into ten million fragments while at the same time he was thrown into the air and dashed back down. Light streamed from all sides, he was caught in a shower of what looked like flying diamonds and his eyes were dazzled by a spectrum of colour. At the same time his psyche seemed to expand exponentially, intuiting a reality far beyond what the senses of his compromised body were capable of discerning. After which – abruptly - he lost consciousness.-----------

My heart is black,
Black as his coal-black hair,
Because he's lost to me.

Chapter fifteen

"Alright my husband – what excuses do you have now? Let him find it, you said, it's his destiny, and then we can take it from him. And so he has found it, and now that ill-formed issue that I once thought had been destroyed, has found him, and may be taking him down into his domain. If you hadn't tried to impede me, if you'd been less of a laggardly sluggard, we might have already ensured our safety by writing finis to his existence once and for all. I've been much preoccupied with dealing, primarily, with that thing I brought about - the convulsion which I at first thought had achieved my aim - and secondly – once I realised that that had failed - with trying to encourage him to self-destruct, but you, you have had more time on your hands. Why, by all the stars above and below, didn't you do your utmost to seize the opportunity once you realised that the Periapt was in his possession? Instead you stood back and let things take their course. It's enough to make me think of quitting this miserable planet for good and all."

"You know we can't do that after all this time, wife, we're bound to both it and the Object-of-Power – so much so that if the latter is removed we'll be lost in the dark for ever."

"Well then, what?"

"I'm coming round to your way of thinking. You have the ear of a trickster who once possessed certain insignificant abilities. I know now that these potencies gave him a sense of such overweening hubris that he thought he was the equal of beings such as ourselves. Through his own folly he ventured into the underworld where dwells that rapscallion you've already mentioned and in order to escape he promised to steal the Treasure from my keepers and bring it back, a promise he never intended to keep. But in his obsessional curiosity, on the way out of the Caves of Bone he explored that nether region; he knows his way around. Supposing you send him below in search of the Thing to which our fates are

tied – I believe that that's where it's going to end up and that he has as urgent a reason as we for wanting to retrieve it."

"***What! the one you said was 'a hollow mockery from which all the juice has been sucked'?! As you mention, I have his ear, but little good it did me recently when he failed miserably to carry out my wishes. Come to think of it, why don't you go yourself? After all, the local apes believe you travel there every winter when the light dies."***

"***That's just a story they've made up to explain the effects of Terra's tilt. We can't go – the dark son is too strong and might reach out and bring about our annihilation. In fact I believe we're running out of options and may be stymied if my latest idea isn't given a chance."***

"My da's got et by a tiger!" lamented Horry, weeping copiously.

"We don' know that," answered Milly who nevertheless had also been piping her eye. "We're not goin' to give up on 'im, you bet your life. Wot does your ma have to say about it?"

But Horry just went on bawling inconsolably while staggering round in a circle, his face screwed into a mask of sorrow.

"Come on," urged Milly, seizing him by the shoulders and giving him a rough shake, "you can't be a nipper no longer – you've got to be a man – you've gotta take your daddy's place. Your ma - 'as she gorn wiv 'im or is she still 'ere?"

Horry lifted a tear-stained face and cocked his ear to one side as if listening.

"Both," he sniffed.

"Boaf?! That don' make no sense. She can't be in two places at once!"

"Yes she can," replied Horry truculently.

"No – it don' make sense – you're talkin' fru yer 'at," repeated Milly with scathing disbelief. She watched as Ralph also ran in circles, gazing up at the sky and whining piteously.

"Wot I fink," she added after a period of intense cogitation, "is it woz someone after that flippin' fing 'ee's got slung roun' 'is neck. I wish 'ee'd never foun' it."

Her face darkened and assumed a ferocious expression much like a wrestler's about to grapple. "If they've 'urt 'im," she vowed, "I'll kill 'em – I'll kill 'em dead!" Then, to Horry, "You talk to your ma an see if she knows anyfink. I reckon we'd better go back an' tell the uvers wot's up. Wot else c'n we do? – we can't fly up into the sky.

You 'elp me get the bike to the top of the slope – then we c'n sit on it an' ride down wivout needin' an engine."

To retrace their steps, manoeuvring the bike between them, proved to be a major undertaking for two such small people, but they brought it off by gripping a handlebar each and throwing their weight forward in unison. Taking frequent rests to recover their breath they eventually arrived at the top of the downward gradient and at this point Milly managed to mount the machine and hold it steady while Horry clambered on behind her. Once astride, the hardest part was getting the bike moving. As soon as they commenced to coast their speed rapidly increased and then it was a case of applying the brakes circumspectly to avoid travelling so fast that they overshot on the turns. In this manner the two of them descended to the plains taking a fraction of the time Dando had employed pushing in the opposite direction. Once on the level, however, the fuel-less bike was of no further use. Far more ruthless than her lover, Milly had no qualms about leaving it behind.

After walking for a few miles, darkness descended and they prepared to sleep al fresco. The tent as well as most of their other assets had had to be abandoned along with the bike for the simple reason that it was beyond their powers to carry anything more than just the essentials.

"Come on 'Orry," encouraged Milly, "let's cuddle up together - Meena and Ralph too. We'll feel warmer like that an' then you c'n tell me wot your ma meant about bein' in two places at once."

Horry obliged with an explanation.

"I asked her," he said, "an' she says she c'n go among the stars. It's such a long long way away that she c'n see everything that's happening – here where we are an' there where my daddy is too – both together."

"OK, go on then," urged Milly after she had waited a while for him to continue, "where is 'e? 'Oo is it wot's taken 'im? Is 'e orl right?" and fiercely, "'ave they 'urt 'im?"

"She says it's the dark brother that's taken him," Horry replied. "She says he's bein' guarded closely by a non-human warder so's he can't escape. She's says she's very concerned that he's going to end up in the Caves of Bone where it will be hard for her to follow."

"Hmm," remarked Milly, "I di'n't unnerstan' any of that but I don' like the soun' of it. Ast 'er where 'e is now an' if we c'n rescue 'im."

Horry stayed silent for some time listening, and then began to cry once more. In between sobs he jerked out, "She says she's very afraid for him - she'd rescue him herself if it were possible - he's out of her reach, an' ours she tol' me. She can't talk to him cos he still can't unnerstan' what she's saying - all the same she'll do her best not to desert him until they reach the cave mouth."

"Not desert him?" cried a scandalised Milly, "wot's she on about – that's no way to talk! We've got to get 'im away! I'm goin' to round up a load of people an' tell 'em wot's 'appened. Surely someone will be able to fink of sompfink to do."

The next morning they came upon a previously unnoticed minor track hugging the base of the Tuscadora Range and, turning along it, they set off in an eastward direction that would, they hoped, eventually bring them to Hayseed Junction and, subsequently, to Rockwell Springs. Milly clung to the idea that someone among those who were presently living there in Becca's house would be able to suggest a way in which her dear lord could be saved. Only through such a belief could she ward off the terrible pain that was beginning to gnaw at her heart.

The day drew on and although they had no time-piece to mark the passing of the hours the two young people could not help but be aware that they had been on the road for a prolonged period. By now they were both dirty and travel-worn while, far from the path returning them to the haunts of men, the hills on their right seemed to be getting higher and the forest wilder. Apart from the track they were following human kind had left no significant mark on this landscape. Milly strode out ahead, in a pother to arrive anywhere at all as long as it was somewhere where she could enlist help for her Lordship while Horry, protesting vigorously, had to run to keep up, his legs being much the shorter ("For gawd's sake 'Orry, put a move on, we 'aven't got all day!"). They were becoming extremely irritated with one another and in need of a diversion to take their minds off their plight, so, when they heard shouts and the jingling of harness to the rear, they both turned with a certain relief to see a string of mules rapidly overtaking them. The train was being driven by two men, one middle-aged, one little more than a kid and the walkers stood aside to make way for this procession.

"You're a long way from home, ain't you young 'uns?" commented the older man as they passed although not as if expecting a reply. A few yards further on however he called a halt and turned back to ask, "where are you making for?"

"Wot's that to you?" replied a hostile Milly. She was thoroughly put out when Horry chipped in with, "The railroad - it's called Hay...

er... Hay... something I think," and even more so when he added, "we're goin' back to get help for my daddy." Although desperate for aid she was not going to trust the first Tom, Dick or Harry to offer assistance.

"You're heading for Hayseed Junction?"

Milly nodded reluctantly, feeling she was taking a risk in giving even this much information.

"Well, jump up. We c'n take you that far. We're on our way back to the depot to reload."

"On the gee-gees?" asked Horry eagerly, charmed by the idea.

"They're mules, not horses, but we've got a vacant saddle and you're both small enough to fit onto the same critter I reckon... That's if the little coloured lady'll agree?"

"Come on Milly," Horry pleaded, "please – please..."

It took quite a bit of persuasion to overcome Milly's deep suspicion of strangers but in the end her desire for speed won out over caution and they were both installed on the back of one of the long-suffering animals. Milly mounted with great alacrity in order to avoid the proffered helping hand.

"I c'n manage," she insisted and once astride rebuffed the mule-skinner's friendly advances with, "I'm warning you – no hanky-panky!"

"Hyah, you ol' jug-head – take a hold there boy! Ho, you lop-eared devil – you bob-tailed rascal! Hey Jenny! Why – you bunch a ring-tailed, leather-necked, sway backed...! Hyah – git along mule – git along there...!"

Once they were in motion the captain spent most of his time sounding off and laying the whip on with a vengeance. Milly flinched each time she heard it land, but the mules themselves appeared indifferent. They clopped along with their heads low, the only indication that they were aware of the two men following behind being the evidence of their mobile ears which, when not flicking away flies, were continually cocked to catch the voices of their human slave-drivers.

Three dogs accompanied the muleteers and a degree of hackle-raising and stiff-legged strutting, as well as curious bottom sniffing, had to be gone through before they and Ralph established some sort of amicable relationship. Meena clung to Milly's shoulder, hissing whenever the unfamiliar canines came near, her pupils dilated and fur on end.

When he was not belabouring his charges the muleskinner seemed pleased to have someone other than his silent companion to talk to as they wended their way along the trail. Milly held herself aloof but Horry cheerfully joined him in conversation.

"Where are you going with the gee-gees?" he asked.

"We're off back to Duquesne to take on another load – our last for the season before we hand over to Bruce's team. These critters need a break, same as us."

"Have you been away long – how far did you travel?"

"We go wherever we're paid to go - 'cross the western desert, up into the hills, over the High Chaparral. Wherever you've got settlers you've got a demand for goods and wherever you've got that you'll find us. What sort of goods? This trip we hefted letters, books, boots and shoes, tobaccky, clothes, medicines, a bridal-dress, a guitar, a kitchen stove – you name it, we've carried it. Sometimes we use a wagon if we're haulin' borax. But now they're talking of bringing the iron-horse westwards 'cross the plains an' even up into the hills. If they do that it'll be the end for us. All that'll be left as a reminder is the picture on the tin – 20 Mule-Team Borax."

"I wish I could come with you."

"Well lad – we're always lookin' for new recruits – but you'll have to grow up pretty fast if you want to catch us before we disappear."

"I am growing up fast," replied Horry.

It was late in the afternoon of the same day when something very strange occurred. The sun went behind a cloud and then, all of a sudden, the hills, the trees, the mules and the winding trail in front of them were leached of colour as a blinding flash of light lit up the sky.

"Hell's bells!" cried the muleskinner as several of the animals began to rear and buck with the result that Milly, Horry and a terrified Meena were unceremoniously dumped into the road. Both drivers flung themselves at the reins in order to prevent the whole train from bolting. As they struggled with the panicking team, the members of which were lashing out at one another with teeth and hooves, a low rumbling noise came from the south beyond the highlands. It came after a significant interval indicating a very distant source, grew in intensity and then died away. Following this, although the day, up to then, had been bright, the landscape was abruptly plunged into stygian gloom and the heavens opened. Humans, mules, dogs and a very frightened cat were soon soaking wet and dripping. It was a tribute to Meena and Milly's bond that the little creature did not take to the hills, never to be seen again. In the midst of this mayhem Ralph and the muleteer's mongrels decided to end their truce of several hours and began the mother of all set-tos, one against three. Milly and Horry jumped up from where they lay sprawled and danced around on the periphery of the action shouting their heads off, but it was not until the captain had got his beasts under control and came to lend a hand with his whip that the combatants were separated. Somewhat the worse for wear the four animals slunk apart but continued to growl and bristle for some time afterwards as the wet, shivering and thoroughly demoralised cavalcade got under way once more.

"Well," said the captain, "you never stop learnin' however old you get. In all my years on the road that's the first time I've experienced anything like that!"

Within a couple of days they arrived at the railroad that ran north through the grain belt and the kindly leader, finding his passengers were completely without funds, gave them a sufficiency of money out of his personal profits. With part of this they paid for tickets that would carry them as far as Rockwell Springs. Milly unbent sufficiently to thank him for his generosity but felt relieved when they were once again on their own. A great stretch of time seemed to have elapsed since they had seen Dando whisked away in front of their eyes and she was missing him more and more. Her mood got darker with every hour that passed but she tried not to despair.

"P'raps they'll know 'oo took 'im, the ones up at the 'ouse," she said to Horry as they left the train having reached their destination. "Surely someone mus' know sompfink about a flyin' car. If we c'n find out 'oo it belongs to then p'raps we'll know where 'e's ended up."

As they walked towards sixty-seven Camelback Avenue she turned to Horry for support.

"You mus' back me up, 'Orry – I don' fink they're likely to take much notice of me on my own. They di'n't used to when I woz 'ere before." The closer they approached their destination the clearer became her recollection of the rather servile role she had played during the last time she had been under the roof of the Paternoster family.

"They don' fink much of black people roun' 'ere," she worried, "although they're 'appy enough to let us do orl the work. But when we tells 'em what's 'appened to *'im* surely they'll stir their stumps an' fink of some way to 'elp. 'Ee's as good as them – better 'n them if truth be told."

“I don't think Uncle Curtis or Aunty Tracy really liked my daddy,” cautioned Horry. “They wanted to know why Aunty Becca let him live in her cabin without paying – they said she was too soft-hearted by half.”

“Well, that's orl in the past,” answered Milly quickening her pace, “surely they won't 'old that against 'im.”

“But what about when he made it catch fire?”

It was Becca who came to the door in answer to their knock and when she saw who was standing on the step she registered surprise which quickly transformed into something suspiciously like disappointment. It was almost as if she had not expected or even wanted to set eyes on them again.

“Shoot!” she murmured to herself, “it's Horace and Milly, returned by themselves without the boy.” - then - “What are you doing here my loves? Where's Dando? I'd ask you in but the place is absolutely heaving at the moment. Ramona has just turned up with her three daughters and one of them is about to deliver. Wait a bit – I know what you can do. Your friend Jack's down at the cabin. Go and get reacquainted.”

“The cabin? But it burnt down.”

“Oh, things have moved on considerable since you were last here. The boys saw to the rebuilding and I told Jack he could try the place out while he came to terms with... er...” She looked in the direction of Bishops Hollow. “Why not go and say hello? It migh put him in a better frame of mind. I'll mosey along later.”

The sound of an altercation within the house involving children's voices claimed her attention and she turned away, about to close the door.

“No!” cried Milly, “'ang on – you 'aven't 'heard wot we've got to say!” while Horry burst into furious tears wailing, “My da's got et by a tiger!”

His piercing lamentations drew several other people into the hall including Becca's eldest son Curtis.

“Heavens to murgatroyd,” he complained, “I can't hear myself think!”

“It's the child that came with me across the Tethys – you remember,” explained Becca. “His father appears to have abandoned him. Alright Horry baby – hush now – I'll look after you.”

“You've got it orl wrong,” repeated Milly, “the Lordship – Dando – somebody stole 'im, right from unner our noses. We needs 'elp!”

"He went up into the air," wept Horry. "It was the man an' the tiger that took him. We wants to know where he's gone!"

"What are they burbling about?" enquired Curtis of his mother. "If they're on about that arsonist I'd certainly like to know where he's at, considering there's a warrant out for his arrest. Come on you two – let's have it - when did you last see him?"

Although probably not intended as an outright threat, these few words, spoken abruptly and in a hostile manner, held such an undertone of menace that both Horry and Milly backed hurriedly away, putting a space between themselves and the angry man. Meanwhile Becca was trying to make sense of what she had heard. "My word!" she exclaimed with a sceptical laugh, "I'm no stranger to the hidden arts, but up in the air? - on a broomstick do you suppose!?"

She stepped towards Horry and held out her hands invitingly. "Your story sounds a bit like a fairytale, sweetpea," she pronounced in honeyed tones, "I'm sure your paw is fine and he'll come back before too long. Meanwhile I'll take care of you until he gets here."

Her attempt at reassurance was accompanied by a rather fixed artificial smile which slipped slightly as she glanced sideways at Curtis, seeking his approval. In response the little boy dodged behind Milly who retreated further, spreading her arms out protectively.

"'E's not yours," she cried, "leave 'im alone! 'E belongs to the Lordship!"

Turning she grabbed hold of Horry and, accompanied by the animals, hauled him away from the house in order to make for the centre of town.

"What's the matter Milly?"panted the boy as they slowed down on approaching the railroad, "why are we running away?"

"I fink they woz goin' to 'ang on to you until the Lordship turned up," she jerked out, "an' then, maybe, they would 'ave shopped boaf 'im an' you to the fuzz."

"But Aunty Becca liked my daddy - she wouldn't want to hurt him!"

"She might if that geezer told 'er to. That Curtis – 'ee ain't nice – 'an she's 'is ma. I reckon 'e's got 'er just where 'e wants 'er. Anyways you'd better keep your distance."

"But where can we go for help?"

"We'll do like she said - we'll go an' see Jack. She said 'ee woz down in Bishops 'Ollow. Come on, it's not far. If we put a move on we can be there an' gone before Becca or anyone else knows what's up."

"Uncle Jack! Uncle Jack! Open the door! It's me an' Milly!"

In no time at all they had descended into the shanty town on the other side of the tracks where they were confronted by a remarkable transformation. On the site of Becca's unlamented tar-stained shambles of a property a smart-looking log cabin had arisen, the timbers of which glowed amber in the late-afternoon sun while the air round about was redolent with the scent of freshly-sawn wood. "Blimey," exclaimed Milly, "they've built that quick. It shows the rest of the 'ouses up sompfink chronic. I fink the Lordship did them a favour by sendin' the ol' place up in flames."

Indeed the adjacent premises looked twice as shabby and dilapidated in contrast to this brand-new dwelling which was even equipped with sash windows and a decorative bell pull by the front door. Milly availed herself of this last and awaited the outcome, but for a long spell nothing happened. Eventually Horry, growing impatient, began to shout while Milly rang once more. As a result of their persistence the door opened a short way and somebody muttered in muted tones, "Who is it?"

"It's me!" cried Horry, at the top of his lungs, "me an' Milly – we needs your help!" but at the same time a perturbed Milly asked, "Jack – are you orl right?"

She had grounds for her concern. Although the Vadrosnian's familiar figure appeared within the half-open door there was something anomalous about his appearance that suggested a profound change had taken place. In the days when he had been mourning his mother's death and later what he imagined to be his lost potency there had still been present, behind his misery, traces of the cocksure Jack they had come to know and love. Now, however, they were faced with an individual quite hard to recognise. Despite the fact that he was wearing his familiar dark glasses and employing a brightly-coloured cane once more, he looked somehow drained and diminished and less youthful than on their last encounter. At first, when the door opened, Milly jumped to the conclusion that the young man was not pleased to see them. This seemed to be the most likely reason for his off-hand manner, but then, because of the strange gloom he was radiating, she began to wonder if there might be a different explanation. After all hadn't Becca said something about his needing to be cheered up? "Are you orl right?" she repeated, but his only response was to open the door a little wider and step aside in order to allow them to enter. It was not until they had walked through into a simple but well-equipped kitchen and sat themselves down at the brand new wooden table they found there that he heaved a long weary sigh and answered her.

"Yes, *I'm* all right," he said, "d'you want coffee?"

It was obvious by the ease with which he navigated his way between taps, stove and larder as he sought to serve them that he had been living in this place for sometime. Milly followed his movements with a troubled gaze. Although she was still gripped by the urgency of their mission and was constantly haunted by visions of Dando's abduction, she was beginning to get a sense that other events of some moment had also happened hereabouts in their absence. It made her reluctant to bring up her own concerns before she had heard more on the subject, yet, at the same time, she was wary of probing too deeply in case she unearthed something painful. Horry however had no such qualms.

"Where's Uncle Fynn?" he demanded. "He used to play football with me. Does he still play football?"

"No, he doesn't," answered Jack abruptly and did not elaborate.

"Are you 'ere on your own?" enquired Milly timorously.

"Yes."

A long silence ensued while Jack produced a cake to go with the coffee or rather milk in Horry's case and also found some titbits for Meena and Ralph. They had finished second cups and he had cleared the china away before he finally said in a strained voice, "He's had it."

"Fynn? You're torkin' about Fynn?"

"Yes – you won't be seeing him again."

"Why? Wot's 'appened?"

Jack sighed once more and cleared his throat as if expanding on this bald statement was an ordeal that had to be faced.

"Well – you may or may not know that he and I decided to go to Belle City a few weeks back," he began, gripping the edge of the table in front of him with both hands, "we went via Harrisburg by train. We'd only been there a short while when Fynn said he wasn't feeling well and he'd have to opt out of what we'd planned to do that day. He was very apologetic – said he was spoiling the visit for me. I said, not to worry, we'd carry on when he felt better." Jack paused as his voice choked up, then, struggling to keep his emotions under control, he continued, "Well... he didn't get better even after several days. Belle City's full of con-artists – everyone's out to make a buck at the expense of everyone else. I called in a quack but didn't trust him. I decided the best thing to do would be to take the kid back to Harrisburg on the train. I managed it, but by the time we got off at the other end he was in a shocking state. We put up at a hotel and I found a doc with a good reputation. He couldn't do anything for him – the lad just kept on going down hill – it was terrible..."

Jack turned his head away, at the same time taking off his shades and putting his hand over the place where his eyes should have been. His shoulders were shaking. After a while he got out a handkerchief and blew his nose, then, banging the table as if to emphasise every word, cried, "Seventeen! Would you credit it?! No more than seventeen – and they say we all get our just deserts!"

Milly and Horry were reduced to speechlessness by this outburst until the black girl summoned up enough resolution to ask, "D'you mean 'ee's dead?"

Jack nodded. "A brilliant conclusion."

"But wot was it? Wot did 'ee 'die of?"

"Your guess is as good as mine – the doc didn't know – although..."

Milly waited. "Although..." she prompted.

"Well," Jack slumped down in his chair, appearing so listless all of a sudden that it was an effort to get the words out, "it was when we were at the Club – before the earthquake – things were apparently going along fine. Then one or two of the kids stopped coming to meetings and somebody said they'd heard they were sick. They never returned. I didn't think anything of it at the time. Before the end arrived he admitted – I mean I got Fynn to admit – that he'd not been really well for ages but he'd kept it from me. I know I'm blind but I should have seen... and he was so talented... I never gave him his due"

Again Jack's feelings seemed in danger of overwhelming him.

"My Grandpa's bin put unner the earth too," Horry remarked unexpectedly.

There was a long pause before Jack sat up straight in surprise as if someone had waked him from a bad dream.

"What...?" he responded.

"'Orry's torkin' about Tallis," explained Milly, "you know – the knight. He had a reely orful accident in Damwey – thrown by 'is mount an' trampled – we couldn't save 'im. Kicked by 'is 'orse and then kicked the bucket."

With an effort Jack switched points and took his thought processes down a different track.

"You're not kidding?! But what about Dando? Losing Tallis must have hit him hard - how did he react? Where *is* Dando – isn't he with you?"

"That's wot we cum to tell you about," replied Milly, while Horry, reminded of their chief concern, wailed, "My Da's got et by a tiger!"

Taking it in turns and sometimes both speaking at once when urgency overcame their attempts at clarity Milly and Horry filled Jack in on the strange events that had occurred on their way south and expanded on the uncertain fate of the third member of their party. After they had given him a rather confused account of what they knew Milly came to a inconclusive halt before adding in a pleading tone, "That's wot I tried to tell 'em up at the 'ouse but I don' fink they believed me." "They thought we was tellin' fibs," added Horry indignantly.

"Well," said Jack gently, "you can't really blame them as it does sound pretty far fetched."

Milly lowered her voice as if about to reveal a secret known only to herself.

"I fink 'ee woz magic," she whispered, "the geezer in the car. I fink the whole fing woz magic. That's why 'e 'ad that tiger animal wiv 'im – it woz unner a spell."

"Magic!" In Jack's tone could be heard the incredulity of a dyed-in-the-wool townee confronted by what he considered to be primitive rural superstitions. "I know I wasn't there but I reckon you'll find there's a perfectly rational explanation."

"You mean you don' believe us eiver about wot 'appened?"

"I believe you're telling me what you thought you saw – but what actually occurred may have been quite different."

"So...?"

"Well, the first thing on the agenda is to go back to where he left you – you may find some traces that'll give you a clue to the real circumstances. Things may not be as bad as you imagine."

"If we do that will you come with us Uncle Jack?" asked Horry. By the tone of his voice he did not seem to have much confidence that the answer would be in the affirmative. Jack's reaction, however, was remarkably positive.

"I don't see why not – I don't intend to leave *le petit oiseau* in the lurch if he's in danger. Anyway I've got no reason to stay here – not anymore – and this side of the tracks is getting pretty anarchic. Night before last there was a fight down at Bo's – everyone joined in – nobody seemed to know what it was about."

"We had Becca's mo'bike," continued Horry, "but we had to leave it behind. The man forgot to fill the tank - daddy was cross. He pushed it all the way up the hill. An' then the man in the car said he had some gas in the back so daddy got in to get it an' the tiger grabbed him and then the car flew away."

"That means we'll 'ave to walk if we do go back," added Milly. "an' we'll 'ave to leave soon, in case those at the house try an' stop us."

"I think I might be able to help you there," said Jack. "You tell me you haven't got Becca's bike but I think I might know where one of her other vehicles is – she had two cars, remember. She bought one for her mother before the old lady got ill and it's recently been moved down here from Camelback Avenue cos they needed to turn the garage up there into a bedroom. Didn't you notice that there's a carport attached to this place? Come and see."

The three of them went outside and sure enough, under a canvas roof at the back of the building, they discovered a little black car similar to the one in which they had occasionally been given lifts during their days at the Magnolias.

"But don' Curtis and Dempsey use it," enquired a surprised Milly. "or any of the uvers in Rockwell Springs? Surely they'd want to 'ang onto it?"

"Too much of an antique for their tastes I reckon," replied Jack, "that's partly why it's down here and not up there sitting outside the house."

"But we can't just take it wivout tellin' Becca!"

"I don't see why not. She doesn't really need it – none of them do, although if we ask to borrow it you can bet your life they'll find some reason to object. We'll leave at night. They won't even know it's gone 'till a lot later – maybe weeks later. We'll bring it back after we've found him."

Milly blinked once or twice, understanding, for the first time, how Jack had earned his nickname *The Chancer*.

"But I don' know the first fing about drivin' a car!" she protested, realising she would have to be the one behind the wheel.

"We'll work something out."

The blind boy seemed to have taken charge, but, as they came back to the cabin, he gave a rare demonstration of his vulnerability. On the way out he had been talking animatedly and not counting steps, with the result that, returning, he miscalculated distance when changing direction, and, despite his cane, walked straight into the wall instead of through the front door. Milly grabbed hold of his arm in order to steady him, causing him to turn to her with a shamefaced expression.

"It's exhausting," he remarked apologetically.

"What you on about?"

"Having to manage without eyes."

This was the first time she had ever heard him confess to the difficulties he faced daily and she was shocked.

"What!? - But you're so good at it – I fort..."

"It wears you down in the end."

Horry had run ahead into the house giving them a brief window of opportunity in which to exchange confidences.

"This illness that Fynn 'ad," asked Milly, "is it one of those fings that people get when they're 'umpin'? Were eiver of you 'avin it orf wiv those nippers at the club 'oo were sick?"

Jack neither confirmed nor denied this but pulled a face, contorting his features into a ferocious grimace. When she asked solicitously, "Could 'e 'ave passed it on to you - are you *sure* you're not feelin' under the wever?" (his manner was so changed that she felt it might be an indication of ill health) he shook his head unhappily as if he could have answered in the affirmative if so inclined. Milly's mind then returned to thoughts of her beloved and she decided it was high time they got back to more urgent matters.

"'E ain't too clever eiver," she volunteered.

"Who?"

"The Lordship – Dando. 'E ain't well - 'e picked up sompfink in that 'orspital. 'E needs me to keep an eye on 'im. I'm doin' me nut worryin'."

"Oh I see." Jack looked troubled but did not seem unduly surprised at this news. "I had an idea something might be wrong before we left to go north but as he never said anything..."

"'E never does."

"I'm just taking 'Orry out for an 'ittwl bit of a walk."

"OK, but don't be long."

Jack did not ask where they were going; he was too busy getting ready for an early departure, having decided that speed was of the essence if they were to make themselves scarce before anyone realised what they were up to. Leaving the brand new cabin Milly hurried the child in the direction of an isolated shack lying beyond the town's limits and situated on the edge of swampy ground, barely noticing that the cat and dog had tagged along behind.

"I know 'e tells us there's no such fing as magic but 'e's wrong. Wot does 'e fink's bin 'appening to you ever since you woz born? We're goin' to see that witchy woman – the one Becca took you to before. P'raps she'll be able to make a spell to find out where the Lordship's gorn."

"Becca gave her money when we went last time."

"I got money – the mule-man gave me money."

The local visionary, Mother Eulalie, proved to be an enormously stout, dignified old black lady who, when she understood that they wanted to consult her in her professional capacity, conducted them into a small back room where she invited them to sit down before pulling the curtains and lighting an oil lamp hanging above a highly-polished table. After staring curiously at Horry and remarking to herself, "It's accelerating," she left them for a short space only to return wearing a dark flowing robe and carrying a kettle in one hand and a metal bowl in the other. She placed the kettle on a small paraffin heater and the bowl on a table mat, at the same time pushing what looked like an offertory plate towards Milly. The girl took the hint and deposited first one, then two, then three bank notes onto the dish. The third donation apparently brought the total up to a satisfactory level and the sortileger prepared to get down to business.

"So chil', what is it you want to ask Mother today? What c'n she consult the Spirits about that'll bring you comfort?"

Milly did her best to explain what had been happening while Horry remained uncharacteristically silent.

"We've just got to fin' out 'oo it was wot's took 'im," she ended, "an' where they've gorn - then p'raps we c'n save 'im."

"Have you got something that he owned or might have kept about his person?"

Both young people thought hard, wrinkling their brows, and were about to answer in the negative when Horry fished in his pocket and brought out a rather crumpled scrap of paper.

"Would this do?" he asked, "Daddy drew it for me. He told me a story about how when he was a little boy he lived in a castle, so I asked him what a castle looked like an' he drew this one for me. He lived there," pointing, "in that tower." The magic-worker took the drawing and smoothed it flat, then held it to her breast for an extended period. As she meditated she seemed to become unaware of the room and its occupants and instead looked inward down long stretches of space and time.

"He was born to wealth and position," she said at last, "but now he walks the earth as a penniless stranger. He has shared the hard times of the outcast and felt the lonely pain of the oppressed. He has been both priest and sacrificial victim and because of this knows what it means to be fully human. He is nearly ready. The world is waiting for him to complete his task but whether the outcome will be fortunate or misfortunate not even the First Comer can tell."

"*To complete 'is task*?!" cried Milly scornfully, making the quotation gesture with her fingers, "'Ow is 'e ever gonna *complete 'is task* when someone 'as run orf wiv 'im an' we don' even know where 'e's ended up?"

"The spirits tell me that his task is to represent the whole of humanity at his final hour," continued Mother Eulalie, ignoring this outburst, "to stand for everyone, both men and women, young and old, black and white, and because of this he must taste all our joys and sorrows down to the last dregs. In the future some will call him the *Universal Child*."

"Yes, an' that's just it – 'e's far too young!" protested Milly who was even younger but, as a result of her own grim upbringing, felt a great deal older, "it ain't fair to ast 'im to do that!"

"His trials have made him old before his time, but in the process he has become wise. The lives of those fated to play a part in the world's destiny are never easy; it seems they have to pay for the privilege of being chosen even if they haven't sought the pre-eminence."

A dissatisfied silence followed this statement until the clairvoyant added, "Do you wish me to continue?" gazing meaningfully at the little pile of notes on the table. Milly added another ten dollar bill. The old woman took a handful of what looked like dried herbs out of a jar and cast them into the metal bowl before pouring hot water over them from the kettle. Then she bent low above the basin at the same time flinging her robe over her head so that it acted like a tent. She breathed loudly and stentoriously causing Milly and Horry to exchange glances. Eventually, when their patience was nearly exhausted, she lifted the curtain of material that hid her from their sight and straightened up, her features running with condensation.

"The light," she wheezed chestily, "if you wish to find him you must follow the light."

"Wot light?" asked Milly but received no reply. Instead, after dabbing at her face, the seer heaved her ponderous bulk out of the chair and waddled through to the front of the dwelling, followed, after a moment's hesitation, by the two young people. She opened the outside door to reveal Ralph and Meena sitting waiting patiently on the step. The animals immediately came to attention at the prospect of renewed action. The woman made a grand gesture.

“These will be your guides,” she said. “Trust the dog – be ruled by the sagacity of the cat.”

“Well,” said Milly, on the way back, “that woz a dead loss – waste of time an' money.”

“She did seem to know who my Daddy was,” said Horry.

“But she d'n't tell us 'oo took 'im or where we could find 'im an' that's what we really wants to know.” “My ma said it was the dark brother that took him an' that he might end up in the Caves of Bone.”

“Well, that could be very useful if I 'ad the faintest notion wot it meant.”

“An' that he had to go unner the earth an' outside. P'raps we ought to look for him unner the earth.”

“You fink so? Well, wot are we s'posed to do then – dig an 'ole?”

Envenomed moon.
Heralding a dark dawn.
Are you fit to reign?

Chapter sixteen

When the date arrived for the shepherding of the flock across to the mine-workings Tyler informed Damask that the children would be coming with them.

"Now you're here you can keep an eye on all four while we're on the move," he explained. "They don' get much chance to meet kids of their own age in the normal run of things. There's quite a number in the houses down by the lake – admin. officers' families. There's usually a birthday party or some such goin' on. I thought we might stay over. You c'n travel with them in the trap. Ryan'll drive."

But this Damask refused to do, not wishing to be landed with the role of a mere child-minder. Instead she insisted on going afoot ahead of the buckboard, stepping closely on the heels of Tyler and his two dogs in order to help chivvy the protesting flock through shadowy passes and alongside hazardous drops. The animals gave voice piteously, they seemed to sense that their time was running out. However everything was going well until on the second day disaster struck. They had reached a stretch of road where the land fell away on one side. Tyler, up to now intent on his task, allowed his concentration to waver, distracted by what was happening overhead.

"Look at that," he exclaimed, pointing upwards, "there's no proper wind to speak of and yet..."

What had grabbed his attention was a bank of storm clouds advancing from the south at an extraordinary pace. Mere minutes passed before the whole sky was covered, the heavens opened and the only source of light came from an ominous flickering beyond the mountain peaks.

"Watch out!" he cried, "the beasts could be panicked if..." but as he spoke it was already too late. Right in their path, between driver and flock, something that could have been a thunderbolt came hurtling down from the stratosphere and struck the ground with a deafening report, throwing out a light so dazzling that for a moment all were blinded. As Damask's vision cleared it was to see several sheep barrelling over the edge of the cliff while the rest high-tailed it up the road as fast as their legs would carry them. They vanished round a curve followed, after a split second, by Tyler and the dogs. At the same time the horse between the shafts of the buckboard reared, backed and then slewed the whole contraption round, by some miracle avoiding capsizing the vehicle or sending it into the crevasse. It took off for home along the way they had just come carrying the children with it out of sight. In the blink of an eye a soaked Damask found herself alone and watched in disbelief as the clouds above thinned, dissolved into wisps and then evaporated, while the sky took on an aspect typical of a serene autumn afternoon.

"By my not-so-sainted aunt," she declared, "what was all that about and what am I supposed to do now?! Shall I wait here? No, I'd better try and catch up. I think the kids'll be all right – that Ryan's got his head screwed on – pity about the animals."

She followed the track northwards, but, by the time dusk approached, had seen neither hide nor hair of Tyler and the surviving members of his flock. Just as she was beginning to anticipate spending a night on her own without food, water or protection against the savage local fauna she heard a grinding of gears at her back and turned to see headlights wavering up out of the dimness. It was a surprise to realise that the noise ricocheting to and fro off the rocky walls was the sound of an internal combustion engine, but then she remembered being told of the truck that conveyed the prisoners to the excavations. This was no lorry however; as it approached she made out a car, an old jalopy, built for staying-power rather than speed, which came groaning and coughing towards her along the road. Damask stepped into its path and held out her hand. The vehicle came to a stop.

"Hi," said the man at the wheel, "you bin stranded?"

"Kind of," replied Damask.

"Wanna lift?"

"Yes please, although I'm a bit damp I'm afraid."

She climbed into the car which smelt of sweat, diesel and cigarette smoke. A light had come on as she opened the door and by its illumination she saw that the driver was a heavily built man, slightly gone to seed, with a shaven head and large stubby hands.

"Where you headin' doll?" he asked.

"The thingy – er – cozerite excavations."

"Snap! What are you goin' to do over at ol' Lake Bravo?"

"Oh – I'm meeting someone."

"Mm – I see. OK – none of my business. It's just you don't get many single women in this neck-of-the-woods."

"So I've been told."

Silence reigned as they set off, then...

"Well – I've got my eye on a nice little earner in that direction..."

"What d'you mean?"

"I'm a promoter – wrestling - I've got a stable..." The man was soon in full flow. "I'm always on the lookout for fresh talent. There's a screw over there who tips me the wink if he sees a likely candidate. I've had two or three good prospects on his recommendation an' now he tells me they're holdin' the best one of the lot. Just goin' to size him up."

Damask glanced again at her chauffeur; he looked by his cauliflower ears and broken nose as if he might once have been a fighter himself.

"D'you mean one of the prisoners?" she asked puzzled.

"Yes, that's right."

"But don't you have to wait a long time before they've finished their sentence?"

"I buy them out. Pricey I know but if they're good they c'n earn it back in a few months."

A faint hope dawned in her heart and glimmered in the dark. "Who's this one you've been told about?" she enquired.

"I don't know what his real handle is – they call him *Carrot Crop* or the *Croppy Boy*. When he fights he goes by the name of *Captain Judd*."

"There's fights in the correctional unit?"

"Cage fights. The guards and the rest of the officers need some excuse to get rid of their pay, otherwise it burns a hole in their pockets. As I 'spec' you c'n appreciate there's not much on offer when it comes to time out."

"But what...?"

"I tol' you – women are in short supply around Lake Bravo. Prisoners have to get things sorted amongst themselves. The new intake's always fair game - you know how it is – or perhaps you don't," looking quizzically in her direction. "Anyway, Carrot Crop wasn't havin' any – stood up to every las' one of 'em. That's how they realised he'd got talent. Now he's a celebrity."

Captain Judd! It could be none other than Foxy!

"You're going to buy him out?"

"Once I've looked him over an' approved."

"But then won't he belong to you?"

"In a way."

"I see. What's your name?"

"Wilson – Chet Wilson."

"I'm Damask."

"Hi Damask."

They shook hands.

Later that night the fight-promoter parked his car under an overhang and chivalrously offered her its use as a bedroom whilst he himself opted to sleep outside wrapped in a rug. In the early hours of the morning she woke and, looking east, saw the waning moon on its back with its legs in the air. This image of helplessness struck her as a somewhat sinister omen.

It took most of another day of travelling (again they saw no sign of Tyler or his sheep) before the road began to descend on the north side of the Craiks and they glimpsed a gleam of water ahead.

Damask and her driver had reached no more than halfway down the steep descent leading to the place known as Lake Bravo when they met a frightened man panting up the hill in the opposite direction. He held up his hands as if indicating that they should turn back, at the same time crying, "There's a riot going on! – the cons are on the loose! – they're holdin' some of the guards hostage! Those that have decided to do a runner are comin' this way!"

"Are they armed?" asked Chet.

"Broke into the magazine after lightening set the governor's house on fire! Some of the warders have bought it. Sorry – gotta scarper..."

He scampered past and vanished into the distance.

Damask and her companion stared at each other in concern, unsure whether to proceed, and while they dithered two more figures came in sight forging up the slope in a determined manner.

"Hey fella," shouted Chet, "is it true that the prisoners are on the loose? How far have they got?"

"You're looking at them," came the reply, " dumped the bee-stripes and made a getaway – there's some still slugging it out down there. If you know what's good for you you'll turn round right now and make yourselves scarce."

When these men had passed by a further mass of escapees came crowding up the hill and they heard the same story more than once. "It was the storm started things off - the screws'll be after us soon as they get things sorted – the army's sent for reinforcements – we're making for Kamloops – if we c'n get to the railroad we'll be well below the horizon..."

Damask, throwing caution to the wind, collared one of the men and demanded, "Foxy – Captain Judd – what is it you call him? Do you know where he is?"

"Eh? - what the hell you on about?"

"Captain Judd – red hair – blue eyes..."

"You mean Carrot Crop, the fighter? No, haven't seen him. That's freaky – should have been in the thick of it with his reputation."

"He's no fool," said a second man, "probably took off soon as the wire went down. Come on Jake – you're wastin' time – we'll be totally buggered if we hang around here."

Damask's driver pulled over to the side of the road to make room for the fugitives who were increasing in number by the minute. It was not long before they became aware of speculative glances being shot at the car by those that passed. Chet shifted uneasily.

"This ain't on," he muttered, "time to vamoose – I'm gettin' outa here 'fore I find m'self havin' to foot it back to Ry-Town."

Taking advantage of a lull in the torrent of absconders he executed a three point turn and then sounded his horn brusquely, intending to clear a path back up the mountain in order to outpace those on foot.

"Hang about!" cried Damask, struggling with the door handle, "I'm not ready to leave – I've got to see what's happening. Let me go!"

"Don't be a chump! - it sounds like it's mob-rule down there – you won't stand a chance!"

But Damask had at last got the door open and climbed out triumphantly, all ready to set off against the current. "I'm gone!" she said.

Chet rummaged around on the back seat.

"Well then," he replied, throwing the car rug in her direction, "if you're determined to be a schmuck wrap yourself in this – it'll be less obvious that you're an attractive woman."

"Oh... er... thanks." Kindness between strangers tended to take Damask by surprise as it was not something she often indulged in. After the car had departed she turned towards the rocky wall and commenced to swathe herself in the large blanket, starting by covering her head and then working downwards. When both her body and her bulky rucksack were wound round in several thicknesses of material a life-like simulacrum of an old hunchbacked woman emerged and provided her with a very effective disguise. She crept downwards giving those coming in the opposite direction a wide berth but at the same time searching their ranks for a familiar face. Eventually she found herself less than a hundred feet above what was obviously an extensive settlement while the flow had been reduced to a trickle. She paused, gazing down, trying to work out what awaited her. Off to the left, partly obscured by the hillside, she could see a wide stretch of still water, obviously one end of the lake which gave its name to this place; permanent resort-like buildings were situated along its margin. Below and to the right lay row upon row of identical wooden huts while further away she made out other temporary-looking sheds, some quite large, intermingled with low crags that had a raw, recently-worked appearance. Large spoil-heaps were dotted here and there, confirming the presence of quarrying or mining in the area. What was immediately obvious was that a number of the man-made structures had been set on fire and that no-one was attempting to quench the flames. In fact, as she stared downwards, she got the impression that the place was almost deserted.

Once she reached level ground she discovered that the huts were surrounded by a high wire fence. Turning alongside this she soon came to a place where it had been cut through. At the same time she began to hear sporadic gunfire in the distance. Finding her movements somewhat restricted and there being no-one else in sight she unwound the blanket and let it fall to the ground, then began to creep towards the source of the noise, doing her best to stay under cover. It was as she peered around a corner trying to see what awaited her that she almost passed out from shock as someone who must have snuck up totally silently from behind, took hold of her by the waist. With a gasp she twisted round only to come face to face with a freckled, pugnacious visage, penetrating blue eyes and tightly-curled red hair. Here he was, that *sniffer-out-of-traps*, *that sly-stealer*, the *Croppy Boy* as they had named him here. It was none other than her lover of a single night!

"Foxy! For heaven's sake! You just about gave me a heart attack!"

"Well, gel," replied the Nablan in a conversational tone, "I weren't a-gooin' ter warn you by shoutin' me head off. What be you a-doin' in such a place as this?"

"Looking for you, of course!" She noticed that his familiar features were somewhat battered but at the same time there was a new poise and self-assurance about him that had not been there previously; she was apparently in the presence of a VIP.

"Why are you still here?" she demanded. "Why haven't you escaped with the rest of them while you had the chance?"

"'Cos it be whooly a waste of time. That lot," waving his hand towards the road she had just come down, "won't git far before they meet the army comin' t'other way. They di'n't even think to cut the phone lines when they first broke out. The screws had time to yell for help before their throats were cut."

"So is that it?" demanded a disappointed Damask, "have you still got this crazy idea of serving out your sentence? Are you going to stick around until you're locked up again?"

"Howd ye hard, gel – did I say that? No – I'm waitin' till dusk – then I'm gooin' to t'other end of t'lake to steal a boot. It's the only way to git away for good an' all. I'm goin' to foller the river down over the border. Then they'll never be able to haul me back agin to make a fewl o' m'self for their amusement."

"There's a river?" exclaimed Damask.

"Come – I'll shew you."

It did not take long for Damask to realise that Foxy was totally familiar with all the highways and byways of this confusing complex. He led her in out and roundabout until they were sneaking along behind the properties on the edge of the lake. The gunfire that she had heard in the distance was much louder now.

"What's happening?" she whispered after they had skirted around the place from whence it came.

"Some of the cons think they're gooin' to discover untowd riches by raidin' the top brass's pleasure palace. They're on a hidin' to nothin'. When the army gits here – BANG – they'll be dead afore you c'n say *duzzy eejits!*"

"Where's this river then?"

"At t'other end of the lake like I said. We'll lay low here till it git dark. Should be easy enough to find a boot then. Mustn't be too big cos we'll hev to carry it roun' the barrier that holds the water back."

"Do you know anything about boats?"

"Not so's you'd notice. Do you?"

"A little."

Fortunately when they set out a while later the sky was clear so that although the moon had not yet risen the starlight was bright enough to see by. Also some of the staithes in front of the properties were lit by artificial light although the owners were probably well away by now if they had not already cashed in their chips.

"How about that'un?" muttered Foxy from where they lurked in the shadows between two adjacent houses, pointing towards a jetty against which several boats were moored.

"Too big, an' the draft's too great," replied a knowledgeable Damask. "Rivers vary a lot in depth. I don't think any of those would do – they're just for playing about on the lake. Let's try further along."

By the time they had almost reached the end of the development Foxy was getting impatient. "Come on gel," he said, "we gotta make up our minds. The longer we hang around here the likelier we are to git caught."

"No – no," replied Damask eagerly, "there – on the last jetty – that's the boat for us."

"Boot? That look like a heap o' ol' balloons tied togither!"

"No – it's a boat right enough - a sort of blow-up raft – it'll be light and buoyant. But we'll need some paddles 'cos we can't carry it an' the motor as well."

A somewhat bemused Foxy helped her to discard the outboard which was attached to the rear of the inflatable, then to shoulder and cart the craft along the path leading to the head of the lake. There the steep shores closed in as the expanse of water narrowed until it appeared that they were walking beside a conduit rather than a mere.

"Hey," exclaimed Damask, "there's a current! It's flowing away from the lake – it really is a river."

"Di'n't I tell you?"

"But what's that ahead?"

"That be what they call a sluice. We mus' git roun' it afor we put the boot in the water."

The path they were following petered out and they had to climb the hillside to get past the obstruction. Once on the other side it was noticeable that the character of the stream had fundamentally altered; here it was shallow and fast-flowing, with patches of foam where rocks impeded its progress.

"Where does it go to – this river?" Damask asked doubtfully.

"I towd you – over the frontier into Caffray . There's a war gooin' on further south 'twixt this side an' a place caller Tartary. The filth won' be able to foller once I gits into another country an' I'll be a free man."

Damask thought about all she would be abandoning if she took the irrevocable step of accompanying him on his journey: she might never see her surrogate son Horry again, or Dando, her twin and life-long confident, or the other friends who had been part of her great adventure. She looked at her companion, her half-brother as she now knew him to be, and made up her mind.

"OK," she said, "let's get this thing launched. We'll sit on either side in order to guide it and keep to the deepest part if we can. It should get easier as we go along. By the way, here's a gun, plus some ammunition, to replace the one you lost."

The weapon she had managed to purchase after the trial and had kept safe through thick and thin was handed over and a delighted Foxy sealed it in a waterproof bag of which there were several in a small compartment located on the inside of the craft, after which the boat was lowered into the river. The Nablan held it steady as Damask climbed aboard. He jumped in after her and immediately it was in motion. Before they could bring the paddles into play they revolved twice in the current but then managed to get the bow headed in the right direction. By necessity, picking up skills at a rate of knots, they were soon steering a fairly straight line between hazards as the stream bore them headlong into uncharted territory, taking them down an unexplored course from which there might be no return.

"Whoopee!" shouted Damask, confident that her voice would be lost in the roar of the rapids, "Caffray, or whatever you call yourself – stand by for boarders – here we come!"

Well, the road is wide, the air mild,
And the light goes before us.
But, tell me, where is he?

Chapter seventeen

Towards the farther end of that galaxy which is home to the small blue-green planet that provides the setting for this narrative a huge assemblage of beings, numerous as the stars that shine on a clear winter's night, had gathered. But this congress did not shine, in fact it darkly filled every cubic parsec of space in the afor-mentioned region and was ranged around an area that could have been described as a celestial amphitheatre. At the centre two lone life-forms took their stand, apparently isolated yet at the same time the focus of tremendous interest and concern from those that looked on. The observers were well aware that a conflict was about to take place and that the couple's adversary would be that fragmented, incomplete creature who had never known what it is to experience normal corporeal joys yet who exercised a great and malevolent power. They also knew that the outcome would be of tremendous import to them all.

"***Stay back pet,***" the male individual cautioned his female companion, ***"put yourself behind me. The one that is coming intends harm to us both, his aim is elimination, but to you in particular. He will do his best to destroy you because something that was once a part of your body and which can only retain its power as long as you continue to exist is protecting both the Catalyst and the young lordling who holds it. When I give the signal exert all the power you have in your possession and I will do the same. I think in the end we will carry the day because we are not alone, there are others who will fight on our behalf."***

"***But Dadda – you always taught I that although I possess the gift I must injure no-one and that we mus' worship and pay homage to the gods of which he is one."***

"***That was before I Crossed-the-Brook pet and in those days I did not fully understand how things are ordered. I thought then that those from outside were far above us in the hierarchy of***

existence but even so, by the end, I doubted that they were gods. Now I know that they are no better than you or I – just farther along the road, and I realise that sometimes it is necessary to use force when we are given no other choice. Get ready sweetheart – see there – see where he comes. It will be a great test of your fortitude to oppose him but with the help of our friends I believe we will prevail."

It was evening by the time Milly and Horry returned to the cabin and Becca, despite her promise, had not put in an appearance. Jack had finished packing the car so they ate a quickly improvised meal, then snatched forty winks before preparing to depart.

"I know how to drive," said Jack, "I learnt when I was just a kid. My grandfather imported a horseless carriage from Armornia – it was the only one in Drossi. It was pretty basic but the principles must have been more or less the same as this one. I suggest you get behind the wheel, Milly, an' I'll sit along side an' tell you what to do. Horry c'n go in the back."

"With Ralph an' Meena," the child piped up.

"What?! We're not taking the animals!"

"Of course we are." It was Milly who answered, sounding determined. "It would be unkind to leave 'em behind - there's no-one here to look after 'em, and besides the Voodoo woman said they might be useful."

Jack made an exasperated noise with his tongue.

"So that's where you went earlier," he said, "while I was having a mid-life crisis trying to decide what necessities to take with us. I could have done with some help in that department."

Milly ignored his protestations but instead insisted they should leave a note for Becca. Then, in the dark hour before dawn, they began their peregrination as the whole town lay asleep. Once Jack had brought the car to life by using a starter handle they took their allotted places, after which they set about climbing the path from Bishops Hollow at a snail's pace before crossing the railroad into Rockwell Springs. As they progressed upwards Milly was subjected to an intense course of instruction from the blind boy during which, despite her teacher's best efforts, she stalled the vehicle on several occasions. At one juncture they were on the brink of rolling backwards all the way to their starting point until Jack seized and engaged the hand-brake.

"I can't do this," moaned Milly as they jerked to a halt for the umpteenth time, "I'm 'opeless."

“No you're not – you're doing fine – better 'n a lot of people. It'll be easier once we're on the flat.”

“Well, which way do we go then to find the Lordship? I still 'aven't a clue.” Without further mishap they had reached the north-south road that cut through the west side of Rockwell and now had to decide whether to turn left or right.

“We'll head due south and follow the railroad as I suggested. Later we'll turn west and make our way to where you lost track of him so we can see if there's any clues to pick up on.”

Very soon, as light grew in the east, they were bowling along through the grain belt on the route that would eventually lead to Hayseed Junction. Milly's confidence was growing by the minute. But now the animals began to behave in a distinctly unorthodox manner: Ralph, his nose pointing almost vertically, started to howl and went on howling despite all their attempts to quiet him, while Meena rose on her hind legs and scrabbled at the side window with her front paws, adding her tiny voice to Ralph's strident one. At last, his patience exhausted, Jack exclaimed, “I can't stand this any longer – I don't care what you say – we're going back to the Springs. We'll leave them on the edge of town for someone to take pity on. Come on Milly – three point turn.”

Even the black girl was finding the noise hard to stomach. Reluctantly she reversed, swinging the car round and set off the way they had come. However, as soon as they changed direction, the howling and mewing died away and the cat and dog appeared perfectly content.

“It's cos we were goin' the wrong way,” Horry offered as explanation, “I tol' you my ma said we shouldn't go south. Ralph and Meena know that – I think they know where my Daddy is, or anyway where we're most likely to find out where he's been taken.”

“That Mother Eulalie did say they'd be our guides,” put in Milly hesitantly.

Jack gave another snort of derision, but when they drove into Rockwell Springs a second time he did not attempt to eject the animals. Neither did he voice any objections when they continued to head north although he was obviously far from happy.

“You realise we're getting into the realms of fantasy here,” he grumbled a little later when Milly and he were the only two left awake, the three in the back having realised a pressing need to make up for lost sleep. “This magic shit reminds me of one of those stories out of the books that used to come in on the packet from Armornia.

I've read loads of them in my time but eventually you get too old for such nonsense."

"Oh blimey," replied Milly, "an' 'ow old are you - a hunderd an' three?"

"Dando liked that sort of thing – he had some that the doctor gave him – the one that cut off his foot."

"Poor Lordship." Milly withdrew into her own thoughts for a while before adding, "I'm really worried about 'im – 'e's still got this corf..."

"Yes, you told me."

"...an' sometimes I fink 'e brings up a 'ittwl bit of blood. 'E tries to 'ide it from me but it's not easy at night when... I mean..." she faltered, embarrassed at what she had been about to admit to, while Jack turned to her in surprise as if he had made a remarkable discovery.

"Are you saying what I think you're saying?"

If Milly had not been so dark of skin and if Jack had not been blind he would have seen that she was blushing. She giggled despite her anxiety and went on in proud and satisfied tones, "I fink you've guessed, so I may as well tell you. Yes, it's true – 'im an' me, we've bin 'avin' it orf for quite a while now – I wasn't too keen at first, but we got on orl right once we started – very orl right."

"Well... well..." Jack was momentarily silenced. Then with complete sincerity he gave his approval. "I'm so glad. I was afraid that that side of things was over for good as far as he was concerned. I'm glad for him... and glad for you too."

"But wot about now?" Milly's momentary happiness quickly dissipated as she awoke to the current situation, "we don' know where 'e is or wot's 'appenin' to 'im. Maybe 'e's getting' more'n'more ill an' me not there to 'elp 'im."

"He may not look it," said Jack, attempting comfort, "but Dando's pretty indestructible. He's already been to hell and back and come through relatively unscathed."

"Unscathed?" exclaimed Milly indignantly, "wot about 'is foot?" and then, a little later, "Wot's this about hell? Do you think there reely is such a place?"

"I wasn't talking literally."

By this time the sun had risen and light flooded the landscape. The new day proved to be fine with a wide blue vault above, just softened slightly by a low haze.

"Wot's that?" Milly was pointing through the windscreen, already sanguine enough to take one hand off the wheel. "Is it the sun? No, the sun's over there. I've never seen nuffink like that before."

"What are you on about?" Jack spoke with weary patience, well used, by now, to the fact that people regularly forgot that he was blind.

"There's a sort of bright patch in the fog – it's sort of coloured on one side – straight ahead of us. I bet the Lordship would know."

Indeed Dando could have informed her that what she was seeing, not far above the horizon, was something called a sundog and that such a phenomenon, from the point of view of an observer, always appeared at the same distance from the sun as the span of an outstretched open hand measured from thumb to pinkie. He would have been genuinely puzzled, however, to observe that this particular example was nowhere near that position, the sun being far off to the right.

"It's still there," remarked Milly a little later after they had covered a few more miles. "Look 'Orry – wot d'you fink that is?"

Horry sat up, yawned and rubbed his eyes, then stared into the distance.

"I s'pose it's the light she tol' us to follow," he said as if stating the obvious. "I think my ma and my other granddaddy must have put it there to show us the way."

Time passed, the journey continued. It was more than a day before Milly made the discovery that the route they were following was already familiar to her.

"Look 'Orry," she said, "I fink we're goin' to end up in the same place we came to las' time; I mean before the Lordship decided 'e 'ad to go souf."

.They had been heading north but had now turned north-west, following the light in the sky, the sun-dog, as it went before them. Although evidently acting as their guide, it was not always visible; the conditions had to be just right. It usually appeared within a type of faint wispy-looking cloud close to ground-level that barely obscured the sky. On the days when it did not manifest the animals soon let them know if they went the wrong way. Ralph barked and Meena yowled, both impossible to ignore, while Horry was always on hand to interpret.

"They're saying you should have chosen the turning we've already passed. No, not here – the one before. This is it. See, Meena's telling you you're going in the right direction now."

Milly listened to Horry with a new respect and a certain amount of awe. This *youth* as he must now more rightly be designated, had begun to display certain abilities that she found virtually mind-blowing. It was in one of the towns they passed through that Jack, with his ready supply of cash, had bought camping and cooking equipment which included, in place of the abandoned yurt, a modern tent, saucepans and a paraffin stove. This meant that each evening it was their custom to pull off the road and set to work making a temporary home for themselves. On one occasion, watching his elders cackhanded attempts to erect their sleeping quarters, Horry had become impatient and stuck in his oar.

"You're not doing it right," he told them, "those twiddly bits don't go on the bottom there – you've got them the wrong way round. You should spread it out and stick the poles through the loops before you try an' lift it. An' you've forgotten this piece. How do you think it'll stand up without putting that on first?"

Jack sighed and turned away while Milly angrily dropped the items she had been trying to connect saying, "Orl right clever clogs – let's see you 'ave a go!"

Horry bent down, picked up various components and then stood completely still for a few minutes staring off into the distance. After that, without apparently making any effort, he began to put the tent together, or rather the tent seemed to assemble itself under his hands like a well-trained circus animal. In no time at all he had it up, functional and ready for use.

"'Ow did you do that?" cried an astonished Milly

Horry looked at her in slight bemusement. "It's not difficult," he said.

Another night, after a day of rain, Jack and Milly were having a deal of trouble trying to light a fire. Despite the fact that they now owned a stove, it was because of a problem in obtaining paraffin along the road that they had gone back to a more old-fashioned way of cooking. Some bread and succotash had been purchased from a road-side stall and that, along with seasonal fruit, was to be their evening meal.

"Sod it," complained Jack, "we'll just have to forget about the fire and eat the food cold."

"I think I might be able to get it going," said Horry, selecting a stick. As Milly watched in incredulous amazement the twig in his hand began to glow a dull red at one end, gradually brightening until the boy thrust it in amongst the rest of the kindling. There was a shower of sparks and a small desultory flame sprang to life before everything turned dull and black once more.

"It's too wet," said the boy, "hang on – let me try..."

He lifted the saucepan containing the food and walked away a few feet where he stood with his back towards them apparently ruminating. Eventually he returned and handed the container to Milly being careful to offer it to her handle first.

"I'll get the plates," he said.

To Milly's astonishment she saw steam rising from the surface of the stew. After some hesitation she spooned out a portion into a bowl and put it into Jack's hands who, receiving it, felt its warmth and remarked, "So you did manage to get the fire going after all."

Later that night when they were in their sleeping bags and Horry had apparently nodded off Milly whispered, "'E di'n't get the fire goin'."

"What do you mean," said Jack.

"'E di'n't light the fire."

"Then how did he heat the corn thing?"

"I don' know – 'ee jus' did – 'ee jus' stood there 'oldin' it an' it sorta got 'ot."

"Impossible."

"You tell me wot 'appened then."

"Well, who knows. He is the son of a genius cook after all."

"An' the son of the girl remember – the Lordship's sweet'eart. The Lordship tol' me once that she woz magic – praps 'Orry takes after 'er. Praps she's teachin' 'im."

Jack shook his head disbelievingly.

"Magic!" he growled.

"Wot about the light – ain't that magic?"

"Remember, I can't see it. For all I know it's just a figment of your imagination."

"Me *an'* Horry's? An' wot about the animals?"

"All right – I don't want to argue. As far as I'm concerned I'm just tagging along for the ride." But this was very far from the truth: Jack troubled himself as much or even more than the other two over Dando's fate.

It was indeed to Damwey that the sun-dog and the flesh and blood dog and cat led them. They even put up once more at Mr and Miss Wapshott's establishment. Entering the town however proved to be a quite different experience from when Milly and Dando had arrived previously. As they penetrated the environs they came upon some swaggering bully-boys who seemed reluctant to let them pass until Jack told them he was returning home to his father and sister and, more to the point, handed over a substantial sum of money. At the guest-house they found a pale-faced Miss Wapshott shivering in her shoes.

"It's not safe here any more," she told them in a low voice. "It's the Brady Bunch and the James Gang; they've been at loggerheads since goodness knows when but now suddenly everything's come to a head. Brady's lot invaded the town last week saying they were taking overall charge but the James boys claimed it as their territory and before we knew there was a shoot-out just up the road which solved nothing apart from making things ten times worse. Now one group are holding the west side while the others are over in the south-east with a no-go area in between. It's not safe on the side-walks, law has broken down and decent folk are becoming victims of all sorts of outrages. What's going to become of us?"

When Miss Wapshott found that her guests were planning to go straight out again and expose themselves to the dangerous environment of the streets she pleaded almost tearfully for them to stay indoors.

"It's worse after dark – you don't know who you'll meet – some of them are completely off their heads on I don't know what – they'll shoot you down soon as look at you."

"But we've got to find out wot we're 'ere for," explained Milly, "an' if we stay indoors the animals will be kicking up a stink by mornin'. Listen to 'em already. But *you'd* better not come 'Orry – you'd better go to bed – can you keep an eye on 'im?" to the older woman.

"What?! I'm not goin' to bed!" declared Horry indignantly, "I'm not a baby any more!" and on the word *baby* his voice suddenly broke and swooped down nearly an octave.

"Horry!" exclaimed Milly in surprise She noticed for the first time that she was looking slightly up into his face; he was going to be tall, perhaps as tall as his father, in proof of which he was already bursting out of his clothes, the second set she had managed to acquire in a matter of weeks. She could also see, despite his Nablan colouring, that there was something about him that reminded her of Dando. If they had only just met how old would she guess him to be? Thirteen? Fourteen? He seemed to be absolutely flying through his life - soon he would leave her behind. He was no longer the child that she had once been able to order around. What was it like being him she wondered. The cat and the dog might be able to empathise; after all, their respective species took little more than a year to reach maturity.

"'Oh orl right," she said in response to his protest and then to her other companion, "'ow about you, Jack?" She was well used by now to the blind boy's scepticism and would not have been surprised if he had cried off the expedition altogether.

"Safety in numbers," he grunted, through which brusque statement she understood that he intended to accompany them.

"We 'ave to follow the animals to get to the centre of town," explained Milly, "that's wot the Lordship tol' me 'e did. Come on – look, they're waitin' for us." and sometime later after a confusing half hour threading the Damwey maze, "Crikey, I fink we're 'ere – the Blue Mountain Saloon – that's the place where the Lordship foun' the ol' man after 'e'd bin chucked orf 'is 'orse an' where 'e picked up the fing wot everyone's tryin' to get an 'old of."

They were standing in the same square to which Dando had been led four weeks earlier, but now the place was transformed. No longer dark, silent and deserted, the tavern throbbed with noise and blazed with light. A huddle of indistinguishable figures in ten-gallon hats stood around the entrance smoking pungent cigars while various anonymous individuals came and went. Meena flew to Milly's shoulder while the two male members of their party hung back, cautious about their reception. The black girl, however, had no such scruples. Saying firmly, "I needs to go to the lavvy - I shoulda gone before we set out," she marched in through the front door. There was no-one at the counter but at that precise moment a couple of women appeared from the back of the premises giving her the opportunity to ask in a conspiratorial tone, "Scuse me missus, c'n you tell me where the loo – no I mean the bathroom - is?"

One of the women pointed behind her and Milly disappeared smartly in that direction, Meena in attendance, while Jack and Horry, accompanied by Ralph, sidled into the crowded tap-room trying to look as inconspicuous as possible. They were met by a scene of ear-splitting, drunken revelry. The place was crowded with men in working clothes, a number wearing chaps and spurs, all with tankards in their hands, all armed. Were these members of the Brady Bunch or desperadoes from the rival James Gang? There was no way of telling and it hardly seemed to matter; whoever they were they looked a dangerous lot. Many of the clientèle were accompanied by flashy-looking women, some black-skinned, some white, all decked out in frills and flounces which did little to disguise large areas of bare flesh. Someone was pounding away at an upright piano, obviously a different one from the complete wreck that Dando had encountered, while four chorus girls did high kicks on the pocket-sized stage. Just as they entered, this act came to an end and was replaced by a lugubrious fellow behind a microphone who launched into a typical cowboy song accompanied by two guitarists and a fiddle player. Ralph went ahead of them towards the bar giving a sharp bark which drew glances in their direction. The place was so crowded that even as they stood waiting their turn they were jostled by those who had purchased brimming glasses of the hard stuff and were trying to get them away from the crush unspilt. Jack and Horry could hardly hear themselves think as their senses were assaulted by booming music and strident voices.

"Look," shouted Horry above the racket, "I spose that's the Blue Mountain."

"What?" asked Jack resignedly.

"Oh sorry – I mean there's a painting along the wall behind the bar..."

"A mural," said Jack.

"A muriel - is that what it's called? It's a landscape with funny-looking buildings in the foreground an' funny-looking trees – an' in the background there's a mountain, painted blue with snow on its upper slopes – it looks as if it's round an' comes to a point."

"A cone," said Jack.

"Oh right – a cone. There's little people in the picture near the buildings, with hats almost the same shape as the mountain. I s'pose that's why this place is called what it is."

By this time Milly had returned from paying her visit.

"Look Milly," said Horry, "there's the Blue Mountain. D'you think it's a painting of a real place? Praps we ought to ask someone."

In response to his suggestion Milly hesitantly approached the woman she had spoken to earlier and made enquiries.

"You'd better try Sarah," came the reply, "she's there behind the bar. If anyone knows about things like that she will. Some say her great-great-granmaw used to work for the Bunyips before they cleared out."

They rejoined the queue and resigned themselves to a long wait, only for Meena to rashly jump from Milly's shoulder onto that of the man in front and from thence onto the bar. Once there she stretched her front paw into the air apparently pointing towards the picture.

"Hey, who owns this animal? Get it outa here!" The bartender was understandably angry. Milly gathered Meena to her bosom.

"Sorry – I fink she jus' wanted us to look at your painting. Can you tell me about it? What do you know about the Blue Mountain?"

The barmaid called Sarah, a very old lady indeed, heard what she said and, turning to the rear wall, examined the mural almost as if she'd forgotten what lay behind her.

"Oh that my dear – that's been here since the year dot or rather since the town was founded. The Blue Mountain Saloon was part of the first building phase; they started on it long before my people ever came into this country. The Inshami, the ones that put it up in the first place, left when the war went against them. You've heard of the Madderhay Wars? That's what Damwey used to be called: Madderhay. After they went no-one felt inclined to live here and it was deserted for many a year. It got the name of Dead-Man-Walking because it was supposed to be haunted. Some people think it still is."

"So you can't tell us where the Blue Mountain is?" said a disappointed Milly.

"Go ask Colonel Wapshott – he's an expert on the history and geography of Pangorland."

"Are we supposed to go an fin' this Blue Mountain?" asked Milly as they hurried back to their lodgings, "is that where the Lordship's bein' taken? The animals seem to fink so."

Jack shrugged; Horry remained silent.

"Wot does your ma 'ave to say about it?" she persisted, addressing the younger boy.

Horry looked grave.

"My mother's not here anymore," he said.

"Wot! - but I fought you said she could be everywhere at once and that she put the light in the sky?"

"Yes - she may have done that, but now, when I talk to her, she doesn't answer. Something's happened."

"Such as wot?"

"I don't know exactly but it was when it got all dark an' the mules tried to do a bunk. Something big changed then far to the south, an' a little while later my ma got involved along with my granddad. I think she's still trying to sort it out."

Horry fell silent and it took Milly a while to absorb this new information.

"Oh 'eck – well we'll 'ave to get along as best we can wivout 'er. This Colonel Wapshott that the lady tol' us about – maybe 'e's the bloke we're stayin' wiv' – I fink 'e's called Wapshott. We'd better ask 'im if 'e knows about the mountain."

They had already discovered that Mr Wapshott, their landlord, who indeed proved to be a retired colonel, spent most of his time in a sanctum on the upper floor of the boarding house, engaged on research into old manuscripts. His niece showed them up after first approaching her uncle to find out if he was amenable to a visit from their current guests. The old soldier stood up as they entered the room and shook hands with all three as if they had only just met, but after that addressed himself exclusively to Jack who consequently became their spokesperson. The boy gave a faithful account of Dando's adventures as recounted by Horry and Milly, but made little attempt to disguise his reservations over the more sensational aspects of the tale. The colonel, however, did not seem fazed by the fantastical side of the story and in fact his interest appeared to grow as it unfolded.

"You say that your friend found the Agent-of-Change here in Damwey?"

"Yes – in a tavern which, at the time, occupied an uninhabited part of the town."

"I knew the Object was believed to be here when the Inshami, the Bunyips as the locals call them, monopolized the place. I never imagined it could still be in the vicinity. Why didn't they take it with them when they left I wonder."

"Dando said it was hidden – hidden in plain sight."

"Ah – clever. Whenever I've read about that nation and about the Thing-of-Power I've always had the feeling that there was a certain person within their ranks whose plans went against those of the majority. Are you sure it was the legendary Key?"

"Evidently it displayed certain occult properties."

"Mmm. And you're interested in the Blue Mountain? Well, it was famous throughout the land at one time. People round here regarded it as a place of pilgrimage – somewhere they went when they had problems to be solved. It was the home of this famous seer and natural philosopher you understand, the one I've already mentioned. He was wise beyond knowing, it was said, and had acquired the ability to live to a great age. But now such a journey is impossible and the local people have to manage as best they can. The mountain is to be found some distance to the east and since the border conflict broke out it's been virtually inaccessible from this side although the philosopher is said to live there still. He went to that place with the remains of his countrymen when the Madderhay Wars reached their inevitable conclusion because the substance he needed for his experiments was to be found beneath it. Unbeknownst to him, though, another - an enemy of mankind called Azazeel – already occupied the strata between Aigea's realm and that of Rostan and this individual's powers waxed as the years rolled by."

The old man, looking concerned, took down a book and began leafing through the pages.

"You say your friend was kidnapped by a man in a flying car?"

"That's right," said Jack.

"Well – see what it says here. *Azazeel, although dwelling in the depths, is renowned for his sky-chariot and often ventures into the upper atmosphere far away from the underworld. Even the Earth Mother and the Father of Winds have to defer to him when he is abroad.* Your friend – does he have a resolute nature?"

"If there's something he believes in you can't shift him."

"That's just as well because if he turns the Key-of-the-Ages at the suggestion of the Prince of Darkness it could go ill with the world."

The man fell silent for some time as if weighing up various options, one against the other. Eventually he spoke. "You intend to go to the mountain?"

"Yes and rescue him if that's where he is."

"You know I find it rather surprising that you've been led here if the mountain is to be your ultimate goal but, on the other hand, I do believe that that's where his abductor may have taken him. Before you proceed, it might be as well to research the place more thoroughly, going beyond what I have been able to tell you. Of course it could be too late to do anything – that is if the Enemy already possesses the Thing-of-Power."

He mused for a while, then began afresh.

"About two weeks ago there was a brief but very violent storm over Damwey which seemed to signal a general transition from one environmental state to another. Since then the border war has intensified, there are rumours of a sickness in the east and we appear to have entered a general period of unrest. I sense that a lot of things have changed and it causes me to wonder if a new age has been put in train. Anyway I doubt you'll get to Caffray on foot but as an alternative you might... I'll just go and see what I can arrange... By the way, I imagine your meal must be waiting for you in the dining room..."

They left him, went down stairs to eat luncheon and when they had nearly finished the colonel reappeared with news.

"You may not know this, coming from a distance, but before I retired I served my time on the eastern front fighting against the

Tartary invaders. I'm still in contact with what goes on there – old comrades' parades, reunions and suchlike. Because of that I've just sent a message to one of my contemporaries who's now running a freelance operation ferrying supplies to the partisans behind the lines. I put in a word for you and in his reply he says that if you present yourselves before his next run he's willing to make a touch down on the other side and drop you off with the deliveries."

"Do you mean...?" asked Jack, swooping his hand up and over.

"Yes, that's right – above rather than through ("We're going up in a flying machine!" Horry exclaimed excitedly to Milly), and my friend – his name's Johnson – can probably provide suitable clothing for when you land which will enable you to blend in with the local Caffray population. However, he won't be able to do anything about your faces – you'll have to keep them hidden as much as possible."

"'Ow do we gets to where this flying thing is?" put in a practical Milly.

"Well, it's a long way and the going is not too good apart from the millitary road – all the same you'd better steer clear of any troop movements. I'll give you a sketch map and my permit – that might be of some use if you get stopped, though it's well out of date by now."

Milly and Horry finished their meal and left the table but Jack stayed on and picked his host's brains as he sat eating, asking various questions. After a while though he felt impelled to interrupt the man's flow of information. Having been told once again about Azazeel and his strange powers he cut in in a tone of withering disdain.

"Magic!" he exclaimed, "as far as I'm concerned there's no such thing."

"Have I mentioned magic?" countered the colonel. "Who said anything about magic? I can assure you that everything we've talked about today is perfectly in accordance with the laws of nature; it's just that the laws of nature are far stranger than anyone has been able to discover up to now. *Magic* is just a convenient term for something people don't yet understand."

Having reached the end of his discourse Colonel Wapshott looked Jack over appreciatively and then issued an invitation. "If you care to come back upstairs," he said, "I've got a number of scrolls dating from the time of the Inshami I'd like to show you. They knew a thing or two, those folk."

"I'm sorry," replied Jack, "but I'm afraid I'll have to disappoint you. As I thought you might have realised I'm as blind as a bat."

"Blind? Oh I see. You manage so well I thought you must have some residual sight."

"None."

The colonel looked put out but then rallied.

"Well, no matter. Come anyway. I'll describe the documents as best I can. You strike me as someone I could hold an intelligent conversation with - in fact we might have a lot in common."

A faint smile played about Jack's lips.

"OK," he said with a slight hint of world weariness, "lead the way."

No breath, no moisture,
And, like a mummy, dead.
Bodies are just useful discards.

Chapter eighteen

Dando became aware of something extremely abrasive being rubbed against his face, something almost rough enough to lacerate the skin. He put up his hand to protect himself only to hear a subdued snarl accompanied by a cold breath that fanned his cheek. Opening his eyes he saw Letty's great mask staring down at him and realised he had been on the receiving end of a revivifying lick.

"Where am I," he asked in clichéd response to the tiger's attentions and then immediately recalled most of what had happened prior to the point at which he had lost consciousness. Looking around he found he was lying at the base of the hill on which the little transparent temple had stood not long before but that the building was no longer there. Instead he found that he was surrounded and covered by crumbs of glass that glittered in the sunlight like early morning frost. Cautiously he sat up and the glass fell away from his body with a sound like the tinkling of tiny bells. He saw that for the first time since his arrival in this benighted place, the sun was shining and small wispy clouds were drifting slowly across the sky, but otherwise things were much the same as before: the lake had not been restored and the shores around its bed remained barren. Yet were they the same? He looked up, following Letty's example – she was gazing at the heavens - only to see a small black dot descending towards them and to hear a faint whine which grew louder by the minute. He put his hand to the chain encircling his throat and then stared desperately around him. Where was the Key? Several feet away he saw a brassy glint on the ground and, ignoring the splinters beneath his knees, crawled forward until he could retrieve the Master-Changer that, despite this particular designation, did not appear to have changed things, other than itself, one iota. He just had time to reinstate it next to the locket before the airborne craft landed close by.

How long had he been unconscious? It must have been for more than a few minutes if Ken had had time to leave and then return. When, a while ago, he had set out to cross the lake bed he had not looked behind to check on his captor's movements. Knowing what he knew now, he wondered if there might have been an opportunity to escape, although Letty's constant surveillance would probably have prevented it. Anyway, now that the car had reappeared the chance was gone. Instead he guessed he had to prepare himself for further weird and wonderful happenings and, although he had no idea what to expect, he was pretty sure that whatever form they took he was in for more unpleasantness. The tiger, surprisingly, seemed to share his apprehension for it got up and paced to and fro giving the occasional roar, seeming to be torn between two conflicting desires:- the urge to flee and the compulsion to remain at its master's beck and call. What Dando had not bargained for was that, for a long time, absolutely nothing happened. As the minutes ticked by the driver sat unmoving behind the wheel of the stationary vehicle while boy and tiger stared in his direction. Dando noticed that the car seemed to have lost most of its newly-minted sheen. At last he asked with a faint degree of hope, "Is something the matter?"

Like an automaton's the man's head turned slowly round and the face that presented itself was that of a corse three days dead. Letty hissed and Dando caught his breath as a horrified nausea rose in his throat. He began to retreat but the tiger, despite its own apparent desire to get away, blocked his path, its paw raised and claws extended. The driver faced front once more and bending down fished a bottle from beneath the dashboard. He took a long swig of whatever fluid it contained and then noisily drank some more, smacking his lips.

"Unavoidably detained," Dando heard him mutter in a voice that seemed to come from deep down in his body, "unavoidably detained."

The young man, guarded by Letty, waited for he knew not what while his captor again partook of the liquid in the bottle and carried on some sort of self-pitying dialogue with himself.

"How was I to know..." he growled from the pit of his stomach, "...unfair advantage... ganged up on me... father, daughter, all those others... lucky to escape... no-one appreciates my situation..." He had obviously made an attempt to eliminate Ann but had been thoroughly trounced by the combined efforts of her father and the other dancers.

After another long interval he looked once more towards Dando, this time, much to the boy's relief, with a living face: the handsome, middle-aged, intelligent face with which he was familiar.

"Get in," the man ordered, opening the door to the front passenger seat, adding, "you can't refuse, Letty's right behind you."

Dando obeyed, knowing he had no choice, while the tiger leapt into the back and took up position as before, while the vehicle lifted into the air amidst a blizzard of flying glass.

"I-Is Letty a zombie?"

Since he had been forced to re-enter the car Dando had been gripped by a feeling of such utter futility that, for the moment, it hardly seemed to matter if he relaxed his veto and spoke to his hijacker. Very conscious of the tiger's cold breath, he recalled a tale that had come his way during his time in Bishops Hollow: one of the older black women that lived there had whispered that someone in possession of secret knowledge could bring the dead back to life and force them to do the spell-binder's bidding. In reply to his question Ken gave a great shout of bitter laughter.

"Letty?! No, it's not Letty who's the zombie!"

He refused to elaborate further.

The car had quit the ground and turned north but this time its driver seemed disinclined to take it into the upper atmosphere. They cruised along at cloud height catching sight, every so often, of the land beneath. Dando saw forests, huge jungles extending over thousands of miles, amongst which were mountains that by virtue of their height shouldered the trees aside. He saw lakes and wide meandering rivers. Sometimes they passed over man-made clearings, sometimes over open country across which ranged vast wandering herds. He asked where they were bound but Ken remained uncommunicative, brooding over some unexplained setback. When he did finally speak, however, it was as if some new train of thought had substantially improved his mood.

"Well," he said in a voice which sounded both husky and unused, "you've really gone and done it this time."

The young man looked towards him and then away, trying to give the impression that he was not remotely interested.

"You turned it didn't you? I saw it from afar. And now I've come back the smell in the air, the look of the sky, the sounds in the wind – they're all different somehow, utterly alien. Aren't you aware? But perhaps it hasn't struck home yet. During most of the reshaping you were out for the count, or so Letty tells me - examine those scratches if you want to know for how long. It's essential that those in the flesh should be conscious throughout the whole metamorphosis in order for the transformation to register – otherwise it escapes notice. This is only the second turning I've experienced since I was just a gleam in my mother's eye and it was you who did it my friend, all on your little ownsome. But you've really put the cat among the pigeons and no mistake. Talk about the eternal dance – this planet will be dancing its bloody socks off before too long – it may even dance itself right out of orbit. Well, at least I've got my own back on those jumped up pretend-divinities who decided I could go to hell. This is the last thing they would have wanted."

The boy continued to ignore him but a vague fear gripped his heart. Ken seemed so triumphant, so gratified, by the change his victim was supposed to have wrought that he already suspected that what pleased this malevolent creature could bode ill both for himself and the rest of humanity. *Have I made a mess of things?* He wondered.

He looked again at the sky and, momentarily, saw the sun as a blood red disc surrounded by numerous protuberances that stretched out in all directions like the legs of a hairy spider - surely that was not how it was meant to be? The next minute however everything appeared normal once more despite the fact that an image had been imprinted on his brain of bare trees bowing and groaning in a spiteful wind while black birds perched, cawing, in those leafless branches and a distant string of mountains belched fire. In the foreground of this vision a forest of stones leant every which-way - tombstones he thought they must be - on which a strange language was engraved.

What am I remembering?" he silently questioned.

As Ken had suggested he ran his hand over the wounds on his shoulders and discovered they were almost healed. His head spun and his grip on reality faltered as he realised that days, maybe even a week, must have elapsed since he blacked out. What had been happening since last he was compos mentis?

I must have been here ages after I... after... Was Letty waiting for me all that time?

"Cats are patient creatures," remarked Ken, demonstrating, heart-stoppingly, that there was no refuge to which he, Dando, could retreat, not even one within the privacy of his own mind. He sank back into his seat, trying to think purely of trivialities.

For an extended period they had been flying over bleak uninhabited moorland that had little or nothing to recommend it, but now Ken abruptly steered to the left and then executed a half-circle manoeuvre so that they ended facing east.

"Look below," he invited. "you might recognise something."

The craft swooped down into a mountainous region, then levelled out well below the height of the highest peaks. For a brief moment Dando glimpsed a circular combe that looked vaguely familiar, the word *Midda* sprang to mind, after which they plunged into a ravine, winging along a few feet above a turbulent stream. His confused senses had only just time to register this enclosed space before they burst out into a wide fertile valley and he knew immediately where he was. This was Deep Hallow! This was home! There it was - the quarry - there was Castle Dan and ahead he saw the town of High Harrow racing towards them!

"What are you doing?!" he cried, clinging on for dear life to the side of the car.

Ken did not reply. With consummate skill he took the flying machine over the roofs of the little burg missing chimneys and steeples by what seemed like inches. Dando caught sight of some of the townsfolk rushing out of doors, of others cowering in the middle of the road and carts being overturned by panicking horses. Then they were past and skimming over Low Town and after that Gateway. At the mouth of the Incadine Gorge they roared skyward, turned round and then headed back up the valley at strafing height. Now Dando saw that besides the absolute mayhem that had been created in the streets of the towns several thin columns of smoke were rising above the rooftops and in one place a flash of bright flame consumed the upper-story of a house.

"Did you do that?!" he exclaimed in horror.

There was a rattle against the car's exterior and he registered the fact that a few bold spirits down below had gone on the attack with their grossly inadequate weapons, but that the arrows, spears and sling-shots they aimed at the invader were just bouncing harmlessly off the fuselage. Then the craft, turning north, was once more amongst mountains and the valley of Deep Hallow had been left behind. Dando realised that Ken was laughing quietly to himself.

"Just one or two miniature grenades that I keep tucked away under the chassis – couldn't resist it – good joke, eh?"

"People probably got killed!"

"But just think – in a hundred year's time the descendants of the majority who've survived will still be talking about the day the dragon attacked their town. We'll go down in history."

Under his joviality Dando detected a mood of sly malice and was appalled.

"This was all on my account, wasn't it?" he cried, "you knew that that was the place where I was born – that there are people down there..."

"Well my boy, if you will insist on defying me you've got to expect the occasional rap over the knuckles. Why don't you decide to co-operate and give me that thing you're hanging on to so obstinately. It's not like it's doing *you* any good; it's not doing the planet any good. You'd be better off without it."

Dando shook his head and covered the Key with his hand. It had become small and nondescript over the last few hours as if trying to hide itself away.

Ken did not remain long among the highlands; he swung his craft back eastwards again as evening approached and soon they were flying above the Kymer Levels in the fading light, looking down on isolated villages surrounded by small areas of cultivation in the midst of miles of monotonous grassland. These scenes were glimpsed through a misty layer and it was where this was at its thickest that a bright flash suddenly lit up the pall from below. Immediately a denser angrier looking cloud began to blossom skywards, cauliflower-like, unfolding into space. At the same time a shock wave caught the flying car and threw it sideways so that the immortal had to fight to regain control. Several seconds later there came a muffled boom that reverberated to and fro from horizon to horizon. Ken looked expectantly at Dando as if hoping for some reaction, but since the recent attack on his homeland the Glept had determined not to be drawn whatever happened and refused to respond. In contrast to his taciturnity the pilot became extremely garrulous. "Glad to see they're making good use of what I supply. Weapons' test - that's what it was; several megatons at least. Yes, I'll fess up – I provide the raw material for the armaments – Xoserite – need you ask. I've acquired customers already: Trewithik's army, the Armornians and the Tartary invaders; probably the first three of many. They're never going to find their own source however hard they try. I've got access to the only genuine reserves on the planet and even so there's precious little to be had - major operation getting it out. That's why when I sell it on, it costs an arm and a leg... mmm... an arm and a leg..." He stretched out his own arm, as if to admire it, turning it this way and that. "Not a bad choice, even if I say so myself. No, dear boy, it's not Letty who's a zombie, if by zombie you mean the continued utilisation of an exanimate body."

Dando sat on, grim-faced and silent trying to appear indifferent; he felt more and more as if he were living out a waking nightmare from which he was unable to escape because Letty's presence, rarely more than a hand's-breadth away, reduced his options to zero.

"You see, my friend," continued Ken, embracing a subject that was obviously of great interest to him, "when those smart-arses decided to create a second generation from their own insubstantiality they gave little thought to the fact that their offspring would miss out on a vital stage in their development. All life-forms, including the so-called *dancers* who are free to roam the universe, start their journey with the coming together of sperm and egg inside material bodies. This means that even those that have transformed carry with them a recollection of the shape they once held - it's called Ancestral Memory. In the early days there were some crazies – just a few – who decided, voluntarily, to return to the flesh, which meant experiencing death for the nth time, despite having broken through and achieved immortality. Unfinished business I suppose."

Ken paused, then resumed in a tone dripping with self-pity: "Because of the manner in which we were engendered my brother and I never *crossed over* as it's called – we've always been on the other side, having been robbed of the common heritage of the living. Unlike those piss-artists who thought they were so clever that they could fashion life out of their own essence we can't make an image of what we once were when we go amongst the earthlings – we have no mental template from which to construct a physical body, so we have to improvise in whatever way we can. Personally my own solution is to borrow, because, after all, I need flesh and blood hands to work these," indicating the controls, "I need a flesh and blood tongue to communicate with you."

He shook his head and brooded for a while, then suddenly grinned.

"Actually, the situation I find myself in isn't really so bad. In fact, as I said, I think that this latest acquisition," touching the top of his head, "was a pretty good choice. Superior brain – makes things easier – and a wiz in his own field. Oh yes – this once belonged to somebody else," proffering his wrist as if inviting Dando to smell a perfume, "perhaps he's still in here somewhere," and he spoke down the front of his shirt, "hello, c'n you hear me?" This was a signal for more raucous laughter which rendered him temporarily helpless. Eventually he made an attempt to clarify further.

"No, seriously – I picked this one up just as he was being expelled – pancreatic cancer you know – galloping – fifty-six years old – unfortunate for him – lucky for me. Of course, they never last long, the bodies. They deteriorate pretty quickly – then I have to go looking for a new one."

Another pause.

"In actual fact," he continued, speaking half to himself, "something really bizarre occurred on this particular globe concerning the act of transformation. In a time before any creature here had progressed enough to reach that stage of evolution, a Thing, an object loaded with enormous potential, appeared not far away and went into orbit around our local star. Where it came from or what its original purpose was no-one has ever been able to tell, but some of that flotsam who crowd outer space – various non-human species known as the Old Ones who, by some fluke, have made the changeover to immortality - managed to ensnare it in a web of their own substance, known by the savants as *dark force*. After that they brought it down to the nearest habitable planet – this one - in order to put it out of reach of other ex-terrestrials and in so doing reversed the evolutionary process as far as they were concerned, becoming surface-dwellers once more. Inevitably they fell out amongst themselves and a long battle for possession ensued. While in close proximity to the material world the Object began to take on form and substance, moving through many transformations, and the planet in turn became charged with some of its power so that the two became inextricably linked. In the midst of the war which raged above and below the earth's crust the Thing became temporarily lost and a creature of the flesh, one of your ancestors I believe, came shambling along, fists knuckling the ground, and picked it up. He jammed it into a nearby hole – in a rock? - in a tree? - who can tell? – thereby committing a transgression of the first order and incurring a debt which has yet to be paid. But as a result of his action it took on the appearance of a Key, the hole became a Lock and, as it turned under his hand, the gates of paradise -a metaphor for the innocence of the early earth - swung open and those within seized the chance to leave that place, not realising they could never return. It was at this point, or rather a mere few thousand years later, that another entity from beyond – my so-called mother – discovered it and I think you know the rest. The greater part of the human race, having quit Elysium, was pitchforked into a state of accelerated development, yet at the same time found itself trapped on the surface of this battle-scarred world as age followed age, prevented by the presence of the Key from reaching the end of their transmogrifying journey."

From this point on Ken's monologue became internal. Where his thoughts took him remained a mystery but it was quite some time before he remembered his prisoner and turned in his direction.

"Ah well," he remarked, "the evening is wearing away – you want to sleep I suppose. We might as well stop here before we reach the coast. Tomorrow I'll take you on a grand tour while I explain things more clearly. I don't want to be forced to become unpleasant, but I'm afraid I'll have to if you refuse to come round to my way of thinking."

The craft came to earth beside one of the few stands of trees to be found on the savannah and Ken climbed out of the driving seat. Dando found that he was permitted to follow and left the car on the passenger side, but as he went to step away his head swam and he fell to his knees. The fact was that he had neither eaten nor drunk since the start of his captivity and the effects were finally kicking in with a vengeance. Ken came round and gazed down with feigned concern. "Hello – aren't you well? - what's up?"

Dando crouched, head bowed, and then temporarily blacked out, keeling over onto his side. The immortal bent over him, noticing for the first time the cracked lips and cheek bones sharp as knife blades.

"Oh, I see – I get it. Bodies need solid sustenance. I tend to forget that. It's probably why mine wear out so quickly. Here..." He brought the bottle he had been drinking from a while ago, lifted the boy (once more semi-conscious), and held it to his lips. His prisoner took a sip and then spat the liquid out – it tasted disgusting and he suspected he was being poisoned.

"Oh dear - not up your street? All the same I've found it remarkably reviving. I suppose I'll have to go and get you an alternative. But first..."

He went to the car and came back with something in his fist that seemed to glow a bluish-white between his fingers. As he shook it out Dando saw that it took the form of a very fine chain, gossamer thin and several feet in length, much more delicate than the one round his own neck which bore both the locket and the Key. Ken stooped and, putting his hands under the boy's armpits, dragged him across to the nearest tree. He then looped the chain several times around the trunk and snapped the ends onto a belt with which he encircled his prisoner's waist and which appeared to be made of the same phosphorescent material.

"Recognise it?" he enquired, "no – you've probably never seen the like. This is the stuff they're all trying to get their hands on – Xoserite – stronger than the strongest steel and that's just a minor attribute. You'd have to speak to one of these modern scientific boffins if you want to hear about its many other surprising properties. As for the chain, it may look to you as if just a single tug would be enough to break it, but if so you'd be deluding yourself. Anyway – I'll be as quick as I can – contain your impatience."

He returned to the car, expelled Letty and took off into the darkness.

As soon as he was left alone with the tiger, Dando, despite what he had been told, summoned up what strength remained to him and pulled hard at the chain, soon realising, however, that if anything was going to give it would have to be the substantial tree rather than the shackle. To deal with that he needed help and so filled his lungs and shouted aloud but his voice sounded small and hoarse in his ears and elicited nothing more than a distant rather unnerving howling. The night air was cold and his deep intake of breath had irritated his chest, causing a coughing fit. Apparently concerned, Letty came and lay down beside him and this might have been comforting if her body temperature had not been way below his own. He propped himself up against the tree and thought of Ann. His dry-eyes pricked as he recalled their last extraordinary encounter, brought about through Milly's generosity. If only they could renew communication he would ask her if there was any chance – any chance at all – of escaping from this desperate predicament in which he found himself and completing the mysterious task he had been set. Overshadowing these thoughts hung the fear that, in turning the Key, he had altered the earth's future in some calamitous manner.

Stars were beginning to peep through gaps in the clouds and a little later the moon rose, not far off the full, and illuminated the overcast from above. Dando remembered that Ann had had a way of describing this beautiful sight: *a dancing floor* she had called it. Staring at the sky he became lost to himself and wandered at liberty for a while in serene contemplation among the wide open spaces above. When he returned he felt calmed and fortified. Again, in the far distance, came a faint disquieting baying, similar to that which he had heard on the journey along the Way of the Shades. He vaguely remembered that as a child he had been told stories about packs of wild dogs that roamed the Kymer Levels, but, apropos of this, Letty had heard the same noise and, raising her head, let forth a low rumbling roar. Dando realised that with her at his side he need fear no other predators.

It was not until the early hours of the morning that a light appeared above the horizon and a wandering star approached that rapidly turned into Ken's airborne vehicle. As it landed the pseudo human clambered out, a carrier bag in his hand full of lumps and bulges. "What a palaver," he muttered grumpily, emptying it out beside the boy, after which he withdrew to the car where he took his place facing the instrument panel and froze into stillness. Dando looked to see what he had been brought and found that the only liquid refreshment on offer consisted of pint cans of a strong porter while the edibles were made up of packets of nuts, pork-scratchings and potato chips. Making the best of a bad job he ring-pulled one of the cans, tore open some peanuts and commenced to eat, finding the nuts extremely salty. Moving on to a packet of crisps he wondered where Ken had come upon this bounty. It looked as if he had raided a down-town bar in some grotty city back street but our ex-restaurateur could have informed anyone who asked that items such as these were not to be had for love nor money south of the Middle Sea. Thinking about his abductor's ability to travel vast distances within short periods of time, the planet's dimensions shrank in his imagination to minor spans that could be covered in a matter of hours. His world, which had once beckoned him towards almost limitless horizons, now metamorphosed into no more than the insignificant pebble floating in space that Ken had described. Envisaging the earth in this way made it all the more precious to him and the thought that it might be in immanent danger as a result of his actions affected him deeply. Three fourths to the wind after consuming several more cans of beer he tipsily ruffled Letty's fur and scratched her neck, attentions she seemed to enjoy, following which he fell into a drunken stupor until long after dawn when Ken, having released him from the Xoserite chain, began shaking him vigorously. At this point he awoke to the realisation of something that had been glaringly obvious for sometime.

"Come on – chop, chop – time to get back on the bus."

I know who you are...

"Hurry up and stir your stumps – I'm not going to carry you and I need to get going. I've unchained you. Bring that food with you, and the drink..."

...you're Pyr and Aigea's child! Their offspring were called Pendar and Azazeel – two brothers who were originally a single individual. You're Azazeel! I was told what Tom once said: '...the

uncomely one she abandoned on a hillside and at the dark of the moon a creature of the night crept out and took the baby down into the underworld.' That was you wasn't it? - you're the bogeyman the Rytonians are so terrified of that they put people to death when they think you've corrupted them. And this stuff about bodies is a load of tosh because Pendar, the bright brother, walked and talked among men in human form - there was nothing about stealing corpses - that was what Tom told Annie and he knew what he was talking about when it came to the immortals. Pendar – he disappeared into the Caves of Bone, didn't he? What have you done with him? Is that where you're taking me? His head, whirling with these revelations and also with a hangover, Dando staggered to his feet and, had it not been for Letty's tolerance in allowing him to use her as a prop, would hardly have made it to the car. Although the chain was gone he was still wearing the Xoserite belt and discovered that bracelets of the same material had been clamped onto his wrists and one remaining ankle. He climbed groggily into the front passenger seat as Ken/Azazeel took up his position behind the steering column. The driver, despite his impatience, paused before taking to the air and gazed inquisitively at Dando. After his two tangles with the tiger the young man's clothes, as already mentioned, were in shreds and his left shoulder was exposed to the elements.

"What's this – a tattoo? A pretty amateurish effort I'd say - OUCH!"

Azazeel had jabbed at the design with his finger but then recoiled as if stung.

"Hell and damnation! - not again! You must be wearing some sort of impregnable armour that shuts me out," and to himself, "might even shut me out after you're unconscious - all the same Letty seems able to penetrate it. Hey Letty – put your paw here," pointing at Damask's smeary attempts to execute the double D. Dando felt the great claws grip his shoulder once more but not hard enough to puncture the skin; in fact, despite her strength, the tiger was being remarkably gentle. "Yes, you see, the embargo doesn't work on her – she'll have to stand in for me in future unless... GRRRR!" The immortal suddenly lunged towards Dando, his yellowish eyes wide and his lips drawn back to show discoloured teeth. His victim attempted to ward off the attack but Azazeel's sheer impetus propelled his hands as far as the boy's throat - he was apparently intent on throttling him. But once again, as soon as he made physical contact with the chain and its two attachments something out of nowhere interposed and he was thrown backwards over the car door, ending up on the ground. He lay there writhing and making curious squealing noises in his throat. Letty meanwhile, greatly perturbed, leapt out of the car and paced to and fro, rumbling and growling. Eventually Azazeel climbed to his feet. Dando saw that his host's body had suffered considerable damage from his fall but there was no sign of blood flow around the contusions.

"Ok – after all I don't have to touch you," the abductor eventually threatened hoarsely, "I could still finish you off by letting you die of hunger and thirst and then get one of my underlings to hand me the Treasure!" If this was meant to sound intimidating it was robbed of most of its menace by the uncertain and desperate tone in which it was delivered.

They dawdled north throughout the day, after which Azazeel came back to earth and reinstated the chain, pinning the ends down beneath a large rock – he seemed capable of lifting enormous weights – before departing in the car. The next morning when the craft returned a strange man was sitting at the wheel: a large muscular individual, over six feet tall, with a mane of sun-bleached hair. He turned his handsome face to the boy and smiled in satisfaction.

"How about this? I've got a talent for choosing good'uns. Came across it just along the coast – washed up on the shore – off one of the ships I reckon. Won't be needing him anymore," and he ejected a malodorous shrunken corpse from the passenger seat with a grimace of distaste. Dando looked at the poor crumpled half-decayed body lying abandoned on the ground and, for a moment, because he was far enough away, felt not revulsion but pity.

Flying north on a clear morning the margins of the Middle Sea soon came in sight, as did the river delta and the large dark smudge at the southern end that was the city of Vadrosnia Poule. What Dando had not bargained for, however, were the hundreds, nay thousands, of vessels clogging up the channels between Drossi and the sea.

Azazeel laughed. "Invasion fleet. That fellow from Pickwah wasn't satisfied with his triumphs along this side of the Tethys. Most of the plunder he promised his troops vanished into thin air by the time he homed in on the bankers' safes and deposit boxes – he wasn't quick enough on the uptake - so now he's set his sights on crossing to Armornia while they're at sixes and sevens because of the mess my so-called mother created as she tried to wipe you off the map. By the way – this is all your doing you know. Trewithik's campaign along the south coast was just a foretokening of the next turning – your turning. There's going to be a lot more of this. When you rotated the Tergiversator you adapted men's mindsets from an inclination towards ingenuity and invention to a desire for spoliation and pillage. Things will start to alter; the new age will be one of violent change, brought about through feverish activity and impulse - the planet itself will become restless – and two of the greatest curses of mankind – warfare and disease - will raise their ugly heads. Shall I go on? Existing conflicts will intensify, fresh wars break out and there'll be civil unrest in densely populated areas. And as for Terra's substance, platelets will shift, great waves swamp shorelines, fire from below will blast into the stratosphere. Hurricanes, tornadoes, floods, extinctions - it'll be pretty lively, I c'n tell you."

"No...! No...!" breathed Dando, suspecting, even as he cried out against it, that what he was hearing might be no more than the unvarnished truth.

"Also those imposters that have wielded power for so long, my so-called progenitors, will find their influence draining away. Because of what's going to happen, their acolytes will loose faith in their authority and eventually even their very existence will be doubted. Serves 'em right!"

As soon as they quitted the coast and headed out across the water Azazeel turned right and brought his craft down to sea level. He bounced from one wave crest to the next, sending up fountains of spray and yelling at the top of his voice. They were both soaking wet before he thought to reinstate the canopy and set windscreen wipers to work. They needed protection not just from sea water but also from the wild weather which had suddenly set in. Gales, thunder and lightening, vicious showers of hail – everything seemed to be thrown into the mix. All that day they forged eastward through the fret, Pangorland vaguely visible on the left and the southern continent just out of sight in the other direction; Azazeel was apparently in no hurry to arrive anywhere. At dusk they came in to land and, on some deserted northerly shore, he clipped one end of another long chain to the boy's waistband and the other to the window-frame of the car's offside door. Then he went back to sit immobile in the driving seat as he had done two nights previously. There was something so lifeless about the still figure behind the wheel that, after a while, Dando got out of his seat and walked forward in order to obtain a better view. What he saw made him retreat to the full extent of the chain. The immortal had departed, he realised, and left something behind that, in its aspect, was the very embodiment of death. This time he did not feel pity. Instead he laid himself down on the cold hard ground as far away from the car as he was able, and, after a while, Letty came and joined him, trampling at will over his defenceless body. He tried to push her off but was reprimanded in no uncertain terms. The tiger stood with her front feet planted squarely on his torso, after which she began padding up and down, kneading his body while rumbling deep in her throat – could she be purring? With all her weight behind it the manipulation was quite painful but he had no choice but to submit, thinking meanwhile that Meena's kittens had performed exactly these movements while at the teat. "I'm not your mother, you fool," he grunted querulously, yet feeling, in his defencelessness, surprisingly aroused. Eventually the animal desisted and settled down, her great chin resting on his shoulder. As a result he woke the next morning chilled to the bone with the impression he had been sleeping next to a block of ice. However, on coming to himself, he understood that his wish, made on the Kymer flood plain, had, in a manner of speaking, been granted: she – Annie – had been with him during the hours of darkness, if only in a dream.

A figure upright amidst the ripening corn; that was the after-image that hovered in his imagination. As in the past, he had seen her standing among gently waving tassels of barley which were swaying and rustling in the warm breath of a zephyr that fanned his cheek and lifted his hair. What else? She had spoken – they had spoken together – maybe he could recapture something of what had been said.

"***My darling,"*** Yes, that was how she had begun, ***"I can't be with you much longer. I've been beside you all the while, right from the beginning when I made the alteration, apart from when Dadda called me away to confront the Dark Brother, but now I'll be left behind at the door. Yet I hope that that which I gave you may continue to guard you from harm."***

Door – what door?

"But Annie, how am I supposed to manage? How can I resist when I've got nothing to defend myself with?"

"***It's your helplessness that will be your greatest strength, my love. You mus' accept what comes. Don't try and fight it. Don't hope, don't despair – accept, accept."***

"What! You mean I should give up the Key!?"

"***Oh no, not that – anyway you'll find the Key looks after itself. But when it come to other choices you mus' do what you think best. And when you're faced with something you can't change, then – sweetheart – you mus' accept it whatever it is."***

"Accept," he repeated.

"It will be hard – the hardest thing you've ever done. But you're strong – stronger than the one who persecutes you – you're strong on account of your very weakness."

"Weak? Am I weak? I s'pose I am. But, tell me Annie, is there going to be any future for us – or is this the end?"

She remained silent for a long time. At last she said, ***"Yes, there will be a future."***

Dando chewed this over for a while.

"But what is it going to be like?" he asked.

"It don' be real."

"What? You mean the place where I'm goin isn't real?"

"None of it be real 'an that's why anything can be born..."

"Oh..." Dando was left thoroughly confused; but then, as with most things he did not understand, he dismissed the conundrum from his mind and held out his arms. She came gladly into them while the golden field streamed and rippled. That was the last thing he remembered from the dream, his loved one in his arms, although there may have been a great deal more which dissipated before he had time to pin it down.

Now, as he thought of Ann he put his hand automatically to his breast pocket where the envelope containing her hair was kept, only to find it gone. His jacket and shirt were in tatters and this particular pocket had been slashed along with the rest. At some time in the last day or two the envelope must have slipped through the resulting tear without his being aware. Frantically he searched around both inside and outside the car, but there was no sign of the thing he treasured. His heart sank into his solitary boot and once more he had to blink back tears. Eventually he reminded himself that he still had the locket and in it the precious tress that Becca had placed there. Nevertheless he began to feel even more vulnerable than he had before this discovery.

"She can't help you – she hasn't been able to help you since she succumbed to the ancient one's enchantment." By this time Azazeel had returned, reoccupied the body of the dead seaman and ordered Dando back into the car, confirming, once again, through this remark, that his prisoner's thoughts were no longer just his own.

"That's not true – she's been helping me all along – she's helping me now," and Dando put his hand to his throat.

"Oh OK – have it your own way. But listen carefully and attend; I'm going to ask you one last time before I get really serious. Remember what I said about Terra being under the dominion of the Key and that as a result the human race has been prevented from taking its final evolutionary step. Well, if you give me the Catalyst I'll convey it far, far away – its power over the earth will fade and your people will go free."

Dando refused to give the slightest indication that he had heard. This time he did not even deign to shake his head. Azazeel paused, but then made a dismissive gesture, miming the undoing of laces at his wrists.

"All right," he declared, "from now on the gloves are off – no quarter."

He swung back to his controls, set the car in motion and spoke no more that day.

The dogs of war
Are straining at the leash.
Fell deeds have choked compassion.

Chapter nineteen

Back on the road Milly was seeing Horry in yet another light. Her eyes had been opened one morning when she was at the wheel of the small car while the boy sat close behind in company with Meena and Ralph as Jack dozed. He was leaning forward, practically breathing down her neck, causing her to recall how in recent times he had been paying her a great deal of attention. Most days he helped her get the meal ready, washed up afterwards, spread the bed-roll for her and frequently offered to bring her nightcaps. A proper little gentleman she had thought. But now, as she drove, his hand crept beneath her left arm and gently cupped her breast. It remained there as Milly was swept by a feeling of total disbelief.

"Oy! Wot d'you fink you're a-doin' of?!" she exclaimed. The boy shrank back.

"Nothing," he muttered and then as if talking to himself, "I didn't think you'd mind."

Milly realised that a certain degree of plain speaking was in order but felt that perhaps it ought to come from Jack rather than herself. She determined to tackle the blind boy about it when they were alone together. However, later that day, a more urgent matter than reading Horry the riot act occurred to her now they were well on the way to their rendezvous with the colonel's colleague.

"D'you fink this 'ere air-plane man'll expect us to give 'im money?" she enquired, only too well aware of her depleted purse, the muleskinner's generous gift having been gradually expended on food along the way. "I've got money," replied Jack. His face wore an inscrutable expression.

"You've always got money," said Milly suspiciously, grateful none the less. After a pause she remembered her first concern and went on, "C'n you 'ave a word wiv 'Orry, man to man like. 'E's bin getting' a bit fresh wiv me lately an' I don' fink 'e understands 'ow 'ee's supposed to behave."

"Man to man!" replied Jack with a rueful laugh. "I'm not really the best person to initiate him into the ways of the world. That should come from his father."

"Well, 'e's not 'ere so you'll 'ave to do."

"Oh, thanks!"

Whether this proposed exchange ever took place Milly was not entirely certain but it probably did because one thing could not be denied; a few days later Jack and Horry's relationship seemed to have subtly changed, they were on a more equal footing somehow and presented a united front when she had the temerity to criticise either one of them. Horry continued to make himself useful to her but physical contact was apparently now out of the question; in fact if she chanced to touch him he reacted as if he had been stung. She found such a response a little hurtful.

"This map'll take you as far as the border," the colonel had explained before they set out, "where you'll liaise with my friend Johnson. The original battle lines were a long way farther east, of course, on the other side of Caffray and it wasn't until much later that the neighbouring country appealed to Armornia for help. Tartary lies beyond Caffray and minor skirmishes had been happening along their common border time out of mind, but about a year ago the more belligerent of the two set out to establish a bridgehead farther west and swept across before anyone was ready for them. By the time they were stopped nearly the whole of Caffray had been swallowed up; in fact here and there they'd even advanced a few miles into Armornian territory and it was then that we got involved. After that it became a game of back and forth with first one side and then the other gaining ground. But now things are hotting up – it's these advanced weapons you see. Before they appeared on the scene we were starting to get the upper hand and if it hadn't been for the earthquake and then this new trouble down south... Anyway our side is going to need everyone with military experience they can lay their hands on so maybe even I'll get a call." He gazed wistfully at a plan of the battlefield which was pinned on a nearby surface.

"The Blue Mountain is somewhere in Caffray," he went on, "over towards the Tartary side I believe, so you'll have to travel through enemy territory. This may help." He took down a small scroll from a shelf, a shelf which contained a number of similar objects, and unrolled it, revealing a rather beautiful, stylised landscape similar to the mural in the saloon.

"Woodblock print," he said, spreading it out before Milly and Horry. "That's the mountain you're looking for. If you come across someone you feel you can trust you can show them this and get directions."

"Are you sure you want to give it to us?" asked Horry, "it looks as if it might be worth quite a lot of money."

"The colonel smiled. "I've got the original blocks," he replied. "One more thing – *Ian Shan* – can you remember that?"

"What's that when it's at home?" asked Jack.

"That's Blue Mountain in the Caffray tongue. *Ian Shan* – Blue Mountain."

They began their journey to the east the very next day and at first the going was easy. The road, a smooth blacktop, gradually descended from the prairies towards the northern shore of the Great Lake. From thence it wound its way through a string of resort towns, towns which at that particular time were providing accommodation in their hotels and guest-houses for a mass of displaced Rytonians who had crossed by boat from Harrisburg. In contrast, after leaving the lake behind, they found that the settlements they began passing through as they progressed farther east appeared peaceful and undisturbed; it seemed that most of them were situated at too great a distance from the coast to become refuges for earthquake victims. But gradually the roads got rougher and less frequented, the ancient automobile started to demonstrate that it was hardly equal to the task they had set it and, at night, there were intimations in the sky ahead, short-lived glimmers that came and went, of what awaited them. As Colonel Wapshott had advised, they avoided the new military road that forged eastwards without deviation, and instead took a more circuitous route through a series of small rather impoverished villages. Eventually they limped into a strangely quiet town where just one or two people were out on the deserted streets. These individuals, ignoring the travellers' enquires, hurried away when spoken to as if reluctant to have any contact with them.

"Wot's up wiv the locals?" Milly grumbled. "That woman looked as if she'd got a really bad smell up 'er conk. An' why 'ave some 'ouses got crosses? Are they goin' to be pulled down I wonder?"

"Crosses?" said Jack sharply, "do you mean there's crosses on the doors?"

"Yers – an' the 'ole place is 'alf empty – unfriendly too. But I fink there's people lookin' at us froo some of the windows. I woz 'opin' to buy our supper 'ere for later. Shall I go an' knock?"

"No," commanded Jack, "drive on. The sooner we leave the better. Don't stop till we're well down the road."

"It's the crosses," he explained a little later when they were in open country once more. "Back when my grandfather was a kid, Drossi was hit by an epidemic that took the form of a pretty lethal sickness. It spread all along the coast, passing from town to town. When a household succumbed to the disease the authorities painted a cross on the door to warn people to keep away. I think that's what might have been happening back there. In those days people were afraid of anyone on the move in case they might be carrying the infection."

"Oh," said Horry, "I thought they were scared of us coz we could have been going to rape and pillage or something."

"You'd like a bit of that then, would you?"

Only a few miles farther on they came upon a barrier across the road bearing a large sign which read: *DISEASE-FREE ZONE! Only authorised personnel allowed beyond this point!!* Several men regarded them from the other side of the obstruction with apparent hostility.

"Shall we show them the colonel's permit?" asked Milly, remembering a similar situation when Loretta had given her a pass to the Transfer Facility.

"He said it was well out of date," replied Jack, "and they might wonder how we came by a millitary permit at all. We might get into trouble."

"Well then, wot's the answer? I ain't goin' to turn back."

"Take to the fields - the car's on its last legs anyway. I think from what you tell me we've come at least halfway to our goal. If we keep walking towards the rising sun we should reach disputed territory sooner or later and then it'll be just a question of finding this runway he told us about. I think we'd better keep away from towns altogether."

"But what about food?" put in an anxious Horry.

"Won't hurt you to go hungry for once in your life."

They retreated for about a quarter of a mile and then, abandoning the car on the highway, shouldered as many of their possessions as they were capable of carrying and took off across country. As they skirted built up areas, progressing on foot through, at first, cultivated but later weed-infested abandoned fields, several days passed and soon all three were utterly ravenous, their rations, such as they were, having been exhausted. But now the animals proved their worth and showed that they had other talents besides their ability to act as guides. Each night they went hunting along nearby hedges and ditches and brought back a variety of prey. Ralph supplied them with several rabbits and even Meena contributed a squirrel or two. These were cooked (they could have done with Dando's expertise at skinning and gutting) and shared equally amongst all five companions. Such small offerings, along with vegetables that they scavenged from the neglected fields, took the edge off their hunger.

It was not long before the aspiring rescuers had further warning of the war zone they were approaching. After dark, lights grew and died behind hills on the horizon, swelling, blooming, flickering and then fading away, all in complete silence. Milly described to Jack what she was seeing.

"It's a bit like when we 'ad to get out of Drossi but not so noisy."

Although, in the beginning, these fitful glares came to them purely as visual impressions eventually they began to be accompanied by bodeful rumblings and the odd muffled boom. During daylight hours the sun-dog had once again taken up its position above the horizon, but now it was slightly off to the left. They turned in that direction and the animals seemed to approve.

The map, the instructions they had received, their non-human companions, the sun-dog that awaited them most mornings, all combined to bring them to one specific location. The fields – untended fields – were left behind along with the occasional deserted farm house, and now they were penetrating deeper and deeper into apparently endless woodland, a muted green and shadowy domain of intertwined branches heavy with foliage that filtered out most of the daylight. The animals went before them as if this remote region were totally familiar territory. Eventually Milly and Horry glimpsed a contrasting brightness ahead, visible through the dim parade of trunks.

"There's a place that's been cleared," Milly explained to Jack who was walking a few yards apart. For most of the trek he had insisted on foot-slogging forward without her help, striding through the undergrowth swinging his cane from side to side in order to locate obstructions.

"How big?" he asked.

"It's long but not very wide."

"Well, we'll soon know whether it's what we're after."

They emerged from the trees onto a green runway and, looking around, the sighted travellers eventually glimpsed the plane for which it had been created, but only after a significant interval. Low at the rear, high at the prop-flanked nose, it crouched at the end of the airstrip like a runner in the slips. Because of its all-over brown and green attire it emerged only very slowly from the forest background, a ghostly manifestation teasing the vision with its uncertain profile. It seemed to be placed in that quiet glade purely for their benefit, for there was nobody else about. They set out towards it and by the time they stood beneath the nose-cone Milly had spotted a hut, equally well camouflaged, half-hidden amongst the trees.

"D'you fink 'ee's in there," she wondered, "the gent's friend? P'raps 'ee's 'avin' forty winks."

"Show me," instructed Jack. She led him to the door, partially ajar, where he stopped stock still, his head raised and tilted to one side as if listening. When Milly declared her intention to knock he pulled her back, grasping her arm as she reached out to announce their presence.

"Don't touch," he warned.

"Why not?" she demanded, somewhat miffed at being manhandled in this way.

"There's something... I'm not sure. I smell... decay."

"Wotchoo on about?"

She tugged herself free then, despite her irritation, took care to avoid brushing against the door as she edged round it. A few minutes later she returned the same way and acknowledged in a subdued tone that Jack's hyper-sensitive perceptions had not deceived him.

"There's a bloke on the bed – I fink 'e's 'ad it. 'Ee's covered in spots an' orl sort of swelled up like. Made me want to frow up."

"Let's get outa here," exclaimed the Vadrosnian urgently.

They hurried back into the open to find that Horry had not been able to tear himself away from the plane.

"Those blades in the front," he said excitedly, "they pull it through the air like a ship's screw drives it through the water and the wings provide lift. An' that bit at the back gives stability I think. D'you reckon there's enough room inside for all of us and the animals?"

"Curb your enthusiasm," advised Jack. "It's unlikely we'll be using that to get us past the conflict. We've just found the pilot and he's in no condition to go anywhere. I imagine this proves it," he continued, turning to Milly. "There's a plague on the loose. We'll be lucky to escape."

"Well, I'm not givin' up," repeated Milly, jutting her jaw in determination.

Horry gazed longingly at the aircraft. "Could *we* fly it do you think?" he said.

"Not in a month of Sahwains."

After a long and fairly acrimonious discussion they decided, or rather Milly decided, that the only option left open to them was to try and cross the lines on foot after dark. Jack thought, at first, that this would be insanely dangerous - "We'll probably get lost and blunder into some no-go area and then get our heads blown off," - while Horry, having been robbed of his chance to take to the air, relapsed into a sullen silence.

"But look," said Milly, "I've got this," and she pulled Tallis' compass out of her pocket. "The needle points north and if you turn it round like that you c'n see which way is east. If it's a starry night or the moon's up we may just be able to read it."

Without saying a word Jack put his hand into his jacket pocket and presented her with a miniature electric torch. She stared at him in amazement. What earthly use could he have for such an object when his world was irredeemably dark? This was not the first time he had surprised her with what he came up with.

At this point Horry emerged from his sulk, minutely examined the compass and torch and then spoke his mind. "You won't be needing those," he said with utter conviction, "Ralph and Meena will show us the way."

Because their plans did not allow for sleep once it had grown dark and because the better part of nine hours still lay ahead before nightfall Milly suggested they should take a prolonged nap within the shade of the plane's wings in order to make the time pass more quickly. Jack was nervous about remaining anywhere near the plague-ridden hut but she was equally unhappy about moving before dusk and, through her stubborn determination to stay put, she carried the day. It was only as they composed themselves for rest that he remarked on how quiet their surroundings had grown.

"They must have declared a truce," he decided, "or at least some sort of temporary cease-fire. I haven't heard any explosions for several hours."

"Good," replied Milly, "p'raps that means we can get some shut-eye."

"When we set out," Jack continued, "we'll have to make ourselves as inconspicuous as possible. Don't wear anything that will show up."

"Pity we can't turn ourselves invisible like I reckon that magic bloke did 'oo 'urt the Lordship."

"Don't talk rot."

One after another all three laid themselves down beneath the plane. Jack was the first to drop off and immediately began to mutter unintelligibly and to toss and turn. Milly was used by now to witnessing these involuntary attacks; she had learned not to interfere, even when he cried out in terror, knowing that after a while his agitation would subside as he entered a deeper level of sleep. Once he had quietened she also drifted into unconsciousness. Horry lay nearby and waited until he was satisfied that the other two were fast asleep. Then he got up and walked a few yards into the open. It was a fine day with not a cloud in sight. He glanced back at the prone bodies he had just left behind before standing on tiptoe and stretching his arms upwards, fingers spread, as if trying to reach the wide blue yonder. He maintained that stance for a moment or two before grabbing and holding – what? There was nothing to be seen between his hands but from his precise movements you could almost believe he had retrieved some kind of large sheet made of sky stuff from the firmament and was carrying it before him across to the sleepers where he spread it with great care over the little black girl. Returning to the same spot he repeated the process for Jack's benefit and then went through the pantomime a third time. During this final assay he swung the unseen fabric round his own shoulders as if he were donning a mantle and in so doing his outline became blurred and unclear in much the same way that the camouflaged plane had merged into its background. Throughout this whole performance the two animals watched with interest from where they sat on the edge of the clearing. He walked across in order to pat Ralph and stroke Meena who rubbed purring round his ankles.

"You two don't need any help from me to stay hidden," he said with a smile, "you c'n manage perfectly well on your own. Given the shields, your assistance and a dose of good luck I think we might make it through."

Later, after sunset, the friends shared a meagre supper, the humans fully aware that this might be their last meal together if things did not go according to plan. Before moving off Jack - still worrying about infection - managed to persuade the other two to tie handkerchiefs over their mouths and noses.

"It may not do any good," he said, "but it's worth a try. Whatever happens avoid contact with strangers – any contact at all."

"Blimey," said Milly once they started, "ain't it dark! - I c'n 'ardly see eiver of you, or the animals, or the way forward, but I don' fink I'd better use the torch."

"Hold my hand," said Jack, "I've had plenty of practice at coping in the dark."

"You'll soon be able to make out the way," Horry informed her, sounding very sure of himself. "The moon'll be up about one. I suggest we don't speak unless absolutely necessary."

As before, Meena and Ralph went ahead trailed by Horry, while Jack and Milly brought up the rear. Milly hung on to the blind boy as if her life depended on it. For the first few miles they travelled through untouched forest and all that was to be heard were the usual hootings, stridulations and faint barks to be expected in a large wood at midnight. But then the moon rose and the heavy fragrance of growing things began to be overlaid by a scorching smell similar to that of an old bonfire. Soon they came to a region where the trees showed signs of damage: branches had been stripped of leaves and were broken off or bent to the ground. Further on they reached a place where there were no standing trees at all: every one they passed had been toppled and lay flat on the ground with just a few splintered stumps remaining. In the midst of this ruined area was a raw circular wound punched into the surface of the earth.

"Bomb crater," said Jack once Milly had described what she was seeing. "It's what the noise was about we were hearing up until yesterday. But where are the troops? Where's the army?"

Soon his question was partially answered. Amongst the twisted trees on the other side of the crater a dark shape loomed. Cautiously investigating they discovered a huge armoured vehicle, silent and apparently deserted, a gun-turret mounted on top, and beside it a body stretched out on the ground.

"Is there any sign of wounds on the corpse or damage to the tank?" asked an anxious Jack.

"Not as far as I c'n see," replied Horry, "shall I take a look inside?"

"For god's sake no – keep away – the sooner we make ourselves scarce the better."

They left the sinister war machine behind and penetrated deeper into the forest. It was not long before they came upon another body lying amidst the undergrowth and then several more. Soon the ground was littered like an outdoor mortuary. Milly, infected at last by Jack's uneasiness and deciding, after all, to use the torch, reversed roles and led the blind boy on a safe route between the dead. A lot of the bodies were Armornian in appearance but there were others of a more oriental cast dressed in outlandish uniforms.

"You remember the Mog," Milly said to Jack, "Pnoumi the Mog – the one wiv the cat show? These geezers 'ave got eyes just like 'im. I reckon they comes from the same place. Cripes – look at that! There's one bloke got 'is 'ands roun' anuver bloke's froat an' the other bloke's got a knife, yet they've boaf snuffed it."

"It's a battlefield," said Jack, "but from what you tell me these people didn't die fighting."

"No," replied Milly, "They looks like the bloke in the 'ut looked. I fink it must definitely be some sort of sickness. Woz this the sort of fing wot your 'ittwl ladyboy had do you fink?"

"I doubt it. Fynn's illness was slow – really slow – but this seems as if it's hellishly fast."

Whilst they were talking they did not register what Horry was up to. The boy had walked a short distance apart, his attention having been grabbed by something half-hidden amidst the ground cover. Gleaming invitingly a few feet in front of him lay a state of the art pistol with a pearlescent handle that had presumably fallen from someone's nerveless fingers. Checking that he was not being watched he stooped and, trying not to admit to himself that he was behaving with total irresponsibility, picked it up and slipped it into his pocket.

A bit further on they were startled by the sound of moaning coming from within some nearby bushes.

"There's one in there wot ain't dead," whispered a wary Milly. She grabbed hold of Horry as he passed her on the way to investigate. "No!" she ordered.

"But someone needs our help," protested the boy, "we can't just leave them."

"Don't you realise you'll probably pick it up – this bug wotever it is – if you gets too close? Wot would the Lordship say if he knew I'd let you take such a risk?" But as she spoke it dawned on her that Dando would probably have done exactly as his son wished to do.

"Come on," urged Jack, who may have been thinking the same thing, "we're wasting time. Do I have to remind you what we're here for?"

Hardening their hearts they walked on eastwards, covering several miles. Eventually they passed an array of tents to which they gave a wide berth and after that apparently left the war-zone behind. Two more days elapsed before the trees started to thin and then, almost without warning, they stood on the edge of a steep escarpment. It was quite early in the morning and in front of them the sun was rising over an open landscape half hidden by luminous ground mist. In the middle distance, sticking up through the haze, were strangely shaped rocky outcrops on the summits of which perched diminutive pine trees and buildings with tiled roofs curled decoratively at the edges. At one spot, just below the place where they were standing, the fog had thinned sufficiently to reveal a small river winding between bamboo thickets and spanned by a bow-shaped bridge. As they looked down a flock of white birds flew low over the water. The whole scene appeared so peaceful and idyllic that it was hard to believe that they had reached the borders of a country suffering under the weight of a foreign occupation.

"Hey," said Horry, waving his hand towards the horizon, "is that it?"

On the very limits of vision a tiny isosceles triangle rose above the mist pointing heavenwards, its white vertex vanishing against the sky.

"Is that it?" he asked again, directing his question towards the animals, but for the first time since starting their long journey their non-human companions seemed at a loss. Ralph put his tail between his legs and whined apologetically while Meena appeared more interested in some small creature hidden amongst the grass at the side of the road.

"We'll have to take a chance and ask directions," said Jack, "or at least show someone the picture he gave us, otherwise we'll probably end up all at sea."

"At sea?" replied Milly, "we've come a long way from the sea by now I reckon. I don't fink 'Orry even remembers it – do you sweetie?"

But Horry was not paying attention. "Listen!" he cried, "there's something coming towards us up the hill!"

Milly looked down and saw a moving column on the zigzag road.

"Soldiers!" she exclaimed, "let's get over there behind those rocks – quick Jack!"

The two of them had just time to conceal themselves in the shadows before the head of a platoon rounded the nearest corner and came marching up towards them. The troops were wearing similar outfits to the unfamiliar uniforms they had seen in the forest but, in contrast to the unprotected dead, these soldiers faces were covered by masks and every fourth man carried a cylinder on his back from which he was pumping spray into the air as they moved.

"They're taking precautions," muttered Horry who, to Milly's consternation, was still standing in full view. She tried to reach out and pull him to safety but he shook her off. When the outfit had passed by without noticing him he turned round with a broad grin.

"How about that!" he said, "I was waiting for the chance to see if it worked."

"Wot the 'ell are you on about?!" scolded Milly.

"Don't be cross – I was just trying out something mum explained to me. She's back again by the way – been back several days. It would've worked for you too, you didn't need to hide. I set up the shields when you were asleep. I'd better lift them now though cos they can start to make you sort of fade away if you wear them too long. Don't you feel a bit see-throughy Jack?"

"Very funny," replied Jack scathingly, "if I had the least idea what you're on about."

"Is this your magic stuff again?" asked Milly, "like when we were on the road to Damwey?"

"It's not really magic," explained Horry.

"If you made it so's we couldn't be seen why can we see each uver?"

"Cos we're all under the shields together."

With a few shrugs Horry appeared to slough off the invisible mantle he had donned back at the air-strip. Next, after going round behind his two companions, he mimed the seizing of something at the nape of each of their necks, tugging it away. Both Jack and Milly were rocked back on their heels and staggered a step or two. They put their hands up to their shoulders in comical accord, thoroughly puzzled.

"Oy!" exclaimed Milly, "do you mind!"

"Come on," said Horry impatiently, not prepared to waste time on further explanations, "Don't you see, there's some sort of building halfway down the hill. P'raps we c'n ask there about the Blue Mountain. *Ian Shan* – isn't that what he told us it was called? We'll ask for *Ian Shan*."

Seen from above nothing more than the roof of this structure was visible, but as the travellers descended the slope an imposing three-storied edifice came into view, built into the side of the hill. At each corner a representation of a gap-jawed winged dragon snarled down at them from overhanging curved eves while two enormous doors - firmly shut - were situated within the frontage. Dwarfed by this entrance an elderly pigtailed man in dun-coloured robes was sweeping the path before the building and as Milly's party approached he leant on his broom and raised a small brown wrinkled visage that seemed to be fixed in a permanent grin.

"'Ere Jack," muttered the black girl, " let's 'ave that picture – the one the colonel gave us. You take it 'Orry an' show it to 'im. See'f 'ee knows wot it is."

Horry walked forward, clearly o'er-topping the man by nearly a foot as he approached. He unrolled the scroll and held it up, repeating as he did so the words that their host had taught them. The path sweeper did not even look at the print, however, he was far more concerned by something approaching from further down the hill and, with a series of expressive and urgent gestures, invited his visitors to follow him round the side of the building.

"Come, come," he implored, "not good stay here. You come – I show you..."

"I think there's another squad on the road," said Jack who, for his part, had also noticed the sound of marching feet, "they're heading this way."

Milly looked about her in alarm, realising they needed to get back into hiding and that they would not be able to make it to the top of the hill before the soldiers approached.

"Wot shall we do?" she gasped, only to find that Horry had already taken up the old man's offer and was treading close on his heels. "Come on," he called back over his shoulder, "I lifted the shields so we'll have to get out of sight."

With a great deal of reluctance Milly grabbed Jack's arm and followed round the corner, through a small side-gate and into a garden where herbs were growing. From there their guide, who seemed to be some sort of mendicant, led them across to a wooden pavilion and slid open a flimsy-looking door.

"Prease to enter," he invited. As he shut it behind them they heard the first soldiers begin to pass the front of the main building.

"You rike nice cup of tea?" enquired their new acquaintance.

The monk, who introduced himself as Lin-ji, served up bowls of pale green liquid accompanied by dishes of cooked rice before disappearing into the lofty main building in order to perform some late-afternoon ritual; they heard the sound of a gong being struck.

"Do you fink 'ee lives 'ere orl alone?" wondered an intrigued Milly, "there don' seem to be no-one else about."

"The last of his order," replied Jack, "I've heard of such things. It's a good job he came forward when we needed him – otherwise we would have been in the soup."

"I reckon he's given other people shelter before now," said Horry. "This place (indicating the pavilion they were currently occupying) looks well used. Perhaps he's on the side of the partisans – perhaps he..." He stopped abruptly and covered his mouth with his hand, but this did not prevent him from suddenly spewing up the rice he had just eaten.

"Horry!" cried Milly in alarm.

The boy doubled up, continuing to heave dryly. "I don't feel well," he groaned.

Milly looked round, seeking assistance, and noticed something in the corner of the room.

"'Ere look," she said, "there's a kind of bed on the floor. Lie down. I'll go an' fin' the bloke. I'll ast 'im to get you a drink. Jack," she whispered, pulling him outside the door, "'is face is orl blotchy - do you fink...?"

"I don't think – I bloody well know," replied Jack. "It was too much to hope that we'd escape something that's achieved a more or less hundred percent head count back there. Next thing that'll happen is we'll all go down with it an' then it'll be goodbye and thanks for all the fish."

"Fish?" replied Milly, "wot you on about?"

Lin-ji, once he had been summoned by Milly, bent over Horry's prone moaning body, examining him minutely, after which he went outside without saying a word to the anxious visitors. He was gone for sometime and when he returned he was carrying a basket full of aromatic leaves while his jaw moved rhythmically. He placed some of this greenery in Jack's hand before holding out a fistful to Milly saying, "You chew." Milly was reluctant to follow this advice until Jack complied, urging her to, "Do as he says." Milly hesitantly transferred one leaf to her lips and bit into it. Her mouth filled with a pungent but not displeasing flavour and a moment later the lights in the room appeared brighter and the colours of clothing and carpets more vivid. A pleasant lassitude swept through her body.

"I make tea for him," said the monk shaking the basket and nodding at Horry. "He must drink – drink orl time – orl through night. We help him, first one, then other."

And so that is what they did, taking it in turns to force beakers of the infusion that the monk produced into the young man's reluctant mouth, before setting about cleaning him up afterwards when he urinated and defecated as a result. In the process they discovered an unfamiliar pearl-handled gun in one of his pockets and, on Jack's insistence, it was rapidly disposed of. By morning the blotches on his face had turned to oozing pustules while mentally he appeared to be far away on some harrowing journey of the mind.

"Poor kid," said Jack, standing close by and listening to their patient's muttered ravings while Milly dabbed at his lesions, "he's really right on the edge."

"Well, he ain't gonna fall off," replied Milly fiercely.

The monk returned at dawn with a fresh container of leaves. He had insisted that not a moment passed during the night without their chewing on the plant which had such mysterious curative properties and by now their lips and tongues had been turned totally numb by whatever nostrum it contained. He stooped over Horry smiling sweetly.

"He live," he pronounced with certitude. "If not that," pointing to the basket, "he dead by now."

And so it proved. Within the next few hours Horry began the long slow climb back to health helped by the vigour of youth and, when he had recovered consciousness, his determination. At the end of week one he was able to stagger to his feet and was starting to eat and drink normally, by the end of week two he had almost gotten his full strength back. However certain things would never be the same.

On the fourteenth day after he had been taken ill he requested the loan of a mirror from Milly in order to examine his face. She demurred. "No luv – I don't fink you'd better do that."

"Oh, come on – I've gotta know the worst sooner or later."

Reluctantly she handed over her powder compact and Horry stared at his reflection for a long time before passing it back without comment.

"It won't notice so much after a while," she comforted, "you've just got to give it time to heal." Her voice lacked conviction.

"Crap! I'm not going to pretend that things are any better than they are. I might as well accept that I look like something out of a bad dream."

Milly wished she could disagree but was unable to pretend. The fresh-faced, even angelic-looking Horry of a few days ago no longer existed. The wounds had left livid scars and in healing had puckered his skin in several places. His good looks had been reduced to a grotesque parody of his former comeliness. Only the vivid blue of his eyes and his thatch of golden hair served as a reminder of what he had been for such a brief time.

"It's not fair," Milly burst out, "an' you growin' up so fast an' all." Then calming slightly, "Anyway dearie you'll never be any different far as I'm concerned."

"At least I've still got my sight," said Horry in a low voice nodding at Jack who was sitting on the other side of the room. Milly looked across and saw the blind boy clearly for the first time in days; she had been taking his presence and help completely for granted while she attended to Horry. With a sense of shock she noticed that although his face was unmarked he too looked somewhat frail. *Not another one on the sick list!* she thought. Her mind returned to Tallis and Dando – one dead, one ailing. The men in her life seemed to be dropping like flies while she soldiered on regardless. *Women are made of sterner stuff* she admitted to herself, coming to the conclusion with surprise and a certain amount of regret.

During Horry's convalescence they were inevitably in constant contact with the monastery's sole occupant but never once did he enquire as to their purposes in entering his country; he seemed profoundly incurious when it came to their origins or their intended destination. It was only as they prepared to depart that he finally asked in his broken version of the common tongue, "Where you go?"

Jack produced the scroll that he kept stuffed into a pocket of his rucksack and displayed the delicate work of art that he himself could not see. *"Ian Shan,"* he said.

The monk examined it appreciatively.

"Velly fine – velly fine," he replied, "but where you go?"

"There," contributed Horry, jabbing the scroll with his finger. "We're goin' there – the mountain – *Ian Shan.*"

For the first time since their initial meeting, Lin-ji's face lost its beatific smile. His brow creased in consternation and he shook his head emphatically.

"That not good! Ian Shan velly bad prace – everybody stay away – *you* stay away."

"Then you knows where it is." Milly was all eagerness. "C'n you say 'ow to get there? Woz it wot we could see from the top of the 'ill?"

"I think you go back home now," the monk advised gravely. "Way to mountain dangerous – way *in* to mountain dangerous – under mountain velly dangerous."

"P'raps I'd better explain..." Jack took it upon himself to give their reasons for venturing into this occupied country where their very presence might get them arrested at any moment and in the process spelt out why they so desperately needed to reach the Blue Mountain.

"...so you see our friend was kidnapped when he was on his way south and we think it was because of something valuable he was carrying. We've been told that the one who's taken him is called Azazeel and that he lives below Ian Shan. Have you heard of him?"

Lin-ji screwed up his face into what could almost be called a scowl.

"In our language – *Nu-mo-wang* – that mean very superior devil – demon first class. And under mountain lots of little devils – velly bad prace – prace where ghosts of people walk when they lose their way – prace where they find rocks that help the Wo-kou win wars."

"Well – never mind all that," said Horry, keen to get started. "C'n you draw a map that'll point us in the right direction?"

"I mus' consult ancestors," answered Lin-ji. "They tell me what true and what not true. You wait..." and he disappeared into the main building. A couple of hours later a bored Horry, wandering across the garden to the door in the fence, came hurrying back.

"Hey – I've just seen Ling Gee or whatever his name is heading off down the hill out of sight. Do you think he's going to split on us?"

"Oh blimey!" cried Milly, all ready to fly into a panic at this information. Jack groped in her direction and put a calming hand on her shoulder.

"Cool it," he said, "no need to freak out. He's up-front, I'd stake my life on it. Give him time. But if he hasn't returned by tomorrow we'd better leave and seek help elsewhere."

Later, however, when they were starting to feel hungry and it was just getting dark the door slid back and the monk appeared holding a tray; he was accompanied by a diminutive figure sporting a coolie hat and dressed in what appeared to be sackcloth. This newcomer hung back shyly, darting inquisitive bird-like glances at the pavilion's occupants. Lin-ji guided him to the low table where the travellers were sitting and both sank to the floor in order to wait politely for the visitors to reach the end of the meal that the monk had just provided. But Milly, too impatient for any delay, laid her chop-sticks aside and demanded, "'Oo you got there?"

The monk glanced at Jack and Horry before launching into an involved and difficult explanation in the tongue with which he was not entirely familiar.

"Ancestors – they tell me what real. They know your friend – they call him *Deliverer*. He written 'bout long ago. They say the world waiting for him. They say he mus' go to *Ian Shan* but it velly dangerous for him. You mus' go too because p'raps you able to help him. They say I mus' help *you*."

From within his robe he brought forth some loops of bleached linen and laid them on the table. All bore mysterious black characters which Lin-ji proceeded to translate.

"This say *The spirit of the magic writing will destroy the ten thousand phantoms. Let it be executed as fast as Sang-po.* This say *Death to the great devil.* These ones for the head, these ones for arms an' legs. You put on when you get to door – they protect you."

"But 'ow we gonna get there if we don' know the way?" protested Milly, "I don' fink even Ralph and Meena know the way." (The cat and the dog had been spending most of their time at the monastery in the herb garden, showing no great eagerness to continue their journey).

The monk touched his finger to the top of the head of the small person next to him, a boy of no more than eleven or twelve years of age.

"This man Bau-zhi – that mean *full of wisdom*. He lead you. He velly clever but he don' speak your language. He take you as far as door. I give you clothes once belong to my brothers. P'raps when *Deliverer* complete his task I can join them and be freed from wheel. P'raps then everyone go free."

"Deliverer," mused Horry later, "does that mean dad's got to deliver something – like a parcel or a baby or something?"

"Don't be an idiot," answered Milly, "it's that fing roun' 'is neck – 'e's got to deliver that, I reckon, an', as far as I'm concerned, the sooner 'e gets rid of it the better."

The next day, newly equipped with monkish robes and pongee masks to hide their faces, our three friends bade a grateful goodbye to Lin-ji and set out. With them went their young dragoman plus the two animals, who, having handed over their guidance responsibilities, opted to bring up the rear. The weather which, during Horry's illness, had been gradually deteriorating, now became thoroughly unpleasant and they descended the remaining stretch of the escarpment along a road running with water from steady relentless rain. The conditions which favoured the manifestation of the sun dog were now entirely absent and in fact it never appeared again during the remainder of their journey. Pretty soon the three foreigners were soaked to the skin. As the day wore away a slight awkwardness, not to say resentment, grew out of having an addition to their party with whom they could not communicate.

"It's all right for him," complained Horry, pointing towards Bau and presuming he would not understand what was being said, "his hat's like an umbrella – the rain misses him altogether and runs off onto the ground."

Contrary to expectations the small person seemed to pick up on his companion's discontent. He doffed the conical head-piece he was wearing and offered it to Horry with a low bow, much to the young man's embarrassment.

"No mate," he protested, "you keep it. It's far too late for me anyway – I'm absolutely drenched."

Milly and Jack having also refused to accept the hat the boy sent it spinning away into the bushes, but he had not bargained for Ralph, the faithful hound, who promptly retrieved it and brought it back to him. This triggered a general laugh which was shared between all four and the atmosphere immediately improved. Nevertheless the interchange caused the Terratenebrans to wonder if they had misunderstood Lin-ji when they thought he had claimed that Bau was unfamiliar with the common tongue.

Hey – over here my lad,
I can explain your hang-ups, I can heal your guilt.
But what's this? Weeping?

Chapter twenty

"Congratulations!"

It was the tenth morning since Azazeel had turned east along the Tethys and they were still spending the better part of each day at sea. As before, each night the man at the wheel brought his craft ashore onto some deserted beach of which there were many in the extensive stretches between settlements along the Middle Sea's northern coast and either secured Dando to a hefty natural object while he absented himself in the flying car or alternatively chained him to the vehicle as he settled himself in the driving seat where he abandoned the body he was currently occupying and took himself off in his non-corporeal form. During both states of affairs Dando was left in Letty's charge with no choice but to make the best of whatever sleeping arrangements were on offer. Because, on his initial capture, he had been whisked from the northern to the southern hemisphere in a matter of hours he could not understand why they were now dawdling along as if the roadster were no more than some playboy's flashy toy. Perhaps Azazeel thought that, if enough time passed, the treatment he was meeting out would wear down his prisoner's resolve and eventually persuade him to yield the treasure he was guarding with such desperation.

On this particular occasion his tormentor had something in his hand as he returned in the car and came over to loosen the chain. Dando was confronted by the incongruous sight of a chocolate-covered cup-cake with a single candle on top. The immortal blew gently on the wick and it popped alight.

"It's your birthday," he said smiling maliciously, "you're nineteen – did you realise? Pity you won't make twenty."

Dando normally greeted everything Azazeel said with the utmost suspicion but in this case he recognised that perhaps he was hearing the truth. Autumn was here and it was feasible that they could be nearing the end of the ninth month. If it really was his natal day then two years had passed since he had become involved in this ill-starred quest – two years of hardship, sorrow and suffering as far as he was concerned, but also two years of joy, revelation and unparalleled experience. Taken all in all he would not have had it otherwise. While this was passing through his mind he was rapidly devouring the food on offer, ignoring the fact that it might well be tainted.

"You're many months away from home now my friend," said his gaoler, demonstrating yet again his mind-reading ability. "This is Tartary. We've bypassed Caffray. We'll head up country from here. I've got an appointment – a secret meeting with representatives of the criminal fraternity – price-fixing negotiations. I supply the regime with the substance they think is going to win them the war and if I pay a sweetener the gangsters don't interfere. As I said before, what the top dogs don't realise is I'm supplying all three sides: Armornia and Pickwah as well as Tartary. There's some caves beside a remote lake to the east of here that connect through underground waterways to the mines under the mountain. The lake is where I transfer the stuff I dig out into run-of-the-mill lorries and carry it overland along byroads to the shores of the Tethys - the locals are none the wiser – brilliant scheme. Come on – don't want to be late."

They left the Middle Sea and for most of the day flew north at cloud height above fields and villages until a haze of pollution materialised ahead. At this point Azazeel brought the car back to earth and they made their way along well-maintained roads towards an extensive urban development. As they reached the outskirts Dando noticed with surprise that pedestrians often bowed low as they passed. The roads were crowded with cars - sleek streamlined models - while the side-walks and overhead walkways were heaving with exotic-looking people. It was just getting dark as they approached the city but the streets were still lit up as bright as day by thousands of signs which flashed and mutated. Dando could not read a word of what was written for the illuminations were all in some strange pictographic script. He looked up. Adverts, if that is what he was seeing, were even being projected onto the haze overhead, for the stars were as invisible here as they had been in Ry-Town. Azazeel seemed totally at home in this metropolis. He penetrated deeper and deeper into the warren of roads, finally drawing the car to a halt in a dead-end alleyway between blank walls. The place was deserted apart from a group of men hanging around outside a doorway halfway along one side. Above the door indecipherable writing gleamed fitfully as a florescent tube switched on and off in an endlessly repeated sequence.

"Here we are," said Azazeel, "the gentlemen I wish to contact make a habit of patronising this establishment. As for me," patting his crotch, "might as well mix business with pleasure – a fully functional body sometimes has its advantages."

He paused, then directed a vindictive smirk at Dando who was sitting in the passenger seat. "There might be something in it for you too," pointing to the doorway, "if you're lucky. I'll introduce you to the Yakuza. Gloves off – remember."

Once more he shackled his prisoner to the vehicle and saying "Come Letitia," walked across to the entrance where the gang round the door rapidly made room for the newcomer and the great animal padding at his heels. The young man watched as he stopped and spoke to the loiterers, pointing towards the car, before disappearing inside. In response to what he imagined had been said Dando's insides began to shrivel and his hands to clench involuntarily. The whole group stared at him in an appraising manner. He thought of opening the door, getting out and putting the car body between himself and the onlookers but gave up on the idea; chained as he was, there was no hope of escape. The crooks, jail-bait to a man he was sure, exchanged banter in a language he did not understand, then the one he took to be their leader began to walk over, followed by the rest. Throat constricting Dando despairingly moaned, "Accept," but with not the faintest idea how he was to put this advice into practice.

The boss-man stood outside the car and regarded him curiously. Dando made an attempt to appear indifferent but could not disguise the fact that he was shaking with fear. The other reached across the door and laid a hand on his bare arm, the shoulder of which displayed Damask's amateurish double D tattoo, in the process demonstrating that his own hand and arm were covered in designs far more expertly executed. As his flesh came in contact with Dando's however he exclaimed in surprise and peered closely at the botched circular depiction in the dim light, stroking it with his fingers. He then retreated to speak to his companions. They talked excitedly amongst themselves for a few moments before, to the young man's astonishment, placing their hands together as if about to say their prayers and bowing towards him in unison. The head yakuza began to speak, apparently asking a question. Dando shook his head.

"I-I don't understand," he said

The leader turned to one of his deputies who stepped forward.

"You holy man?" this underling asked in the common tongue.

"H-holy man?" replied a confused Dando, " no – not at all. Although..." he was struck by a sudden thought, "I-I was ordained priest once – is that what you mean?"

The leader said something else which the deputy translated.

"My kyoda think you look hungly. You want eat?"

"Well – yes. I am very hungry."

"I get you food."

The gang member hurried off along the alley, presumably making for the nearest local takeaway and came back carrying several packages. When these were opened and their contents spread out on the driver's seat Dando ate his first square meal in four weeks.

As they set out at ground level once more, leaving the city behind and heading north, Azazeel was in a very bad mood.

"You needn't think you've gotten away with it," he growled, "because that was just intended as an opener; in fact I told them not to harm you. But I'm fed up with farting around - we'll go straight to the mountain, my mountain, and get down to things in earnest – should cross back into Caffray soon after dawn."

"They've always been called the Caves of Bone – the Haunted Caves of Bone," he explained as they drove, speaking initially in a grudging manner but soon warming to the task – he seemed to enjoy showing off his erudition. "I'm talking about the caves under Ian Shan, the Blue Mountain. It's not because they're made of bone of course - it's just their shape and the way they're arranged. The prehistoric race who used to live there gave them that name after finding that the whole set-up suggested that a giant's skeleton had once been encased within the rock and had crumbled to dust leaving cavities, tunnels and shafts in the places which it had originally occupied. At the top, inside the mountain itself, is the skull – a huge empty space presently occupied by my tenant – a useful chap to have around – he made this for me," patting the car's bodywork. "Below the scull is the jaw as you'd expect, and that's followed by the neck – several smaller caves one below the other. Then, of course, comes the spine – a long lift-shaft of caves plunging down, down to where the whole formation opens out into what I call the pelvis. That's where my chief seat of operations is located and the place where I put my little ghosts to work. Below that, who knows? If you carry on downwards you're supposed eventually to reach the place which Rostan rules - not my scene at all – far too hot. But before you get there - *Deep, too deep to delve are the haunted caves of bone that swallowed the Wayward Son, long lost to the world.* Does that refer to me or to my brother do you think? Even in my realm you'll find monsters, ghouls, baleful creatures, just waiting for a denizen of the upper air to fall into their clutches."

"Ghosts?" interjected Dando shakily, "I don't believe in ghosts."

"Well what else would you call them? They're members of your species that have got lost between lives – p'raps *lost souls* is more up your street. They wander through the subterranean honeycomb that exists beneath the surface of this planet. Oh yes – as I thought you knew - Terra is mostly eaten away below the surface as a result of the great conflict that took place here thousands of years ago – you saw a small example when you visited the Oracle at Toymerle. Anyway I've rounded up a fair number of these *lost souls* and put them to work digging out the Xoserite – don't have to pay them – a free workforce can't be bad. You'll work along side them."

"How can ghosts dig?"

"Ancestral Memory – don't you remember what I told you? They think they have bodies, ergo as far as they're concerned they actually *do* have bodies, ergo they dig."

"Is this Purgatory you're talking about?"

"I suppose that's what some people might call it. Anyway you'll soon have to say goodbye to all this," waving his hand heavenwards, "no more stars, no more moon, no more sun, no more clouds. Unless you relent you'll never see the sky again."

They were following a long straight road which gradually climbed. Eventually at dawn they reached a saddle and gazed across lowlands towards something so sublime that it made Dando catch his breath. Solitary in its cone-shaped simplicity, dominating everything else within the surrounding landscape, the Blue Mountain fully lived up to its name. Its base, although thickly wooded, glowed a luminous azure, while the silver purity of its snow-covered summit sparkled against the clear sky. If this was the location of Azazeel's lair then its outward appearance utterly belied its true nature. Most of the country surrounding the lonely peak consisted of a patchwork of vary-coloured fields but these did not extend all the way to the mountain's foot. Before reaching the trees that grew on the lower slopes there was a zone of uncultivated land. He sensed something else, a faint – so faint that he wondered if he was imagining it – fume rising from the apex of the cone. The whole panorama shimmered with light while the early-morning clouds dazzled his eyes. He gazed hungrily at the scene well aware that the clock measuring his chance of ever witnessing such beauty again was tickling down to zero.

He was being taken into the dark, so how could he prevent it from becoming an overwhelming cerebral darkness also? There was only one solution, he must fill his mind with an illumination so strong that it would cancel out the gloom. He began to list things that, over time, had lit up his life. He though of the peace and timelessness he had found inside the Ministrant's temple and also, on occasions, within the valley of Deep Hallow itself; if he could just hold that mental state in the forefront of his mind he would have some protection against whatever horrors were being prepared. He thought back to scenes of his childhood that at the time he had almost taken for granted but which now held a jewel-like quality in the memory. For example he recalled how the fruit trees in the orchards on his family estate came into delicate pink blossom in the spring and how those same trees, once the fruit had ripened and been harvested, flamed red and gold until the leaves fell; he remembered the pure clear voice of a thrush in the hush of early morning before the full dawn chorus chimed in; he remembered rowing his boat in amongst the branches of a weeping willow growing beside the Wendover and how he had sat totally still behind the green curtain in order to watch the secret life of the river flowing silently by. Yes, such things could act as armour against whatever frightfulness lay in store.

And what else? How about when the snow had been so deep round the castle during his sixth winter that it had come over the top of his first pair of boots, the time when the two sturdy cobs that normally pulled the family carriage had been yoked to a venerable sleigh, a completely novel experience as far as he was concerned. Also, more recently, he could not forget mornings in that ancient house in High Harrow when he had lain watching the constantly changing patterns of light and shade made by the sun on his bedroom wall as it shone through the leaves of a breeze-blown tree in that residence's enclosed garden. These were just small glimpses from the past but they furnished his imagination with brightness and provided a lasting solace.

From here he moved on to thoughts of the people he had loved as a child and who had loved him:- Potto, Doll, Tom and – at least from his side anyway - his father. He thought of the companions who had shared his journey: Damask, the sister who was his complete antithesis yet who had always been there for him; Tallis, the master to whom he still felt linked by an indissoluble bond; Foxy, his sometimes troublesome but always respected half-brother; and of course Horry, the young son who had been gently worming his way into his heart in the days before they were so cruelly separated.

Lastly he thought of his lovers: Milly - dear Milly – the loyal lieutenant who had cared for him so tenderly and had freed him from his demons, Jack and the coupling which, despite everything that happened later as a consequence, had ultimately enriched his life, and of course Annie, his beloved other self who had shared that happy, holy time when they were learning about sex together. He could imagine her now, standing almost within arms reach, waist-deep amidst the golden corn, looking back towards him and beckoning. All these memories he would take beneath the mountain, along with the blue of the heavens, the faint pink flush of early dawn and the wondrous vision of infinity to be savoured on a clear starry night.

"Hello? - what have you got to smile about!"

Azazeel glanced sideways and then swung round towards him with a hard calculating stare, for a moment failing to concentrate on his driving so that the car swerved across the road. Dando tried to assume a stone face that gave nothing away but could not disguise the fact that, for the moment, he was feeling fortified and defended, in fact briefly invulnerable. His captor turned back and mooched along at a snail's pace for a certain distance until, snorting in disgust, he put the car into overdrive and the engine climbed up the revs.

Straight as a die the road they were following cut through fields and across streams making a beeline for their destination. In no time at all they were a mere half a mile from the lower slopes of the mountain. Passing between two tall gate posts crowned with stone gargoyles Dando discovered that branches now obscured the wider view and all that could be seen through the windscreen was an avenue, a tunnel hemmed in by dense woodland. The car surged forward and suddenly he was desperate to do anything in his power to halt the onward rush. The fact was, he had recognised something familiar about this place and as a consequence thought he knew what was to come. A dark orifice awaited him he believed, a gaping mouth foreshadowing a downward-slanting shaft *wide enough to take three carriages abreast* out of which, when they reached it, a dank gale would be blowing smelling of unlife. This Gehenna had apparently been lying in wait for him ever since that recurring nightmare presaged its existence in his boyhood. Consolation and dread cancelled each other out in his mind and emotionally bankrupt for the moment he stared stupidly forward as they approached the anticipated entrance which must also be the door past which Ann told him she could not follow. When they were about twenty yards distant a portcullis-like barrier clanked upwards to allow them passage before dropping back into place once they had passed under it. There was no question but that they were now within the rock and, despite the pervasive sterility of the air, he saw there was life in this underground environment: cobwebs caught in his hair, a few bats, disturbed by the noise, flew low overhead, while, in the beam of the headlights, small rat-like mammals scuttled to safety.

The light of day was soon left behind, headlights were employed and the engine noise redoubled as it echoed off rocky walls on either side. They continued to travel downwards, the tunnel becoming narrower and more claustrophobic, until all at once the car burst out into a huge open space, a cave much larger than the basilica at Toymerle which Dando had once thought must be the biggest underground chamber in the world. The floor of this enormous cavity was level enough to drive across and he could actually see a host of smaller vehicles in the distance busily darting to and fro around the base of a huge mysterious object. It was this towering construction, the focus of all the far off mechanised activity, that grabbed his attention and caused him to gaze upwards open-mouthed. The structure was presumably man-made, a column of metal hundreds of feet high, and it dominated the centre of the cave, supported by a spider's web of scaffolding and surrounded by a complex network of walkways and staircases over which tiny figures clambered. Looking upwards he was unable to see the top of the edifice because it disappeared into a gap in the distant roof of the cavern which apparently connected to the outside world. Faint daylight was filtering down from above, adding to the illumination provided by banks of floodlights situated all around the subterranean hub, while the huge object also appeared to be shining with its own interior light. Azazeel brought the car to a halt and Dando stood up in order to get a better view.

"The skull," explained his driver with an expansive gesture which took in the cave and all it contained, "the resemblance is obvious I think. I lease the space out – have done for years. Quahaug's his name – I let him have it for a nominal rent in exchange for certain favours. I also have an arrangement over the Xoserite he uses - that's what that machine - that *space ship* as he insists on calling it - is made of. He tells me the mineral also provides its means of propulsion although I don't understand the processes involved. He's got the notion that, once completed, it's going to take a surface-dwelling creature to places where none have ever ventured before, places where not even those who've made the *Change* dare to go – sounds a bit far fetched to me."

"Who are they, these people?" asked Dando in a toneless and barely audible voice, pointing towards the operatives and feeling that he already knew the answer.

"They call themselves Inshami. They turned up here way, way back. Evidently they originally came from some place on the same continent that you hail from. There's not many left now – they're not that good at reproduction."

"Belturbet,"sighed the young man, watching as a faint hope of rescue disappeared over the horizon. He was remembering how, at their final meeting, the Ministrant had told him about that ancient race from Terratenebra who, when the war went against them, had gone east to live beneath a mountain. He had been nursing the idea that this was the very place and that, if any descendants of the original emigrees still existed, they might possibly come to his aid. But now it seemed that, although they *were* here, they were hand in glove with his persecutor.

"Belturbet - yes – you're right," Azazeel was obviously anxious to get moving, "but I think you've seen enough for now - we can't hang around just for your benefit. Time and tide wait for no man you know and you haven't yet been exposed to a fraction of my little kingdom – I believe you're going to find it highly educational."

Azazeel selected first gear and shot off towards the periphery of the cave jerking Dando back into his seat. The car entered a curved, descending passageway which brought them out into another large cave directly beneath the previous one, but this time low-roofed and dim, the only illumination apart from the car's headlights appearing to come from the rock; he saw seams of silvery deposits around the sides glowing with a faint blue light.

"You get traces at this level," said Azazeel, pointing towards the brightness within the walls, "but they're not abundant enough to be worth extracting. We have to go much deeper. Looks like the elevator's at the bottom of the shaft – it'll take a few minutes to raise it. That's another thing Quahaug did for me – he's a clever chap when he confines himself to practicalities."

The cave floor here was as level as the one above but in the centre Dando saw a wide pit from which both indistinct fumes and a monotonous muffled thumping noise emerged. As they drove across and parked beside this hole the emanating miasma penetrated deep into his lungs causing him to cough helplessly until he became aware, once again, of the salty taste of blood in his mouth.

"Oh dear," commented Azazeel with feigned concern, "the air in this place doesn't seem to suit you. Here – hold this over your nose," and he offered the same stained towel that he had tendered nearly a month before when Letty launched her first attack.

After a fairly long wait, a platform, looking as if it had been specifically designed to accommodate the flying car, rose from the depths and Azazeel drove onto it. Bizarrely, along with the elevator came a swarm of small creatures, apparently disturbed by its progress: among these were a few bats, but there were also tiny transparent humanoids, some with wings, some using the bats as mounts. They buzzed to and fro, mosquito-like, and a number of times Dando felt the pathetic rags which were all that was left of his clothing being tweaked and his hair pulled. Azazeel slapped at the air, trying to drive them away.

"Gerroff! Gerroff!" he muttered.

"What are they?" exclaimed his astonished prisoner.

"Gurkies, Hoikendorfs, Nac-Ma-Feedles – you name 'em, we've got 'em. I've tried calling in pest control but the little devils just laugh at their charms and cantrips. It's the element that draws them – they can smell it several miles away. They ingest it, would you believe – they think it boosts their powers."

As the platform started to move downwards the little people followed in its wake, circling round and round within the shaft. The lift was equipped with an array of lights which enabled Dando to catch glimpses of their surroundings as they descended. He saw caves apparently made of sparkling crystal, caves with what looked like fossils in the walls and others containing large reflective pools. There were dark recesses within some of the adjacent spaces harbouring moving shadows which were rendered more sinister by being unidentifiable, and a place where, briefly, two enormous fiery eyes blinked at him out of the darkness. The thumping noise became increasingly insistent the further down they travelled, resolving itself into a raucous, driving, relentless beat underpinning the sound of amplified guitars and strident brass. Dando could not help but screw his face up into a grimace of pain, causing the lord of the underworld to chuckle maliciously.

"Doesn't turn you on?" he sneered. "What? - a young bloke like you? Didn't realise you were such a square. You'll have to put up with it I'm afraid - got to keep the employees happy."

The platform eventually halted beside some double doors.

“We're not at the bottom yet,” explained Azazeel, “but there's a few little tasks I have to perform at this level. You'd better accompany me. Heel Letty.”

Dando, unchained and having no choice, left the car and followed the immortal through the doorway, the tiger close behind, only to find himself in a large well-lit space equipped with wide benches fixed against the walls and in the centre a table on which stood various items of glassware and scientific apparatus. Although he had never personally encountered such a place before, knowledge gained from his reading caused the word *laboratory* to spring to mind. On the far side of the room he saw banks of cages containing small animals, rats and mice mainly, and opposite them shelf upon shelf of large brown bottles, each bearing a label describing its contents: *Acetic Acid, Hydrochloric Acid, Sulphur Dioxide, Hydrogen Chloride, Calcium Oxide* and so on.

“This is where I come for recreation,” the other told him. “In my spare moments I amuse myself by investigating the miracle material – its possibilities seem endless. Quahaug's given me a few pointers and I've taken it from there – sit ye down a minute while I just update a few things.”

Azazeel soon became totally absorbed in his research. Dando watched as he removed rats, one at a time, from the cages and either injected them with fluid from a syringe or took blood samples which he then examined under a microscope. The rats, carried around by their tails, squeaked in fear and struggled fruitlessly. Azazeel then went to a different cage, selected one particular rat, and killed it by breaking its neck. He bent over the central table and proceeded to dissect it, separating out its various organs while Dando looked on in disgust, reminded of the examination he had undergone at the Transfer Facility.

Is that me, he thought in despair, *is that how I'm going to end up – spread out on a slab, waiting to be slit open? What point is there in continuing to hope? All the same,* defiantly, *I'm not giving in as long as I've got life in me – whatever he does I'm not giving up.*

Eventually Azazeel appeared to lose interest and, licking the blood from his fingers, ushered his prisoner back to the car. Before he left, however, he took down one of the bottles and, unscrewing the lid, offered it to Dando.

“What do you make of that?” he asked

Unwisely Dando stooped and took a small sniff. The fumes slammed into his nasal tissue with the violence of a physical assault while at the same time the vapour streamed down his throat and took possession of his airways. He gasped and spluttered while tears streamed from his eyes. Azazeel displayed the bottle's label; it read *Concentrated Ammonia*. "Pretty strong stuff!" he said, slapping a choking Dando on the back and laughing deliriously. As the elevator plunged downwards once more the young man gradually recovered, but at least an hour passed before he felt he was breathing normally again.

When they finally reached the foot of the shaft it took a moment or two to get used to one G after being partially weightless during the long descent. His captor drove the car off the platform and along a sloping passageway until they came to a place where the rock music that had been a constant on the way down was partially drowned by the sound of rushing water. When they turned a corner he discovered the source of this noise and was taken aback. Out from a tunnel on the left hand side burst a black watery flood, at least fifty feet wide. It streamed past in a channel just a short distance from where the car had come to a halt and then disappeared into another dark opening, thousands of gallons flashing by every second without a break.

"I'm afraid this is where we have to abandon the love-machine," explained Azazeel, giving his car's bodywork a slap. "Hey Sindbad! – chop, chop – over here!"

Dando saw that on the other side of the watercourse, up by the outflow, a boat was moored with a figure sitting motionless beside it. It took several shouts on Azazeel's part before this individual responded to their presence and even then his movements were those of a sleepwalker. Eventually the boat set off across the underground river sweeping downstream on the current so fast that it only narrowly avoided vanishing into the exit tunnel. Dando examined the boatman curiously as he arrived and noticed that his expression was strangely blank as if cognitively he had strayed far away into some remote mental wilderness. Having towed the craft upstream after landing the man helped them to board before motoring across once more, but made no other attempt to interact with his passengers. "Thankyou," said Dando as they alighted after their short voyage but received no answering civility.

"Here we are," said Azazeel with the pride of ownership, pointing to a glowing archway ahead of them, "you're now about to enter the enterprise's main sector. Just one more rabbit-hole to negotiate and then... Oh bugger..! Hang on..."

What caused him to grab Dando's arm with some urgency was the wailing of a siren emanating from within the tunnel.

"We'd better stay put until..." His last words were drowned out by a deafening explosion which caused a shower of rubble to fall from the roof, followed by a gradually dying rumble as the rocks surrounding them settled back into immobility.

"Sorry – should have remembered it was time for the four o'clock blast. Better give them a few minutes to pick up the pieces. Come round this way – I'll show you some of the later stages."

After just a few yards the passageway they were following opened out into an expanse of such enormous complexity that Dando gasped in amazement. He could see naves, aisles, transepts, galleries, staircases on many different levels, and in the floor two great cavities, hundreds of feet across, plunging to unknown depths. All were suffused in a blue incandescent glow that emanated from the craggy walls. This was more than just a cave – this was a sequence of interlinked, interconnected caverns with roofs so remote that they resembled part of the night sky and chambers that retreated on and on into the misty distance. The whole area reverberated and re-echoed to the continual noise of machinery: crushers pounding rocks into fragments, conveyor belts passing over, under and across one another, hoists lifting rubble up onto the belts. As if this was not enough, the same heavy rock music he had heard on the way down – but in this place amplified to a deafening pitch - accompanied the din. Dando pressed his hands over his ears, unable to bear the cacophony, at the same time noticing that in the midst of all this uproar people were working.

"Voilà the ghosts," yelled Azazeel, "look real enough, don't they. I believe there's a new intake just arrived. You might as well join them."

The same gaseous smell that had caused Dando's coughing fit at the top of the shaft pervaded the air down here and this had grown stronger since the explosion. He tried not to inhale too deeply. Azazeel conducted him up flights of steps and along walkways until they were on a level with the moving belts. He saw that standing on either side of these bands were rows and rows of individuals picking over the detritus that was passing by. It was apparently their job to spot and discard anything that was not pure Xoserite, a task which required intense concentration. If their attention wavered even for a moment they incurred severe punishment from guards who hung at their backs equipped with whips and batons. These task-masters were not human.

"Baldangers," shouted Azazeel, pointing to one group, "and those across there are Wodwoses. They'd evolved down here over many millennia, but to what purpose I have no idea. Up until I moved in they were leading completely pointless lives. I think they get a kick out of working for me – the whole set-up functions like clockwork."

Dando stared in the direction of these extraordinary creatures. The Wodwoses presented the appearance of animated tree-stumps, their skin bark-like, their brows heavy and their greenish hair more like a coating of moss. The Baldangers on the other hand were slender, two-legged, billygoat-like creatures, priapic, nude, their sex prominently on display. Parts of their bodies were covered in a scanty coating of hair, small horns sprouted from their foreheads and their backward-jointed legs ended in hooves. Both species laid their scourges on enthusiastically with scant regard for their victims' health and welfare. In overall charge were a few heavily-built men, undeniably human, of oriental cast and virtually naked apart from a wisp of cloth round their loins. They were wearing smog-masks over their noses and mouths.

"Superannuated wrestlers," Azazeel informed him.

After having gazed his fill at these strange life forms Dando's attention was then drawn to the prisoners employed at the belts. He noticed that they covered a wide age range: some mere children, barely tall enough to do what was required of them, a few well along in years. What was immediately obvious was that many had suffered severe damage to their bodies - he saw smashed heads, lacerated flesh, severed limbs.

"What's happened to them?!" he cried appalled.

"Didn't I explain? These are the ones that have become lost between incarnations. That usually occurs when death is premature. Although some will have died by their own hand most perish in accidents long before their destined time and the normal progression from life to death and back to life again never takes place. They carry the injuries that killed them."

So these are the dead, thought Dando, awestruck, *but how can you tell they're not alive? They move, they groan, they cry out, they breath. Or do they breath?* He could not be sure. What did strike him was that all bore the same bewildered, stupefied look that he had seen on the face of the boatman who had carried them across the river.

"What do you feed them on?" he asked.

"Feed them? Nothing of course - this stuff keeps 'em going." Azazeel bent and filled a metal cup from one of several barrels in the vicinity, before offering it to Dando - it was the same nauseating liquid which he, Azazeel, drank to sustain the reanimated corpses he occupied. “Anyway,” he added, “imaginary food is good enough for imaginary bodies.”

“Their bodies are real enough to carry out your dirty work,” said Dando indignantly, gesturing towards the rows of drudges.

“Dispensable,” replied his captor, “dispensable, every last one.”

“I think things will have settled down by now – I'll take you to the face and then hand you over for training.”

Azazeel led him into a more chaotic region. In this area the ground was littered with debris that had obviously fallen from the roof at the time of the explosion. The light in the rock was stronger here and grew in intensity as they advanced. Soon large boulders impeded their progress and the air was full of the sound of metal on mineral as gangs of phantoms wielded picks and shovels in order to break these into manageable pieces. Others piled the rubble into heaps while a digger scooped up the results of their efforts and tipped the raw material into huge buckets that were carried away suspended from a cable. Dando was shocked to notice the occasional body casually abandoned beneath a rock-fall, some still feebly moving. “Aren't you going to do anything to help him!” he demanded as they passed one of these unfortunates.

“Oh he'll just get dumped in a sink-hole. There's a particular hole we employ that is reputed to be where the giant's dinglum-danglum used to hang, but if that's the case the monster's anatomy must have been really freaky. A discard like this one'll be left there along with the other rejects and he'll probably just fade away, although some actually recover enough to be of some use. And then of course there are those who retain such a strong body-image that they putrefy - creates quite a stink.”

Dando noticed that it was not only when the explosives were detonated that the rocks quaked. Every now and then the ground quivered like the surface of an enormous blancmange and each time this happened more stones fell and the atmosphere thickened, affecting the lungs of anyone still in the land of the living and not wearing masks. Soon they came upon a crowd of captives being guarded by one of the strongmen.

“Here they are,” said Azazeel, “the new guys – those you'll train with. I've just received an important message (showing him a small communication device) – gotta dash - Letty'll keep an eye on you. Remember – the gloves are off – I know what you most fear...”

Dando, left alone amidst strangers in an alien and hostile environment, was suddenly overcome by a feeling of utter confusion: *Letty – Letty who? What is this place? What am I doing here? What's my name? Who am I?*

To drink his health
You must go down among the dead men,
For that's where he's at.

Chapter twenty one

The diminutive figure of Bau-zhi stood between the gargoyle-topped gate posts and pointed ahead along the dark avenue. He then stepped aside and motioned for them to pass. Once they had done so he put his hands together and bowed deeply.

"Ain't you comin' wiv us into the mountain?" asked Milly.

The little boy shook his head and backed away.

"He ain't comin'," explained Milly to Jack.

"Well, I don't spose we'll be needing him from now on." The blind boy's response was nothing if not brusque. "We c'n find our own way from here. We'll say goodbye and then take ourselves off."

"I fink we ought to give 'im sompthin' for orl that 'ee's done," Milly whispered.

"Of course – he's not going to leave empty-handed."

Jack held out several gold coins that he had somehow managed to acquire along the way but their guide refused the proffered payment, waving it aside while looking slightly affronted.

"'Ee don' wan' them," Milly interpreted for her friend's benefit.

"Fair enough," said Jack.

It was not long after they had left Lin-ji's monastery that it became clear that Bau-zhi, despite what the monk had told them, understood perfectly well every word they uttered. When it came to speech, however, vocalisation seemed way beyond his powers. Even when encountering his fellow countrymen he communicated solely by graceful, dance-like hand gestures of which he had a large fund. There were many reasons to be grateful to him, for throughout their journey he proved to be an invaluable and necessary companion. War-torn Caffray at that period was a hazardous place even for its regular inhabitants, but when it came to those who risked being exposed as Armornian spies or covert partisan sympathisers it became rapidly lethal. They passed many horrific sights: gibbets hung with rows of bodies swaying in the wind, villages burnt to the ground and, on one occasion, a glimpse of condemned men stretched on their backs in a town square, pinioned hand and foot to stakes and left to die slowly at the mercy of the local vermin. Bau was constantly on the alert and steered them away from locations occupied by the millitary or from areas where troop movements were common. He knew the best places to hide and the more unfrequented routes across country. During their time on the road they experienced atrocious weather and oddly this proved to be a distinct advantage because it kept most of the locals, who might have identified them as strangers and then reported their presence, indoors. They made good progress towards their goal but apart from that one unverified sighting from the escarpment above the monastery, they did not get a glimpse of the Blue Mountain for some time. It was only when they came over the same saddle of land, on one of the rare fine days, surmounted previously by Azazeel and his prisoner that they were rewarded with a view of what they were seeking, for there it stood - *Ian Shan* - splendidly isolate, a remnant of some prehistoric upheaval, now broodingly counting down the centuries, awaiting its time.

"We can't be far from the foot," said Horry as they left the gates with the gargoyles and walked forward between dense stands of trees. "This probably leads to the entrance but how we're ever going to get inside without being seen I've no idea."

"Get ready to hide if you hear anyone coming," cautioned Jack.

"Oy, wait a minute – look at the animals..." Milly's attention had strayed to what was happening behind them. For most of their journey across Caffray, Meena had spent the time curled up in the neck of the black girl's rucksack while Ralph padded tirelessly at their heels, loyally in attendance, but now both cat and dog were standing at the entrance to the avenue making no attempt to follow into the dimness. "I don' fink they fink we ought to be goin' this way," she said.

Horry stood looking back, a frown on his face. "Maybe they realise we'll get on better without them," he suggested.

"Well, that's certainly true." Jack was quick to agree. "With them around we'd certainly be advertising our presence to all and sundry. We'll pick them up on the way back."

"D'you fink they'll be orl right?" asked a concerned Milly.

Not many minutes later they were given a possible reason for the animals' behaviour. The grand portal to the underworld came in sight ahead but it was immediately obvious that it was barricaded against them.

"It's like the gate to the Lordship's castle," said Milly, "that 'ad bars that went up an' down. Someone 'ad to turn an 'andle in order to make them shift. The people outside rung a bell."

"Well we won't be doing that," replied Jack. "I don't think it would be advisable to knock and ask to be let in,"

They crept closer and the sighted ones peered through the barrier, becoming aware of a wide descending passageway, dark, silent and deserted, disappearing into blackness.

"D'you fink the Lordship's down there?" asked Milly in a small scared voice, "'ow on erf are we goin' to get 'im out?"

"I think we ought to go back," said Horry with sudden conviction, "I think maybe the animals know a better way."

Jack sniffed his disbelief at this idea but did not seem to have any alternative suggestion. After a brief hesitation they turned and retraced their steps to the beginning of the avenue where, instead of Ralph and Meena, they found the young Caffrayan boy Bau-zhi sitting on the ground and leaning against one of the gate posts, evidently waiting for them.

"Where are the animals?" Milly asked and, meeting an uncomprehending stare, "you know – the puss-cat," pointing to her shoulder, "an' the doggie," bending as if to pat an invisible head. Bau shook his own head in reply and then, using eloquent sign language, asked what they had found at the far end.

"The entrance to the mountain is blocked," said Horry, "is there another way in?"

The boy got to his feet and pointed skywards.

"What's he doing?" demanded Jack.

"'Ee seems to fink we c'n go up in the air." Milly was derisory. "We ain't got no air-plane luv an' anyway we wants to go down not up."

"I know what he's saying," cried an excited Jack, "he means we've got to climb. That'll maybe bring us to the back door – a vent of some kind at the summit going way down inside."

Bau nodded vigorously.

"Do you think we c'n do that?" doubted Horry. "climb the mountain I mean. It looked devilish steep up near the top."

"I'm willing to give it a go!" Jack was suddenly all eagerness. "Perhaps the kid'll show us the easiest route up."

"But what about the animals?" worried Milly

"Well, maybe they've gone ahead." It was Horry who answered her, having rapidly come round to Jack's way of thinking. "If we hurry we'll probably catch 'em up."

When it came to scaling the side of *Ian Shan* they soon discovered that, although Jack's spirit was willing, after a very short time his body began to let him down. He gasped and stumbled, refusing to give up, despite becoming increasingly exhausted. Milly looked at him in concern. By rights at his age, which she thought must be around twenty four by now, he should be coming into his full strength. Instead he appeared even more enfeebled than when she had rescued him, half-starved and traumatised, from the depths of that precipitous ravine alongside the road from Toymerle.

"Wot's the matter luv?" she asked.

Jack sat down heavily on a rock and shook his head as if making a last ditch attempt to deny what was all too obvious.

"I don't know," he said, "and I don't really want to speculate."

"Wot d'you mean?"

"Nothing. Let's pretend things are normal for as long as possible."

"I c'n help you get up the mountain," offered Horry.

Milly looked from Jack to her young charge. She was used by now to the fact that Horry was tall – as tall or even taller than Dando. Now she saw that in the last few weeks he had begun to fill out. His Nablan heritage was giving him bodily strength to go with the height that he had inherited from his father. He looked all of eighteen – perhaps older – and would soon become a fine figure of a man, despite his ruined face. Almost without realising it she felt the first stirrings of an interest that was no longer entirely maternal.

It took a while for Jack to decide to forego his independence, always fiercely fought for, and reluctantly submit to being supported as the gradient became yet steeper. Even so he still found the climb an ordeal, especially when they got amongst the snows on the higher slopes.

"Blimey, it ain't 'alf cold up 'ere," complained Milly.

"But look," said Horry, "near the top the ice seems to have melted."

"That's a good sign," panted Jack, "it probably means there's warm air coming through some outlet that leads to the interior."

"Yers," said Milly, "but what about the animals? They're nowhere to be seen. I 'opes they're orl right."

As they scrambled up the almost vertical last hundred feet it was true that they were treading on bare rock and when they came over the rim at the summit there was a distinct rise in temperature, but it was what awaited them once they had o'er-topped the highest point that grabbed Milly and Horry's attention. A wide, completely circular crater lay before them and in the centre a huge gaping orifice plunged to unknown depths. Milly described the scene for Jack's benefit.

"...an' there's this whacking great pot 'ole in the middle. But there's sompfink sticking up out of the 'ole – I don' know what it is but it looks reely peculiar."

"There *is* something there," contributed Horry. "It's similar to the nose-cone of the plane we came across in the forest, but much, much larger. I think we ought to investigate."

Throughout the climb Bau-zhi had forged confidently ahead in order to show them the way, as if he had made this ascent many times before. Now he indulged in a piece of mime that initially they did not understand. First of all he touched his brow and then circled his hand around his head, after which he followed this up by pointing to his wrists and ankles.

"It's those bits of clorf wiv the writin' on them that the monk gave us," cried Milly, tumbling to what he was trying to say, "I fink 'ee wants us to put 'em on. I reckon praps we should 'ave bin wearin' them all along. They're in your pack, ain't they Jack?"

Jack produced the bands and handed them round. Obediently his companions placed them on their heads and extremities.

"Are they meant to make us go invisible?" wondered Milly.

Horry stared hard at the pictograms, turning his wrist this way and that. "No – not invisible," he explained, "it's more of a disguise. Down there they won't see you for what you are if you're wearing these – they'll see what they expect to see."

"An' are you goin' to do your magic too – like you did by the flying machine?"

"No – you can't have two continuities happening simultaneously and my advice would be to go with the bands. I've got a feeling that they represent very deep local knowledge - deeper by far than I could manage."

"Oh," said Milly sounding somewhat nonplussed.

As mentioned, the day up to that point had been one of those rare fine ones that were becoming less and less frequent since the world had entered upon its new dispensation, but now, almost instantaneously, everything changed as a dense cloud layer descended over the mountain peak reducing visibility to zero.

"It's gorn orl foggy," Milly explained to Jack, "I c'n 'ardly see me 'and in front of me face. 'Ow on erf are we goin' to find the 'ole now wivout fallin' into it?"

"If you'll trust me," said Jack, "I think I could locate it for you."

Milly nodded slowly. "Yers," she said, and then to Horry, "it's true – 'ee's good in a fog – 'ee woz brilliant when the 'orspital fell down."

"OK, lead on McDuff," said Horry and subsequently they deferred to Jack's superior directional skills, even Bau who had less past evidence to rely on than the others. The blind boy walked steadily forward probing the shallow soil in front of him with his cane before coming to an abrupt halt.

"Better go carefully from here on in," he warned, "this ground's been well trodden – I think we're getting close."

Sure enough they soon saw something pale and massive looming through the fog, projecting up out of darkness, and realised they were approaching the brink of the pit.

"There's a ladder I think," whispered Horry, "goes down between the wall and the missile."

"Missile?" Milly whispered back.

"Well, isn't that what it is?"

They were speaking in lowered tones because a dark silhouette, a man in uniform, had just emerged from the shaft, apparently on sentry go, and they were extremely anxious not to advertise their presence. Bau, however, walked boldly forward and they were amazed to hear the guard address the little boy in a respectful tone before stepping aside to allow him entry to the nether regions. Bau turned and beckoned to the other travellers before setting foot on the topmost rung of the ladder.

"They seem to know 'im," muttered Milly, full of suspicion.

"It's the bands," explained Horry, "they're seeing something familiar – they probably think Bau is part of their set-up and they'll think the same about us if we introduce ourselves."

"What do you say, Jack?" asked Milly nervously.

"I don't reckon we've got much choice if we want to get inside." Jack, for once, was being uncharacteristically fatalistic. "Whatever their reaction we'll probably end up by being taken below as long as they don't shoot us first."

And so it proved. The guard ran his eye over the three of them and then gestured towards the ladder without saying another word. As they started to feel their way downwards he brought up the rear and when they reached a platform on which another uniformed man was standing he barked, "Delegation to see Project Manager," after which he scuttled aloft once more. This set a precedent. Gradually threading a series of metal stairs, gantries and walkways they were handed on from one escort to another and thus were given no chance to guilefully lose themselves among the maze of intricate scaffolding. As they clambered downwards, they were constantly aware of the great glowing machine in close proximity to their left, which was being laboured on by numerous technicians dressed in protective clothing. It was not long before the shaft that encircled them came to an abrupt end and they emerged into the upper regions of an enormous cave just below roof level, where their ears were immediately assaulted by the sound of mechanical drills, automatic hammers and other heavy machinery of various sorts. At this point in the descent a substantial viewing platform had been built on which a range of huts was positioned. At the door of one of these stood an elderly man with long grey hair and beard, a sheaf of papers in his hand.

"Delegation to see Project Manager," repeated their latest minder before giving a full military salute and hurrying away. The man in the hut doorway smiled vaguely and bent his gaze downwards.

"Ah, Bau-zhi," he said, adding something quite extensive in the local Caffrayan tongue which they were unable to understand. To their enormous surprise Bau, after making an obeisance, answered him vocally in the same language, proving, at this late stage, that he had a voice and could use it perfectly well when he chose to do so. Eventually, the boy, having apparently received instructions, turned towards them and introduced his new acquaintance.

"This Master Manfred Quahaug - he great man of learning – natural philosopher - velly old. I tell him who you are. Perhaps he help you, perhaps not. You ask him nicely. I go back now."

"You're going?" cried Milly, dismayed at this second abrupt leave-taking. She had become totally accustomed to Bau's presence and placed enormous reliance on his route-finding abilities.

"I don' know way from here. I help you all I can. You talk to man – he know lots of things."

"Oh, orl right – but we mus' thank you somehow – you've been a real peach, ain't 'ee boys."

Horry and Jack both voiced their agreement.

"I help you," answered Bau earnestly, "you help *Deliverer* - *Deliverer* help the world - then everything velly good. I go now."

Acting on impulse Milly bent and kissed the little boy. Bau, blushing furiously, fled up the steps they had just negotiated and disappeared into the shaft above. That was the last they saw of him.

"An extremely unusual child," commented the old man, demonstrating that he was as fluent in the common tongue as he was in Bau's language, "come into my office – I think we need to talk."

Milly and Horry looked at each other with raised eyebrows but Jack, showing no fear, followed in the scientist's footsteps, thereby making a decision for all three.

"Bring us some tea Vera."

Once inside Quahaug's sanctum the noise of construction was left behind and peace reigned. The room was obviously efficiently sound-proofed because, although work could still be seen continuing on the other side of a large picture window, it was taking place in what seemed a dream-like environment while, inside the hut, all was quiet. The old man stared at them with a piercing gaze which appeared to penetrate any dissimulation and rendered the disguising bands ineffective. Then, without any further preliminary greetings he launched into an elaborate explanatory discourse, proudly waving his hand in the direction of the glass, outside of which an abundance of activity was taking place.

"Xoserite has smashed the old rules that we all thought were set in stone," he began, "such as the speeds we are able to achieve between heavenly bodies, the length of the journey undertaken, even which direction we travel in time; they've all been rewritten. Pretty soon I would have been able to offer proof – the craft's already space-worthy – if the circumstances had been different. The problem is I can't find anyone willing to pilot it – the fools all think it'll be a death sentence, and maybe it will but that hardly matters when the gain in knowledge will be so great. Unable to go myself – have to stay here and respond to incoming info – needs two to tango you see – I designed it that way. Of course I still had Orlando in those days, my great great grandson – he was keen. Suffocated in the vacuum chamber during a spacesuit try-out – when we realised what was happening it was far too late. That *diabolus* likes to pretend the boy's down there now in his factory of the damned, working on the rock-face, but that's just a story he's concocted so's he can tighten the screw – as far as I'm concerned I don't owe him a thing – especially now he's persuaded Ursula..."

During this rather rambling speech Milly became visibly more and more impatient. Eventually, unable to contain herself, she burst out with - "Where's the Lordship?! Where's Dando?! What've you done wiv 'im?! 'Ave you 'urt 'im?!"

She gave the man no chance to reply but pounced on his defenceless body - a second Meena in fighting mode - and the next moment had grabbed handfuls of his hair and beard and was attempting to pull them out by the roots. Horry and Jack hurled themselves into the fray and managed to drag the spitting snarling girl off while at the same time apologising to her shocked victim.

"...stop it Milly! He's not the one who's taken Dando! You know that perfectly well! Calm down for heaven's sake! I'm awfully sorry – are you ok? - can I fetch you something? She's all worked up because our friend was kidnapped and brought here against his will, or so we believe..."

Quahaug did not call for assistance or attempt to have them ejected, although he would have been perfectly within his rights to do so. Instead, after gathering his wits and drinking another restorative cup of tea brought to him by the faithful Vera he sat back down and invited them to offer a fuller explanation of their reasons for entering his domain. Eventually he gave a half smile and remarked ruefully, "I suppose the little lady's reaction was no more than I deserve for regularly consorting with the Devil."

"The Devil?"

"Azazeel – the Lord of the Underworld some call him. His realm is below here – a considerable way below. Personally I think that what goes on down there earns the place the epithet *Hell* if anything does. If you're here for any length of time you'll see that he passes through my scene of operations quite frequently in the toy I built for him – that car was part of the deal we struck back in the dim and distant past." He gestured towards the window. "On one occasion recently he did have another with him but I couldn't say if it was the person you're looking for. All the same tell me a little more about this thing your friend's supposed to be carrying."

Milly, slightly shame-faced, recounted what she had learnt concerning the Key's history and Jack contributed what he knew, while Horry explained as far as he was able the message his mother had given him about *going outside* and *under the earth.*

"Yes," said Quahaug after they had finished, "I thought so – it's the same. *Tergiversator, Catalyst, Age-Fomenter, Master-Changer, World's-Bane, Periapt, Talisman...* the list goes on. Why does it have so many names? I think the answer is to be found in the fact that no-one's able to solve the riddle of its true nature and so nobody is quite sure what it's actual function is. My people had it in their possession at one time – in as much as it can be possessed – but we woefully mistook its purpose and were arrogant enough to think we could exploit its power – we were justly punished. I was actually the one that spoke before the council against the idea that it should be prevented from carrying on in its current direction – spoke all those years ago when I was still a young man. As I handled it briefly at the time, along with several other members of my race, it has prolonged my life well beyond the normal human span, although, finally, I think I'm nearing the end. I suppose you realise that I was also the one who stole it from where my fellow councillors had squirrelled it away and then left it in the centre of the city of Damwey where no-one would think to look for it. I then departed for the mountain, meaning to return when I had devised a way of separating it from the earth. Over the years, because I became so absorbed in my project, I lost sight of my initial intention, but now..." he paused as if reviewing what he had just said and then continued in a voice of suppressed excitement like someone who has discovered proof of a long-abandoned theory: "Thinking about what you've told me I'm reminded of why I was originally inspired to build this craft," gesturing towards the window. "If you find the young man bring him to me straight away."

"D'you mean the Lordship?," demanded Milly, somewhat tearfully, "But *'ow* are we goin' to fin' 'im? We don' know where 'e is or what's 'appenin' to 'im."

"Can you show us the best way to reach Azazeel's realm?" asked Jack. "We've been given these bands which are supposed to help us go unnoticed – do you think they'll be effective?"

"Let's have a look. Mmm - they will if you encounter run-of-the-mill personnel but probably not if you meet the fellow himself or some of his more erudite henchmen. As for getting there, the lift down the spine that I built is out of the question of course but the right arm might suffice – if you're really keen I'll take you to where the clavicle connects with the humerus."

"Clavicle – humerus?" queried Horry.

"Oh - I thought you understood – you've surely heard why these caves are called the Caves of Bone. The whole system is enormously complicated and extends to unknown depths - there are subterranean lakes and rivers – it's a place where it's very easy to get lost. But if you want to locate your friend go to the mine workings – the Xoserite workings – if he's anywhere at all he'll be there. Once you arrive you'll need these," handing them small devices that looked like deaf-aids. "They act as an antidote to the amnesia-inducing music. You'd better have two each – the batteries only last a few hours."

"She's been left behind," said Horry later, when they had once more embarked on their search, "we're out on our own from now on."

"I don' get you."

"My ma – she said she'd have to stay behind when we came down here – she told me a while ago that she wouldn't be able to follow once we passed the door. Azazeel's pitched a hex on the mountain that keeps the dancers out – he didn't extend it to those still in the flesh or the ones stuck between lives because they're useful to him. Anyway, she can't tell us where dad is, she doesn't know anymore than we do. By the way, can you hear something?"

"There's a faint beat," said Jack, "it's coming from below – I've been listening to it for some time."

"Do you think it's anything to do with the mining he talked about?"

Earlier Quahaug had loaded them into a small run-around that he took from a vehicle park close to the construction site and had then driven through a series of passageways on a slightly lower level to that of the cave known as the skull. These became more and more deserted the further they travelled although faint outlines of figures depicted on the walls suggested that in the distant past the tunnels had once been the scene of human activity.

"Here you are," he said when they reached the end of the final passageway, "we're now at the far limit of the right shoulder; the right arm extends downwards from here. The left arm is to be avoided at all costs – that's where Gorth has his lair and as a consequence a lot of other nasties have taken up residence in the same place. When you reach the wrist and after that the hand you'll be on a level with Azazeel's netherworld. I think you'll find fissures which should enable you to move through into the main network."

"But how do we get down?" asked Jack, "we're not rock climbers, you know."

"You'll find there are steps cut, although I understand that in some places they've crumbled and are rather tricky to negotiate – I've never used the route myself. As I said, if you discover where your friend's being held and manage to rescue him, bring him back to me – I believe I may have something he's in need of." Without more ado he reversed the car, turned and drove away, leaving them in darkness only slightly relieved by the beam of the little torch that Jack had lent Milly several moons ago.

"Are we gonna do wot 'ee said?" the black girl asked.

"Might as well," said Horry, "what other choice have we got? But we must remember which way we go so that we'll be able to retrace our steps when we come back."

"When!" exclaimed Jack, "you mean *if* we come back."

Making an inventory of their possessions, and leaving behind anything they thought unnecessary for the task in hand, they set out. It did not take long before they discovered that the route downwards - besides seeming to go on for ever - was indeed tricky, while to complicate matters the torch battery began to fail. However, as they descended, a faint glow started to radiate from the rocks and this grew stronger the lower they went. Also growing stronger all the time was the pounding monotonous techno-beat which seemed to be emanating from the very walls and floor and which soon drowned out any other noise.

"Rad!" was Horry's enthusiastic verdict, but after a while even he was finding the unrelenting reverb hard to take. "It sorta gets inside your brain," he complained, "an' makes it hard to think straight."

"That's probably what it's intended to do," said Jack. "I reckon the time has come to put those things in our ears that Quahaug gave us."

On their long climb downwards Jack had to be guided, Horry going ahead and Milly bringing up the rear. He thanked them grudgingly but as usual found accepting help humiliating, (this present situation was of a different order from his time on the road with Dando when the aid had been reciprocal). Eventually the chimney they were descending connected with another parallel shaft and they found themselves clinging to the side of a much wider space with a further choice of several lower routes.

"I reckon this must be what he meant by the hand," said Horry, "and look - there's a sort of window over there with light coming through it. Is that one of the fissures he was talking about?"

"Let's go an' see," replied Milly, "we c'n get round on that ledge I fink."

When they arrived at the opening it did indeed prove to be the viewpoint of a most remarkable scene. They were gazing into another extensive cavern, brightly illuminated, where they overlooked what was apparently an underground dockyard. A wide pool took up the greater part of the cave floor and that was being fed from a stream which flowed out of a gap in the rock on the left while a virtual river disappeared into a crevasse on the right hand side. Around the watery expanses were a series of quaysides on which were situated rail-tracks and cranes, while moored against concrete jetties they could see numerous barges being loaded with piles of gleaming rock which they guessed to be raw Xoserite. At least that is what had been happening up until quite recently but now all activity had come to a halt. The attention of everyone below was currently focused on a small inflatable raft floating in the middle of the huge pool. In the boat were two figures, one sitting and one on its knees. This second individual – a male - was holding a small firearm in both hands and balancing precariously. He was aiming at a man with a megaphone on the nearest quay who was shouting something hard to distinguish because the cave's echo distorted his voice while the rock music attempted to drown it. As they watched, a dingy emerged from behind a wharf and set out towards the raft. The seated figure - a female - called a warning and the other swung round towards this new threat and fired, but in doing so lost his balance causing the shot to go wide. In answer another report rang out – they saw a man on the far side of the pool with a rifle at his shoulder. Almost immediately the intruders' craft began to deflate, fill with water and sink, dumping its occupants in the drink. They struck out for the bank but the dingy overtook them and they were hauled aboard. In a matter of minutes it brought them to the wharf just below the natural window in the rock where our onlookers were standing and Milly put her hand to her mouth as she saw how the prisoners were treated once they came ashore. The man, who made a determined attempt to resist when his waterlogged gun was confiscated, received a blow which knocked him to the ground, while the woman was grabbed and her arm bent up behind her back as she tried to go to his aid. She shrieked and struggled causing much amusement amongst the surrounding dock-workers. Horry let out a sudden exclamation.

"That's my Dammy!" he hissed, "Dammy - my second mother. It *is* her! An' that's the man she took up with – the foxy fellow! Bloody hell!"

"You're right – it's Damask and Foxy!" gasped Milly, "how on erf did they get 'ere? What c'n we do...?" but Horry had already acted. Putting his hand to his brow to check that the disguising headband was in place he climbed through the gap in front of them and marched down a ramp to the quay below.

"What's happening?" asked Jack urgently.

"It's Damask and Foxy," replied a horrified Milly, "they were in the water an' now they've been captured an' 'Orry's gorn barmy an' thinks 'e's goin' to rescue 'em."

"Well, come on," said Jack, "he needs back-up!"

"The authorities are aware of the situation - an order has come down the line – the detainees are wanted for questioning – they're to be handed over unharmed – I'll escort them to headquarters. Give me that gun."

The Supervisor of Lading who had been attending to the binding of the two captives turned round in surprise. Confronted by the speaker of the above he saw someone in complete contrast to the shabbily-clad, pock-marked youth who actually stood before him. As far as he was concerned he was face to face with one of Azazeel's main henchmen accompanied by two of his enforcers – thugs to whom, if you preferred to stay healthy, you would accord the utmost respect. Ingratiatingly he handed over Foxy's weapon, bobbing his head and saying, "Certainly – certainly – they're all yours."

"Untie them," ordered Horry.

The man looked mystified but complied and then, in an attempt to curry favour, offered the use of a nearby vehicle to those he imagined out-ranked him. It was Milly, rapidly coming to terms with the situation, who got behind the wheel and found, to her relief, that its controls were of the simplest. Once the others were on board she made a quick getaway along a track that followed the watercourse into the upstream tunnel, turning on the headlights as they left the dockyard behind.

The two who had been rescued seemed far from overjoyed at the way things had turned out. They sat with heads bowed but with one eye on the weapon that Horry had stuck in his belt. It was not until he tried to talk to them, wondering why they were so unappreciative of their deliverance, that he realised where the problem lay. With a grand gesture he divested himself of the charmed bands at head, wrists and ankles, saying as he did so, "Fee Faw Fum! Open Sesame! Abracadabra!" The thunderstruck expressions on Damask and Foxy's faces as they became aware of the true state of affairs were worth a hundred words of gratitude. He displayed the bands and tried to explain their purpose before putting them back on.

"They provide a disguise – people see what they expect to see. This is really Jack in front of me and that's Milly. I'm Horry by the way – long time no see. Yes – now you know what's happening you c'n tell it's us, can't you? But what are you doing here – how do you come to be beneath the Blue Mountain?"

Damask was the first to recover. "Blue Mountain?" she said, "Is that what this place is called? I could ask you the same question."

"We're searchin' for the Lordship," said Milly over her shoulder.

"Dando? - is he around? I thought he was still in Rockwell!"

"An I fort you'd gone norf - norf of Damwey where Foxy was goin' to be locked up," added Milly, "'ow d'you get orl the way over 'ere?"

"I *did* go north to the mine-workings but then there was a riot and this chap," putting her arm around her companion, "stole a boat and... anyway, it's a long story – too long to tell just at the moment..."

"The mine-workings across the Craiks be where they be lookin' for this here cozerite," said Foxy slowly and deliberately as if trying to get something straight in his head. "They foun' all sorts of other stuff there but none o' that. Then the las' few days the river be taking we through tunnels where the walls be all bright wi' light inside the rock. At the mine-workings they say cozerite be like that – that it shine. So do this be the place where it be? Is this where they're digging it out? Who be in charge?"

"Yes," said Damask, backing him up and getting down to basics, "you say this place is called the Blue Mountain but what makes you believe Dando's here? As for us, since the river went underground, we've just been trying to find a way back into the light of day. But praps you'd better explain a bit more about what's going on..."

Munch knew a thing or two,
Put the scream into their mouths -
The ones destined for Hades.

Chapter twenty two

A dank blanket of incomprehension had descended over Dando's mind. It was with a total lack of understanding that he found himself lined up between two other unfortunates, handed a pickaxe and goaded towards a wall of partially disintegrated rock by Azazeel's underlings where a row of mostly naked workers were already hacking away with picks at the larger detached pieces while others shovelled up the results of their efforts. None of these chattels appeared to realise that they were wielding weapons the equal of or superior to those employed by their tormentors and could have retaliated in kind, given sufficient resolve. Accompanied by continual barked exhortations and belaboured by whips and batons, our hero was subjected to several hours of backbreaking toil, accompanied by the mind-numbing music and the continual radiating glare from the surrounding walls. It was not until he was about to drop from exhaustion that the constant activity came to a halt and he and the other grimy drudges were allowed to fall to the ground and snatch a couple of hours rest before they were kicked awake and set to work once more.

It so happened that as his shattered body folded downwards the chain around his neck rode up and the locket - one of the two objects it bore - came to rest against his temple. At once his brain cleared, he repossessed his psyche and remembered the circumstances which had brought him to this place. He pressed the mind-quickening jewel to his brow as he took in his surroundings with a clear understanding of what was happening for the first time in several hours, uncertain, now he was compos mentis again, whether to curse or be grateful. Looking around at the nightmarish world of which he was at present a part he noticed two dark-skinned children linked to his Xoserite belt by delicate metal tethers and these were evidently brother and sister on the evidence of their almost identical features. He saw that they were both already fast asleep. Stretching away into the distance and lying in an interwoven weariness were other comatose bodies, some in such close proximity to his that he was able to ascertain that, indeed, these living dead did not breath. Not far away sat a group of heavily-muscled men, the ones in overall charge, noisily playing cards and smoking through holes they had torn in their smog masks. Further off he saw a shape he recognised: Letty, sphinx-like, patient, was stretched out on top of a rock, gazing down, and he remembered that Azazeel had ordered her to guard him during his absence. From her high perch she was acting as his keeper, ready to thwart any attempts at escape, yet her presence felt oddly reassuring.

He took the locket off its chain and fixed it behind the stud in his left ear, the stud placed there by Jack on the occasion of the Sahwain talent contest. In this position it rested permanently against his scull. Then he surrendered to the sleep that was insisting on taking over his body, thereby rendering himself temporarily insensate once more. The next thing he knew he was back at the rock-face, unaware of how he had gotten there, and being forced into more punishing labour. Although his brain was now working comparatively normally some areas remained clouded. At the back of his mind lurked the memory of a dream concerning Ann that he believed might have been relevant to the present situation but the more he attempted to recall it the more it eluded him. This was to set a precedent during his time in Azazeel's domain; he was forever trying to remember intangible but important things that hovered just out of reach. He swung the pick and the children he was chained to employed their small spades to heap up the pieces of rock he managed to dislodge ready for the mechanical shovel that came by at regular intervals. He wanted to know who these fellow prisoners were but did not get a chance to ask until a trolley brought round a barrel of the disgusting liquid that was all the slaves were given for sustenance during their travail and they were allowed five minutes' grace to drink a cupful. When he spoke to them the young ones stared at him stupidly, obviously with no understanding of what he was saying. He crouched down close to the older child, a girl, so that the locket came in contact with both her head and his own and repeated his question. This time she replied, explaining, quite lucidly, that she and her brother hailed from an agricultural community located in the south-west of Terratenebra. From the way she spoke he discovered that she thought she was still close to her native village and that neither child realised they were no longer alive; it seemed to have escaped her notice that the little boy had an arrow permanently lodged in his back.

"Some bad men attacked our town," she told him." daddy went to fight them. Mummy told us to go and hide by the river so we went down to the lock just by our house but Spatch fell in when he climbed over the gate an' I jumped in to save him. He's Spatch and I'm Ennis - what's your name? We were all alone in a dark place an' a man came by an' said he had some work for us to do. Do you think we'll be able to go home soon?"

"I hope so," said Dando, trying not to let his sadness show.

When the next period of toil began and the Wodwoses with their sticks and the Baldangers with their whips passed to and fro behind the prisoners he tried his best to protect these little ghosts with his own body. After a while though this no longer became necessary. The whips and batons were employed less and less frequently in their vicinity until in the end he and his two companions were left completely unmolested by the slave-drivers. Observing the behaviour of these strange creatures Dando could not help but suspect that the reason for this dispensation lay in the fact that the blows aimed in their direction had travelled back through the grips and stung the wielders of the weapons; he saw one or two exclaim in dismay as they dropped the scourges and shook the hurt out of their hands. Because of this he mouthed a thankful prayer to his unknown god and touched the protective locket in acknowledgement.

Beneath the mountain there was no evidence of either day or night so that the only indication of time passing came once every twenty-four hours when the siren sounded its warning and there was a very brief period in which to find shelter before a charge went off that brought down a fresh fall of rock and exposed new surfaces. Dando tried to keep count of these explosions but gave up after they passed twenty. How long he remained in that place was forever vague in his mind; all he knew was that, whilst there, the only thing that stood between himself and total physical and mental collapse were precious past memories. A prolonged period passed before he saw Azazeel again. The Lord of Misrule seemed disinclined to stay in his underground kingdom for any length of time. On his eventual reappearance he was in a foul temper.

"Where is it?!" he yelled to his underlings who cowered away, huddling together in trepidation. "Where's the Key?! Didn't I tell you to get it off him?! Look, there it is – still round his neck!"

Yes, though Dando in astonishment, *the Key! That's what this has all been about! How could I have forgotten?* He put his hand to his throat and located the object in question which by now had shrunk to the size of a pin.

The humanoid brutes groaned and whimpered under their master's scolding, shifting uneasily, while the men in charge looked on sulkily.

"You tell me you're unable to relieve him of the Object-of-Power," continued Azazeel in a more reasonable tone, "but why not get him to give it to you! Make his life so unendurable that he'll plead with you to accept it! You have the skills – use them!"

And so, in short order, Dando was parted from his recently acquired little friends, much to their distress, and hauled off to a series of stuffy caves in a remote part of the system where the Baldangers existed when not on duty. In this inimical place he found the ground littered with faeces, while mangers full of hay were placed at regular intervals, their contents provided not as bedding but for nourishment. He saw also, for the first time, the female of the species. These beasts went on all fours and appeared indistinguishable from nanny-goats, while clinging to their teats were brute-like young of both sexes. Dando was thrown into a pit and a grating banged down over his head. There he was abandoned for several hours to repent of his sins and to anticipate what might yet be in store for him.

When at last they pulled him out by his hair the first thing his tormentors did was remove his prosthesis. They then began to employ various well-worn and unoriginal methods of persuasion. Beforehand, however, they made it clear that he had only to say the word and they would stop what they were doing, as long as this meant that he immediately surrendered the precious thing he had in his possession. Once this had been established they set to work. He was strapped to an inclined board with his head at the lower end, after which a rag was spread over his face onto which they began to pour water. Such a procedure was apparently intended to give him the sensation of drowning and cause him intense suffering. The rag, however, became mysteriously impermeable and the water ran off on either side, leaving his face completely dry. Other cloths were tried with no better results. Next they stripped him of whatever clothes he had left, lifted him up and spread his arms out above his head, suspending him from an iron bar. They tried administering a beating but this ended in the same fiasco as had occurred at the rock face; they then attempted to burn him with cigarette ends but the butts burst into flame before they could be employed, scorching the hands of the perpetrators. Lastly they applied electrodes to various parts of his body but the current reversed and the torturers became the tortured. This was the final straw as far as the Baldangers were concerned. They made it quite clear they had had enough of this farce by stampeding away on their little hooves, bleating piteously.

Three of the ex-wrestlers who had stopped by to watch and who were annoyed at being deprived of their expected entertainment took Dando down, bound him securely and threw him into some out-of-the-way corner before contemptuously urinating on his body, leaving him in a pool of foul-smelling liquid to think over the error of his ways. As he lay there, completely helpless, he was suddenly seized by a recurrence of the cramps that had plagued him ever since his near-death experience on Hungry Island. This was a far worse agony than anything the Baldangers had tried to inflict on him. Unable to move and thereby ease his pain he cried out in despair and then lay with his eyes tight shut, given no choice but to endure. After a while though someone came to his rescue. First of all he was aware of a great rough tongue licking his dirty skin and at the same time heard a low throaty rumble. Then two enormous paws mounted his torso and began, as once before, to rhythmically pace up and down. His iron-hard muscles were thoroughly kneaded and under these administrations the pain eased and eventually disappeared. Yes, it was Letty, and now she set to work to make a thorough job of cleaning him up, just as if he had been one of her tiger cubs, before lying down companionably at his side. He felt enormously comforted and for once did not object to the chill that radiated from her body.

"You bad cat!! bad cat!! it's the bottles for you!!"

Dando had slipped into a temporary state of oblivion but now awoke with a start to see four men hauling Letty away on a chain while Azazeel glowered nearby apparently beside himself with vexation; he was breathing hard and hitting out at anyone who came near him, regardless of who they were. In a voice that was barely under control he addressed his prisoner.

"So, you've gotten away with it yet again!" he hissed, "well this is the end! I think this time it'll have to be for real, although I hoped we could avoid going this far - I like you, you see – you weren't aware of that were you? All the same I know what you most fear and you know what I'm talking about. Come on – give it me – I'll let you go. You'll never see hide nor hair of me again."

The boy had enough sang froid left, despite his recent maltreatment, to return stare for stare and, with an ultimate attempt at defiance (outwardly at least), shrug his shoulders.

"OK – so be it. Come here you lot," to the Baldangers who had reappeared and were standing in a timorous huddle nearby, "who's game for a bit of rumpy-pumpy?"

He walked towards his lackeys who initially looked apprehensive but became greatly excited as they listened to what he had to say. Eventually, at a wave of his hand, three of them broke away and came over to Dando. They untied him and then forced him onto hands and knees with his naked buttocks uppermost. Meanwhile the rest selected a candidate from amongst their ranks – they picked the most generously endowed - and stood back to watch the fun. The chosen one strutted forward, his erect penis bouncing proudly ahead of him as Azazeel shouted hoarsely "Fuck him senseless! fuck him till he bleeds! till it's coming out of his ears!" The Baldanger was obviously only too eager to obey these commands but when he crouched and attempted to thrust into the waiting body something very extraordinary happened. Instead of penetrating as he intended, his member paled, taking on a chalk-like hue. It appeared to calcify, became brittle, and then, with a sharp snapping sound, broke off at the root. A momentary pause, a gasp and the would-be rapist fled away screeching, leaving a red trail on the ground behind him.

It took a while for those assembled to recover from the shock caused by such a bizarre occurrence and then when they examined the intended victim they found that the boy had fainted dead away; in fact Dando was so deeply insensible that at first it seemed that his spirit had fled his body. Even with their scapegoat in this comatose state the Key was still out of reach; when they attempted to lay hands on it, they were repelled in no uncertain manner. It was a long time before they managed to bring the young man back to life and when he came round it was slowly and hesitantly as if he were reluctant to return to a world that contained such cruelty.

Eventually he opened his eyes to see Azazeel regarding him in complete bafflement and frustration. Then the Overlord's expression marginally changed as one of his more reliable strong-men whispered in his ear.

"Oh, do you think so?" he replied somewhat dubiously, "you reckon that would work? It would never have occurred to me. Well – all right – give it a go; anything's worth trying."

A prolonged period of consultation followed, after which Dando was hauled upright and made to stand on his remaining foot with a guard supporting him on either side. One of the ghosts, a man, was then brought in looking completely bewildered and they proceeded to do to him everything that earlier they had attempted to do to Dando. Azazeel, who had positioned himself next to the boy, leant over and spoke in his ear.

"If you want this to cease, you know what is required," he confided.

"No... no...!" cried Dando, deeply distressed at witnessing the man's suffering, but equally determined not to give in. After this they produced a woman and subjected her to various forms of sexual abuse. Even though she was just a phantom she screamed like one of the living and Dando wept. When finally she was removed he waited with enormous trepidation for what was to follow. All too soon a boy and a girl stood before him, young children who gazed around stupidly, apparently still under the influence of the brain-deadening music. He recognised them immediately: it was Ennis and Spatch, his little work-mates who had shared his labour at the rock-face. Dando turned to Azazeel, putting his hands to the chain around his neck.

"Stop!" he cried, finally defeated, "you mustn't... you... here - take it – take it!"

In desperation he fumbled with the chain's clasp, all fingers and thumbs, but as he struggled to give up his sacred trust it was as if he were struck over the head by a planet-sized bludgeon and went out like a light.

Milly's party, having become somewhat confused as they threaded the underworld's network of passages, had halted and, during this temporary lacuna sat listening to Damask as she spoke for herself and Foxy, giving a brief account of the exploits that had brought them to that place. Horry, meanwhile, returned the gun he had acquired to its owner and the Nablan immediately began to take it apart in an attempt to get it working after its immersion.

"We left Lake Bravo in the inflatable raft we borrowed," Damask told them, "that's where the river begins that brought us all the way here. You wouldn't believe some of the rapids we came down – the boat capsized loads of times – by rights we should have drowned but instead we're both pretty good swimmers now. The country we passed through was in the middle of harvesting – it's much later in the north – and we helped out in exchange for meals and beds on dry land. It was a good time. We both enjoyed it so much we didn't want to stop. But then Foxy said that if we went back to the river and drifted far enough down stream perhaps we'd find our way to the Big Water. However, when we followed his plan, we got into canyons and then into these tunnels which were pretty hairy at times. We kept going in the hope that we'd come back into the open air but it just went on and on and we were starting to feel pretty desperate when all at once..."

"So you ain't bin back to Rockwell Springs," interrupted Milly.

"No, no way. Too busy going on the game, getting married and springing this dyed-in-the-wool villain," replied Damask with a grin. "I thought Dando was still there but you say he's here – how did that happen?"

Jack summed up recent events as far as their experience went but in a tone that suggested he was not expecting to be believed.

"I thought they were having me on when they told me about a flying car," he ended, "but since coming to these parts I'm beginning to think there just might be some truth in the story."

(Milly smacked him over the head in exasperation at this, crying, "O' courst it's true!")

"Yes, but what *is* this place," repeated Damask again, "who's in charge?" She was certainly finding some things hard to swallow, especially that the tall heftily-built young man with the damaged face was her baby Horry of less than a year ago.

Milly felt they were wasting time. "Come on," she urged, "let's get movin' an' I'll explain as we go along."

"But which is the right way?" demanded Horry, "we've got to have some idea of where we're going."

"Quahaug said that Dando would be where they're digging the Xoserite," contributed Jack. "I'd take the beat as a guide - I think it's used to control the workforce - go towards where it's loudest - These two'll need earpieces."

A couple of the spare devices that acted as antidotes to the brain-scrambling sound system were handed over and then Milly started the run-around's engine. Every time they came to a choice of routes they picked the one where the noise was at its most insistent and in so doing began to feel they were on the right track. The caves and passageways became increasingly populated the further they went and although many of the supervisors they passed stared curiously, no one tried to stop them; they were obviously still being seen as an official detachment escorting prisoners.

Eventually they came out into the vast underground complex that Azazeel had once compared to a pelvis and gazed awe-struck at the hoists, the diggers, the huge lumbering trucks laden down with ore, and at the swarming mass of weird beings that were continually occupied in seeing the work go forward.

"Blimey!" gasped Milly, "'ow we goin' to fin' the Lordship among all this lot? I wouldn't know where to start."

"We won't," said Horry bluntly, "we'll have to run someone to earth who's in the know. I've got an idea. A little way back we passed an opening – there was a sign on the wall saying *no entry*. That's where we we ought to go, I reckon. Perhaps we can persuade someone to talk." He stared fondly at Foxy's gun.

For want of any better suggestion the others agreed to follow his advice and, in a short space of time, found themselves back beside the sign that only Horry had noticed. Disregarding its warning they drove into the forbidden tunnel but soon came to an obstacle across the path. A pair of doors made of a gold-coloured material, intricately decorated and lit by two softly gleaming carriage lamps, blocked the way. The lamps shone with a mellow yellow light, the garish silvery-blue glare of Xoserite being wholly absent from this location. In the centre of the door hung a large polished knocker in the shape of a wickedly grinning satyr's head.

"What are we s'posed to do now," muttered Milly, somewhat unnerved by this very opulent-looking obstruction.

"Well," said Damask, climbing out of the car, "where there's a knocker I presume you're supposed to knock," and, suiting the action to the word, she did just that, much to the others' consternation.

"IDENTIFY YOURSELF! STATE YOUR BUSINESS!" came a loud robotic voice from behind a small grating let into the door frame. Damask put her mouth close to the intercom.

"The Lady Damask of the family Dan, landholders in the Valley of Deep Hallow, wishes to enquire of Lord Azazeel as to the welfare of her brother, the Lord Dan Addo, second son and heir to the Clan Chief of that kinship. Can you tell him I'm here?"

There was no answer but very shortly they heard a click and one of the heavy doors swung slightly open. Damask put her foot in the gap and pushed. Her expectation was that someone would be waiting for them on the other side within the dwelling, but this proved not to be the case. Although she paused for some time no-one appeared, so, after a decent interval, she stepped over the threshold and with a jerk of the head invited the others to follow.

"D'you fink we should?" asked Milly in a hushed whisper.

"Why not?" replied Horry squeezing past her.

Milly took Jack's arm and followed rather reluctantly, describing what she could see for his benefit, while Foxy brought up the rear, still fiddling with his gun. What met their eyes as they entered would not have disgraced the interior of a house on millionaires' row in some great city. The decoration and furnishings were elegant in the extreme, some of the items obviously of great value, and the whole scheme was in the *best possible taste.* They walked along a hallway passing several rooms to left and right, greatly impressed by what they saw. Eventually they came to a wide staircase.

"You'd never know we were miles underground," said Damask, as overawed as the rest despite her familiarity with the luxury of Castle Dan. "Except for the lack of windows we could be in one of the palaces on the Grand Canal. Shall we go up?"

They mounted the stairs, their senses on the alert for anything unexpected, and arrived at a landing surrounded by several closed doors. It was here that they became aware that the suite was not unoccupied. From one of the rooms came a series of the most extraordinary noises: grunts, groans, shouts and the occasional bang and crash as if someone were throwing heavy weights around. Damask looked at her companions, eyebrows raised, before tapping at the door. "Excuse me...!" she called.

"That'll do no good," announced a voice to their rear, "he's entirely unresponsive when he's having one of his episodes. Can I be of assistance?"

Horry and Foxy swung round, ready to defend themselves, but were hideously disconcerted by what greeted them. A beautiful girl stood there, dressed in a few items of diaphanous underclothing that left nothing to the imagination. To their eyes she was glamour incarnate with a perfect figure as well as make-up and hairstyle to die for. Damask felt a pang of jealousy and glanced suspiciously at Foxy, wishing she herself was not looking such a total wreck. The two sighted young men were completely tongue-tied and it was Jack who answered this new arrival.

"We're searching for my friend Dando," he explained. "He's been brought to this mining complex against his will through some fundamental misunderstanding. We're concerned about his welfare because we know he's not in the best of health and we're anxious to be reunited with him as soon as possible."

The girl looked at them non-committally, giving nothing away. "Come with me," she said, crossing the landing and entering a corridor that ended at a low door which she opened, beckoning them forward. They obediently walked as far as the threshold, then, after a pause during which they peered suspiciously within, squeezed one at a time into the room beyond. There they found space at a premium, so much so that Horry had to remain outside.

"Is this who you mean?" the girl enquired pressing a button and pointing to a small monitor in the midst of a great bank of screens, all showing constantly changing images. As there was just one chair in front of this display they were obviously in some sort of mission control centre designed to be operated by a single individual. The wall next to the screens was covered in dials, flickering lights and strange symbols. Milly bent to take a closer look and then turned, exclaiming joyfully, "It's 'im! It *is* 'im – the Lordship!" But then, stooping for a second time towards the tiny screen, her body became rigid and her voice seemed to stick in her throat as she cried, "What're they doin' to 'im?!"

"You're watching a recording," their guide replied, "probably several days old. You obviously don't know it but that young pain-in-the-arse has been the direct cause of..." she gestured back through the doorway to the place from which strange animal noises were still issuing. "Azzy always ends up like this if he can't get his own way. Can last for days. All he was asking was to borrow that thing round your friend's neck which would have freed him from his age-old banishment and given him the ability to live permanently on the surface of this planet, but he was denied it in no uncertain terms. I'm the one that suffers – I get the brunt when his plans go awry."

"By *Azzy* I presume you're referring to Azazeel," said Jack dryly, " and *live on the surface of the planet* is a euphemism for *rule the world* I suppose. What does your great-great-grandfather think about your being a kept woman?"

"What?!" The girl stared at him in astonishment. "How do you know about my grandfather?"

"We met him during our descent."

"But what makes you so sure you know who *I* am?"

"It's in the way you speak – people who're related often have similar ways of talking. Your name's Ursula isn't it?"

She brooded over this for a moment before bursting out, "I don't care what he bloody well thinks! I don't care about the bloody ship he's building! Orlando my brother cared, he was going to pilot it and look what happened to him!"

Their conversation was suddenly interrupted by a deafening explosion which made everyone jump out of their skins. As their heart-rates slowed they saw Foxy holding a smoking gun, a sheepish expression on his face.

"It be the magazine spring," he said in extenuation, "I was trying to push it back into place and one of the cartridges went off."

"Listen," said Horry, speaking from the landing beyond the door, "the music's stopped."

The rock music to which they had become so accustomed that they had almost ceased to notice it had suddenly cut off leaving an uncomfortable ringing in their ears.

"The screens have all gone blank too," remarked Damask. It soon became clear to everyone that a missile from Foxy's weapon had smashed into the instrument panel causing goodness knows what catastrophic damage.

"Did you do that deliberately?" Quahaug's great-great-granddaughter was suitably outraged. "This is the nerve-centre of the whole flamin' operation – his nibs built it for Azzy at the start of their relationship. Without the mind-controlling audio the ghosts'll go wandering off and the extraction will stop. Everything'll fall to pieces, especially now he's out for the count an' no-one's holding the reins."

"But the Lordship!" cried Milly, who during this interchange had been getting increasingly desperate, "where is *'e*?!"

"Oh him? I believe they threw him away."

"Threw 'im away!" Milly was almost lost for words and for a moment could only parrot what the girl had said. "Wot d'you mean?" she finally gasped.

"Well, at first they tried all sorts of ways to get him to give them what he was guarding so jelously until finally he passed out and they couldn't revive him. That's when the boss went gaga and wasn't around to tell them what to do, so they stuck him down the sink-hole where all the rejects are put – him and his lucky charm which they still couldn't lay hands on even when he was out cold. I reckon someone's going to be in deep trouble over that when my sweetie's back in charge."

"But do you mean they thought he was...?" Jack's concern was palpable.

"Dead? That's more than likely."

"Where is this place?"

"It's close to the limits of your actual Caves of Bone but just a bit further on. Somewhere fairly remote was chosen for the dump because of the stink, but they didn't want to lose track of the bodies completely 'cos a number are able to repair themselves."

"But how do you get there from here?" The blind boy's voice had taken on a note of rising urgency.

"I could have shown you a hologram if this idiot," pointing towards Foxy, "hadn't gone and queered my pitch. It's beyond the shafts they call the left arm."

"We came down the right arm to get here," said Horry.

"Then you'll just have to keep going in the same direction and you should come across the sink-hole sooner or later. If nothing else the smell of rotting bodies'll tell you when you're getting near. And now if you don't mind I'd like to be left alone. If you know what's good for you you'll be long gone before my lord and master recovers his senses enough to start seeking recompense for the cockamamy mess you've just landed us in."

The one we revere
Says that the body is negligible,
If the will be strong.

Chapter twenty three

"I feel odd husband – in fact several revolutions ago I was struck by a strange malaise that made me imagine I'd suddenly grown old. Did the same thing happen to you? We can't be old, surely – we've already been through all that when we were in the flesh?"

"You know perfectly well why we've been affected, wife, it's because the Epoch-Initiator has been deployed for the first time in five thousand orbits. It's been turned by that nonentity while under the influence of our dark progeny and in the process has gone beyond our control – we've become superfluous."

"But what about the long-lived one? On your suggestion I sent him to retrieve it. Once we get it back..."

"I'm afraid I've changed my mind yet again. As I originally thought we can't place any confidence in that ancient no-hoper; he's a broken reed and will fall apart if faced with any determined opposition. No, we must look in another direction, to Azazeel himself – our own issue. We know he hasn't managed to possess the Key so far – otherwise day would have become night, north become south and he'd have emerged into the world as its one and only ruler. In fact I believe he's reached as great an impasse as we ourselves have done and might be open to suggestion. How about if we summon him? We'll tell him that three heads are better than one – he might see the sense in that. Send one of your yes-men – a dispensable one – into the dark places to organise a meeting. And if that can't be arranged perhaps, after all, we'll have to go there ourselves..."

Why so quiet? Is this a grave? Am I truly dead this time?

When he finally came to himself the first thing Dando noticed was the absence of noise: someone had turned off the incessant rock music. A few seconds later he awoke to the fact that his nostrils were being assailed by an overwhelming stink of decay. Urgently he put his hand to his throat and found that the chain around his neck still bore the Key and also that the locket was still fixed above his left ear. At this late stage he at last remembered what Ann had told him in a dream about the aforementioned Key – that it was capable of looking after itself. Perhaps if he had paid more attention at the time and taken this on board he might have been prompted to act differently. A much more fundamental idea suddenly struck him. Everything that had happened therefore, from the very beginning up until the moment he had tried to surrender the Object, had taken place under its auspices. Why – why? He went through the sequence of events that remained in his memory and first of all recalled how he had been allowed to remove it from the peg in Damwey's Blue Mountain Saloon. And then he had been allowed to carry it far to the south where the Land of the Lake had once existed. Finally he had been allowed to instigate a fourth turning despite, at the time, being under the power of the Dark Brother. So could the whole timeline have been part of a plan, drawn up to fulfil some mysterious purpose, or had it been just a means of testing him? He floundered, totally perplexed.

But where was he? He could not work out what he was lying on; part of the surface beneath him felt soft and yielding while elsewhere it was hard and bony. Yes, bony! He raised himself slightly and instantly knew the worst. It was apparent that he had been cast into a charnel house, that sink-hole Azazeel had told him about where workers past their usefulness were disposed of. Below lay goodness knows how many strata of rejects. The light was dim but to the side of him he could just make out various body-parts: arms, legs, torsos, heads, tumbled together in complete confusion, and quite close by a hand in the grip of rigor mortis raised stiffly in the air as if in one last desperate appeal for help. Some of the carcasses were only half visible - they were gradually fading away into insubstantiality - while others were obviously putrefying. The most sinister aspect of this necropolis was that there was still the occasional movement among the corpses. His situation was hideous and he felt totally repelled, yet he could not summon up the resolution to move. He lay there wondering if this was to be his final resting place – if so he would have plenty of company. But then, in the distance, he heard something really strange. Laughter came echoing down to him from above accompanied by a noise somewhere between a squeal and a roar as if some animal were being grievously tormented. He had never heard her make this sound before but he was immediately convinced that the one in trouble was Letty. The more he listened the more he became certain that something really bad was happening to the magnificent animal that he had begun to realise was just another victim, like himself, of Azazeel's malice. And so, for the sake of a fellow creature with which he was starting to identify he achieved the thing he thought he could not accomplish on his own behalf: somehow or other he summoned up his depleted resources and began to haul himself out of the pit.

One thing he discovered as soon as he started to move was that those who had despaired of taking what they wanted from his body and had therefore discarded it had done the same with his prosthesis. He came upon it lying a few feet away as he groped his way to the side. The climb upwards was long and gruelling and steeper by far than he would have thought himself capable of, but he managed it, drawn on by great bellows of distress that could not be ignored. As he finally gained the edge of the cavity he found himself facing the deserted entrance to a tunnel. The noise was coming from somewhere along its length and he got the impression that there was quite a number of people involved. Voices rose and fell, sometimes dissolving into merriment, sometimes bursting into yells and shouts, continually accompanied by a leitmotif of angry and agonised animal protest. Dando strapped on his artificial foot, straightened up and crept along the passage to the point where it opened out into a medium-sized cave, the light in the walls augmented by flaring torches. He arrived behind a row of backs, mainly those of Baldangers but with a few Wodwoses interposed, while in the air above a swarm of the miniature winged humanoids that seemed to haunt this place flitted to and fro. Because of his height he was able to look over the heads in front of him and discover what was happening.

He had already realised that this additional cave system was part of the Baldangers' realm and presumably not far from the place where he himself had been abortively put to the torture; the overpowering animal smell he recalled from that ordeal was much in evidence. Now he saw that Letty was chained by her collar to a free-standing rock in the centre. She was constantly in motion, leaping to and fro to the full extent of her tether, her muzzle pulled back into a permanent rictus snarl, huge yellowish fangs exposed. Her deafening cries were both defiant and terror-stricken. The reason for this tremendous agitation was not hard to see: surrounding her but just out of reach crouched several of the muscle-bound ex-wrestlers that

Azazeel employed as minders in his underground realm and each was holding one of the large brown bottles that Dando had seen and sampled in the Dark Brother's laboratory. They appeared to be taking it in turns to shake the contents and then shoot it forward so that it splashed onto the ground right under the tiger's feet. It did not take much imagination to guess what effect this was having on the butt of their cruel sport; Dando remembered the fumes from the ammonia that had practically asphyxiated him. With scarcely a moments hesitation, and with no thought for his own safety, he pushed his way through the outer and inner ring of spectators in order to confront the sadists.

“Stop!” he cried, “what do you think you're doing?! Leave her alone!”

The fighters had only a startled moment to register the presence of this pale, skinny, stark-naked young man before he was past them and stooping to unbuckle Letty's collar. A second later the tiger was free to launch herself at the nearest of her foes. With one blow she knocked the bully down and then dispatched him by seizing the nape of his neck in her jaws; there was not a cat-in-hell's chance of escape. The crowd did not wait around to see what she would do next: the cave emptied quicker than if someone had shouted *fire!* in an armaments factory. Letty set off in pursuit but soon became confused as to which fugitive to follow. She returned, disconsolate, to the scene of her liberation only to find that her saviour was in deep trouble. In going close to the rock Dando had been exposed to at least twenty times the concentration of fumes he had experienced in the lab. As a result he had been seized by a crippling fit of coughing so prolonged that his body had folded up into an involuntary spasm and he had fallen to the ground, the ground that was already swimming in a lethal mix of chemicals. As he lay there his already damaged lungs finally rebelled at the way they were being treated and a large gush of blood spewed from between his lips. This could have spelled total disaster, for, taking into consideration the recent rapid decline in his health, it seemed likely that he might have remained in that toxic atmosphere, unable to find the strength to move, until he died. However, before that could happen, a large soft mouth seized him by the shoulder and dragged him away.

The tiger was really no more than an over-sized betty and therefore not greatly endowed with reasoning power but in this instance she seemed to know what to do. She pulled him across the floor leaving a long smear of blood and fluids behind, not stopping until she reached a place where the air was fresher. Then she commenced to lick his ensanguined body from top to toe with her abrasive tongue. As the spell-bound creature absorbed the young man's blood into her system the frigidity of her breath gradually transformed into a life-affirming warm exhalation while her body temperature crept up to whatever is normal for a fanged tiger. Letty, sensing her deliverance, raised her muzzle and gave an exultant roar.

"D'you know Letty, I believe at last I understand what I'm supposed to do. I've got to go back to that place inside the entrance to the underworld. But I can't walk - c'n you help?"

The voice was faint but utterly resolute; it was the voice of someone who had recently had an unparalleled schooling in tenacity. As soon as he was no longer affected by the chemical miasma emanating from the ground beneath him Dando had made strenuous efforts to stand but on each occasion weakness had reasserted itself causing him to collapse once more. It was obvious that his ability to match deed to intention was failing fast and it seemed that if he wished to complete the task he had apparently been set he was going to have to act now or not at all.

"Can you lie down here beside me?" he asked, "I think I might be able to climb on your back if you've no objection."

Letty may not have understood what he was saying but his words were accompanied by a series of gestures and these evidently meant something to her. When, in response, she lowered herself to the ground he twisted his fingers into her thick coat; then, using all his remaining strength dragged himself across her spine, clinging there unsteadily as she began to rise. As soon as he was sitting astride and she was on the move things became easier and they got along together pretty well; he found that such an arrangement was not that different from the days when he had ridden Attack bare-backed. As a result he relaxed, at first allowing Letty to choose their route, hoping against hope that she had understood where he wanted to go and might even know the way. It was not long, however, before a problem presented itself. The tunnel they were following opened out into another large low-ceilinged cave and there, stretching away before their feet, lay a wide expanse of still water - an underground lake - lonely and brooding. Dando looked to see if there was a path round the edge but the mere appeared to fill the cavern from wall to wall. Ahead, on the other side, he could see boats tied and the mouth of another passage faintly lit.

"I'm pretty sure we've got to go straight on," he said, "otherwise we'll probably end up back where we started. Can you swim Letty?"

While in Pickwah recovering from his injuries he had become quite at home in the hot springs by the edge of the sea, but now he wondered if he had the strength to make it even halfway across.

I must do this, he said to himself and, slipping from the tiger's back and onto his knees, began crawling towards the water before continuing on into the lake until he was afloat, while Letty side-stepped, bobbing her head and rumbling in her throat, as if trying to work out how she could follow without getting wet. Although she was obviously very reluctant to commit, he had only taken a few strokes out from the shore before she launched herself from the bank with a tremendous splash and swum alongside, enabling him to get a grip on her fur and be towed forward. In this way they crossed the dark tarn together, leaving smooth slowly widening ripples in their wake, and, although the silent listening quality of the place caused Dando to wonder if some enormous denizen of the deep might suddenly rise up and punish them for disturbing its peace, they reached the other side in safety. But now, having climbed onto Letty's back once more, he decided it was up to him to choose their direction.

Over the next few hours he experienced a mixture of fear and utter frustration as they penetrated deeper and deeper into this skeleton-shaped warren, wandering, apparently, completely at random, without finding a way upward as he hoped. In the end he passed out from sheer exhaustion and slid to the ground.

A velvety sensation, as of hair brushing lightly against his cheek, brought him back to consciousness. He turned his head in response and saw two cornflower-blue eyes gazing into his own from less than a foot away. They regarded him with an aloof, typically cat-like expression, before softly closing in the feline equivalent of a smile.

"Meena!" he croaked in astonishment, then focussing further off, "and Ralph too! How on earth did you get here - how did you find me?"

The dog, on being addressed, came bounding over and began making a tremendous fuss of his beloved human while Meena feigned indifference: she apparently considered such overt demonstrations of affection rather vulgar.

While overjoyed to see them Dando was baffled at his non-human friends' reappearance in this remote underworld. Where had they come from? How had they managed to get all the way to this place when he had last seen them back at the crossroads in Armornia as he was being whisked away in Azazeel's flying car? So were Milly and Horry near by? He looked around hopefully but drew a blank. The animals' arrival was a complete mystery but an extremely fortuitous one; Ralph, he knew, had a directional instinct to rival migratory birds.

"I've got to get out of here," he told them, "sooner rather than later. Do you know the way to the surface? Can you lead me in the right direction?"

It was at this point that Letty put in an appearance. She had not deserted him but had been some way off drinking from a pool of fresh water with both ears open so that she would be ready to return when needed; she came grumbling onto the scene causing immediate consternation amongst the two smaller animals: Ralph growled and showed his teeth while Meena arched her back, her tail like a bottle brush. For a short spell there was a complete stand off until the little cat, sensing an affinity between Dando and the tiger, made up her mind that the great creature might not be such a bad proposition after all. She smoothed her fur and went to touch noses – a comical enough sight as Felis Catus, tiny but indomitable, reached up towards her enormous cousin. Ralph, understanding that his companion had decided to call a truce, was likewise more accommodating. Dando watched with relief. "All friends together," he grated hopefully.

The dog and cat looked on as the young man attempted to mount Letty for the third time. Ralph wagged his tail half-heartedly but also whined deep in his throat; he seemed to realise that something was greatly amiss. Once in place Dando tried to put a brave face on the situation.

"Come on troops," he urged, "quick-march – show me the way."

Meena and Ralph set off purposefully as if they knew where they were going, yet an hour or so later were still threading passageways on the same level as that on which they had started. Dando's confidence in their expertise began to evaporate. It was at this point that he saw, partially concealed, an archway through which steps were visible.

"Hey, hold on," he tried to shout, his voice coming out in a husky rasp, "how about this? There's stairs – it's a spiral staircase like the one at Toymerle. It must go somewhere. Could it be the way out?"

Ralph stopped in his tracks but refused to turn back. He gave a sharp bark and then walked on a few steps while looking over his shoulder. Meena kept pace with him.

"But it goes up," Dando pleaded, "isn't that's what we want?"

Ralph whined and then barked again – a double bark that seemed to say *Trust me – I know what I'm doing.* Dando pretended not to understand.

"Well, you c'n please yourselves," he croaked crossly, "Letty an' I are going this way – aren't we girl?"

It was impossible to remain astride the tiger's back once she started to climb. Dando slid off and stumbled along as best he could, hanging on to her tail. After a short interval he saw that Ralph and Meena had decided to follow. No-one appeared to have used this route for some time judging by the undisturbed layers of dust and the tangle of cobwebs stretching across their path. This, perhaps, should have acted as a warning, but Dando, determined to climb, chose to ignore the implications and urged Letty onwards. The animals sneezed and shook their heads while he puffed and wheezed, the intake of each breath accompanied by an audible whistle. Eventually the stairwell came to an end and they stepped out into a small gloomy cave where they came across the spinners of the webs. Meena was the first to spot one: she ran, pounced and the next minute was holding down the largest spider that Dando had ever seen. "Watch out!" he warned, "big ones like that can be dangerous!" It did not take long to discover that the walls and floor were crawling with the brutes and in whichever direction they turned, sticky exudations wrapped them round. Dando had to tear the webs away from his face before he could even see which way to go.

"Look - over there," he gasped, holding onto Letty with one hand while pointing ahead, "there's some more steps, going up – hurry for heavens sake – let's get out of here!"

This new staircase disappeared into darkness; the light from the Xoserite deposits had been getting dimmer the higher they climbed and he began to anticipate a time when he would be as blind as his friend Jack with no choice but to navigate by touch. *Well – if he can do it...* he thought.

The spiders were left behind but this did not mean they were entirely free from local wild-life. On one occasion Dando was startled by a movement above his head as a long sinuous shape slithered away around a ledge, while the next moment something bulky but close to the ground came scuttling out of the gloom and ran past, trailing a long tail. He got the feeling that small creatures were fleeing away in front of them as they progressed upwards, becoming more numerous the higher they went. In the caves they passed through they caught glimpses of what these might be: bats, rats and creepy-crawlies for the most part but also less identifiable entities that could have been the strange little ariel people that seemed to permeate this underground region. Eventually the cramped shafts opened out into a large hollow space where life appeared to be absent, although the place had a markedly organic smell and Dando could have sworn that some creature lurked nearby. He was reminded of the Baldangers' quarters but here the excremental aroma was overlaid by something far stronger - the nearest he could come to it was to liken it to the stink of the furnaces at the Dans' Deep Hallow ironworks.

As the young man and his companions penetrated the underground cavern they discovered that it was truly enormous. For Dando, going ahead with Letty, it seemed likely that, as at Toymerle, it had been enhanced by the hand of man and might be the interior of some ancient temple dedicated to gods whose names had long been forgotten. With Letty's assistance he walked beneath its soaring arches in the murk looking for a way out, all the time feeling a prickling up his spine as if he were being watched. For some reason his mind went back to his descent on Azazeel's platform and he remembered the fiery eyes that had momentarily gleamed at him out of the blackness. Now he turned and as he did so registered those same eyes staring down at him from a great height. Their glare was so bright that the light which they emitted rebounded off the walls, reflecting back onto the body of the beast, revealing a reptile at least ten times larger than any living thing he had ever encountered in his life before. He also saw that this lizard-like creature had wings and that, as it breathed, smoke curled lazily from its nostrils, obviously the source of the burning smell. He began to back away just as the animals moved forwards. Before he could stop her Letty had gone on the offensive giving a challenging roar, while Ralph and Meena, ignoring the huge disproportion in size between themselves and the cave's inhabitant, prepared to do battle.

"No!" cried a terrified Dando, "it's too big – it must be a dragon or something - leave it alone!" but all that this achieved was to excite the creature's aggressive instincts. It lowered its head, opened its jaws and, with a sound like a forest blaze, poured forth a flow of burning mucilage in his direction. Despite the fact that it did not quite reach him his brows and lashes were singed, while his skin was badly scorched and his hair actually caught fire for a moment. He batted at the flames gasping, "Leave it! Leave it!" but at this stage the animals had their own agenda. The cat and the dog sprang forward in retaliation and in the blink of an eye under Dando's horrified gaze were snuffed out in a dazzling flash of combustion that left nothing behind but a few floating flakes of soot. Letty, a bit slower on the uptake, also came to his defence, and, although she passed through the same sheet of flame, managed, by making a great leap, to clamp her jaws around the neck of the monster, causing it to rear up in agony. Noises reminiscent of a major conflagration issued repeatedly from the creature's throat and echoed round the cave as the tiger's body was swung violently to and fro. The conflict became a furious fight to the death and one that the bigger animal should have easily won but for the fact that Letty must have pierced some essential blood vessel as she bit with her deadly fangs. The vital fluid came gushing forth from the wound like a stream of larva, spattering everything within range, until eventually the dragon sank down, laying its long neck along the ground, and the light went out of its eyes.

Dando staggered forward, dwarfed by the massive body and heedless of danger. He knelt down next to Letty, desperately calling her name. Although the tiger was still alive he knew at once that there was no hope of recovery: she had suffered nearly a hundred percent burns to her body, and her skin was blackened from nose to tail, her hide beginning to flake away leaving only her jewel-like eyes unaffected. She stared into his with a calm otherworldly gaze and, after an interval during which time seemed to hang suspended, gave up the ghost. Dando crouched beside her corpse for a long time before eventually struggling upright and staggering away across the floor. At first he stood gazing unseeingly ahead, his mind a blank, unable to take in what had happened, until, like an incoming tide, realisation swept through him. Then he gave vent to a great howl of grief before throwing himself flat on the ground where he tore at his smouldering hair and sobbed with complete abandon.

"You know it was the left arm that Quahaug told us we must steer clear of," said Jack as they made their way towards their destination, "something called Gorth hangs out there."

"Well we're not going up the arm, " replied Horry, "we're going beyond it. We're going to see if dad's down this hole."

Resuming their journey they had not progressed more than half a mile from the luxurious apartment where they had encountered the girl Ursula before the going in the tunnel became too rough for the Lader's buggy and they had to leave it behind. Milly was worried about the effect this would have on their ability to avoid capture.

"If she tells that Azazeel bloke about us," she said, "'e'll be after us like a shot, you betyer life."

"Well, that can't be helped, we're going as fast as we can."

Having skirted the main mining area they entered more passageways and caves that appeared to progress onwards, one after another, ad infinitum. In the end they had to call a halt in order to snatch an hour or two's sleep before continuing.

"'Ow are you s'posed to know when it's bedtime?" complained Milly as she woke, and after they had been travelling again for some time, "Do you fink we could 'ave missed it – this 'ole fingy?"

"The mawther said our noses'll be tellin' us when we're near," commented Foxy grimly.

It was Jack, tapping with his cane against the tunnel wall, who discovered the archway and the spiral staircase.

"There's a way up," he told them, "it's probably the left arm that Quahaug was on about. If so then we've nearly reached the extent of the Caves of Bone. The pit where they throw the redundant workers is supposed to be a bit further on."

"But listen," interrupted Damask, "can't you hear something?"

Everyone stood still, breath suspended, as, faint but unmistakable, the sound of battle played out above their heads. Echoing down the staircase came the evidence of a fight so violent that, despite its remoteness, the very walls seemed to vibrate. As it ran its course a sequence of furious cries mutated into yells of pain which then gradually subsided into moans and finally into an uneasy silence.

Horry let his breath out gustily. "What the fuckin' hell was that?!" he muttered.

"The Left Arm," replied Jack, "lots of nasties he said – avoid at all costs."

"It certainly sounded nasty," agreed Damask, "come on, lets take his advice and give it a miss."

"No – we've got to go an' see," insisted Milly, sounding suddenly utterly determined.

"Eh?!" The others stared at the normally rather cautious black girl with open mouths.

"We got to go an' fin' out if the Lordship's up there."

"But why should he be, Milly?" asked Jack disbelievingly.

"It's just a feelin' I got but we gotta look – *I* gotta look."

It took quite a lot of discussion and Milly's utter determination to go it alone if needs be before the rest were even prepared to wait around while someone else explored.

"Let me test out the ground," volunteered Horry. "It'd be safer if just one person has a quick shufty before the rest of you appear on the scene."

"No - I'm comin' too," proclaimed Milly emphatically.

And so the boy and the young woman started up the stairs, neither aware that Jack had also passed through the archway and was following on behind. They came to the cave of spiders and groped their way across before ascending further.

"Someone's been this way quite recently," said Horry, pointing to foot and paw prints just visible in the dust.

"Surprise - surprise!" replied Milly in a told-you-so kind of voice.

Eventually they ran out of steps and peered cautiously forward into a vast dimness.

"We'd know it by the smell, she said," whispered Horry, "but I don't think it was meant to smell like this." The aroma that assaulted their nostrils combined the scent of burning embers with a weird stench of cooked meat, both overlaying the general smoky ambience. "There's a huge heap over to the right," he continued, "an' something else sorta white a bit further on. I don't know about you but it looks like a body to me. I think you might be right - I think it might be..."

He stopped abruptly and shot a concerned glance in Milly's direction. Together they stared at the slender form stretched out on the ground, appearing so very pale in the enveloping darkness and lying so very still. Although they half knew what it was they were seeing they both felt a great reluctance to investigate further. Milly began to weep silently causing Horry to put his arm around her and pull her to his side. It was at this point that Jack arrived at the top of the staircase and without a moment's hesitation walked past them, homing in unerringly on Dando's prostrate body. His friend was lying prone in the semi-darkness so Jack knelt down and very gently rolled him onto his back, revealing the burns on the boy's upper torso which he sensed but could not see. Then he put his own face close to that of his leman's and brushed the other's nose and mouth with his lips.

"Well chickadee," he said with great tenderness, "what's all this about?"

Horry had been watching the blind boy's movements anxiously. Now he called, "Is he...?"

"It's all right," Jack shouted back, "he's alive – come over here."

"He's alive, Milly," said Horry, "Jack says he's alive."

Milly raised her tear-stained face and looked towards her lover. "He ain't got no cloves on," she exclaimed indignantly, "'Orry – you'll 'ave to lend 'im your trousers."

By the time Damask and Foxy arrived on the scene those that had gone before had discovered that not only was Dando alive but he was alert enough to respond to questions. However when an answer was required he reacted merely with a shake of the head or a nod; he made no attempt to reply in words. Whether this was as a result of some kind of emotional trauma or because he just did not choose to speak was not clear. Milly helped him sit up and she and Damask tried to ascertain his state of health.

"There's blisters," said Milly, "an' see, 'is 'air is orl frizzled. Behind the burns 'e looks 'ellish pale except for 'is cheeks an' they're sorta pink. That don' look right to me."

They inspected their patient simply for signs of infirmity but Dando stared back at them out of haunted eyes that seemed to tell a much more complex tale. By the condition of the cavern it was obvious that some decisive battle had taken place there less than an hour before. Horry and Foxy went to investigate and now the younger of the two came running back hardly able to contain his excitement.

"That mound over there is a sort of dragon, believe it or not!" he informed the others self-importantly, "an' there's another animal as well – they're both dead! The bodies are surrounded by this sticky stuff that must be blood, but it's really, really hot! Did you fight it?" this last directed in awe towards his father, only for disappointment to reign as Dando shook his head.

At the same time Milly's interest was caught. "Dragons are s'posed to be wise," she said, "we 'ad a dragon at the circus for a little bit but it weren't a real one. Did you ask it questions?"

Again Dando shook his head.

"Don't bother him with stupid talk," said Damask. "We've got to decide what we're going to do. We're trying to get back to the surface Dodo - is that OK with you?"

Dando frowned painfully, then nodded.

"'Ave you still got that fing wot woz hung roun' your neck?" asked Milly. "Is that it? - it looks different some 'ow. But where's the 'ittwl case wot 'ad your sweet'eart's 'air in it?"

What none of them had noticed until now was that since they had been reunited Dando had been clutching something small and apparently important to him in his left hand, holding it to his breast.

Now, as he opened his fingers, they saw a locket set with a stone in which nameless colours had once swirled but which was now covered in fracture lines as if it had been through a furnace; the setting too had suffered extensive damage and was bent and discoloured. Dando forlornly released the catch and held it out for Milly's inspection. Inside, instead of the tress of flaxen hair it had previously contained, she saw just a tiny pool of greyish ash.

"Oh, Lordship," she breathed, immediately becoming aware of what this must mean to him. She put her hand on his knee trying to think of some words of comfort she might offer and eventually realised how things stood. "But it's still 'er!" she said with great conviction. "It's like when people take someone they love oo's died to the crem and then afterwards they collect up the ashes an' keep them safe. You keep it safe like you've always done, cos, whatever it looks like, it's still 'er," and she closed the locket and handed it back to him. Dando stared towards her for a long time before nodding and kissing the stone.

During this interchange Jack had been standing by. Now he bent to speak in his friend's ear.

"On the way here, spatzi," he said, "we met this scientific fellow, Quahaug by name, who was building some sort of flying machine. He said that if we happened to find you we should bring you to him. Do you know anything about that?"

Dando delayed his response for so long that Jack wondered if he had misheard. Eventually the boy gave a minute acknowledgement.

"So shall we go to see him on the way out?"

Again Dando gave an infinitesimal nod.

"OK - then I s'pose we'd better get going..."

It was not until Dando made an attempt to rise that the others truly appreciated how weak he had become. They watched in concern as he crumpled to the floor.

"Well Dodo," said Damask, "looks like we're going to have to carry you."

"I'll carry he," offered Foxy.

"But he's taller than you," objected Horry, thinking that perhaps this was a task more suited to himself, "won't he be too heavy?"

Foxy stooped and picked up Dando as easily as if he had been lifting a one-year-old child.

"He don' be heavy," he grunted, "he be my little brother," and in so saying demonstrated once and for all that he had learnt of his and the young aristocrat's true relationship somewhere along the road, probably from his half-sister.

"*And I know he will not encumber me,"* sang Jack, much to the others' surprise. "Oh that's just an old hit song I remember," he explained with a smile but there were tears on his cheeks.

"So," said Damask, "up or down?"

"Up, of course," replied Horry.

"All sorts of nasties in the left arm..." Jack reminded them.

"...which are now dead," added Horry, gesturing towards the dragon as he completed the sentence.

"Come on then," said Damask, "I think the stairs carry on over there."

They left the vast cavern, Damask going first holding Jack's faintly shining torch with its rapidly dying batteries which Milly had handed over. Foxy came next, Dando in his arms, while the black girl followed close behind. Horry and Jack brought up the rear. The climb went on without interruption until eventually they reached level ground, not in another cave this time but at the end of a passageway that led off to the right.

"I reckon we're at the left shoulder," said Horry, "just the same as the right one only the other way round. If we carry on along the tunnel we'll get to the cave under Quahaug's place and then we're nearly out."

At this the rescuers spirits rose for it seemed they had achieved their main objective: they had managed to retrieve Dando and make good their escape without any deadly misadventures occurring along the way. But now, as Damask shone her fast-fading torch ahead of them, it picked out something untoward. They were all startled to see the figure of a man gradually materialising as he hobbled into the light with the aid of a stick. This apparition appeared to be in the last stages of decrepitude, but to Damask, Dando and Milly there was something familiar about him, something about his oddly patterned apparel and his ossified appearance that rang a bell.

"Gammadion!" breathed Dando, the shock of recognition bringing about what the solicitude of his friends had been unable to achieve, namely the restoration of his voice. "Put me down Foxy!" Foxy complied and, supported, the young man managed to stand upright for a moment and prepare himself to meet the one who through guile and witchcraft had caused him and those he loved so much suffering. The wizard stumbled to a halt and ran his eyes over the group in front of him before focussing on Dando.

"Ah, there you are," he muttered in a voice that sounded as if it might be issuing from a graveyard. "She *said* you were to be found in the Caves of Bone. I've been looking high and low – very high - very low. And she said you'd be carrying the Treasure if the Dark Brother hadn't taken it from you. He hasn't has he? It's there within reach and however much it transmutes I still recognise it and feel it's power. You know it's rightfully mine, don't you, and that it's your duty to restore it to me."

"It's certainly not yours!" croaked Dando.

"Perhaps I can give you a persuasive reason to change your mind. One thing you can't deny is that this hulking hobbledehoy," pointing towards Horry, "is your son; a great big boy for such a weak and feeble father. I see that the process I put in train is happening far faster than I ever thought possible so how about if I finish what I started?" He lifted his arm and stood poised, staring at Dando as if willing him to respond. When the other failed to do so he stretched out his long-fingered almost fleshless hand towards Horry in a menacing gesture that could not quite disguise the tremor of extreme old age. The boy turned to his father, a helpless look of appeal on his face, while at the same time Jack, seeming to know what was required of him, stepped close to Dando, on his other side, and put his arm supportively around his body.

"Hold me, Jack!" cried the young man and in one swift movement bent and unstrapped his prosthesis. The twisted blade was now greatly altered from the time when it had first been purchased. The metal of which it was composed had become so honed and abraded with use that it had acquired an edge as sharp as a machete and could well have been mistaken for a weapon of war. Lifting it chest high he sent it spinning through the air towards the wizard, proving as he did so that he was not quite so weak and feeble as his opponent imagined. Whether Dando intended it or not, in the mid-point of its trajectory it sliced into Gammadion's neck before he had time to duck and in one smooth movement severed his head neatly from his torso. The separated appendage then fell heavily to earth in company with the prosthesis before rolling across the ground and into the shadows while the headless trunk rocked to and fro for a moment until it also tumbled into the dust. As it fell something small and glittering flew off and landed plumb at Dando's feet: it was the mysterious jointed manikin that had always hung round the wizard's throat.

For a moment all the companions stood frozen to the spot. Then Horry staggered back against the wall clutching his chest.

"I feel strange," he gasped, "everything's come to a stop."

"***No – it hasn't stopped. It's just that for the first time in your life you've begun living at a normal pace.***"

"What?! - Who?!"

The voice they were hearing had issued from within their own ranks and the companions fell back in confusion, uncertain as to what was happening. A human form, luminescent, larger than life, had appeared in their midst and only Dando and Jack stood their ground as the others retreated, staring at this glowing apparition. The vision that confronted them took the form of a strikingly handsome adult male in the full vigour of manhood. His image was partially diaphanous so that the wall of the passage showed through his outsized body. Although he seemed to have no trouble standing the lower half of his left leg was missing.

"What's going on?" demanded Jack, picking up on the general mood of consternation yet completely at sea as to its cause.

"It's the wizard's mascot," said Dando in a detached tone of voice totally devoid of emotion. "You know the little silver man he wore that always seemed to be struggling to break free. I-I believe that now he's dead it's been liberated – it's become..." he broke off as the elemental turned his face towards him with a look of profound understanding and sympathy.

"***Yes - you know who I am,***" he said gently, "***don't you.***"

"I-I do, my Lord," replied Dando, his slight stammer more pronounced than usual. "Y-you're Pendar – Azazeel's brother - the brother who d-disappeared – the one that Pyr goes looking for each midwinter..."

"***If he ever did come looking,***" said the immortal with a wry smile, "***it was in the wrong place and at the wrong time.***" Then, turning towards Horry, "***You're beginning to live normally at last, but because of the machinations of that...***" he spurned the headless body with his foot, "***You've been cheated out of the major part of your childhood and youth. Your life has been greatly curtailed.***"

"I know what you mean," said Horry, making a brave attempt to adjust to his temporal transformation, "but if I hadn't grown up really fast I wouldn't have been in time for..." and he gazed half in embarrassment, half adoringly at Milly.

Pendar stood absolutely still for a considerable period and as he did so his image solidified, becoming less transparent, while his radiance became stronger and lit up the whole surrounding area so that there was no longer any need for Damask's dying torch. When he eventually spoke to Dando he did so as if the two of them were alone together.

"Do you understand what you have to accomplish?" he asked.

"I-I think so," said Dando, "but I don't know if I'll be able to m-manage it alone." Since his haemorrhage he was finding every breath painful and his remaining strength was ebbing away more and more rapidly with each passing minute.

"I can help you if you'll let me – but what I do may ultimately hasten your end."

"I don't care – as long as I'm given time to finish what was started all those years ago."

Pendar moved to his side and laid his hand softly on the young man's head. Immediately Dando got the impression that radiance was streaming into his cranium and rushing down like a waterfall through his entire body, filling every cavity with illumination and ending at last at his fingers and toes. The intolerable weight of flesh which he had been finding, over the last few hours, almost impossible to carry lightened and became virtually unnoticeable while his muscles regained their suppleness and his lungs began to function normally for the first time since leaving the hospital. He stood upright and when Horry brought him his artificial limb he strapped it back on and took several experimental steps, finding he was able to walk unaided.

"Thanks," he murmured, ashamed that the only suitable word was totally inadequate.

"I'm the one who should say thankyou," replied Pendar. ***"For me it's been a long enslavement but now I've been freed because of your actions and I can go forward – we can both go forward. Will you accompany me to where the great engine stands?"***

"Yes," answered Dando, "I know now I've got to take the thing entrusted to me very far away and perhaps it's by means of that that I'll do it."

Before leaving, he bent and arranged Gammadion's body into the simulacrum of an effigy on a tomb, bringing the head from where it lay and putting it back in its rightful place. Even in the short period since death had overtaken him the wizard's flesh had begun to shrink and crumble until the basic skeleton started to show through. Dando stood staring down for a long time trying to fathom this man's role in the grand scheme of things and to imagine what course the Key's history might have taken if he had not played a part in its story. Pendar waited patiently. Finally the boy sighed and turned away.

This is not quietus,
This is not dying,
But merely the end of the beginning...

Chapter twenty four

"If you head to the Cave of the Skull I'll accompany you and explain certain things on the way which I think you ought to be made aware of."

Pendar and Dando, having already formed a liaison that was rapidly becoming a permanent alliance, set out together while the rest of the awestruck company followed in their wake. It was the revivified Dando who spoke first as they made their way along the tunnel, unable to contain his curiosity about his companion's past.

"How did Gammadion manage to trap you?" he asked.

"It wasn't him – the culprit was my dearly-beloved brother. He bound me by trickery and then handed the wizard the figurine in which I was imprisoned; he said it would enhance his spell-binding abilities. The truth was he gave it as a bribe to encourage him to steal the Key, but the necromancer chose to double-cross him and take the Master-Changer for himself, so there was trickery on both sides."

"But how did you loose your leg?"

"Oh, it's not really lost. It's just that my body image is incomplete. My brother and I started off at the beginning as a single individual. When we were separated things didn't go entirely smoothly. Nevertheless I'm sorry Gammadion used the apparent non-existence of my limb to rob you of yours."

Dando thought ahead to what awaited him when he reached Quahaug's construction.

"I know I've got to take it outside - the Key - but what does that actually mean? - where should I aim for and how long will it take?"

"I'm not sure I entirely understand Manfred Quahaug's original motivation in building the craft he's been working on for centuries but it seems that the sage's latter intention is to explore one of the remotest places of all – a place where the rules that govern the universe as we know it no longer apply. That's why,

since his great, great grandson passed on, he can find no-one prepared to sit at the controls and follow his spoken instructions as the machine streaks at unimaginable speeds through short-cuts within the fabric of space towards the heart of darkness. They all say that to do so would be certain death be they in the flesh or of the 'dancer' persuasion. However I feel that, if it ever reaches the place for which it was intended, the Object will find its true vocation and will cease to trouble those it leaves behind. I believe someone must come to its aid and take it there if this planet is to find peace."

"Should it means death," said Dando in a lowered voice, "I think I'm heading that way already unless the Key prevents it After all it was you who warned me that things might speed up."

"***But does it mean death? No-one has ever been to find out. The old man's descendant was prepared to run the risk and I'd go myself if I thought I could carry it that far. But for those on the other-side like me the Key becomes an almost impossible burden after a very short time - why do you think Aigea and Pyr, once each had turned it for a new age, passed it on to their earthly keepers, the Nablar and the Lake Guardians? It's because it would have destroyed them if they had held onto it. Even you find it difficult to carry, don't you?"***

"Yes I do," answered Dando, "it rubs me raw. But Azazeel thought he could control it"

"***Azazeel is deluded: he thinks a borrowed body would be enough to enable him to hold it for all time but in fact you need the flesh in which you were born in order to keep it with you or to take it any distance, and this time the distance may be improbably large. As you know, neither he nor I ever occupied a fleshy body."***

"Wot d'you fink they're on about?" whispered a suspicious Milly to Horry as they tagged along behind. "I 'opes this geezer ain't persuadin' the Lordship to do sompfink stoopid."

"My da won't do anything unless he thinks it's absolutely right," replied Horry with utter conviction. "but you – I mean we – may not be able to follow where he's going. I think we've got to get used to the idea that he may not be with us much longer."

"Don' talk rubbish!" scolded Milly, but there was a note of uncertainty in her voice to go with the bleak look of despair on her face. Jack who had been listening in to their exchange turned back to squeeze her shoulder.

"We've all got to be strong for his sake," he said, "and put our own personal feelings aside."

"Look," cried Dando, "I think we're coming to the end – it's bright ahead – in fact it's very bright – oh, crumbs, it's...!"

The cause of his alarm had appeared around a bend in the tunnel: a wall of flame, swirling and seething, swept towards them as it ate up the distance between; in a matter of moments it would be upon them. In that millisecond Dando thought that annihilation had come much sooner than expected. But then Pendar shouted ***"Take cover!"*** and threw himself towards the threat, holding both arms out in front of him, fingers spread. The blazing curtain ceased its forward rush; Pendar's muscles bulged and, at the same time, his commanding posture, revealed as his figure was silhouetted against the glare, gave the impression of a man holding back an avalanche through sheer fixity of purpose. One minute, two minutes, three minutes passed as the discarnate immortal's body shook with the tremendous effort he was making. At last the fire began to die: the flames flickered, guttered, sank down and in a trice were gone. Pendar fell forward, saved himself, then turned towards his companion while brushing his hands together as if rubbing off contamination.

"Child's play," he said with a grin.

"But what was it?!" exclaimed a stunned Dando.

"I can't be sure, but I think that at the end of this tunnel we may find a reception committee waiting – it's been on the cards ever since certain passé loosers failed to get what they wanted by any other means. Be on your guard when we get there – hang on to that thing round your neck for dear life and to your lover's relict that's been protecting you, although I have my doubts as to whether it will work anymore against these particular no-hopers. Let me do the talking. If anything happens to me the ship-builder's your man – he'll put you on the right track."

"Might something happen to you?" asked Dando, dismayed, but Pendar had already gone ahead along a gradually brightening passageway that promised genuine egress this time. Dando looked back but could not locate his friends in the gloom. Where were they? The Key hung heavy around his neck reminding him that its fate was his responsibility and no-one else's. He felt very alone. *Surely the story must be nearing its end,* he thought to himself. *When I get rid of this Thing then maybe I can rest. I won't be able to go on much longer – even with Pendar's support I feel so weary...* There was a small passage, little bigger than a burrow, branching off from the main tunnel at the point he had reached. For a moment he hesitated, tempted to turn aside while he was unobserved and crawl away. But then thoughts of Ann, without whose care and protection he would never have been able to get this far, of Tallis whose quest he had shouldered through duty and love, and of Tom, his mentor, who had made the ultimate sacrifice on his behalf, convinced him that he owed it to all three not to waver. His sense of responsibility re-awoke and he followed Pendar through the opening at the end of the passage into the floodlit Cave of the Scull.

What he had been expecting to see as he emerged was nothing like what actually confronted him. Instead of the great glowing space-ship standing in the centre of the vast cavern, all latent promise and, as yet, unfulfilled potential, what he actually laid eyes on were two gigantic figures, large enough to completely obscure the machine before which they stood. They appeared to be expecting him. He remembered what Pendar had said about a reception committee. The one on the right stepped forward and, bending down, stretched out a huge pointing finger, the skin of which flickered as if flames were running over its surface.

"I thought you said he was a formidable opponent wife," came a voice that rang a bell in his memory and which might have been generated within the eye of a hurricane. ***"Now I see him up close for the first time, he's just one of the local apes and a poor specimen at that."***

Dando shrank back, staring heavenwards. The towering figure wore glittering armour and had a golden helm on its head. He tried to make out the facial features but they seemed to be continually in flux. As with the hands the rest of the body also appeared to be swathed in fire. With one quick movement the giant's fingers closed around Dando's waist and hoisted him high in the air turning him every which way as if to satisfy a long pent up curiosity.

"How dare you!!"

Up until that moment the immortals had been unaware of Pendar's presence. Since entering the cave he had somehow managed to blend into the surroundings and virtually disappear. But now he became visible, standing facing the two colossi – considerably smaller but with a much greater presence.

"How dare you molest the liberator father and try to interfere with his task! Leave him alone! A new age has dawned and your time is long gone!"

Pyr - for of course it was he that had a hold on Dando – was just reaching out with his right hand for the chain around the boy's neck. Instead he was startled enough by this intervention for his left hand to lose its grip so that his victim fell heavily to the floor.

"***Idiot!***" cried the second great figure who stood beside him, ***"can't you do anything right?!"***

Dando, despite being bruised and shaken, managed to pull himself into a kneeling position and looked upwards, recalling a vaguely remembered scene out of the past. A long time ago in the freezing cold of an early late winter morning he had watched from the edge of Castle Dan's grounds as a beautiful woman with a garland in her hair had come drifting down Spring Road on the way from Lady Wood. And now he saw the same image and heard the same words he had heard then.

"***Well met my lad,"*** the giantess said smiling beguilingly, and then in honeyed tones - ***"Come."***

As she spoke she reached out her hand and beckoned. But Dando was now a very different individual from the seven-year-old boy who had been lured away to the troy-town on Judd's Hill and had nearly lost his life. He gazed directly into Aigea's eyes, penetrating her disguise, and shook his head. At once all pretence of beauty vanished. In response her face, distorted with rage, changed to that of a beldam - an ancient of days – and from there to something completely alien. She glared daggers at him through extraterrestrial eyes as her lips writhed back from greenish gums, exposing a mouth containing strange ridges instead of teeth. Then lightning bolts flashed and he was once more slammed full length onto the ground feeling as if his weight had quadrupled. Despite being in this parlous state he was conscious that Pendar had also been thrown down but that the bright brother was making prodigious attempts to rise. It did not take long before, with a shout of triumph, his protector threw off the invisible bonds that were holding him and leapt to his feet.

"***It's no good, mother!"*** he cried, ***"you can't command the earth as you used to – the planet is no longer yours to bend to your will. Get up Dando – she won't harm you now - have a good look at my progenitors – dead-enders the both of them."***

Dando struggled upright, gasping for breath, and saw that the stature of the two pseudo-divinities had shrunk by a significant amount. The upper section of the rocket had come into view and now there was also a glimpse of someone else who until then had been hidden behind the immortals' bulk. Aigea and Pyr were half turned towards this third entity and were apparently receiving advice.

"***What new trick are they going to pull?"*** asked Pendar sardonically. ***"Give 'em time and they'll go through the whole gamut. Whatever they try don't be taken in – they're the most consummate liars this planet has ever known."***

The two immortals turned back towards Dando. All their attention was concentrated on him and they ignored their own offspring completely. The young man bravely withstood their scrutiny but was then amazed to see them continue to shrink before his eyes until they dwindled to just half his size. As they diminished their aspect changed and they took on the appearance of children, but it was a caricature of childhood with which he was presented: their eyes appeared over-large and their heads enormous in relation to their tiny bodies so that the whole effect was grotesque in the extreme. They stretched out their pudgy little arms towards him and in shrill penetrating voices pleaded in perfect unison:-

"***Have pity! - Have pity kind gentleman! Unless we hold the Catalyst in our hands once more we are going to die! Our predecessors were wrong to bring it here – we were wrong to use it to gain dominion - but because we did so our fate is tied up with its existence. Give us just a touch - a touch every few years is all we ask – more than that and it would burn us to cinders. If you have any compassion in your soul please lend it for a moment – we'll give it right back ...***"

Dando, confused, looked at Pendar, and received a half-smile in return. The odd shadowless life-form who only existed as a result of these two elementals' unnatural congress seemed to be awaiting his reaction with purely speculative interest. Dando turned back to the eldritch children with a heavy heart.

"I tried not long ago to hand it to someone," he explained earnestly, "but it wouldn't let me. And anyway I'm supposed to take it far away from here. I'm afraid it's not mine to give." He could think of nothing more to say but instead put his hand protectively over the Thing-of-Power.

Immediately the two immortals cried out in rage and came barrelling up to seize what they were denied, but as they rose, arms outstretched, they continued to shrink until they were indistinguishable from the tiny homunculi that infested this paranormal underworld. Deftly Pendar reached out and caught them between finger and thumb before they could do any further mischief and then held up the protesting mites in front of his eyes.

"***Well, my parents – looks as if the hour has come to say goodbye. I think you'd better make yourselves scarce before I decide to squeeze the life out of you right here and now.***"

He tossed them into the air and the two tiny creatures fled squeaking and twittering into the tunnel that led to the elevator shaft's cave.

"For the time being they'll take their rightful place among the wraiths that haunt the lower regions," he explained, ***"that's where they were headed ever since they came to this world."***

"Don't you care about them at all?" asked Dando.

"Why should I? Remember I've never known what it was to have a heart."

The young man shook his head at this, as it was beyond question that he had been on the receiving end of silent empathy from this weird being.

"Ho brother – are you there? Come out of the shadows and show yourself."

Pendar, having disposed of two of his relatives, walked across to the scaffolding that surrounded the base of the rocket, picked up a hammer and banged on one of the metal supports, creating a tremendous din.

"Come out, come out wherever you are. I think we've got a score to settle. Don't say you're afraid to meet me? Shame on you for an arrant coward..." and he redoubled his percussive efforts. After a long pause the third figure of the trio that had awaited them began to move and in doing so revealed himself: it was Azazeel.

"What the devil, brother!" Dando's gaoler sounded thoroughly put out. "Why are you creating such an unholy racket?! Do you want to wake the dead?!"

"Not especially," replied Pendar, ***"and besides I believe you've already done quite a good job in that direction yourself. You appear to be occupying one of them right now – in fact you seem to make a habit of reanimating defunct corpses and lurking inside them like a flesh-eating worm. Is it strictly necessary, I ask myself? I've always managed perfectly well without."***

"You've never known what it was like to be rejected," replied Azazeel darkly, his voice redolent with several thousand years of resentment, "I was cast out from day one while you... you were their blue-eyed boy."

"I was their bone of contention, you mean," countered Pendar, ***"pulled first one way, then the other. I never knew if I was on my head or my heels."***

"Bullshit! And why are you helping that thief? I've been flogging my guts out in order to lay my hands on the Treasure and now you turn up and undo all my good work."

"Who are you trying to deceive? You're never going to handle the Periapt. Don't you realise it's gone beyond our control? -

beyond you – beyond me – beyond every last person on this earth except one – and he is only favoured because he'll be able to show it the way it has to go to achieve its destiny. The most courteous thing we can do now is to remove ourselves entirely from the scene so that this young man can finally complete his mission unimpeded by abnormally conceived dinosaurs like you and me. Come and give me a hug brother – let's make up and call it quits for old time's sake," and Pendar advanced with arms outstretched as if to embrace his sibling. Azazeel also held up his hands but in an attempt to ward the other off. "No! No!" he cried, backing hurriedly away, only to practically trip over the base of the rocket's gantry. Pendar seemed about to draw the reluctant Lord-of-the-Underworld to his breast but at the last minute looked back. ***"Take heed Dando,"*** he called, ***"think before you commit yourself - it could mean total annihilation."*** The next moment he had completely enveloped his brother and the two appeared to blend into one. Then they were gone leaving, as the only evidence of their existence, the dead body of the fair-haired seaman that Azazeel had currently been inhabiting which swayed to and fro and then toppled to the ground.

"Lord Pendar!" cried Dando starting impetuously forward, hardly able to believe he had suffered yet another devastating loss, only to find himself grabbed from behind by two small determined hands. At the same time his weakness reasserted itself with a vengeance and he collapsed into the arms of his friends.

"See 'Orry," came Milly's indignant tones, "I tol' you 'ee needed us. Why on erf did you stop me from 'elpin' 'im?!"

"He needs us *now*," Horry sounded as if his patience was wearing thin. "If you'd put your spoke in earlier you'd probably have made a complete mess of things – wouldn't she folks?" (appealing to the others). There was a murmur of agreement from Damask and Foxy.

"Well I fink you're all a load of scaredy-cats!" scolded a furious Milly.

Dando looked up and saw Jack's face above him. He reached out and took his hand.

"Jack," he whispered, "what can I do? People keep getting themselves killed on my account."

Jack squeezed his hand. "It's not because of you, my love," he said with conviction, "it's because of that thing round your neck – the sooner you get rid of it the better."

"Then I must go to the rocket – can you take me to the rocket?"

With Jack on one side of him and Foxy on the other Dando was able to stand and even walk, but his feet dragged. They made their way across to the great column of metal in the centre of the cave, followed by Damask, while Horry and Milly, who were still arguing in low voices, brought up the rear. As they approached its base a small figure crawled out from under the skirt of one of the boosters. "Have they gone?" asked Quahaug in a quavery voice.

"We've returned, sir," said Jack politely, "and brought our friend with us – the one you wanted to meet. This is he."

Quahaug surveyed Dando, assessing and evaluating. "You look ill," he stated bluntly.

"I'm well enough to do what's required," replied the Glept, making a great effort to appear normal. "I believe you're trying to find someone to pilot your ship."

"That's true. We've been working on it flat out over the last few days. It's as ready as it'll ever be. Are you volunteering?"

"Yes," said Dando without equivocation.

"Well you'd better come to my office and give me some details so I can judge if you're suitable." Quahaug could barely contain his delight. Everyone – Dando relying on Jack and Foxy's help - climbed up to the platform where the administrative facilities and nerve centre of the operation were situated but when they arrived the scientist insisted on interviewing his prospective pilot alone. The door was shut against the rest and they waited outside for at least half an hour before they were given permission to enter. Once inside they found Dando settled in an armchair and Quahaug standing beside him, both looking quite at ease in the other's company.

"I'm going," the boy said in answer to their unvoiced questions before they even had time to open their mouths.

"You're goin' up in that fing?" cried a disgusted Milly, gesturing towards the window where a great shiny metal wall loomed ominously. "Why can't you jus' put the fing on board an' send it orf on its own?"

The young man looked at her with tender solicitude. "I'm afraid that's not possible, Milly – at this late stage we can't be separated – I've already proved that. It needs me you see – or so I've been led to believe..."

"But *where* are you going Dodo?" asked Damask.

Dando turned helplessly towards Quahaug. "Can you explain?" he pleaded. The scientist was nothing loath.

"I've always been interested in the night sky," he began. "I built myself a telescope when I was just a boy – several telescopes – I sent up balloons – I learnt what conditions were like in the upper atmosphere. Then I studied the motion of the stars. The sun – Sol – is just another star deeply embedded in an arm of our local galaxy. You know what a galaxy is? Well – it's an island really, but an island floating in space made up of a multitude of heavenly bodies. After a while I began to wonder about the composition of our galaxy and whether there are other galaxies farther away and if they are different from our own. I asked myself how we could escape from our immediate locality into deep space. One way would be to build a ship that could contain everything necessary to sustain life for hundreds, nay thousands, of years – the distances are immense between us and even our nearest neighbours. But when I examined the heart of our particular island I came across something really peculiar. In the centre where the stars cluster thickest I realised that there was a gap - an opening - perhaps a passage into an alternative cosmos. I thought that if we could make it that far it might be possible to go through the gap and come out somewhere entirely different. Then Xoserite appeared on the scene and I understood that space travel was no longer a matter of centuries – not within this galaxy at any rate – but of days or even hours. And so I designed and built the craft you see before you using the substance that *I* discovered and of which only *I* understand all the properties. The thing is, if the vehicle enters the hole and survives to emerge on the other side, will there be any hope of a return? I have my doubts – even I don't understand all the forces involved. My great great grandson was as enthusiastic about the project as I was and seemed really eager to pilot the ship, but both he and I knew it wasn't a job to be taken on single-handedly. So my idea was I would issue instructions from here based on information gathered from those aboard, as well as collating all the other less relevant data by means of my network."

"How old was he?" asked Dando.

"Orlando you mean? Only just entering his third decade when he..." Quahaug stopped abruptly then went on in a voice that appeared to have aged several years. "He said he was prepared to take the risk... he said it was worth it because of what we would learn..."

"...an' now that you've finished 'im orf!" cried an incandescent Milly, "you're goin' to do the same fing to the Lordship! Why don' you go yourself?!!"

"You don't understand," replied the scientist somewhat fretfully, "the ship, although it's under the control of a pilot, is designed to be guided from earth. I have to stay here and follow its progress using my instantaneous intra-spacial communications system in order to give directions based on whatever eventualities arise. This young man is a godsend – I'll be eternally grateful..."

"...and like I told you – the Key and I can't be parted," added Dando, "not at this late stage."

"Well, I fink e's just too scared to go," muttered Milly darkly but only to herself.

Quahaug mused for a moment then continued in a low voice, "I've been getting the strangest feeling recently that perhaps I originally intended this for a grander purpose than mere exploration. Does that sound crazy?"

"Not at all," answered Dando. "Who among us can be sure of the true motivation behind our actions?"

"But 'e can't go!" shouted Milly suddenly, reanimated by her desperation, "'e mus'n't – you'll kill 'im!" She was on the verge of hysteria. Dando reached up from where he sat and laid a hand on her arm. Immediately she quietened - his very touch seemed to calm her.

"Milly – please try to understand – I have to do this. Once I believed I was born to help govern a small remote valley although I wasn't too keen on the idea. Then I decided it was my job to please people's taste buds and invent new ways of eating. And then, after he died, I decided I must fulfil my master's wishes by completing his quest. But now I think all those things were just childish dreams and it was this I was really meant to do."

Milly stared at him and was granted a sudden revelation: she saw that in his worn and weakened state her lover was no longer a boy – that he could not even be described as a young man. No – he was purely and simply a human being – and an exceptional one at that: such a one as appears when the times demand a single individual who will act on behalf of the whole of humanity. In that moment all her aggression drained away. She nodded in reluctant acquiescence and then began to weep long and bitterly.

Although the ship's construction was complete Quahaug explained that it would take several hours to ready it for actual take-off. When the time arrived everyone except the pilot would have to take shelter, either in the cavern below the Skull or in reinforced structures built around the periphery of the main cave. The newcomers were welcome to join the other workers by the top of the elevator shaft he said; there they should be well protected. Quahaug went off to set the whole process in motion. Once he had gone Dando gave his friends some advice.

"There's no point in your hanging around," he said. "I think it would be safest if you got right away from the mountain before the rocket goes up. I don't like the thought of you too near as it fires. I'll come and see you off – no need to prolong the agony. Have you decided where you're going to go?"

This speech brought home to them the realisation that the time had almost arrived when their little group would be permanently fragmented. The thought put everyone in a sombre mood – even Horry. Damask went off to tell Quahaug of the change of plan and came back with the information that they could borrow the motorised run-around in which three of them had been transported once before.

"I think it's just as easy to manage as the dock boss's buggy," she said, "it'll get us along the tunnel to the entrance in double quick time – that's the entrance you told me was barred against you when you tried to find a way in Milly. The old man says that when we come to the gate there's a control panel on the wall. You press a green button to make the barrier open – then when you're through it shuts automatically," and turning to Dando, "He says to tell you that you must be back by dusk for the take off."

Dando offered to drive the car and the others crowded in beside and behind him, discussing in low voices their plans for the future. The Glept, whose future was going to be severely curtailed if he understood the situation aright, stayed silent, feeling somewhat extraneous. As they approached the end of the tunnel they saw daylight for the first time in days – several weeks in Dando's case – and by the length and direction of the shadows it looked to be early morning. They stopped short of the entrance beside the panel that raised the portcullis and everyone climbed out except for the one who was to remain behind. Conversation died and they stood around awkwardly exchanging embarrassed glances. Then Milly launched herself back into the car and flung her arms around Dando, burying her face in his neck. He returned her embrace, patting her consolingly. "Where are you all going to end up?" he asked the others over her head.

"Me an' the woman be a-gooin' ter fin' the river where it do come out of the mountain further down stream," said Foxy with determination. "It should be a-comin' out onto the surface somewheres over that side. We be a-gooin' ter follow it an' see where it do goo."

"Yes," chipped in Damask, "we think that as it's flowing east it must eventually reach the ocean – we want to see if all the stories they tell about that place are true. Is it really as big as they say? Are there really islands where everything is made of gold? Are there monsters beneath the waves?"

"How about you?" asked Dando of Milly, but she just cuddled closer to him, unwilling to speak. Horry answered for her. "I think Milly an' I will be travelling together – that is if I can drag her away before... I mean..." he broke off, for the moment too embarrassed to continue. Then, following a long pause and not meeting his father's eye, "I tol' her I wanted to see that castle you made a drawing of - the one you said you lived in when you were little – an' she said it were called Deep Hallow..."

"It's the valley itself which is called Deep Hallow," replied Dando with a small compassionate smile. "Here..." pulling the heirloom worn by every Dan's second son from his finger (somehow the ring had survived all his vicissitudes), "show this to those you meet when you get there. Tell them I gave it to you, and explain who you are. You may not receive a very warm welcome but it's worth a try."

The only member of the group whose intentions remained a mystery was the blind boy. Dando gently extricated himself from Milly's embrace and whispered something in her ear. They both climbed out of the car. Then he turned towards his male lover with an ache in his heart. "Where are you going, Jack?"

His friend cleared his throat and spoke in a voice that shook slightly.

"I'm hitching up with Damask and Foxy. I've always wanted to see the Big Water. I just hope I last long enough to get there. If I'm ok I might even enlist on a ship."

"*See* Jack?"

"Yes caridad, there's other ways of seeing besides using your eyes."

Now nobody had anything more to add and yet they seemed unable to drag themselves away. Eventually Dando, supporting himself against the car door and on the verge of tears, muttered, "Go! - for God's sake go!" This was enough to break the paralysis and one by one the company stepped forward rather stiffly for a formal leave-taking.

"Are you doing the right thing Do-Do?" asked Damask, giving him a sisterly peck.

"Yes, this time I think I am."

"Well, do it for both of us then."

"Surely."

"Bye Dad," cried Horry, trying to grin but looking more as if he was about to burst into tears, "I wish I was coming with you."

Dando shook his head. "You've got your own life to live," he answered.

"'Till we meet again, my love," murmured Jack.

"No, I'm afraid not," replied his friend.

"But I have to tell myself we will, otherwise I couldn't bear this."

All Milly could managed was to stand stock-still with wide eyes, mouthing, "Lordship, Lordship," over and over again. Eventually Horry pulled her towards the entrance.

Foxy gave Dando's hand a shake then pushed the portcullis's button which rose, only to descend again once the company had passed through. They walked - backwards for the most part - along the avenue of trees until they reached a bend in the road where they stood and waved before vanishing from Dando's sight. He got back into the driving seat of the stationary run-around and stared through the windscreen at the scene in front of him while the hours ticked by, watching as the day wore away. There was a brisk wind out and about that morning tossing the treetops around and sending the last of the autumn leaves swirling. Clouds streamed overhead. Sunshine came and went and once or twice there was a heavy shower. Eventually, towards late afternoon, the rain set in in earnest. He shut his eyes and sat listening to its gentle pattering while breathing the cool mountain air; he might even have fallen asleep for a short spell. At last he roused himself and, starting the engine, turned the vehicle about before heading down once more into the dark.

The bearer of the Signifier lay strapped into a chair tilted back ninety degrees after having been sealed within the poky flight-deck of the scientist's vessel. The pilot had not been provided with much room for his activities despite the fact that, beneath him, on the other side of a bulkhead, a large unused empty compartment extended downwards for some distance. This had originally been intended to serve as a cargo-bay. Below that again the propulsion units were located.

"I once meant to provide enough equipment for a stay of several years when I thought a base might be established on another planet but that idea fell through," Quahaug explained.

Dando was dressed in a cream-coloured space suit minus the helmet which lay beneath his one remaining foot. The outfit was a pretty good fit; Orlando and he must have been much of a size. In front of him, filling most of his vision, were a number of screens but with no obvious switches or buttons to operate them. Four of the screens, labelled *Rear-View, Forward-View, L-side* and *R-side,* were grouped around a fifth showing a chronometric display plus various other esoteric data, while clamped to his head a pair of headphones carried the sound of Quahaug's voice as the ship's designer went through a complicated launch sequence. Earlier he had spelled out what would happen during the various take-off stages.

"She uses conventional boosters to lift her into orbit,"he explained. "They're jettisoned as soon as she enters zero gravity and then the Xoserite drive kicks in. When that happens she should achieve hyper-speed in a matter of minutes and be taken right out of the local system and into a space-time warp. Everything is controlled through the panel. I'll be able to see how she's riding and then give guidance. We'll be in communication all the way to the target area so you'll just need to carry out occasional adjustments by means of the screens according as I tell you. The external instruments will be sending a continual stream of info back to earth and this will be invaluable for my research. Of course I don't know how long they will continue to function once she enters the singularity; I hope long enough to solve the mystery of what lies beyond..."

In other words, Dando mused, silently completing the man's train of thought, *despite what you said earlier about your true purpose in building the ship you're still mainly hooked on the idea of exploring this weird opening in space you keep going on about, and so a certain person will be totally dispensable once he's managed to get the machine through the portal. Well, at least it might mean that I can rid myself of this cursed thing that's weighing me down and preventing everyone else from doing what they were born to do.* Having a fairly realistic view of the state of his consumptive body he had come to the conclusion that under normal circumstances he would probably be at death's door or through it by now. *When he helped me, Pendar said that what he did might hasten my end,* he thought, *so it must be the Key that's keeping me alive, just as it did Gammadion. If I dispose of it maybe the ordeal will be over. But what will happen then? Will I be born into another existence as lots of people believe happens after death or will I go 'Over-the-Brook' like Annie, Tom and the Ministrant? Perhaps I'll become one of the ghosts that wanders in the underworld. More likely it'll be the final curtain - Pendar warned me that that might be the case. Well, if in the process I can rid the world of the blight that's been plaguing it for thousands and thousands of years p'raps even that might be worth the sacrifice.* These were noble sentiments indeed but accompanying them came a feeling of atavistic terror, a new kind of dread that he had not experienced before, despite the fact that this was not the first time he had faced the possibility of death since starting his journey. Like a frightened child he longed for the impossible, which was to find himself once more within the safety of Annie's arms. “Help me,” he whispered, but the surrounding macrocosm was either deaf or indifferent to his plea.

Bringing his mind back to the present he listened as Quahaug proceeded with the count-down and for a long time waited in vain for some morale-boosting words to be thrown in his direction. It was not until the controller conducted a final check on the preparedness of various personnel that he heard himself mentioned.

“Pilot?” said the voice on a note of interrogation.

“Yes?” He was not sure what was required of him.

“Are you ready?” slightly impatiently.

“As ready as I'll ever be.”

“This is no time for joking – are you ready?”

“Yes – I s'pose I am.”

“Stand by.”

That was all the encouragement he was given. At last he heard the words *starting ignition sequence,* which were followed by the classic *ten, nine eight, seven, six...* He braced himself. On *one* something exploded beneath him and went on exploding. A roar filled the whole of the area within the shell of the craft while an intense shuddering invaded everything around him. He found himself gripped by forces that bound him to his seat and threatened to re-dislocate his already much-abused limbs. As had happened in the past when he had been at the mercy of multiple Gs it became impossible to breath and, on this occasion, he passed out.

His moment of unconsciousness must have been extremely brief for, when he opened his eyes, the reading on the time display had barely changed, yet, as he came to himself, the suffocating pressures were gone, the screens had sprung to life and on the one marked *Rear-View* he saw evidence of the rocket's exhaust flow and a view of the earth rapidly receding. But what riveted his attention, what drew his eyes, was a dense cloud expanding up towards him. Within seconds it had filled the whole of the screen and was apparently threatening to envelope the ship. For a moment cloud and craft were engaged in a race, then the machine won out and, at the periphery of the VDU, part of the blue-green planet came into view once more although the centre was still obscured by billowing smoke. Dando looked on in horrified disbelief. He did not want to give the thing credence yet could not deny what he was seeing. Apparently the thrust of the boosters had reached deep below ground and penetrated some underlying magma chamber. *Ian Shan* had been handed a sharp kick in the fundament and, in response, had awoken from a centuries-old slumber. It was undeniable that beneath him an extinct volcano was at that very moment erupting. Because of this he was presented with a vital yet unanswerable question: had his friends been able to get away? Fervently he prayed (to whom?) that they had. But Quahaug and Quahaug's construction team...? The 'phones were still clamped over his ears and before his mouth was positioned a tiny microphone. “A-are you there?” he stuttered, and then more urgently, “Quahaug – where are you – answer please – I need a response!”

He fell silent, listening intently, but the only noise that came over the headset was a faint hissing sound interrupted by muffled thumps. Meantime things around him were rapidly changing. The rearward camera showed an earth shrunk to no more than a pinprick in the blackness of space while the sun could be recognised for what it really was – just a minor star. The outer planets flashed past and then the whole system was gone – nothing more than a fading memory. The vessel progressed exponentially as it carried its solitary crewman and the tiny fateful Mutating-Object that he bore into an uninhabited region between two of the galaxy's arms.

Quahaug said that his ship was designed to go where the stars are at their thickest, Dando remembered, *where I'm heading now can't be right.*

Timorously he reached up and laid his hand against the forward-view screen, but as he had no idea what he was doing felt he could be making a huge mistake. As a result of his action the few points of light visible on the other screens swung violently from left to right before vanishing completely and when the whole thing settled once more there was even less evidence of tangible matter ahead. Feeling totally helpless he almost abandoned hope, convinced he was now set on a course that would carry him further and further into the void and that the Key would drag his unendurable life out to the limits of recorded time. He made one last desperate appeal into the microphone. “Please, if anyone can hear me, tell me what to do, show me how to steer this thing!”

The hissing noise stopped, the earphones crackled, and there was the momentary suggestion of a human voice before the line broke up into a series of bangs and whistles that made him flinch in discomfort. Despite this he anxiously requested, "Try again – try again – you almost got through."

There was a long pregnant pause before the 'phones clicked once or twice, squealed and then came alive with what appeared to be the second half of a message, the meaning of which was ambiguous to say the least.

"...to the other clever ones and they say I should ask the Banatees cos they know all about such things but they say I should goo to the ones that come from the outer planet in their system an' then one o' they..." but at this point Dando interrupted with an exclamation of joy because he recognised the speaker.

"Annie!" he cried, "is that you?!"

"O' course it is, bonny lad," came the loved voice, leaving no room for doubt.

"Oh Annie! I can hear you at last! Where are you – are you near?"

"We... all aroun'... help... I be with you my love..."

The sound kept cutting out and Dando had great difficulty in understanding what was being said.

"But Annie – I think the mountain blew up – I think Quahaug's been killed – and he was the only one who understood how this ship worked. What am I supposed to do?"

"He don' be killed – he just be crossed over cos, although he be way too long in the life of the flesh, he still be able to make the change. Shall I ask he?"

"Oh please Annie. Ask him what I should do to make the ship go in the right direction. Where is he now?"

"Those that goo Over-the-Brook usually find theyselves on the surface of some empty world while they get used to being on the other side an' where they c'n learn to live among the stars. Dadda will show I the place. I'll have to leave 'ee my love but I'll be back. The others will stay wi' you while I be away. Don' be afrighted..."

"What others?" asked Dando but the intercom had already gone dead, or so it seemed. However, a little later he realised he could still hear a very faint hiss coming through the headphones and this gradually mutated into the unthreatening sound of water running, a sound that conjured up a picture in his mind's eye of the little River Wendover flowing gently through his home valley. To reinforce this vision came the accompanying sound of water birds: the call of a moorhen, *kr-r-ck, kr-r-ck, kr-r-ck*, followed by the cheeping of a family of ducklings and the muted splash of a diving kingfisher. With this mysterious fluvial background to steady him he managed to sit out the long hours of waiting that otherwise would have become unendurable.

"***I be back bonny lad!***"

Dando opened his eyes to the awareness that Ann's voice was once more in his ears.

"Annie!" he cried, full of gratitude, and then, as he came more fully awake, "did you find him? What did he say?"

"***Master Quahaug be a-restin' a long ways from here but when I tell he what you wan' he remember what be happenin' an' he say you mus' touch the front screen to steer the machine.***"

"But that's what I did a while ago and everything just went haywire."

"***He say you mus' only give a little tap – lots of tiny taps on the side you wan' it to turn to until you be pointin' in the right direction.***"

"I'll try." With great trepidation Dando extended one finger and briefly touched the forward-view screen on the left-hand side. There was no noticeable effect. After a long pause he repeated the manoeuvre and this time two tiny lights appeared on that side of the screen, travelled forward a short distance and came to rest a third of the way across. Gaining in confidence he tried again, tried several times, and soon the view became populated by a number of motes that must surely be the representation of stars. These were congregated most densely towards the base of the screen and he realised that, as a result of his actions, the spaceship had shifted into a new alignment. Experimentally he tapped close to the bottom edge and immediately a blazing mass of heavenly bodies swung upwards towards the centre, the monitor displaying a cluster that became increasingly clotted and brilliant as it became more visible, the blazing conglomeration outshining everything else of lesser magnitude in the vicinity. "I've cracked it, Annie!" he cried triumphantly, "It's the heart! – the hub! I believe she's making for the centre of the galaxy now."

"***Good,***" came his loved-one's reply, "***But there be something else Master Quahaug tol' I. If you keep a-travlin' like you be a-doin' now it will take many lifetimes to arrive where you wan' to go. To get there quicker you have to cross the wall – lots of walls. He say you mus' wipe your finger downwards from the top of the screen – c'n you do that?***"

With his index finger Dando swiped as instructed, feeling he was becoming quite an expert at this game, but was then startled to see a row of icons appear along the top.

"There's some pictures Annie," he said, "what do I do?"

"Do you see one that looks like a door?"

"There's a symbol a bit like a doorway with a half-open door. Is that what you mean?"

"He say you mus' touch that to make the machine goo through the wall. Then when that ha' happened you mus' do the same thing again – do it four times altogether."

"Ok." Feeling very confident, Dando complied but was taken aback when, as a result of this procedure, the whole ship shuddered like a train hitting buffers at speed, the images on the screens flared and mutated, and he got the feeling that the vessel had leapt forward across an enormous distance and rematerialised in a quite different region of space.

"What was that," he gasped, "what happened, Annie? - Annie? - Are you there? - Answer me!" but it seemed that when it came to distances to be crossed and speeds employed in the crossing even dancers have their limitations; it was apparent that during this last manoeuvre his soul-mate had been left far behind and that now he would have to cope alone. The screens in front of him blurred – he was looking through tears – while a huge lump formed at the base of his throat. "I hardly had a chance to say hello before it was time to say goodbye," he lamented, "what's the point – what's the bloody point..." Briefly he felt like abandoning the whole crazy enterprise and retreating into a kind of self-induced amnesia. But then, with a great gulp, he nerved himself to repeat the touch screen procedure, resolutely insisting, "No – no - I owe it to her – to them. Four times, she said - I have to do it another three times."

He suited the action to the word and once again the craft leapt, but, after this strange transmogrification had occurred thrice more, the space ship's speed settled down, although it appeared to continue at many times the pace it had been travelling previously.

Pendar had told him that there was something black at the heart of the galaxy but the vessel appeared to be penetrating into light rather than darkness. That it was moving unimaginably fast was obvious by the perceived behaviour of the surrounding phenomena. Having been used all his life to the idea that the night sky was fixed and immobile Dando saw that in his present situation this was not the case; in fact all was in flux. Bodies ahead of him appeared to part company in order to let the ship slip between, only to slide inwards again once it had passed. More and more stars blinked into view in the central area and rapidly increased in intensity, demonstrating a huge variety of types and colours. Time too seemed to have gone into overdrive and to be increasing incrementally outside the ship or, rather, slowing down within it. Things that should have taken vast ages to achieve their final potential were happening in the blink of an eye. He watched as young stars formed from gas clouds, blazed for a moment, then expanded into red giants before shrinking finally into dwarfs. He saw planetary systems come into being, comets speed to oblivion, super-novae light up the whole of space for a brief second. He also saw the formation of mysterious dark spheres – spheres that were invisible except when superimposed against a brighter background. All the while the vastness was becoming more and more populated so that, despite the enormous distances involved, he began to fear that his craft might be involved in a collision before it reached its objective. As far as he was concerned there was nothing he could do now but sit and wait, yet he was too nervous to remain static for long. Feeling trapped, he undid the straps that bound him to the pilot's chair and immediately parted company with it, floating slowly up towards the ceiling. He felt rather like a bubble in a stale glass of beer, (it was noticeable that the air *was r*ather stale; Quahaug's life-support system did not seem to be working all that well.)

In that weightless environment there was just one thing that exerted a downward pull. Apparently giving the lie to a state of zero gravity that should have been universal the Key continued to drag at his neck and eventually became heavy enough to reverse his direction of drift and bring him back to the floor. He undid the chain (this time there was no retaliatory knock-out blow) in order to examine the Object-of-Power in more detail and saw, to his surprise, that it had actually increased in size, was in fact growing bigger by the second. Its shape was also altering: the ring at one end was beginning to merge into the shaft while the teeth at the other were transforming into some kind of knob. As it became larger it lost all resemblance to a key and in fact was beginning to look rather like a... he blinked and laughed nervously wondering whether madness had at last claimed him. But no – it was not just a crazy illusion - it really had taken on the appearance of – what was the polite word for it? - oh yes, a phallus – a sculptural representation of the male member. Another thought struck him. According to Quahaug the ship was heading for a great hole in the centre of the galaxy. So was that it? - *the Key hurtles through space in order to keep a date with its heavenly bride?* What a weird notion! He grimaced humorously imagining how Jack might have put it: *the Prick-of-the-World on its way to fuck the galaxy's cunt.* The whole thing became too impossibly ridiculous to believe yet he could not deny what was happening in front of his eyes. Over the next hour or so the strange priapic symbol went on enlarging until it filled half the cabin, leaving him scant room to move. Suddenly becoming aware of his danger he pressed the button that opened the door to the cargo bay and managed somehow or other to push the thing over the threshold into the much larger space beyond. Then he strapped himself once more into the chair, shaking violently from the effort he had made.

Staring fixedly ahead so that his eyes became thoroughly dazzled he thought for a moment he saw the phenomenon that Quahaug wished him to explore: there was a gap amid the brilliance, a missed out place where things were not; it was as if space had been perforated and in the resulting breach natural law was suspended. But at that moment the screens went blank before blinking hesitantly back on at a much lower intensity, the lights failed and an ominous metallic creaking from nearby gave notice that the ship was in trouble. It was not hard to guess what was happening: the Thing he had undertaken to carry far from the earth must have swollen to such an extent that it was now threatening to burst the vessel's outer framework, totally destroying it in the process. At the same time he experienced a sensation utterly unfamiliar and inexplicable. It was as if a great hand had wrapped itself around his frame and was beginning to squeeze every part of him from the top of his head to the tips of his five remaining toes. He struggled to break free but the invisible force increased, paralysing his limbs and constricting his throat so that he was not even able to scream as excruciating pain invaded his body. However, before he became completely immobilised he managed to raise his right arm – it was like lifting a ton weight – and for a few seconds his hand hovered, shaking, in front of the forward-view screen. Because of what had happened when he first tried to steer the ship, he guessed that if he laid it on the surface for any length of time the vessel would swing right round and might even head back the way it had come. Perhaps, if that happened, everything would go into reverse and he would continue to exist, maybe for years, maybe for ever after. But:- “No, no!” he gasped, “I mustn't!” - refusing to be beguiled by this final temptation to abdicate his duty and, as a consequence, ceasing to fight against the forces that were about to overwhelm him. Then – in any case - it was too late to do anything. Under enormous pressure from within, the ship's Xoserite shell finally gave way and burst asunder so that fragments, both organic and inorganic, flew outwards and dispersed in total disorder into the vacuum awaiting them. Dando himself was not immune - as consciousness failed, his body was ripped apart along with the rest, and it was thus that, if a debt had been incurred at the first turning, it was finally paid. One object, however, retained its integrity in the midst of chaos; the Ultimate-Reality that had once rested long ago on Morvah's palm in the shape of a tiny ornamental key, but which had now become larger and more powerful than the rocket it had just shattered, ploughed ahead towards its objective, continually increasing in size. How much time passed before it reached its goal was irrelevant – it could have been minutes, it could have been more than a hundred years – but, inevitably, discovering its purpose at long last and achieving the correct dimensions for what was to come, it penetrated the hole awaiting it and realised intergalactic fertilization. Immediately the fruit of this union switched from one substantiality to another, to a place so utterly remote that up to now nothing had existed there: no matter, no space, not even time itself. The inseminated zygote which both procreative elements had combined to produce, issued forth in this new location apparently unremarked and unheralded, with none to welcome it into the world. It was smaller than an atom, this embryo – smaller than the smallest particle - yet it was humming with inchoate unrealised energy. The labour that was about to result would be prodigious, the inflationary pangs gargantuan but, at the beginning, before expansion commenced and while the actual birth lay still in the future, a new universe came into being.

When the may was almost in flower
His spirit showed like a sword out of the sheath,
Called forth by love.

Chapter twenty five

"Oh, Mrs Goodhousen, how be the old man these sad times? The other day my Fred say he hear he be proper poorly. It mus' be a real worry for thee an' thine."

Doll was on her way back from the Castle after completing her work for the day. She had been to collect her father's retirement allotment - various food stuffs and a ration of beer – and was thinking about cooking the evening meal when she had the unwelcome experience of being waylaid by the local gossip. Saphira Emily Norbut was famous for being a real nosey-parker and it was taken as read that anything spoken within her hearing would be all round the neighbourhood in a matter of hours.

"Mr Applecraft be nicely, thankyou," said his daughter between gritted teeth before hurrying away (past experience had taught her that Saphira was incapable of any genuine concern).

"As long as he don' be suffering from the pest," the woman's voice called after her, "we don' wan' ter be losin' another one..."

Would that you might succumb to this pest we keep hearing about, thought Doll uncharitably, *then perhaps you might stop interfering in other people's business!*

Over two years before, when the Dan was assassinated whilst in pursuit of his errant son, the scene on the road had been one of utter confusion. The chieftain's head tracker and his second in command were riding just behind their leader and had seen the Nablan on the rock as he stood up to fire and also the loosing of the arrow. The rest of the troop further down the slope did not have a clear line of sight but all heard the THWACK! as the missile hit home. At first none of them was quite sure what had happened because, for what seemed like an age, the Dan stayed upright in the saddle, although his hand went to his breast. Then slowly he keeled over sideways and fell to earth, lifeless before he hit the ground. The whole party leapt from their saddles. The tracker knelt beside his master while the rank and file, after letting fly arrows in the general direction of the rock, went hot foot on the heels of the killer, followed and soon outdistanced by the dogs. It happened to be the morning of the weekly chase and the pursuit, although they did not know it, was going to be a fox-hunt after all, although one in name only. The Dan's second-in-command, having ascertained that his master was well and truly dead and that therefore he was now in charge, grabbed two or three of the tail-enders to carry the corpse.

"We must get 'im back to the Castle some 'ow or other. We'll make a sling with a couple of spears an' a' 'orse blanket. They'll put 'im on show I reckon."

This was indeed the case. Early the next morning the Dan's body lay on a bier in an open coffin within the Great Hall; plans were afoot for a grand funeral. But first, when the soldiers returned and the Castle learned to its consternation that its Leader was no more, a deputation was sent to wait on Dantor in order to hail him as the new Clan Chief. In fact as soon as his father died his heir ceased to be the Lord Dan Attor, the number one son – it was a case of *the Dan is dead, long live the Dan!* Later that day the rest of the hunting party came straggling back, their quarry having apparently vanished into thin air; even the dogs had lost the scent.

The new Dan, spectacled, unprepossessing, a mere twenty one years old, had already had the reins of the Dan estates in his hands for over a year because of his father's mental state. Although acknowledged by all to be a brilliant administrator he was otherwise thought to be of little account; in other eras and in other places he would probably have been labelled a *nerd.* But cometh the hour, cometh the man – the new chief, at this moment of crisis, showed unexpected qualities. To everyone's surprise, his first display of original thinking was to refuse to move his young wife, his baby and himself from their comfortable little flat near the gatehouse into the Dan's cavernous gloomy suite. He then set about disbanding his father's troop of mercenaries and rendering them weaponless before sending them packing out of the valley. The new incumbent declared an amnesty for all prisoners within the Dans' jurisdiction, abolished the death penalty and other draconian punishments and began to emancipate the nibblers, initially by using their correct name: Nablar. Over the next few months he gradually altered the status of all servants under his rule, giving them freedom to leave his employ if they so desired or granting them a living wage if they chose to remain. Most of them decided to stay. Also it was declared that ancient retainers, after many years of faithful service, would not be cast adrift to fend for themselves when of no further use but would be supported in their old age. These were radical changes indeed and would have a profound effect on that isolated community. The Dans were the most influential family in Deep Hallow, and where they led others might follow. How the two races would react to such seismic shifts was as yet unknown but there was no question that a new age was dawning.

Although making for home Doll was not heading for the old hut in the warren at the back of the Big House where she had once lived. Another innovation undertaken by the former Dan Attor as part of his new order was to arrange for a brand new hamlet to be built outside the walls of the castle with the purpose of providing housing for all the Nablans who were currently serving his family. The dwellings were small and spartan but well constructed, and had facilities such as running water, toilets and separate kitchens, things that had been no more than a dream in the old days. With the change of regime Doll had been given a job as chambermaid and would have been well satisfied with her lot had it not been for her continuing anxiety concerning her father. During the last two years Potto had gradually lost the will to live and now spent much of the time in his bed while she was absent. She could not deny the fact that he was heading for decrepitude at a vastly increased rate and there was nothing she could do about it. It seemed that the main cause of his malaise had been his rough treatment at the hands of the mercenaries on the day of the murder, but another contributing factor was definitely the distress he felt at hearing the rumours that circulated concerning his former master, the Lord Dan Addo, after the boy had vanished on that very same day. These rumours began in remote parts of the valley where the inhabitants were not so well acquainted with the soldiers' report that the killer of the clan chief had been a stocky red-headed fellow and his weapon a longbow, something no nobleman would think of wielding. Although, at first, the lower orders at Castle Dan bruited it about that the killing had had a supernatural origin – that it was the Mother's revenge for the slaughter of her priest and the desecration of her temple – elsewhere a belief grew, shared equally among the dominant and subject races, that, having fallen foul of his father, the second in line of succession had had a hand in the crime, after which he had fled the valley and was now in hiding somewhere along the Great River.

"He be a-meetin' wi' those o' our folk who chose to leave and now live down on the plains. They be bringin' fighters to the valley to send they incomers packin'." This was the rumour that was circulating among a rebellious core of Nablans, the ones who had belatedly responded to Foxy's urgings and had begun to flex their muscles since the lessening of their servitude. To them Dando was a hero.

"The Old Dan's army has gone in search of him. They'll arrest him and haul him back to face the music." This was the opinion of the majority of Glepts for whom the runaway was nothing less than a murderer.

Right from the off Potto would have none of it.

"My young Lord wou'n't kill his own father," he insisted, sounding greatly perturbed, "how c'n they say such a thing? He be a good boy – whatever his parent do to him he wou'n't want to hurt he!"

"Don' take on so dadda," Doll replied, trying to calm things down, "you an' I know well enough my lad ain't like that, whatever they duzzy eejits say. Don' pay them no heed." But Potto could not ignore the slander, especially when eventually the same rumour began to circulate within the Castle. "They all be turnin' agin he," he mourned, "an' he be better 'n the lot o' 'em put together."

As she returned to her little house Doll thought of the last sentence that had been flung after her by Saphira, that sentence which had contained the significant phrase: *suffering from the pest.* Several mysterious deaths had occurred in the Valley over the last few weeks, the victims being mostly people in the prime of life and coming from both races. The only explanation for this increased mortality appeared to be that there was an infection on the loose. After all it was only a short while since rumours had come from the north about a rampaging plague on the other side of the Middle Sea, whilst locally everyone had been frightened out of their wits by a flying monster that had appeared overhead one day and bombarded them with flames and smoke before disappearing the way it had come. It was now suggested that perhaps, in launching the attack, it had also brought sickness with it, this despite the fact that the bodies of the victims showed no sign of disease. When these corpses were discovered it was seen that most of them were either sitting composedly in a chair or lying serenely on top of their beds as if they were willing participants in whatever had taken place. This type of fatality was on the increase and Doll had a secret fear that her father might become one of them.

"Cooee," she called as she entered through the door, attempting a forced cheerfulness, "I'm back – I be a-gooin' ter cook you somethin' real nice for supper. Be you a-gittin' up?"

"Sweetie-pie," came Potto's voice in reply, "come you in here a minute. I got somethin' to say."

Doll entered the bedroom to find her father wide awake for once, his face completely transformed. Instead of the sad resigned expression it had worn over the past few months it was now suffused by a sort of eager childlike excitement.

"Tom ha' bin here," he told her. "He want me to keep company wi' he - he say he could help me goo over - but I say I couldn' goo wi'out you so he say he be a-comin' back later."

"Over what?" asked a thoroughly confused Doll, "Tom who?"

"Why Tom Tosa, o' courst - you knows who I mean. He say we c'n all goo *Over-the-Brook* now acos o' somethin' my young lord ha' done. I knew he be a good boy."

"I don' know what you be a-talkin' about," replied Doll, a faint feeling of panic rising within her; this sounded like the first stages of dementia.

"You wait an' see – you'll get a surprise – jest like I did."

"Well, me – I be a-gooin' to cook the supper – I don' hev no time for sech piffle."

It was when the meal was almost ready that she again heard Potto's voice from the bedroom, apparently in conversation with another. She put down the ladle she was holding and stood listening. Yes, she was sure she could hear two people talking. Taking the pot off the flame she went to investigate.

"Look daughter," said Potto, "I tol' you so – he's here – don' it be won'erful..."

Standing by the bed was a figure – a figure lit up in an unearthly kind of way yet immediately recognisable: it was her old friend Tom Tosa Arbericord, Culdee to the Nablar – one she had imagined long dead. He turned to her – the same pleasant-looking, slightly worn young man that she remembered – and gave her a welcoming smile.

"***Hello my dear – I'd better explain...***"

It was not until late the next day that Saphira, the gossip, could interest anyone in the fact that Mrs Goodhousen had not been seen to set out for work at her usual time that morning. When at last she persuaded someone to go to the length of breaking into the father and daughter's small dwelling Potto was discovered lying on the bed, apparently insensible, while Doll sat as still as a statue beside him holding his hand; in the kitchen they found a saucepan containing a cold untouched meal. Neither father nor daughter were breathing and when the coroner arrived they were both pronounced dead. Saphira was called in to lay out the bodies and, because there were no other members of the Applecraft or Goodhousen families remaining in the castle, the new Dan himself made arrangements for the funerals. Afterwards, back in his apartment, he confided in his wife, the only one with whom he cared to share his innermost thoughts.

"Well, Cuddlebuns," he said as they lay in bed together, "I'm really sorry to lose two such good people. It seems like the end of an era. Applecraft was Dando's man you know, right from when he was old enough to have a servant of his own. They really loved one another I think. And Doll was a second mother to us all of course. Strange that both deaths should occur at the same time like that. There's been quite a few pass away recently but these are the first in the castle since father died."

"You know, Danny Boy," replied his wife, "I was down in Gateway last week to see about the stores and I got talking to a merchant from Drossi. He told me there'd been quite a few deaths in the Delta City as well but that some people from over the sea have been saying that the victims didn't actually die – that in fact they weren't victims at all but, because of some change that's taken place, they had been able to shed their earthly bodies and move on to a new stage in their development. It sounded like complete nonsense to me."

The Dan, as was his wont, remained silent for some time, mulling this over. Eventually he spoke in an introspective manner.

"Certain people talk of the Key-of-the-Years, the Key that's supposed to set each new age in train, and, concerning that, I heard something a while ago from Tom the cobbler, just before... well, you know what I'm talking about... I was studying traditional tales at the time and I asked him about Nablan legends. He gave me several examples and among them was one to do with a Thing that came down from the skies and had a baleful effect on the earth and its people. According to this tale we're still being prevented, even now, from going in the direction that was originally intended for our species and we won't be free to follow our preordained course until the Object is banished. Perhaps, after all, there might be some truth in what you heard."

His wife kissed him vigorously on the cheek and tugged at his earlobe.

"Come on Fudgekins," she said, "I know what you're like – you'll start to worry yourself sick about it all if I let you. We've got better things to do than pay attention to old stories..." and she enfolded him in an embrace.

It was a bright and breezy spring morning as Foxy and Damask stood high on a hill many thousands of miles from Deep Hallow staring eastwards. They had just lowered a litter to the ground on which lay the young man from Drossi, by name Jack Howgego. The paved road before their feet fell away in a series of curves, winding down through a small coastal town. Beyond the buildings, stretching to the horizon, lay a vast expanse of open water gleaming in the sunlight. They were far enough up the hill to be able to look down on the elaborately tiled roofs of the houses below them and further off on those of the boat sheds nearer the sea. Although the streets appeared meticulously clean there was a pervasive smell of fish. Where the shore could be glimpsed they could see boats - junks and sampans for the most part - none of them more than moderate in size. It was just a small port this settlement, much too modest to accommodate the huge ships that plied the Tethys and occasionally circled the globe, yet the larger of the humble vessels anchored or moored at the quayside had a workmanlike air about them which suggested they were equipped to undertake longish voyages.

"There it is," said Damask, waving her hand towards the place where sky and sea met, "the Big Water. I wonder what name they give it round here?"

"There be one o' they Bridge Houses," said Foxy, gesturing off to the left where a brand-new building dominated the town, "one o' they places where people goo, so they say, to *relocate*. Even the little villages we passed through seem to be building 'em."

"Ug!" shuddered Damask, "not for me – not yet. I've got a whole lot more things to do in this life before I think about moving on to the next."

Meanwhile Jack had struggled to his feet and they guided him to a seat that had been thoughtfully provided nearby. It was when they had had to abandon the river as a means of transport after it went underground once more that he had been forced to face up to the fact that, due to his weakened state, when walking he was unable to match the others' pace or to keep going for more than an hour at a time. He had had little choice but to accept Foxy's suggestion that he and Damask should acquire a stretcher and carry him between them.

"We be pretty strong, the gel an' I," the Nablan boasted, "an' you be no weight at all."

Reluctantly Jack acquiesced and from that point on was forced to accept the humiliating role of semi-invalid. Being reliant on others came as a blow to his self-esteem for since his blinding he had always prided himself on remaining independent.

Now Damask suggested they should make their way down to the waterfront.

"I want to ascertain if there are any boats due to sail in the near future," she said, "and if so where they're going and if they take passengers. I'd like to head out to sea as soon as possible. In a place like this they must know something about what lies beyond the horizon. Then we'd better find somewhere to spend the night. Are you coming Jack?"

"I'll just sit here for a while and admire the view. I'll joint you later."

"Oh, ok." She was used, by now, to his mocking take on his disability.

When his two companions' footsteps had died away the blind boy remained for a while deep in thought as if nerving himself to make a decision. Finally, employing the foldable walking stick that had recently replaced his cane, he hauled himself to his feet and shuffled in the direction of the building Foxy had referred to. This brand-new construction was built in the style of a traditional Tartary temple. It was a large imposing edifice with overhanging eaves and in the centre of the front wall a wide doorway minus a door where fluttering ribbons hung from the lintel. Jack, using his highly-tuned senses of hearing and smell, found his way to this opening and was greeted by an ostiery who stood aside to let him pass. The young man walked forward and almost collided with a statue just inside the entrance. "What's this?" he asked the gatekeeper.

"That? That Deliverer of course – all *mahouno-hashi hausa* have shape of Deliverer at the door."

Jack investigated the image by touch and at the same time thought about what they had learned on their recent journey. Soon after escaping from the Blue Mountain eruption – it had been a near thing, they had made a run for it with rock fragments raining down around their ears and a flow of larva at their backs – they found the countries of Caffray and later Tartary in a ferment of excitement. First of all word had come that the war with Armornia had ended and also that the new power in charge south of the Tethys no longer posed a threat. Evidently, at the same time as the rain ceased and the sun came out from behind almost permanent clouds, the troops, taking their cue from the clement weather, had thrown down their weapons and embraced their foes as brothers. Universal rejoicing followed. But then it was discovered that twice as many people were dying each month as had died in the war and a new epidemic was feared. It was not until a voice came from the western boundaries of Caffray that the panic subsided. A young boy who it was claimed possessed the gift of prophecy, began passing through village after village telling everyone that the Deliverer, the being who had been awaited for so long that his advent had been almost despaired of, had finally come to earth and then left again in order to complete his task. He had taken the World's-Bane into his keeping and carried it afar off and by so doing had managed to nullify the jinx under which mankind had been labouring for millennia. In gratitude, the boy said, there will soon be a declaration of intent by the most senior sanayogi. The constellation of winter stars, up to the present day known throughout the land as the Hunter will be renamed the Deliverer in his honour. Now that the Object-of-Power had been banished from the planet it had cleaved to for so long the weight of it would no longer fetter humanity and in future every person would be free to realise their destiny, maybe to move to a new incarnation after death, or to avoid death entirely by beginning a life of eternal blessedness beyond the earth. The boy also told them to build houses - Magic Bridge Houses - *Mahouno-hashi Hausu* - where those that were ready to go through the Change could wait in peace for their apotheosis, and the fleshy shell that remained after their departure would be disposed of in a dignified manner. The people of Caffray that knew him personally informed everyone that the words the boy uttered must be true because, as far as they understood it, since birth he had been unable to speak and only now, when he was required to utter divine verities, had he found a voice. Jack thought of these things as he explored the statue's contours. From what his hands told him he conjured up a picture of a typical far-eastern sage with slanting eyes, drooping moustache and pigtailed hair. Below its head the figure was decked out in long flowing robes and open-toed sandals.

Oh Dando, my dear, he mused, *you're going to be revered from one end of this benighted planet to the other as long as any remnant of the human race still exists on its surface and in each community you'll have a different image and none of them will look anything like the real you.*

This idea filled him with a great and regretful sadness.

As he penetrated further into the building an official met him on the stairs – already a civil-service grade had been created entitled *Keeper of the Magic Bridge* – in order to offer him the choice, among other things, of counselling, a meal and a room to himself. He turned down everything except the last option. Having achieved temporary sanctuary and having slumped onto a low-lying couch (he felt weary all the time these days but could get little relief even after prolonged rest) he thought about the concept of going *Over-the-Brook*. The whole idea would have been repellent to him until a few months ago. As a result of his ingrained scepticism he had imagined Horry was indulging in wishful thinking when he insisted that his mother and grandfather had gone through this mysterious transformation and he found it almost impossible to believe that the boy was receiving actual advice from a disembodied Ann. But now he supposed he had to accept the idea of metamorphosis as fact because everyone seemed to be getting in on the act. So how was it to be achieved? Could you bring it about by taking a narcotic he wondered or did you make it happen through meditation? He had heard of out-of-body experiences, had even met with something of the kind when he had been hooked on Dr Good's. Well, it seemed unlikely that a similar change could happen to such as he in the normal course of events so it looked as if, at present, he must resign himself to just taking a restorative nap on the comfortable couch before going back to join his friends. He sighed, tried to relax, and eventually drifted into sleep.

"Capitaine, mon capitaine – wake up – like it's time to go!" Jack shifted uneasily. He was having a strange dream, a dream of his little lover from the Posse who had died so tragically from the sickness that now had him in its grip. "Go away," he muttered and sought to return to blessed oblivion, but the voice came again. ***"Capitaine – like you're not dreaming! I'm real – I'm here – let me show you the way!"***

Jack suddenly sat bolt upright, wide awake and in shock, because he could SEE! He could see the boy, or at least a bright glowing image of him that illuminated the walls and ceiling of the room.

"Fynn! – is that you? What are you doing? How did you get here?"

"I was in a dark place – a place with lots of other people. I was there a long time. But then someone came and pulled aside a curtain an' we all came out an' I recognised you an' somebody said

you were ready to go. Come mon capitaine – take my hand – Make the Change."

Jack got up without effort - he seemed to float upright - and stood looking towards his former bed-mate. He saw (SAW!) that there was a great gulf between the two of them but also that there was a bridge across that gulf. Was this it then? Was it really going to be this simple? For a moment he hesitated – uncertain - still only half believing – then, reaching out, he took hold of the boy's hand and stepped forward. In no time at all he found himself on the other side, surprised to discover he still had a body and that that body was apparently in rude good health. Fynn was beside him, arm around his waist, steadying him, encouraging him. Jack raised his head and stared upwards, joy beginning to flood his discarnate heart.

"I can see!" he cried in triumph, not caring if he made a complete idiot of himself, and then on a quieter, more awe-struck note, ***"I can see them! - I can see them clearly! Look Fynn, there, up there – I can see the stars!"***

A couple of months wore away before Milly and Horry reached the culmination of their epic journey back to the valley where this story began. The last stretch up the Incadine Gorge proved a hard slog for both of them. Things had changed somewhat during their period in transit and, over time, their relationship had deepened and matured. At her parting from Dando the black girl had felt such pain that she was convinced she was about to die. However, as they set out and the days passed, the presence of the son of her idol went some way to assuaging the agony. Horry did his best to stand in for his father and also to divert her mind from its misery by making her concentrate on the task in hand. When she had rashly promised to accompany her charge back to his forefathers patrimony Milly had not given much thought to the distance they would have to travel or to the fact that her direction-finding abilities were of the haziest. In the end it was Horry who suggested that, if they went due south from the mountain, they would be bound to come to the Middle Sea and then, if they could beg a passage on a Terratenebrian ship, they would eventually make landfall not far from where he understood the ancestral home he had never seen was located. This plan they duly put into practice over a period of weeks until they came ashore on a thinly-populated part of the southern continent to the east of the River Kymer and its flood plain. Here they wandered, confused, for more than two months, in a hilly region where the people spoke a strange local dialect divorced from the common tongue. At last they were rescued by a travelling salesman who told them that he was on his way back to the Great River and the town of Vadrosnia Poule. For a while they joined forces with him but, having been put on her guard by her experiences in Rytardenath, Milly, despite being a dyed-in-the-wool townee, felt nervous about once more entering an intensively-populated urban area so they gave the Delta City a miss and, bidding farewell to their guide, spent the last of their money on a ferry trip across the upper tidal reaches of the Kymer. After that they begged their way slowly from village to village, accepting the occasional lift when it was offered, sleeping in barns or out in the open under the sky, despite the cold and occasional snowfall. The places they came to had a disturbed, uneasy air about them.

"There ain't 'arf a lot of funerals goin' on," pronounced Milly after they had passed their third hearse of the morning, "is sompfink up do you reckon - is it like when we woz on the battlefield?"

Nervous of encountering some new contagion, they avoided mixing with the local population as much as possible, so that, when they finally made it to the Stumble Stones late on a chilly spring day, they were still in total ignorance of the huge transformation that was sweeping the planet.

"Nearly there," said Milly as they toiled upwards alongside the Wendover. "It's weird that there's no-one else on the road. 'Ave we got our sums wrong do you fink – is today a rest day?"

"Don't know," muttered Horry, his mind on other things.

"There's only free towns in Deep 'Allow," panted Milly as they stopped for a breather, "'Igh 'Arrow up at the uver end, Low Town in the middle an' Gateway – that's the one we'll come to first. The Lordship woz there when 'ee woz learnin' to be a soldier but it orl went wrong an' 'is dad got real angry wiv 'im. Then the knight turned up wiv the Lordship's sweet'eart an' they decided to go along o' him an' then Foxy shot 'is dad dead an then... Well, it's a long story an' I wozn't there for most of it - I woz off wiv the Majesty doin' actin' an' rescuin' Jack from the cliff an' workin' in the circus."

"Um..." said Horry. During the last hour or two he had spent a lot of the time gazing ardently at Milly's curvaceous backside as she climbed ahead of him up the gorge. At several points on their journey he had indicated by a shy caress that he thought the moment had come for their relationship to move beyond mere friendship, but on each occasion she had wriggled out of his embrace, giving him to understand that although she was not adverse to carrying things a little further the time was not yet ripe. "Let's wait 'till we c'n get a bit more comfortable, dearie," she had suggested gently, "I don' wan' ter start takin' me duds off in orl this frost." And so, at night, he had to content himself with a fully clothed Milly cuddling up against him for warmth.

Gateway, when they reached it after midnight, was silent and dark, the streets empty, but then that was to be expected at such an hour. Milly took the narrow path out of town running parallel to the main highway. This alternative route followed the base of the valley's northern wall and passed the place at which the Shady Way set off on its long mountainous odyssey.

"This is where the Lordship an' the others turned north," she said pointing along the path, "we went the wrong way, the Majesty an' me. But it's the road we're on that'll get us to the factory that makes the stuff they take down to the sea, an' after that we'll come to the back of the Castle."

It was early afternoon by the time they passed the iron-works of which she had spoken but all was as silent as the grave; there was no sound of water-driven hammers, no roar of furnaces.

"It *mus'* be a rest day," concluded Milly.

They progressed onwards to the Castle which frowned down on them as they made their way round the periphery to the front entrance having found the back gate locked and barred. The black girl turned to Horry, a nervous light in her eyes. Now that she believed they were on the verge of encountering her former employers she was beginning to wonder what sort of reception awaited her.

"I don' honestly fink they'll remember me - I woz just the Majesty's maid after all. If they do remember I don' 'spec' they'll be orl that pleased to see me cos I reckon they were pretty miffed about us runnin' away." Then sizing up her companion, "You looks more like a nibbler than one of them toffs. Get ready to show them that ring the Lordship gave you. Uverwise they'll never believe you're 'is son. Well, in for a penny, in for a pound..." and so as they rounded the corner of the house and made their way to the archway that led through to the main bailey she steeled herself to face a certain degree of hostility from whoever was keeping the gate. What she was not prepared for was that there would be absolutely no one in sight. Because the portcullis was raised there was nothing to stop them from walking through the passage into the inner quadrangle, but nevertheless they hesitated for sometime and it took a deal of courage for Horry to tug at a rope connected to a large rusty bell high on the wall, causing it to toll several times. The sound it made was startlingly loud in that silent place, a place where normally there would have been a hubbub of clattering hooves, pacing feet and clamorous voices. Even after this solitary summons had rung out, still nobody appeared.

"There ain't a soul about," exclaimed an astounded Milly, "where've they orl gorn?"

"Let's go an' find out."

The Great Hall, the Dan's apartments, the gynaceum, the chapel, the kitchens, the barracks, even the Punishment Yard - they searched high and low but wherever they looked they were met by the sight of empty rooms, unpeopled living quarters and dusty corridors.

"Joo realise," said Milly at last, "we ain't seen a single person since we started up the gorge. I fink p'raps the 'ole Valley's empty – I fink they've orl scarpered."

"Or died," suggested Horry with relish.

Milly flinched. "Don' be rotten," she muttered, and then, "anyway, there'd be bodies."

"Well, perhaps some died and then the rest of 'em got scared and did a bunk. Anyway, looks like we've got the place to ourselves which could be fun. I'll be the king of the castle an' you c'n be the dirty rascal."

"That's just plain nasty!"

"Oh all right. Well, how about you be the lady of the manor, swanking around in gorgeous frocks, an' I'll be your very 'umble servant."

"'Orry! This ain't funny. Those poor people – if sompfink's 'appened..."

By this time they had returned to the bailey where the inner bastions of the castle towered over them. "You know," said Horry, "what you haven't shown me yet is the place where dad used to live. How do you get to it?"

"You mean the tower? If we wanna go there I reckon we'll 'ave to go out the front an' roun' the outside. I don' know 'ow to get to it from inside – I never bin."

They went back through the main entrance and Milly led him to the right along the exterior wall until they reached a door. Again they found the entrance unsecured. Within, a flight of stairs climbed past several floors on which they discovered kitchens, servants quarters, a nursery, a schoolroom, bathroom and a magnificent playroom cum living-room with tall windows.

"Was this all just for him?" asked Horry, astounded.

"'Im an' 'is sister. The uver towers woz lived in by the boss's children too – 'ee 'ad ten of 'em or more – but the Lordship was special cos 'ee woz number two."

Horry became absolutely fascinated by the possessions he came across in his exploration of his father's childhood abode:– books, toys, clothes, pictures; these small abandoned items seemed to bring his young father very close; but by this time it was getting late and they had been awake for nearly thirty six hours. After sharing some bread and cheese from Milly's backpack, all they were interested in now was finding a place where they could lay their weary heads.

"How about bedrooms?" asked Horry, "there must be bedrooms somewhere."

"The stairs go further up," she replied, "I 'spec' they're up there."

The two travellers investigated. When Horry opened a door at the top of the next flight they both gasped in amazement. A king-sized four-poster met their eyes, canopied with gold-embroidered brocade and hung with richly patterned curtains. The mattress was spread with silken sheets and coverlet, while the headboard bore the Dans' escutcheon.

"Crikey!" blurted out Milly, and "Wowee!" contributed Horry who had known many different beds and none at all in his short life, "I reckon we'll sleep pretty well tonight – though if you don't want... I mean..." He tailed off, shooting a sideways, slightly embarrassed, glance at the girl he adored, uncertain of her reaction. Milly, however, quickly set his mind at rest.

"I'll never forget the Lordship - 'ow could I. But you an' me luv – I reckon this is the right place for it – the place where 'e used to sleep. I fink 'e'd be pretty pleased if 'e knew what we woz up to - p'raps 'e's even lookin' down on us now from where 'ee's gorn. Me an' you – it sorta seems right it's ended this way..."

"You're telling me!" replied a fervent Horry, and started to help her undress.

Blue sky – small white clouds above tangled branches – cumulus fractus – fair-weather clouds. Birds – birds high above, soaring, wheeling – birds lower down, darting, chasing each other, calling. Where on earth am I?

Dando pushes himself up into a sitting position, brushing leaf-mould from his body, and rubs his eyes. *Goodness – what a view - I'm halfway up a mountain! There's a huge valley down below – look at those cliffs! But it's not all rugged – there's lakes and water-*

meadows and lots of trees – it's beautiful. He gets easily and unthinkingly to his feet then gazes round in confusion, realising he is just above the margins of a small wood and that close by a substantial stream is hurrying through a gully. He starts to walk downwards, following the stream, catching glimpses through the trees of wide-open spaces, while hearing rustles around him in the undergrowth and briefly spying some creature on the bank of the watercourse – otter? - beaver? - he cannot be sure. But then a thought causes him to halt abruptly and he stands frozen to the spot.

I got to my feet – both feet! I'm walking on two legs, flesh and blood legs with heels and toes, ankles, calves – how can that be?! It must be a dream, yet it can't be - my imagination could never invent a place like this. He looks at his hands – four fingers and a thumb on each – he touches his nose – perfectly straight! *Was it all in my head then? Did none of it really happen?*

He carries on, amazed to find that he is also pain-free – he has almost forgotten what that feels like - and comes to the brink of one of the towering cliffs over which the stream is launching itself into space. At his feet some steps have been gouged into the nearly vertical rock-face and these disappear downwards out of sight. He stares at the vista through volumes of crystal-clear air and sees herds of deer far below, peacefully grazing. He watches as one group scatters, spooked by something that could be a hidden predator. The enormous glen presents the appearance of a uninhabited world – uninhabited by human beings at least. But now as he looks more intently he glimpses a roof near the edge of the valley floor in the midst of a small open area of golden grass. A domestic dwelling is visible down there in that edenic place giving the lie to the idea that it has never been visited by his own kind. He can see the front door. Someone is standing outside in the sunshine and even at this distance of more than a mile he thinks he recognises who it is. Impetuously he begins the hazardous descent beside the waterfall, aware that these steps, hewn out of solid rock, are further proof that the valley has been occupied at sometime or other by a hominid species.

When he reaches level ground he can no longer see the building - it has become hidden amongst the trees. He wanders at random for a while feeling increasingly forlorn until suddenly the cottage appears before him, but now with no-one outside it. Testing the door, he discovers that it is firmly shut. Timidly he raises his hand and raps softly on the wood. After a short wait he hears footsteps and then – wonder of wonders – *she* is there before him.

"***Annie!***" he cries, his voice breaking as he grabs her into his arms.

"***My bonny lad,***" she answers and the next moment he is overwhelmed by the whole spectrum of her physicality, the warmth of her, the feel of her body, her very essence.

They have made love in the small clean bedroom on the upper floor and now they are sitting on a bench outside the cottage in the sunshine, holding hands, leaning against one another.

"***Wherever are we, Annie?***" he asks, ***"I don't understand – I didn't think I was intended to go on at all after I had taken the Key to the place where it was supposed to be."***

"***Well, my love, as the Deliverer you had to share in all human experience and that included death, but it also includes life – life among the stars. You may not be aware yet but you too have become a dancer.***"

"***But what is this place Annie?***"

"***I don' be knowin' exactly where we are my love, but it be a long, long way from our starting point. When you touch the picture of the door on the ship's screen an' the great machine be taken through walls while the Thing-of-Power be gettin' ready for its wedding day I be lef' behin', but I tell my friends what happen an they promise to look for you. Very soon one of they foun' you a long way away. You ha'n't stopped existing completely like I think you were afraid might be the case, but you'd become lost between lives the same as others who have been hurt so bad that they died. Most o' those escaped as the heavenly marriage took place and became dancers but not you. As fast as I could, I come to where you be, an' put my arms arou' your very centre while I carried you Over-the-Brook to save you from wanderin' in the dark for ever. But then we get caught up along o' the About-to-be-Born an' get sucked across all sort of walls until we end up here – somewhere altogether different yet almos' the same.***"

"***Another continuum perhaps,***" says Dando dreamily, remembering something Quahaug had said during their conference together.

"***At the las' minute you be snatched from my grasp an' once more I thought I'd lost you but you don' be far away – jus' a little ways further up the mountain. This planet be the like o' the earth back home but here everyone ha' passed over long ago so now it belong entirely to the animals an' mayhap someday one o' they be clever enough to follow where the people goo.***"

"Did you say animals?!" cries her lover in astonishment, *"look over there by the side of that pool – I could almost swear..."*

Two quadrupeds are coming towards them out of the shadows under the trees, one wolf-like and grey-coated, one much smaller with dark points.

"It's Meena and Ralph!" exclaims an amazed Dando, stooping to greet the new arrivals as they get within arms' reach.

"Yes sweetheart. But these don' be the same Meena and Ralph that you knew - every world like ours ha' a Meena and Ralph in it. I make friends with these ones an' they be a-gooin' ter stay wi' you when I be not here."

"Not here! What are you saying? Don't leave me again Annie when I've only just found you!" He clutches her as if he would prevent her from departing by main force.

"No, sweetheart – I don' be a-gooin' just yet. But I hev things to do. You mus' remain until you be ready to join the dance. If I goo I'll always be comin' back I promise."

Dando relaxes slightly.

"Join the dance? Perhaps I'm ready to do that right now." He stands up and attempts an experimental pirouette but it feels strange doing it with two good legs.

"Annie," he asks, *"why have I got my leg back? Why can I feel an' smell an' taste just as if I've got a real body? Why can we make love?"*

"After people goo Over-the-Brook an' leave the flesh behind their bodies are just part of their minds. It's your mind that tells you you c'n feel – that you hev two good legs – if your mind say one leg then that's what you'd hev."

"Ancestral-Memory," murmurs Dando, recalling the term that Azazeel had once used. *"D'you know,"* he goes on, *"I tried so hard to protect the Key and stop it falling into that Dark Brother's hands but then in the end I found it was able look after itself just as you'd told me it could. Was what I did all a waste of time?"*

"No, my love – I see now it need a living person to set it on the right road, otherwise it would ha' carried on being the immortals' plaything just as it was in the beginning when it first come to earth. You shew it the way – you remind it of what it were sent to do an' then you help it to goo to the place where it were meant to be right from the start."

"Does it think then? Is it alive?"

"There be only One in the whool of everything that know the truth o' that."

"Annie, tell me, would it have been better if I hadn't turned it – the Key? That's what I keep asking myself."

"Don' 'ee fret, sweetheart. You turn it out of love for your master an' that be whooly good. The final turning had to be made – it were long overdue - afore the Key leave the earth - there be no profit in wishing it undone. What follow straight after were bad acos you were in the power o' the Dark Brother, but in taking it outside you make everything alright for always."

"Always?"

"Well, for a long long time."

"My master, he died in Damwey - is he Over-the-Brook too do you think?"

"He don' be among the dancers – not yet. I believe he hev further lives to live afore he be wise enough."

"Poor Tallis," says Dando with a sigh and lapses into silence. Later he asks, *"What happened to the others – did they escape the mountain?"*

"They all goo in different directions. The blind boy, cos he be ready, ha' made the Change same as you; your sister an' Foxy be gooin' adventurin' an' Milly an' Horry be back in the valley where we started from. They be a-cosyin' up together."

"Oh yes of course – Milly and Horry," and Dando smiles with tender approval.

They talk on and off for the rest of the day while Ralph and Meena sit close by. At some point in their conversation Dando asks what he thinks will be his last question.

"What about all the rest of those Old Ones that have been ruling our planet for so long? Will they become dancers again like they used to be?"

"The Old Ones who come to the earth and the Great Ones the same – it be too late for they to break away. They be a-gooin' to fade until they take the place of the ghosts who've been freed now the Key ha' foun' its true purpose. They be a-gooin' to creep like lost mice through the passages unner the earth."

"That sounds hard – do they deserve such a fate I wonder?"

They move indoors and with the approach of evening, because the little house is well supplied, Dando enjoys concocting a sumptuous feast designed to be shared between themselves and the animals.

"Who bought all this stuff?" he asks, *"is it real?"*

"It be already here when I arrive. That be all I c'n tell you. O' courst it be real."

At the conclusion of the meal Dando gets up from the table, stretches and holds out his hand. ***"Come on – let's go to bed – the washing up can wait 'till morning."***

At dawn, the young man wakes to find himself alone apart from the cat and the dog who are curled up on top of the coverlet beside him.

"***She said she'd return – she said she'd return...***" As he gets dressed he tries to convince himself of the truth of this statement by continual repetition. Not feeling like eating he leaves the cottage accompanied by the animals and hikes through the valley in the early-morning light. About two miles from his starting point he comes out of the forest into a grassy clearing and catches sight of a dark shape slinking into the shadows on the farther side. For a moment he is reminded of the black and menacing creature that visited him when he was hung in the tree on the Dark Island. He walks forward until he reaches the centre of the glade and as he does so all colour leaches out of the surrounding landscape and a great silence descends. The animals crouch down at his feet, very much afraid, but Dando stands straight and tall ready to accept whatever is to come. The silence deepens – it takes on the form of an alternative dimension in which the whole spectrum of sound is negated. Then in that absence, pits are dug, excavations are delved representing words which in their unspoken purity no longer need verbalisation to communicate their meaning.

"WELL DONE!" Dando understands that this is what is being conveyed. He sinks to his knees.

"***I t-tried,***" he replies.

"RISE MY CHILD – DO NOT KNEEL TO ME – YOU HAVE BROUGHT HARMONY TO YOUR SMALL CORNER OF THE MULTIVERSE. I WILL NOT FORGET."

Dando regains his feet staring around him in awe. ***"I don't understand,"*** he exclaims, ***"who are you?"*** And after a wait of some minutes during which no answer is forthcoming: ***"Master Tallisand said someone from beyond the earth spoke to him at the start of his journey but never again, an' I heard a voice when I was in the tree, but thought it must be a dream. Are you one of the Great Ones?"***

"YOU KNOW WHO I AM, DAN ADDO - YOU CARRY MY LIGHT ON YOUR FOREHEAD AND MY MARK ON YOUR SHOULDER. WHEN YOU ARE READY THERE ARE FURTHER BRIGHT JOURNEYS TO UNDERTAKE BUT FOR NOW YOU MUST REST – REST AND RECOVER. TAKE

PLEASURE IN YOUR STAY UPON THIS PLANET – THIS THIRD FROM THE SUN – ONE OF MANY THE SAME..."

It is Dando's turn to remain silent – silent for so long that he appears to have run out of words, - then: ***"Thank you,"*** he finally replies, laying his hand on Ralph's head to soothe him and bending down to reassure a frightened Meena. ***"Thankyou – I will."***

The surrounding countryside gradually regains its sound and colour in proof of which first one and then several birds begin to sing. Deciding that normality has been restored Dando turns and begins walking back towards the cottage followed by the animals, suddenly feeling very hungry. Perhaps Ann will have returned; perhaps he can cook her some breakfast. He immediately begins to plan the meal they will share and is filled with delight to think he may be able to serve her in this way. "Please be there," he whispers to the firmament above and the drifting clouds, "please don't stay away too long."

All is calm, all is quiet, within a corner of a certain remote spiral galaxy. Silence reigns - the kind of silence that is only to be found between the stars. But one being, one of the many who have made the Change and who has the ability to hear even where there is no atmosphere to transmit sound, catches, as she passes, faint anthems emanating from the surface of an insignificant planet, lost in immensity, where the majority of the events recounted in this history took place. As she listens - in the brief period she is within range - melodies of such light-hearted exuberance come to her ears that she, and all the other souls whom she consequently summons and who later darkly fill the apparent emptiness all around, cannot help but swear that the very rocks of which this little world is composed are singing for joy.

THE END

Printed in Great Britain
by Amazon